TERRORISTS
AND THE
TERCHOVA TREASURE

IN MY BROTHER'S PLACE

GEORGE BANAS

Copyright © 2010, 2013 by George Banas

All rights reserved. This book or any portion thereof may not be reproduced or used in any manner whatsoever without the express written permission of the publisher except for the use of brief quotations in a book review.

This is a work of fiction. Names, characters, businesses, places, events and incidents are either the product of the author's imagination or used in a fictitious manner. The history is real.

Printed in the United States of America

ISBN: 978-0-615-91016-1

George Banas
5378 Candlewood Court
Lisle, IL 60532

Book design: Judy Maenle; www.mosaicbookworks.com

*I dedicate this book to my wife, family, friends,
neighbors, and colleagues for their inspiration,
encouragement, and help to make this book possible.*

*More broadly, I dedicate my work to all the military
and civilian defenders of this country
from its inception to the present day
whose commitment, devotion to duty,
and personal sacrifices marked the path
to our freedoms and signaled our ever-present
responsibility to guard and maintain them.*

Lynn —

I hope you enjoy my story.

George Bunas
January 3, 2015

REVIEWS

"... Action, adventure, mystery, international intrigue, politics, a treasure hunt ... it feels like there is an adventure or plot around every corner ... all these exotic locales come to life with a touch of historical fact and details that the reader just knows comes from experience. I enjoyed turning the pages not only to follow the adventure, but also to explore the world, my world, and the world of Joe Legion...."
~Judge, Writer's Digest 21st Annual Self-Published Book Awards

"Even from the first couple of chapters, it's hard not to suspect that Banas has insiders' knowledge of international intrigue."
~Janet Wilmoth of the Lisle Sun

"Banas builds his story on a strong, historical foundation, sharing details of actual events to create for his readers an authenticity and realism that puts us all at the 'front' in the war on terror."
~Reviewer Ron Logeman

"You get the excitement of the story along with important historical information that all of us should never forget."
~Reviewer Pete Earleywine

"This novel uses fictionalized real characters to convey dozens of true meaningful messages to the readers."
~Sean Ely of the Owosso (Michigan) Argus Press

"The character of Joe Legion is highly memorable, and the dialog is inspired, smart, philosophical, and funny."
~Professional Editor Chris Yurko

"I enjoyed your book immensely. Your characters Hassan and Vasily would be great in a spy thriller on TV."
~Joanne, cancer patient

ACKNOWLEDGMENTS

I wish to recognize the following individuals, groups, and organizations for their cooperation and support for this project:

Reverend Jude D. Randall, O.S.B., President, on behalf of the administration, faculty, students, and alumni of Benet Academy in Lisle, Illinois.

The administration, scientists, and staff of the Fermi National Accelerator Laboratory in Batavia, Illinois.

The residents of Aurora, Downers Grove, Lisle, and Naperville, Illinois for their support of my literary efforts and my special project to help area veterans in need through my donations from book sales.

I'd like to acknowledge the management and staff of Mosaic Book Works in a special way, particularly Judy Maenle whose expertise, commitment, advice, and knowledge of the publishing field is unrivaled. Without her, this book, cover, and interior formatting would likely never have come together.

I also wish to thank the following publishers and other organizations for their permission to use their organization's resources, publications, or copyrighted materials as reference sources for this book: Alpha Books, Associated Press, Bantam Books, Barnes & Noble Publishing, Inc., Berkley Books, Brandt & Hochman Literary Agents, Inc. on behalf of the Estate of Charles B. MacDonald, Brookings Institution Press, Carnegie Endowment for International Peace, Chicago Tribune, Council on Foreign Relations as publishers of *Foreign Affairs*, Fodor's Travel Publications, HarperCollins Publishers, Little, Brown and Company, Lonely Planet Publications Pty. Ltd., Massachusetts Institute of Technology, New York University Press, Oxford University Press, Penguin Group (USA), Princeton University Press, RAND Corporation, *Scientific American*, Stanley Karnow, author of "Vietnam: A History," The Random House Publishing Group, and WGBH Educational Foundation.

TABLE OF CONTENTS

PREFACE   1

Chapter 1   IBERIAN ESCAPE   5

The Return Ferry to Madrid 5 • An Unexpected Invitation 6 • First Time to Morocco 8 • Hassan's Companions 9 • Incident in Casablanca 10 • Heading Back North 11 • Portuguese Detour 14 • Fatima on the Fateful Day 14 • Disaster at Home 16 • Finding Our Way Back 17 • Unexpected Help 18 • Return to a Changed Homeland 19

Chapter 2   JOE LEGION AND PURPLE   21

Early Days 21 • The Walk of Despair 22 • Getting My Records 23 • Very Bad News 24 • Searching for Answers 27 • My Decision 29 • Tuning Up 30 • First, Master the Self, Then Master the Weapons 32 • Alice Introduces Herself 33 • The Reservation 34 • The PURPLE People 36 • Partner Down 38 • Alice's Rescue 39 • In Appreciation—Nothing 41 • Conversion to Civilian Life 42 • Marika and Unresolved Questions 44

Chapter 3   HASSAN AND THE RUSSIANS   46

The Chance Encounter 46 • British Intelligence and the Lost Camera Bag 46 • Russian Reconnaissance 50 • Getting to Know Hassan 53 • Minor Miscues 55 • On to Moscow the Hard Way 58 • Hassan's Gulf War Experience 60 • Arrival in Moscow 69 • Second Encounter 70 • Roast Duck 72 • On to St. Petersburg 78 • Fooling Around with the Fleet 79 • Russian Farewell 80 • Balkan Briefing 81 • What Next? 85

Chapter 4 Janosik and the Treasure 87

Back to My Day Job 87 • Our European Roots 89 • The Legend of Janosik 92 • Beginning Thoughts of a Treasure Hunt 94 • Scenic Diversion 95 • Exploring the Caves 99 • Casual Counseling 99 • Still More Caves 103 • On to Trstena 105 • Meeting Aunt Maria 106 • Aunt Maria's Warning 113

Chapter 5 Sujaya and the Indian Earthquake 116

International Responder 116 • Dr. Sujaya 118 • R & R (Rest & Religion) 119 • The Man Without a Number 122 • Assigning Myself a New Job 123 • Our First Real Break 123 • A Walk on the Beach 124 • Holy Man in Rome 125 • The Lessons Continue 127 • A Final Bit of Buddhism 131 • Karmic Change of Plans 132 • Gathering Intelligence for the Hunt 136 • Deadly Business in Delhi 139

Chapter 6 Rounding Up Roberto 147

March Toward Mumbai 147 • Mumbai Mlecchas 148 • Searching for Didymus 153 • Tough Going in Goa 156 • Taking Chances in Chennai 157 • Too Many Hoods 160 • Vasily Remembers 162 • Assessment 165 • Recruiting for the Future 171 • Painful Good-bye 176

Chapter 7 Latin American Lesson 178

Peru This Time 178 • Volunteering for Trouble 182 • Campus Recruiting 184 • Onward to Miraflores 189 • Master of the House 192 • A Business Proposal 196 • Testing the Gringo 198 • Breakfast Invitation and Drug Quiz 199 • Trouble Brewing 201 • Blaming Uncle Sam 202 • Temporary Reprieve 207 • The Tingo Maria Ranch 208 • My Personal Milagros 210

CHAPTER 8 JENNY AND THE MISSIONARY MISSION 215

Checking with Chauncey 215 • Mormons Again 216 • Puerto Maldonado and the Missionaries 221 • On Light Ground 224 • Fire! 227 • Returning Stateside 230 • Helping Angel Moroni 231 • Lightening the Load 234 • *Dos* 235 • Texas Two-Step 236 • More Help for Moroni 239 • Undiplomatic Negotiations 241 • Moroni, Butch, and Sundance 248 • Scout Down 253 • Paying My Respects 257

CHAPTER 9 REPAIRS AND RECRUITS 261

Time Out for Repairs 261 • Defining What We Knew 262 • End of Debate, Almost the Start of Action 265 • Getting to Know Amy 269 • Recruiting and Logistics for My Second Coming 272 • The First Scout Candidate 276 • The Second Scout Candidate 280 • The Real Job Requirements 284 • One Little Indian 286

CHAPTER 10 UNFINISHED BUSINESS 288

Rescheduling the Raid 288 • Señora's Surprise 289 • More Little Indians and Some Big Dogs 292 • Grenade Party 294 • Command Jitters, Nothing Serious 295 • Helping Hand from the Neighbors 295 • The First Assault 298 • First Assault Success 301 • Next Objective 302 • Second Success 303 • Organizing the Third Assault 304 • Activating the Plan 305 • Ranch Justice 305 • Samurai Showdown 307 • Crossing the River 313 • Manco's Intelligence Briefing 316

CHAPTER 11 TANGO AT TINGO 321

Custom-Made Hostage 321 • Official Arrival 323 • First Campesino Drug Test 325 • Second Campesino Drug Test 329 • Debriefing with Advari 333 • While You're in the Neighborhood 336 • A Chicken's Way Out 339 • Passenger Disarmament 340 • Disbanding My Army 342

Chapter 12 A Doe, a Doc, a Declaration 344

Visiting My Scout 344 • Agreement with Alexandra 348 • Answers for Andrews 351 • Gathering Clouds 354 • Declaration of Total War 358

Chapter 13 The Omen—A Fight on Home Ground 360

Prologuing the Past 360 • Ron's Early Morning Surprise 361 • Beginnings of a New Game Plan 363 • An Omen of What? 365 • Fossil Therapy 366 • No Fluff, Just the Facts 368 • Patton and Amy, A Fine Combination 370 • Amy's First Standing Order 371 • Arming My Scout 372 • They're Here! 374 • Audacity in Action 376 • Dialing Up More Audacity 382 • The Chief, the JASONs, and the Deal 385 • Cutting to a Different Chase 392

Chapter 14 Ambush at Amy's Place 395

Yard Work 395 • Reluctant Runners 397 • Amy's Arrival 403 • Paramedic Parade 406 • Scout Supremacy 411 • Edging Toward the ER 416 • Uphill All the Way 419 • Medical Pit Stop 420 • The Morning After 428 • Clearing the Air 433 • The Twenty-Year Mystery 440

Chapter 15 Operation Hercules 443

Preparing for My Personal Parousia 443 • Plane Talk 445 • The Talk Gets Treasonous 454 • Meeting the Marshal 461 • No Rain in Spain, Only Advari 462 • Diplomatic Detour 464 • Hunting for the Real Hassan 468 • Personal Connections 471 • Hitching Hassan to Hercules 476

Chapter 16 Marketplace Madness 488

First Target 488 • Getting the Details Right 496 • The Plan Goes Awry 499 • Moroccan Style Audacity 501 • Restructuring the Plan 503 • Confiscating a Scanner 505 • Full Employment 509 • Lining Up a Lifeline 511

CHAPTER 17 WESTERN WAR 515

Dinner Conversation and Wet Pants 515 • Moroccan Magic 518 • Motoring to La Montagne 522 • Intermission for Admonitions 525 • Tangier Terrain 527 • Farid and the Fantasias 528 • An Audacious Cavalry Trot 532 • Unbridled Success 535 • Accounting for Casualties 536

CHAPTER 18 EASTERN EXTRACTION 540

Surveying the Landscape 540 • Bath Water and the Baby 546 • No More Nice Guy 549 • Night Fight 556 • Too Good to be True 562 • Crashing the Border 564 • A Friend Left Behind 566 • Catching Up With Beth 569 • Cobra Convention 570 • Debriefing 574 • Penetrating Questions 576 • One More Encounter 579 • Another Good-bye 582

CHAPTER 19 GHOSTS AND REGRETS 585

Ron's News Coup 585 • Followed by a Lecture 588 • Followed by a Death Notice 589 • Back to the Lecture 591 • Scout's Honor 593 • Calling Mr. Right 596 • Promises 598

CHAPTER 20 MARIKA AND ST. GEORGE 600

Mending Fences 600 • Double Dealing 605 • Scheming 609 • Deadly Details 610 • No Harassment, Just Family Fun 613 • Beth's Proposed Itinerary 614 • My Proposed Itinerary 616 • Errant Apple 617 • Marika Invites Herself 619 • Itinerary Change Payoff 621 • Sermon by the Sea 622 • Recruiting Accomplices 624 • Gauging the Penalties 626

CHAPTER 21 UNFAMILIAR KIND OF WAR 631

Belgrade Beginnings 631 • Old School Chums 635 • House Hunting 643 • Natural Forces at the Bridge 645 • Flaming the Dragon 647 • Party Time 652 • Uninvited Guests 654

• Dance Partner 657 • Love's Ultimate Sacrifice 658 • Enough for One Night 662 • Home for the Holidays 664 • In-Flight Inquisition 666

CHAPTER 22 TRANSITION TO NEW PROBLEMS 669

Late Arrival 669 • Not Quite an Auld Lang Syne Conversation 670 • The Alpha and the Omega 676 • A Reminder of Jeremiah's Promise 681

APPENDIX LIST OF CHARACTERS AND ORGANIZATIONS 683

BIBLIOGRAPHY 689

PREFACE

On September 11, 2001, my wife and I learned of the tragic attacks on the World Trade Center and the Pentagon while traveling between Tangier, Morocco, and Madrid, Spain. Similar to many Americans traveling abroad at that fateful time, our first thought was to return to the States as soon as possible. Our second thought was to determine how to protect ourselves from a yet unknown enemy. For me, a third thought was to protect my extended American and European families and to fight back against anyone responsible for an attack on us whenever and wherever such an attack occurred.

Although my story nominally begins in September 2001, the actual start of my training as the second Joe Legion and preparation for the events that preceded and followed September 11, 2001, occurred many years earlier when I was growing up, going to college, serving in the Army, and pursuing my professional career while maintaining a hidden life. I write in a fictional mode and mix facts and fiction in the events I describe. Doing so allows me to maintain privacy for my family, friends, neighbors, and colleagues who are not public figures, but who participated in actual events. I also maintain confidentiality where necessary for my past actions and for future plans and actions against my known and future adversaries. In my story, we will meet many characters. The names of my characters and brief descriptions of them are listed in the Appendix. In all cases, except for the identities of public and historical individuals who are associated with actual places, locations, and historical events, the names of my characters have been changed, including mine most of the time, as you will discover. Thus, any similarities between the names of non-public characters portrayed in my story and the names of actual persons living or dead are coincidental. Reference sources concerning historical characters and events are identified in notes at the end of each chapter.

Unfortunately, tragic circumstances such as the New York and Pentagon attacks on September 11, 2001, natural disasters such as the devastating earthquake in India in January 2001, and the equally devastating earthquake in Peru in June 2001 have dates, times, locations, and human suffering attached to them. Similarly, the circumstances and public figures involved in historical events such as the Iran hostage crisis, the Iran-Contra affair, and the First Persian Gulf War are not changed. Equally unfortunate, I cannot expose or wish out of existence all the misfortunes caused by corrupt public officials, the powerful and unscrupulous rich, national and international terrorists, and crime networks of every description. I have addressed these people and associated events for the lessons they teach all of us rather than merely holding them up to my personal criticism. Often, national and international people and events generate macro consequences on the collective lives of others, particularly those who are chronically impoverished or politically disenfranchised. Conversely, individual actors may generate consequences far beyond their regular spheres of influence. You will meet some of each category.

Also, you will travel with me to various locations in the United States, Europe, India, Central and South America, Russia, and North Africa. Readers who have traveled to these locations and who have engaged the local people and their cultures may recognize familiar places and customs. When I relate events that occurred during my military service or my activities outside the United States, I cite the time using the twenty-four hour clock, e.g., 1330 is 1:30 p.m. in U.S. time.

As for the treasure, Juraj Janosik was the early eighteenth century, real-life, Slovak equivalent of England's Robin Hood. He remains a national hero, particularly in the towns and villages along the mountainous border between Slovakia and Poland. Janosik may have had more expenses, or may not have possessed the generosity of Robin Hood in sharing his bounty with poor peasants. Hence, legend has it that much, if not all, of his treasure remains hidden, perhaps in the hills and caves of the Terchova area, or in countless other places. Readers will learn how I use the legendary existence of the treasure for other purposes among my Slovak relatives and terrorist adversaries.

My story involves considerable conflict with evildoers of every stripe and inclination as well as people who are dedicated, helpful, or simply handy when I needed them. As in real life, my primary conflict involves my personal battle with good and evil and how I interpret these characteristics in others. Although I am not always successful, I resist the urge to preach because I frequently authorize myself to inflict maximum harm on my adversaries before, or immediately after, their best efforts to inflict maximum pain and suffering on my family, my associates, and me. As in real life, I am able to escalate insignificant events into major problems, or ignore people and events that are in crisis. Some events that I perceive as important evaporate while others resurface after long incubation periods. Again, as in real life, my objective is to determine which actions or options are important enough to pursue in the present circumstances, in the foreseeable future, or not at all.

As you read my story, I hope you profit from my efforts to inform you about the people, places, and events of the world that have been part of my life, albeit under changed names and scrambled circumstances, as I mentioned above. To a lesser or greater degree, similar people, places, and events may have shaped your world too. If so, we share a common bond in our continued struggle against evil in whatever form we encounter it.

CHAPTER 1

IBERIAN ESCAPE

THE RETURN FERRY TO MADRID

The date was Sunday, September 9, 2001. The ferry *Ibn Batouta* (named for a fourteenth century Muslim traveler and explorer) was about two hours out of Tangier. My wife, Beth, and I were retracing the route northward to the Spanish port of Algeciras, from which we had sailed to Morocco five days earlier. But, unlike our previous crossing, today was clear and crisp with only a small chop as the ferry's broad bow bullied its way through the dark blue Mediterranean water. Hassan, who I regarded as my unequivocal Kuwaiti friend at the time, came out onto the starboard deck to join me as I watched the endless chain of westbound freighters and container ships steering out of the Gibraltar Straits into the Atlantic.

"*Jebel Tarik*," Hassan shouted to me against the steady wind while pointing to the ever-growing landmass on the horizon ahead.

"Yes, Tarik's Rock," I shouted back, equally enthused. "We call it Gibraltar now."

"Do you know about Tarik?" Hassan asked, hoping to catch me without an answer.

But, I was ready.

"Tarik bin Ziyad was a Berber general who crossed the straits from Africa to raid Spain in the year 711," I replied confidently, although I knew Hassan had vastly superior knowledge of Arab and Spanish history. "If I recall my history correctly," I continued, "the early Islamic raids on Spain really were initiated by North African Berbers rather than Middle Eastern Arabs."

"*Touche*," Hassan conceded at my quick follow-up. "Although you heard or read that rather recently, I think," he parried. "But, who brought Islam to the Berbers?" Hassan queried to re-ignite the conversation as his frown changed to his more usual wide smile.

Taking the offensive again, I asserted, "The Berbers didn't need to know about Islam to forge swords and sail boats across the straits to plunder the Spanish countryside."

At that, Hassan gave a quick laugh that generally ended our verbal sparring on any topic. I was glad he did so now for two reasons. First, although I could have continued discussing Spanish and Moorish history for a while longer, there was no point to it. We both knew that Hassan ultimately would win any Muslim history challenges. But, more importantly, this was the first time in a while that Hassan displayed his sunny disposition. He had been irritable and distracted since we left Marrakesh for Casablanca three days earlier. In all the time I had known him, Hassan had never kept his smile under wraps for so long.

As Hassan silently joined me at the ship's rail to take in the magnificent view, my thoughts wandered back to the chance reunion with him six days earlier in Slovakia, his invitation for my wife and me to accompany him to North Africa, and the events of the past few days.

An Unexpected Invitation

The excursion from Slovakia to Morocco with Hassan had been a spur of the moment decision. Beth and I were visiting relatives near the Slovak capital city of Bratislava on the east side of the Danube River across from Vienna. After the former Warsaw Pact countries declared their independence from the Soviet Union in the early 1990s with the subsequent split of Czechoslovakia into the separate countries of the Czech and Slovak Republics, we reunited with our relatives scattered throughout Slovakia. Despite political independence, they were having a rough time. The men died early from a combination of work and worry. Of the eleven families related to us, widows headed the five households that we visited regularly. We scheduled our European visits to coincide with the annual harvest season to give them a hand and to arrange for additional help from neighboring farmers.

Replacing Nazism with Communism had not been kind to people who worked the land for generations in Central and Eastern Europe. Many of our other relatives were either dead or had emigrated to Australia, Canada, or the United States. Among those who stayed, neighbors had stopped trusting and helping each other despite collective farm production quotas issued by central government bureaucrats. But, after following our planting and harvesting suggestions for several years, our family and their neighbors accepted our "Western way" of more efficient farming. We progressed to the point where we could initiate the harvest and leave the family and neighbors to finish while we visited other family members, or roamed the countryside by ourselves for a few days.

On Sunday, September 2, 2001, we decided to visit Piestany, a Slovak spa town. We invited my cousin, Daniela (age twenty-eight, or thereabouts), who had worked in the Chancery Office for Metropolitan Cerveny (the Slovak equivalent of an archbishop) of Nitra to be our guide. Because he had been a frequent visitor to the United States, particularly to Nitra's sister city of Naperville, Illinois, Metropolitan Cerveny's and Daniela's English skills were highly polished, and better by far than my self-taught speaking and writing skills in Slovak. Daniela now was employed in Slovakia's Foreign Office, and she knew her way around both geographically and in dealing with international people and their customs. We realized later how important her skills would be as future events unfolded.

Piestany was about eighty kilometers northeast of Bratislava. The town was not widely known to tourists, which would make it ideal for us when we needed relief from people stress. Roman legions had discovered its mineral springs when they waged war against Germanic and Slavic tribes in the first century AD. During the fifteenth and seventeenth century Islamic invasions of the Hapsburg Empire in Austria and Hungary, Arabs rediscovered Piestany's springs.

While the second Islamic invasion of Europe was halted at the gates of Vienna in 1683 by a coalition army of Europeans, recent archeological studies revealed that the Arabs had free run of the country on the eastern side of the Danube. The foraging Islamic horde probably came across Piestany's mineral springs at that time. Although most of the Arab invaders retreated from Vienna, some of them and their descendants settled peacefully in the neighborhood. Others return to visit Piestany's springs periodically to the present day. Thus, the town retained an Arab enclave for centuries. This is where we unexpectedly met Hassan and his family on Monday, September 3, 2001.

Beth and I first met Hassan in the summer of 1993 while in Russia as members of a multi-national consulting contingent. Our group advised government officials, business and union leaders, and university professors when Russian leaders were newly interested in global market concepts and how to more effectively manage their work and employees. Hassan had been schooled in England. His English was impeccable, and his smile was infectious. I found myself frequently teaming with him to spread the free-market gospel to the former Soviet organizations and governmental agencies that the group leader scheduled for us each day. Beth and I had enjoyed Hassan's company after business hours too. We learned that he worked for a major Kuwaiti oil company and that he had many contacts across Europe and other countries.

At his grandmother's insistence, Hassan brought his family to the Piestany spa at least annually. Although we corresponded with him regularly after our Russian adventure, we had met Hassan only for short visits since then—until he recently re-entered my hidden life. Still, after eight years, his trim features, wide smile, aviator sunglasses, and his richly tailored suits made him stand out in any surroundings. At dinner that night, he informed us that he had business to conduct in Morocco and invited Beth, Daniela, and me to accompany him for several days while his family remained at the Bily Kun Hotel in Piestany. The first hint of uneasiness should have stirred in me then because of my natural survival instincts and my military training to recognize impending danger long before it arrives. But, how could we forego a chance to visit exotic Morocco with an old friend, especially when he insisted on making the last-minute arrangements and paying our expenses?

First Time to Morocco

Very early the following morning, Tuesday, September 4, 2001, we drove from Piestany to Bratislava in Daniela's baby-size car and flew from Bratislava to Seville, Spain. Upon our late morning arrival in Seville, we rented an adult-size car and drove to the ferry dock at Algeciras. (The car rental manager would have had severe chest pains if he knew where we took the car after leaving his parking lot.) The ferry fought a stiff west crosswind, turbulent currents, and a cold rain that made our southbound crossing from Spain to the Moroccan port of Tangier anxious and unpleasant. But, the weather cleared by the time we arrived in Tangier in mid-afternoon.

Hassan insisted on driving south to the old capital city of Fez before we all collapsed into our hotel beds very late that night. The next morning and every morning while we were in Morocco, Hassan identified places of interest, pointed us in the right direction, and then set off separately on his personal business. Aided by the location of towering minarets across the city, my old Army compass, other knowledgeable tourists, and helpful Moroccans amused by our frantic Western sign language, Beth,

Daniela, and I explored the main squares or marketplaces (*medinas*), palaces, and shops (*souks*) of Fez, Marrakesh, Casablanca (the *Casbah*), and the new capital city of Rabat. As avid photographers, Beth and I had plenty of new people and places to capture on film. A camera in Beth's or Daniela's hands also helped them avoid or ignore overzealous Moroccan street merchants. In the evening, we usually met Hassan at the hotel and recounted our adventures of the day with him over dinner in a non-touristy restaurant that he selected.

Hassan's Companions

The only variation to this routine occurred in Marrakesh. As Beth and I walked through the market square, we noticed Hassan talking heatedly to three Arab men dressed in Western suits. I didn't think the group was worth a photo, but, fortunately, Beth and Daniela took several shots of the men capturing them in various backgrounds and sunlight. I was glad that Hassan didn't observe them photographing his group because earlier he had told us that Arabs ask tourists for money to "ransom their souls that are lost in the camera" if they see foreigners photographing them without their permission. By that evening, I had forgotten about the incident, but Beth mentioned it during that night's dinner conversation. Hassan was frowning when we first sat down, and the frown deepened upon his hearing that news. But, after a few moments, he let it pass without comment.

On the way back to our room after dinner, I asked Beth why she had taken the photos in the first place, and why she told Hassan about it. The answer I expected was that she thought it was a good idea at the time, or that she wanted to finish the roll of film.

Surprisingly, she said, "I saw several men in that group before, particularly the one in the straw hat with a red hatband. They made me uncomfortable then, and they still do, especially the Red Hatband Man."

"From where I stood, the sun was in my eyes. I didn't get a good look at anyone. Are you sure?" I questioned.

"I saw them plainly," Daniela interjected. "Beth is right. I'm positive that I saw the men at the hotel in Piestany—especially Mr. Red Hatband."

Too tired to grill each other further on the significance, if any, of the location and apparel of Hassan and his friends, we turned in for the night. As I closed the drapes in our room that overlooked the hotel's patio, I observed Hassan and the same trio of men standing in the dim moonlight talking excitedly to each other. Again, I could not see them plainly, but I noticed that when another person or group came close to them, they stopped talking until the intruders passed out of hearing range.

INCIDENT IN CASABLANCA

After we checked into the Royal Mansour Hotel in Casablanca on the afternoon of Thursday, September 6, 2001, another unusual incident occurred, although we did not fully connect the events in Marrakesh and Casablanca until much later. This time, I was opening the drapes in our room. (Europeans and North Africans tend to close windows and drapes to keep the room as cool as possible—with or without air conditioning. In the absence of air conditioning, Americans typically open windows to get any breeze available regardless of the outside temperature. Here, in the westernized hotel with central air, the windows did not open.) I flung back the drapes to discover that we had a view of the street on the east side of the hotel. A number of men were seated around tables and benches on the stone patio of the restaurant on the opposite corner. Arab women generally were not invited to these men-only social gatherings. Nonetheless, an Arab woman in a black *burka* that covered her from head to foot stood near the restaurant doorway accompanied by a young boy about four years old who I assumed was her son. Abruptly, she glanced at her wristwatch, left the boy unattended, walked out to the curb, and began looking in the direction of oncoming traffic as if she were expecting someone. Meanwhile, the boy began walking among the restaurant patrons seated on the patio. His unsupervised wanderings attracted the men's attention, and, whether planned or not, the boy distracted them from closely watching the woman now pacing back and forth along the curb. By this time, Beth had joined me at the window just as a small black car pulled up and stopped about ten meters beyond where the woman waited.

"What are you watching?" Beth asked as she looked more closely out of the window.

"I don't know yet, but keep your eye on the woman in black over there," I said as I pointed in the woman's direction.

The woman stepped off the curb into the street, walked quickly to the left side of the car, and handed the driver a bulging envelope that had been hidden in the folds of her *burka*. She completely ignored the impact she had on traffic as she stood in the middle of the street.

"I think she's trying to get herself run over," Beth noted.

At that point, my attention turned back to the boy whose antics were engaging the entire group of men on the patio. Beth's focus stayed with the woman and the car, and she saw the driver pass a briefcase to the woman. In doing so, the driver's head moved into the waning sunlight, and Beth exclaimed, "The man in the car is Mr. Red Hatband from Marrakesh. I'm positive!"

After the car drove off quickly and weaved through traffic, the woman collected the boy, who by then had reached the far end of the patio, and they both disappeared around the corner.

Fortunately, Beth had her camera ready and took a few photos before they were out of sight.

We looked at each other and said almost simultaneously, "We just saw an illegal transaction of some kind!"

"Do we contact somebody?" Beth asked. "Should we call the police, the hotel manager, the consulate, anybody?"

"Not unless you want to stay in Casablanca answering questions for a long time," I responded while trying to convince myself one way or another. "But, that was a strange event, wasn't it?"

"What was strange?" Daniela asked as she came into our room to check on our progress in getting settled. "Is it my being unpacked before you two for once?"

We told her about what we had just seen.

"That is strange," Daniela concurred. "Usually, Arab women are very protective of their children. They don't allow their child to run loose that way."

"Unless the boy was not her son," I added hypothetically. "Or, perhaps an Arab woman was not in that *burka*."

On second thought, my hypothesis might not have been that farfetched. Hers or not, the child had done a good job of distracting the restaurant patrons from observing the exchange between the woman and the driver of the car. Later events would fully enlighten us concerning the connection of this incident with those in Marrakesh and the far more dramatic events yet to come.

HEADING BACK NORTH

Several horn blasts from the *Ibn Batouta* brought my mind back to the deck of the ferry and out of my reflections about our Moroccan visit. Hassan stood upright from leaning on the rail.

He patted me on the back, then rested his hand on my left shoulder as he said, "In Piestany, Daniela told me that you and your family were hunting treasure before we met. What kind of treasure are you hoping to find in such a poor country like Slovakia?"

"Before I tell you that, no, I'm not carrying my handgun now," I replied. "You could have asked me instead of patting me down. My pistol is in my luggage."

Hassan laughed heartily and withdrew his arm from around my shoulders. "We cannot escape our history or destiny, can we?"

"History depends on who records and interprets it, and for what purpose," I responded. "Your people and mine probably are fighting the Crusades yet and don't know it. If so, our mutual ignorance, intolerance, and the lack of respect between Christian and Islamic worlds will collide some day soon in my opinion."

"We should save that philosophical and theological debate for another day," Hassan said softly with his head uncharacteristically down. "For now, let us talk of more pleasant things like your treasure hunt," Hassan shifted the conversation back to the hunt as he did vertical push-ups against the rail.

"Okay," I started reluctantly, "do you know about Juraj Janosik?"

"You mean the Slovak bandit from the early eighteenth century?" he replied. "Of course. I could not have visited Piestany all these years without hearing about Slovakia's favorite outlaw."

"You mean Slovakia's favorite patriot," I corrected him.

"Okay, patriot," Hassan replied obligingly, "tell me more about his patriotism if you must."

Despite his wide smile and warm friendship, I suddenly felt that I did not want to tell Hassan more about our family treasure hunt. Not now, not ever. My thought process was a little delayed, but it occurred to me that Daniela had no reason or opportunity to tell Hassan about what had begun as our family's casual interest in Janosik's legendary treasure.

Fortunately, just then, Beth came onto the deck, causing Hassan to turn toward her as she approached, which effectively interrupted our conversation.

Hassan addressed her with his usual Islamic greeting, "*Assalamu alaykum*" (Peace be upon you).

Now that we were seasoned Moroccan travelers, Beth knew the appropriate Moroccan Arabic response of "*Wa 'lekum salam*" (And upon you), which differed slightly from the Middle Eastern version of *Wa alaykum assalam* and surprised Hassan that she had picked up the local *darija* dialect so quickly.

Following these formalities, Hassan continued, "I was about to tell your husband that if you have time, I would like to show you some of Portugal and Spain before you go back home or return to Slovakia. Would you enjoy that?"

Beth's standard answer to any travel invitation is an immediate "yes," regardless of the status of our finances, clean clothes, previous commitments, or travel plans. As I anticipated, she gave Hassan her standard answer.

"Good, it is settled then," Hassan proclaimed. "I will make the arrangements now," he said as he moved quickly toward the gangway to go inside.

"Did I do what I think I just did?" Beth asked me.

"You arrived without time to spare. You not only extended our free vacation, but broke up what was becoming an uncomfortable conversation," I stated thankfully. "The only downside is that I have only one more change of clean clothes with me. But, let's go inside," I said and grabbed her arm as the ferry turned into Algeciras harbor, making the starboard deck uncomfortably windy. Another uncomfortable feeling that I did not share with Beth was my gnawing uneasiness that something big, something unusually big and terrible was set to happen soon.

After we cleared Spanish Customs at dockside, we drove to Seville and checked into our hotel. We had just settled into our room when Hassan knocked on our partly opened door, came in, and carefully closed the door behind him. Although he tried his best to compose himself, he looked uncharacteristically ruffled.

Somewhat regaining his equilibrium, Hassan reported, "I have just phoned my colleagues in Portugal, and I need to be in Lisbon early tomorrow morning. Do you mind if we get an early start?"

"Does that mean before or after breakfast?" Beth chided as she picked up the dining menu from the desk.

"Okay, we can have a quick breakfast, and, if agreeable, we can stop somewhere along the way," Hassan responded almost pleadingly.

"It's your rental car and your *peseta*," I said, encouraged by Beth's saucy rebuttal. "What time do we need to be on the road?"

"We should leave about 0630 at latest," Hassan answered.

"We also should tell Daniela to sleep in the clothes she wants to wear tomorrow. Her twenty-four hour clock usually starts at 0900. At least, she will be modestly dressed when we haul her into the car with the luggage," Beth observed.

Portuguese Detour

Surprisingly, the next morning we were on the road at 0615. As we started out, Daniela was clothed and vertical, if not fully awake. But, she was comatose again before we cleared the hotel's parking lot. The early hour and the arid *Extremadura* countryside did not promote conversation. The time and distance went by with each of us in our private cocoon of sleep, meditation, or road hypnosis. Eventually, the increasing traffic as we approached Lisbon restored our normal heartbeat, respiration rates, and survival instincts. It was almost midday in Lisbon, Tuesday, September 11, 2001, and about 5:00 a.m. on the East Coast of the United States. The "something terrible" I had premonitions about earlier had not yet occurred.

While Hassan conducted his business in Lisbon, Beth, Daniela, and I thought we would lounge around the hotel, take a leisurely stroll through the nearby upscale shops, then amble down to the magnificent harbor that were all within easy walking distance. But, we were out of luck on our plans for a leisurely day. Before he departed, Hassan gave us instructions and tickets to take a bus tour to Cascais. ("*Cash-kai-ish*" is the closest my Portuguese will get me to the correct pronunciation of the name of this beautiful, but expensive, resort town on Portugal's Atlantic coast.) Within two hours, we had exhausted our budget and all the touristy things we wanted to do there. Beth spotted a brochure in a travel shop about the shrine at Fatima. Fatima is located near the town of Vila Nova de Ourem, and, on our map, it was only about three centimeters north of our current location. We didn't know what that translated to in actual kilometers, but we decided to go anyway. With Daniela's European driver's license and international connections in the form of the correct currency, we rented a car and were on our way north to the shrine within a few minutes.

Fatima on the Fateful Day

Fatima is the location of a little grotto in which the Virgin Mary is believed by faithful Catholics to have appeared to three Portuguese children (Lucia, Francisco, and Jacinta) several times in 1917. During the apparitions, the Virgin Mary instructed the children to pray the rosary for world peace and to inform others of her request. Now, a stunning white cathedral with gold trim, a paved square, and religious shops replaced the quiet wooded grotto. But, the devotion of the faithful still prevailed.

A pathway was painted on the tarmac surface of the square for those who wished to approach the holy shrine on their knees. I estimated the pathway to be almost a kilometer long. Had we known that at about this same time in New York and Washington, D.C., hijacked planes were crashing into the World Trade Center and the Pentagon, we would have been on our knees too instead of merely reciting a few short prayers while standing comfortably in the shade. When we went to the outdoor rack to light a candle for our personal petitions, so many other candles were aflame that the inferno forced many pilgrims to back away. Ironically, the flames and smoke engulfing the stricken World Trade Center and the Pentagon were causing occupants and rescuers there to similarly flee from danger.

After the obligatory purchases at the gift shop, we headed back to rejoin Hassan in Lisbon, still unaware that terrorists had struck a devastating blow to our country. We arrived at the hotel about 1700, went to our rooms, and changed clothes for dinner. Hassan was nowhere in sight, but we assumed that he would arrive as usual to select a restaurant for the evening. After almost an hour of aimless conversation in our room, we decided to find some food for ourselves and left a note to inform Hassan of our intended destination.

The television set in the hotel lobby was tuned to a Portuguese news station. The volume was barely audible (louder Portuguese would not have helped us anyway), but the scene of a large plane hurling into a tall building was shown several times. The idea that we were viewing film footage of actual events in New York was so incomprehensible that we concluded the news program was reporting on some action movie that was being shown locally. Or, at worst, it was an accident similar to the B-25 bomber that crashed into the Empire State Building on July 28, 1945, that resulted in fourteen deaths and comparatively little structural damage. The B-25 crash was bad enough, but that was not an unimaginable terrorist attack on our country. The attack on the second tower and the collapse of both buildings were not yet being shown. We proceeded on our way to dinner without being traumatized by the visual news that we would see later.

We found a restaurant close to the hotel where our collective pointing at various items on the menu produced favorable results. After two hours, we decided that Hassan was not coming. We kept putting paper money and coins on the table until the proprietor was satisfied that we had paid our bill. Then, we walked back to the hotel.

Disaster at Home

The TV set in the hotel lobby was still showing scenes of planes crashing, with added footage of buildings falling, dirt and debris clouds billowing everywhere, people running, and emergency crews and police trying to restore order. *This couldn't be real, could it? Could this be the terrible event that had been gnawing at me for the past several days?* We sprinted to an unoccupied elevator, hurriedly pushed the button for our floor, and then ran down the hallway to our room. After bursting through the door almost before it was unlocked, we kept punching numbers on the TV remote control until we found an English news channel. Then, like millions of others across the world, we learned the full impact of the terrorist attacks on the World Trade Center, the Pentagon, and the crash of the hijacked plane in Pennsylvania. We sat and watched the scenes replay hour after hour without speaking to each other. We felt no fear, no panic. Strangely, our only emotion was disbelief. Shakespeare had it right in his play *The Tempest* when his character Ariel said, "Hell is empty, and all the devils are here."[1]

The first hint of dawn was breaking on Wednesday, September 12, when we heard a hesitant knock on the door. It was Hassan. His face told us that he knew as much as we did, if not more, about the events revealed on the TV screen the night before.

He said rather calmly for the occasion, "If the United States declares war, Lisbon is the best place for you to be. If you remember, Portugal was a neutral country during World War II. Surely, you will be able to fly home from here. I will help you."

After another day of inactivity and debilitated by the scenes of death and destruction constantly being replayed on the TV screen, our brains had no room for logic. All I could think of was the 1942 movie classic in which the principal characters struggled to acquire letters of transit to flee from Casablanca to neutral Lisbon where they could escape the Nazi occupation. With that in mind, I accepted Hassan's offer to help us return to the States from Lisbon. Not knowing what other action to take because all air traffic to the States was grounded, we went to bed. There was no immediate escape to home and safety from Lisbon or anywhere else.

Finding Our Way Back

The next morning, Thursday, September 13, we confirmed that air traffic over the U.S. gradually would resume. Planes in the air had been instructed to land at the nearest airports immediately after the attacks. Beth and I were scheduled to fly back to Chicago from Slovakia on Saturday, September 15. But, we quickly ruled out flying eastward to Bratislava from Lisbon, which would put us further away from our U.S. home. When we did not know whom the enemy was or how to defend ourselves, any action we took to increase the distance from home did not appear logical. At that point, we agreed with Hassan that Lisbon was the best place for us to wait for further developments. They were not long in coming.

Not surprisingly, Hassan initiated them. He did not leave a message and did not show up for breakfast or any other activity on Wednesday and most of Thursday. We could barely call ourselves active as we sat glued to the TV set in our room hoping for confirmation that planes were flying and that international travel was safe again. Just before dinner on Thursday, we heard Hassan open the door to his adjoining room, and, shortly after, he knocked on our door. He looked extremely fatigued and nervous—totally unlike the Hassan we knew.

During dinner at the hotel that night, he advised that we might have a better chance to fly back to the States from Madrid rather than Lisbon. He explained that because U.S. air traffic had been grounded wherever it was at the time, planes and crews were scattered all over the globe. The airlines would need time to re-orient U.S. crews and planes before normal flights could resume. However, if we were booked on a major European airline with planes and crews ready for direct flights to Chicago, we should be able to get home on the earliest available flight. Further, Hassan reasoned that Lisbon was too small to have available planes and U.S. flight priority. He said the best place for us now was the Madrid airport. This large city had direct flights to Chicago's O'Hare International Airport. Once again, we put ourselves in Hassan's hands. We threw our luggage into the rental car and drove to Madrid.

Early Saturday morning, September 15, after many hugs and words of comfort, we sent Daniela off on a flight to Bratislava, and hoped that she would be safe. Now, we needed to arrange our flight to Chicago. This was strictly business. We had no time for any emotion other than an increased determination to survive. If Beth felt fear, she did not show it.

Like everyone else in the Madrid airport, we pushed and pulled ourselves into a line we believed led to our destination. After two hours, we recognized that we were in the wrong line. We corrected our error by pulling and pushing toward another line. An irate American man ahead of us advised that we had cut into the middle of a line in which he had been waiting for several hours. We explained that we had much in common, but he became unruly. As his verbal abuse grew louder, I saw Hassan motion to the *Policia de Securitas* officers, who quickly encircled the man and led him away. We never saw him again. Moving a few centimeters at a time, we finally reached the luggage inspection station. Despite all our time in line, I had not thought of a good explanation for having a handgun in my luggage.

Unexpected Help

But first, the inspectors had to deal with Beth's suitcase. On this trip, she had far too much time for shopping. Like an inflatable raft, the contents of her suitcase opened and expanded exponentially as soon as the *Policia de Securitas* unlocked her case. I gave the three officers credit for trying diligently to discover contraband in that collection of clothes, books, itineraries, gifts, and other unidentifiable items. After their search, the officers tried with equal diligence to repack the contents and to close Beth's case. Eventually, they succeeded with everyone involved perspiring profusely, and everyone in line behind us applauding enthusiastically.

Now it was my turn. I handed the *Securitas* officer my passport, and turned to open my luggage. The officer looked at me, glanced at Hassan who was standing a short distance away, motioned to me not to open my case, handed back my passport, and signaled me to follow Beth to the ticket counter. I recalled that Hassan had offered to help us, but I didn't expect him to have that kind of influence. The officers confiscated pocket knives, razors, and scissors from other passengers while I skipped through Madrid security with a loaded handgun because of a nod to the *Policia de Securitas* from my Kuwaiti friend. Some day, I would need an explanation from Hassan, but not today. I only wanted to get on flight 7463 to O'Hare. Besides, I still needed to invent a witty response if U.S. Customs officers in Chicago inspected my luggage without Hassan being there to intervene.

To distract myself from these thoughts when we settled into our seats on the plane, I took out a booklet I had bought at the Fatima bookstore.

It was a treatise on individual choices to help form a better world. More likely now, the world would experience collective fear, anger, revenge, and war through a Christian crusade, an Islamic *jihad*, or both in response to the terrorist attacks. A better world would have to wait.

My theological musing was interrupted when Beth opened her eyes, looked at me, and said firmly, "No more traveling to Europe until the world is safe again, buster."

Although I did not answer her, my prior thoughts began to coalesce. Sooner or later, we needed to return to Slovakia to ensure the safety of our European family. I needed to learn more about Hassan's apparent influence with officials outside his country and his interest in our family's treasure hunt. *More importantly, what did he know about the attacks, and where and when would the unknown enemy strike again?*

RETURN TO A CHANGED HOMELAND

But now, we had to deal with more immediate matters. The airline crew was distributing U.S. Customs forms for re-entry into the States. Beth was busy tallying her European purchases. I concentrated exclusively on scripting an explanation for the handgun in my luggage because a U.S.-made .44-caliber Magnum is difficult to hide. No explanation surfaced. The plane "vectored for a landing" as the pilot described it, and then we were on the ground. I was still in a cranial coma regarding firearms.

Nobody talked as we and the other passengers walked down the long hallway toward the U.S. Customs stations and the luggage carousels. Everyone looked straight ahead. Then, we turned a corner, and the customs booths came into view. Soon, everyone was talking. Everyone was cheering. It was great to see uniformed U.S. Customs officers! For the first time in my travels, I believed that the officers truly were glad to see us too. But, life in the States was different now. Changes had occurred in the three weeks we had been away. A new seriousness and determination had enveloped both passengers and customs officers as the officers inspected and stamped passports and travel forms.

Security officers and dogs met passengers at the luggage carousels. They moved in and out of the crowd with precision and purpose. At that time, passengers didn't seem to mind the increased security activity. One dog kept leading his handler back to me, or vice versa. The officer extended the leash and let the dog sniff. *What does a handgun smell like to a dog?* I thought. My body odor should cover up the scent because I had been standing in endless lines since early morning. Then, I was sandwiched into a middle seat on a crowded plane for more than eight hours.

Finally, our luggage appeared on the carousel. I retrieved our cases while Beth guarded our carry-on bags. Nobody asked me to open our luggage for inspection. The security officers and dogs were at the other end of the hall. We loaded our belongings onto a cart and vectored for the nearest exit. We had escaped! We were in Chicago! We would be home safely in a short time! *Was this the end of the story?* As we were to discover, our arrival home was an interlude before we encountered terrorists again and a more deadly treasure hunt commenced. The hunt would require survival skills that I had learned in the U.S. Army and over a lifetime in other roles. *Would that experience be enough?* I would find out shortly.

At the closest point of the Straits of Gibraltar, only nine miles separates Muslim North Africa from Christian Europe. As I just related, Muslims and Christians were interacting in everyday activities up to the time of the attacks without checking each other's religious credentials or family history. *Would the attacks now create a larger gulf between Muslim and Christian nations with no solid land bridge between us? Or would people see themselves as citizens of a larger world, and maintain boundaries of reason and tolerance despite the efforts of terrorist predators and purveyors of hate?*

Chapter Notes

1. "The Tempest Act I Scene II," *William Shakespeare The Complete Works* (New York: Barnes & Noble Books, 1994), p. 1138. By permission of Barnes & Noble.

CHAPTER 2

JOE LEGION AND PURPLE

Early Days

To understand the implications of September 11, 2001, and its aftermath for my family and me, I first need to recount the almost inconceivable convergence of people and events that came together over time. Some of the reasons for this convergence go back only a short time. Others go back further, but not quite back as far as the pre-Cenozoic era over 65 million years ago when a few stray dinosaurs still roamed the earth as my grandkids reckon my lifespan to be, but close. My personal war against terrorists started on July 14, 2001, although I did not understand it in those terms then. In any event, I am convinced that none of the people I met or the events that occurred prior to or after September 11, 2001, happened by chance or without a purpose—despite my lack of recognition or comprehension of the purpose at the time.

I had graduated from college in the early 1960s. Similar to many other graduates, I looked for professional work. I had been a decent student and had no problem obtaining interviews with recognized companies. But, my Selective Service classification was 1A. Employers did not hire draft bait, particularly at the beginning of the Vietnam buildup under the Kennedy and Johnson presidencies. I took destiny into my hands and enlisted in the Army as had my older brother Joe three years earlier. That's where our sibling similarity began and ended. He trained to be a Special Forces Advisor in Southeast Asia with whatever went with that role. I was satisfied with a less strenuous career. I intended to serve my military time faithfully and return to civilian life in one piece at the end of my enlistment.

I completed my basic and advanced training and reported to my first duty station at a headquarters unit "across the wide Missouri." One day, as I was standing in line at the base post office with my buddies, the sergeant major walked by, called me over to him, and instructed me to report to his office after I finished sending my letters. The old military standard that if anybody over the rank of master sergeant knows you by sight or name you are in big trouble instantly occurred to me. I put my fate in the hands of St. Jude (the Christian patron saint of hopeless cases), gave my letters to one of my buddies to mail for me, and headed for the Western Sector Command headquarters building on the double.

The Walk of Despair

When I arrived at the sergeant major's office, the door was open, and I saw three platoon sergeants seated in there talking with him. I stepped back out of their line of sight, adjusted my gig line (aligned my shirt, pants, and belt buckle), stepped forward to be seen, and knocked. The sergeant major instructed me to enter. He then asked the three sergeants to wait while he escorted me down the hall to the commanding officer's suite. Many years later, my granddaughter would coin a phrase that described that walk precisely. When she didn't do well in a swimming meet or other activity, she called the walk to the car following the event her "walk of despair."

As the sergeant major and I walked silently toward officer country, I mentally scrolled through my recent military sins to decide whether to request a court martial or non-judicial punishment. Within twenty paces, I decided that I was destined for the stockade; so any plea-bargaining didn't really matter. As far as the Uniform Code of Military Justice was concerned, I was a classic case of *"de bien et de mal."* I would put myself in the hands of the colonel "for good or evil." I had no other options.

Upon our arrival, Colonel Andrews, the commanding officer (CO), who was an Airborne Ranger in spades, instructed us to enter and to close the door. (I thought it was the stockade for sure by this time.)

He gave us an "At Ease," pointed to his guest chairs, and came around his desk to sit with the sergeant major and me. Things appeared promising until the CO looked at me sternly and said, "I have your latest performance report from your platoon sergeant."

I quickly interpreted that to mean an immediate transfer from the stockade to the firing squad. A lame "Yes, sir" came into my head and exited my mouth in the same instant without much thought in between. In my mental rambling, I barely heard the CO tick off some positive comments and state something about an opportunity to train for a different kind of role. At that point, any alternative to imprisonment or death appeared good to me. I thanked the CO for his confidence in me and moved into position to stand up and leave.

The CO observed my movements and said, "Not so fast, soldier. The operative phrase here is 'to qualify.' Your first test is to report to my quarters at 2015 and bring your 201 personnel file with you. Dismissed."

The sergeant major and I got up and left. As we retraced our route through officer country, the sergeant major said nothing, but I noticed a wry smile on his face as we arrived back at his office. The three platoon sergeants were still waiting. He instructed me to be seated and launched into a rambling conversation with the three sergeants that had nothing to do with my new role or me. It was now 1900, and most of the command staff were long gone.

Abruptly at 1930, the sergeant major ended his conversation, dismissed the three sergeants, turned toward me, and said, "You better move out quickly too. You don't have much time to get your personnel records and report to the CO's quarters. Any questions?"

"No, Sergeant," I responded. "I'm on it," I said confidently although I was about as "on it" as riding a Brahma bull.

Getting My Records

By then, I had internalized that part of the CO's "test" was to determine how well I would respond under pressure to conflicting demands and without official help. The first thing I needed to do was get my 201 personnel file. The Military Police (MP) station was down the hall from Personnel, so I couldn't simply break into Personnel's file cabinets and walk out with my records past the MPs—*or could I?* As I stood in the hallway contemplating my next move, an MP and one of the personnel specialists who had drawn guard duty that night entered the headquarters building.

I shouted down the hall to the specialist, "Hey Slick, I just received a TDY assignment from the CO. I need a travel advance *pronto* and beneficiary change forms to go into my file tonight."

"Slick" was short for "Slick Sleeve" because he had trouble retaining stripes of any kind for long. (The term "slicks" later described the helicopters without door guns used in Vietnam to haul supplies and the wounded. But, the term didn't have that definition yet.) Slick was a friend, and I needed help from any friend I could find. Everybody knew that temporary duty (TDY) assignments at this post involved travel, and, generally, the assignments were issued without much prior notice. So,

I was not asking for anything out of Slick's domain, and nothing that required MP involvement. Slick told his MP partner that he would be down the hall in Personnel with me for a few minutes.

While I kept Slick busy in an adjoining room hunting for beneficiary forms and preparing a travel voucher, I "borrowed" my file from the open drawer and put it into a mail pouch addressed to the Subsector Command Office in an adjoining building. Because of the late hour, Slick had to personally deliver my travel voucher to the finance officer on the floor above to receive cash. In Slick's absence, I locked the file drawer with the keys he had left on his desk, and then hid the keys under a pile of papers on the personnel sergeant's desk. Anything on or near the sergeant's desk was off limits to Slick, so I knew he would not look for his keys there.

When Slick returned with my travel money, I thanked him profusely, and told him I would deliver the Subsector Command pouch as a return favor. When he tried to put my revised beneficiary forms in my file, he became aware that he had misplaced his keys (not thinking that I had misplaced them for him). By that time, the MP was hollering down the hallway for Slick to start guard duty. He had no choice but to deal with his missing keys later. I walked out of the building with Slick, the MP, and my file. *Not bad for dealing with a last-minute situation*, I complimented myself. The CO should be pleased with my resourcefulness if not my theft of government property, fraud, deception, and breach of security. Those skills would be valuable later, if not immediately.

I showered, changed my uniform, grabbed my file, and was on the CO's front porch precisely at 2015 as ordered. His wife answered my ring, and led me to the colonel's study. The CO was still in uniform. I gathered that a serious conversation was ahead of me. He nodded in the direction of the file in my hand as if he had no doubt that I would show up with it (so much for my big impression), pointed me to a chair, and moved his desk chair closer to me.

Very Bad News

Colonel Andrews started the conversation by repeating that he, other officers, and the sergeants in the command observed that I had demonstrated some unique skills (probably the same list of unlawful skills I mentioned above), which, again, he did not enumerate. He said that these skills along with others that I could be taught would help me qualify for the new role he had in mind for me. If I agreed to the training program but quit before I completed it, he would bust me back to a private (at least Slick would have a companion at the bottom of the military food chain), and otherwise make life miserable for me. If I finished the training program, I would perform my usual duties in the command, and, initially, I would receive other assignments directly from him. My duty station would always remain in the U.S., and any foreign travel would not qualify as foreign service. As expected, I was not to inform anyone concerning this conversation, the existence and nature of any later conversations, assignments, missions, or people involved in them under penalty of court martial, or a fatal accident. I already had a "Top Secret" security clearance in process, so that requirement wasn't a problem. *So far, so good,* I thought. In a few sentences, the CO had taken away opportunities for foreign service credit, hazardous duty pay, official performance recognition, and free time to study or sleep. He had replaced them with a greater likelihood of reduction in rank, hard training, life imprisonment in a military facility, or death. The bonus features of this new role kept piling up. *How could I ever gripe about dull military service under these conditions?*

But, there was more. I would have another identity and a ghost personnel file. In case of an emergency, the CO would be my only contact—maybe. Because the CO was scheduled to transfer to another post soon, he expected me to be ready for assignments before then, and an unidentified "source" would be my new contact. Otherwise, I would be on my own, and I would be disavowed if any operation failed—my fault or not—if I was still alive to worry about such minor details.

I would never be held hostage under those conditions. Tortured and killed, yes, but not held hostage. No written record of the assignments would be made or retained. To the rest of the world, what I did never really happened. My first assignments would test my abilities in communications, diversion, deception, covering, or delaying operations. If I performed well on my initial assignments, I would be given "hotter" ones. Once involved in this kind of work, the CO asserted, I may be asked to continue in a similar role beyond my active military service— not that I was expected to survive long enough to reach that decision point. The CO continued that I would commence training with the three platoon sergeants in the morning. I would be sent elsewhere as needed for specialized training.

I had the highest respect for the three sergeants. They were former Philippine Scouts who survived the sixty-mile Bataan death march in

World War II. Of the approximately 10,000 U.S. and Philippine prisoners who started the march, they were three of only about 3,000 who survived. (A measure of military justice was served when Japanese General Masaharu Homma was executed on April 3, 1946 for ordering the march.) These three sergeants enlisted in the U.S. Army after their release and rehabilitation from their ordeal in Japanese prison camps. Although the physical conditioning and survival skills they would teach me would be helpful, the most important lessons I would learn were to be mentally prepared, to study and understand as much about my opponents as possible, and to think and react quickly under adverse conditions.

I was jolted back to the present when the CO cleared his throat and said sternly, "Finally, if you agree to these conditions and complete the training, you will have an alter ego, another identity." With that, the CO leaned forward in his chair and asked, "Well, what is your answer, soldier?"

My initial reaction was to stall a decision until my enlistment period expired. Instead, I heard myself reply, "Anything you think appropriate, sir. You know the job better than I do."

"That's a good answer, soldier. In that case, your new name for these purposes will be Joe Legion."

I was taken totally by surprise. After missing several heartbeats, I recovered sufficiently to respond, "I don't understand, sir. My older brother is a lieutenant who does classified work for the Army. That is the name he uses in his work."

"Yes, I know, soldier. I have some very bad news for you. Your brother died bravely a few days ago. Now, we need you as his replacement, and, initially, using his working identity."

"But, that can't be, sir. My brother is a career soldier. By comparison, I just want to put in my time and return to civilian life. Where is he? Do I have your permission to attend his funeral? How did he . . . die? How do you know I can be as good a soldier as he is, especially for the role you described?"

My questions kept coming. Colonel Andrews let me ramble until I was exhausted. I didn't understand how I could replace my brother who was an ace at everything he did. I couldn't comprehend that he was no longer invincible—a mere mortal, and now, not even that.

"Soldier, you may not believe me now, but you are good enough," the colonel interjected to end my conversation with myself. We will make you good enough to take your brother's place. In fact, your brother recommended you as his replacement if anything unfortunate happened to him."

"But, how do you really know that I am good enough for this kind of work, sir?" I asked the colonel and myself for the seventy-fifth time in the last minute and a half.

"I know because in all your stress and confusion in learning about your brother you never stopped thinking and you never lost control of yourself. We can teach you all the other things that you need to know, but we cannot teach you how to think, how to keep going, how to fight back, and how to stay alive. When I commanded your brother's unit, he told me that you don't quit. Nonetheless, he warned me that in a tough situation, you have, as he said, 'unconventional ways of doing business.' We will find out shortly. That is all for now, soldier. You are dismissed."

"Once again, sir, I request permission to attend my brother's funeral."

"That is not possible, soldier. Your training starts tomorrow. You will find that we can be unconventional too."

"Then, I'd like to be by myself for a while if I can."

"Certainly, but remember, your training starts at 0600 tomorrow morning. The beginning may startle you a little bit, but don't let it bother you. We need to do it that way. And, I am truly sorry about your brother. He was a good soldier. I was proud to serve with him."

"Good night, sir."

"Good night, soldier."

SEARCHING FOR ANSWERS

As I left the colonel's house, more questions began to fog my thinking. My brother was stocky, with bushy dark hair and dark eyes. By comparison, I was a string bean with light brown hair and goofy green eyes. *How could I fit the description of Joe Legion who my brother's colleagues or opponents already knew? Or, didn't my physical appearance matter? Why would it not matter to the contacts my brother had met personally?* They would see the difference immediately. My brother and I shared some similar mannerisms, but we weren't identical in our thoughts, actions, mental agility, and physical strength. He was five years older. He had all his marbles and most of mine. *Would that matter?* By now, I realized that my brain had taken me hostage with all these questions, but I still couldn't stop.

As I approached the Post Chapel, more serious thoughts crossed my mind. Although no one was around at that time of night, I went in, sat in the back pew, and let my mind wander as I thought about my brother.

The first thought that came to me was how he had adopted the name "Joe Legion." Joe was his first name, of course. But, he took the name "Legion" from St. Luke's account in the New Testament about Jesus expelling demons from a man in Gerasa. When Jesus asked the man his name, the man replied "Legion" because he had so many devils in him. I guess that was the way Joe felt about intelligence work with the Army at the time. I already had enough devils in my life. I wasn't searching for more to have easy access to my feeble aspirations for immortality. In my search for the slightest confirmation of a correct decision about my new role, I picked up a Bible in the pew. I didn't have a particular passage in mind. As I flipped through the pages, they stopped turning in the Book of Jeremiah. There, I read:

> "What I have built, I am tearing down; what I have planted, I am uprooting; even the whole land. And do you seek great things for yourself? Seek them not! I am bringing evil upon all mankind, says the Lord, but your life I will leave you as booty, wherever you may go." (Jer. 45:4-5)[1]

That was a partial answer I supposed. Somehow, the world order was changing. I could sense that despite my young age and lack of life experience. I should not expect fame and fortune. That was fair enough if my life was spared. I flipped pages again. When I stopped, I was still in Jeremiah. This time, I read:

> "Thus says the Lord . . . write all the words I have spoken to you in a book . . . Behold, I will deliver you from the far-off land . . . for I am with you . . . to deliver you . . . I will chastise you as you deserve, I will not let you go unpunished . . . Your pain is without relief . . . Yet all who devour you shall be devoured . . . All who plunder you shall be plundered, all who pillage you I will hand over to pillage . . . 'The outcast' they have called you, 'with no avenger.' The anger of the Lord will not abate until he has done and fulfilled what he has determined in his heart . . . When the time comes, you will fully understand." (Jer. 30:2-24)[2]

Those were strong words for me to accept. Until now, I had been casual about practicing my religion, as were many of my friends. I didn't see myself regaled in armor as God's avenger, or Him as my Special Protector. I had no strong feelings about any causes or a zealous need to right every wrong that I encountered, especially if it involved going out of my way to help someone. I had been truthful to the colonel. Until now, all I wanted to do was to finish my enlistment and return to civilian life. Maybe it was the stress of learning about my brother's death. Maybe it was the temporary thrill of being singled out for a different kind of military role. Maybe it was part of growing up. Maybe it was just plain hubris! But, at that moment, I accepted my brother's former role as Joe Legion—whatever that role meant and wherever that role would take me.

Being the second Joe Legion would continue to affect my life in unexpected ways long after my active military service ended, and long after my complete personnel file "disappeared" from Army archives. I didn't know it then, but Joe Legion's rebirth would introduce me to a variety of international characters and events over the years. Later in life, I also learned that sometimes family, friends, and colleagues suffered, or got left behind in order for me to complete an assignment. The most frustrating times were when partners were left behind, and I never knew what the real mission was or if I had succeeded in my part of it. I might have answered the CO differently if I had known that events leading up to and after September 11, 2001, were to be a part of my Joe Legion legacy.

In Jeremiah's words, my purpose was to help others through completing my assignments and surviving so that I could write about my experiences both for my personal redemption and understanding, and to instruct others. But, a very long time would pass before I picked up the Bible again and renewed my Christian faith, introduced myself to the teachings of the Koran, and explored the principles of Buddhism and Hinduism. It would be longer still before I picked up a pen to write my observations of the events of that night and my life thereafter. When I finally did, I had been discharged from active military duty for many years. I had watched my family grow, and I had observed, as many other people did, unsettling changes in the United States and in many other countries around the globe.

My Decision

As I got up from the pew and put the Bible on a shelf, I realized that my first assignment was to get my military body into my military bed to prepare for the beginning of training the next morning. As I stood in the chapel aisle, I opened the mail pouch and pulled out my file. A handwritten note from Slick that I had not seen earlier fell out of my file. It read, "This afternoon, the CO told the personnel sergeant and me to give you your personnel file. If you had asked me, I could have saved you a lot of time and energy. But, you demonstrated a nice array of diversionary skills. Don't forget to return your file to me tomorrow and the $250 travel advance to Lt. Milton. Good luck in your training, Hotshot."

"Thanks, Slick," I said half aloud. "My new career has started with several breaches of security already. I wonder how many other people know about this."

I couldn't do much about it now. I was committed to the rebirth of Joe Legion.

Tuning Up

As usual, at 0500 the next morning, the command formed ranks in the street in front of the headquarters building. I was usually straight and typically didn't receive negative comments about my appearance and military bearing. The morning's events were unexpected despite the colonel's warning to me the previous night. Colonel Andrews inspected the troops personally that day. When he came to me, he did not like anything about me. My fatigues were not starched enough, I needed a haircut, my shave was not close enough, my boots and brass were not polished enough, and on and on. He was not going to tolerate such sloppiness in his command. Before he moved on to the next man, he summoned the three platoon sergeants to finish the inspection of my body and equipment because he could not bear to look at me.

By that time, I had caught on to his act, but the fat lady had not sung yet. The three platoon sergeants picked up the colonel's theme. They had me knock out several series of push-ups as an example to any other trooper who might be inclined to disgrace the uniform and shame his fellow soldiers. This exercise allowed the colonel to finish inspecting the remainder of the command and return to me for an encore. His verbal harassment recommenced to the consternation of my buddies whose personal hygiene and appearance generally were a notch or two below mine. The colonel's tirade continued. In a voice loud enough to echo into the mountains and canyons beyond the parade ground, he announced that the three sergeants would take me under their wing immediately and make a soldier out of me because obviously basic and advanced training had not been sufficient to convert me from a sloppy civilian into a sharp soldier.

That was the opening salvo of my training program. It was a clever ruse because otherwise everyone would be curious as to why I was receiving different treatment. The colonel took care of that loophole by announcing that anyone who interacted with me except in the line of duty would be subject to disciplinary action. His warning ensured that even the most fanatically curious soldiers and headquarters civilians would keep their distance.

My solo training started in the exercise area at 0530, a half hour earlier than the colonel had announced—and without breakfast. The sergeants didn't need much daylight to watch or hear me do endless push-ups and other strength-building exercises. As the longer daylight hours of summer approached, the training became more rigorous, if not enjoyable. The sergeants displayed their sense of humor by putting a scorpion on my back to ensure that my low crawl was both fast and fluid. As my skills improved, "Scooter" the scorpion seemed to enjoy the rides, and he stayed in one place in the middle of my back. Camouflaging me with poison ivy was another one of the sergeants' delights. Booby-trapping me with live grenades sent them into ecstasy for hours while I tried to extract myself without propelling my body into the hereafter.

Evening skull sessions were devoted to military strategy, tactics, philosophy, and mental preparation. Knowing when not to act was as important as knowing when to act with audacity and skill. Despite all that the sergeants had endured at Bataan, we studied and discussed the codes of the *Bushido* warrior and the *samurai*. The writings of the sixteenth century Zen master Kenshin Uyesugi appeared particularly applicable to our task and were not very different from the words of Jeremiah:

> "Those who cling to life die, and those who defy death live. The essential thing is the mind. Look into this mind and firmly take hold of it, and you will understand that there is something in you which is above birth-and-death and which is neither drowned in water nor burned by fire . . . Those who are reluctant to give up their lives and embrace death are not true warriors."[3]

In addition to military metaphysics and philosophy, we discussed and practiced more mundane but necessary skills of ambush, taking out sentries, hand-to-hand fighting, and improvisation—over and over. I began to be jealous of snipers who could simply walk away from danger after hitting a target 700 to 750 yards out. But, gradually, ever so gradually, I began to execute the techniques properly. It was noticeable in less laughter from the sergeants and fewer rips in my fatigue pants.

After my body was satisfactorily "conditioned" (bruised), we moved to the rifle and pistol ranges. I spent most of my time on the pistol range.

My weapon was not a standard military issue .45-caliber automatic, but a short-barreled .22-caliber revolver. I knew what that meant—more "close contact" training—within an arm's length of my opponent. In several of our evening sessions, we talked about one shot, one kill, and quick escape. I practiced one shot, one kill, and quick escape. I never enjoyed it, or felt expert at it, but I learned it as a survival skill.

First, Master the Self, Then Master the Weapons

Eventually, the time arrived for archery training. One would think that nearly everyone could master this ancient weapon with relatively little instruction and practice. That would not be my experience with the sergeants. I didn't touch a bow for the first week. Again, the sergeants reverted to the *samurai* techniques of their former Japanese captors. The wise Zen masters had identified eight critical steps to achieve mastery of the bow. These included positioning of the feet and legs for alignment with the trunk of the body, and deep abdominal breathing exercises to keep the upper body undisturbed and relaxed. Only then was I allowed to learn the proper way to nock an arrow, raise the bow skyward to draw the bowstring, and pull the string while lowering the bow back to eye level. Once that was accomplished, the next secret was to attain a state of *zashin* before and after release of the arrow, and to listen to the harmony of the bow and string to determine if I had made an accurate shot without looking. If the shot were executed correctly, my shooting hand would release the arrow without effort or my conscious movement. The target was not my real enemy, but mastery over my own ego-consciousness. In making the shot, I would have to give up my "self."

A martial arts master described this approach much better than I can:

> "Success in *kyudo* (the Way of the Bow) does not mean hitting the target . . . Success, if that is the correct word, is firing of the bow while being in the desired frame of mind. This state is one in which the archer is not driven by the wish to succeed. His mind should be empty of intention and filled with pure awareness of the present moment."[4]

The archery training was longer and more difficult than I expected. I was not simply building arm strength. I was developing the frame of mind for the arrow to "release itself" without my mind interfering with its accurate flight. To achieve "oneness" in my first week of shooting would have required a target the size of a battleship. With additional practice over the next few weeks, I shrank the target to the size of a tank. Several weeks later, I was hitting a regulation target consistently—with or without wind—from greater distances. Then, one morning, I was introduced to a Cherokee Indian who fitted a custom-made bow and arrows to my body and arm specifications. The hand-tooled arrows cost $8 apiece, and I was instructed not to attempt to split my first arrow with a second one, as Robin Hood did. At that stage of my training, there was little danger of my putting two consecutive shots in the same place, either by "oneness" or sheer luck.

In late summer, Colonel Andrews' replacement arrived. I had completed the initial stage of my training on time. So, I expected to have contact with Colonel Redmond, the new CO. But, it didn't happen. *Who would give me my assignments, or was my exercise now terminated with the change in commanding officers?* Colonel Redmond inspected the troops the day he officially took command. I looked sharp, but I presented a rifle to him that the armorer had given me moments before we formed ranks. The new CO wouldn't see sunlight through that dirty barrel on the equinox. But, to my relief, he moved on to the next soldier.

ALICE INTRODUCES HERSELF

Several days later, we all learned that the new CO brought a new civilian secretary on board named Alice. The guys inspected the new secretary. She was a full-blooded Navajo. We guessed she was in her mid-twenties. The guys declared Alice Bright Feather attractive but unassailable and incorruptible, and they stayed away. One evening, as I entered the headquarters building to pick up my gear for that night's training session, Alice was coming out. She deftly handed me a small envelope, and continued on her way without speaking. I put the envelope inside my shirt to read later. In my quarters that night, I finally had a chance to open the envelope and read her note—actually a short rhyme:

> "Earth and sky both know me, that's all I need of fame; 'Scout' is what you call me, Alice is my name."

Through Alice, my orders and assignments began coming from PURPLE, an unknown person or organization. Obviously, PURPLE had to be someone, a representative of someone, or a group of "someones" who had knowledge and authority. I wanted to know, but I knew better than to ask Alice directly. She was far too committed to the "cause" to disclose anything like that to me. As my Scout, Alice made arrangements for my travel, identification, proper attire—including weapons if required, briefcase if needed, documents if any, and last-minute inspections to ensure that I didn't carry my dog tags or any personal items that could identify the "real me" and compromise whatever I was doing. As we gained confidence in each other, I began asking about PURPLE in nonverbal ways. Alice did not know PURPLE's identity, she said, nor would she tell me if she knew, no matter what. I saw her at the pistol range one day. She had been well trained by someone. In my mind, she had earned her position as a Scout.

Eventually, I stopped asking Alice about PURPLE and concentrated on my assignments. In due course, I completed my probationary period and started doing real stuff. *How did I know I was doing a good job?* The assignments became more difficult, and I was not dead. Most of the early assignments involved delivering envelopes, documents, and briefcases. Later, I personally began to deliver other kinds of messages. The "postman" didn't have to ring twice. My training was effective for getting the job done the first time.

One late Thursday afternoon, Alice was waiting for me as I came in from the pistol range.

"Would you like to go to the Navajo reservation with me over the weekend?" she asked.

"Is it part of my training?" I inquired in return.

"No," she said, "I thought you might like to relax and spend time with my family to understand our life on the reservation. My father is the chief there. Would you like that?" she asked.

"Certainly," I responded, "I don't know as much about Native American culture as I should. I am genuinely interested. How do we get there and what do I bring with me?"

The Reservation

"I will pick you up in front of headquarters at the end of the workday tomorrow, okay?" she declared. "Bring comfortable civilian clothes. I will have you back before Monday morning formation. The colonel already gave me permission to take you."

"Great," I said, trying to be cool while I scattered a box of ammunition on the ground. "I will see you then."

The drive to the reservation was longer than I expected, but my civilian clothes and the absence of my ever-present pistol belt and archery harness made me feel lighter. Alice drove, so I had nothing to do but watch the night sky become clearer as we got closer to the reservation. My night training was usually too intense for me to marvel at the brilliance of the Western sky, even when I spent most of the night beneath the same canopy of the moon and stars that I was viewing now as if for the first time. Alice knew about the magic of the night sky. She drove steadily, kept the radio off, and didn't speak. I noticed her glance at me now and then to be sure that I was absorbing the healing effects of nature. I was. When we arrived at her family's house, neither of us was sleepy. Alice got some blankets while I selected a rocking chair on the porch that I soon discovered had only one arm. It was too late to change my selection. With her superior knowledge of the terrain and furniture, Alice took possession of the swing, wrapped herself in a blanket, and fell asleep. I stayed awake to contemplate the night and my future as Joe Legion until I finally dozed off.

The next morning, Alice's father and I bonded immediately. He talked about the history of his tribe, how the Navajo people survived on the barren reservation, how they honored nature, family, and country by helping others, and how they identified a person with a true heart. He showed me the tribe's ceremonial dress, weapons, tools, and implements. He described tribal customs and rituals. By the end of the weekend, I was not only invited back, but I was adopted into the tribe as "Joe Quick-To-Learn," a title I cherished as a great honor.

I did not see much of Alice during that visit. On the way back, I expected her to quiz me about what I had seen and absorbed over the weekend. She did not. I tried to talk about the natural beauty of the open country in contrast to the sparse lives of those who chose or who had no other option except to live on the reservation. That conversation went nowhere. Then, I did the right thing and listened to my mind and heart talk to me until we arrived at headquarters as the flag was being raised. Alice stopped the car just short of the assembled troops, covering them with a cloud of dust. I grabbed my gear, and hurriedly bailed out of the car to join the formation.

"Thanks, Alice, for the great weekend," I said over my shoulder. "I enjoyed meeting your family very much. I think I understand your heritage better now," I said with genuine feeling.

"If we have time," she replied, "I will take you again. You still have much to learn," she smiled faintly and drove off.

I didn't have a chance to think about her last comment then or throughout that day. I was a soldier again, and I should have been in uniform and in ranks at least ten minutes earlier. As it was, I was the only one in ranks in civilian clothes. Colonel Redmond was waiting for me. When he came to my position, he announced to the assembled troops that after a number of weeks of "special training" under the former CO, I had not yet learned how to tell time or to be a soldier. He would not tolerate such an oaf in his army. Therefore, he ordered the three sergeants to step forward to escort me away from the command. I would receive further training and discipline at a location of his choosing. Then, the colonel asked the assembled cohort to join him in displaying the highest degree of ridicule for someone as unruly and undisciplined as I was.

As I was being "led away" by the sergeants, I glanced at the sky for a moment. The sky was not as brilliant as it had been on the reservation. As I stood there "under arrest," *I wondered why our society dampens and blurs everything we want to hold dear in nature and in our lives.*

Usually, we make outcasts of those who follow the true path of their hearts and minds. Did my brother feel this way while he was training? These were strangely humane thoughts for someone who had spent so much time training to survive—and now to kill, if necessary.

I was sent to three locations along the East Coast for several months of training. I either started a week later or left a week earlier than the course schedule. That way, I never appeared on the training or graduation rosters. When I returned to my old quarters late one evening, everyone glanced up. My closer friends nodded or said hello, but nobody stepped forward to greet me, or to ask me any questions. Both of the COs had done their job well in isolating me from my former friends. Strangely, their reactions didn't bother me much because I had changed too. Indeed, now I was the "outcast named Joe with no avenger" that the Army wanted me to be and who Jeremiah had foretold I would become.

The Purple People

The next day, I received orders for my first "partner" assignment. It took us four travel days to reach the target. My partner's name was Dick. That's all I knew about him other than to assume that he was at least minimally qualified for the job. Under those circumstances and prospects, we connected quickly on how to get our job done for our mutual protection.

During a short break en route to our final objective, Dick surprised me by asking, "Did you go to your high school prom?"

I was too startled to answer other than truthfully.

"No. I asked a neighbor girl, but she said her mother wouldn't let her go. So, I stayed home and waxed my car. Then, I heard that she went with another guy. They were arrested for underage drinking. I didn't drink or smoke, and her mother knew that. If you figure that out, Dick, let me know. Of course, I didn't dance very well which probably was a date buster too."

"That probably was the real reason," Dick assured me. "Mothers are very protective of their daughters if they date guys who can't dance well."

A few minutes later Dick asked, "Do you intend to go to your class reunions?"

It was time to start concentrating on the objective. I was annoyed with Dick's questions, but I stayed calm.

"Sorry, Dick, I haven't thought about that very much, but right now I'd say I probably won't. Why do you ask, and what has that got to do with our assignment?"

"I just wanted to know how disappointed you'd be missing those events if we get ourselves killed here," he replied.

Now I understood where he was going with the conversation. He was trying to relieve his pre-action jitters. Fine, that was okay with me, so I continued.

"Until recently, I thought that insecure people go to reunions to check themselves out against their former classmates hoping that somebody there is in worse shape than they are. Then, they can go home and feel justified for otherwise messing up their own lives."

"So, you don't need to justify yourself to your former school friends?" Dick continued to probe.

"Assuming we make it out of this assignment alive, how successful do we need to be in our own minds to match up against the jocks who stayed home?" I responded. "We haven't changed underwear, had a shower, or eaten a hot meal in almost a week. But, we're mission-ready and willing to defend each other. Nobody back home will understand what we're doing, and we won't be able to tell them. We took an oath to defend our country, and then volunteered for this status. We knew what was expected when we started, or at least, we knew by the end of our training. So, if I return home, I'll wax my car, stay out of trouble, and let my former peers think I'm socially dysfunctional. Probably, they and the rest of the world will be better off that way."

"Oh, yeah," Dick asserted, "where are all the jocks and social swells when we need them?"

"Who says we need them?" I replied as I rammed a cartridge clip into my rifle. "We are pretty close, so noise discipline starts right now. And, Dick, don't worry, we'll make it out of here," I assured him and myself to end the conversation.

I recalled Jeremiah and hoped that the passage about my personal protection applied to this assignment.

Partner Down

The assignment didn't go well. Dick and I should have alternated our movements and covered each other. We didn't get to our target. The target was ready for any intruders. Clearly, someone had done a bum reconnaissance job because defenses appeared to have been in place for some time. As the "first among equals" partner, I called off the operation by hand signal to Dick. Our movements back from the target were supposed to be coordinated the same way as going in, but now we were taking fire. Dick was way out of position to my left. I couldn't cover him, and he was hit in the neck. In my attempt to get to him, I ran into a barbed wire fence that broke my nose, and made divots in my face from ear to ear. I could see blood spurting out uncontrollably from Dick's neck. I was bleeding profusely too, but I'm sure that my wounds looked worse to Dick than they really were. We were dead ducks if we stayed in our present positions. We knew what had to be done. The first standing order was to complete or protect the assignment. Dick looked at me with the blood gushing from his neck wound with each heartbeat and waved weakly. He put the barrel of his pistol in his mouth and pulled the trigger. That was his way of protecting the assignment we couldn't complete. To this day, I think he moved further left to draw fire away from me so that I could escape. When I was finally evacuated, the chopper had room for only one passenger. That further confirmed my belief that his actions were intended to protect the assignment and me.

As far as survival priority was concerned, we were equals. Dick didn't have to provide special protection for me. *Was Dick's action what Alice's father had talked about in helping others*, I wondered. *Is this what Alice had taken me to the reservation to learn? Did Jeremiah's promise to me cost Dick his life, and if so, for what purpose? Had Dick mistaken my superficial wounds for life-threatening ones that led him to conclude that both of us would die? How would I live with that thought for a lifetime? How many more like him would I see die on joint assignments? Could I carry that kind of burden and resume a normal civilian life?*

When I returned to command headquarters, I wanted to write to Dick's family and tell them that he died trying to save me. Even today, I don't know if I wanted to console his family, or to cleanse my personal guilt by writing to them. I asked Alice for his address. Alice reminded me that he had been my partner for only a week (a lifetime for us). Others would provide official notice and assistance to the family. She also reminded me that I needed to prepare for the next job. The more I thought about it, the more I realized that Alice was right. His name was Dick, and he was from Muscatine, Iowa. That's all I knew about him, and maybe his name really wasn't Dick, the same as me not really being Joe. But, I couldn't stop thinking about him. I raged at God, at Alice, and myself. Alice held up best under that barrage. Alice Bright Feather was a full blooded Navajo all right, and I learned that Navajo women hold up in tough times. So do mothers of servicemen in Iowa, I hoped. Now when I think of Dick, I also remember that neither of us ever went to a class reunion. I hoped the world was better off for it.

My next solo assignment took me to a part of the world that I would not choose as a vacation site. My meeting with my contact misfired, and I had to wait until he arrived the next day. During the night, the hotel where I stayed was shelled. The roof caved in pinning the other guests and me under the debris. Fortunately, I had just turned over on my stomach in bed when two ceiling beams came down—one on the back of my neck, the other on my lower back. The brass headboard of the bed caught and held up one end of the beams. Otherwise, the second Joe Legion's career would have ceased that night without an avenger. Even so, the beams and other falling debris peeled the skin from my back and shoulders and left some deep cuts. I tried to reach my pistol but found that I couldn't move my arms. Then, I passed out.

ALICE'S RESCUE

When I regained consciousness, I was in a hospital somewhere, and Alice was standing over my bed watching me intently. Rather than her usual business attire, Alice wore a traditional Navajo blouse with a wide skirt, and she carried a colorful beaded bag. With the restraints and bandages on my neck and back, I found it difficult to turn to look at her. I was groggy, but not so groggy that I forgot the lessons "Joe Quick-To-Learn" had absorbed on the reservation.

"Hand it over," I told Alice weakly.

"What do you mean?" Alice replied softly and wide-eyed.

"Whatever you have on you that is intended to ensure that I don't compromise the assignment," I responded more forcefully.

I hit the jackpot. A pistol with silencer came out of her bag, and a bone-handled knife came from somewhere in her skirt.

"Slip the automatic under my pillow," I told her. "There's no need for silencers on the reservation. You keep the dagger. It goes with your father's ceremonial outfit, and he really will be upset if you lose a tribal heirloom. Thank you for honoring me this way, but I am not ready to meet the Great Spirit yet. And, I'm not going to compromise the assignment if you help me get back to the States."

"I'm sorry, but—" she stammered. Then, she laughed a shy little laugh. "You really listened closely to my father, didn't you?" Alice acknowledged. "You have a clear mind and strong heart. But, are you sure you belong in this kind of work?"

"The Great Spirit may take exception to your evaluation," I said. "Besides, you're the one who gives me these bloody assignments."

I could tell immediately by the tightening of her body that I had said too much. Personal integrity, family honor, and tribal bonds meant a great deal to Alice. I tried to win her back.

"I'm sorry," I tried to reassure her. "Rules are rules, and the house always wins. You're only doing your job. Now, what do you know about my medical condition, and how do we get out of here?" I asked trying to become action oriented as fast as I could to relieve the tension.

"It's okay, really," she replied.

But, she wasn't telling the truth. It was not okay. In her mind, I didn't have the faintest notion of what she felt, what she wanted me to understand, and how unappreciative I was toward her.

Nonetheless, Alice told me that the doctors had informed her that the ceiling beams had bruised and chipped several of my cervical and lumbar vertebrae. The available medical equipment there was inadequate to resolve the problem. Additional imaging and surgery would be conducted stateside. A concussion from the fallen debris was the cause of my headache and dizziness. I would be moved quickly because the doctors were concerned about infection setting into the large area of open flesh on my shoulders and back. I would be flown to San Francisco, and, against standing orders, Alice promised that she would accompany me the entire way.

About this time, Dr. (Major) Hanes came through on his rounds of other injured soldiers in the ward with me. "How are you doing today?" he asked me.

"Fine, sir. Thanks for your concern. I'm ready to roll," I responded in the best military tradition I could muster.

"Liar," he replied, "you're a mess. We cleaned up your back as well as we can here, and while you were sedated, I also cleaned up the barbed wire scars across your face. When did you get those?"

"Those are souvenirs from a previous trip," I said and left it at that.

"Yeah, right. But, they should heal eventually and not be as visible," he reassured me. "I almost used up my entire supply of chromic catgut on you. It's a good thing you have a prominent nose. Otherwise, we would be picking barbed wire out of your tonsils. Your nose will be crooked from now on, but at least you won't have to breathe through your ears. Good luck, soldier."

"Thank you, sir, for all your help," I said earnestly as he moved down the line to look at his next patient.

The next day, Alice and I were on a military aircraft bound for the States. After all we had been through, I thought that Alice would open up and talk more during the flight. But, I had touched a very sensitive nerve by reminding her of the conflict between her personal and cultural beliefs to cherish and preserve life versus her duty as a Scout to take mine if needed for assignment security. She would not allow me to do that to her again. She found a place among the medical supply boxes, took out a book, and stayed there for most of the flight with only occasional glances at me as I bounced and groaned with every movement of the plane.

In Appreciation—Nothing

The three sergeants had done their job well. They taught me fighting and survival skills. They also taught me to suppress my emotions so that I could perform and go on to the next assignment. That was the necessary, and, as I then realized, the easy part. For me, the sergeants had reinforced behaviors and attitudes that I had already learned while growing up.

I began to realize that Alice had taken on the harder task. She didn't simply receive the assignments from PURPLE, hand out the equipment, and drive me to the airport. She interpreted the assignments and put the equipment in the highest state of readiness—weapons oiled, knives razor sharp, maps and photos in priority order, documents checked and secured. She gave me every possible edge to survive. Then, she waited. Not the impatient wait of a person anxious for a bus in the rain. Not the raucous wait of teenagers in line for a movie. She had to endure the tortured empty wait for the return of the person she was responsible for, someone she had delivered into harm's way, and now whom she was trying to rescue while disregarding PURPLE's protocols that she had sworn to uphold.

It didn't matter that Alice and I were from different cultures. But, it mattered to Alice that I did not recognize her feelings and commitment when I left on an assignment, and I didn't recognize her contribution to the success of the assignment after I returned. That didn't happen just once. It happened every time I went out and came back. And now that I was injured, I wanted her help despite her sworn duty to act otherwise.

I was delivered to the Letterman Army Medical Center at the Presidio of San Francisco for further treatment and recovery. Within a short time, I returned to my headquarters unit, but I didn't receive any PURPLE assignments. My external wounds healed. Alice went about her business as secretary to the CO, and I went about mine as a soldier. During this time, we didn't encounter each other much, and I think both of us found convenient ways to avoid meeting.

Conversion to Civilian Life

When my enlistment was up three months later, I cleared post and flew home to resume civilian life. Specialist Slick gave me a left-handed salute and a firm handshake. He had not been busted in over four months. Alice was not around when I left, and I never said good-bye to her. I didn't know what happened to her. I never tried to find out, or to contact her again. She had done her job well. *What more could one ask of a person?* I wasn't sure if she had notice of my last assignment when she took me to visit the Navajo reservation, but the ideas and inspiration I had acquired that weekend helped me through my recovery.

The three sergeants had volunteered for duty in Vietnam, moved their dependents to wherever they would call home during that time, and left the post several weeks before my departure. We shook hands warmly, but we knew that, most likely, we would never see each other again. Years later, on a business trip to Washington, D.C., I visited the Vietnam Memorial. Their names were not listed, and I was pleased that they survived that agonizing war. "Scooter," my scorpion, had been returned to the desert long ago having done his job in motivating me during my training.

The Army doctors told me that my injuries were not life-threatening, but they could be troublesome later in life if I didn't take care of myself. Sometimes, on cold winter mornings, the tingling and stiffness in my shoulders and lower back remind me of Alice, her Navajo heritage, and the assignments I had so long ago. We didn't accomplish every assignment, and, apparently, it didn't matter in the larger scheme of things. For a long time after returning home, nothing really mattered to me. I told myself that I would have to drop that attitude and get on with life.

Despite my responsibilities for a young bride and new baby, my initial transition from military to civilian life proved difficult. As I had told Dick, my family wouldn't have believed what had transpired during my active military service even if I could have told them. Then, as the Vietnam campaign became more unpopular with Americans, protests grew, and returning veterans were shunned, I found it easier not to say anything about my military service. However, after being an active player whose performance made an immediate impact, I now had to be satisfied being just another civilian cog in the egocentric wheel of corporate America.

During this period of working full time and attending night school on the GI Bill, my international activities were largely dormant. Understanding the words of Jeremiah and my larger purpose in life had to wait. I had a family to support, and I was trying to catch up to those who stayed at home during the years I had been a soldier. They had learned corporate survival skills in an environment more vicious than anything I had experienced in my military career.

Over the years, though, I learned other survival skills, became more aware of world events, and discovered my European roots. At first, I became involved in small international projects that I could do from home. On the few assignments in which I needed one, I experimented with other code names. I was the Angry Dragon (my Chinese astrological sign) when I worked in the Orient. I was Napokon (the Ultimate) when I was involved in Eastern Europe and Russian projects. Nonetheless, in all these projects, I continued to report to PURPLE. I never knew, or to my knowledge, I never had direct contact with the person or entity that initiated my assignments. However, I suspected that someone or some office in the Pentagon knew a great deal more about me than I did about PURPLE.

Marika and Unresolved Questions

Marika became my new Scout. As a Serbian medical professional, she was experienced and tough. I could as easily have been her Scout after she became familiar with living in the United States. Because of her family's connections and her medical training, she had important European contacts and became more than a Scout to me. Within a short time, she became my teacher, counselor, confidante, guide, and healer. I had learned about Navajo culture from Alice, but she had been reluctant to disclose her own personality and beliefs. Through Marika, I received a full dose of European history, culture, politics, conflicts, and attitudes. She was not hesitant about expressing her opinion on any topic. Soon, she became a PURPLE Operative based on her merits and performance. Yet, nothing we discussed could have prepared me totally for what was ahead in the events leading up to and after September 11, 2001.

In the early 1990s, as my international horizons expanded, I accepted an invitation to participate in a human resources consulting group to Russia. But, I didn't expect the consulting assignment to directly introduce me to my arch adversary and to an unreliable ally in my future activities as a civilian PURPLE Operative.

Over the next ten years, I became aware of a number of international smuggling networks and their movement of money, drugs, weapons, and people as their activities intersected my assignments. I also learned that major European and U.S. law enforcement agencies were uninformed or reluctant to tackle these networks, and turned a blind eye to them. I wanted them shut down. The human wreckage these networks created was too much for me to ignore. Through Marika, I pestered PURPLE to let me try to find, disrupt, and destroy some of the networks. Eventually, PURPLE relented. Using the cover of a vacation with my wife to Slovakia in early September 2001, I started my first of several unaided excursions into the realm of illegal networks. This is why the pistol was in my luggage when we returned from Morocco and Spain.

Following the events of 9/11 and that trip, my unanswered questions to myself were: *How did Hassan know about the contents of my luggage? How did he know of my family's treasure hunt, and what was his interest in this activity that had nothing to do with PURPLE's business? Had Hassan changed allegiances since I first met him in Russia in 1993?* Probably, most important in my mind was *would my military training and survival skills be sufficient to finish what I had started, and could I rely on PURPLE to support me at critical times?* I was starting a new phase in my PURPLE career squarely behind the eight ball, and I had asked for it.

Chapter Notes

1. *The Holy Bible, New American Catholic Edition* (New York: Benzinger Brothers, Inc., 1961), p. 809.

2. *Ibid.*, pp. 792–793.

3. Winston L. King, *Zen and the Way of the Sword* (New York: Oxford University Press, 1993), p. 175, citing D.T. Suzuki, *Zen and the Japanese Culture* (Princeton, N.J.: Princeton University Press, 1959), p. 78. By permission of Oxford University Press, Inc., and Princeton University Press.

4. *Ibid.*, p. 244, citing Paul Crompton, *The Complete Martial Arts* (New York: McGraw-Hill, 1989), p. 59. By permission of Oxford University Press, Inc. Rights currently held by Roxby Publications, Ltd. *Zashin* (alert concentration) is the desired frame of mind for the Way of the Bow, while *mushin* (the mind that knows no stopping) is the desired mental state for the Way of the Sword.

CHAPTER 3

HASSAN AND THE RUSSIANS

The Chance Encounter

As far as my family was concerned, the Iron Curtain collapsed when Czechoslovakia declared its independence from the Soviet Union in November 1989. By the time Czechoslovakia split peacefully into the two independent countries of the Czech Republic and the Slovak Republic on January 1, 1993, Beth and I had reconnected with our Slovak relatives. Also, by that time I had reactivated my dormant connection with PURPLE. My first major European assignment was in March 1990. Despite Marika's presence, the new PURPLE operations were not as smooth as I had remembered them. Due to mediocre intelligence, I almost lost my tail feathers on my first field assignment. This caused my civilian boss to get a glimpse, but only a glimpse, of my renewed involvement in international affairs.

Nominally, we were touring the Slovak region. Beth and I actually were there for a few days but a piece of my PURPLE assignment took me to Paris. When I completed my work, I contacted Beth to meet me there. She did. Although we had been to Paris and London several times, we always found something new in those two cities. Everything was calm until I encountered a former colleague in the Musée d'Orsay. The meeting was troublesome because I was sure that she would contact my boss when she returned to the States several days before I intended to return. One option was to accelerate our return schedule. Beth and PURPLE did not like that option. The second option was to return as we had planned and deal with my colleague and my boss then, if necessary. We also decided to move on to London the next day.

British Intelligence and the Lost Camera Bag

In the two days we were in London, we met an elderly American couple who stayed at our hotel. We encountered them frequently in our comings and goings. We noticed that the wife had health problems, so we didn't mind giving them information about things to do and see within easy range of the hotel. As we were checking out of the hotel to return home, the couple was departing for another destination in Europe. Because we were all going to Heathrow Airport, the couple asked if they could share a taxi with us. I should have nixed the shared ride, but I didn't. I did not see the harm in it until later.

At Heathrow, the couple got out of the taxi first at the European terminal. The driver helped them haul their luggage inside while Beth and I stayed in the taxi. That finished, we drove to the International terminal for our flight home. As soon as the driver opened the boot (trunk), I knew the shared ride had been a mistake. My camera bag was missing. We had time before our departure, and the driver agreed to take us back to the European terminal to find the couple. Upon arrival there, we spread out to find the pair. We asked ticket agents, security people, lost-and-found clerks, passengers, and drivers. Nobody had seen the couple. It didn't occur to us that the wife had felt faint, and emergency aides had taken her to the medical station. While his wife was there, the husband discovered that he had my camera case and turned it in to the lost-and-found unit of his airline, which was not the same unit that served the entire terminal let alone the International terminal. But, by then, it didn't matter. We were now pressed for time, and left the European terminal to catch our international flight home.

When we checked in for our flight, we informed the clerk of our camera bag problem. A supervisor standing nearby came over to hear our story again, excused himself, and said he would be back promptly. He returned with some official-looking, non-airline types who said they would like a private word with me. Just then, a general announcement was broadcast that passengers should be mindful of their luggage and that all unattended luggage would be confiscated. *I had a nice camera,* I thought as Beth and I took our places in the parade of officials heading toward the staff office area. Nothing lasts forever, but my camera could have survived longer if I had been a jerk instead of a gentleman with the couple and told them to find another taxi.

Beth was asked to wait outside while I was escorted into an inner office without windows. The two senior officials introduced themselves as Chief Inspector Harley of Scotland Yard, and Mr. Robbins of the MI-6 branch of British Intelligence. I told them I would like to stay and chat, but I had a plane to catch. Like Queen Victoria, they were not amused. Robbins did most of the talking from that point.

"We have a situation, here," he said. "Within the last hour, we arrested two Iraqis and one British citizen with contraband devices in their possession. What do you know about it?"

"Nothing," I replied truthfully, "but, thanks for thinking of me. I was on vacation in Slovakia with my wife, and now we're going home."

"But, you spent a few days in Paris and London too," Robbins continued.

"Yes," I concurred, "and we enjoyed ourselves immensely as we always do. I hope your observers were pleased with where we went."

"Do you enjoy yourself more with a pistol in your camera case?" Robbins asked as Harley produced my camera bag from an adjoining office. "The weapon is clean, but it has been fired recently."

"I use it as a backup when the flash attachment on my camera doesn't work properly," I answered smartly. "Thanks for locating my bag for me. Now that you and I have everything in order, I can be on my way, and you can get on with your work. Cheerio, I've enjoyed our little chat, but time presses onward," I said as I got up from my chair to leave.

"Apparently, you do not know the entire story, so let me enlighten you and ask your cooperation. Otherwise, Inspector Harley will find accommodations for you downtown that may be less enjoyable than those you have become accustomed to in London," Robbins declared.

"I'm listening," I said less composed than I was earlier.

"Earlier today, our people intercepted a shipment of forty capacitors bound for Iraq that can be used as triggers for nuclear devices. We captured the person carrying the triggers and those who were to receive them. We also know that a backup team led by a Russian military officer was working with the Iraqis. U.S. authorities are cooperating with us, and they were responsible for surveillance and control of the backup team. Now, I ask you again, what do you know about this operation?"

I considered my situation a minute and decided that I did not have any better story than telling the truth.

"The only thing I know for certain is that you need not worry about the Russian officer. He is a colonel, by the way."

"And you dealt with him here?" Harley interrupted.

"No, on the continent," I stated emphatically, "and not with my revolver. By the way, I only used it for target practice in Slovakia. My assignment was to ensure that the Russian officer would not participate in any events of interest to you in the next three days. The last time I saw

Colonel Vasily, he was tranquil, in the back of a truck, er—a lorry to you Brits—and bound for Toulon."

"Was that your only involvement with Colonel Vasily and members of the surveillance team?" Robbins inquired, greatly relieved but apparently wanting me to reassure him once more.

"The assignment was not presented to me as a team effort," I responded. "If anyone else is involved from the U.S., or if any other targets were identified in Europe, I don't know who they are."

"Thank you for your cooperation," Robbins said, offering his hand. "Your story confirms information we have from other sources. By the way, the moniker 'Napokon' is a nice touch. It is European, yet with an American panache. You and your wife are free to go now. We have held the plane for you. If you don't mind, we would like to keep your camera bag and return it to you later. Have a pleasant trip home."

"I expect the bag and contents to be returned in their present condition—no dust, no rust, no fingerprints on either the camera or the pistol," I stated with determination.

"By all means," Robbins agreed. "We have people who will take good care of your equipment for you."

With that, the meeting broke up, and I met Beth outside the office.

"What was that all about?" she asked curtly.

"They wanted to tell me personally that they found my camera bag," I replied briskly. "We'd better hurry now, or we'll miss our flight."

"Do you have the camera case?" Beth asked not ready to board the plane without all our possessions.

"The British have an airplane devoted exclusively to carrying American cameras and related equipment," I told her. "They want to show their appreciation by returning it to us in their own way. Don't worry, everything will be okay, you'll see."

Without giving Beth a chance to continue the conversation, flight attendants swarmed around us and hustled us to our seats before a passenger revolt broke out because of the delay in getting us aboard. Then, life improved for everyone. The pilot announced that he could make up the lost time in the air, and he did.

Apparently, my former colleague wasted no time in contacting my boss at home about our chance meeting in the Musée d'Orsay in Paris.

When I arrived at work the following Monday, my boss commented, "I thought you were going to Slovakia? How did you and Marcia meet in Paris?"

"I was in Slovakia," I replied. "But, I needed to transact business with a French bank. We had time before our return flight to Bratislava, and Beth wanted to go to the museum in Paris, so we did."

At that time, Europe was awash with people trying to buy back or retrieve property that had been confiscated by the Nazis or Communists during and after World War II. The Jews in Europe lost plenty, including family members, but they were not the only ones. My boss knew of my interest in repurchasing family property through French financiers. If my comments misled him about what I was doing, I couldn't help what he thought. Also, he knew that, because I wasn't a European citizen, I had to buy the property in the name of my Slovak family members, which complicated the transactions. To help me through the legal morass, I retained a former KGB attorney. The inside information I obtained on the KGB alone was worth the price.

Several weeks later, the British Consulate in Chicago called to advise that my camera case and contents were available for pickup. That day, my boss had scheduled presentations to several incoming executives. He freaked out when I told him I had an appointment at the British Consulate, but I would do my best to return for the presentation. I picked up my camera bag without any problem and got back to work on time. Now that Napokon was active again, my boss needed to be more flexible and understanding about my unpredictable private activities. This episode alerted him for my next surprise when we were on a business trip to Washington, D.C.

While in D.C., I made an appointment at the Czech-Slovak Embassy for the same time my boss and I were scheduled to have a group dinner with his superior and other company executives. Fortunately, the ambassador had a meeting of his own at the U.S. State Department, so he and I conducted our business quickly. I got back in time for most of the executive dinner. The moral fabric of the world was disintegrating while corporate America evaluated executive potential by the suits, dresses, ties, and party manners the favored few displayed. With those criteria, Slick could have been executive material.

Russian Reconnaissance

In early 1993, a colleague gave me a brochure that he had received from an organization sponsoring an international group of Human Resources (HR) professionals to consult with counterparts in Russia concerning Western management principles and practices. By this time, my boss was almost fully enlightened about the advantages of my international contacts and allowed me to accept the consulting trip to expand my professional and international horizons—as if he had any choice after I informed PURPLE about my possible access to Russian government and business leaders. PURPLE agreed that this was a golden opportunity to gather intelligence using the host country's invitation as cover. The instructions I received were simple—take your wife and leave your weapons home. (PURPLE's instructions also should have included a warning to avoid Russian dairy products that were not refrigerated for several hours before the meal, but that's another story.) I had one more approval to get—from Beth. I didn't think I would have a problem. I had married a traveler, but this would be the longest distance and most time away from home for her.

After several nights of observing me reading even more than usual, she asked, "Where are you going now, and can I come?"

> I didn't answer her directly, but said, "Did you know that following the Potsdam Conference at the end of World War II in July 1945, the United States and European countries recognized that Russia intended to continue its expansion into Central and Western Europe? To counter that threat, in April 1949, the U.S. and nine Western European countries drafted a mutual defense agreement that led to the creation of the North Atlantic Treaty Organization (NATO). As a countermeasure, on May 14, 1955, the Soviet Union and eight Eastern European nations signed the Warsaw Pact to provide for their mutual defense against attack from the U.S. and Western European countries. The 'Iron Curtain' between Eastern and Western Europe became a reality as Winston Churchill had predicted at Potsdam. The Cold War between East and West that we feared would separate us from our European family did exactly that."

"Yes, I know that story, so stop fooling around. Which NATO or Warsaw Pact countries will we visit?" Beth asked with hands on hips.

"Slow down," I replied. "You must listen to the preliminaries before I tell you the travel plan."

"Go ahead, get it out of your system while I start packing," Beth parried.

"Geez, you always make it difficult for me to convince you to travel, but here goes straight from a PURPLE information sheet. After twenty-nine years in power, Joseph Stalin died on March 5, 1953, but the Communist stranglehold on Eastern Europe continued under the Warsaw Pact almost into the 1990s. But, on March 11, 1985, Mikhail Gorbachev succeeded Constantin Chernenko as the Communist Party General Secretary. The old line Soviet hierarchy had died. During Gorbachev's term in the late 1980s, the words '*glastnost*' (openness) and '*perestroika*' (reconstruction) signaled the loosening of the Communist grip on Eastern Europe. How's that for an abbreviated history?"

"Yeah, great, I remember all that, but where are we going?" Beth repeated.

"Okay, let's see if you remember this," I continued. "Since the beginning of the 1980s, President Reagan turned the heat on the Soviets under the Strategic Defense Initiative (SDI). Reagan's 'Star Wars' plan eventually led to his challenge to Gorbachev to tear down the wall separating East and West Berlin. The wall, which Nikita Khrushchev had ordered built in August 1962, was intended to keep Europe, and, especially, Germany divided. But, the people in Russia, Germany, and Eastern Europe were ready for change. The wall could no longer confine those who demanded freedom and self-determination. The wall would have to go, and it did on the night of November 9, 1989. Coincidentally, that was the fifty-first anniversary of *Kristallnacht*, the night that the fledgling Nazi Party in Germany looted and burned Jewish synagogues, businesses, and houses in a prelude to World War II. Beginning in 1990 and 1991, Communist Russia itself imploded, giving birth to new republics that formerly were satellite nations under the Soviet Union. On July 10, 1991, Boris Yeltsin became the first elected President of Russia. Ready or not, Russian military and business changes occurred quickly with corresponding changes in national attitudes. For the first time since the 1930s, Russian government, military, and business leaders looked to the West for ideas and systems to manage people and operations in their new market economy."

"Would it have been so hard just to say that we're going to Russia, when, and for how long?" Beth scolded.

"It would have been agonizing for me without the proper buildup," I replied, collapsing onto the couch. "You don't want us to be ignorant

Americans on a trip like this. And, oh yeah, you have two days to pack and tell your boss that you will be away for a while. Our passports and visas are current."

"With all your preparations for the trip, you must really be tired," Beth responded. "Here are a few pillows for you."

Beth launched two pillows in my direction, which I immediately returned, initiating subsequent volleys in each direction to confirm that she was coming with me despite my long speech and short notice.

The U.S. contingent of the HR consulting group gathered from various parts of the U.S. in New York. The flight from New York to London to Frankfurt, Germany, was uneventful, but long. The next leg took us from Frankfurt to Riga, Latvia, where the consulting assignments would begin. The Latvian airport was small compared to Chicago's O'Hare, but equally modern. The airport's security officers had modern guard dogs and modern automatic rifles. The bus ride into the central city was informative. The buildings on the outskirts of town were in poor condition and depressing, even in the warm July sunlight. But the central area of Riga was clean and majestic. The Russian bullet holes in the Latvian Ministry's walls were silent but strong evidence of the Latvian people's determination to be independent despite Russian military force. The Hotel Latvia on Elizabetes Street was cosmopolitan and as good as anyone could expect east of the Danube River in those days. Hassan and the European members of the consulting group joined us there. Guides were available to entertain the spouses while the group members consulted with bureaucrats, university professors, business people, and union officials. Hopefully, we would do some good. The Latvians were more than cordial. They were friendly and genuinely glad to see us. The feeling was mutual. They left a very favorable impression on us with their hospitality and eagerness to learn.

After a full day of consulting, we dined as a group at the hotel or were invited in small groups to private houses to mingle with "real" Latvians, depending on the consulting agenda for the following day. Hassan, who was traveling alone, generally came with Beth and me to these private dinners because the three of us could fit into a Latvian minicab if no other transportation was available.

Getting to Know Hassan

Hassan was at least ten to fifteen years younger than Beth and me. He was of average height with a slim build topped by dark hair, a trim mustache, and equipped with his ever-present aviator sunglasses and smile. He also enjoyed photography, which gave us something to talk about immediately. His equipment was new and lightweight. Ours was ancient by comparison and built to last. We examined each other's cameras and noted the different features, advantages, and disadvantages of optional settings and things to push and pull. As we became more acquainted with each other, we began to examine each other's personalities and habits. We were pleased with what we discovered in Hassan, although he seemed more like a Midwestern American with a suntan rather than the Middle Eastern Arab we expected.

On the first night in Riga, the consulting group dined at a long table in a private room of the hotel. Hassan was seated directly across from me about a quarter of the way in from the right side of the table. None of the Americans smoked, while all of the Europeans did. Hassan didn't.

In Eastern Europe, alcohol is an important part of the menu—sometimes it was served for breakfast, lunch, and dinner. As a Muslim, Hassan didn't imbibe—even away from home. I didn't either, although I wasn't bound by any particular moral scruple or dietary code. Almost everyone accepted a small glass of vodka. I filled Hassan's and my vodka glasses with mineral water, and we joined the toasting with our colleagues. The lady to Hassan's left asked why our vodka bubbled while hers didn't. I told her to hold the glass tightly, and let the heat of her hand warm the vodka to make it bubble like ours. Hassan was impressed. After watching the woman unsuccessfully squeeze her glass for a few minutes, he was even more impressed with my ability as a con artist. Shortly thereafter, though, she was no longer receptive to our pranks. We needed to find another source of amusement for ourselves.

Until the meat course arrived, the two of us were an island of nonconformity bisecting the table and interrupting the usual flow of toasting and conversation. When the waiters brought Hassan a specially prepared plate without meat, my side of our island capitulated. I went with whatever meat the main course offered. Hassan was still impressed with my tomfoolery.

"Are you dieting?" he whispered politely.

"Not that I know of," I replied. "It's just something I learned from three Philippine sergeants long ago."

"What was that?" he inquired.

"Always eat and drink less than anybody else when in unfamiliar surroundings," I answered quietly.

"What does that do for you?" Hassan continued.

"Besides making my tummy more comfortable, it aggravates the other guests. They think I know more about the menu and local customs than they do," I answered.

"Do you enjoy aggravating people?" Hassan gushed.

"Only when I have a good chance of getting away with it like now," I said. "Look how many people are watching us wondering what we'll do next."

"What will we do next?" Hassan asked playfully.

"I thought I'd tell you to remove your elbow from the lady's salad to your left because apparently you have already dipped your other elbow in the lady's salad on your right," I responded, thoroughly enjoying the moment.

"I think you are a very dangerous man," Hassan laughed as he wiped the salad dressing from his jacket sleeves.

"Not as dangerous as the waiter standing behind you with a water pitcher," I quipped. "Do not let him give you tap water," I continued. "Otherwise, you will entertain the medical staff of Riga's hospital for a week or more."

At that point, the group leader saw his chance to disrupt our antics by standing and announcing the assignments for the following day. In the morning, we would meet with officials of a combined labor union. In the afternoon, we would meet the president of a brewery in his official role as head of an employers' association that negotiated with the union officials we would meet at the morning session. I suspected that both groups were composed of drinkers. If that proved true, collective bargaining east of the Danube could be an occupational hazard to one's liver. Reaching an agreement would be a matter of determining the other party's alcohol capacity before slipping difficult provisions into contract negotiations. By the end of the first day, my suspicions about our hosts were confirmed.

Minor Miscues

In both morning and afternoon sessions, I contributed to the discussions by proposing collaborative rather than confrontational labor negotiations. I proposed that collaboration could be productive when rapid technological changes occurred in various industries. Irina, our Latvian interpreter appeared confused. She looked at me for what seemed like a long time. Then, she launched into an extended dialogue with our hosts. After she finished, the union leaders turned in my direction and smiled politely.

"What technological changes?" they asked through Irina. "We do not have technological changes in any industry here."

"Excuse me, I must be a little ahead of myself," I replied. "But when technological changes come, they will occur rapidly in a market economy. You may want to keep the collaborative negotiation concept in mind for such future occasions," I assured them.

Irina shifted from one foot to another while our hosts continued to smile patronizingly at me. Several agonizing seconds went by before Irina translated my comment. The result was more smiles and a few nods. Then, finally, I was off the hook. The discussion proceeded to a different topic. The same thing happened with the employers' association representatives in the afternoon session. *So much for collaborative collective bargaining*, I concluded. *It rarely works in the U.S. market economy. Why did I think I could sell it in Latvia after forty years of Communism?*

Fortunately, the afternoon session was shortened to provide time for sampling the brewery's products. Although we did not participate in the sampling, Hassan and I examined the brewing vats and other equipment. I noticed that the main control panel of the brewery had been manufactured in Czechoslovakia.

"Hey, Hassan," I half whispered as I pointed to the nameplate, "my European relatives were here. Or, at least, those who are not employed in assembling weapons were here."

As he came over to examine the nameplate, Hassan asked, "Which part, the Czech or Slovak part?"

"I can't determine from the equipment. Both Beth's and my relatives are in Slovakia. But the borders changed so frequently that some of the family believe they are Polish, others Hungarian, and still others Austrian," I told him. "The Russians think that my mother was Russian because she was born in a Russian province at the time. Sometimes, it's useful to let officials proceed without updating their information. Regardless of my family history, every region has a different dialect, and the people have adopted words from neighboring countries. That makes for a challenging evening of conversation."

Hassan caught me by surprise when he said, "I know Slovakia fairly well. I take my family to the Piestany spa every year. Do you know about the spa?"

"I know about it, but I haven't been there yet," I answered casually.

I was anything but nonchalant internally because the surprise conversation reminded me of PURPLE's instructions for me to keep my eyes open and lips zipped. I shouldn't disclose information about my family and myself to strangers so readily—especially with so many HR people around.

That evening after the group dinner, Beth, Hassan, and I were invited to the home of a prominent Latvian physician. Actually, the invitation was from two prominent physicians because both the husband and wife were physicians, which meant that the family was financially comfortable and respected in the community. We spent most of the time with the wife and two daughters in their nicely furnished apartment in a residential district of the city. The oldest daughter, Nita, announced that she was home for the summer from college in the States.

"Really, where?" Beth inquired in earnest.

"A university in Southern Illinois," Nita answered with a Midwestern twang. "I study music there. I hope to be in the Latvian opera someday."

"So, you know Chicago?" Beth continued.

"Oh yes," Nita replied. "I fly to Chicago, then take the train south to Carbondale."

The notion of a small world occurred to me. But, the real message was that if Nita had requested a student visa when Russia controlled Latvia a year or so earlier, her application probably would have been denied. Nita's hopes of being an opera singer may never have been fulfilled. World politics, terrorism, autocracy, failed government programs, and other factors continue to cause unnecessary hardships and missed opportunities for millions of people around the globe. *How do we stop it?* I thought to myself at the time. *What can I do to stop it?* I asked myself more directly.

Hassan saw me fidgeting, and his glance in my direction indicated that he was having similar thoughts. Meanwhile, Nita had moved to the piano. She accompanied herself in singing several operatic pieces that delighted all of us. She certainly had talent that could be appreciated by the other tenants through the paper-thin walls of the apartment building.

When Nita's father arrived, the musical part of the evening ended. Apparently, he had been briefed on our backgrounds before his arrival because he knew about my professional experience in healthcare. Within a short time, he left no doubt that he was interested primarily in me, and in what I possibly could do for him in creating for-profit health clinics in Latvia. I told him that I would pass along his proposal to my superiors, but my organization did not provide funding for private enterprises, foreign or domestic. He looked extremely disappointed.

However, I did better on his next proposal. The doctor said that Latvia currently had a surplus of young physicians. All of them could not be placed in the Latvian healthcare system, and he was upset that their talents would be wasted in other occupations. That wasn't a problem, I told him. According to Beth's cousin, who was a nurse in the Orava region of Slovakia, Slovak hospitals had an acute shortage of physicians. I was certain that the Slovak Health Ministry would be glad to arrange positions for any Latvian physicians who were interested in establishing practices in Slovak hospitals. I gave him the phone number of my contact at the Health Ministry.

On that happy note, we recognized that it was long past our curfew. We said good night to our hosts and thanked them for an informative and entertaining evening. They were pleased and called a taxi for us. While we waited outside the apartment building in the cool Baltic breeze, I realized that if a taxi didn't come, we had no alternative means of getting ourselves back to the hotel. Fortunately, before uncontrollable panic enveloped me, we saw the lights of a small vehicle approaching us. We were doubly fortunate because the driver was friendly, especially for that late hour, and he knew where our hotel was—even if we didn't. Now assured that we could get back to our hotel, we all relaxed and listened as the driver told us in his best English about his relatives in Chicago. The underlying message that we are all connected to each other's lives made a deep impression on us.

Upon our arrival at the hotel, we didn't linger with Hassan, nor he with us. We had to get some sleep and pack because tomorrow the group was to fly from Riga to Moscow. We could talk to Hassan during the flight. Beth and I said good night to him and headed for our room. Being seasoned travelers, we knew to pack as much as we could that night. Mornings were hectic enough for us without causing ourselves additional problems. Unbending schedules and group peer pressure on latecomers also were effective incentives to be on time for group travel and events.

ON TO MOSCOW THE HARD WAY

The next morning, everyone was on the bus promptly, and we left for the airport on time. Now that we knew some of the people in Riga, the buildings on the outskirts of town didn't look quite as dingy. We knew the Latvians had been through a tough time, but they had the determination to succeed in restoring their buildings and heritage. That did not prevent us from being the recipients of some quirky events before we left their country.

At the airport, our first duty was to weigh our luggage. When I didn't move fast enough for her, the middle-aged lady in a blue airline uniform hoisted both Beth's and my luggage onto the scale at the same time. To avoid an overweight penalty, they needed to be less than ninety pounds combined. The lady's forearms were larger than my thighs. In fact, every muscle group on her was larger than mine. Fortunately, we were under the baggage weight limit, and I didn't have to wrestle with her.

When the weigh-in exercise was completed, the group moved toward the ticket counter. The weigh station lady now became the ticket agent and took her place behind that counter. With everyone's passports and tickets in order, the group was ushered into a small room with no windows. All we saw was two locked steel doors — one ahead of us and the other that just closed tightly behind us. In those claustrophobic quarters, I pondered if anyone in the U.S. would know our fate if nobody opened the door in front. *Who in the U.S. would mount a search for HR professionals under any circumstances?* After what felt like a ten minute eternity, I promised my Guiding Hand that if somebody opened a door, I would never talk about collaborative collective bargaining again—ever. A few minutes later, the door opened, and we were escorted to our plane by the modern guard dogs and the modern security officers carrying their modern automatic weapons assembled in a modern factory in Slovakia.

Upon boarding the plane, we were greeted by a flight attendant with a familiar face and body. Yep, she was a triple-career person—weigh station operator, ticket agent, and now flight attendant all tucked into one large blue uniform. At this point, the airline gave her a break because she did not need to present preflight safety instructions in multiple languages. The plane had empty spaces where emergency air bags should have been. *If the plane had no safety equipment, the passengers did not need safety instructions—a very economical, market-driven concept,* I thought.

During the flight, Hassan would be seated across the aisle from us. He was usually efficient in taking care of himself and his belongings. This time, he was having trouble getting himself together. It gave me a chance to needle him a bit.

"Hey, Hassan, do you plan to stand during takeoff? Nobody from the airline will mind, but you may want to plant yourself in a seat for your personal safety. I haven't seen our lady friend for a while. Maybe she is the pilot too."

Hassan closed the overhead bin, looked back over his shoulder at me, and responded with a smirk, "If she is driving this plane, I should climb into the overhead bin and put my luggage on the seat."

"Lead him not into temptation," Beth scolded me, but Hassan took the orthodox approach and fastened himself into his seat.

"Do whatever works for you, Hassan," I started my aggravation assault anew. "Living as close as you do to Iraq, I'm sure you know how to take care of yourself."

Hassan's Gulf War Experience

"By the way," I continued, "what were you doing when Saddam Hussein and his army paid your country a visit in August 1990?"

"Seriously?" Hassan asked.

"Yes, if you don't mind," I responded. "We certainly have time. The way the engines cough, this plane needs to taxi about 400 kilometers before we become airborne. We may as well think of something other than our untimely demise."

"Initially, we were okay," Hassan began. "We live outside Kuwait City, where most of the military action took place. Eventually, Iraqi troops came to our town and searched every house. Officially, they were looking for men my age who might cause trouble, and, unofficially, they searched for whatever valuables they could steal for themselves."

"Did they find you?" Beth inquired.

"Fortunately, no. I was hiding in an upstairs closet."

"You should have hid in a closet in Saudi Arabia. The Saudi border is only about forty kilometers from your town," I exclaimed.

"Lucky you," Beth chimed in while poking me in the ribs for my remark.

"Well, not so at first," Hassan said quietly. "I discovered too late that my eleven-year-old son was still downstairs watching television rather than hiding as I had instructed him. But when the Iraqi soldiers came into the house, saw him there, and my wife coming home from work through the garden, they assumed that nobody else was in the house. One of the Iraqi soldiers told my son that he had a boy like him at home. So, although they made trouble for others, the soldiers did not harm my son or wife, or completely search my house. I waited a while longer, and then I came out of the closet to see if they were okay."

"Were they?" Beth asked.

"Yes, they were fine. My son was watching television. He said the soldiers asked him if he liked Hussein, meaning Saddam, of course. For a minute, he was really frightened because I taught him never to lie about anything. But, he told them he loved Hassan (meaning me), and the soldiers did not distinguish the difference in his pronunciation of Hussein and Hassan."

"What about your wife?" Beth asked keenly. "The soldiers could have treated her very badly."

Hassan smiled. "Yes, I know, but they did not harm her," he said. "She asked the soldiers if they wanted something to eat. She is not a good cook. They took one look at what was on the stove and decided to eat elsewhere."

"Is that why you are so trim?" Beth inquired.

"Not entirely. I travel and eat away from home a lot," Hassan answered. "Otherwise, I would be thinner than I am."

"If your wife hears you tell that story, the next time Iraq invades Kuwait, your wife may show the Iraqi soldiers where you are hiding," I offered.

"And you will make a point of telling her if you have a chance, won't you?" Hassan replied.

"Absolutely," I said. "I wouldn't let an opportunity like that go by without my input. More seriously, though, how long were the Iraqis around?"

"The invasion started in early August 1990 as you stated correctly, and the British did not come until February 1991, so almost six months," Hassan stated matter-of-factly.

"The British contingent of the coalition liberated your town, correct?" I inquired to continue the conversation.

"Actually, the Iraqis left in a hurry before the British troops arrived. But, yes, the British troops were the first ones into our town after the Iraqis left," Hassan said with a sigh. "I was glad that the war ended."

"I'm sure you were," I agreed. "But, you were luckier than you realize because, from your description, the Iraqi soldiers in your town were not the Republican Guard. The Guard would have been tougher on you and everyone in your neighborhood. Do you know what Iraqi units were in your town?"

"No, not really," Hassan replied. "All I wanted was to see them get into their vehicles, and sometimes even into our vehicles, and go north. Is it important to know the units that were there?"

"The details are important only if I want to beat you in a history debate. Are you ready?"

"Can I avoid it?"

"Not unless you want to get off the plane ahead of schedule."

"Okay, I will listen and learn this time, but be prepared for unconditional surrender when I get a chance on another topic."

"Well, you had a big selection to choose from besides Republican Guard units," I started. "From my research, I understand that south of the Burqan oil fields, as the Iraqis called your oil fields and your province when they assumed title to your part of Kuwait, the Iraqis had at least three armored divisions—the 10th, 12th and 17th, plus four infantry divisions—the 25th, 27th, 1st, and 48th.[1] In the early days of the war, everybody was south of Basra and the Rumaila oil fields in Iraq. If international negotiations had not resulted in ending the shooting war after four days, coalition forces may have been able to trap more Republican Guard troops including the Tawalkana, Medina, Hammurabi, Adnan, and Nebuchadnezzar divisions before they got back into Iraq with all of their weapons. Then, Saddam would not have had anybody to talk to or to guard his palaces after the war."

"Yes, certainly that is true," Hassan asserted. "Burqan once again belongs to Kuwait. It took a long time to put the fires out and for us to breathe fresh air again."

"With the sand blowing around all the time, do you ever breathe fresh air?" I jabbed.

"With all the industrial pollution in Chicago, do you ever breathe fresh air?" Hassan countered.

"You have me there, my friend," I said. "God only knows what goes into our lungs these days. Actually, Saddam gave Kuwait double trouble during his retreat, didn't he?"

"If you mean destroying our desalinization plants for drinking water, yes, he caused us problems that could not be repaired quickly," Hassan responded woefully. "That sent us another message because, at one time, Saddam offered Kuwait water rights from the confluence of the Tigris and Euphrates Rivers at the Shatt-al-Arab waterway, which flows south into the Persian Gulf, in exchange for two Kuwaiti islands and some land near the Rumaila oil fields in Southern Iraq. The Kuwait government refused the offer."

"Everyone remembers watching the burning Burqan oil fields on television. But, to my knowledge, the water treatment plants did not make the news, although the water facilities had more immediate importance to the Kuwaiti population, did they not?" I asserted.

"That is true," Hassan responded. "Saddam is not finished with us yet if the United Nations (UN) gives him another opportunity to invade by not enforcing the sanctions that the United Nations Security Council imposed."

"He has some history on his side to validate his claim to Kuwait though, doesn't he?" I continued.[2]

"Then you know that Kuwait was part of Iraq dating back to the Ottoman Empire, yes?" Hassan conceded.

"Yeah, I know some of the Ottoman-Persian history, but you know more pertinent details than I do," I replied. "Tell me what you know."

"Okay," Hassan stated. "A previous border dispute between Iraq and Kuwait goes back to 1962. Iraq claimed all of Kuwait from Ottoman Empire days, but Saddam also added the two islands of Bubiyan and Warbah, which, if under Kuwaiti control, could interfere with free access to the Iraqi port of Umm Qasr and the nearby city of Basra.[3] In 1973, Iraq created another dispute involving three kilometers of the border along the Rumaila oil fields. To break the deadlock, Iraq proposed a land and water swap elsewhere for the oil fields and the islands. Would you trade oil fields for desert land?"

"With oil revenues, I could buy water whenever I was thirsty. No, I wouldn't exchange oil fields for desert lands unless Saddam had a gun to my head," I said.

"Exactly my point," Hassan continued. "Saddam used these old land and water disputes to partly justify his invasion of Kuwait."

"Saddam came into power as the Iraqi President on July 16, 1979, so he could have had personal issues for the balance of his justification for war, true?" I asked, not wanting to end the history conversation yet.

"If Saddam had succeeded in invading Kuwait, he would have been able to influence the price of Middle East oil like the Saudis do now, and, maybe, he would have used those oil revenues to repay Iraq's huge war debts to European countries. Then, he would have had the funds to renew his nuclear weapons program, possibly pose a missile threat to Israel, and thereby upset the balance of power in the Middle East to the detriment of the U.S. and its allies."

"So, potentially, he could have created considerable trouble for Arab countries, Russia, Europe, Britain, and the U.S., among others. Good thing that the U.S. military planners were foresighted enough to recognize that static warfare conceived for Cold War Europe would not work in desert combat. At least some U.S. flag and field commanders converted and trained our military forces to use the mobile tactics needed to overrun the Iraqi forces in their fixed defenses before opposing forces were deadlocked in prolonged military action," I reasoned.

"I agree wholeheartedly," Hassan concurred.

(Looking back, I remembered how strange this conversation with Hassan was in light of the U.S. invasion of Iraq on March 19, 2003 when our military tactics for urban warfare were nowhere near as effective as our tank warfare in the desert had been. But, initially, the battle plans were good enough to permanently end Saddam's regime. After that, political and military solutions eluded the Bush administration regardless of U.S. tactics, hardware, or diplomacy.)

"Did it all work out for you after the war?" Beth asked to bring a different perspective to the conversation.

Hassan nodded. "This year, the United Nations Security Council used a 1963 Iraqi-Kuwaiti agreement which placed the Kuwaiti border 2,000 feet north of the existing one.[4] This shift gave Kuwait additional land in the Rumaila oil field and eleven more oil wells in the Ratga field that Iraq had drilled during its occupation of Kuwait. In addition, Saddam had to recognize Kuwaiti independence to avoid UN sanctions, not that he is good at obeying sanctions."

"Then, in his mind, Saddam believes that he has some unfinished business in your country, doesn't he?" I remarked.

"Yes, we will need international help, and especially NATO or U.S. assistance if Hussein starts trouble again. Kuwait is determined to remain independent, but we do not have the military resources to resist an unchecked invasion by Iraq."

"I'm sure the U.S. will keep Saddam off your street if he pays a visit to Kuwait again," I declared. "After all, some war commentators believe that the U.S. was responsible for Saddam's invasion of Kuwait in the first place."

"Now you are telling me something I do not know," Hassan stated as he leaned closer. "Explain how they arrived at that conclusion," he asked eagerly.

"This description is convoluted, so bear with me while I construct the landscape," I advised. "First, Ayatollah Khomeini declared Iran an Islamic republic in April 1979 after Muhammad Reza Shah Pahlevi was deposed. In September 1979, the deposed Shah, who was living in Egypt under U.S. protection, came to the U.S. for cancer treatment. Between April and September 1979, the Ayatollah and his followers pressed furiously for the Shah's return to Iran for his trial or death, whichever came first. Not succeeding in their diplomatic efforts for the Shah's return, Khomeini loyalists in the guise of 500 students captured about ninety U.S. diplomats and other staff members in a raid on the U.S. Embassy in Tehran in November 1979. Some hostages were released, but fifty-two of them were held for 444 days until they were freed under the Algiers Accords on January 20, 1981, the day President Reagan took the oath as U.S. President."[5]

"Are you saying that the Iran-Contra affair started Saddam's war with Kuwait?" Hassan interjected anxiously.

"Not the affair itself, but the events leading up to it," I continued. "I think you are confusing the Iran hostage crisis that President Carter's administration encountered versus the Iran-Contra affair that belonged to President Reagan's administration. President Reagan's turn at dealing with Iranian hostages would come soon enough. Going back a bit, in April 1980, President Carter had to decide if he should initiate military action against Iran to recover the hostages, or continue diplomatic approaches and sanctions which had been unsuccessful to that point. The problem with the war option was that Russia invaded Afghanistan in December 1979 to gain access to Persian Gulf oil. Iran was the sole buffer country that could oppose Russian advances in the event that Russia overran Afghanistan."

"If the U.S. invaded Iran, in effect, the U.S. would play into Russia's hands by destroying the only remaining roadblock preventing Russian access to Persian Gulf oil. Is that what you are saying?" Hassan asked.

"That's a good summary of the theory, yes," I said. "Iran would go from U.S. ally to U.S. enemy overnight, if it wasn't already an enemy of the U.S. because of its opposition to an Israeli-Palestinian peace plan. Also, Iran would portray any U.S. invasion of that country in terms of 'U.S. versus Islam' to draw support to itself from other Islamic Middle East countries."

"Possibly Kuwait would balk at assisting the U.S. under those circumstances too," Hassan added.

"Very possibly," I concurred. "And we wouldn't be sitting here discussing the current independence of your country. Fortunately, in that respect, disaster struck the U.S. plans for a secret incursion into Iran to rescue the hostages."

"How?" Hassan asked.

"Do you remember hearing about Operation Eagle Claw in April 1980?" I answered with a question as a polite reminder to Hassan.[6]

"I think I have some information about it," Hassan recalled. Was that the clandestine Delta Force rescue mission that went awry when the U.S. helicopters and transport planes ran into each other in a sandstorm in the Iranian desert?" Hassan asked to verify his understanding.

"Yes, if the mission had not failed in the desert, can you imagine what would have happened to the hostages if the Delta Force units engaged in a rescue firefight in downtown Tehran?" I asked as I let Hassan reflect on the military and diplomatic implications of those events for a moment.

"But, all that took place in 1979 through 1980. How does that connect with Saddam's invasion of Kuwait in August 1990?" Hassan inquired pointedly.

"Saddam became President of Iraq in July 1979 as I stated earlier (that was a busy year for dictators and invaders). In 1981, Saddam invaded Iran, comforted by U.S. neutrality in the matter. Nonetheless, Iran pushed Iraq back to within twelve kilometers of the Kuwaiti border, which really got U.S. and British attention. The war dragged into 1989, although, by then, Saddam had the fourth largest army in the world (not the fourth best, just the fourth largest). Supposedly during that time, Saddam developed his nuclear and chemical warfare programs. President Reagan's administration criticized President Carter's earlier blind eye to Saddam's weapons development program although President Reagan perceived Iranian religious extremism as more dangerous to U.S. and Middle East security than Saddam's more secular Iraq. According to President Reagan's position, President Carter's administration could have forced Saddam to abandon his nuclear ambitions much easier in those days and still have helped Iraq defeat Iran."

"In 1989," I continued, "Iraq 'won' the war with Iran, and Saddam emerged as a hero among the Middle East countries. But, like other heroes, he was broke and looked at Kuwaiti oil to restore his finances. As you mentioned, land and water issues were also involved. The U.S. Ambassador to Iraq at the time was instructed by President George H.W. Bush to caution Saddam against starting a war against Kuwait.

Unfortunately, the U.S. Ambassador at the time was a woman. Can you imagine Saddam being persuaded by a woman—any woman—to avoid war if he wanted war?"

"Not for a moment," Hassan responded sadly.

"Right you are. Saddam interpreted the U.S. Ambassador's polite message that the U.S. took no position for or against an invasion as an open invitation to invade your country without any worry of U.S. intervention. That is how the U.S. helped Saddam invade Kuwait. Then, we had to build a Gulf War coalition to force Saddam out, and we devastated your country in the process. After four days, President G.H.W. Bush called a cease-fire before coalition forces could close the gap on the retreating Iraqi army. Iraqi soldiers who did not surrender went back home with whatever Kuwaiti loot they could carry. I won't ask you to thank America and the coalition countries for defending your country for four days then allowing the Iraqi soldiers to loot Kuwait on their leisurely retreat home."

"The U.S. and coalition soldiers fought hard for us though," Hassan asserted.

"True, the military operation was well planned and executed, but U.S. diplomacy failed," I asserted. "Any adversary knows U.S. tendencies favor soft diplomacy going back to the Cold War era."

"Such as?" asked Hassan.

"Such as not thinking about future consequences in terms of an adversary's long-term intent and interests, our unwillingness to take casualties—especially after Vietnam, the inability or unwillingness of our government to explain to the U.S. people what really needs to be accomplished by military or other actions, our dislike for a war of attrition which takes longer than a week, and our relative ineffectiveness in guerrilla-type warfare, which tends to neutralize our superior technology. Our enemies and potential adversaries probably know more, but that gives you an idea of how the U.S. beats itself time after time."

"Does that mean Saddam gets another shot at us someday, even though Kuwait wraps itself in the U.S. flag?" Hassan asked dejectedly.

"I don't know," I stated my belief accurately. "Crazy things happen in the Middle East. You mentioned the Iran-Contra affair.[7] In 1983, members of an Iraqi group called *Al Dawa* were arrested for a number of truck bombings in Kuwait. *Hezbollah*, the group's ally in Lebanon took thirty hostages, including six U.S. citizens, to use as bargaining chips to have the *Dawa* bunch released from prison. Among the six U.S. hostages was a Catholic priest from Beth's and my hometown who was administering the Catholic relief organization in Lebanon. Yes, Hassan, foreign wars can become very personal for us in America too."

"Between 1979 and 1983," I continued, "the U.S. gradually reversed its position from supporting Iraq to supporting Iranian moderates in the Iraq-Iran War. Iran needed arms, and the U.S. needed Iranian help to arrange release of the American hostages held by *Hezbollah* in Lebanon. So, the U.S. sent arms shipments to Iran through Israel. A portion of the arms revenues the U.S. acquired was diverted to buy arms for the *Contra* army fighting Daniel Ortega and his *Sandinista* rebels who, in turn, were fighting to depose the Samoza dictatorship in Nicaragua that the U.S. previously supported and armed. Do you have all that?"

"You were right when you said the story was convoluted. Why didn't the U.S. send arms or money directly to the *Contras?*" Hassan identified the primary issue.

"The U.S. Congress forbade direct support to the *Contras* through the Boland Amendment to the U.S. Neutrality Act of 1939 that prohibited arms shipments to belligerent countries. So, the Marine officer who was the lead adviser to the National Security Council had to find another approach that President Reagan could credibly deny if the scheme was discovered. That approach worked until November 1986 when the Lebanese magazine *Ash-Shiraa* released the story. Then, the officer and a number of other high-ranking officials in the Reagan administration had to answer to the U.S. Congress and to the U.S. Federal Court following the Tower Commission hearings. In 1992, Reagan administration officials found guilty in the affair had their federal convictions overturned, or they were pardoned by President G.H.W. Bush when he was elected. But, the convictions and pardons were preceded by President Reagan's fuzzy admission of knowledge and ultimate responsibility for the entire affair."

"The bottom line was that the U.S. hostages were eventually released, and the U.S. maintained a 'perfect record' of not negotiating with kidnappers. The *Contras* continued operating a drug network to fund additional arms purchases while the CIA turned its back and allowed drugs to pour into the States. I may have missed a few points, but that's a summary of the Iran-Contra affair as it relates to U.S. activities in the Middle East that you easily can find on the Internet and in history books if you want. Once again, war can become personal and have unintended consequences for years to come," I concluded my dialogue.

"And where do you fit in?" Hassan asked without hesitation. "Certainly, the average American does not have that kind of detailed knowledge in his head without some interest or involvement in such activities. Do you work for your government in an intelligence capacity?"

"No, I work in healthcare, as you heard me tell Nita's father the other day," I shot back almost too quickly. "Beth can confirm that my life has little or no connection to intelligence."

"Then I don't understand how you retain all the miscellaneous pieces of information you have," Hassan followed.

"Miraculous, isn't it?" I needled him.

Just then, the pilot (a man's voice instead of our triple-career lady) announced that everyone should buckle up for landing. Until the last few minutes, we had enjoyed our conversation with Hassan, who seemed pleased that we were interested in him, his family, and his country. Soon enough, I would have a different view of Hassan's interest and role in international activities. For now, I was spared identifying myself as anyone other than as a member of the HR consulting group.

To our relief, the flight to and landing at Moscow's Sheremetyevo Airport (not to be confused with the crosstown Domodedovo Airport, if that matters to anyone not needing to differentiate between international or domestic flights in and out of Moscow) was otherwise uneventful. Within minutes, modern guard dogs and modern Russian soldiers with modern automatic weapons similar to those we witnessed in Riga arrived to greet us. But, one look at the terminal building itself was sufficient to inform us that all elements of Russian commerce were not yet ready for change to a market economy. Apparently, nobody in Moscow did windows (at least on public buildings at that time) because it appeared that the windows on the terminal building had not seen a cleaning rag since Napoleon left town.

Arrival in Moscow

Our group leader advised us that the Russians took security procedures seriously, and we should avoid aimless chatter while waiting in line for passport clearance. We arrived in the middle of the day with bright sunshine, but everything went coal black when we entered the terminal building. The only light was a single bare bulb a long way down the hallway. The hallway ended at a table occupied by two uniformed officers accompanied by the ever-present, modern guard dogs. The two passport *gendarmes* hassled a few of our group, but they didn't harass Beth or me. In the darkness, I couldn't tell if the officers stamped our passports or the backs of our hands, but we claimed our luggage and boarded the bus to the Radisson Slavjanskaya Hotel that would be our Moscow home. (If you have to ask the hotel's star rating, you have never stayed in a Russian hotel.) Beth ensured good service by leaving our "floor mom" Marianka a bribe of cosmetics every day before we left the room. If Marianka did not use these items herself, she could always sell them for food or rent money. Barter was the market currency in those early free-market days in Russia.

The group's consulting regimen was the same in Moscow as it had been in Riga. We visited universities, trade unions, government agencies, and private organizations. Hassan and I encountered one unusual organization that would continue to have a bearing on future events. "Transition" was an organization that sought to find civilian jobs for former Soviet military officers. That was a worthwhile objective because those officers' skulls had classified information in them about Russia's nuclear program. The officers' relatively meager pensions provided financial incentive for them to collect arms that they could sell surreptitiously to the highest bidder on the black market. That meant real trouble for the Russian government and the world at large. Later, I discovered that it meant direct trouble for PURPLE and me.

Second Encounter

Now holding the rank of general, Vasily was the military officer in charge of Transition. I instantly recognized him from intelligence photos and our previous encounter in Paris when he was only a colonel and I had sent him on an involuntary tour of Toulon bound and gagged in the back of a French truck. On that occasion, I met him from the rear in the dark, so he had no opportunity to recognize me as his tour guide to Southern France.

The Transition office was located in a residential section of Moscow. Not that it mattered. Space was always at a premium in Moscow, and zoning was not a government priority. A cigarette factory as easily could be located in an old villa next to a school as it could be adjacent to an art museum, a munitions plant, or missile site. Transition's office accommodated three desks and three guest chairs. Once inside, a visitor had to stay inside unless one had made prior arrangements to exit. Svetlana, our Russian interpreter, two other consultants, Hassan, and I went in and stayed.

General Vasily looked at Hassan and me and said boldly in Russian, "Well, what is your proposal?"

"What proposal?" I whispered to Hassan, my colleagues, and to myself. Neither PURPLE nor the group leader had authorized or discussed a proposal or informed us that any team members might have one. I was almost right—Hassan had a proposal. Hassan informed Vasily that his employer, a Kuwaiti petroleum company, could offer management positions to Transition officers. If those positions were unsatisfactory, Hassan had connections with other Middle East oil companies that had management vacancies. Obviously, Hassan had something working for him that the remainder of the group didn't. *Okay, Hassan, whose agent are you? Who is your real employer? What is your real job? Why are you offering jobs to Russian officers who provided Iraq with technical information on Russian-built, Scud missiles launched toward Kuwait during the Gulf War?* It was only a little over a year since that event. *Was Hassan out of his Kuwaiti mind?*

But, I had to give Hassan credit for strategic boldness. Russia wanted access to Middle East oil to supplement its own reserves. Meanwhile, Kuwait, which was still recovering from the Iraqi invasion, could use any country's money, technology, and protection. That kind of hands-on deal was infinitely better than any United Nations resolutions for international protection, sanctions, trade, or reconstruction. If any of the Western powers protested the deal, Kuwait, at its pleasure, could use Russian presence to negotiate more favorable business terms and government concessions from Arab countries, the United States, Britain, and Europe. *I knew something like this would happen if I left my weapons at home—I just knew it!*

General Vasily liked Hassan's proposal so much that he forgot himself. He did not wait for Svetlana's interpretation. (I put Vasily's revelation about his foreign language skills in my cranial files for future reference.) With his English skills uncovered, Vasily wasted no time in inviting Hassan and me to lunch while dismissing the other HR group members. I knew why Vasily invited Hassan and suspected why he invited me. I had been too cool and collected during the office discussions. Although I didn't have a proposal, Vasily sensed that I wasn't present merely to absorb Russian culture. With his experience and instincts, he knew that my presence had a purpose beyond HR conversations, and that, in all probability, my trip report would land on the desk of a U.S. government official in the Pentagon whose job included knowing about Russian influence and activities in the Middle East. Vasily would enjoy lunch and make me sweat. Single-handedly, Vasily would attempt to destabilize the existing Middle East balance of power while I choked on my borscht and roast duck.

ROAST DUCK

On the walk to the restaurant (spelled *pectopah* in the Cyrillic alphabet if you find yourself hungry in Russia with no golden arches in sight), General Vasily was the grand tour master as he pointed out buildings and other points of interest in the neighborhood. We were away from the Kremlin and the usual places tourists go, so Hassan and I observed the lives of middle-income Moscovites who we might not have encountered otherwise. I noted that traffic police walked a beat or manned traffic towers at busy intersections. When they blew their whistles, traffic offenders (and sometimes non-offenders with guilt complexes) stopped and pulled over to the curb. There were no police chases of traffic offenders in Moscow. All the cars looked ninety years old, and many were on the side of the road for mid-summer repairs. I could only imagine what winter driving was like in Moscow.

When we placed our orders at the restaurant, the waiter was terrified when he saw Vasily in uniform. I passed on the borscht but selected roast duck, which was a little tough. As I predicted, I choked on it, but only once. Before the food arrived, we took turns introducing ourselves. Vasily said that he had been in the Soviet missile program, and he was unable to discuss the details. I believed him, but I wouldn't let him off that easily.

"Where were you stationed?" I asked.

"In the Ukraine," he answered tersely. "With the 1987 INF treaty, START II talks, and Ukrainian control of the missile sites, Russian officers are no longer needed there," he advised.

"I agree that the 1987 Intermediate-Range Nuclear Force (INF) treaty is in effect, but do you really believe that the Duma (Russia's lower house of parliament) will ever ratify the START II missile reduction program?" I asked to slyly inform him that I had done more than my HR consulting homework.

"Approval by the Duma concerning any issue is always doubtful," Vasily responded with little hesitation.

"That is my point exactly. Why should you resign your military commission when the Duma has not acted on any proposed missile treaty that might result in military staff reductions?"

"There are other considerations," Vasily replied vaguely, hoping that I would end my aggressive questioning.

Even under the new Commonwealth of Independent States (CIS) form of government, Russian political and military leaders would not let unreliable former satellite countries play with their missiles. But, I let his answer die unchallenged. Soon, Vasily would have his shot at me, so why should I stir up trouble prematurely? Besides, I needed to learn his real reason for inviting me to lunch.

"Were you in Afghanistan?" I asked trying to draw him out on an easier topic. Russian involvement in Afghanistan ran from 1979 through 1989. If he had been a politically disconnected field officer, he would have spent considerable time there in the mountainous terrain being shot at from all sides by regional warlords. On the other hand, he could have been involved in opposing U.S.-supported Pakistani training camps for *mujahedeen* fighters. That activity would have been consistent with his intelligence and counter-insurgency background.

"Only for a short time early in the campaign," he continued his terse replies.

"That was a smart move for you," I concurred. "The purpose of the Afghanistan campaign for Russia was to gain access to Middle East oil. Hassan just offered you free access to Middle East oil in his proposal. I applaud you. You have executed a bloodless coup."

After a short, but electrically charged pause, I asked Vasily, "Did you serve in Serbia or Bosnia?"

"I am sure you know that the Balkan engagement is a conventional war with guns, planes, and politicians with territorial ambitions. They do not need my services," Vasily countered sharply.

"I might disagree with you," I replied, barely containing myself. "Russia and Serbia have had close relations since World War I. If Russian civilian or military leaders told the Serbians that genocide would not be tolerated anywhere in the former Yugoslavian territory, President Milosevic would have listened. That would have been a powerful statement that could have saved many lives and hardship for everyone—Serbs, Croats, Slovenians, Bosnians, Kosovars, Albanians, and Europeans in general," I argued forcefully. "Russian action would have been received very well in the world community. I think Kremlin leadership missed a golden opportunity to receive favorable comment from all interested nations."

"You know as well as I that Russian leaders have no regard for world opinion in their decisions."

"Okay, I will let that go," I conceded. "But, if you didn't serve in Serbia, then perhaps you had experience in the Katyn Forest?" I challenged, knowing full well that he was too young to have been a soldier in World War II.

The general roared with laughter.

"You are a bold one," he answered, still laughing. "But, you have your historical dates confused. I was a baby then."

The Katyn massacre of Polish officers and other prisoners by the Russian NKVD (predecessor of the KGB and FSB) on Stalin's orders in World War II was not a laughing matter, and I purposely ignored historical dates. I wanted to be bold, even fierce in drawing Vasily out. In April 1990, Russian leaders finally accepted responsibility for the massacre of 8,000 Polish officers, plus 14,000 Eastern European intellectuals and political prisoners in the Katyn Forest. Previously, the Kremlin had blamed the Nazis for the execution of the prisoners.[8] I served notice to Vasily again that I was current on my Eastern European history, and that I knew Russia's longstanding tendencies to create unnecessary havoc when the situation was already running in its favor, or to ignore a situation when timely words or actions could easily help avoid harm to other nations and people.

At that point, the food arrived and interrupted any chance for Vasily to comment on my latest jab. It was just as well, because Vasily still hadn't disclosed his real purpose for inviting me to lunch. The general toasted us with the standard before, during, and after meal vodka while Hassan and I replayed our mineral water routine that we had perfected in Riga. With our newly minted cordiality, I hoped that Hassan, who had been silent, would pick up the conversation. He did, but Hassan didn't want to offend his new friend. So, Hassan related stories about his family and some of the milder events of the 1990–1991 Gulf War. He did not mention Russian arms shipments to Iraq and Iran or Russia's inability to build the necessary infrastructure to capitalize on world markets for its own sizable oil reserves. Instead, Hassan set up an appointment for Vasily to meet him in Kuwait City to proceed with the general's Kuwaiti employment opportunities.

Now, it was Vasily's turn to interrogate me. The cordiality had to end sometime.

Vasily started by saying, "Your name is not European, but your features are. Did your family change its name when it emigrated to America?"

That was a loaded question for me, but I decided to answer. "My grandfather or U.S. Immigration Officers tired of writing our European family name, so one or the other dropped a sizable number of consonants at the Ellis Island entry facilities in the early 1900s. American employers still couldn't pronounce the remaining alphabet stew, so my grandfather totally Americanized the family name shortly thereafter."

"I would say that you are from Central Europe, perhaps Poland or Czechoslovakia, certainly?" Vasily pressed his query.

"Careful how you say Czechoslovakia, General," I answered. "That is an old Russian name for a satellite country. Slovakia is independent now."

"Oh, yes, yes, by all means, excuse me," Vasily said with a wave of his hand in dismissive agreement. "Because, you are truly American now, I excuse myself if I offend."

I began to feel the noose tightening, but I said, "Yes, certainly, I was born in America."

"I thought so," Vasily countered, "because Americans always want to appear to have the high moral ground on every issue, like you. But, in reality, the U.S. supports oppressive regimes around the globe, particularly in Africa and South America. Those countries are worse off than any Socialist or Communist governments ever will be. And, both my country and yours have enough nuclear capability to destroy civilization, so who are you kidding with your American morality?"

"Over the years," I replied, "my family and the U.S. have learned that we had to play both high and low moral games in dealing with the Soviet Union and now the Russian Commonwealth of Independent States. For example, my mother had to hide in the basement of a relative's house for three days before she could evade Russian soldiers to escape to America. In October 1944, Russian soldiers invaded Czechoslovakia when the U.S. was providing food for the Russian troops and the Russian population to fight Nazi Germany. In June 1948, the Berlin blockade started and the 'Iron Curtain' closed travel between Western and Eastern Europe. In May 1955, the Kremlin pressured Central and Eastern European countries to sign the Warsaw Pact to make sure that the 'Curtain' stayed in place. The Soviets invaded Hungary in 1956 to maintain power there. In 1968, the Kremlin used the Warsaw Pact again to drive tanks into Prague to crush the Dubcek government's hopes of putting 'a human face' on Communism in Czechoslovakia. The country was not ready to declare its independence, but the Soviets forcefully put down a reform movement that probably would have stopped short of open revolt against Russian occupation. So, Slovakia's independence had to wait until President Reagan put the heat on Mikhail Gorbachev to tear down the Berlin

Wall in 1989 before Slovakia's seeds of independence finally sprouted. Only in 1991 did the Czechs and Slovaks jointly gain independence from Russia when the Warsaw Pact dissolved, and another two years passed before Slovakia stood on its own as an independent nation separate from the Czech Republic. Oh yes, I am well acquainted with Kremlin morality too," I answered heatedly.

"Spoken like a true patriot," Vasily said patronizingly while clapping loudly to the annoyance of other diners seated around us and without appearing to take offense at my criticism of Russian politics. "It is good that you know who you are. But, there is the matter of a certain U.S. agent with the code name 'Napokon' who has been particularly active in the past several years. Others know of this Napokon too, and they may not be as understanding of his patriotism as I am."

Although my heart was pounding, I tried to appear calm. If he knew about my activities as Napokon, he was not merely a Russian field officer looking for a new career in Kuwait. I had smoked him out for my purposes. He was KGB or FSB, whatever the intelligence agency now called itself under the Russian Commonwealth. By exposing himself, Vasily also was warning me that my activities were known to Russian intelligence agencies. I would have to be extra careful in any activity in Eastern Europe. At the same time, Vasily knew that when I returned home, I would identify him to U.S. intelligence agencies through my PURPLE report. *What was the real game here?* I thought. That's when I choked on my roast duck.

If Hassan understood the implications of my conversation with the general, he didn't show it. He had concluded his business, had his lunch, and was relaxing while observing Vasily and me verbally sparring with each other. Nonetheless, Hassan helpfully announced that it was now time for him and me to rejoin our consulting group for the afternoon sessions.

Vasily wanted to play with me a bit more. When the check came, he insisted that I pay it as the junior military person in attendance. I counter-argued that I was a civilian, and, under those circumstances, the host should pick up the tab. With Hassan's intervention, we compromised by each paying our own bill. That was probably the best choice because it allowed me to cool down while I was engrossed in counting out the correct combination of paper *rubles* and coins for my food and tip. Outside the restaurant, we said our professional good-byes, and Hassan and I caught a taxi to our hotel. I didn't say anything important to Hassan during the taxi ride (Russian taxi drivers have ears), but I knew that if Vasily had that much information about me, we would meet again as adversaries.

When we returned to the hotel, everyone wanted to know what happened to us. Hassan did not know what to say, so I told the group that it was a case of mistaken identity. The general thought that Hassan and I had Russian roots and wanted to learn more about us (sure, and I was the Queen of Sheba). But, that answer ended the group's inquiries for the moment. The afternoon sessions were rescheduled, which allowed us free time to visit the Kremlin, St. Michael's Cathedral, St. Basil's, and the GUM (Glavni Univermag Moskvi) department store. Red Square was alive with people. In those days, many were standing in line to view Lenin's tomb and his mummified remains that were still displayed. Newlyweds in their best attire were taking photos of themselves and their wedding parties, including the Orthodox priests who always seemed to tag along to visit the sites. Americans perceive Russians as dour and unemotional, but with the warm summer sun and with clowns and mimes to entertain the kids, their world looked brighter that afternoon.

No photography was allowed in St. Michael's Cathedral, where the czars and czarinas held their respective coronations until that practice came to a screeching halt with the assassination of Czar Nicholas II and the beginning of the Bolshevik Revolution. Uniformed security ladies patrolled the cathedral to ensure that no cameras were used. I couldn't resist that challenge, especially with the husky patrol lady standing next to me. The movement of the subdued crowd was sufficient to cover the click of my camera shutter. While I was turning, looking at the ceiling, and occasionally looking straight at the guard, my camera, which was positioned on my right hip, was getting a 360-degree sweep of the cathedral. The Philippine sergeants had taught me well—just hide in plain sight and nobody will see you. However, I don't recommend imitating my cathedral actions. I imagine confiscation of film and cameras are only the beginning of bad things that can happen if one is caught taking photos inside St. Michael's. During our stay, the group saw some of the public parts of Lubyanka Prison, and I do not recommend its accommodations, despite its downtown address.

The group continued its consulting activities for the remainder of our Moscow stay. As promised, I didn't mention collaborative collective bargaining. When our Moscow assignments ended, the group took the midnight train from Moscow to St. Petersburg. We were a sufficiently large group to have an entire train car to ourselves. Shortly after pulling out of the station at midnight, we realized that at this time of year near the sixty-fourth parallel, the night sky is not totally dark. Rather than sleep, most of the group stayed awake and watched the forests, villages, and countryside go by in the half-light of the Russian summer night. Most of the houses in the villages we passed were not painted on the outside, but each had lace curtains in the windows that attested to the tatting (lace-making) skill of the mistress of the house.

ON TO ST. PETERSBURG

As we approached the suburbs of St. Petersburg at dawn, we were joined on the tracks by commuter trains that took turns stopping at various stations to pick up passengers just as they do in suburban Chicago. In the villages, people were starting their daily work—tending their goats and cattle, riding their bikes to the market, or hanging out the wash. Basically, people are the same everywhere. Only politics and religious fanaticism separate us from realizing our full potential, and our common needs and wants. *Matka Bozia* (Mother of God)—what a revolutionary thought that is!

Our home in St. Petersburg (renamed Petrograd and Leningrad at various times in its history) was the Pulkoskaya Hotel, a relatively modern building on the outskirts of the city. Across the wide boulevard was a forest of Cold War-era apartment buildings that were depressing even in the warm sunlight. In addition to our consulting duties, the group visited the Hermitage (the winter palace built by Catherine the Great), St. Ivan's Cathedral, museums, art exhibits, and attended musical concerts. Or, we strolled the streets to see the workmen rejuvenate the former Czarist villas to their former grandeur as in Peter the Great's time from 1689 to 1725. This certainly was Peter's town and his window to the West, through which he intended to push the Russian people to interact with other European centers of commerce and culture. When the Russians retreated to their isolationist habits, Catherine the Great gave them another Western push during her reign from 1762 to 1796. Napoleon caused great hardship for the French Army and for the Russian people during his 1812 winter occupation and retreat from Moscow during the 1801 to 1825 reign of Czar Alexander I. Following World War I in 1917–1918, the Russians retreated within their borders again. This time, the Russian windows and doors were closed tightly during the Bolshevik Revolution against Czar Nicholas II, the last of the Romanov family to rule "all the Russias."

But now, the world was here once more to make friends with the Russian people and to break their isolationist chains. Russia was trying, but some segments of the nation were not trying very hard. Russia had a large army that it could house and feed, but not train. Russia had a modern navy bristling with missiles and other armaments. But, when we were in St. Petersburg, many ships from Russia's Baltic fleet were anchored facing upstream in the Neva River between the Hermitage on one shore and Sts. Peter and Paul Cathedral on the other side. They had no fuel to patrol Russian territorial waters in the Baltic.

Fooling Around with the Fleet

On our final evening in St. Petersburg, the group had a party on a tour boat. If the Russian Navy didn't have fuel, neither did the tour boats. Instead of taking us up or down the Neva River, the tour boat kept circling the anchored naval vessels. This was even less of a challenge than taking photos in St. Michael's Cathedral in Moscow. I kept taking photos of the ships with their bows pointed upriver. In an emergency, they would have had to turn around in the narrow channel, refuel, and only then set sail into the Baltic. The Russian Navy was not prepared to challenge any nation on land or sea that evening.

After about the fifth time around the fleet, an officer on one ship spotted me taking photos and raised the alarm. Instead of sounding battle stations, the crew congregated on the rail to have their portraits taken. I kept my camera with its telephoto lens clicking. I'm sure that PURPLE and U.S. intelligence agencies had plenty of photos of every type of Russian vessel, but now they would have mine too. Ironically, one vessel was named *Nepekon*, perhaps the Cyrillic equivalent of my European code name. General Vasily was wrong. I didn't always have to be "the Ultimate." I only needed to be in the right place at the right time. If we had circled the fleet one more time, I would have fallen overboard from dizziness. Some of the Russian sailors were uneasy now as they milled around the deck waiting for orders that, fortunately for me, never came.

Equally fortunate, the camera klatch ended before someone got hurt, namely the tour boat captain or me. Other members of the HR consulting group were dizzy from the vodka. Inexplicably, Hassan was not around. I looked for him all night. I heard him come back to his room well after the group had returned to the hotel. *Could he have had a date with Vasily?* I asked myself.

At the airport the next morning, the group said its good-byes to its European members and Hassan. Besides meeting new friends in the various countries, friendships also blossomed within the group. Hassan came over to Beth and me, and threw his arms around me in a big bear hug.

Russian Farewell

"Good-bye, my friend," Hassan said. "I really enjoyed your company during this trip."

"I am glad you gave me the bear hug rather than to my wife," I answered. "Otherwise, I would not only have had to tell Saddam where you hide during his invasions, but that you have corrupted all the Russian generals to support Kuwait in any future Middle East war."

Before he let me go, I could feel him slip something into my sport coat pocket. He then went to Beth and gave her a more subdued, but warm, hug.

"Take care of yourself and your crazy husband," he cautioned Beth. "Stay in touch so that I can know where he is at all times. He is much too dangerous to leave out in the world by himself."

"Too late," Beth replied. "He knows how to unlock the door and let himself out of the house when I'm not around. But, we will stay in touch. Say hello to your family for us."

Then, we reran the preflight Russian drill with the modern soldiers, modern dogs, and modern weapons for the last time as we boarded our flight for our return home. Hassan and the Europeans took whatever flights would get them to their destinations. This plane had all its air bags in place and was in operating order according to the preflight safety presentation in forty-five languages—with English being the last one. If the plane went down, the English-speaking passengers would have been the last to know. But that wouldn't be necessary. We had a short stop in Helsinki, then on to Amsterdam, and continued from there to New York. Upon arrival, the group separated. Beth and I flew to Chicago. Probably, we would never see most members of that group again.

Earlier, on the leg of the flight from St. Petersburg to Helsinki, I had reached into my pocket to retrieve Hassan's note. It was a passage from the Koran that read:

> "They who believe, fight on the path of God; and they who believe
> not, fight on the path of Thagout; Fight therefore against the friends

of Satan. Verily the craft of Satan shall be powerless! And He hath ordained for them a term; there is no doubt of it; but the wicked refuse everything except disbelief. And it is not for the believer, man or woman, to have any choice in their affairs, when God and His Apostle have decreed a matter; and whoever disobeyeth God and His Apostle, erreth with palpable error." (Koran 4:78, 17:103, 33:36)[9]

Yes, Hassan, I thought to myself, *I have no choice but to continue as Joe Legion, the Angry Dragon, or Napokon, as bidden, wherever the road leads. Thank you for letting me know that you are aware of my hidden identity too. I suppose that my wife is the only person on earth who doesn't know about what I do in my spare time. What will be my next destination in the ongoing conflict within myself and between my opponents and my building a better world one brick at a time? Was Alice Bright Feather right after all these years? Was I really cut out for this kind of work? Would I meet Vasily again?*

I had no doubt that Vasily's and my trails would cross again. It was only a question of where and when. As Shakespeare wrote in *Hamlet:* "If it be now, 'tis not to come; if it be not to come, it will be now; if it be not now, yet it will come; the readiness is all . . ."[10]

I promised myself that I would be ready when the time came.

BALKAN BRIEFING

The consulting trip to Russia had taken most of the summer. Within a few days of our return home, I sent my report on my interactions with General Vasily to PURPLE through Marika. I did not expect, nor did I get, a reply because any response might have given me and interested others a clue about PURPLE's identity and its level of interest in Russian activities. I expected my report to get channeled with others for future reference or action. Future events confirmed that my assumption was correct. That is all I thought I needed to do or to know about that subject then. But, when I told Marika of my meeting with Vasily, she had a lot more to say on the subject. She was no longer a Scout, and I sought out and welcomed any information she could give me in her new role as a fellow PURPLE Operative.

"Did you ever encounter a Russian Army officer named Vasily in Serbia?" I asked her.

"Yes, our paths crossed several times," she said. "He was a major then. He was KGB now FSB, you know," she added.[11]

"I thought so, but I didn't know how to approach the subject with him," I replied.

"Do you know anything about the dissolution of the former Yugoslavia into separate states?" Marika asked with her eyes blazing and her fists clenched.

"Not as much as you're about to tell me, I suppose," I answered as I pulled a chair alongside her desk.

I anticipated that this conversation would take some time, and it did.

"You know that the United States is largely to blame for what happened there," Marika started.

"No wonder Vasily became excited when I blamed the Kremlin and him for the trouble," I answered partly to see how disturbed she would get. I definitely hit a raw nerve.

"I was a Communist student in the early days," she began. "Of course, Marshall Tito ran Yugoslavia as a non-aligned, Communist country, so what could I do? What could anyone do? After he died, the government was still Communist, but a power vacuum was building in the country that could not be controlled. Other political parties were formed under the Yugoslavian Communist League. Slobodan Milosevic began consolidating his power as early as 1989 when he engineered reduced autonomy for Vojvodina and Kosovo. Then, in the 1990 elections, non-Communist governments came into power in Croatia and Slovenia. Bosnia was not Communist either, but it had three ethnic groups who continually agitated each other—Croatians, Serbians, and Muslims. Milosevic was elected Communist Party President in Serbia. He saw his chance to grab power and took it."

"And that started the Balkan trouble, I suppose?"

"Yes, certainly," Marika replied. "But you are ahead of my story."

"Sorry," I said apologetically, "I won't interrupt again."

Marika nodded and returned to her story. "Shortly after Croatia and Slovenia separated from their Communist regimes, they began to agitate for independence from the Yugoslav Federation. The Yugoslav Constitution called for rotating presidencies. But, when Milosevic's term ended, he did not relinquish the presidency. That, in effect, was a Serbian coup of Yugoslavia. In response, Croatia and Slovenia declared independence."

"And that started the war," I interjected again, which Marika noticed immediately.

"I thought you promised not to interrupt me," Marika said. "Be patient, or you will miss important facts. You Americans are always in a hurry, and then you don't know what you are doing with anything important."

"Okay, no more interruptions. I double promise," I acknowledged as I sat up straighter in my chair.

"Now, once again," Marika continued, "Milosevic should have relinquished the presidency on May 15, 1991, but he did not.[12] Croatia and Slovenia declared independence on June 25, 1991. The next day, Milosevic sent the Yugoslav Army, consisting mostly of Serbs, to invade Slovenia. The Slovenian Army put up a tremendous fight and defeated the Yugoslav Army. So, Milosevic had to recognize Slovenia as an independent country. Do you understand this so far?"

"Yes, I think I have that straight," I answered. "Please, go on."

"Then, Milosevic sent the Yugoslav Army into Croatia. Now, things were different there because a large part of the population was Serbian, and the people turned against the Croatian government and joined Milosevic's army. So, within a short time, Dubrovnik was surrounded, the Dalmatian Coast was cut off, and Vukovar and Osijek were under siege for eighty-seven days with 2,300 confirmed dead. But, no one knows truly how many were killed there. Some bodies were never found."

I thought that Marika was so excited and involved in her story that she would never come up for air, but I didn't dare interrupt her. She continued without hesitation.

"Finally, in November 1992, the United Nations brokered a truce. But, by that time, the former Yugoslav Army still comprised mostly of Serbians had control of one-third of Croatia and over 10,000 were killed there. God only knows how many were wounded and maimed, and 730,000 refugees were all over the country trying to escape the bloodbath. Yet, the fighting did not stop even with a truce because Europe did not send any soldiers to enforce it. So, where were the Europeans and the Americans all this time? Russia was there. Vasily was there telling Milosevic to go ahead and kill them all—meaning all the Muslims because he did not expect the UN and the U.S. to intervene. Do you understand what I am saying?"

"The United States was still in Kuwait and Iraq or moving the VII Corp back to Germany from there," I offered as an excuse for lack of action by the U.S. "We were not ready for more war."

"The United States proclaims to everybody that it is a superpower. Can't it do more than one thing at a time, or instruct Europe or the UN to get involved to save lives?" she asked insightfully, but hopefully, not expecting an answer from me. "The U.S. has some excuse because, in 1992, the European Community (EC) should have intervened. For the first time, Europe wanted to take action without U.S. involvement even though Europe cannot tie its shoes without U.S. approval, true?"

"You know what's true better than I do on that subject," I said hesitantly because I couldn't rationalize anything better.

"And, now I will tell you about Bosnia."

"Oh, God," I mumbled, "I forgot Bosnia wasn't included in what you already described. In the U.S. we received filtered news so that we didn't really understand what groups were involved and how bad conditions were there," I tried another unsuccessful apology. Fortunately, Marika ignored my interruption.

"But now, because genocide occurred, Europe finally woke up and worried about the war spreading beyond former Yugoslav territory, especially into Albania and Greece. The European Community sent a mediator from England, and the United Nations sent another from the United States.[13] Both were ineffective because of previous alliances made after World Wars I and II. The Russians, British, and French favored the Serbians, while Germany supported Croatia and Slovenia. So, what were the European Community and the UN going to do? Absolutely nothing," Marika answered her own question. "But, on December 23, 1991, Germany on its own initiative recognized Croatian independence. Then, the European Community recognized Croatian independence three weeks later. In February 1992, the EC had a referendum for the independence of Bosnia-Herzegovina. If that referendum held, the Yugoslav Federation would be officially dead. If at that point, Europe and the U.S. had sent troops, or even warned Milosevic not to continue aggression, Serbia would have been forced to abandon the war. On April 6, 1992, the EC officially recognized Bosnian independence. On June 7, 1992, the U.S. recognized the independence of Croatia, Slovenia, and Bosnia."

"That should have ended the conflict, right?" I asked because I was losing track of the sequence of events.

"Absolutely not," Marika continued. "A few days later, the bloodbath in Bosnia reignited because Milosevic did not need Vasily to tell him that Serbia could start ethnic cleansing of Muslims in Bosnia at any time without intervention from any other country. Europe only wanted the level of war to go down low enough so that the EC did not have to send any soldiers. The U.S. did not want to send troops to the Balkans because they returned home from Kuwait only a short time earlier. The U.S. government was still shaking in its boots from Vietnam, and the U.S. people did not want any more casualties. So, newspapers all over the world were full of stories about the atrocities going on there, but nobody came to help. Some thought President Clinton finally would do something. I really do not know what else anyone could do. I will tell you, though, that if you saw Vasily in Moscow, he was probably home for the holidays from Serbia or Pakistan. That "Transition" organization you talked about probably is a front for the KGB or now FSB because Vasily is not out of work, believe me."

WHAT NEXT?

I agreed with Marika that General Vasily was not inactive or without a source of income. I also believed that my report would now receive more attention than I initially anticipated. *When would that document generate another assignment for me from PURPLE, I thought. What would that mean, if anything, to my European family and me? What hidden network would I discover if I pursued Vasily across Europe? How effective would I be in identifying and destroying such a network?* Marika's history lesson generated more unanswered questions than I could handle at the time.

CHAPTER NOTES

1. Tom Clancy, *Into the Storm* (New York: The Berkley Publishing Group, 1998), p. 552 *et. seq.* By permission of Penguin Group (USA) Inc.

2. Geoffrey Kemp and Robert E. Harkaavy, *Strategic Geography and the Changing Middle East* (Washington, D.C.: Brookings Institution Press, 1997), p. 95, 101, 416. By permission of the Carnegie Endowment for International Peace.

3. *Ibid.*, p. 95.

4. *Ibid.*, p. 95.

5. Wikipedia contributors, "Iran hostage crisis" *Wikipedia, The Free Encyclopedia*, http://en.wikipedia.org./w/index.php?title=Iran_hostage_crisis&oldid=314534141 (accessed June 9, 2009). pp. 1–13.

6. Wikipedia contributors, "Operation Eagle Claw," *Wikipedia, The Free Encyclopedia* http://en.wikipedia.org/w/index.php?title=Operation_Eagle_Claw&oldid=315236166 (accessed August 18, 2008). pp. 1–6.

7. Oscar Avial, "A Cold Warrior's Revival," *Chicago Tribune*, November 3, 2006, pp. 1, 24. By permission of the Chicago Tribune Company. Also, Wikipedia contributors, "Iran–Contra affair," *Wikipedia, The Free Encyclopedia*, http://en.wikipedia.org/w/index.php?title=Iran%E2%80%93Contra_affair&oldid=315992388 (accessed May 7, 2008). pp. 1–8.

8. Monika Scislowska, Associated Press Reporter, "Putin Puts Blame on West for WWII," *Chicago Tribune*, September 1, 2009, p. 14. By permission of the Chicago Tribune Company. Also, Wikipedia contributors, "Katyn massacre," *Wikipedia, The Free Encyclopedia*, http://en.wikipedia.org/w/index.php?title=Katyn_massacre&oldid=318046324 (accessed September 22, 2009. pp. 1–13.

9. John Medows Rodwell (translator), *The Koran* (New York: Bantam Books, 2004), pp. 59, 201, 302.

10. "Hamlet Act V Scene II," *William Shakespeare The Complete Works*, (New York: Barnes and Noble Books, 1994), p. 710.

11. In World War II, the regular Russian police force, the People's Commissariat for Internal Affairs (NKVD) was expanded to include the secret police. The NKVD evolved into the Gulag and the Main Directorate for State Security (GUGB) which subsequently became the Committee for State Security (KGB).

The KGB is the predecessor organization of the Federal Security Service of the Russian Federation (FSB). Although espionage activities are the responsibility of the Russian Foreign Intelligence Service, I use the acronym "FSB" to encompass both foreign and domestic intelligence and espionage agencies for the Russian Federation.

Wikipedia contributors, "NKVD," *Wikipedia, The Free Encyclopedia*, http://en.wikipedia.org/w/index.php?title=NKVD&oldid=317553602 (accessed October 7, 2009). pp. 1–8. Also, Wikipedia contributors, "Federal Security Service (Russia)," *Wikipedia, The Free Encyclopedia*, http://en.wikipedia.org/w/index.php?title=Federal_Security_Service(Russia)&oldid=316993879 (accessed October 7, 2009). pp. 1–9.

12. Christine Spolar, "Old Divides Plague Bosnia," *Chicago Tribune*, May 14, 2007, pp. 1, 16. By permission of the Chicago Tribune Company.

13. Noel Malcolm, *Bosnia A Short History* (New York: New York University Press, 1994), p. 229 *et. seq.* By permission of New York University Press.

CHAPTER 4

JANOSIK AND THE TREASURE

BACK TO MY DAY JOB

Upon my return to my regular job following the Russian rendezvous, everyone was glad to see me, including my boss—at least for a while.

"We have some business to talk about after you debrief with your staff," he said as he passed my office on his way to his corner domain one early morning.

"I'll be there as soon as I finish," I replied.

"Make it 9:30 sharp," he instructed over his shoulder. "I have other meetings scheduled."

A spectacular mountain of paperwork, correspondence, and professional magazines had accumulated in my absence, threatening to bury any unlucky passer-by under an avalanche of paper. I congratulated my staff for being able to stack the stuff that high without sorting it or resolving any critical items that might be contained therein. But, I considered the stack a good sign. I wouldn't need to undo any errors that may have been committed in my absence. Buoyed by that happy thought, I headed for my manager's office at 9:29:30 a.m. and arrived on time. The door was open, but he was on the phone, so I withdrew to a professional distance and waited. Within a short time, the conversation ended, and he called me in.

"How did it go?" he asked as he swiveled his chair in my direction. "We didn't hear about any revolutions or uprisings, so you must have behaved yourself for a change."

"No revolutions," I replied. "But, you may get varying views on my behavior during the Moscow part of the trip."

"How so?" he asked gingerly being fully acquainted with my propensity to ignite an unpredictable event without advance notice.

"Have you ever seen Boris Yeltsin appear in public without a coat and tie?" I started.

"Not that I recall," he responded. "What did you do to the poor guy? He has a country to run for God's sake."

I think my boss had an idea of the general direction my conversation would take because in the twenty some-odd years we had worked together, he usually saw me with my suit coat off and wearing a short-sleeved dress shirt with tie—in any kind of Chicago weather. This was my interpretation of my Second Amendment right to "bare arms." For reasons of their own, several board members had adopted the same style. Nonetheless, my boss accused me of corrupting these board officers and starting the business casual fashion trend long before corporate America officially adopted it. I took exception to his charges of my corrupting any board members or executives, either professionally or sartorially. They had sufficient individual or group potential for personal corruption without my intervention or support.

"I was only in Moscow for three days," I told my boss, "when Yeltsin appeared on national television standing on a tank in a short-sleeved shirt and tie. We live in different orbits, so I'm not taking the hit for his fashion statement due to my influence."

"Based on my observations over the years," my boss said, "Pavlov would take a distant second place to you when it comes to generating negative behaviors in humans and animals within a short time. Speaking of short time, three days is all you have to develop the agenda and draft reports for the autumn board meeting. Let's see how fast you complete that," he continued.

"That time frame will require expedited mail service from Slovakia because that's where I'll be three days from now," I countered.

"You just got back from vacation," he responded with a little edge to his voice.

"Absolutely incorrecto," I held my ground. "I returned from a business trip. The organization received substantial publicity and goodwill from my being a part of that HR consulting group. Now, I'm taking vacation. I promised my family on both sides of the Atlantic that I would be there for the annual harvest. Besides, I will have the draft agenda on your desk today, and I'll have time to prepare the reports when I return."

My boss knew that I wouldn't fail to complete the board reports because that would be career suicide for both of us. He also knew that both of us had rescheduled or lost vacation days many times due to management pseudo-crises over the years. Like many other professionals, we took vacation when we could, if at all. Before he could formulate a rebuttal, I was on my feet and out the door.

"Don't fall off a tractor or horse, whatever they have," he shouted after me by way of granting his imprimatur without officially sanctioning my absence if anything went wrong during that time. "And buy me an icon of St. George while you're there to remind me of how you should behave both in and out of my presence. Remember that your performance appraisal is due when you get back too."

"St. George isn't as big in Slovakia as *slivovice* (plum brandy). Will you settle for *slivovice*? I may accidentally wander into a religious store to buy the icon, but I'll guarantee that I will go to a store for your *slivovice*," I called back. "You have ten seconds to decide before I get out of range of your voice," I added to maneuver the high-pitched conversation away from my conduct and job performance to his personal needs and wants.

"Buy the icon for yourself and the *slivovice* for me then," he answered while I was still within hearing range. "That way I'll know you spent some time in a religious environment. If the plane goes down on your flight back, God will determine where your heart and mind were and decide your career in eternity from that."

"If I have *slivovice* with me, God will want me with him. Maybe, I should buy two bottles of *slivovice* and get the icon on another trip."

I didn't hear any further comment issuing from the corner office; so, for my purposes, he had capitulated. He always did, eventually. Otherwise, I never would complete any PURPLE work.

When I returned to my office, I called Beth to tell her that we were traveling unrestricted by any pending work. My disposition always improved under those conditions.

OUR EUROPEAN ROOTS

As for our European families, I began corresponding with three of my wife's relatives in April 1992. Although Czechoslovakia was then an independent country, its separation into two independent republics would not become effective until January 1, 1993. At that time, the former regions of Bohemia and Moravia formed the Czech Republic, while Slovakia itself became the Slovak Republic. Fifteen million people called the Czech Republic home, and five million proclaimed their allegiance to the Slovak Republic. That didn't bother me if it made sense to them, although the economic advantages were definitely with the Czech Republic. Other observers and commentators agreed that Slovaks hurt themselves economically by breaking away from Prague and the financially and politically stronger Czech Republic. But, after waiting nearly a thousand years for any kind of independence, the Slovaks would not be denied full independence when it became available to them.

The split of the two republics created some quirky situations though. The precise location of the border caused some initial problems when the Czech and Slovak measurements differed by fourteen kilometers. For at least one farmer, the border decision was important because the disputed measurement placed his house in one country while his barn was in another. (Call me a traditionalist, but I believe that a farmer and his cows should have the same citizenship.) I don't know how the situation was finally resolved. It didn't matter to the world at large, but it probably mattered to the farmer and his cows, especially at tax time.

As my Slovak writing skills improved and my U.S. family discovered more old photos and archives, the number of Slovak families in our regular correspondence pool expanded to six on Beth's side and five on mine. Life would have been too easy if they were all located in close proximity to each other. That way, I would only need to use one form of writing or speaking. But, Slovaks recognized three regional dialects and writing styles in their country—Western, Central, and Eastern. Additionally, because borders changed frequently due to wars, treaties, and more wars in this part of Europe, most Slovaks had to learn several languages if they wished to live in peaceful harmony with their neighbors. This introduced me to Polish, Ukrainian, Russian, Hungarian, and German words in addition to approximately nineteen different Slovak dialects. I adopted the Western Slovak dialect in writing and speaking and dared the remainder of the family to understand what I wrote, or spoke with a Chicago accent. Fortunately, I selected the style that ultimately prevailed in an independent Slovakia. The Slovaks looked to Western European and American culture, or to its absence, in every business transaction or cultural endeavor in the early days of independence. In retrospect, they should not have, but retrospection is frequently as faulty as introspection.

Direct flights from Chicago to Bratislava were available several days a week with only a few more minutes of flight time than a flight to Vienna. Daniela and her mother met us at the small, but modern, Bratislava airport. Daniela was more attractive than her photos with light brown hair and slender frame. Her chatty outgoing personality made our first meeting comfortable. Her mother's face showed the strains of recent widowhood, but her greeting was warm and cordial.

Daniela's exposure to the West through her Slovak Chancery and Foreign Office work in Nitra and Bratislava not only gave her a command of English (British-accented English), but a cosmopolitan presence that immediately let us know that she had the majority of her life under control. I wanted to rent a car to avoid imposing on the family's school or work schedules. Daniela would not consider it. As far as she was concerned, the only option available was her car and her persona as our official chauffeur. I don't recall what we did with the luggage in a car that small, but after a long drive east from the airport, we and our luggage arrived simultaneously at her mother's house near Presov in the Saris region.

After being surgically removed from the back seat of the car, Beth and I were engulfed by a large body of people of all sizes and ages who professed to be related to us. Out came the vodka, *zubrovka* (herbal vodka), *slivovice* (plum brandy), *griotka* (cherry liqueur), *marhulovica* (apricot brandy), and *becherovka* (herbal, don't ask) before I was allowed access to mineral or well water. I had no alternative drink for the hastily prepared toasts: to health (*na zdravie*), to family, to independence, to our respective countries, to the neighbors, to the living, to the merciful dead, and so on for a long time. Well past everyone's bedtime and alcohol tolerance limits, we were escorted to the master bedroom. Again, Daniela advised that no other options, including sleeping on the couch or in the second bedroom, would be considered. I don't recall being in any condition to resist. The next few days were reruns of meeting and greeting people, eating too much, and trying to find other sources of liquid refreshment besides alcohol. But, Beth and I would not have traded those moments for a kingdom. We loved all of our relatives there. They were our family who stayed behind when our grandparents and parents decided to come to America. Years of Hungarian, Nazi, and Communist oppression could not change family ties. They remained our family, and we were theirs—for better or worse.

Within a few days, we met three million of the five million people in the country. I believe that the other two million were in the States visiting their U.S. relatives. If I had met ten more relatives, I could have taken over the government in a peaceful coup. Fortunately, the day finally arrived when the adults had to go to work (those who had jobs with the country's 20 percent unemployment rate), and the kids had to return to school. After a good night's sleep, I dressed and strolled into the kitchen where Daniela's mother was baking doughnuts (*pampuchy*, *kobilky*, *paczeky*, *venceky*, *paczki*)—pick whatever dialect or Central European language you want. She gave me one. When her back was turned, I tried to steal another, but she caught me.

"You are Juraj (George) from America, but I think that you are also Juraj Janosik, the bandit too."

THE LEGEND OF JANOSIK

As Daniela came into the kitchen while braiding her hair, I greeted her with my respectful *dobre rano* (good morning), and asked her to tell me about Janosik.

Daniela pushed me into a chair, gave me the doughnut I had attempted to steal earlier, and replied, "Janosik was a Slovak outlaw in the early 1700s who now is our national hero for fighting against foreign oppression and taking care of the poor."

"A Slovak version of the English Robin Hood?" I asked.

"Yes, both Slovak and Polish," she replied. "And, unlike Robin Hood, we know from court records that Janosik was a real person."

"You have all my attention; tell me more about him," I lied because the jelly on my mouth and hands was distracting me.

Daniela poured herself a cup of coffee, sat down at the table with me, and began her story:

> "Janosik was born in 1688 in Terchova, northwest of here near the Polish border. When you visit your wife's relatives in the Orava and Trencin regions, they will show you where that village is located. His parents were peasants, and they were bound to the land and to the Hungarian landowners under the feudal system that had been in place for centuries. At that time, Slovakia was part of the Austrian-Hungarian Empire, and the Hapsburg family ruled from Vienna when the Turks were not after them. Details differ, but the common thread holds that, in 1711, Janosik was in the Saris region here as a freedom fighter in the service of Frantisek Rakoczy, a Hungarian noble who joined some of his peers in rebellion against the Hapsburgs."
>
> "At some point," Daniela continued, "Janosik joined or was forced into the Hapsburg army, which put down the rebellion within a year. Janosik's parents had to pay a ransom for his

release. Before he arrived home, his mother became ill and died. His father, who tried to care for her in her final illness, subsequently was beaten to death by the Hungarian landowner for leaving his work in the fields without permission. When Janosik returned to Terchova to find his parents dead, he joined a band of outlaws, particularly with Tomas Uhorcik, a renegade who Janosik met when he was a guard in Bytca while Uhorcik was a prisoner. Briefly, that is the story of how Janosik became an outlaw. Other versions claim that he was away at the seminary when his parents died."

"Whatever version of the story one accepts, I understand that those were very difficult times in Slovakia," I proposed.

"Yes, truly," Daniela agreed. "Although some Hungarian aristocrats revolted against the Hapsburgs, most of the actual fighting occurred in Slovakia, particularly in the north. So, Janosik began stealing from the Hungarian lords and landowners and giving money to the peasants who otherwise would have nothing. He was not the only former soldier who turned outlaw, but he is the most remembered for his good deeds to the poor on both sides of the Slovak-Polish border."

"Did he always give his 'income' to the poor?" I inquired having succeeded in wiping most of the jelly from my face.

"Because he was not married, it is said that sometimes village girls were seen wearing jewelry that was too expensive for them."

"So, like every free-market businessman, he had overhead and customer service expenses," I commented slyly.

"Yes, that is a very good description of his business methods, I would say," Daniela confirmed as she laughed her quiet little laugh.

"How long did that go on?" I asked.

"Only about two years," Daniela recounted, but stories are told about him in Moravia, Silesia, Poland, and Hungary, in addition to Slovakia. Apparently, he moved around easily. Mostly, the outlaws were active in the summer, and they hid in the forest and mountains around the King's Plateau in the Tatras (the range of the Carpathian Mountains between Poland and Slovakia). In the winter, they came down and lived in the villages among the farmers who protected them. In that way, the Hungarians could not track them through the snow back to their mountain hideouts."

After pouring herself another cup of coffee, Daniela continued.

"In 1711, Janosik was captured in Klenovec, but he escaped. In 1712, he was captured again in Zvolen or Liptov; it is uncertain where exactly. This time, he did not escape from Vranov Castle."

"Was he given a fair trial and then executed, or did he receive the abbreviated version of Hungarian justice?" I asked.

"Court records of a trial survive, thus we know that Janosik was given a trial. We do not know how fair it was because he never killed anyone. But, the sentence of hanging applied to both theft and murder, so the court did not have to deliberate long to reach its fatal decision."

Daniela slapped my hand away from requisitioning another doughnut as she finished her story.

"Wow, you are tough on crime around here," I said rubbing my hand from the sting of her hearty slap.

"What was the verdict for Janosik?" I asked while almost certain of the answer.

"Guilty, of course, for both you and Janosik. After all, it was a Hungarian court," Daniela replied.

"And Janosik's sentence was?" I proceeded.

"Actually, he had two," Daniela continued. "First, he was tortured on the rack for theft and then hanged by hooks through his ribs in the town square as an example to other outlaws. Some say he died in one day. Others say he died after three days. It was a horrible death regardless," she sighed.

"Based on the sentence, I believe the court wanted information that he would not divulge," I conjectured.

"It is said that he gave the names of his companions, but he did not divulge their hideout," Daniela declared. "And, he did not tell the authorities where his treasure was buried. So, Slovaks search for it to this day, especially when we have high unemployment," Daniela concluded.

"Has any treasure been found?" I asked as synapses of possibilities fired wildly in my head.

"Some people claim to have found pieces, but we do not know if it was Janosik's or another bandit's treasure. The hunt goes on," Daniela assured me.

BEGINNING THOUGHTS OF A TREASURE HUNT

"If the treasure hasn't been found with all the people looking for it over the centuries, several possibilities exist," I suggested. "One, no treasure survived Janosik. Two, the hunters are looking in the wrong places—perhaps, it was not hidden in Terchova. Three, natural or man-made conditions such as a rockslide or construction may have changed access to the treasure. Or four, some party found it and isn't telling anyone."

"Those are all good possibilities, but Slovaks fantasize that one day, Janosik's treasure will be found," Daniela asserted.

"Good, the family will find it, or, at least, search for it," I declared. "From now on, we will spend some of our future vacations looking for the treasure—in Terchova and elsewhere, if necessary. We will involve the entire family in research and in actually searching. At least, we will draw their minds off *vodka* for a few hours. The family may enjoy the search activity, take pride in themselves, and find happiness in their independent Slovakia."

That was my rationale in 1993 when the idea of a family treasure hunt began.

Scenic Diversion

"For now, though, we should move your mind away from doughnuts and go tramping in the *Slovensky Raj* (Slovak Paradise) today and in the *Kras* (*Karst*) area tomorrow," Daniela proposed.

"The Slovak Paradise area sounds great to me," I agreed. "I have seen photos of people climbing steel ladders to enter the caves. Am I correct?"

"Yes, good, you know something about the country already. Also, bears still roam in the mountains and in the national park where I will take you. If we see one, and if you can outrun it, you will have excitement for a lifetime, and I will have excellent photos to prove it," Daniela teased. "Otherwise, we will have a nice burial of whatever is left of you," Daniela laughed while grabbing my arm and pulling me off the chair. "But, you will have no more doughnuts, or '*Old Pyzdra*' will catch you for sure."

"Is that the bear's first or last name?" I asked. "I want to be polite if such an event occurs. Also, what is a Polish bear doing in Slovakia? Anything he wants, yes, I know that line."

"Actually, that was the name of the first gamekeeper he devoured many years ago. No one remembers how long ago that was. But, the national park service became aware that a young bear was killing sheep and goats on both sides of the border. The park rangers in Poland were the first to actually see him, and they tranquilized him so that they could place an electronic collar on him to survey his movements. Ranger Pyzdra was careless or slow because the bear woke up before the ranger was out of reach. All that was found of Ranger Pyzdra were some bones and his boots. Consequently, the people call the bear *Old Pyzdra* to this day," Daniela related.

"Why can't the Polish or Slovak park rangers catch the bear if he is dangerous, especially when he has the collar?" I continued my inquiry.

"The strangest thing about the collar is that when *Old Pyzdra* comes into Slovakia, the collar operates. When he goes back to Poland, the collar is silent. The Slovaks do not want to kill him because he has not hurt anyone on this side of the border, and the Polish rangers do not know where he is when he crosses the border into Poland. So, *Old Pyzdra* has lived a long time, and he knows how to avoid people. He has enough sheep and berries to eat without bothering people if they leave him alone," Daniela related while taking a jacket from the closet.

By that time, Beth arrived in the kitchen and zeroed in on the doughnuts. That was good because she does not consider mountain hiking, cave spelunking, or outrunning bears as three of her favorite things. We left Beth in the good company of Daniela's mother while we drove west on E50 toward Poprad and then south to the *Raj* area not far away.

As we drove, Daniela said, "You appear to be in good condition. But, I should warn you that the rolling hills ahead are deceptive. In the heart of the *Raj*, the limestone valleys, canyons, and waterfalls are very high. The trail is difficult, although the ladders, chains, and steps will help us. But, if we are caught in the rain, the trail will be treacherous."

"You sound cheerful about the prospect of me falling off a ladder or cliff," I teased.

"You are right," she said playfully. "Perhaps you should let me carry your wallet. Then, if you fall into one of the deep crevices, I will not have to search for you. I can go home and tell Beth that the wallet is all *Old Pyzdra* left of you. Then, Beth and I can go shopping."

"You don't know how relieved I am knowing that my money will be well spent while my bones rot in a hole in the Slovak Paradise area," I replied sarcastically.

We picked a good day for tramping. The weather was warm, and the parking lot was only half full, or half empty—depending on your point of view. For Daniela, the day was even better. As we got out of the car, a handsome young park ranger walked through the parking lot. One look, and it was instant mutual attraction. The ranger reversed his direction and headed straight for Daniela. From that moment, I ceased to exist. Even my wallet was no longer valuable. The ranger's name was Marek, and he proved to be as helpful as he was handsome. He apparently had some rank because he was able to reassign other rangers to various locations and duties while he devoted his time to us—correction, to Daniela. I continued not to exist.

At the *Sucha Bela* climb, one steel ladder that was bolted onto the rock had about fifty rungs leading to a rock shelf where another ladder ascended a similar distance higher on the cliff. The sight was spectacular. No camera could capture that awesome work of nature. Marek showed us a climbing technique that proved helpful and efficient. The rule to keep in mind, he said, was to maintain three points of contact with the ladder. We were to move only one hand or one foot at a time and to anticipate our next move. He saw me hold onto some rock outcroppings or reach into crevices several times to gain a firmer foothold and suggested that I cease and desist that practice. Sometimes, he advised, snakes (including the poisonous European viper) sun themselves in those crevices. I was impressed with the way Marek handled himself as he avoided letting his interest in Daniela totally disable his brain.

Fortunately, young lovers get hungry. Marek showed us a "nicer" place to eat. He suggested that we tour the *Dobsinska ladova jaskyna* (Dobsina ice cave) in the afternoon. During lunch, Daniela told Marek a little about herself and me. Marek and I seemed to relate to each other well enough, although he was not especially pleased that I was not Daniela's father or legal guardian. Little did he know of the fire and brimstone I could unleash if provoked. I told him about my idea for a family hunt for Janosik's treasure. He was eager to join our band of adventurers and believed that he could help us by gaining access to caves not open to the general public. When he informed me that Slovakia has over a thousand caves (most in the central part where Janosik chiefly operated), I appreciated his offer even more. If Marek needed an excuse to call on Daniela again, he certainly had a thousand good reasons available from the start.

"If you were seriously hunting the treasure among the many caves that Slovakia apparently has to explore, where would you start?" I asked him.

"You already know that Janosik hid in the mountains close to the Polish border northwest of here," Marek summarized. "Tradition says that he hid the treasure somewhere close in the *Horne diery* or *Dolne diery* (mountains or valleys) between Podziar and Stefanova. That is where most people have looked for the treasure over the years. You could start there," he replied helpfully.

"Maybe I will do that to give myself perspective on his location and habits, but with so many people looking for the treasure for so long in the same place, I believe that someone would have found the treasure by now if any treasure was still there," I responded, half thinking aloud.

"You really are serious about this treasure hunt, aren't you?" Marek commented.

"I'm more serious about finding a way for my European family to regain hope and joy in living after all these years of oppression and privation," I stated forcefully. "I don't know how long the Slovak economy needs to create jobs for all the unemployed people here. Meanwhile, if I can cause my family and others to regain their spirit by recalling Janosik as their national hero, then I will keep them hunting treasure until they stand upright as human beings again, especially when I'm not here with them. Do you understand my purpose?"

"You are remarkably complex yet direct," Marek said. "I can see that you think like an American. You think like a man who is accustomed to independence. No Slovak man has that perspective or feels that courageous in expressing his independence despite strong feelings."

"Thanks for the compliment," I said, "but don't let my charm carry you away. When I was a boy and my great-grandfather saw me doing something stupid, which was more frequent than he or I wanted, he would tell me that I was like a Russian running through a forest with a ladder. Then, he would put his hands out as if he were holding the ladder horizontally in front of him so that he would hit every tree in the forest. I got the message. Because of him I try to make it through the day's forest of activities without hitting every tree; either by carrying my ladder of stupidity off to the side or leaving it at home where it belongs. The Russian government insists that my mother was a Russian citizen, having been born when that part of Slovakia was a Russian province. So, I return their intransigence by telling my great-grandfather's story. Anyway, I hope my great-grandfather is proud of me now in my later years. That's what life is all about, you know. Each generation struggles to understand life and improve on what previous generations built. I hope the day comes when Slovaks and other countries around the world throw off their burdens, regardless of the source and live as God and nature intend. Maybe that will happen in your generation. Mine has largely thrown away its opportunities long ago. But, enough of that; let's have a look at your ice cave."

Exploring the Caves

I was totally awed by the Dobsina ice cave despite Marek's earlier remark that it was nowhere near the most spectacular cave in Slovakia. Daniela had toured the cave several times, she told me, and she knew that the cave was cold regardless of the season. She had advised me to bring a jacket. I recalled her getting her jacket from the closet before we left home, but she wisely left it in the car. When she began to shiver, Marek gave her his ranger jacket to wear. She glanced over her shoulder to determine if I would be an accomplice in her ruse. I had learned long ago never to interfere with a hunting lioness. I signaled with a nod that I was a neutral party, not her father or priest. That was all she needed to know. I think that her father would have approved. We would worry about her priest later.

While the pair chatted happily, I busied myself enjoying the ice and rock formations and repeating the Czech/Slovak tongue twister Daniela had taught me to help my American tongue pronounce my native language properly—*strc prst zkrz krk*—which roughly translated means to "stick your finger through your neck." I also tried to picture myself as Janosik searching for a place where he could have access to his treasure while keeping it safely hidden. I couldn't decide. I needed to see more caves. We had the *Slovensky Kras* (Slovak Karst) on our schedule tomorrow. That area of about 800 square kilometers had four major caves. When finished, I would be either caved in or caved out. Daniela would come as my guide, and I had no doubt that Marek would find reason to serve as hers. We agreed to meet at the entrance at 0900 sharp.

Casual Counseling

On our drive back to Presov, Daniela asked, "Did you enjoy the day?"

"I would have been an idiot not to," I replied. "The sights were magnificent, and *Old Pyzdra* did not attack me."

A few kilometers of silence later, Daniela asked, "Do you think Janosik hid his treasure in a cave and that we truly can find it?"

"Several elements are necessary for our success," I replied. "The hiding place needed to be accessible to Janosik without exposing him to danger, and the treasure within its hiding place had to be secure from untrustworthy gang members as well as outsiders. Another element was the nature of treasure. What kind of treasure did he have? Stealing a pig or chicken from a local *margrave* or *hajduk* (hereditary noblemen of the

Holy Roman Empire) does not count as treasure to me. But, before you ask me another question about the treasure, ask me the question you really want to ask," I stated so abruptly that it caused Daniela to momentarily lose control of the car.

After another moment's hesitation, she asked, "Do you like Marek?"

"If you're asking me, do I think you are wise to like him, I believe it is too early to tell. However, I believe you are proceeding the right way. If you ask me if he likes you, I believe so. Further, I believe he is behaving properly. I observed the way he treated his subordinates, and my impression is that they consider him to be a good person and supervisor. We probably will spend most of tomorrow with him, and you can learn more about him then."

"What is the right way for me to learn more about him?" Daniela inquired.

"Charles Varlet Marquis de La Grange once said, 'When we ask advice we are usually looking for an accomplice.'[1] Do you prefer to have me as your advisor or as an accomplice?"

But, her question was too serious to be overrun with a quick sarcastic answer, particularly when she no longer had a father to counsel her. I gave myself a few minutes to collect my thoughts.

A few kilometers later when I felt as ready as I could manage, I said, "I don't know if one way is better than another. I don't know if I can provide anything useful from my vast experience of one courtship and one marriage, but I will try. I think a couple first experiences an initial period of attraction when everything seems wonderful. Then, a period of withdrawal or hesitancy occurs as if the pair believes the experience is too good to be true, and they fear that something hidden might be wrong—either within themselves or in the other person. Often, nothing seems to go right during the second period. Sometimes, the two are trying too hard to please and are embarrassed when something awkward occurs. If the pair survives to the third period, they begin to learn more about each other to confirm that the relationship is a good fit. If the two want to get into trouble around this time, one persuades the other or they mutually agree to experiment or to over-extend the boundaries of appropriate conduct without any commitment or thought about the future."

"You mean in a sexual way, don't you?" Daniela asked, taking her eyes off the road to look at me.

"A French proverb expresses it best: 'There is the one who kisses, and the other who offers the cheek.'[2] A woman should know when to offer. The woman always controls the third period of the relationship, or should, in my opinion. That's not easy, particularly for a young woman who is still trying to discover who she is, let alone evaluate a potential marriage partner."

"What else do I need to know?" Daniela inquired softly.

"A next step might be reaching a mutual awareness that your feelings for each other are genuine and lasting, and that you want only unselfish good for the other person. You realize that responsibilities accompany those feelings, and you are ready, or soon will be ready, to take on those responsibilities. Does that makes sense to you?" I asked to test her comprehension.

"Then, you lose yourself in the other person?" Daniela asked, which I interpreted to mean she was focused properly on my infinite insight into marital bliss.

"Now you made me think of my military training with a bow and becoming 'one' with the weapon while emptying myself of my ego at the release of the arrow. Although that may be a good analogy, I am resigning as your counselor. I recommend that you have a quiet talk with your mother whenever the timing works for you. I believe that a person does not merge or submerge him or herself into the other. Both parties unite in a new 'being' through a unique bond created by them. In some ways, this bond separates them from everybody else on the planet. They pledge this unity to each other exclusively, for a lifetime, with mature knowledge and free will. Marriage is hard work. A priest in high school told my class that, if a partner believes he or she is putting more into the marriage than that person is getting out of it, that partner is contributing about the 'right amount' to the marriage. At some time during a marriage, the parties will experience their highest hopes and worst fears. If they are not together when those events happen, life can be very difficult. I conclude my lecture here because, if you recall, I resigned my counselorship at least five kilometers ago."

"How did you feel the first time you met Beth?" Daniela continued, not yet willing to accept my resignation.

"Are you recording this conversation for the Slovak Secret Police (SIS), or are you merely interested in learning how it feels to be in love?" I chided.

"*Prosim*, Juraj—I mean—please, George," she begged while recovering her English, "do not be cruel to me now."

"Okay, if you need a factual account of the beginning of our courtship, here is what I recall. It was Labor Day, a holiday we have in the

States on the first Monday in September. My father and I were putting shingles on the roof of our house following a bad hailstorm. My sister belonged to a political club, and she brought Beth, who also was a member of the club, over to the house for lunch. Why she did that, I don't remember. My father and I had already eaten lunch, but I climbed down from the roof to have another lunch with the girls. So, if you ask me how I felt to be in love, I would say I felt hungry, then full."

"You are absolutely no help, Juraj," Daniela protested.

"Well, let me finish my story. The next weekend, I took Beth to a football game—American football—not soccer. We were late, so I had to park my car in a field relatively far from the stadium. Beth walked with me through the muddy field with her good shoes. Then, as the game progressed, the wind became stronger, and the temperature dropped. The colder it became, the closer she sat to me, and the warmer I became because the wind was blowing from her side of the stadium. I thought that if she walked through the mud and kept me warm on our first date, she would be my partner for life. To confirm my feelings, I don't remember which team won or lost."

"That advice is even worse, Juraj," Daniela said, trying to cry and laugh at the same time.

"I guess a woman just knows when the right partner enters her life. Your body and spirit tell you that your feelings are genuine for each other. It is very personal, and nobody has to tell you when it happens. You just know," I closed my dissertation gently.

"*Strc prst zkrz krk*," Daniela said, finally giving in to the laughter inside her.

"That's easy for you to say," I responded.

It was after dark when Daniela and I returned to her home and Beth and Daniela's mother had eaten already. Daniela buzzed around fixing something for herself and me.

"What have you done to my daughter?" Daniela's mother asked, watching her daughter's high-energy ballet from the stove to the refrigerator and back again.

"Nothing," I said. "She is suffering from subterranean psychosis. Observe her dilated pupils, giddiness, shortness of breath, sweaty palms, hyperactivity, and well-timed chills during the day. One would think she was in love if she hadn't been in the caves with me most of the time. If she can get food and oxygen now and sleep tonight, she will be fine tomorrow and for a long time after that, I think."

"*Strc prst zkrz krk*," Daniela mouthed at me while making a face behind her mother's back.

"Yes, everything will be all right," I repeated. "Otherwise, it will be my neck for sure."

I was up early the next morning, but Daniela already had fed the chickens, milked the cow, and finished her breakfast before I came into the kitchen.

"How do you milk a sleeping cow?" I asked in lieu of a *dobre rano* (good morning).

"If you had sympathy for me, you would have helped. Then you could have seen for yourself," Daniela answered.

"I have plenty of sympathy for you and empathy for the cow and chickens too, but if you notice, the sun is not up yet. I would have stumbled over the cow and hurt myself. Besides, I am weak and hungry from all the cave activity yesterday. But, never mind, I know where things are, and I will help myself," I exclaimed with pseudo pathos.

I was glad to help myself because this was the second day without alcohol for breakfast. Some feeling was returning to my arms and legs again.

"To restart our day on a more civilized level, what do young married couples do in Slovakia for work and housing? Where do they live? Where do they find work?" I asked earnestly.

"Young people here sometimes delay getting married until they have jobs and some money. Others live with parents until they can afford an apartment of their own. Sometimes, one or both of them work in another country for a while. They see each other only on holidays until they can find work here," Daniela said soberly. "Life for newly married couples in Slovakia is not easy."

"No, that doesn't appear easy. That makes choosing the right partner very important. One or two days do not make a lifetime of happiness here or anywhere else. But, let's enjoy the day and see what happens. I will drive so that you can be well rested for the day's adventures."

STILL MORE CAVES

Driving to the *Slovensky Kras* took longer than I expected. But, following Daniela's instructions, we started south toward Kosice, and then took E571 southwest toward Roznava almost to the Hungarian border. We arrived at the *Kras* well ahead of the 0900 opening time. Even so, Marek was waiting for us. The *Slovensky Kras* is the largest *karst* region in Central Europe complete with gorges, cliffs, valleys, ice grottos, castles, and caves. We started with the *Gombasecka jaskyna*, the easiest cave to explore. The cave has unusual formations with stalactites (forming from the cave's roof) only about three meters long and about a half centimeter wide, more like thin straws rather than thick legs. Marek told me that the cave has no draft, which allows the water to drip in the same place for years producing the thin formations. He also advised that the black stalactites are made from oxidized manganese in the dripping water, while the red stalactites result from oxidized iron in the water drops. The cave was interesting and unusual, but nothing I saw remotely related to a possible hiding place for Janosik's treasure.

Next, we scouted the *Domica jaskyna,* which was a better prospect. Some say it is one of the fifteen largest caves in the world. Most of the cave is closed to tourists, but the biggest part of the cave stretches from Slovakia below the Hungarian border. *Now we are getting somewhere strategically,* I thought. Although the location was well southeast of his usual haunts, Janosik was known to have been in the Saris region while in the service of Frantisek Rakoczy. He could have learned about *Domica jaskyna* then. Later, as an outlaw, if Janosik wanted to raid one of the Hungarian border towns, this cave would have given him protected access. But, the cave was too open and accessible to be a good hiding place for treasure. When Marek said that archeologists found human and other remains from the Neolithic period in the cave, he confirmed my suspicion that the cave had been too closely examined for treasure to still be there. We rode a small boat along the river Styx, which runs underground along part of the cave. Hiding treasure in the little stream would not have been a good idea either.

The third cave, *Ochtinska aragonitova jaskyna,* was west of Roznava and was of no strategic importance to us as a hiding place for treasure. This was not a *karst* cave shaped by glaciers and other surface forces. Hydrothermal vents rising from below altered the surface limestone into crystal formations that resembled flowers. Again, nature did a magnificent job in displaying powers beyond the ability of mankind to comprehend or duplicate.

We did not bother to examine the *Jasovske jaskyna* cave because it wasn't close to the other three caves, and, by that time, Daniela and Marek knew what I had in mind when I talked about strategic locations. We spent the remainder of the day visiting castles or climbing steep hillsides to inspect their ruins. Several times, I sat on the remains of stone walls or outcroppings and enjoyed the view while Daniela and Marek strolled the nearby hills. Sooner than they wanted, it was time to leave.

As Daniela gathered her things, Marek came to me and asked if he could call on Daniela again. I told him, that using the American approach, he should address his question directly to Daniela. Further, I was not her legal guardian, but if permission was necessary according to local custom, he should discuss that with Daniela's mother. Lastly, I promised Marek that I would speak to Daniela's mother and put in a good word for him. As payment for my services, I told Marek that I would write periodically concerning the prospect of certain places being worthwhile to explore for treasure. Then, he could take my letters to Daniela to translate. Beyond that, he was on his own in developing a relationship with her.

I told him that, in my judgment, he was a fine, intelligent young man whose company I enjoyed very much. He started pumping my hand so vigorously that I thought we would strike water at any moment. Retrieving my hand and arm from Marek's grasp, I started down the hill toward the car, and let Daniela and Marek tag along behind to say their personal good-byes to each other. In some respects, I believe the two of them had already found their treasure in each other. We would all have to wait and see what the future held in store for us. As far as I was concerned, the hunt for Janosik's treasure was just beginning.

ON TO TRSTENA

The next day, Beth and I said our good-byes to Daniela and her mother. It was time for us to meet members of Beth's family in the Orava region south of the Polish border. During the bus ride from Presov to Trstena, I told Beth about my cave explorations while she shared her shopping adventures with me. I already could feel the difference in the comparative weight of our luggage resulting from her shopping.

In Trstena, we stayed with Beth's second cousin, Veronica, her husband, and two young children. They were a typical late-twenties Slovak couple struggling to make ends meet that Daniela had told me about. Veronica was a nurse, and her husband was an accountant. With the income from two professional positions, they should have been relatively comfortable financially, but the transition from Communism to a market economy was a struggle for the entire country. If the 20 percent unemployment rate didn't cause enough problems, the 25 percent annual inflation rate did. Still, they had a nicely furnished apartment, recently purchased appliances, a phone, and television with cable. As visitors, we might consider cable service extravagant but no other communication infrastructure existed in the former Communist bloc. Cable was their window to the West. Perhaps, cable TV more than any other communication media led to the collapse of the Soviet Union and to the breakout of Warsaw Pact nations from Russian dominance. Through television, the Central and Eastern European people saw the freedom and material goods Western countries had. Good or bad, they wanted that kind of freedom, future prospects, and material goods for themselves and their children. They would not be denied any longer—even if they did not understand fully how democracy and a free market economy worked. They had enough of suffering and privation. They wanted something else for themselves and future generations.

MEETING AUNT MARIA

During the day, Veronica and her husband worked while the children went to school. Beth and I set out to find Aunt Maria, who lived in a retirement apartment within walking distance. From her letters, we knew that Aunt Maria was in her nineties, that she maintained her own apartment, walked to church each day, and did her own shopping. We did not quite know what to expect from a lady of that age, who, as a young widow, had survived two world wars. It took us a while to find the apartment building, but we had no problem after that. Everyone in the building knew Maria. We knocked on her door and waited for a response. We heard footsteps inside coming toward us. The door opened, and there she was—a vigorous stocky lady with gray hair who looked thirty years younger than her chronological age. Aunt Maria immediately encircled Beth in a huge bear hug with lots of kisses and words of endearment in both Slovak and Polish. *Oh no*, I thought, *another dialect. I hope we can communicate.* I didn't get much time to think because now it was my turn for the big hug. *Old Pyzdra* the bear could not have done any better. Chiropractors must have a booming business in this town when people visit Aunt Maria. Breathing what I thought was my last breath I heard cheers from the small group of residents who had followed us up the stairs. Without a moment to spare, I was released from the bear hug and dragged into the apartment. Aunt Maria had a nice apartment with a little balcony that contained flowerpots and hanging flower baskets of every description. She also had a spectacular view of the mountains on the other side of the village that we could now see was centered in a long valley.

Beth and I were no sooner situated on the couch than Maria brought out plates of pastries like the ones that we had seen our grandmothers make years ago. Aunt Maria offered *slivovice,* but we declined. Then, she brought out the teapot. *Excellent,* we thought, *this lady is cool.* She was cool. With her cable TV, Maria knew about U.S. professional basketball. Her favorite player was Mikhail Jordansek, as she called him. She sang the "Star Spangled Banner," which she had learned from watching U.S. sports and the Olympics.

Eventually, I got around to my interest and family involvement in searching for Janosik's treasure. Aunt Maria knew about Janosik as intimately as if she had lived in his time. If she had been a contemporary of Janosik, he never would have stolen anything from her and lived to boast about it. Maria said that if we took Veronica to work tomorrow and borrowed her car during the day, she would guide us to Terchova and some of the caves in that area. *How old is this lady really?* I thought. She had not lost any voltage to old age. I was certain of that.

The following day, we arrived with Veronica's car at the appointed time, but it was raining hard, and Aunt Maria was not up to traveling that day. As substitute entertainment, she began to quiz me on what treasure I expected to find. She made me realize that I had not thought about the project nearly enough.

"So, Juraj," she started, "what do you expect to find? What kind of treasure could Janosik possibly acquire in the poor border towns of Slovakia and Poland? Certainly, he could steal the livestock of the Hungarian landowners, but what else?"

"I hope coins and silverware, perhaps."

"That is a good start, but think bigger. Think geography first. What is north of here?"

Oh, brother, I thought; *this lady is in her nineties, and she is testing me on European geography and early eighteenth century history?* Then, some of my brain fog lifted.

"The first Polish town north of the border on the Dunajec River is Chyzne, and we know Janosik was in Poland around Novy Targ a little northeast of there."

"Good guess," Maria said encouragingly, "now think further north."

"Krakow is directly north on E77, which is the main route from Krakow to Budapest."

"You are a geographical genius so far. This may be difficult for you, but think a little northwest of Krakow now. The Polish people consider the place especially holy."

"Until you said that, I was thinking of Oswiecim (more widely known for the Nazi prison camp of Auschwitz-Birkenau), which is west of Krakow, but the Poles do not consider that a holy place at all. Nor would the small number of Polish Jews who survived it."

"Try again," Maria urged.

"Oh-uh, the Black Madonna, the Shrine of *Jasna Gora* (Bright Mountain), and the town of Czestochowa, yes, Czestochowa, I remember, we were there," I recited in short bursts as if I were a quiz show contestant.

"Good, now who were the rulers in the late seventeenth and early eighteenth centuries? Remember, I am ninety-two, so do not take too much time to decide. Start with Russia." Aunt Maria continued to give me clues while distracting me at the same time.

"Oh, gee, Peter the Great, I think."

"Next, try Poland, please," Aunt Maria chimed in without letting up.

"I guess Augustus II the Strong, only because Poland was a client state of Russia at the time."

(I recalled that he was called "the Strong" because he sired over 300 children, not because he was a weight lifter or great ruler. People should have called him Augustus II the Tired, but whatever worked for the locals was fine with me.)

"Excellent guess. How men learn anything is beyond all reckoning, but now try Sweden."

"Sweden? How did we get to Sweden? You will have to help me on that one."

"I will give you Charles XII of Sweden if you give me Prussia," Aunt Maria continued relentlessly.

"Can we come back to that one? You are talking about a time when the United States or the Colonies did not exist yet."

"No, you must go on. Try Austria-Hungary," Aunt Maria instructed.

"Austria-Hungary? You are talking about a Hapsburg before Maria Theresa. Let's see, her uncle was Joseph I, who died in 1711 and was succeeded by her father, Charles VI, in his role as Emperor of Austria, and, I think, the Holy Roman Emperor."

"Now, go back to Prussia," Aunt Maria pressed.

"Hmm, if Charles VI as Holy Roman Emperor also was king of Austria-Hungary, and possibly Bohemia at the time, I believe Germany was still divided, and Frederick the Great as the king of Prussia paid homage to Charles VI, who had titular power over Germany as a whole."

"Excellent. Now, if you concentrate, you can identify the rulers of Western Europe by yourself. After you have those, you can tell me what took place in Europe at the time. Then, you can determine what could be in Janosik's treasure," Maria said as she tried to focus my thoughts.

"You have more confidence in me than I do. I am thinking in English and talking in Slovak. That's not easy for me, but I will try."

"Try the Sun King." Aunt Maria all but gave me the answer.

"Certainly, you mean Louis XIV of France, but late in his reign. His *'L'etat c'est moi.'* I am the state was quickly replaced by *'Apres moi le deluge.'* After me the deluge. The deluge came quickly after his death. Oh-ah, yes, okay, um, you want Queen Anne of England, and Charles II of Spain too. I have it, the War of Spanish Succession ran from 1701 to 1714."

"Good, but that is not all. How did the outcome of the war affect Central Europe?"

"You really are relentless. Let me think. I haven't had this tough a history exam since high school. Europeans talk about events 200 years ago as if they happened yesterday. When we visit from America, you give us liquor for breakfast and expect us to know European history before we unpack our luggage," I stalled shamelessly.

"I think that your brain is gathering dust. Once again, how many years do you think I have left in these old bones?"

"Nothing is wrong with your bones or your brain. Okay, I am ready. Philip of Anjou was Louis XIV's grandson, and Philip was in line to succeed Charles II of Spain, who had no male heirs. But, that proposal would put the Bourbon family on the thrones of France and Spain, which was unacceptable to England and most of Europe. A second proposal was to have the Hapsburg Holy Roman Emperor Charles VI become king of Spain too, which was totally unacceptable to almost everyone because the Hapsburgs would control Austria, Hungary, Bohemia, Germany, and Spain, which was a decent chunk of European property by anyone's measure."

"How was that resolved?"

"Let's see. The Peace of Utrecht in 1713 allowed Philip of Anjou, as a Bourbon, to succeed the Hapsburg Charles II of Spain as long as France and Spain were never joined as one monarchy. I believe that Duke Philip of Anjou became Felipe V of Spain, which was a good example of being in the right place at the right time. Having a family network already in place to promote his job search certainly helped him. He did not need a résumé and outplacement assistance under those conditions."

(Had I recalled the Peace of Utrecht of 1713 when Hassan and I were talking on the deck of the *Ibn Batouta* while approaching Gibraltar, I could have impressed him by reciting that under the terms of the treaty, Spain ceded Gibraltar to Great Britain. Then again, Spain allowed Britain to conduct slave trading to the Spanish colonies in the New World under the same treaty, which in hindsight was more shameful than impressive. My memory lapse at the time was a blessing in disguise.)

"Meanwhile, what was going on in Central Europe?" Maria returned to her previous question.

"While we were in Presov, we talked with Daniela about Janosik being in the service of Hungarian or Transylvanian nobles who wanted an independent Hungary separated from the Austrian-Hungarian Empire and the Hapsburg family."

"Good, you are almost there. What happened in the north?" Maria continued.

"If Peter the Great was the Russian Czar, then Charles XII of Sweden was raiding Poland, Russia, and the Baltic Coast while Peter was expanding Russian territory in the south along the Black Sea. Is that close to being accurate?" I stalled with a question again as I noticed my palms were sweaty.

"Now, the last item you probably do not know. Although Jasna Gora was the site of a Polish church, it was founded and administered by Pauline monks from Hungary. For a while, Charles XII of Sweden was unstoppable until he reached the Jasna Gora church and fortifications at Czestochowa. The Jasna Gora fortress was attacked in 1702, 1704, and 1705. Where would the Jasna Gora monks send the gold and silver chalices and other church valuables for safekeeping?"

"I suppose back to Hungary or Austria; perhaps to Estergom, Buda, Pest, or Vienna," I guessed.

"Good, you know the distinction between the current city of Budapest from the former two cities of old and new Buda with Pest on the other side of the Danube. I may have misled you on your answer, but we can clear that up. What was the significance of the Battle of Mohacs Fields?" Maria slipped in a bonus question.

"The Ottoman Turks defeated the Hungarian Army there in 1562, but I do not know the significance for Slovakia," I confessed.

"Let me tell you then. The part of Hungary not held by the Turks became part of the Hapsburg Empire, and the Hapsburgs moved the Hungarian capital from Budapest to Bratislava, or Pressburg as it was named in those days. Between 1563 and 1830, ten Hungarian kings and eight queens held their coronations in Bratislava instead of Buda. You mentioned Estergom as the seat of the Hungarian archbishopric. Where did the Hungarian archbishop go to evade the Turks?" Maria reignited her verbal grilling.

"The Slovak archbishop resides in Nitra in the Trnava district now; possibly there?" I truly hoped for my continued sanity.

"Yes, Trnava was the residence of the Hungarian archbishops until 1820. If the Jasna Gora valuables never got to Nitra, Estergom, or Vienna, or, likewise back from there to Jasna Gora, who possibly could have intercepted them?"

"Possibly, Janosik? The church caravan would have had to pass through his territory to and from Czestochowa whether it came or departed from Budapest, Nitra, or Vienna. By searching for Janosik's treasure, are we really chasing the Holy Grail of the Hapsburgs?" I asked hoping against hope for Aunt Maria's mercy.

"With Jasna Gora regularly under attack in the early eighteenth century, continual fighting between Protestants and Catholics, and then two world wars, who can say what records survived, or what church treasures may have been misplaced at various times by Bohemian, Swedish, Prussian, Austrian, Hungarian, and Russian invaders, or intercepted between Czestochowa and other places by outlaws. The Church would not announce that it lost valuable items when the peasants in Central Europe were starving. If you find Janosik's treasure, you may find a 'Big Holy Grail' from Jasna Gora or other cathedrals, or only 'little holy grails' from smaller churches, or both," Maria summarized her conclusion.

"Are you sure?" I asked, dumbfounded.

"No. You may find nothing, similar to so many others who have searched for Janosik's treasure. I am guessing, as you did during most of your history quiz. We have no record or legends of Janosik stealing from churches. The only way to be sure about what he acquired during his outlaw days is to find his treasure."

"We looked at several caves near the Hungarian border when we were in Presov. What caves or other hiding places were available to Janosik along the Polish border?" I took my opportunity to quiz Maria.

"Two principal caves in this area you should try are the *Demanovska ladova jaskyna* (Demanova ice cave), and the *Demanovska jaskyna slobody* (Demanova cave of liberty). You will find tourists there, and, probably, no treasure. However, the system has about twenty kilometers of caverns, and it will give you some ideas of the caves in that area. Both are located in the Demanova Valley not far from here. At the floor of the valley, the ice cave is the oldest known cave in Slovakia. The upper part has regular limestone formations, while the lower part has permanent ice formations from the underground river. The Cave of Liberty is higher in the valley and has limestone formations and small lakes. During the Slovak National Uprising in August 1944, Slovak partisans hid their food and weapons in the Liberty cave. It did no good, because the leader of the country then, Josef Tiso, was suspected of collaborating with the Nazis, and the uprising known as the *Slovenske Narodne Povstanie*, the SNP, was put down in two months. Both partisans and Jews were sent to concentration camps, and they were never heard from again. So, it would be good for you to see where they hid the weapons and fought for freedom. The most important treasure you will find there is your heritage," Aunt Maria counseled.

"Thank you for the information, Aunt Maria. If we do not see the caves on this trip, we certainly will view them at another time. (I did not tell Maria that I had already viewed those caves with Daniela and Marek because Maria had added the historical information about the partisans' hiding place that the young people did not know.) I also will correspond with Marek, a park ranger we met while staying in Presov about other possible caves in that area and around Slovakia."

"I urge you to be careful about who you give information and your confidence to in this and other business you conduct here. Many have not forgotten their old ways of informing the authorities about what you are doing so that they can gain favors for themselves when you get into trouble. I do not want to spend my last years bringing you food in prison."

"Thank you. That is good advice, although I would not mind eating what you cook for me at any time. I will keep you informed of what we intend to do, and you can counsel me if I am leading myself and the family into trouble."

"You also should know that Slovakia has iron ore, copper, lead, zinc, and manganese mines in the Slovak Ore Mountains. The *Slovenske Rudohorie* range is south of here. In Janosik's time, gold and silver mines were active also. You might look for an abandoned gold or silver mine as a place where he could hide his treasure. I do not know where they are, but we have uranium mines too. The Nazis and Russians were very interested in exploiting our uranium deposits when they controlled our country. They did not stay here simply because they liked our music or my pretty face. So, Juraj, you have many places to look, and many opportunities for trouble. If you find treasure, you will have trouble keeping it from all the bandits who roam the country in addition to the bandits in our government. If you tire of looking for Janosik's treasure on this side of the border, you can always shift to the Polish side, which also has caves and mines. Do you know why the Silesia region is famous?"

"Coal mines for certain because we saw many coal trucks on the road going in all directions in that area and coming into Slovakia through Zakopane," I answered.

"Yes, and the Picniny region is as mountainous on the Polish side as it is here. You will need two lifetimes just to walk around the possible hiding places let alone actually finding Janosik's treasure."

"You are making me hungry with all the walking."

"Good, I was beginning to think that you and Beth never eat. Now, I will feed you so that you do not go away with empty hands and empty stomachs."

Aunt Maria's Warning

As later events demonstrated, Aunt Maria knew what she was talking about when she warned me of possible trouble, but I would have plenty of help trying to find the treasure, some of it unwanted.

The rain continued for several more days. That allowed Beth and me to visit other relatives and share our ideas about efficient harvesting methods. We did not visit any more caves during that trip, which was fine because I needed time to devise a search plan with that many caves and other hiding places in the area.

When we returned to suburban Chicago after our vacation, I began to review European history of the late seventeenth and early eighteenth centuries. It was a great time for banditry at all levels of society. The events of the period were as interesting and as complicated as the personalities involved. Peter the Great was trying to bring Western European commerce and culture to his country while building a Baltic fleet to challenge Sweden in the north and to extend Russian influence south to the Black Sea. Charles XII of Sweden invaded Poland as far south as Krakow. The other European rulers were engaged in one way or another with the War of Spanish Succession. The intrigues, entanglements, actions, and royal ambitions were still being played out during World Wars I and II, the Cold War, and, in many respects, global politics to this day.

Our family treasure hunts from 1993 to 2001 had a set pattern. I researched possible areas while at home, corresponded with relatives and Marek to solicit their opinions about the best places to search, and then I scouted caves and mountain areas by myself or with relatives on our annual visits. While Daniela was busy obtaining copies of Janosik's court records and other documents that might aid us in learning his habits and whereabouts prior to his capture, Marek was helpful in obtaining passes to caves not open to the general public or in exploring restricted caves himself. Although we saw interesting sights or had something new to discuss in each letter, I recognized that family interest in the project would wane, particularly if we did not discover anything of value soon. Meanwhile, we were learning more about each other and drawing closer, which was my primary objective from the start of the project. The year 2001 would accelerate that process for all of us.

Through this period, I often reflected on Aunt Maria's words to me as we left her apartment for the last time.

"Juraj," Aunt Maria called out to me while the neighbors surrounded Beth with their bouquets of flowers. I went back to where she stood. She put her hand on my arm and said quietly, "At my age, the next time you come to Trstena, I will not be here. My days flee from me. You are the 'different one' in the family who your great-grandmother foresaw many years ago. Everyone depends on you. Your days will be long in their service. That vision also had been foretold to me many years before you came to visit me."

"Aunt Maria," I told her calmly, "if the family and others see salvation in me, they are sadly misinformed."

"No, Juraj," she said, determined yet equally calm. "You know what I am saying is true. You have a different life than the other men in this family. I know it will not be an easy life for you. Already you have your head in the lion's mouth. But, if God allows me to protect you through my spirit until your work on earth is finished, I will be at your side until we meet in Paradise."

"Thank you, Aunt Maria, I understand your words. Yes, my great-grandmother prophesied the same to me when I was fifteen years old. I did not fully understand then. In fact, I do not fully understand now, but

I accepted her message and began preparing myself for that life. Goodbye. I will not forget you, my heritage, or my purpose in life. But, you might want to wait in the vestibule rather than in Paradise for me. I may not have a ticket to go inside."

Over the years, I would not forget Aunt Maria's words as I would not forget similar words from my great-grandmother. But, I was never sure that I captured the level of understanding that Jeremiah promised to fulfill my destiny. My one certainty was that I would be tested many times in whatever roles evolved for me. Oh well, if the family and the world were going to observe and test me, I may as well be both entertaining and proficient. I may not resolve problems the way my brother would have approached similar situations, but I was headed toward events with no precedents among my family or anyone else.

Chapter Notes

1. John M. Shanahan (editor), *The Most Brilliant Thoughts of All Time* (New York: HarperCollins Publishers, Inc., 1999), p. 2.

2. *Ibid.*, p. 169.

CHAPTER 5

SUJAYA AND THE INDIAN EARTHQUAKE

INTERNATIONAL RESPONDER

The year 2001 was the Year of the Snake according to Chinese astrology. The year was appropriately titled for a number of reasons. Astrologers claim that people born under the sign of the Dragon, such as me, do not excel in Snake years. Unfortunately, I had plenty of company in the United States and across the globe. Nothing seemed to go right for any of us almost from the start. But, in January, nobody foresaw the main event to occur later that year. We went about our lives, as we perceived them.

All soldiers learn something about first aid and lifesaving techniques during basic or advanced training. My first aid training was enhanced by my sojourn with the three sergeants, although, at times, I could not determine if they were interested in saving my life or taking me to the eternal brink. Over the years as a civilian, I allowed my first aid skills to rust. For some inexplicable reason, I took refresher courses in 2000 to re-qualify as a First Responder. PURPLE was ecstatic, partly because it (they) didn't pay the tuition. But, primarily, as an International First Responder, I could gain legitimate and quick access to countries and people in trouble. PURPLE, the United States, several host countries, and I did not have long to wait for clients.

On January 26, 2001, one of the deadliest earthquakes recorded in India struck the town of Bhuj and the surrounding area of Gujarat state. The quake registered 7.6 on the Richter scale but did more damage than even that high number suggests because of the construction materials used and the large number of people living in the quake zone. The statistics tabulated later counted 19,727 dead, 166,000 injured, 600,000 people left homeless, 348,000 houses destroyed, and 844,000 houses damaged.[1] The Indian government estimated that the quake affected over 16 million people. U.S. media ran stories for several days, and then promptly forgot about the long-term impact to India and its displaced people, as the American press does for most human tragedies outside the United States.

International First Responder teams from the U.S. and around the world did not know the statistics when we reported to our respective embarkation points. All we were told was that the situation was bad and that the Indian people needed everybody and everything.

Onboard a military cargo transport, my group leader advised that the Bhuj time difference was 8.5 hours ahead of Eastern Standard Time. For us, the first stop before the earthquake zone was New Delhi's Indira Gandhi International Airport, which is about 350 miles northeast of Bhuj as the crow flies. The airport is about twenty-five miles southwest of New Delhi itself. Other flights would go into Mumbai (formerly Bombay) if the New Delhi airport could not handle all the incoming air traffic. Then, the crows and us would be transported to the quake zone by helicopters because most of the roads were impassable. Also, communications from the quake area to the capital were spotty, at best. As if going on my first International First Responder assignment was not challenging enough, PURPLE gave me its agenda in case I became bored or overwhelmed by all the death and destruction around me. Jenny, my new Scout, advised that PURPLE encouraged me to bring my weapons of choice. This notice confirmed my view that conditions in the quake area were extremely bad and that recovery rather than rescue work would be our primary concern when we arrived. PURPLE's agenda also signaled that I should not expect to spend all my time in humanitarian activities. Upon arrival, actual conditions were much worse than my most pessimistic expectations.

Bhuj is (or was) a town of 200,000 located on a remote, drought-stricken peninsula called the Rann of Kachchh on the northwest coast of India just south of the Tropic of Cancer and west of the seventieth meridian (23.399 degrees north, 70.316 degrees east, to be precise). If you accept the analogy of India being shaped like an ice cream cone, Bhuj is about where the ice cream emerges from the cone on the Arabian Sea (the west side of India). That location guarantees heat and humidity most of the year. The weather was especially warm for Responders coming from the Midwest in January. That included former military types who, like me, trained for years to ignore the weather and concentrate on the job to be done.

Some more experienced Responders complained about our initial destination of New Delhi rather than somewhere closer to the quake zone, such as Ahmadabad, the old capital of Gujarat, or Gandinagar, the new state capital located about twenty miles further north. Both cities were still over 200 miles east of Bhuj. Other Responders thought that Karachi, located northwest of Bhuj across the Pakistani border, was a closer landing site. The group leaders explained that New Delhi was selected because the areas surrounding Ahmadabad and Gandinagar were damaged in addition to almost 300 villages in the area between Bhuj and those two towns. My team leader stated that our personal safety was as important as our aid mission. Some team members shuffled their feet at that remark, but nobody verbally dissented. The group leaders eliminated Karachi because they argued that valuable time would be lost clearing Responders through both Pakistani and Indian Customs, then, rebooting us onto Indian transportation to the quake site. We were rescue workers bound by laws and treaties, not insurgents who ran across borders almost at will in early 2001. Pakistan and India were not caring neighbors, and no natural disaster would change their lingering feud over the unclear partitioning of the Kashmir region which was unresolved from British colonial days.

Lastly, when the group leaders advised that serious earthquakes occurred in the Bhuj area in 1819, 1845, 1846, 1856, 1857, 1869, and 1956, any residual whining stopped. The winning argument for me was that the ground was still shaking no matter where we landed. I kept my mouth buttoned, cleaned my equipment, read a little, and slept whenever I could. I did not quite know what to expect, but I assumed that this was not a recreational tour.

DR. SUJAYA

Upon our arrival in New Delhi in the middle of the night on January 28 (virtually all flights from the U.S. arrive during the night), we disembarked from our plane and immediately were grouped by teams and loaded onto helicopters for the flight southwest to Bhuj. I was no stranger to helicopters, but trained U.S. military technicians maintained those choppers. The Indian choppers ran rougher, and we were still on the ground. Just before we departed, an ambulance roared out of the darkness up to the helicopter pad and skidded to a stop just beyond reach of our whirling rotor. A slender, dark-haired, light-complexioned, Indian lady in her late forties (I guessed), carrying what appeared to be a medical bag emerged from the darkness and dust and ran toward our chopper. My seat was closest to the starboard door—a lesson learned from long ago. As she approached, I reached out, grabbed her hand, pulled her into the seat next to me, and we were off. Over the noise of takeoff, she shouted in my ear that her name was Sujaya. Her last name was lost in the rotor noise. If I had guessed that her family name was Jain, Gupta, or Patel, in this part of India, I would have been correct 99 percent of the time. When the initial takeoff noise subsided, she told me that she was a gynecologist, but, in this emergency, the government ordered all available medical personnel to the quake zone.

The four hospitals in the area had all been badly damaged, killing both medical staff and patients who were unfortunate enough to be there at the time. That explained why what looked like a large tent had been deposited on the floor of our helicopter moments before Sujaya arrived.

Upon touchdown at daybreak on January 29 on the outskirts of what remained of Bhuj, the Responders assembled into work teams, and the teams started digging in the rubble for survivors or human remains. In our immediate area, the prospect for survivors was slim, as I expected from the briefing. Three days had elapsed since the initial quake, Responders had mobilized from around the world, and we were pleased to see elements of India's emergency response team on the scene and working hard. India's governmental bureaucracy did not have a reputation for moving quickly on anything. Later, we learned that the rescue effort was being coordinated by international and private relief organizations, which moved more efficiently than local officials. Even so, the sense of urgency and ability to respond were different in this part of the world. Most buildings were made of brick, stone, or masonry heavy enough to crush those inside when buildings collapsed. Sujaya asked me to help her set up a medical tent close to the center of town and to assist her with initial triage of the patients, if we found any survivors. The initial call for our services came from workers who were injured or exhausted from moving debris and carrying bodies from the wreckage. Nobody slept that night despite jet lag and working in the heat all day at this difficult job.

R & R (REST & RELIGION)

After dark, Sujaya and I took our first break. We exchanged basic information. I told her I was from the U.S. Midwest, and she told me that she received an Ivy League medical degree. Similar to many Indians, her language skills were a product of former British colonialism, flavored by her U.S. education and vacations in New England. Introductions concluded I opened another serious topic. Other Responders and I had general knowledge that the victims may include both Hindus and Muslims, but we could not accurately guess their religious affiliation simply by looking at the bodies. The Hindus and Muslims treat their dead differently. I asked Sujaya if she could help us distinguish between them. The question was important, because we learned that a sizable number of Muslims lived in Gujarat state, and we wanted to treat the victims as respectfully as possible.

"Actually, India has three major religions," Sujaya said. "Buddhism is strong along the Tibet and Nepal borders, but we may find some Buddhists here too. We have a few Catholics in central India from the days of Portuguese exploration and colonization in the fifteenth century," she advised.

"Can we make life simpler for us foreigners? Who do we bury and who do we cremate?" I asked.

"That may be difficult because public health concerns may outweigh normal religious practices with this many bodies. But, if we have a chance, we may set aside the Hindu bodies for cremation and bury the others. Let me explain briefly the religious practices which may help you and the other workers."

"Thank you, we could use all the guidance we can get. I'm certain that we have offended half the surviving population already."

"I will start with Hindu practices and beliefs that you may already know," Sujaya answered with real concern. "First, Hinduism is the oldest religion in the world. Hindus have the ancient writings of the Veda (which is four times as large as the Christian Bible) to guide us. But, our religion is based more on our personal striving for self-knowledge than group performance of religious rituals. To us, only one god exists, although identified within three forms, or the *trimurti*, similar to the triune persons in God of Christianity to represent specific divine characteristics. The Hindu *trimurti* includes Brahma the Creator, Vishnu the Protector, and Shiva the Destroyer or Liberator.[2] The devil does not exist in our religion. Rather, ignorance of one's spiritual nature is the source of evil in the world. Hindus try to acquire the correct knowledge and spirituality through personal enlightenment in daily life. We should shape our lives to be without material expectations, we should devote our lives to selfless service to others rather than to our own wants, we should concentrate on our duties rather than on any individual rewards, and we should continually strive for unconditional love. These principles are not much different from other religions, but getting ourselves to the level of perfection of a yoga master is a lifetime effort. If we do not perform well in our attempts at perfection, our immortal souls are reincarnated into other mortal bodies for subsequent attempts until we gain the required perfection. Yoga practices are designed to enlighten both the mind and body to strive for this perfection. Statues, relics, and a host of living and deceased saints also help us on our journey toward spiritual perfection. Upon death, we do not care about the mortal body. That is why we tend to cremate Hindu bodies rather than bury them. Is that enough information on Hindu beliefs for you under these conditions?"

"Yes, well almost," I answered hesitantly while deciding to display my ignorance now rather than be embarrassed later. "I noticed that when you boarded the helicopter, you wore a wide long dress or skirt under your medical smock instead of a sari. Now you have slacks. Do you have more freedom in your dress and conduct as a Hindu than Arab women do under Islam? Or, did the U.S. corrupt you with our collegial fashion code when you were an Ivy Leaguer?"

"The demands of my medical practice and the weather dictate what I wear more than religious practices or the corrupting influence of being an Ivy League graduate. Women here are allowed to wear *kurtas*, the tunic and long pants outfits you have seen, and the *salwar kameez*, the long-sleeved dress and pants that I frequently wear. Our apparel should always be modest, but we wear more jewelry and brighter colors than Muslim women. Also, we do not cover our faces in public like the Arab women. Arranged marriages are still common, but we have greater freedom for education and professional careers. Here in Gujarat, tensions are high between the Muslim and Hindu religions. I often fear that war will break out between the two primary religions in India, or between India and Pakistan, where Muslims are in the majority. But, returning to my earlier point, I believe that Vishnu recognizes my deeds and good heart more than my apparel. If not, I may be reincarnated as your neighbor and let weeds grow in my yard to irritate you so that you can gain perfection by not noticing them."

"My neighbors have less tolerance for weeds than I do. But, if you were my neighbor who often baked pies and let them cool in your kitchen window, I would feel obliged to confiscate those pies as soon as I became aware of them so that my family and neighbors would not be tempted."

"I can see that you are a man of deep convictions—deep in your stomach. Do you have any particular preferences for your temptations or intolerances?"

"My intolerances are far ranging, but apple or strawberry-rhubarb pies are the primary offenders."

"I will alert all my relatives and friends in the Chicago area of your propensity toward dessert crimes and intolerances."

"We have Indians, Africans, Chinese, Koreans, and Vietnamese in our neighborhood. They are nice people, family-oriented, and work hard for a better life. I respect them, and I have not stolen any pies from them so far. Tell me more about reincarnation."

"To a Hindu, life is cyclical, not progressing toward some future point as in Buddhism, Judeo-Christianity, and Islamism. These life cycles are identified as the *Krita, Treta, Dvapara,* and *Kali Yugas.* Unfortunately, we all are now only 5,000 years into the *Kali Yuga* cycle that will last about 432,000 years, according to Hindu teaching. In this cycle, people are at their worst, and selfishness, hatred, and self-delusion prevail."

"Will the human race survive under *Kali Yuga* conditions?" I probed.

"No, and especially not you," Sujaya replied.

"Why am I here then?"

"Because I need your help. We better get back to work," Sujaya said to conclude our conversation for the moment.

The Man Without a Number

At the next morning's roll call, I noticed that my Responder badge number had not been called for the second time when teams were being assigned. Previously, I tagged along with Sujaya, but I didn't expect to be assigned to her permanently. With the grim task facing us, nobody noticed or seemed to care that I was a badge orphan. That's when I looked closer at my badge. It didn't have a number. Before the group left the States, Jenny gave me my International Responder badge in exchange for my U.S. badge. This was my first Responder trip and the first assignment of any kind with Jenny. I should have double-checked everything my rookie Scout did, but we were moving fast. Credentials were a lower priority for me than thoughts of rescue work and PURPLE's assignment. Even though it was her job to prepare me for whatever action PURPLE had in mind, I didn't blame Jenny for this apparent foul-up. *Wherever you are, Alice Bright Feather, I hope you are proud of me,* I mused. Joe Quick-To-Learn finally absorbed one of the lessons you tried to teach me so long ago, i.e., to take leadership responsibility and any blame directed at my subordinates—whether I was personally guilty or not. After considering my situation for a few minutes, I convinced myself that Jenny or PURPLE may have been divinely inspired in giving me an unnumbered badge because when I needed to disappear from the rescue scene and commence my PURPLE assignment, I would not be missed at morning roll calls.

Assigning Myself a New Job

As our work progressed along Bhuj's narrow streets, the Responders encountered more rats in the rubble. Shortly after the rats emerged, the snakes followed. As my triage responsibilities diminished, I loaded my .410-gauge shotgun and attacked any unwelcome critters in the rubble. If I couldn't save any residents, I may as well help the aid workers cope with the vermin. As it turned out, I didn't need to justify my actions to the relief workers. They appreciated my services. However, some local workers who were members of the Jainist sect of Hinduism were horrified at my killing any living creature. They did not appreciate my services and told me so through Sujaya. But, from another source, I heard that rats are considered a delicacy in some circles. I didn't investigate, but I noticed that when I returned to certain areas later in the day, my previous kills had disappeared. Motivated by health concerns, I decided to continue my rounds until someone unequivocally told me to stop. My conspicuously doing something other than digging through debris or carrying body bags served an unexpected purpose. When I eventually left the rescue area, I had a second reason to slip away without raising questions among my co-workers.

Our First Real Break

Near sundown on the second day, our group was notified that something resembling a road had been bulldozed to the nearby coast. If we wanted, we could be trucked there to bathe, eat, rest, and get the smell of death out of our lungs in the cool ocean breeze. The shower and food were welcomed, but as tired as we were, few of the group slept. Everyone found a spot on the beach and watched the waves come ashore. Fortunately, the epicenter of the quake had been nine to forty kilometers underground, and the shifting earth did not produce a *tsunami* (tidal wave) on that occasion. We were so tired that we didn't think about the possibility of tidal waves, and we would have been unable to evade an oncoming wave if we had. The principal remedy for us was to gather around a fire on the beach and talk until the trucks returned to take us back to the quake area the next morning. Other individual rescuers and groups also came to the beach to meet old friends among the Responders and to share whatever information they had about recovery operations.

I sat on an outcropping of rocks and stared out over the water thinking about the famous or unheralded Portuguese explorers who had sailed along this coast looking for the exotic trade goods and spices of India and the Orient. Vasco da Gama and his crew finally sailed around the southern tip of India at Cape Comorin and up the east coast to Calcutta in 1498. For better or worse, after the Spice Route to the Far East was discovered by the Portuguese, the British government and its surrogate East India Company quickly followed and opened India and China to all of Europe. During its colonial period, the British left a heritage of many people speaking English in addition to the multitude of Hindi and other dialects prevalent in India. The ability to communicate was helpful to all of us now in this emergency, but, before English colonialism, India saw a number of invaders come and go, including the Harappan civilization between 4000 to 3000 BC, the Aryans around 1700 BC, and Alexander the Great in 326 BC, followed in turn by Mongol, Hun, and Persian raiders.[3] Hinduism formed as a religion between 1700 and 500 BCE (before the common era), and the Emperor Ashoka brought Buddhism to the country during his reign around 323 BCE. Islam came gradually with Muslim invaders during the ninth and tenth centuries. India, as an old country, had more religious and military stories along one coastline than the entire United States could claim as a comparative infant in world history.

Sujaya interrupted my personal musing when she joined me on my rock perch. A group of Responders and several missionary students initiated a lively discussion about basic tenets of Hinduism, Islamism, Buddhism, and Judeo-Christianity for the infidels among us. I noticed Sujaya shake her head a few times at their interpretation of some of the more profound Hindu principles. She was more disturbed by the missionaries' dreams for Christian converts in an already deeply religious land where Christianity was not widely embraced. Nonetheless, the students worked as hard as the Responders at rescue and recovery consistent with the highest principles of any religion.

A Walk on the Beach

"Rather than continue to watch you become upset, let's walk along the beach, and you can lecture me on comparative religions," I suggested to

Sujaya. "I am beginning to feel cold sitting here after our high level of activity in the heat for the last two days."

"When did you become interested in religion?" Sujaya inquired politely while climbing off the rocks.

"I don't know if I'm interested in religions with their rubrics, rituals, public worship, politics, social agendas, and faults as much as I am in trying to connect with my Creator and Guiding Hand. And, don't ask me how I know I have a Guiding Hand because, without one, I wouldn't be walking on this beach after some of the life experiences I've had. It would be like telling you that I don't have a younger sister."

"Do you have a younger sister?" Sujaya responded while trying very hard not to laugh at my analogy. "I got the impression that you might be the caboose of the family given your apparent personality."

"Early in my life, my sister was older, but she stayed at age twenty-nine for so long that I caught up and passed her years ago. At least that's her version of our chronological ages."

"So now you will go to your grave or funeral pyre as her older brother," Sujaya said surrendering any attempt to contain her laughter. "In the medical profession, one does not usually encounter that level of male sibling devotion."

"Unless I post her birth certificate on the church door similar to Martin Luther, I can't publicly undo her repeated assertions over the years about our chronological history at this late date—after all, she is my sister."

HOLY MAN IN ROME

"But I can relate a recent and more mature interest in religion, or, at least, a religious experience. In September 2000, my wife and I were in Rome. Our hotel was not far from the Vatican. On a Sunday morning, we decided to attend Mass in St. Peter's Square with a couple from Arkansas we had met earlier. Because it was warm and Pope John Paul II was ailing with Parkinson's disease, we weren't certain that he would preside at Mass that day. Customarily, if he didn't preside at Mass, he would bless the crowd from his apartment window. Frankly, that's all we expected, if that. Fortunately, we were early enough to get four seats among the few folding chairs that were available. Within a short time, an array of cardinals emerged from St. Peter's Basilica followed by Pope John Paul II. Despite the heat, the length of the ceremony, and the number of communicants, the pope made it through the entire Mass. Then, he climbed into his Popemobile and circled St. Peter's Square, blessing the crowd as he went. He started in front of us, and my wife and I were immediately transfixed. The Polish contingent was next to us. When he went by them, they all cheered and waved Polish flags. I thought the ovation would never stop. As he drove around St. Peter's Square, I looked at our Arkansas couple, who probably were not Catholics, maybe Southern Baptists, but certainly not Catholics. They were as moved by the experience as we were. Later, the husband confirmed that he was not a Catholic, but he said, 'You know, I have a lot of respect for that man,' meaning Pope John Paul II. Those were very powerful words coming from a non-Catholic who sat in the hot sun with me for more than two hours."

"Ever since then," I continued, "I've studied the implications of his feelings and mine, our closeness to a holy man such as Pope John Paul II certainly was, and our presence with thousands of others in the sacred site of St. Peter's Square. All this occurred while we were asking for divine forgiveness of our faults and protection for our families and ourselves. Our brains are so small. We cannot comprehend the Being we call God let alone be worthy of forgiveness and protection. So now, I devote time to being a student of the deeper meaning of life and the role I should play, am expected to play, or destined to play with or without my Guiding Hand pointing me to where I belong each day."

"Are you a good student?" Sujaya asked while scurrying to avoid an incoming wave.

"That depends on the subject matter. The other day, I finally deciphered a geometry problem that had been aggravating me since high school. So, I am motivated and persevere despite being a little slow in achievement sometimes. Does that sufficiently define my mental capacity for you?"

"Can we go back and sit on the rock while I think of an appropriate answer?" Sujaya proposed.

"I believe you're too late. Someone else took our seats already. Besides, I haven't spent much time in the presence of an Ivy League graduate lately. I could use some East Coast *karma*. The only way I could have been on an Ivy League campus was with a rake or shovel in my hand, so you should tell me what I missed."

"I watched you during the last two days. Whatever you missed in the classroom, you certainly picked up quickly by yourself, good or bad," Sujaya teased.

"Like a magnet without a conscience, right? Am I a good example of a bad example? That's me for sure."

"Strange analogies, but I will accept them from the mischievous mysterious person you portray to others. But, I think you are someone who cares more about people and what affects their lives than you are willing to admit. You carry feelings of past experiences that you do not share with anyone, including your sister. Am I right?"

"By that, I think you mean that you are cold, and you want me to give you my jacket," I answered obliquely, although signaling that her descriptive arrow hit fairly close to the mark.

"Precisely, thank you. See how observant and caring you are even when you do not intend to be?"

"Commence the lecture before tuition increases, please. All I have left is the shirt on my back."

The Lessons Continue

"Where shall I resume?"

"If I recall correctly, you were describing the major differences between Hinduism and Islamism. I find it strange that the religion perhaps most different from yours prospers next door in Pakistan and to a lesser degree here in India. Of course, China, Tibet, Nepal, and Buddhism aren't very far to the east. Unfortunately, religious differences often fuel political and territorial policies that push countries that can afford them to pursue nuclear weapons. These in turn threaten global peace rather than encourage individuals to strive for spiritual perfection."

"You really dive right into the heart of a subject, don't you?" Sujaya observed.

"I subscribe to the old Bulgarian proverb, 'If you wish to drown, do not torture yourself with shallow water.'[4] Life to me is multi-dimensional, deterministic, and always amazing. Whenever I think I have disciplined myself sufficiently to gain internal harmony or peace with others, the old dualism of good versus evil emerges. I'm always forced to make a choice. But, I believe events happen for a reason, not by chance. So, tell me about Islamism. Perhaps, I can find some relief there," I said, surrendering the conversation to Sujaya.

"We probably both know that Muslims strongly believe in one God and that Muhammed is his prophet. The Muslim prayer '*La ilaha ill Allah*' meaning that '*There is no God but Allah*' attests to that.[5] To Muslims, Allah is the same God as recognized by Jews and Christians, but to Muslims, Jesus is not the Son of God, but one of his prophets, and Muhammed was the last prophet. Because Allah is the one God, Muslims have no need for the Christian Trinity or for multiple personifications of God as the Hindus believe. Muslims believe no purpose existed for Jesus to be born as the Son of God and to die for peoples' salvation because there was no original sin to forgive. To Muslims, sin is personal between Allah and individuals rather than inherited through Adam and Eve. Further, Allah had no need for a consort to give birth to a son. Allah is all-powerful in his own Being. Allah can forgive sin on his own without the help of others. Jesus is venerated as a prophet, and Mary is respected as his mother. On a more earthly basis, Muslims do not believe in images of God, and despise Hindu and Christian statues depicting God and saints, which we venerate to guide our thoughts toward the divine. Like Hindus, Muslims should not force belief in their religion on anyone. But, some passages of the Koran have been interpreted by non-believers, and, at times, by Muslim believers who favor an offensive *jihad bis sayf* (striving by the sword) to authorize the use of force against unbelievers, or to defend Muslim territory. Muslims believe in Satan, death, and a final judgment. For them, life on earth is a test for entry into eternal life. The Five Pillars of Islam are also familiar to many people, including the declaration of allegiance to Allah through the *Shahadah*, the daily *salat* or prayer five times a day for the truly devout, charity of at least 2.5 percent of annual income through the *zakat* collection, the *Ramadan* month of fasting, and the *hajj* pilgrimage to Mecca for those who are able to travel there."

"I can accept that," I acknowledged. "But, despite the striving for personal or community perfection in the various religions, much of the world is now concerned about the continuation or expansion of *jihad bis sayf*, the armed Muslim struggle or strife. Can you imagine the hardship thousands of people will suffer if an offensive *jihad* ignites in the Arab countries similar to the way the *mujahedeen* soldiers carried it out in the Balkans, Afghanistan, and Chechnya? Even Muslim fundamentalists and moderates argue about the correct interpretation of when an armed offensive or defensive *jihad* is permitted. If Islam is intended to perfect the shortcomings of Judaism and the perceived misinterpretation Christians give to the role of Jesus as the Redeemer, then Muslim *imams* should teach their followers the way to perfection, not warfare. If Muslims believe in personal accountability for their acts, I fear that we will see how accountable the Arab population in the Middle East is very soon. That's my lecture, so tell me about the conflict between the Sunni and Shiite sects of Islam."

"At the time of Muhammed's death," Sujaya started, "the Shiite minority held that Ali, Muhammed's son-in-law, followed by his direct successors, should be the only legitimate line of caliphs to govern the Muslim faithful. Conversely, the majority of Sunnis believe that a devoted disciple, Abu Bakr was the duly elected caliph after Muhammed, and that this precedent allows any devout Muslim to be eligible for election as caliph. The different interpretations have been a source of dissension among Muslims since Muhammed died in the year 632 CE."[6]

"That dispute involves a temporal question of succession rather than an article of faith. A similar issue in Christianity involved Henry VIII separating the Anglican Church from the Roman Catholic Church because he could not father a healthy son by six wives, not because the Church of England differs dramatically from the Vatican's teachings. How many people have been slaughtered over the centuries because of just those two questions? Muslims, Anglicans, and Catholics had plenty of time to resolve governance and succession issues and return to more important questions of morality and religious practices. Or, if we cannot do that, at least we should all agree not to unleash chemical, biological, or nuclear weapons on each other."

"It's interesting now that you mention it, that Christian, Jewish, Muslim, Hindu, and Buddhist countries all have nuclear weapons. When countries decide to become nuclear powers, all nations are adversely affected. Is that what God or any religion intends for us, or are we acting in defiance of religious instruction and our better selves in such cases?" Sujaya asked both rhetorically and in anticipation of an answer.

At that point, we ran out of beach as we headed north, so we turned and retraced our steps back toward the rescuers on the rocks.

"I read somewhere that hydrogen and stupidity are the most common elements on earth. Muddled thinking, defiance, and ignorance are always available alibis for a wide range of conduct including warfare. You reminded me that we haven't discussed Buddhism. I'm also reminded that when I was training in archery during my military service, I used some Buddhist *mantras* and mental exercises to improve my skills through focusing my mind. I didn't realize it at the time, but I was personally subverting religion for military purposes similar to samurai warriors of sixteenth century Japan or the *kamikaze* pilots of World War II. To make matters worse, I was taught this methodology by three Catholic sergeants from the Philippines who suffered terribly at the hands of their Japanese captors on Bataan. Distress or bad *karma* were not sufficiently available from our own religion, so we borrowed what war tactics we needed from Buddhism and Shintoism."

"You did remarkably well to maintain your sanity, let alone your faith under those conditions," Sujaya suggested.

"Are you asserting your gynecological opinion that I am still sane and able to distinguish between right and wrong?" I rebutted her assertions.

"Perhaps I am too hasty in my assessment. A second opinion on your mental condition would be valuable in your case," Sujaya said with mock seriousness.

"Isn't it strange that we are joking about sanity when we are only a short distance away from death and destruction beyond our comprehension and almost beyond our ability to cope with it? Within an hour or so, we'll go back there to find more bodies. What purpose was served when those nameless thousands lost their lives in minutes? Is that sanity? Is my God sane in allowing such things to happen to people who already do not have much hope in life? Is God just trying to reshuffle the Hindus into other bodies and hope for a better deal the next time around despite the presence of a *Kali Yuga* cycle? Or is this disaster nature's way of thinning the herd, to speak very crudely of human life?"

"You're not like the other Responders, are you?" Sujaya observed. "They help us, we thank them, and they go home feeling satisfied that they have done something both useful and necessary. You do all that, and then want to know the meaning of it all. You want answers to unanswerable questions. Why?"

"A long time ago, I accepted a role in life on the assumption that my Guiding Hand promised me that I would fully understand my purpose on this planet someday. The youthful days of quick answers are long gone. I'm still searching for a deeper understanding. Meanwhile, I believe my Guiding Hand continually expects more from me than he does others, and he reminds me of his expectations every day. I always have to face the dual choice between good and evil, or at least between my personal comfort and helping someone else. I don't always make the right choice, even after all these years. I haven't read enough of the Koran, the Veda, the Dharma, Jewish scriptures, or even the Bible to be assured that I get total forgiveness by merely asking for it after I make a bad choice. I do know that the Lord's Prayer of Christianity contains the phrase 'Forgive us our trespasses as we forgive those who trespass against us.' That statement is a powerful assertion that I don't get a free pass. I didn't read the small print when I signed on for my role in life. According to the prayer and my own imperfections, I only get forgiveness to the degree that I am willing to forgive. So far, I always come out with less than full value. Every time I think I've found harmony within others, my Guiding Hand, and myself, something always disrupts that harmony. Then, I'm back to the old choices between good and evil that are externally imposed or that I impose on myself. Good and evil are twins for me. So, I have a difficult time identifying and choosing between them."

"But you keep trying don't you?" Sujaya asked reassuringly.

"Sure, but at the rate I accumulate negatives, I won't have enough lifetime to achieve a positive balance under any religion's accounting system. I'm not Mother Teresa of Calcutta, you know; I don't forget and forgive everything. I get brain cramps on a regular basis. I don't always fully embrace members of my family, my friends, and my colleagues, let alone care for the untouchables as she did. I always hold a little back to gnaw on years later. Even my Guiding Hand's promise of complete understanding someday isn't always enough to keep myself under control and allow me to totally forgive others all the time. My Guiding Hand is very smart. At the time he and I made the deal, he knew what kind of bandit I was. Now, he and the devil have me chasing myself with my own moral posse."

"I think you're exaggerating more than a little bit. Everyone struggles with choices between good and evil. As an example, you may need a posse and a very large army in this part of the world if you believe your mission is to stop evil, ignorance, and poverty through good deeds. Too many things are already in motion for one person to prevent war and bloodshed in the Arab countries, and possibly here in India," Sujaya suggested as a conversational escape for me.

After that, we walked a few strides in silence.

When I couldn't tolerate the silence any longer, I said, "I think we're overdue for a change of topics. Is my jacket warm enough for you? You look uncomfortable. We're almost back to the group, but, we can walk faster while you tell me about Buddhism."

A Final Bit of Buddhism

"Yes, I am fine, but the wind is picking up beyond my comfort level. At any rate, Gautama Budda was born Prince Siddhartha in Nepal in about 560 BCE.[7] He rejected his life of ease to pursue truth and knowledge about the human cycle of life and death. He traveled the country as an ascetic for six years before coming to Bodh Gaya here in India where he sat under a *bodhi* tree to meditate. While he sat under that fig tree and contemplated his prior life and the cycle of life and death for all humans, he reached a state of *nirvana* in which he transcended all pain and suffering. Although he did not force his beliefs on others, he encouraged them to take a similar path toward enlightenment. When he died in 486 BCE, Buddhist monasteries and temples were being erected for his gathering flock. Budda saw a person's 'awakening' as the middle way toward understanding that life is temporary, and we are not separated from the living people, animals, and things around us. He came to believe what are now called the noble truths. These truths proclaim that unless believers follow the right path, life will continue to produce dissatisfaction (*dukha*), dissatisfaction results from unneeded cravings (*trishna*), that the end to these cravings brings (*nirvana*), and the way to achieve *nirvana* is through the right path (*marga*).[8] The right path is acquired through meditation, wisdom, and morality. The right path also involves eight steps: the right view, the right thought, the right speech, the right action, the right livelihood, the right effort, the right mindfulness, and the right concentration," Sujaya explained.

"Like other religions, after Budda's death, his followers created additional interpretations so that now we have the *Himayana*, *Mahayana*, *Tantric*, and *Zen* Buddhists. Happily, fully engaged Buddhism preaches nonviolence, but as you say, military skills and martial arts are also major components of Buddhist training. Originally, the martial arts were taught so that Buddhist monks could defend their temples from robbers and brigands. As Buddhism spread throughout the Orient, Japanese *samurai* warriors adopted the teachings as their rules of engagement. As principles of religious faith and practices were re-interpreted to accommodate warfare, innocent people suffered or perished. The human race has become very good at misappropriating codes of conduct for its own dark purposes. Do you agree?" Sujaya concluded her commentary with a question.

"Although we didn't cover all the precepts of the various religions, I agree with you," I said, "but in my life experience, while I am sitting in a lotus position contemplating universal truths, someone is sneaking up behind me to steal my wallet, or worse."

Karmic Change of Plans

A few minutes later, we returned to our Responder group. My Guiding Hand must have been listening to my complaining about his promise of

TERRORISTS AND THE TERCHOVA TREASURE

understanding and the continued duality between good and evil in my life. No doubt about it, my *karma* was about to change. As we collected our gear for the return trip, a Bhuj police officer drove up in a vehicle that could no longer be identified by make, model, or original paint. He asked for Sujaya and advised her that according to a message received from the New Delhi police, unknown parties had kidnapped her husband yesterday. The officer said that supply helicopters were currently unloading at Bhuj, and she could ride back to New Delhi on their return trip. The officer agreed to drive her back to Bhuj to ensure that she arrived before the choppers departed. A car would be waiting at the New Delhi airport to take her to the police station. I stood silently while Sujaya processed the bad news.

"Will you come with me?" she asked.

"Yes, if you think I can help," I replied in earnest despite knowing that I was already delinquent on my PURPLE agenda, and that my boss in the States was expecting me to appear behind my civilian desk sometime soon—perhaps a guest visit on payday, at least. Once again, the news took care of my latest bid for harmony and unity between my divine versus human dynamic. I was back in the duality of real life. Besides, Sujaya still had my jacket with my passport in it. I may as well go with her because it was now obvious that I could become involved in more trouble at a faster rate in New Delhi than I could by continuing to do good deeds in Bhuj.

Ravi, the police officer, managed to get us back to Bhuj without driving on the road for more than a few seconds at a time. Without seat belts, Sujaya and I were in continual motion in the back seat. Fortunately, she did most of the talking. Even then, a protective mouthpiece to guard my irreplaceable collection of natural teeth would have been helpful. Under the circumstances, conversation was limited to short sentences. So, I spoke first.

"Tell me about your husband," I asked, as I slid toward her side of the car.

"Roberto is a nuclear scientist. He works at the Bhabha Atomic Research Center near Mumbai, which you may know from your geography lessons as Bombay."

"Missiles? Bombs? Energy?" I inquired in one-word questions.

"All three, I think. He also teaches at the university there, and guest lectures at the university in New Delhi."

That was a fairly long reply under those driving conditions. We must have had one of our rare moments driving on the pavement.

"Wait a minute. You said your husband's name is Roberto?" I asked finally catching up to her first sentence.

"Yes, he's Portuguese. His family is quite wealthy. They have been merchant sailors since the sixteenth century. His brothers have homes in both India and Portugal, and the family owns ships in the Mediterranean, Atlantic, Pacific, and Indian Oceans."

"That covers the major water trade routes of the world and identifies at least two motives for his kidnapping—money and nuclear information. What else?"

"Lately, he has been distracted as if something is happening at the center that does not please him," Sujaya related.

"Could some shady nuclear transactions be involved? Nuclear weaponry is not a field for the faint-hearted, especially in the Middle and Far East."

"If so, as his way of protecting me, he would not tell me. I have no value as a hostage. We both agreed long ago that I do not need to know secret missile information any more than he needs to know about my patients."

"That sounds reasonable and professional. How does he interact with his superiors and colleagues at the center and at the universities?

"He is the most intelligent, sensitive, and caring person I know. He treats his colleagues, students, and friends as if they were members of the family. I never know whom he is bringing home for dinner or as an overnight guest."

"I hate lovable people who get kidnapped. Just once, I'd like to have a real jerk get kidnapped so I wouldn't feel bad about not rescuing him or the family not paying the ransom."

"What? I did not hear you," Sujaya shouted over the noise of squealing tires as the driver executed a right-ditch, paved road, left-ditch maneuver in under five seconds. "I think our driver is on lunch break rather than driving."

"Where does his family live while in India?"

"Oh—" Sujaya began.

"Never mind," I interrupted.

I noticed that the driver was becoming more interested in our conversation than he had a right to be given the obvious and ongoing conflict between his driving skills and road conditions.

"I'm sure we will find him," I declared as I motioned toward the driver with my eyes.

Thankfully, Sujaya got the message without my need to redial her memory machine.

"Officer," Sujaya shouted toward the driver as she tapped the back of the seat, "I want to contact the New Delhi police chief before we leave Bhuj to determine if the police have any additional information about my husband."

"Yes, by all means," the driver answered over his shoulder. "I will do better than that. I will accompany you to New Delhi and be in contact with the police while we are in the helicopter."

Why didn't I like the sound of Ravi's offer? I thought. But, I'm sure I'll obtain more information than I need shortly, given the way I was hemorrhaging good *karma* as we bounced toward Bhuj.

Sujaya saw my frown and asked, "Is something wrong?"

"Nothing in particular, but maybe a lot in general based on my experience. Despite India's deep religious heritage, poverty is also a major player here. First Portuguese, then British colonialism simultaneously helped and harmed conditions for the Indian people and their country. Under similar circumstances, people and countries everywhere do strange things to survive even years later. I'm still chewing on the motive for Roberto's kidnapping. I'm asking myself if his kidnapping is in response to his wealth, professional knowledge, or his heritage."

"I will let you decide the motives. I just want him back," Sujaya answered defiantly.

"I'm sure you do. But, determining possible motives helps me decide if and how I can retrieve a client and the best way to proceed."

This part of the road was particularly bad which made further conversation impossible. I kept myself occupied with my own thoughts and survival instincts as we bounced around in the car. During the flight to India, I had read that the country is about one-third the size of the United States, and it struggles to feed its population of about one billion. The country is advancing its economy and literacy through an emerging middle class, partly as some of my PURPLE colleagues explained to me, from outsourced U.S. customer service and computer related jobs. These jobs are prevalent near Bangalore, which is a long way south from Delhi. Like its neighbors, India has acquired the technology, fissile materials, and equipment to be a nuclear power. Again, like other nations, India sets aside its religious ideology and ethics in its dealings with Russia, the United States, or whatever other country is willing and able to offer assistance in weaponry. Pakistan and China, India's frequently adversarial neighbors may be ahead in certain areas of missile development, and that generates high stakes in national policy and diplomacy games. Consequently, kidnapping a key scientist such as Roberto to extract critical information, or crimping a rival's nuclear program, is all in a day's work in this part of the world.

My accompanying Sujaya back to New Delhi was one thing. Recovering her scientist husband, if it meant more than her paying a ransom to some rogue pirate or local gang was another matter entirely. I knew I was asking for serious trouble by accompanying Sujaya. I didn't know precisely what kind and how much. But, I rolled my mental dice and committed to the project.

The outskirts of battered Bhuj appeared on the horizon. We arrived at the medical tent followed immediately by the overwhelming cloud of dust that we created on the gravel road. Sujaya and I jumped out of the car and immediately began to collect our things from the tent. A black cobra was coiled up on my bow case. If I weren't in such a hurry, I would have been troubled by this unwelcome omen. He came to attention and spread his hood when I disturbed him. I grabbed a towel from the wash line and threw it over him, yanked my bow case away, and went to help Sujaya pack her medical equipment. We were ready in ten minutes, and the helicopters were revving their engines for the return run to New Delhi in eleven. The choppers kicked up another dust storm with their whirling blades, but we jumped in. I made sure I had my outboard seat on the starboard side. The Birkenhead Drill of women and children first in an emergency applies only to sinking ships (in my lexicon). On a crippled or poorly maintained chopper, I let the suicidal or neophytes take inboard seats.

We no longer looked like we had showered and changed our clothes a short time ago. *Nirvana* and good *karma* were nowhere in sight as we lifted off. Ravi, the Bhuj police officer went forward, hopefully to use the radio to contact the New Delhi police as he promised. That gave me a chance to ask Sujaya additional questions about her husband and his possible whereabouts.

Gathering Intelligence for the Hunt

"I know this is a bad time for you, but do you have any idea who may want to snatch your husband?" I asked Sujaya methodically.

"Under present circumstances, it could be Pakistanis, Iranians, Russians, or common Indian criminals," Sujaya answered broadly.

"You may be right, but let's explore the possibilities more closely. Pakistan and Iran may find his technical information valuable, but I doubt that they would use this method for obtaining his cooperation if he is regarded as a true patriot of India with a Portuguese heritage. Besides, these countries already are exchanging information and equipment with Russia, China, and, maybe, North Korea, all of which might be further ahead of India in some aspects of missile development. So, they don't need your husband for that information. The only reason why they might kidnap him is to keep him from using his skills here in India or in another country interested in developing nuclear arms. Hmm, China is equal or superior to Russia in first strike capability. With its fixed sites and mobile missiles, China can wipe India off the map. But, if Pakistan or China launches missiles, they know that India has retaliatory capability to make life miserable for them too. They certainly know that India might have both countries outgunned in conventional airpower. So, China or Pakistan won't risk a war just to hold one man who likely won't cooperate. The possibility of North Korean involvement is even more remote because Kim Jong Il gets help from Beijing. He doesn't need Roberto either. Whatever is going on doesn't seem rational to me from a missile technology perspective. How trustworthy and competent are the New Delhi police?" I asked Sujaya following my soliloquy. "I only know what I hear, and that information isn't reassuring."

"The gossip you hear is fairly close to the truth as far as the New Delhi police are concerned. Corruption and incompetence are rampant throughout most government bureaucracies here. You noticed that the Indian and international emergency relief teams from distant countries arrived at the quake site at about the same time. I really am worried because I don't know who will help me."

"On our way to Bhuj, I started to ask you where Roberto's relatives live while they're in India. Now that the driver doesn't have his ears in our conversation, perhaps you can tell me."

"Roberto's parents stay in Goa when they are in India, which is about half the time. His family has a large plantation near there. Goa is an old Portuguese settlement on the coast south of Mumbai. Many Portuguese and other Europeans have plantations in and around the city. One of Roberto's brothers, Paolo, occasionally stays in Goa. But, most of the time, Paolo takes care of family business from Lisbon. Miguel, the third brother goes back and forth between Portugal and India as family business and his personal whims require. He is not much of a businessman, so the family keeps him traveling to prevent his meddling in important matters."

"You said the family house is in Lisbon?" I asked to confirm Sujaya's information.

"Yes, they have large houses in the hills overlooking Lisbon. They have houses in the resort town of Cascais on the coast a short distance from there too."

(Little did I know I would hear the name of that town again within a few months.) I was about to ask another question when Ravi came back from the cockpit to talk to Sujaya.

"A car will be waiting for you at the airport, madam," he stated without emotion. "The car will take you to your house. The police will come to your house to tell you what they know and to ask you questions which may help them locate your husband."

"Who informed the police that her husband was missing in the first place?" I interrupted.

"That I do not know," Ravi replied.

"If you don't know that, you certainly don't know if later contact was made by the kidnappers, who they might be, and what they might want for ransom. Am I correct?" I stormed at Ravi.

"Yes, you are correct. I have no details about the kidnappers at all," Ravi said pleading ignorance.

"I am sure you are being as helpful as you can," Sujaya reassured him. "Thank you."

I was not as certain as Sujaya about the extent of Ravi's knowledge of recent events and innate helpfulness, but we didn't have much choice other than to accept his statements at face value. This case had too many loose ends, and, if their reputation was accurate, the New Delhi police might not be able or feel inclined to work hard enough to sort through them. The other big question for me was whether PURPLE wanted me to be involved. At the moment, I had no opportunity to contact Jenny or PURPLE. I really didn't intend to request clearance from PURPLE anyway.

As we approached the airport, Ravi went forward to take a seat nearer the cockpit crew. That gave me an opportunity to open my bag of tricks and start hiding little weapons and gadgets that I might need. I knew it would have an unsettling effect on Sujaya, but I had no choice if I wanted to help her without knowing more about the status of her husband.

"You look like you intend to stay with me," Sujaya noted as she watched my movements.

"You raise a good point," I said. "After we learn the details of your husband's status, I may need permission to become involved in retrieving him. My travel papers don't authorize me to run around your country as an armed posse of one. Meanwhile, I will help you all I can."

When Sujaya saw me take the big pistol and shoulder holster out of my bag, her eyes opened really wide. Her eyes became larger still as she watched me strap on the shoulder holster and put my light jacket over it. It was hard to hide a .44-caliber Magnum, even in a country with a billion people.

Deadly Business in Delhi

We made a hard landing near stockpiles of relief supplies for the quake area. Through the whirling dust, I caught a glimpse of a civilian car with a driver waiting a short distance from the landing pad. For now, Ravi's conversation appeared to be on the level. Ravi told us that he would stay with the chopper and help load for the return trip to Bhuj. He said goodbye to Sujaya, smiled, and did a half wave to me. By that time, I had learned the Indian custom of not touching in public, especially with the left hand, which is reserved for religious or sanitary purposes. So, a half wave from Ravi appeared genuine to me too.

The new driver was gracious enough to get out of the car and open the trunk, but not gracious enough to help us put our stuff in it. No problem, we had bigger concerns now. We drove east from the airport toward the city. Sujaya told the driver to head for the Sunder Nagar district, and she would direct him from there. He responded that he had been informed concerning the location of her house, but he would appreciate directions from her if traffic required any deviations from his anticipated route.

New Delhi is an ancient city that keeps growing beyond its previous boundaries. The result is a conglomeration of old and new districts. Theoretically, tourists don't see the most destitute areas in which the poorest 30 percent of the Indian population resides. What I saw was wretched enough for me. But, the Sunder Nagar district was a nice mix of shops and upscale residences befitting the solid income that Sujaya and her scientist husband probably commanded. Over the years, friends and former travelers to India warned me about "Delhi belly," even in the nicest hotels and restaurants because of the bad water throughout much of India. Supposedly, over 110 cities with populations exceeding 50,000 pour raw sewage into the sacred Ganges River every day. If I planned to stay to help Sujaya for a few days, being in her private residence might help me avoid local intestinal ailments as well as the skin sores also attributed to polluted water.

The driver stopped in front of an elegantly understated house. Inside, the rooms were simple and uncluttered with only a few Hindu figurines of various gods in what appeared to me as mysterious poses. I already confirmed my ignorance of the Hindu religion to Sujaya during our walk on the beach. If I did or said anything inappropriate now, I hoped she would recognize my actions were unintentional and inform me not to repeat the offense. In any event, I was here at her request to help her recover her husband rather than to traumatize her Hindu gods.

When we arrived, the New Delhi police weren't there as scheduled. That was more traumatic for Sujaya at the time than anything I did. I wasn't happy with that situation either. With Sujaya and me in the same room, I couldn't contact Jenny to advise PURPLE that I wasn't following the approved program, and tell her to obtain PURPLE's authorization for me to pursue this potential nuclear adventure with Sujaya.

About an hour later, three plainclothes police detectives arrived at the front door. Although their late arrival gave me time to shower and change clothes, the delay built up additional angst in Sujaya from not knowing the status and whereabouts of her husband. In a similar situation in the U.S., the family would have been phoning the local and state police, FBI, and any other law enforcement agency within reach to demand action. But, this was India. Sujaya knew the Indian system of waiting patiently until the police overcame their inertia before initiating action on a potentially difficult case such as this. The trio of detectives flashed their badges too quickly for my liking, although I frequently used the same technique. But, Sujaya accepted them as authentic. I was a guest in her home, and not a very informed guest at that, so I kept quiet.

"Tell me all you know about my husband's situation," Sujaya started.

The tallest most muscular one of the bunch who seemed to be the senior officer spoke up.

"First, I want to express our deepest concern for your welfare, and we pledge our best efforts to return your husband to you safely."

At any other time, that might have been a good opening statement for the police. But, Sujaya had waited too long for information about Roberto.

"Thank you, I appreciate your concern. Now, tell me about my husband and what you have done thus far to find him."

"Yesterday, we received a call from Director Rajiv of the Bhabha Atomic Research Center informing us that your husband left the facility at lunchtime and did not return. The director advised that he had lunch with another party, and, when he returned, the receptionist gave him a note stating that your husband was being held pending payment of three million British pounds."

"Do you have the note?" Sujaya asked firmly.

"I am sorry to say that we do not at this time," the chief officer stated. "It is in the hands of the Mumbai police."

"Do you know how and when the ransom is to be paid?"

"We do not have those details, madam," the chief admitted.

"Are the Mumbai police more informed about my missing husband, and are they searching there? Should I contact the Mumbai police directly?" Sujaya continued to interrogate the officer.

"We have contacted the Mumbai police, but they have no more information than we do at the present time," the chief officer answered.

As this conversation proceeded, I noticed that the other two officers were nervously shuffling around, regularly looking out the window, and listening for any activity from servants who might be working in or around the house. They were not interested in looking through the house for potential clues, missing clothing and other items, or setting up a communications network. This did not look good to me, and the chief's last comment lit a torch under Sujaya.

"If you do not intend to do anything to help me locate my husband, thank you for your time and information. I will go to Mumbai myself and look for him there."

"But, madam—" the chief protested.

"No, please leave now, I will find my husband myself," Sujaya shouted. "Please leave now!" she repeated as she started for the front door to show the trio out.

"I must object to your request, madam," the chief said as he and the other two officers drew their handguns.

Officer number one beat Sujaya to the door and let in a familiar person. It was Ravi, our alleged police officer from Bhuj. He hadn't taken the helicopter back to Bhuj after all. The second officer leveled his handgun at me while the chief grabbed Sujaya and slapped her hard across the face. My intuition was right; trouble found us quickly. At least, I had time to shave and shower so that I would look my best when it did. Sujaya recovered quickly only to get slapped again, harder this time. I didn't have to guess that these guys were serious about whatever they had in mind. While showering and putting on clean clothes, I had emptied my pockets of all my weapons. One lifelong belief I hold is that timing in life is everything. I hoped I could recover from my apparent bad timing in this situation for Sujaya's sake and mine.

The trio would separate us any time now for further "interrogation" if my three sergeants had taught me correctly. I'd have to decide quickly if I needed to invent a story or tell them the truth, which was that I didn't know anything including what Roberto looked like. My problem was that I didn't know what effect those two choices would have on their treatment of Sujaya.

"Take him into the other room," the chief instructed no particular colleague while he pointed his weapon at me.

Officer number two and Ravi started in my direction. I backed up into a little alcove, grabbed the brass statue of Vishnu the Protector (I think), and nailed officer number two as hard as I could with it. He went down in a heap, but I couldn't recover quickly enough to avoid Ravi's charge. He hit me across the forehead with his weapon and drew blood. I tried to remain conscious, and I did, but Ravi controlled the situation. He half dragged me into an adjoining parlor, and threw me against the far wall (just like the three sergeants used to do, but with more malice). I involuntarily went to the floor. I was still receiving neurological aftershocks when Ravi kicked me in the ribs. He lifted me by my shoulders into a chair, but did not tie me. *That was a mistake, Ravi,* my misfiring brain synapses calculated. *I will get you for giving me an opening when the time comes.* Then, Ravi made a second mistake, although I was not in a position to put everything together at that instant. He cocked the hammer of his pistol and put it to my head.

"Where is her husband?" he asked.

Then, he hit me with his fist in my stomach, and again to the side of my face. I was still thinking because it registered with me that he was right-handed. I wondered what was on the menu besides my blood as it trickled down my face into my mouth. I thought that my dentist would be very upset if she had to replace my natural teeth. As it was, she had enough trouble getting me to bite in the same place twice. Now, Ravi relocated my jaw a few notches further out of alignment.

"Where is her husband?" I heard Ravi ask again.

"I can't help you there, sweetheart," I heard myself answer. "I've only been in the country for three days. Working me over isn't going to get you information that I don't have, angel face."

Some of my blood had congealed, and I was moving my mouth and lips trying to move the clots out of the way. Ravi mistook my slumped shoulders and mouth movements as weak attempts to say something more, and he leaned closer. *Remember, Ravi, you gave me this opening. I hope you enjoy it.* I exploded out of the chair and butted him with all my strength on the jaw with the top of my head. As he reeled backward, I grabbed for his automatic and wrenched his right arm across my left forearm while my right hand twisted the gun toward Ravi's head. Simultaneously, I pulled the slide back so that the weapon would not discharge until it was pointed away from me. I had leverage now, and Ravi had only two choices. He could remove his trigger finger and let me release the slide to fire the gun myself. Or, he could hold on, allow me to break his finger inside the trigger guard, and pull the trigger when I released the slide. To gain additional leverage, I stomped on his foot, scraped his shin with my heel, and gave him two quick knee lifts to his groin. Ravi chose option two. I heard his finger snap, and I quickly released the slide (just like the three sergeants taught me years ago). The weapon discharged instantly. Ravi would not feel the pain of a broken finger. He would not feel any pain again in this incarnation.

Now, I needed to take on the chief and officer number one without getting Sujaya or myself killed. They couldn't see who had been shot, and I had my blood and Ravi's all over me. I staggered to the doorway as if mortally wounded with Ravi's weapon hidden behind my back. As I staggered through the door, officer number one and the chief stood transfixed watching my movements. Officer number one was off to my left by himself. The chief was just a shade to my right, but he was holding Sujaya partially in front of him. I would have to execute quickly which created two tough shots.

In that situation, my body was taught to respond, not evaluate the possibilities—good or bad. My first shot hit officer number one in the neck, my second quick shot hit the chief above the right eye before he could adjust and use Sujaya as a complete shield. As was true so many times in the past, the postman didn't have to ring twice. Both messages were delivered the first time. Sujaya just stood there with her hands over her ears. She started to shiver, so I moved toward her. As I rounded the dining room table, I looked at officer number two who was still on the floor from his earlier encounter with Vishnu. I felt his neck and wrist for a pulse, but couldn't find one. Vishnu had enrolled him as a reincarnation candidate. I had hoped to question at least one of them about why we were attacked, who was behind it, if there were others—if so, where, and what did they want? If the genuine New Delhi police were involved, I served notice that I took no prisoners that day. I didn't have the time, patience, backup, or lockup facilities needed for Geneva Convention rules of engagement.

By the time I got to her, Sujaya was slowly sinking to the floor. I caught her and eased her gently into a chair. Then, I found a seat for myself on the floor near her and audited my body parts by the degree of pain they presented. I had a superb headache and my jaw was sore, but I wasn't bleeding or missing any body parts. My brain was scrambled. I allowed myself to think that Sujaya had a well-built house—four shots from a 9-mm pistol, and nobody came running from inside or outside to see what happened. Either that, or the neighbors knew better than to become involved in somebody else's problems, even in a nice Indian neighborhood. That was fine with me. Sujaya and I were not ready for guests. Ironically, I had killed four men to possibly save the life of one man whose knowledge of nuclear weapons could wipe out thousands. I went through the gunmen's pockets. Except for phony police badges and ID cards, they had no other useful identification.

After fifteen minutes of staring at the wall or ceiling, Sujaya began to stir. "With all of them dead, now we will never know where they have my husband," she moaned.

"Maybe not. Before Ravi committed handgun *hari kari*, he asked me where your husband was. If Roberto was at the receiving end of a kidnapping or hostage situation, I think somebody in Mumbai bungled the job, or your husband escaped. The ransom amount was the only piece of information all our visitors knew. All the other facts of the kidnapping had changed, and nobody created another cover story. Somebody instructed our unwelcome guests to take you hostage with the intent of using you to recapture your husband. We need to discretely clean up your house and go to Mumbai. I hope we can recover Roberto before the party of the second part in this situation learns that you are still loose. The thought of going back to my regular job in the States is becoming attractive to me again, assuming I still have one. We'd better get going on this venture before I miss another payday."

"Do you really think Roberto is alive and safe?" Sujaya interrupted my rambling.

"He may not feel totally safe, but the way Ravi asked me the question leads me to believe that 'they,' whoever 'they' are, don't have him. You mentioned some family homes in Goa. Perhaps, Roberto is there, or at least close by in a safe haven. If the New Delhi and Bhuj police are involved as a group or as individuals, we need to be very careful about whom we deal with in trying to find your husband. We don't know why he's a target, who the 'they' are who want him, and to what lengths 'they' will go to retrieve him."

"Will you help me?" Sujaya asked with a spike of renewed energy.

"Being around you is getting hard on my wardrobe and ribs, but, yes, I'll help if I can find a clean shirt and find a way to carry weapons wherever we go."

"What should we do with these?" Sujaya asked, waving at the collection of bodies in her otherwise spotless parlor.

"Do you have any friends with a van?"

Sujaya got on the intercom to the servant's quarters in the carriage house behind the main residence. Shortly after her call, two of her men came in with old sheets and bundled the bodies for transfer after dark, I presumed. When the men finished removing their baggage, three women servants appeared with water and rags to finish tidying up the house. Sujaya posted another man to patrol the yard during the night to warn us of any other intruders. I went to the guest bathroom to wash my face again and to look at my ribs where Ravi had kicked me. For a moment, I celebrated my victory. Then, I remembered Jeremiah's warnings, and I asked my Guiding Hand for continued safe passage for Sujaya and me on the work ahead of us. I asked Sujaya for alcohol to put on my open cuts because I didn't want Ganges River water to do more damage than Ravi already had done to me. Then, I went downstairs one last time.

Everything was tidy, but the house still smelled like an arsenal after all the gunfire. I hoped that legitimate New Delhi police were too busy to pay us a visit until the gunpowder scent dispersed. With my inspection completed, I went back upstairs and crashed on a conveniently positioned bed until I heard Sujaya knock on my door the next morning.

Chapter Notes

1. Fiona Dunlap, *Fodor's Exploring India* (New York: Fodor's Travel Publications, 1998), p. 78 *et. seq.* By permission of Random House, Inc.

2. Linda Johnsen, *The Complete Idiot's Guide to Hinduism* (Indianapolis: Alpha Books, 2002), p. 14. By permission of Penguin Group (USA), Inc.

3. Dunlap, *op. cit.*, p. 32.

4. Shanahan (editor), *op. cit.*, p. 222.

5. Yahiya Emerick, *The Complete Idiot's Guide to Understanding Islam* (Indianapolis: Alpha Books, 2002), p. 40 *et. seq.* By permission of Penguin Group (USA), Inc.

6. *Ibid.*, pp. 334–337.

7. Gary Gach, *The Complete Idiot's Guide to Understanding Buddhism* (Indianapolis: Alpha Books, 2002), p. 5 *et. seq.* By permission of Penguin Group (USA), Inc.

8. *Ibid.*, p. 79.

CHAPTER 6

ROUNDING UP ROBERTO

MARCH TOWARD MUMBAI

Earlier than I expected, Sujaya was packed and ready to go. I think that was her way of getting my ribs to move despite the lingering soreness.

"Are we taking a train or plane?" I asked.

"We have a private jet because someone may be watching public transportation. Is that okay with you?" Sujaya replied as if everyone worldwide had a private jet at their disposal.

"That is fine with me. I hope you didn't call anyone to tell him or her that we're coming. We know less about the situation in Mumbai than we do here. We shouldn't announce our travel plans to anyone."

"I did not call the research center or my brother-in-law, Miguel, in Goa. I hope he is there when we arrive though," Sujaya affirmed.

When I went downstairs ten minutes later, the smell of breakfast had replaced the gunpowder vapors from the previous night. Money, manners, and a little help from the servants can go a long way toward tidying up a large house. By the way Sujaya treated them, they were more family than servants. I suspected that she had more servants than needed as her way of keeping a few New Delhi families from going hungry. I tried several *masala dosa* (puffy rice pancakes) and remembered to use only my right hand to feed myself according to Hindu custom.

"Where are our guests this morning?" I asked Sujaya.

"Assuming they are Hindus in need of additional perfecting through reincarnation, they are on their way to a funeral pyre in Gujarat as earthquake victims," she replied.

Terrific, that's all I needed to know about their passage to eternity.

With all the servants busy at other things, we hauled our luggage to the garage where an array of cars awaited us. Privacy was welcomed because we would not be able to explain our bruises, and I could not equip myself properly for this trip on a commercial flight. I instructed myself never to be unarmed in any situation during this enterprise after my major gaffe of leaving my weapons upstairs last night.

In New Delhi traffic, our drive to the airport seemed longer than our later flight to Mumbai. The flight crew was ready, and the eight-passenger plane allowed room for our luggage and my toys. Sujaya and the crew interacted with precision, indicating that they were accustomed to conducting Western-style business. We were airborne within a few minutes.

Recalling my earlier imagery of India as an ice cream cone, Mumbai (previously Bombay from the Portuguese Bom Bahia meaning Beautiful Bay, and now from the Indian Goddess Mumbadevi) is located about halfway down the western side of the cone south of Bhuj. The flight would take several hours—mostly spent circling the Mumbai airport waiting for clearance to land. Mumbai is India's largest city, located in its most industrialized state of Maharashtra. If people cannot find what they want in Mumbai, it doesn't exist, or it hasn't been requisitioned yet. Place an order with the right supplier, and the goods will be delivered within forty-eight hours—anywhere—guaranteed.

Along the way, Sujaya leaned across the aisle from her seat and said, "Thank you for your help in New Delhi. Perhaps, we can discuss what we need to accomplish at the research center."

"Your husband reports to the director of the center, correct? Is the director trustworthy?"

"Until this happened, I believed so without question. Now, I am not certain of anyone. No, I still must believe that Director Rajiv is a long-time friend. He is trustworthy, but he may be unaware of what happened. Or, someone may be holding him captive too."

"If the director is a trusted friend, he knows about the family houses in Goa and elsewhere, right?"

"Yes, he has been to our house in Goa many times."

"When we meet him, don't give the director our proposed itinerary until we evaluate his knowledge and involvement. If the director is not at the center and nobody knows where he is, we have bigger problems."

Mumbai Mlecchas

We received clearance from the tower, landed, and taxied to the private aircraft section of the airport. While the pilot stayed with the plane, the copilot brought a car around and assumed his alternate role as our chauffeur. I brought my big gun and derringer with me, and left the remainder of my toys on the plane. The distance to the research center was not far, but the map did not show the mass of humanity one needs to pass through to go anywhere at any time of day in Mumbai. We arrived at the center at 1145. Sujaya and I walked into the administration building with our hearts and adrenalin pumping higher than normal. The receptionist contacted the director in his office. *So far, so good, my Guiding Hand was aware of my presence in India.* Director Rajiv came to the reception area to greet us. He was short, but distinguished-looking, graying at the temples, and well dressed with a slight frown, probably from managerial frustrations and from not always wearing his glasses in public. He got off to a good start with me by suggesting that we walk and talk outside rather than return to his office.

Outside, a number of employees milled around on their lunch break. Several came up to the director to remind him of something they thought was important, or just to be seen. I suggested that we go to the car and instruct our combination copilot and chauffeur to take a brief hike while we talked. Apparently, the driver was accustomed to taking hikes. He knew where the cafeteria was and didn't mind being evicted from his vehicle. By the time we reached the car, Director Rajiv and I were properly introduced. He informed Sujaya in no uncertain terms that he was concerned about her safety as well as Roberto's.

"What happened exactly?" Sujaya asked the director when we could communicate freely in the car.

"Several months ago, a Russian representative previously unknown to us presented a lucrative proposal for high-energy uranium equipment and technical assistance if India stopped its public opposition to Pakistan's aid to the Taliban and to other Muslim fighters who use Pakistan and Afghanistan as training sites and safe havens. The Russian technology could give India a clear advantage over Pakistan in its nuclear development program. Everyone spoke in favor of the proposal except your husband. He wanted Russian assurances to control Pakistan's continued insurgency against India in the Kashmir region. The Russian representative would not give those assurances because Pakistani aid to the *mujahedeen* fighters kept NATO occupied in the Balkans protecting Bosnia, and the U.S. tied down in the Middle East protecting Israel. The U.S. had been eager to help the *mujahedeen* against Russia in Afghanistan and Chechnya. Now the shoe was on the other foot, and Russia saw its opportunity to tie down the U.S. in multiple locations while extending Russian reach into India. With the U.S. preoccupied elsewhere, Russia had more time to rebuild its military arsenal and regain superpower status. In the 1990s, U.S. strategists believed Russia could rebuild itself as a threat to the United States in ten years. Unimpeded, Russia could rebuild its military and political power in less time. Consequently, your husband's opposition to the proposal did not please the Russians," Director Rajiv concluded.

"From that, do you believe the Russians have my husband or that they are involved in his disappearance?" Sujaya asked the director shrilly.

"A part of me fears that is exactly what happened. Yet, another part of me believes your husband was able to escape and is hiding. The ransom of three million British pounds is miniscule compared to Roberto's importance to India's nuclear program. If the Russians are involved, they want him silenced, not ransomed. In that case, a ransom is merely a ruse for us to disclose his whereabouts. I cannot decide if Roberto's kidnappers are Pakistani insurgents, Russian FSB agents, opportunistic international provocateurs, or amateur Indian criminals who unluckily for them have allowed Roberto to escape. I have not been contacted by anyone since Roberto's disappearance, which strengthens my belief that he is not in the hands of his captors now."

Sujaya and I then described to Director Rajiv the events that transpired in New Delhi and our belief that an attempt had been made to take Sujaya hostage primarily to force her husband out of hiding. I noticed relief in the director's face when our information coincided with his belief that Roberto probably was free and hiding somewhere.

"Do you know the details of Roberto's departure from the center?" I asked the director.

"At lunchtime two days ago, Roberto stopped by my office to invite me to lunch with him. I told him that I had other commitments, but we could talk after lunch if he had something important to discuss. The logbook at the main entrance shows him signing out at 1215. That is the last anyone has seen or heard from him."

"Could we see his office?" I inquired. "Perhaps Sujaya can identify some helpful clues about where he might be."

"Certainly," the director responded. "We can go now unless you have further questions."

"We may have further questions after we see his office, but I think we have finished what we can do here," I assured him. "Oh, there is one thing, perhaps two. Do you think that the Mumbai or New Delhi police are involved, or, perhaps, the Pakistani Inter-Service Intelligence (ISI) agency?"

"Only the highest level of India's secret police are informed, and they are searching for Roberto. I truly believe that an unknown third party employed your visitors in New Delhi. Although their methods appear amateurish, I do not believe they were acting on their own," Director Rajiv confirmed.

"Have you had any incidents or attempted break-ins at the center recently?" I continued.

"None that are known to me. Is that important?" the director asked for clarification.

"I was attempting to confirm that our adversaries, whoever they might be, are after Roberto personally and not for any documents or information he might have. Has anyone inquired about him since his departure?"

"Again, not to my knowledge. No, wait—the Russian representative asked about him yesterday."

"Does the Russian representative have a name?"

"He is a military man, General Vasily. Yes, Vasily. Do you know him?"

"Unfortunately, yes. We met several years ago in Moscow. In addition to his military past, add FSB to his connections. Or, in this case, he may be acting entirely on his own. Be careful in your dealings with him. Ben Franklin and my grandfather shared an old saying, 'There is no little enemy.'"[1]

"We certainly will. Sujaya, what kind of person have you brought to us?" Director Rajiv asked, nodding in my direction.

"We do not know what kind of *mlecchas* (non-Hindu foreigner) he is yet. But, he has helped me a great deal in the last few days," she verified my legitimacy.

With that, Director Rajiv escorted us to Roberto's office. The clutter was consistent with a scientist's workplace. The safest spot to put classified material was on his desk. No one would ever find it there. With the director observing us, Sujaya and I went through every scrap of paper in Roberto's office. We gave the director any sensitive documents we found for his safekeeping. In the middle of one stack of papers, we came across a hand-drawn map that sketched a rough line from New Delhi to Mumbai to Goa. We set it aside and continued sifting through other stacks of papers because Sujaya said that the map was not in Roberto's handwriting.

About an hour later, Sujaya, who was sitting in Roberto's chair, leaned back and accidentally bumped the keyboard of his computer. When the screen came to life, a map similar to the hand-drawn one we had found earlier appeared. The computer map had additional details on it including a line from Goa southeastward to Chennai (or Madras as the Portuguese previously called it) on India's east coast. It also had the words "MANAS," "SAMADHI," "DIDYMUS," two crosses, and the phrase "*In solo Deo salus*" typed in near Chennai.

"What does that mean?" Sujaya asked looking at Director Rajiv.

"I have no idea," he said. "It is not a code for any programs we have here. Try to open other screens or programs."

Sujaya tried other simple entry codes such as birthdays, addresses, and wedding dates, but the computer quickly shut down. Fortunately, I had copied Roberto's message on a piece of paper before the computer crashed. Roberto had done his security homework well on any information related to the center. We could not get into his computer, nor could the director using official passwords. Nonetheless, Roberto wanted Sujaya or someone he trusted to see the "map" screen, interpret its meaning, and take appropriate action. My bet was that Vasily had seen Roberto's computer screen and had hand-drawn the incomplete map we found on the desk, either to keep others such as us from searching further, or because he had been interrupted. With the hand-drawn map on the desk, we would have stopped our search for Roberto in Goa, and we would not know where else to look for him.

"I'm no cryptologist, but probably Roberto gave us all the information we need to find him," I asserted. "Let's try making sense of the words he used. What is MANAS?"

"The manas is the part of the brain that processes sensory data and thinks," Sujaya replied. "That certainly would be a word familiar to me as a physician."

(I was glad of that because I would have misled everyone, including myself, if I had guessed the Manas airbase in Kyrgyzstan used later by the U.S. and NATO forces to supply troops in Afghanistan.)

"Okay, Roberto wants us to use our brains here. Now, what is SAMADHI?" I asked because I didn't have a clue otherwise.

"That is an intense state of concentration," both Sujaya and the director answered.

"Hmmm, he already told us to use our brains. Why would he repeat that if he was writing a cryptic message in a hurry, unless he felt our first guess would be incorrect without further reflection?" I pressed them.

"The word can also mean a saint's burial place," Sujaya suggested.

"Good, let's go in that direction a bit," I stated, getting more enthused that we had a good start in decoding Roberto's message. "Now, try

DIDYMUS. That doesn't sound Hindu to me, but what do you think?" I asked them.

(I had an idea, but I wanted to compare their answers with my assumption.)

"I agree, the word is not Hindu," Sujaya replied with the director nodding his head in agreement. "But, I have no idea what else it means."

"I may take a wrong trail here, so don't lose sight of what we have already," I said. "The only reference I recall in my life experience is that Didymus means 'the Twin.' Whenever I heard it, the word referred to Thomas, one of Jesus' apostles. Does that make sense to either of you?"

Sujaya's face looked blank. "Was Thomas the Apostle a twin?"

"We have no precise information about Thomas' siblings," I responded. "But, St. John's Gospel refers to Thomas as the 'Twin,' and that name has been handed down in the Catholic Church for centuries."

Then, Director Rajiv spoke up hesitantly, "Christians in Chennai believe that Thomas the Apostle came to Southern India to convert people to Christianity."

I nodded. "Now that you mention it, I recall reading or hearing about 'Doubting' Thomas the Apostle coming to India to preach. It's impossible to prove one way or another. Some speculate that Jesus also came to India or Egypt before he started his public ministry to learn about the ancient religions such as Hinduism and the Egyptians' worship of the Sun God, Amun Ra. These religious beliefs existed in India for thousands of years before Christians arrived. Another story my wife and I heard in Glastonbury, England, is that Jesus visited there as a young man along with Joseph of Arimathea. Joseph of Arimathea allegedly became Jesus' foster father after his traditional birth father, Joseph of Nazareth, died. Also, the ruins of Glastonbury Abbey allegedly hold the graves of King Arthur and Queen Guinevere. So, the accuracy of tradition can be slippery. But, if you only want a pleasant afternoon, a cup of tea in the restaurant across the street from the abbey, or to buy a souvenir, absolute truth in a conversation is not as critical as it may be to us here."

SEARCHING FOR DIDYMUS

"Tell me again how you connected Didymus and Thomas the Apostle?" Sujaya asked.

"Actually, I cheated. I have a constant reminder. A St. Thomas the Apostle church is not far from my home. My son and his family go there. My wife and I do too when the grandkids have a special religious event. Besides, the last phrase appears to be Latin. I merely followed my intuition and my four years of high school Latin when neither of you offered anything different. I also assume that Roberto is a Catholic given his Portuguese heritage."

"Yes, you are right," Sujaya confirmed. "We did not ask each other to give up our families or our religions when we married. In fact, I understand that in the days of the Portuguese explorers, the Catholic Church wanted Portuguese sailors and soldiers to marry Indian women to increase Christian converts."

"Pardon my smirking, but, requiring fifteenth and sixteenth century sailors and soldiers, or current ones, to increase church membership by marrying the women they encounter while they are on shore duty seems the absolute hardest way for a church to boost membership. Having Portuguese inquisitors make house calls in the middle of the night may be an infinitely more efficient and persuasive method for building a congregation, at least until the Portuguese ships leave the harbor. But, we need to return to deciphering Roberto's message. What are the two crosses—another reference to the 'Twin'?"

Director Rajiv contributed again with his knowledge of Chennai.

"Actually, two churches there are dedicated to Thomas the Apostle. Both are near the Armenian Bridge and the Chinnamalai shrine in the cave where tradition holds that Thomas lived. The Portuguese built one church in 1551, and other missionaries built the second church in 1971. So, we have two choices in Chennai."

"I suspect that Roberto being Portuguese and knowing the language would select the first church to find sanctuary. As a clincher, the Latin phrase 'In solo Deo salus' means roughly 'Safety in God alone,' which is a warning for us not to share our information too widely. Agreed?"

Both Sujaya and the director nodded their heads affirmatively.

The director added, "Your conclusions appear plausible for now. In addition, Roberto might go there to more easily reach the safety of Portuguese government offices."

"Perhaps, Roberto may not feel totally safe in Goa because it is too accessible to Vasily. Otherwise, Goa is closer to Portugal and apparent safety," I suggested.

"Both Goa and Chennai have airports. We can stop in Goa first to check if Roberto is or was there and if his brothers, Paolo and Miguel, have any information. If not, we can fly on to Chennai," Sujaya recommended.

"One thing is certain. Vasily has a head start on us in trying to locate Roberto. We should be prepared to deal with him somewhere in our travels. By the way, was Vasily in Roberto's office alone at any time?" I asked the director.

"He asked to use the phone. I was interrupted by other business several times. He could have been in Roberto's office longer than I now believe was wise for me to allow him access to Roberto's personal papers and classified documents."

"I don't know if Vasily is acting on his own or as a representative of the Kremlin. I urge you both again to be wary in any business transactions or other encounters you might have with him personally or with anyone connected to him. After our incident in New Delhi, he has four vacancies among his colleagues, but I don't know how many other collaborators he might have on his payroll," I cautioned.

"Yes, thank you. I will remember your advice," Director Rajiv nodded as we shook hands. "Take care of Sujaya for us."

"I will do my best. Contact Sujaya in Goa in the next day or so if you hear from Roberto. That may save us time and worry. If we don't find him in Goa by then, we will move on to Chennai."

"Certainly, yes, good-bye, and good fortune in finding him," the director replied positively.

That conversation finished, we left the office to retrieve our copilot-chauffeur for the ride back to the Mumbai airport. We found the driver talking to an attractive young lady who looked like a potential convert to any religion.

As we walked toward the car, I asked the driver, "Were you a sailor or soldier before taking this job?"

"I was a navy pilot, sir," he replied, "why do you ask?"

"No particular reason. I'm merely following up on an old Portuguese military practice for increasing religious converts in India," I answered as Sujaya rolled her eyes at me.

"You men never let up, do you?" she remarked, smiling despite her anxiety for her husband.

"I was merely trying to relax you and myself before life gets tough for us in Goa or elsewhere. You heard the director. Vasily was in Roberto's office for a long time. That is too cozy for an arm's-length business transaction at a nuclear research facility, or even a personal visit. Something has or will happen that we don't know about yet. But, if betting is allowed in India, I'll bet your husband is involved in some way that is now unhealthy for him."

"But, he is a good man. He would never do anything illegal or disloyal to this country!"

"I believe you. But unexpected situations can overwhelm good men too. Look at me. I came here to help people recover from an earthquake. Hindus do not believe in the devil, so I must be a good man. At least, I was when I left home. So far, I've reduced the Indian population by four men in the last twenty-four hours. I certainly didn't expect to team up with you buzzing around the country searching for your husband. Once again, I'm engaged in the never-ending duality between good and evil. Hindus and Buddhists proclaim that duality is only a reflection of my mental state and doesn't exist elsewhere in reality. The bullets that were flying around your house yesterday were real enough for me. But that's my problem. I shouldn't bother you with my ethical conflicts and deterministic belief that everything happens for a reason."

We got in the car, and drove back to Mumbai's Chhatrapati Shivaji Airport as fast as traffic allowed.

TOUGH GOING IN GOA

We must have caught the Mumbai control tower by surprise or on a good day because we were airborne toward Goa within a short time after taxiing to the end of the runway. If current circumstances were different, I could become accustomed to having a chauffeur drive me to my private plane and pilot me to wherever I wanted to go. Goa was tropical and touristy and maybe too westernized for those looking for the "real" India. But, it was fine with me. I could understand why the Portuguese did not relinquish control of this area until 1961. We drove southeast from the airport to Roberto's family house. Actually, it was a plantation with one grand house and several smaller residences in the compound for use when other family members or business guests came to visit. The principal crops on the plantation were spices. I recognized cinnamon trees but not turmeric, lemongrass, or other spice crops. I could only identify those by reading the labels on the small spice bottles in the grocery store back home. Roberto's brother, Paolo, wasn't there when we arrived in late afternoon, but he was expected shortly. That gave us a chance to have our first meal since breakfast, which seemed to be four centuries ago. I passed on *vindalho*, which is spicy pork or beef marinated in garlic, chili peppers, and vinegar. This was the first time I saw meat on the menu since my arrival in India. I finally elected *bangra*, which is a mackerel, and I caught the cook before he dipped my order in *balchao*, a hot curry and onion sauce. I only wanted to eat, not set the plantation and myself on fire. If the Portuguese explorers had this menu on the ship, I could understand why they stopped at so many ports along the Indian seacoast.

Paolo was the youngest brother, but he received a full ration of family brains and energy. He had the training and skill for his profession that only a member of an old maritime merchant family can acquire over generations, and he conducted himself as if he expected only top quality results from himself and others. Yes, Roberto had been here two days ago. Paolo argued against Roberto's decision to go to Chennai because he believed that Roberto had more options for fight or flight in Goa. But, once the decision was made, he supported Roberto in any way possible. No, he had not heard from Roberto since his departure. We didn't waste any more time. After Paolo's private conversation with Sujaya, we were back in the car, back to the airport, and flying southeast to Chennai located on India's east coast in the Bay of Bengal.

As we shook hands prior to our departure, Paolo told me, "Sujaya said that you can be trusted. This may be more than you can handle. Roberto had several transactions or agreements between Vasily and him go bad, and now Vasily is looking for him. Bring Roberto and Sujaya back to us safely, please. I will stay here and contact you if Roberto or Vasily reappear in Goa."

"What was the nature of the transactions?" I asked.

"Something to do with the research center; that is all I know. That is all I would tell you even if I knew more. Good luck in finding my brother."

Taking Chances in Chennai

In the air on the way to Chennai, Sujaya saw me looking silently into space and asked, "What are you thinking?"

"When we arrive in Chennai, I need to make a phone call if we cannot locate Roberto or Vasily within a short time."

"That should be easy to do. Why are you anxious? Do you need anything else to help us?"

"Sometimes, when I'm not sure what's happening, I invent my own games to see who comes to play with me. Then, I can deal with the situation on my turf and terms. I may need to do that here."

"What makes you feel that way now? What do you think happened between Roberto and Vasily?"

"I think in the trade it is called a failed fissile materials exchange."

"Should we obtain more experienced help?"

"We don't have time unless you want to get your husband killed and ship me home in a Christian casket for good measure. Besides, name someone who we can trust to help us in this kind of work. Whatever was on the agenda at the center didn't occur as scheduled. My guess is that Vasily intends to pin the tail on Roberto for something."

That ended the conversation and set Sujaya to wringing the life out of her handkerchief for the remainder of our flight.

It was dark when we landed. I was tired from the long day and the longer day before that. I hoped I wouldn't need to be at my best until morning. Before leaving Goa, Sujaya had arranged for a car to be waiting for us at the Chennai airport. As in Mumbai, the copilot doubled as our chauffeur while the pilot stayed at the airport to supervise maintenance and security of the plane in case we needed to make a quick exit. We checked into the New Woodlands Hotel. I made my phone calls but couldn't contact Jenny. I assumed that I was still acting without PURPLE's authorization. Under those circumstances, I decided that a quick tour around town was more productive than crawling between the sheets. Sujaya agreed with my priorities.

Within a few minutes, we set out for the two churches near the Armenian Bridge. (Apparently, Chennai has an Armenian enclave in addition to other non-Hindu groups.) We searched diligently and frantically among the hotels and shops, but we found no trace of Roberto. We had no choice but to go back to our hotel and get whatever sleep we could. Before I turned in, I called around one last time to the other hotels in town. Nobody had a booking for Roberto or Vasily. I suggested that Sujaya engage the hotel manager to find some street boys to attempt to locate Roberto. The night manager liked the intrigue and the possibility of earning additional *rupees* without any work on his part.

The next morning, when we went down to the lobby, the night manager was not on duty. Nor was he anywhere around the hotel. We had breakfast and drove out to the two churches near the Armenian Bridge again. We hung around the shrine at Chinnamalai, and the cave where tradition holds that St. Thomas lived while in the area. St. Thomas and Roberto were not seeing us or any other visitors that day. We retraced our drive from the city toward the airport to a little hill called St. Thomas Mount where believers say that St. Thomas was martyred. We hung around the little St. Thomas church there. We stayed so long that I found myself saying a prayer for help in finding Roberto. A monk told us that a cross encased in the wall of the chapel had once bled, and many people considered the cross to have miraculous powers. We could have used a miracle. It was late afternoon. We had frittered away almost the entire day without a sign of Roberto—or Vasily for that matter. We decided to go back to the hotel to check if the night manager had learned anything from the street boys.

On our way back, we drove past a stately building with one large onion-shaped tower and several smaller ones.

"What is that building?" I asked the driver.

"I believe that is the High Court building," he responded.

"Very nice," I commented.

We drove a bit more toward the seacoast and the outdoor marketplace nearby. Everyone simultaneously and silently realized that we had not eaten since breakfast. But our work wasn't completed. We hadn't found Roberto. Another large edifice loomed in front of us near the beach.

"What is that building?" I asked the driver again.

This time he didn't know. When we stopped for pedestrian traffic, I told him to ask the market boys what the building was. I don't know why I did this, but I did.

One of the market urchins shouted back, "That is San Thome Basilica where St. Thomas the Apostle's relics were kept for a while. I can take you on a tour of the basilica for twenty *rupees*!"

I opened the door, grabbed the kid, and pulled him into the back seat with me. We took off for the basilica, no longer mindful of pedestrians or the going rate for our newly acquired guide. He looked frightened until I gave him a fistful of U.S. dollars as a down payment. For that price, he would follow me home to America, he said. Then, he saw the pistol bulge under my jacket and started to count the money again. He was too late to renegotiate the price of being my tour guide. By that time, we had exchanged money although we had not exchanged mutual promises to perform the terms of the contract. Nonetheless, he had an airtight verbal contract as my guide with no escape clauses as far as I was concerned.

In nanoseconds, we roared up to the basilica and parked in the middle of the street. We ran into the dimly lit church just as the monks were making their way in procession to the main altar for Vespers, the evening prayer. As my eyes became accustomed to the dim light, I saw a few people scattered throughout the immense church. Over in a small left aisle pew, I could make out Vasily's silhouette. *Roberto had to be somewhere close, but where?* I told our copilot-driver to escort Sujaya out of the church as quietly and discreetly as possible before Vasily spotted her. Once outside, they could hunt for Roberto on the grounds or in the surrounding outbuildings. If Vasily saw Sujaya, he would never lead me to Roberto or permit Roberto to leave the basilica alive. With me, it didn't matter. Vasily last saw me in 1993. He would not expect us to collide in this church, in this country, on this continent. Besides, my hairline had changed significantly since our last encounter. After Sujaya left, Vasily glanced at me briefly without recognition and without identifying me as a potential threat. His eyes swept the church again, looking for his quarry. His actions told me that he had not located Roberto yet.

Too Many Hoods

I assumed that the monks had their hoods on for ceremonial reasons because it was well beyond warm in the church. I remembered Shakespeare's line from Henry the VIII, "But all hoods make not monks."[2] I couldn't see their faces, and it occurred to me that Sujaya's presence would have been helpful in identifying Roberto by his gait, height, posture, or mannerisms if he was impersonating a monk. I looked for contradictory information. Initially, I counted ten monks. Then, I had eleven when I included the organist. According to the cornerstone, the basilica had been constructed in 1896 in a neo-Gothic style that included plenty of side altars, statues in little alcoves, and countless nooks and crannies in which someone could hide. I counted the monks again. Now, I had thirteen. Everyone was about the same height. Two were stooped with age. *Good, I was back to only eleven again.* I looked for designer shoes. Everyone had sandals. I looked for new sandals, squeaky sandals, or different colored sandals. I had no luck there. I looked for skin color. If Roberto normally wore shoes and socks, his feet might be paler than the other monks whose feet were exposed to sun and dirt all day. Everyone had the same Portuguese-colored feet and hands. I looked for expensive watches. None of the monks had watches that I could see. I looked for the twinkle of a wedding ring—the universal marker that every married man forgets to take off when he meets a chick in a bar, or wants to impersonate a monk. In the dim light, I couldn't detect a wedding ring. I wasn't getting anywhere. The 1830 closing time was near, and the monks were concluding their rituals. I presumed the monks would soon gently ask everyone to leave, and I still hadn't identified Roberto. The only thing I could distinguish was each monk's general shape—large or small, thin or round. I subtracted the round ones; that left me with six. I recalled a photo of Roberto that Sujaya showed me in their New Delhi home. In the photo, Roberto was seated at his desk holding a pen in his left hand. *Okay, wizard,* I told myself, *look for a left-handed monk*. That wasn't easy. All the monks had their arms crossed with their hands up their sleeves, unless they actually were holding something.

Services were over now, and the monks scattered throughout the church to perform various maintenance tasks. Only Vasily, the monks, and I remained in the basilica. Nobody appeared interested in chasing us out, so I stayed watching for an identifying sign of Roberto. The monks' activity level picked up—monks get hungry too. I had a hard time keeping track of the six monks who most fit Roberto's general frame. One monk in the right side aisle finished vacuuming and began wrapping the cord onto the machine. (Beth is left-handed. She always wraps the cord on our vacuum cleaner at home counterclockwise. When I use the vacuum, the cord snarls into a bird's nest because I coil or uncoil it in the opposite direction.) My monk was winding the vacuum cord counterclockwise. *I finally found you, Roberto!*

I glanced in Vasily's direction. Vasily had found him too. Vasily was on his feet and heading across the nave toward Roberto. I was closer to Roberto, and, with luck, I could intercept Vasily before he reached Roberto. As I got to my feet, Roberto observed Vasily and my movements and recognized that unwelcome guests were present. About the same time, several monks came from the back of the church and stopped to chat in my aisle, blocking my way to Roberto. I moved down another pew, but I was losing time. Vasily would get to Roberto before I could.

Meanwhile, Roberto was not idle. He moved swiftly, but monk-like into a confessional along the right wall of the church. Both Vasily and I slowed up on the assumption that Roberto was trapped without any means of escape. But, the Portuguese monks who built the original church recognized that they were missionaries in a hostile country. They were in India only as long as the population or government allowed them to remain. Vasily was the first to discover that the confessional's primary purpose was not to hear and absolve the sins of the congregation, but to provide an escape for monks under siege. Vasily opened the door of the priest's section of the confessional to find it empty. In his anger, he slammed the confessional door, spun halfway around in the direction of the side exit of the basilica, pulled out his pistol, and ran outside without taking any notice of me about twenty pew lengths behind him.

Until I reached the confessional, the other monks stood transfixed in their places and watched the proceedings in silent amazement. Roberto apparently had alerted them about the possibility of Vasily coming to the church. I had not yet drawn my gun. Fortunately, the monks perceived my efforts favorably. My Catholic *karma* was working. As I opened the confessional door, several of the closest monks came forward to show me how the escape mechanism worked. The priest's section was solid, but the exquisitely carved side panels moved. If I interpreted the monks' gestures correctly, the left panel led to a passageway going outside. The right panel led to a passageway leading downward. All I had to do now was pick the correct passageway. If my *karma* held, I might be able to keep Roberto from falling into Vasily's hands.

Which panel should I choose? I didn't have time to process the data logically. When in doubt, I reverted to the reliable American system of dumb luck. Roberto was left-handed, so I took the left passageway leading outside.

The passageway was narrow, made of stone, longer than I expected, and probably the coolest place in India. I exited into a little outbuilding at the back of the basilica. Roberto was about thirty steps away, facing me with his hands raised. Off to the right with his back to me was Vasily, holding Sujaya tightly around the waist with his left arm while holding a pistol to her head with his right hand. The copilot-driver was nowhere in sight. This could be tricky. I pulled my pistol from its holster.

Vasily Remembers

As I cocked the hammer, I squatted down, and shouted, "Hold it, Vasily!"

I hoped his first instinct would be to wheel around, look for a target standing upright, and shoot. By squatting down, I was temporarily under his gun radar when he pivoted. Hopefully, he would be late in adjusting to the small target I presented. If so, I would have a slight advantage if I needed to shoot. But, Vasily was a professional. He would adjust quickly, and I would have to angle a shot over Sujaya's head. Vasily did exactly as I anticipated—until a small stone hit him on the side of his face. The impact was not hard enough to knock Vasily out, but it drew blood, and spoiled any chance for him to shoot at me. It also informed me that my advance payment to a certain little tour guide had paid big dividends. The boy had a bold and accurate slingshot technique in addition to his street smarts and guide skills. He also had a few more stones in hand if additional artillery was required, and he appeared unafraid to launch them in Vasily's direction. Meanwhile, Sujaya wrenched herself sufficiently free of Vasily's grasp to give me a bigger target. That still left Vasily and me facing each other with our respective weaponry.

"Who are you?" Vasily asked angrily.

"Someone who knows that you stole a shipment of uranium from the Ukraine that you intend to sell here in India," I replied. "Perhaps we should put our guns away and have a private chat while Padre Roberto gets reacquainted with his wife. Or, we could just shoot each other. If you are lucky, you will make my widow financially secure. She will be on a plane to Paris with the insurance money twenty minutes after my funeral. However, if I am more fortunate, you will be just one more piece of debris floating down the Ganges. My trigger finger hasn't eaten all day, and it's a little jumpy waiting for your reply. So, don't test its patience."

"We have met before, I presume?" Vasily fumed.

"Oh, now that hurt, Vasily. To be your current target is vexing. Not to be remembered is unforgivable. Try "Transitions" in Moscow in 1993. I know I look slimmer, and you look a lot older, but you still should remember me."

"Yes, now I recall. You were the American cowboy with Hassan and the consulting group. I know you. We know you now as Napokon, the self-righteous American gnat," Vasily sneered, spouting verbal venom in my direction.

"Careful, Vasily, I am a very sensitive self-righteous cowboy. So, mind your manners. My trigger finger is allergic to harsh criticism. It twitches uncontrollably when you call me names and become impertinent. Besides, I was on my best behavior that day in Moscow. Well, I behaved myself most of the day. On second thought, maybe you're right. Perhaps you weren't around for the part of the day when I behaved. That doesn't matter now. I will count to three. Then, you will release Sujaya and hand her your weapon. If you don't, my little friend here has reloaded his slingshot. Somewhere between the whirring of the slingshot and the cocking of the hammer of my pistol, if you listen carefully, you might hear the sound of a .44-caliber slug coming your way, which may scare all the monks and certainly spoil your profile when it arrives. We wouldn't want that to happen on hallowed ground, so here goes—one, two," I counted in quick succession.

Vasily quickly released Sujaya and handed her his pistol. She took it and immediately ran to Roberto who embraced her and finally took off his hood. The copilot-driver came running around the opposite side of the basilica where he had been searching for Vasily. When he observed that I was armed, he stopped in his tracks a short distance behind where Roberto and Sujaya stood. He was too late to be anything but an observer now.

"Wow!" I exclaimed. "In all my years in this business, that is the first time I've been able to use showdown psychology successfully. Thanks, Vasily, for restoring my confidence in my military training long ago. Consistent with my born-again confidence, my little friend will take your boot gun and bring it to me. If you try to use him as a shield or hostage, I am still sharp enough to put a slug between your creepy Cossack eyes."

Vasily blanched when I guessed correctly that he carried a backup weapon, and he lowered his arms to his side careful to keep his hands in view.

"My name is Advari," my little slingshot-wielding guide said as he proudly removed Vasily's second gun from its boot holster and carried it to me.

"Thank you, Advari," I said, "you are very brave. Now, the lady over there, Sujaya, will give you some *rupees*, and you can go back to the market, go home, or stay out all night with your friends if you don't attend school. If you hear a big bang, tell the policeman on the corner that you put firecrackers under a bucket. Give him some of your *rupees* and tell him that there is nothing for him to worry about behind the church. Okay? Do you understand me?"

"Yes, I understand you," Advari said, "and I understand *rupees* very well," he added as he collected his reward from Sujaya and disappeared around the side of the church before I had time to blink.

"Sujaya, Roberto," I said as I turned a little to address them. "I need some private words with Vasily, and then, we will take Roberto home. You can start walking back to the car now. Vasily, you and I should walk along the beach for a few minutes, after which, the remainder of the night is yours to do with as you please as long as it doesn't involve my friends, their family, and me."

Vasily and I finished our walking and talking, and I was back at the car in less than ten minutes. I left Vasily on the beach to consider our discussion and my terms for continuing his wretched life. I was certain that he would not cause trouble for Roberto, his family, or the research center during the remainder of my stay in India. I felt equally certain that he would cause trouble for me the next time we met, but not there, and not then. Given the current situation, that was the best I could do short of killing him.

Back at the car, I jumped into the front seat with the driver and sat silently as we went to the hotel to collect our luggage. A short time later, we drove to the airport for our flight back to Goa.

In the back seat, Sujaya and Roberto filled in the blanks that occurred in their lives during the past several days.

I told the driver, "I know you are curious, but the less you know about today's events the better. Understand?"

"I understand fully," he acknowledged, "but some day when I am very old, I may tell my grandchildren about what I saw today behind the Basilica of San Thome."

"I will give you Vasily's backup gun as a souvenir so that your grandchildren will believe you," I added. "And tell your grandchildren to stay away from the priesthood. It is a dangerous occupation in India—at least when Vasily and I are in town."

Assessment

On the return flight to Goa, Sujaya was asleep before the pilot brought the wheels up. My internal clock was so fouled up, it didn't matter if I slept or not. Hopefully, the crew or the autopilot was functioning properly in the cockpit. The interlude gave me a chance to talk to Roberto. Actually, he started the conversation.

"Thank you for rescuing my wife and me. I cannot thank you enough," Roberto said gratefully.

"Cling to that thought because I have a list of possible ways for you to thank me."

"Sujaya told me that you are different, no, eccentric, she said. I should have rephrased my expression of gratitude more precisely."

"Don't jump out of the plane yet. You can handle my requests with minimal effort."

"Okay, I will at least listen to your proposals."

"The first thing involves the four men who attacked Sujaya and me in your New Delhi house. These men were Indian, and I don't care if they were Hindu, Buddhist, Muslim, Shinto, or agnostics. They were hired guns, but they were not professionals. Fortunately for us, they did not excel in their line of work. Probably, they didn't deserve to die, but I didn't have time to negotiate with them. I believe that Vasily got them to do what he wanted because they were in desperate straits. If you find out who they were, and if I'm correct about their family situations, I would like you to donate some money to their families so that their widows and children have a decent home, education, and food on the table for as long as they need a helping hand. Do you think that's possible?"

"I will do it if I can find their families. That may be difficult for me."

"In that case, send someone to Chennai to get Advari, and put him on their trail. With that kid's street knowledge, he should find them in a short time."

"Okay, consider it done. What else?"

"When Advari finishes that job, teach him your family business, or get him into a good school in Portugal and off the streets here. He is too intelligent and courageous to waste his life hanging around the Chennai marketplace."

"Okay, but if he is unruly or unacceptable for any reason, I will discharge him at my discretion. What else?"

"Fine, if he can't do anything else, make him your bodyguard and give him a lot of stones. My next item may be more difficult, but I will present it to you. Someday soon, I may need your help or a loan of family resources. Vasily and I are not finished with each other. Even without Vasily, my life still drifts into different orbits than most people. Tell me how you got involved with Vasily, and I will outline my next request."

Roberto collected his thoughts a moment, and then started, "Beginning with the partitioning of the continent in 1947 between India and Pakistan, religious and territorial tensions have always been high. Each country controls a part of Kashmir and wants to control that entire area. If the British had clearly defined the borders at the initial partitioning, perhaps our lives would be more peaceful. Now, we have to be a nuclear power to defend ourselves against our neighbors. Because of Professor Abdul Qadeer Khan's work in Pakistan, we know that the Pakistanis have nuclear capability. Their capability may be equal or superior to ours in some aspects. Certainly, Pakistan is prepared to sell its nuclear technology to other interested nations such as North Korea."

"So, India wants to restore the nuclear balance or get an edge on Pakistan, correct?" I presumed.

"Yes, certainly, and the Indian government doesn't particularly care if the technology that gives us an edge comes from Russia, the U.S., or elsewhere. But, we look primarily to both the U.S. and Russia for most of our military purchases."

"The way computer and customer service jobs have been flying out of the States to Bangalore and other Indian cities, the U.S. will look to you as its supplier someday. Your multiple supplier policy must be fun for Indian pilots. On an emergency scramble, half the Indian Air Force jumps into U.S.-made fighters while the other half flies off in Russian MiG-23s. Then, they shoot at each other while Pakistan and China lob missiles at important targets all over India. I am exaggerating, of course, but I can see that your country has problems."

"You are correct about China," Roberto agreed. The Chinese CSS-2 and CSS-3 missiles have about a 4,750-kilometer range, which can blanket India from Chinese bases in Jianshui, Datong, Liujihou, Delingha, Da Qaidam, or Chuxiong.[3] Those are fixed bases. They also have mobile missile sites with shorter-range missiles that can hurt us badly too."

"It might be easier to name the missile sites in China that cannot reach India, if such places exist. But, you have a vigorous, second-strike capability with twelve to fifteen kiloton payloads that you can ratchet upward if you use your Agni missiles. They have a 3,500- to 5,000-kilometer range when launched from your sites at Ambala, Jodhpur, Tezpur, Jhansi, and Secunderabad.[4] That should rattle some cupboards well beyond Beijing and Karachi, and, perhaps, generate sufficient deterrence for China and Pakistan not to use their first strike capabilities. Missile launches in either direction will cause Sherpas in the Himalayas to duck as the missiles go overhead. If you want to send a chemical or biological message to China or Pakistan, dip your warheads in the Ganges River before launch. The source of your sacred river may be pure melting snow from the Himalayas, but with everyone using the river as a 1,600-mile latrine and as a place to float dead bodies before it reaches Varanasi where your Hindu pilgrims drink and bathe in it, India has a potent population reducer if there ever was one. Fixing the Dharavi slum in New Delhi may be a useful project too if you want future generations to thrive."

"Obviously, with the kind of information you have on our missile sites and the condition of our major cities, you are not merely a rescue worker. You are an adventurer or agent, perhaps?" Roberto probed.

"I am not an adventurer, and not much of a rescue worker given the way I performed in the quake zone a few days ago. But, I read and observe. So, think of me as an observer. Most of what I just mentioned is in open source reports and publications in the States."

"What else have you observed about our country?" Roberto continued.

"I observed that the U.S. initially wanted a nuclear-free zone in the Middle East in order to more easily defend Israel. But, Israel decided to pursue its own nuclear program at its Dimona facility and not depend totally on U.S. policies or national interests for its defense. Initially, the U.S. wanted to know every detail about Israel's nuclear capability. Then, both the U.S. and Israel realized the advantages to both countries if the U.S. and other nations did not know exactly what nuclear capability Israel has. As George Herbert once accurately noted, 'One sword keeps another in the sheath.'[5] The unknown capability has a deterrent effect on Israel's neighbors. For example, in the 1991 Persian Gulf War, Iraq lobbed some missiles at Israel but didn't unload its entire arsenal because it didn't know what the Israelis would send in Iraq's direction in retaliation. Fortunately for Saddam Hussein, the U.S. instructed Israel to stand down, take the relatively few hits, and not escalate the conflict into a larger-scale war. Similarly, when India exploded three nuclear devices in its 1998 tests, the U.S. and the rest of the world knew that India was a new member of the nuclear arms club. The U.S. backed off some of its demands for Israel and India to sign the Nuclear Non-Proliferation Treaty (NPT). As Charles de Gaulle once remarked, 'Treaties are like roses and young girls—they last while they last.'[6] I suspect that India believes it has advantages in maintaining an opaque nuclear program along with Israel. I also think that to maintain an opaque program, India believes it should play both its Russian and U.S. supplier cards. That's why your research center pursued Vasily's offer of high-energy uranium. How close am I to what you and Director Rajiv intended?"

"You are not far off. The situation is complicated, as you can imagine. Opaqueness has many advantages for India. We do not have infinite resources, and some military spending must be used for conventional forces. Also, if our adversaries do not know our capability, we do not have to rush our technological development. We do not have to depend as much on Russia or the U.S. as our weapons suppliers and technical advisors. As a superpower, the U.S. can be overbearing in its dealings with other countries. We do not see the U.S. as a threat to India, but U.S. national interests are not always harmonious with ours. When we and other nations differ from the U.S. agenda, the U.S. bullies us and other countries to follow its plan or directives. India perceives its future as a stable multi-ethnic state with potential for greatness. Perhaps we are premature in this belief, but we do not appreciate the U.S. telling us that we are a second-tier nation, and then begging us to help maintain nuclear deterrence capability and trade balances in the Middle East and Asia every time some Palestinian boy throws a rock at an Israeli soldier."

"Boys slinging stones help sometimes, though, don't they? But, I can understand your strategic defense situation more clearly now. When Russia comes to you with what appears to be an excellent proposal for missile technology, your research center is willing to listen, right? So, tell me how you became involved with Vasily."

"A few months ago, Vasily presented himself as a Russian representative with a lucrative proposal for technical assistance and nuclear equipment. As a condition of purchase, I wanted Russian assurances not to help Pakistan in its continued insurgency in the Kashmir and Gujarat regions. Vasily and the Kremlin would not give those assurances because Russia is giving the U.S. the same treatment that the U.S. gave Russia when Russia was fighting in Afghanistan. When Russia was fighting the Afghan rebels, the U.S. helped the *mujahedeen* fighters with weapons and technical assistance. Now, Russia sees its advantage in helping the Muslim insurgents maintain their training facilities in Afghanistan with Pakistani assistance in order to keep the U.S. off balance in the Balkans and in the Middle East. The U.S. must be careful to ensure that its anti-insurgent activities in the Middle East are not perceived as anti-Muslim. Otherwise, it will provoke a larger war involving other Arab nations. That would further destabilize the Middle East and pose a real threat to Israel."

"Your story coincides with what the director told your wife and me about the Russian proposal when we were looking for you at the research center in Mumbai."

"There is more to that story," Roberto added. "A short time after the initial proposal, Vasily appeared at the Bhabha center to speak to the director and me privately about an additional 'sweetener' if we urged favorable consideration of the proposal to top government officials in New Delhi. Vasily directly offered the center an unspecified quantity of high-grade uranium at a bargain price. At the same time, U.S. representatives were in New Delhi urging India to sign the NPT, or at least to adhere to the spirit of its terms. I told the director that we could not ethically sign the treaty if the center purchased uranium from Vasily. The director was very upset with me for my continued opposition. At the time, we did not know that Vasily was acting on his own initiative with respect to the uranium sale. From what we know now, Vasily illegally obtained the uranium from somewhere in the Ukraine. He knew how to obtain it because of his prior experience as a military officer there. When Vasily learned of my continued opposition to the initial proposal and uranium deal, I believe he decided to kidnap me, or hold me hostage until he had a firm deal with Director Rajiv. Again, Vasily was acting entirely on his own."

"Fortunately, as you said, he did not hire experienced kidnappers," Roberto continued. "I was able to elude them for a time. But, Vasily is cunning and persistent. When he found that his men did not have me, he decided to kidnap Sujaya as a means of forcing me out of hiding in Chennai. If you had not intervened, he would have succeeded. Even so, he caused me to change my sanctuary from the churches near the Armenian Bridge to the basilica. With all the trouble he caused, I do not understand why you did not shoot Vasily when you had a chance at the basilica. You shot all his associates in my house," Roberto argued.

"In New Delhi, Vasily's men attacked your wife and me. I did not have much choice except to use extreme measures. The reason why I did not take Vasily down in Chennai involves my last request of you. Let me give you some background first, and then I'll tell you what I may need from you."

"Very well. I will be patient."

"Vasily and I met in Moscow in 1993. I didn't like him then, and I despise him more now with good reason. I always believed that he was capable of dealing off the bottom of the deck with his own country, so he certainly has no loyalty to any other nation, government, cause, or person. I made a few phone calls at the hotel in Chennai, which confirmed that Vasily was operating alone on most of his proposal to you. I learned that the uranium he pilfered from the Ukraine originally was destined for another country. He had the uranium moved out of the Ukraine into my native Slovakia to make the next phase of the shipment easier, and, supposedly, there it sits hidden somewhere. The original buyer lost the capability of buying and secretly moving the uranium out of Slovakia, so Vasily tried to sell the uranium to your center without informing you that free delivery was not included in the sale price."

"What did you tell him at the basilica to make him walk away from trying to recapture me?"

"I told him that I knew where the uranium was, I had proof of his involvement in the theft, and I would inform the Russian, Ukrainian, and Slovak governments that he was responsible. However, if he abandoned his pursuit of you and Sujaya, I would not contact anyone for the moment."

"Do you know where the uranium is, and do you trust Vasily's word sufficiently to let him walk away without harming us?"

"Let's say that I was 'fingering the *ricasso*' on that one."

"What do you mean?"

"In sword fighting, one swordsman may try to gain an advantage by moving his index finger forward on the blade to obtain additional control of his stroke. The downside is that a good opponent will take the swordsman's finger off when he sees it exposed outside the hand guard. So, it's a risky move, but sometimes it works. I haven't confirmed that all the uranium came from the Ukraine, that it's in or out of Slovakia now, or that Vasily controls other hijacked materials. But, I intend to find out. Based on his initial acceptance of my terms, I must have fit enough of the puzzle together to make him leave you alone for now."

"Is that all you told Vasily on the beach?"

"No, there's one other thing that will remain between him and me."

"You enjoy this kind of sparring and risk taking, don't you?"

"Sometimes, but I don't take risks for the thrill of it. I certainly don't enjoy putting other people at risk such as you and Sujaya. But, I believe Vasily needs to sell the uranium in Slovakia with his fingerprints on it more than he needs to continue to harass you now that he knows I'm in the picture and you won't cooperate with him. My replacing you on his hit list is okay with me as long as I know his intentions and whereabouts. Sometimes, I feel that I should confront Vasily personally because his activities are not widely known to any U.S. intelligence agency. Often, I have as much, if not more, information than they do about former Warsaw Pact countries. By the time other agencies identify Vasily as a threat, the damage is done."

RECRUITING FOR THE FUTURE

"Can we help you on that score?" Roberto asked.

"Perhaps. Starting in 1993, I gave my European family the task of looking for eighteenth century treasure that possibly is hidden in one or more of Slovakia's 1,000 caves. In doing so, I became familiar with some of the traditional and unusual hiding places for weapons and other items in that country. My knowledge was just enough to convince Vasily that I could put my hands on his uranium stockpile. Frankly, I don't know how big or heavy a load is involved. It could fit into a backpack or a fifty five gallon drum. If I find it, I may need help from you or Paolo to move it to a safe place. By safe place, I don't mean Russia, the Ukraine, Pakistan, China, North Korea, or India."

"You likely will encounter opposition in relocating it, assuming you find it," Roberto cautioned.

"Absolutely. Russia, the Ukraine, Slovakia, or Pakistan may not be particularly skilled at safeguarding nuclear materials, but they don't like strangers running through their countries with unauthorized nuclear parcels in their hands," I stated my position firmly.

"You play a dangerous game," Roberto advised.

"Dangerous and foolhardy, I imagine to some people," I answered.

"Why foolhardy?" Roberto asked for clarification.

"When I first learned of it, the deal seemed far-fetched to me. I understand that the U.S. is negotiating or has reached an agreement to reimburse the Kremlin for expenses that Russia incurs in retrieving unsecured high-energy uranium (HEU). Russia will attempt to recover HEU that it previously sold to its former provinces and to rogue countries in addition to any of Russia's own spent fuel which has not been properly stored and protected. After learning about the related U.S. legislation, nothing is far-fetched to me anymore. Unless more is involved in this story, the U.S. knowingly and stupidly is funding Russia's return as a nuclear superpower disguised under a plan to keep nuclear materials away from terrorists. I can't control congressional stupidity, but, with your help, if I can get a bundle of uranium away from Vasily, that reduces the risk of his bundle of HEU falling into unsafe hands. That certainly will save lives and U.S. tax dollars. Considered on its own, the U.S.-Russian agreement makes as much sense as having the class scholar do homework for the class idiot and then charging the scholar for the idiot's ignorance and incompetence."

Fortunately or unfortunately, a number of other Russian-U.S. interactions were tied to the HEU recovery program. On May 28, 2004, a bilateral agreement between Russia and the U.S. was signed in conjunction with the Nunn-Lugar Cooperative Threat Initiative dating back to November 2001 along the lines I had described to Roberto.[7] In 2008, bankrolled by U.S. dollars to recover and reprocess nuclear waste from its former satellites and by *euros* for selling oil and natural gas to Europe through Ukrainian pipelines, Russia returned to the world stage as a belligerent nation intent on pursuing its former dictatorial agenda. After Russia's incursion into South Ossetia and Abkhazia in August 2008 to block the Republic of Georgia's attempt to reclaim its breakaway provinces, the U.S. quietly suspended payments to Russia under the nuclear waste recovery program. But, a report sponsored by the European Union released in September 2009 proclaimed that Georgia started the war with its attack on South Ossetia. The report also blamed Russia for interfering with Georgia's internal conflict with its breakaway provinces. However, the report's equivocation was sufficient to reinstate U.S. payments to Russia under the nuclear waste recovery program, even though a year earlier, Russia charged that U.S. and NATO nations had assisted Georgia in the five day war.[8] If that wasn't enough to reinstate U.S. payments, in June 2009, a Russian-American summit between President Barack Obama, Russian President Dmitry Medvedev, and Russian Prime Minister (translate as the real Kremlin leader and former head of the KGB) Vladimir Putin confirmed recommencement of U.S. payments for Russia's recapture of loose uranium from Russian and former Russian satellite facilities. Also, the U.S. needed an alternative route to re-supply U.S. and NATO troops in Afghanistan when the Taliban closed off former supply routes through Pakistan and the Khyber Pass. Thus, renewed nuclear cleanup fees were the payment method for Russian permission for U.S. arms and supplies to flow over or through Russian territory to Afghanistan. Coincidentally, the U.S. restructured the Central European missile defense plan which was proposed as vital by President George W. Bush's administration to protect the U.S. and Israel against Iranian long-range missile attack. Russia had perceived the defense plan as a threat to its national security. Poland and the Czech Republic perceived the U.S. conversion to an intermediate and short-range missile defense program a threat to their national security. Time will tell if Central Europe is more secure if Russia and the U.S. have normalized relations, or if the U.S. has a more aggressive defense program deployed through Central Europe. Some of that difficulty was alleviated when President Obama declared that Iran had constructed secret nuclear facilities, and he called upon multi-national support against further nuclear development by Iran. The last component of the Russian-U.S. chess game is for the two nations to work toward the reduction of nuclear weapons in an agreement to replace the 1991 Strategic Arms Reduction Treaty (START I) that expired in December 2009.[9]

For me, the issue is more than U.S. taxpayers taking another hit in their international wallets. The bigger issue is survival of the United States as a strong nation. We had no business giving rise to and supporting the *mujahedeen* in Chechnya and in the Balkan countries of former Yugoslavia. We had no business supporting the Taliban or its predecessors in Afghanistan when Russia was occupying that country from December 24, 1979, to February 15, 1989. Now that the U.S. and NATO are bogged down in Afghanistan, Iraq, and the Middle East because of the failed diplomacy, bad intelligence, and miscalculated military programs of prior administrations, do we really think that the Russian Bear will go senile in formulating its own foreign policy and be forgetful about our past and present adversarial and ill-conceived actions? What will be the true monetary and diplomatic cost of "resetting relations" with Russia as President Obama proclaimed? Will the U.S. wake up one day to realize that we have used the wrong strategies and resources and harmed both the people we fought for and ourselves by supporting corrupt regimes? Or worse, will we realize that we are now a bankrupt former superpower? Will we continue to be a beacon of hope for an otherwise messed up world? The answer is not self-evident and depends on what we do with ourselves as a nation, and whom we select as our future leaders.[10]

Meanwhile, Roberto responded, "I'm not sure U.S. foreign policy will lead to the results you suggest, but I am certain that, with your disruption of his scheme, Vasily will not rest until he finishes you."

"I don't doubt that for a minute. But, I told you that I have another major concern with him."

"Once again, I have to say that you missed your opportunity to get rid of him at the basilica."

"My grandfather told me an old Bulgarian proverb. If I translated it correctly from Slovak, it goes something like this, 'You are permitted in time of great danger to walk with the devil until you have crossed the bridge.'[11] Vasily hired four men to attack us. Who knows how many others he has working for him on various projects? As much as he hates me and yearns to be an important drug and nuclear arms player, he doesn't have sufficient personal capital to do both. If he operates independently of the FSB, or the Kremlin, at least part of the time, someone bigger must be financing his operations and helping him in other ways. As good as he is, he had help inside and outside the Ukraine to get the uranium into Slovakia. The reason I didn't terminate him at the basilica is to use him to discover his money trail and determine whom his financial backers and potential buyers are. My plan may backfire on me, but I have a few eyes and ears to help me watch him in Europe when I'm not there. In your opinion, who has large sums of money to finance terrorism and international weapons transactions?"

"I believe rogue governments and drug dealers," Roberto answered.

"We agree. So, if I killed Vasily at the basilica, I might not find his money trail by myself because U.S. intelligence is unaware of his operation and is busy watching other trails. Now, do you see my motivation?"

"Again, you could be making a dangerous choice."

"That's why I may call on you or Paolo sometime to pick up a package in Central Europe, provide firepower if I am pinned down by Vasily, or exercise your diplomatic or business muscle, including contacting Interpol or a foreign consulate to help me against a Vasily-led terrorist operation, a drug network, or a money-laundering scheme that I might uncover."

"I still think you should have ended your dance with Vasily and let future events take care of themselves. But, I will give you my business card with my home address, e-mail, and phone in Lisbon and here. I will tell my brothers, Paolo and Miguel, to help you without question if you ever need anything. Further, I will inform my office staff at the center to provide anything you need at any time."

"Including weapons and free passage to where I need to go, if necessary?" I added more items to my wish list.

"Yes, anything we can legitimately provide!"

"Other than a good night's sleep, I couldn't ask for more. Something tells me that Sujaya won't be awake when I leave in the morning. Say good-bye to her for me, please. I saw her work very hard at the earthquake site. She is a good woman and a good physician. Where did you meet her?"

"When she was at the school next door, I was at MIT. We met and dated almost immediately. Unlike my brothers, I always wanted to go faster than is possible on ships. That's why I became interested in missiles. With our professional schedules, we really have to fight to find time to see our families, but we manage. Unfortunately for us, children are not possible."

"At times, I might be too hard on my country," I mused aloud. "The U.S. still is the country of hope and opportunity for many people around the world. Unfortunately, many of our own people don't have the opportunities for education and health services that wealthy foreigners are given, or are able to buy in the States. But, I won't hold that against you if you permit me to suggest one more thing that may save your family and your life."

"What's that?" Roberto asked.

"Put your wedding ring back on before Sujaya notices your bare finger and makes you a permanent monk," I responded as we both laughed.

Painful Good-bye

The next morning, to my surprise, Sujaya was awake and insisted that I go back to New Delhi with her and Roberto in their private plane. Roberto instructed his secretary at the center to arrange my flight from New Delhi to the States. My ticket would be waiting for me at the New Delhi airport. *What more could I ask?* Actually, there was one more thing. Sujaya noticed that I was holding my left shoulder at an awkward angle and with apparent pain. My shoulder started hurting during the night as the adrenalin rush of the past few days subsided. After wiggling it around a bit, she declared that I needed an orthopedic surgeon to examine it upon my return to the States. Her diagnosis would lead me to the first of several shoulder surgeries and interaction with my Scout, Jenny, in her professional capacity as a physical therapist.

Passing through Indian airline security could have been a hassle if Roberto had not intervened by providing me with identification as a scientist at the Bhabha center. With all the excitement and travel to catch up to Roberto and Vasily, I didn't have time to clean my shotgun and pistol. The Indian security dog associated me with the scent of gunpowder before I entered the airline terminal. Otherwise, the flight home was uneventful, and I almost was glad to return to my civilian occupation—almost. But, the year 2001 was the Chinese Year of the Snake. Events soon would propel me into the international arena again, sore shoulder or not.

Chapter Notes

1. Shanahan (editor), *op. cit.*, p. 280.
2. "King Henry the Eighth Act III Scene I," *William Shakespeare The Complete Works* (New York: Barnes and Noble Books, 1994), p. 1176.
3. Ashley J. Tellis, *India's Emerging Nuclear Posture* (Santa Monica: RAND, 2001), p. 49 *et. seq.* By permission of RAND Corporation.
4. *Ibid.*, p. 551 *et. seq.*
5. Shanahan (editor), *op. cit.*, p. 288.

6. *Ibid.*, p. 276.

7. Bill Richardson, "A New Realism," *Foreign Affairs*, Volume 87 Number 1 (January/February 2008), p. 150. By permission of Foreign Affairs. Also, Frank N. von Hippel, "Rethinking Nuclear Fuel Recycling," *Scientific American*, Volume 298 Number 5 (May 2008), pp. 88–93. By permission of Scientific American.

8. Megan K. Stack, "Report: Georgia, Russia Both at Fault," *Chicago Tribune*, October 1, 2009, p. 14. Also, Desmond Butler, "EU Report: Georgian Attack Started War with Russia," *Associated Press*, September 30, 2009, pp. 1–2. Also, Denis Dyomkin and Margarita Antidze, "Russia Says U.S. Mercenaries, Others Fought for Georgia," *Reuters*, November, 24, 2008, pp. 1–3.

9. "Russia: Putin Offers Ban on Nukes," *Chicago Tribune*, June 11, 2009, p. 18. Also, "Kyrgystan Deal Reached on U.S. Base," *Chicago Tribune*, June 24, 2009, p. 17. Also, Jeff Mason, Guy Faulconbridge, and Michael Stott, "Russia Lets U.S. Fly Troops, Weapons to Afghanistan," *Reuters*, July 6, 2009, pp. 1–3. Also, Alla Burakovskaya and Grace Chung, "U.S., Russia Agree to Missile Cuts, But Tensions Remain," *The McClatchy Company*, July 6, 2009, pp. 1–4. Also, Christi Parsons and Megan Stack, "Summit Opens in Agreement," *Chicago Tribune*, July 7, 2009, p. 12. Also, "Obama, Medvedev Agree to Pursue Nuclear Reduction," *Associated Press*, July 6, 2009, pp. 1–4. Also, Julian E. Barnes and Greg Miller, "Obama Ditches Bush's Missile Shield," *Chicago Tribune*, September 18, 2009, p. 16. Also, "Obama: Missile Defense Decision Not About Russia," *Associated Press*, September 20, 2009, pp. 1–3. Also, "Biden to Reassure Poles During European Trip," *Associated Press*, October 20, 2009, p. 1. Also, Christi Parsons, "Nations Set Goals to Cut Nuclear Arms," *Chicago Tribune*, September 25, 2009, p. 25. Also, "Obama's Iran Disclosure Likely Part of Clever Chess Game," *The McClatchy Company*, September 26, 2009, pp. 1–4. Even if the New START treaty, the successor of the 1991 START I Treaty (which expired in December, 2009) signed in Prague on April 8, 2010 by President Obama and Russian President Medvedev is ratified by both the U.S. Senate and the Russian Duma and Federation Council, each country will retain at least 1,550 long-range missiles after seven years of missile reductions. That still is sufficient armament to annihilate civilization regardless of who fires first. The new treaty allows upgrades to each country's stockpile to ensure that the remaining missiles are more deadly. The treaty also allows Russia to renounce the pact if it feels threatened by U.S. defensive missiles deployed in Central Europe to guard against missile attacks from Iran or North Korea. Paul Richter and Christi Parsons, "U.S., Russia Sign Arms Treaty," *Chicago Tribune*, April 9, 2010, p. 12.

10. Chris Brummitt, "10,000 Marines Deploy in Start of Afghan Surge," *Chicago Tribune*, June 9, 2009, p. 12. Also, Laura King, "General: We Must Protect Afghans," *Chicago Tribune*, June 16, 2009, p. 15. Also, Liz Sly, "Milestone and Crucial Test," *Chicago Tribune*, June 30, 2009, p. 4. Also, Julian Barnes, "Resources Shift in Afghanistan," *Chicago Tribune*, July 30, 2009, p. 12. Also, Editorial "Afghanistan, the Sequel," *Chicago Tribune*, July 30, 2009, p. 18. Also, Laura King, "Afghan Race at the Wire," *Chicago Tribune*, August 18, 2009, p. 10.

11. Shanahan (editor), *op. cit.*, p. 214.

CHAPTER 7

LATIN AMERICAN LESSON

Peru This Time

The Snake Year struck again on February 13, 2001 with a 6.6 magnitude earthquake in El Salvador, killing over 400 people only a month after an earlier quake on January 13, 2001, killed over 800 people in the same region. I was out of position to help on either of those quakes, but my turn came again on Saturday afternoon, June 25, 2001, following a magnitude 7.9 earthquake around Arequipa, Peru.[1]

Loss of life and property losses were lower than the quake in India but bad enough for Peruvians. The epicenter of the quake was in the Pacific Ocean about 120 miles offshore. The shifting underwater tectonic plate generated a tidal wave large enough to cause additional structural damage and beach erosion around the nearby coastal town of Camana, but the plate's movement did not create a *tsunami* strong enough to threaten Peru's entire Pacific coast or other countries. Nonetheless, the tremor was felt in neighboring Chile to the south and Bolivia to the east. Ecuador and Colombia to the north were spared any destructive effects of this quake. As an International Responder, this was my second country that did not have everyday resources of clean drinking water or sufficient plumbing to accept toilet paper (if the latter could be found). For me, it was another environmental wake-up call. I hoped somebody in the U.S. Environmental Protection Agency was taking notes on what not to do to our U.S. plumbing infrastructure.

During the time between Bhuj and Arequipa, I followed Sujaya's advice and took my sore left shoulder to Dr. Scott, an orthopedic surgeon of superb and unpretentious skills. He and the MRI technicians began the first of several journeys through the inner world of both my shoulders. Meanwhile, my shoulders busied themselves hiding the full extent of internal damage. What began as simple arthroscopic procedures led to extensive surgeries followed by therapy and my introduction to Jenny in her professional capacity as a physical therapist. She had better skills than many more experienced therapists. My shoulders responded to treatment but were not fully healed when the Arequipa earthquake struck. I decided to go anyway. Jenny and her supervisor Alyce made me as ready as they could. Prior to my adventure in Bhuj, Marika contacted Jenny coincidentally, or purposely—I never learned the details, and she enlisted as my Scout. I raged when I first learned about it, but accepted PURPLE's decision as I weighed the evidence. Jenny was conscientious, thorough, and dependable. She would overcome rookie mistakes. On the other hand, she was a small town Iowa girl with no background in the deadly world I inhabited. I allowed myself one thought about my former Army partner, Dick, from Muscatine. Then, I expelled further thoughts about any Iowa curse from my mind. *That was a long time ago,* I reasoned. *Jenny would be all right. I would guarantee it,* I promised myself.

Jenny's therapy salon was on the other side of town from my workplace, but convenient enough for me to have a therapy session and catch the train home. To avoid interrupting her while she had other patients, we arranged pickup or delivery of documents by slipping them under the stair runner on the back stairway—the third step from the top. I fretted about the possibility of sliding a document too far under the carpet for either of us to retrieve. Fortunately, that and the associated problem of explaining why we were ripping up the stair carpeting to a security guard were unnecessary. Something more damaging than that would occur before this trip ended.

But now, other U.S. Responders and I loaded our gear onto two military cargo planes for the long flight south, actually southeast. With about seventy aftershocks ranging up to magnitude 6.2 on the Richter scale before our departure, I expected that we would fly into the capital city of Lima's Jorge Chávez Airport and then drive or chopper to Arequipa. I soon learned that by traveling overland, we might arrive in Arequipa for the next earthquake, but not for this one. During our refueling stop in Lima, an experienced Responder told me that a bus ride on the Carretera Panamericana Highway from Ecuador at the northern border of Peru to Chile at the southern border takes more than twenty-four hours on an exceptionally good day. Locals could not recall the last exceptionally good day in Peru. When the other Responders and I unloaded and stood near the plane, the ground was still shaking. As I learned more about the country and the general condition of Peru's buses, highways, and rest stops, I accepted statements about extended travel times at face value.

Piling onto choppers, we headed directly for Arequipa about 465 miles southeast of Lima, and to the Arequipa airport around six miles northwest of the ruined city itself.

I couldn't discern from its shape on my map, but Peru is the third largest country in South America. I read in my travel book that Peru's long and narrow perch on the Pacific coast gives it an unbelievable diversity of beaches, rivers, jungles, deserts, volcanoes, and high mountains. Peru's climate resembles Chicago's, although at different times of the year—too dry (June to August), too wet (January to April), too hot (December to March), or too cold at any time at higher elevations in the Andes Mountains.[2] Those were the only weather choices available. We had dry weather for the majority of my time there.

In the Central and Southern coastal areas, residents endure the *garua*, a persistent fog from April to December. (That will be important later in my story.) Local time lags five hours behind Greenwich Mean Time. Daylight Saving Time is unnecessary because Peruvians are casual about time, schedules, and appointments. With half the population living in poverty, time doesn't change their social rank, economic status, or living conditions. The poorest people in the Northern Hemisphere are rich by comparison. In the U.S., we do not understand lifetime economic imprisonment. After observing Peru's poverty, other Responders and I could climb aboard a plane, arrive home in a relatively short time, and lose track of 28 million Peruvians as soon as we returned to our watches, cell phones, and computers. In the U.S., we believe our lives are important while others are not, but we imprison ourselves with "time." We overrun people on our expressways to get to our all-important next appointment. Worse, we run over fellow worshippers as we leave our church parking lots if they don't move fast enough.

For most Peruvians, *fiesta* is the only event that brings relief from their grinding poverty. An earthquake reduces further what little possessions they own and what little joy or hope they secretly acquired in their hearts since the last calamity.

For me, the Indian earthquake would not be the sum total of my Peruvian experience. As we flew low over Arequipa, I observed that conditions were substantially different. On this assignment, U.S. Responders traveled from summer in the States to the colder Andean nights. The temperature ranged from mid-thirties to mid-sixties Fahrenheit and colder at higher elevations. Arequipa is (or was) a city of 750,000 people inland a bit from the Pacific coast, and relatively close to the Chilean border at an elevation of about 7,600 feet. The mile-high elevation required some acclimation before our lungs took in sufficient oxygen for any movement let alone vigorous rescue and recovery activities. Arequipa is known as the "white city" because its buildings and homes are (were) constructed of luminous volcanic blocks called *sillar*. The town is nestled in an area surrounded by active volcanoes, thermal springs, high deserts, and very deep canyons. In other words, this area was asking for seismic trouble with *sillar* not being a quake-resistant construction material.[3] The Spaniards re-discovered the town on August 15, 1540 (translate as "confiscated it" from the Incas and other native tribes). Thus, the town name could be derived from the Aymaran "*ari*" meaning "peak" and "*quipa*" meaning "lying behind," or from the Inca "*ari, quipay*" meaning "yes, stay" because of its beautiful natural surroundings.

From Arequipa, Lake Titicaca, which Peru shares with Bolivia, is to the northeast. Machu Picchu, the lost city of the Incas, is a shade northwest. La Paz, the capital of Bolivia, is due east. That seems like a lot of geography for a poor country, but my adventures would cause me to spend considerable time (that word again) in various Peruvian locations.

Finally on the ground in Arequipa, the volcanic peak of El Misti rose over 17,400 feet and framed the cathedral in the rear when I faced what remained of its twin towers across from the Plaza de Armas. The peak of Chachani was to the left at over 20,000 feet, and Pichu Pichu to the right at about 18,400 feet. (Later, I learned that every city in Peru has a Plaza de Armas, which became a handy reference point.) At this elevation and distance from the ocean, Arequipa was not a hostage to the coastal *garua* fog that I described earlier. For Arequipa, June is relatively dry and the beginning of the high tourist season for skiing and other winter sports. Unfortunately for the Arequipeños whose livelihood depended on it, the tourist season was suspended in 2001.

With its unstable and varied terrain, Arequipa shares a similar seismic history with Bhuj. Major earthquakes struck Arequipa in 1687, 1868, 1958, and 1960, with the addition of a volcanic eruption of El Misti in 1600. On May 30, 1970, earthquakes devastated areas in central Peru leaving a death toll surpassing 50,000 people. The small town of Yungay accounted for 18,000 deaths when it was buried under 15 million cubic meters of rock and ice that gave way from the west side of the Huascaran Norte slope and reached the town fourteen kilometers away at a speed of 300 kilometers per hour, another confirmation that disaster is no stranger to Peruvians.

Arequipeños have learned from this history. They began building only one- or two-story *sillar* structures, with the exception of the high-vaulted La Cathedral, which has its twelve pillars dedicated to the twelve apostles constructed of Italian marble. As a testament to the congregation's zeal, La Cathedral initially erected in 1656 burned down in 1844 and was reconstructed in the 1840s and 1850s only to be leveled again by the 1868 earthquake. Despite its propensity to collapse, the townspeople loved their cathedral, and reconstruction commenced on its twin towers almost before all the rubble and bodies were picked up elsewhere from that quake. The low-rise residential and business construction kept loss of life this time to about seventy dead and about 1,000 injured despite damage to over 70 percent of the buildings in the immediate area.

Unlike in Bhuj, the Arequipeños were not immobilized by the overwhelming loss of life and destruction, and they were working hard to provide medical attention, restore power, set up shelters, and distribute food before we arrived. Nights outside were bloody cold at this altitude for both natives and us. The International Red Cross had overall authority for organizing the rescue project. Other members of my team did all they could in Arequipa within seven to ten days. By then, I had made the first of several major mistakes that would have severe consequences, as I will relate shortly.

Because of downed telephone lines and loss of all communications, Peruvian officials feared that the town of Moquegua, about sixty-five miles southwest of Arequipa might be hit hard too. It was. In the afternoon of my first day in Arequipa, I volunteered with other Responders to helicopter to Moquegua to distribute relief supplies and airlift the injured.

Volunteering for Trouble

My mistake wasn't in volunteering. My mistake was not informing Jenny and my new civilian boss that I would not be in Arequipa at all times. Or, I should have ignored both of them and maintained my communications security. With an experienced Scout and my old boss, my precise location wouldn't have mattered. They wouldn't expect me to notify them of every small change in my location, nor would PURPLE want a lot of unnecessary chatter between my Scout and me when I was in the field. With new people who were uncertain about their responsibilities and priorities, my lack of communication was calamitous. To them, Moquegua simply was not Arequipa. To make matters worse, I didn't tell them that

TERRORISTS AND THE TERCHOVA TREASURE

I was on several air evacuations to the hospital in Tacna, which was even further south from Arequipa. The Tacna area was part of the quake zone, but the area between Moquegua and Tacna was mostly desert. Consequently, less structural damage and fewer injuries were encountered in that area. In addition to my unannounced movements, nobody could have found me anyway with my unnumbered Responder badge, including the Red Cross project director—even if I stood next to him, which I did on several occasions. As far as my boss and Jenny were concerned, I was officially reported missing, and according to them, the world needed to know. To me, it didn't.

But, on the third day, I rose from the dead and took a few minutes to inform both parties that I was okay and to please stop unnecessary communications. In addition, I informed Jenny that I was not on my PURPLE assignment. Jenny understood. My new civilian boss didn't. She could not locate a file she wanted, which was in the top drawer of my desk and plainly marked. At the moment, the file was her problem, not mine. With my whereabouts now clearly identified to both parties, I accompanied several unplanned air evacuations to Lima. Once again, my jittery boss and Jenny listed me as missing, precipitating my second unsecured phone call, which breached all PURPLE security protocols. If anyone was monitoring my calls, I had identified Jenny twice in as many days as my immediate PURPLE contact, which was absolutely forbidden. Serious consequences would result, but they were not apparent to any of us yet.

In India, I never activated my PURPLE assignment. Nonetheless, when I related my actual experiences through Jenny, I received a "well done" from PURPLE with a "but don't lose contact again" warning, which may have contributed to Jenny's current insecurity. Upon my return from India, I had informed PURPLE for the millionth time of my belief that drug and other contraband trails existed that responsible U.S. government agencies still had not adequately mapped or pursued as far as I was concerned. Victimized by brain anorexia at the time (which sounds clinically superior to being stupid), in forgetting that June was not summer in Peru and land travel was a nightmare, I requested and received PURPLE's permission before my departure to explore possible uncharted routes for drugs, weapons, money, humans, and any other contraband I could find. In return, PURPLE instructed me to maintain coded communications while I engaged in relief work or my freelance travels. I agreed, because coded communications are initiated by me, not by PURPLE or my Scout. Those security measures were now undone.

Campus Recruiting

Following a medical evacuation to Lima, I decided that I had fulfilled my Responder obligations in Arequipa. I needed to activate my PURPLE-approved search for contraband, particularly anything with an intended destination in Central or Eastern Europe. To do that, I needed a guide, a *companjero*, an *amigo*, or better yet, an accomplice. I wanted a person who was intelligent, active, knowledgeable, and trustworthy. But, as a stranger in this country, I would settle for anybody. I couldn't go to the U.S. Embassy or to the Peruvian Policia and ask for someone who knew drug traffickers. I couldn't go to the cathedral and ask for someone who had street smarts. But, I could start my search at the Lima campus of the Universitario San Marcos, and troll for my sidekick among the *estudiantes* (students).

In my experience, students are universally informed about all illegal activities within the galaxy, whether they are active participants or not. My experience also demonstrated that the secret of a successful fishing trip is the quality of the bait and its presentation. I took my wallet from my thigh pocket, extracted everything valuable except a $10 bill, threaded a piece of rawhide through and around the wallet's middle crease, and attached the rawhide ends to the inside bottom of my back pocket with a large safety pin.

Some professional thieves in South America are skillful enough to cut through pockets to swipe valuables, but I was fishing for a competent amateur, not a professional. Besides, I would be anticipating a hit, unlike distracted tourists who are spit on or jostled prior to being relieved of their valuables. Also, I had my two-shot .22-caliber derringer up my sleeve for protection.

To preserve valuable time in luring a petty thief into my web, I needed a likely spot for contact. I set up shop on a bench near the College of Law building and pretended to doze. With the activity of the last few days, my dozing became more real than fiction. A stiff wind blew uncomfortably enough to keep me awake, and I didn't have long to wait. If thieves aren't circling or attending a law school, the only other place to look is in a courtroom or in jail, and I didn't want to shop in the latter places for a guide with potentially adverse means, motive, and opportunity toward my personal safety or savings. The change of classes brought student traffic near my bench. After the initial bunch hurried by and scattered among the university buildings, I felt a light tug on my wallet, followed closely by a more vigorous and frantic one. I whirled around, grabbed the extended arm, and pinned it against the bench. Then, I put my left thumb into the back of my *pisces du jour's* (fish of the day's) hand and forced him onto his knees, where he caught his first glimpse of my derringer pointed at his head.

"*Buenos dias*," I said in greeting. "*Me llamo Joe. Como se llama? Habla Ingles?*"

"*Me llamo Jorge. Si*, I speak a little English, *gringo*," he answered with his lips curling a bit as he added the ethnic slur toward the source of his anger, pain, and embarrassment.

"You were doing well, Jorge, until you stumbled over the *gringo* word. Until we know each other better, my name is Señor *Gringo* to you. *Entiendo?*" I asked as I pushed the back of his hand harder with my thumb.

"*Eeeii, si, yo entiendo*, I understand, Señor!"

"Good, now come around and sit down with me unless you have a class to catch. You are making a spectacle of yourself kneeling on the ground like that."

I let go of his hand and put my derringer in my coat pocket as a gesture of goodwill as he walked around the bench and sat down. I also buttoned my back pocket because I only needed one fish today, not the entire "school" (or university) of them.

"Well, Jorge, depending on what information you offer about your skills, Santa Fortunata may smile on you today."

"What do you mean?"

"For help from you over the next few days, you may have an opportunity to earn some *gringo* dollars for yourself. Are you interested?"

"*No me gusta*. I do nothing illegal."

"How can you not like it? I haven't told you what I want yet. And by the Mother of God, I don't want to do anything illegal in your country either, *si?*"

"Okay, what do you want from me, Señor?"

"I'm glad you caught on to the 'señor' part quickly. I'm gratified to hear it. I came to Peru to help with earthquake relief in Arequipa. I accomplished all that I can do there. Now, I need help on another project. I have relatives in Central Europe, in Slovakia, if you know where that is. I'm certain that the flow of contraband goods is increasing in that neighborhood, and U.S. federal agents, the Slovak SIS, and Interpol, among other agencies, are not intercepting these shipments. I want to stop as much of that illegal traffic as I can, or inform law enforcement agencies about it. Believe it or not, some of that contraband may come from your country. I need a local person to help me find that trail. Are you interested?"

"How much will you pay, how long do I need to work, and where do you want to go?" Jorge asked stubbornly.

"Spoken like a true law student, Jorge. I'm beginning to despise you already. *Madre de Dios*, any amount I pay is more than you're earning now! I can't devote more than a week, so a few days at most. Where we go depends on where you tell me the action is, *si*? And before you refuse, remember that when we met, your hand was in my back pocket."

"Okay, but can I have a small payment in advance?" Jorge asked boldly.

"You were ready to steal ten dollars from me, so I will give you that as an advance payment if you come with me now. If you have other classes to attend, I will rip the $10 bill in half, and give you the other half tomorrow when we meet here again. We can discuss the details of your employment package then. It's up to you."

"I have finished classes for today. I am ready, but I need to pack some clothes. Probably, we should eat here before we travel because we may not find a good place on the road, or you may not like our food."

"I wasn't planning any gourmet meals, but you have a point. Good thinking. We can talk more while we eat. Lead the way, Jorge."

As Jorge pointed the way through the campus maze to the cafeteria, he asked, "Would you have shot me if I stole your wallet, Señor?"

"*Si*, I was very serious about that. I'm also serious about you not calling me *gringo* too. Remember, I'm your employer for the next few days."

Jorge grinned and said nothing further until we were in the cafeteria. Like every other college student, he was busy meeting and greeting his classmates along the way, especially the prettier ones.

"Do you know what you want to eat?" Jorge asked as we waited our turn in line.

"I know what I don't want to eat if that helps put us in the correct line. Do they serve ham and cheese sandwiches here?"

Then, I saw *papa a la Huancaina* posted on the menu, and I knew I could survive this meal at least. The *"papa"* dish is a boiled potato in a creamy sauce of cheese, oil, lemon, and egg yolk with the obligatory chili peppers. I would have been elated if they dispensed with the chili peppers. But, I didn't complain and hoped that my stomach wouldn't complain either. Peruvians were the first to recognize potatoes as food, so I assumed that menu item should be okay for me. The man or woman who invented hot chili sauce probably died on the spot before anyone could record his or her name and the date of that devilish invention. I suppose our lives must go on without that bit of information.

Jorge and I found a table in a quiet corner. He aimed for the chair that would give him the best view of *la ninas* (the girls), but I beat him to it. I needed to see the crowd more than he did. In a public place, this *gringo* always sits with his back to the wall. The only time Wild Bill Hickok didn't observe that rule in Deadwood, he was shot in the back while holding a pair of aces and eights (forever after known in poker as the dead man's hand).

When we got settled, I asked Jorge, "What made my wallet attractive to you? You seem to be prosperous enough?"

"Yes, I have a scholarship, but I have two brothers and three sisters at home. My family needs all the income we can get."

"Isn't family size something your parents should consider in their leisure time so that their sons will not have to become *banditos* or law students to survive?"

"Tradition of large families is hard to break in Peru, Señor. What are you looking at?

"I saw three Middle Eastern-looking men come in. Is that unusual?"

"Not really. We have Arab and Israeli teachers and businessmen visiting Lima regularly. They usually stay at a hotel which caters to them in town."

"These guys look more like *pistoleros* than businessmen. Turn around and take a look while they have their backs turned."

Jorge took a quick look over his shoulder and shrugged, "I know them. I see them all the time. They have business connections with the Barrantes family."

"What line of work is Señor Barrantes in, and how do you know his business associates?"

"He is in international trade. He has done very well for himself and his family. I work for him on his *ranchero*, and he pays some of my school expenses."

"But, between your scholarship and your *ranchero* pay you still do not have enough to send *pesos* or *nuevo soles* home to support your family? Is that why you supplement your income by visiting my back pocket? Is that a fair statement of my case against you?"

"Unfortunately, yes. You are the first one to be quick enough to stop me."

"I believe that everyone should have backup skills with international unemployment being what it is. My backup specialty happens to be keeping people's fingers off my wallet. But, let's get back to business. What crops does Señor Barrantes grow on his *ranchero*, coca leaves and poppies?"

"I do not know exactly. I only work at his house and villa here in Lima."

"You just said you work at his *ranchero*. Which is it, *casa, villa, ranchero* or all the above? And, what kind of work do you do for him? Your hands do not look like they do *ranchero* chores?"

"Please, Señor, you are making it difficult for me."

"I think you just told me that Señor Barrantes is in the drug trade, if not more. Is his villa the large colonial house in the Miraflores area south of Lima that everyone talks about?"

"He has a city *casa* in old Lima, and his villa is in the Lima suburb of Miraflores, *si*. He also has other houses and property in Peru and Bolivia in addition to his *ranchero* near Quillabamba."

"You just pronounced the two L's in Quillabamba as two L's. Did I miss something in Spanish class?"

"No, Señor. That is an exception to the rule to pronounce the two L's as a Y, but I do not know why."

"Perhaps, the person who named the town missed Spanish class that day too. But, go on, tell me more about Quillabamba."

"That area is one of Peru's major tea-producing regions," Jorge explained.

"Somehow, I knew you would say something like that. I suppose, if I let you, the next thing you'll tell me is that Señor Barrantes enjoys a hardy cup of herbal or green tea after a hard day in the saddle supervising his *ranchero's* far-flung harvesting, production, and shipping operations in coca leaves or paste. But, time and my compulsive personality press onward. If you're finished eating, we can pick up the clothes you want. Then, I would like to start our tour at Señor Barrantes' villa in Miraflores. Do you have any objections, counselor?"

"Will I be in any trouble with the *policia* and PIP if I show you these things?" Jorge inquired tentatively.

"What is PIP?" I asked in return.

"PIP is the *Peruvian Investigative Policia*. The unit specializes in drug-related crimes."

"I told you I'm interested in finding any weapons or drug trails that lead through Central Europe which may endanger my family there. I don't intend to cause trouble for you or your family if you help me obtain the information I want. In fact, because you told me about your family, I will be extra careful to keep both of us out of trouble. If I ask something unduly risky, you must tell me promptly to keep us both out of harm's way with the Barrantes family or the *policia*. We may have the same problem from my side if we run into any undercover CIA or DEA people from the States. *Entiendo?*"

"*Si*, I understand. *Muchas gracias.*"

ONWARD TO MIRAFLORES

"*Bueno*, now let's go to Miraflores."

"I usually take the bus there from school."

"*Madre de Dios*, unlike Francisco Pizzaro and the *conquistadors* of old, we're going into battle riding on a bus? You're breaking my heart. Please, get your clothes and at least call a taxi for us," I admonished Jorge.

The taxi reminded me of Ravi's police car in Bhuj. The vehicles had more than a passing resemblance, but we eventually arrived at the front gate of the Barrantes villa. An impressive stone wall encircled the property, guarding an equally impressive Spanish colonial house inside. Signs were posted, and I could hear dogs barking from behind the enclosure. It reminded me of a warning sign on a fence in my neighborhood, "Our dogs can make it to the fence in three seconds. Can you?" Señor Barrantes must be very prosperous. His yard was the only one I saw in Peru without a coca tree growing in it. The taxi driver did not have change for my twenty-dollar bill, so I made Jorge shell out some of his *nuevo soles* for the ride. He put on his sad look until I told him to keep track of his expenses and I would reimburse him. To keep him from thinking I was a walking ATM machine, I told him that I would only reimburse expenses he could verify with a receipt or expenses he incurred in my presence. We then walked to a side gate away from the dogs, opened it, and there we were on the property of a bona fide, dirt bag, drug lord.

"What do we do now?" Jorge asked.

"Now that we're here, I'm not sure," I replied. "If Barrantes isn't around, introduce me as a new employee and show me the sights. We will improvise from there."

But then, another approach struck me.

"Jorge," I said, "does Barrantes entertain any of the visiting Middle East professors you were telling me about?"

"*Si*, many of them. Why?"

"He appears to be an advocate for higher education. I'm determined to know why. On second thought, introduce me as a professor from the States who is here on the earthquake relief team and that we coincidentally met on campus. You thought my background would be of interest to the señor. If Barrantes is here, that may obtain our entrée to him despite these rags that I've worn for the past three days."

"Are you sure you know what you are doing? What kind of professor will you be?" Jorge wanted details.

"*Quimica*, *historia*, or *ciencia*s, whatever," I assured him.

"Chemistry, history, or political science? You are a lunatic! Barrantes will kill us both on the spot," Jorge whined.

"Careful what you call your employer, Jorge. A quick look at your personnel records with my firm shows that your seniority is only about three hours long, and that's stretching it. I appreciate your honesty, but, in my civilian life, I always encounter trouble when I'm too candid about what I think and say to my boss, even when I'm ultimately proven correct. Besides, if Barrantes doesn't believe me, I can always show him my .22-caliber diploma."

With those preparations made, we entered the side door of the villa.

Fortunately, Barrantes was not there because we probably weren't as ready to meet him as I professed to Jorge. Equally fortunate, his private pilot was finishing lunch in the kitchen prior to leaving for the Barrantes' *ranchero*. Sometime in the future, Jorge would make an excellent lawyer because under the pressure of the moment and without rehearsal, he convinced the pilot that I was a professor who Barrantes would be eager to meet. This breach of security violated everything in the drug traffickers' handbook about how to discourage strangers who drop in without an invitation, cash, trade goods, or a plan. Meeting the pilot was a stroke of undeserved luck because travel times and distances by land are deceiving in Peru, as I mentioned earlier. A traveler needs to account for vertical as well as horizontal and circular distances over, through, and around mountains, rain forests, glaciers, and other natural impediments in addition to unpaved roads through villages with few restaurants or service stations. Timely business travel is severely impaired for those unfortunates without access to personal aircraft in Peru's tea-growing area. When I observed that Quillabamba was actually where tea is harvested in Peru, I became more receptive to the information I received from Jorge about the country. I also learned that the coca trees are grown much further north in the central highlands close to the borders of Ecuador and Colombia in the Amazon basin.

When we arrived at the airport, I found that Barrantes not only had a pilot and a plane, he had a hangar full of assorted aircraft. I had my eye on his personal jet, but the pilot steered us toward a tired freight plane. I guessed we were considered cargo, not passengers. We would arrive at the *ranchero* inauspiciously as possible with the groceries and other supplies. It was still better than a bus ride. Jorge and I should have talked during the flight, but the bouncing of the plane and the rigors of the last three days put me to sleep before we cleared the outskirts of Lima. More vigorous bouncing as we approached Quillabamba woke me up in time to see some of the local surroundings. The town of approximately 16,000 people was located southeast of Lima and northwest of Arequipa in south central Peru on the eastern slope of the Andes at an elevation of about 3,450 feet. The western edge of the Amazon basin was not far off. Women going through menopause would like it here. Walking uphill in the cool central highlands would take care of hot flashes. Walking around town or to the edge of the jungle would take the edge off any chills. Like downtown Chicago, the wind blows dirt in your face no matter which direction you walk. On our approach, we saw several Andean condors circling the town. I quickly put thoughts of their symbolism out of my head.

The Quillabamba municipal airport was unnecessary for this *ranchero*. Barrantes had his private airfield. Probably, most other successful drug lords did too. Supposedly, Peru has over 350 registered airports and about forty unregistered fields. Of the total 390 airstrips, less than sixty are controlled by civil agencies while less than 10 are under military control. Having over 320 unregulated airfields was a boon to drug trafficking. Tighter security could have meant employment for a few Peruvians, if not more effective control over what kind of people and stuff entered or left Peruvian airspace. *But, I was visiting the impoverished country for the first time, so what did I know?* Corrupt government officials at all borders in concert with cooperative CIA covert operations and DEA inaction meant few law enforcers knew what was really going on or cared to learn. U.S. banks that loaned the banana republics tons of money had to know that the only way for the loans to be repaid was through drug trade profits. The banks were less concerned about the impact of readily available drugs on the streets of Chicago, New York, Los Angeles, Philadelphia, Detroit, and other major cities across the States than they were about timely loan repayments—from whatever South American financial source.

We circled the ranch to land into the prevailing east wind. A pickup truck was waiting for the supplies and us. The ranch hands who helped us unload the plane asked the pilot where he picked up the *exceso de equipaje* (excess baggage, meaning me), but otherwise they were cordial enough. They also confirmed that Barrantes was here. There was no retreat now for Jorge and me, plan or no plan. With the supplies piled high in the pickup, and assorted workers and guests hanging on wherever we could, we completed our bouncing journey from the airstrip to the ranch house. After helping the crew unload, Jorge suggested that we go to the bunkhouse for a shower and shave before we approached the main house. The pilot stayed behind to inspect and service the plane, but before we changed into fresh clothes, word came from the main house that Señor Barrantes had invited the pilot, Jorge, and me to join the family for the evening meal. Apparently, the pilot was someone with influence in this operation. Or, perhaps, his description of me to Barrantes before landing piqued sufficient interest to get us invited to the main house. I only hoped that Jorge and I were not on the menu for some ancient Inca sacrificial ceremony.

Master of the House

Alfonso Barrantes was a *mestizo* (of mixed Indian and Spanish descent) in his mid-forties, husky, about six feet tall, and with flashing dark eyes that could bore through iron. His wife, Juanita was mid-thirties, with dark hair in a braid down her back to her waist, but with a fairer complexion than her husband. Her sparkling dark eyes spoke of a more pleasant disposition and of a more genteel Spanish heritage that was accustomed to wealth and the authority it commands, but absent any associated heavy-handedness unless absolutely necessary. I also detected a hint of sadness, perhaps, from the enforced isolation away from her family and friends because of her husband's occupation. But with three daughters who looked like copies of her at ages three, six, and nine, I

TERRORISTS AND THE TERCHOVA TREASURE

couldn't envision her being involved in the drug trade in any way. She had enough work attending to the education of her daughters and management of the main house. Then again, I could be wrong. I had been wrong on a few occasions in the past, but not recently.

For me, it was love at first sight. Not with Señora Barrantes, but with her youngest daughter. Much to her mother's consternation, halfway through the soup course, impish Isadora decided to finish her meal and part of mine while seated on my lap. I was pleased. My well-honed skills of corrupting kids and pets worked equally well in both the Northern and Southern Hemispheres. I could feel Señor Barrantes' eyes piercing my skull, but he indulged Isadora her simple pleasures. Even wealthy kids have a hard time growing up in this Andean country. With my attention focused on Isadora, I don't remember what was served after the *sopa a la criolla* (a mild noodle soup with a fried egg and pepper slices floating on a piece of toast) other than some potatoes, meat, and mixed vegetables.

Almost on cue before the dessert course, I saw Isadora's eyelids droop and felt her body relax against mine. The *camarera* (maid) appeared from somewhere to take her to bed, but Isadora did not want maid service that night. Her mother was equally unacceptable. With Señora Barrantes accompanying us, I carried Isadora upstairs to her bedroom. With me standing nearby, Isadora allowed her mother to unbutton her fancy dress and get her into her nightgown. We listened to her prayers and quietly left the room. Three steps away from Isadora's bedroom, Señora Barrantes was about to say something to me when we were ambushed by the maid and the other two girls on their way to bed. I was not needed this time, so I went downstairs.

The men had moved to the game room. On the way there, I adjusted my derringer under my blazer sleeve following my dinnertime tussle with Isadora and joined the men. For openers, I expected the conversation to turn to man talk—business, politics, and how I happened to arrive on Barrantes' doorstep. Isadora had given me temporary relief from the harshness of her father's profession and the duplicity of my PURPLE activities, but now it was time for me to return to reality and conduct business. Just because I had dined at his table did not mean that Barrantes would hesitate to kill me before the night was over if he perceived that I posed any threat to him, his family, or his profession.

Upon entering the game room, I couldn't help but notice that Inca and Amigo, two very large and irritable German shepherd dogs had Jorge pinned against the far wall. In the opposite corner was Nina with her basket of recently born pups. I walked toward Nina as calmly as I could. She bared her teeth savagely the first time I put out my hand, then more casually on my second attempt to be friends. By then, I was in talking and petting range, and she quickly calmed down. After a few more minutes of stroking her and telling her how beautiful she was Nina was ready to introduce me to her new rowdy family of one female and three male pups. Inca and Amigo released Jorge from captivity in the corner and joined Nina and me to receive their share of petting and roughhousing, Inca as the father, and Amigo as the proud uncle of the energetic pups. I could feel Barrantes' eyes burning a hole in the back of my head as he watched the proceedings. Barrantes spoke first.

"Jorge told me that you are a very resourceful man, Señor. Now, I have seen it for myself. First, you captivate my daughter, and now my dogs. What else do you want of me tonight?"

Before answering, I allowed myself a glance at Barrantes' hunting trophies, gun collection, and other masculine toys around the room. Under different circumstances, I could have enjoyed myself in the game room for hours.

"Hopefully, nothing that you will not give me freely," I answered. "First, I want to thank you and the señora for the fine dinner and the opportunity to meet your family. Your hospitality is far more than I as a stranger in your country expected. (If Barrantes was going to kill me tonight, I decided that it would not be because I displayed bad manners.) By now, you know I came to Peru to help with earthquake relief. In the course of an air evacuation to the hospital in Lima, I encountered Jorge. The next thing I knew I was on your doorstep."

"So, you go wherever the wind takes you? That could be a dangerous approach to life here," Barrantes cautioned.

"I agree, but I have a serious purpose for my actions. Jorge tells me that you are an international businessman. I have family roots in both the States and in Central Europe. As you probably know, after ten years, some of the former Russian satellite countries continue to have difficulty trying to establish efficient markets and economies. I told Jorge that I was eager to learn if you or some of your colleagues have any interest in establishing trade networks there, if such networks do not already exist."

"What kind of trade networks do you have in mind?" Barrantes asked with mounting interest.

"I expect them to be small at first, and then larger as the customer base, resources, and business expands."

"What kind of products do the people need there?" Barrantes continued, as I had hoped.

"At this point, anything that they can eat, wear, or whatever can produce income, preferably lawful products such as food, textiles, and forest products. You are in the tea-growing area, so we can talk about those items as examples of future possibilities. Like many in the world, men there need to support their families, and high-paying jobs are hard to find. Yet, the people are educated, and look to the West as a source of help. When they have no opportunities, they may be less selective about their careers."

"Do you know what kind of business I am in, Señor?" Barrantes asked with a harsh edge to his voice.

He gave a head movement toward Jorge and the pilot, and they promptly disappeared.

"I believe I have deduced your primary product. The *Sendero Luminoso* (Shining Path) guerrilla movement started in Ayacucho southwest of here and then moved toward Cuzco. Despite ten years of killing and banditry in this area, your *ranchero* looks prosperous and well maintained. I noticed that the security men walking on the patio and around the house are equipped with automatic rifles, and that you have a machine gun stationed in the turret on top of your main barn. The best rifles are made in Slovakia, so you have some access to European goods already. The weapons, uniforms, and the planes you have are not gifts you bought for your children on your last trip to Miami. They are indicators of a lucrative international business. The only commodity that can support a large operation here at the edge of the jungle is coca leaves. How accurate is my assessment, Señor?"

"You are quite perceptive, Señor. But, so were many *desaparecidos* (disappeared ones) in the old days. Unfortunately, they saw and talked too much. I hope you do not share their bad habits."

"I hope I do not share their fate either. I came to your country to help in its time of need. If I disappear, a brash reporter somewhere in the U.S. will write an article about me that will cause U.S. politicians or human rights groups to petition for a search or inquiry about me to gain favorable press for themselves. That will force a federal agency to send a representative here to interrupt your operation for a few days. My disappearance is not worth the trouble it will cause you. All I ask is what can we do to help support my family in Europe. They will do as they are instructed after fifty years of Communism. If you can do nothing for my

European family and me, Señor, I will return to my home in the States and find some other means for my European family to survive."

A Business Proposal

"That is a touching story, but you told me what I might possibly do for you. What can you do for me?"

"My information may be inaccurate in places, but, currently, I assume that you send a variety of products to Europe. You need secure air transport through Colombia, Costa Rica, or Guatemala, then to Miami or New York, and finally on to Spain or Morocco for final shipment in smaller quantities to Central and Eastern Europe. That route requires a considerable amount of handling and intermediaries along the way. Perhaps I can shorten the route, increase the security of the shipments, and eliminate some of your overhead." (If I was ever "fingering the *ricasso*" and taking a risk, I certainly had my entire sword arm unprotected with this proposal.)

"How do you propose to ship my products safely?" Barrantes asked fully engaged in the conversation now.

"I would ship by air through Chicago so that I could supervise their movement, and have deliveries in Central Europe the next day. I assume you already have a safe route between here and Chicago. If not, I can help you with those shipments too. I believe the critical connections are between here and Mexico. They are dependent on how tight Mexican customs inspections are, and how many *pesos* or *nuevos soles* it takes to lubricate the network's machinery."

"What if I told you that I want to move my products in bulk by container ship? How can you improve on that when the United States only inspects about three percent of the eight million containers coming through U.S. ports annually? I have negligible risk under those conditions already," Barrantes countered my proposal.

"You have a good point. I understand that an inspector takes about three hours to inspect one container. That means most containers are not inspected if the shipper gives assurances that the products match the items on the bill of lading. Usually, a customs officer initiates an inspection when a tip is received about illegal goods. Why should you risk having a disgruntled or overly zealous worker alert U.S. Customs about a shipment that may jeopardize your entire network? Why do you need to send container shipments through ports in Central America and the States in the first place? When I was involved in earthquake air evacuations from Moquegua to the hospital in Tacna, I learned that the nearby city of Ilo, a little southwest of Moquegua, is a duty-free port open to merchants from both Peru and Bolivia. If I arrange container shipments for you with a Portuguese company (I assumed here that Roberto, Paolo, Miguel and international authorities would cooperate with me until I had Barrantes and his colleagues arrested with evidence of contraband) to pick up your containers and route them through the Panama Canal or around Cape Horn without U.S. inspections, would that be helpful? Depending on your volume, you may combine your shipments with your Bolivian colleagues, or send yours separately. The choice is yours. I will not interfere with your current arrangements for getting your products from the factories to the docks at Ilo because I am sure that you already have satisfactory local arrangements. If you want to go north through Colombia, I will need a little more time, but I believe the same Portuguese shipping company will quote you a reasonable price while resolving many of the difficulties you have with too many middlemen between you and an Atlantic port. The company also has trucks to move merchandise to and from deep-water ports if you need them. All it takes is a few phone calls to have a formal proposal to you in a few days," I concluded my *a capella* presentation.

"You have more knowledge than I expected and some interesting innovations. I will consider the possibilities in more detail before I give you my answer."

"Certainly, I understand fully. May I ask you several questions that may help me anticipate your needs?"

"Yes, of course," Barrantes agreed.

"Is my presumption that you go into Central and Eastern Europe through Morocco or Spain correct?"

"Yes, for now."

"Do you have any return shipments from Europe such as weapons, people, documents, money exchanges, and incentive payments for officials which are highly sensitive by their nature?"

"From time to time, we have reverse shipments of weapons, certainly, but that is not the major part of my business now that guerrilla operations here have declined. Money for officials and documents are transported by individual couriers when necessary, or through normal banking operations."

"My last question, Señor, do you need alternatives to your current financial arrangements?"

"We have adequate financial arrangements for now, but I will listen to any reasonable proposal you have," Barrantes reported.

"I should remind you that Muslim nations such as Morocco, Pakistan, and India, to a degree, have informal financial networks through the *hundi* or the *hawala* (informal banking and loan systems) if you are interested. Otherwise, the last and most reasonable proposal I have for you tonight is for you to allow me to get some sleep. I have had a long day, and our discussion happily has covered more than I expected. I think we both need time to consider the possibilities," I summarized with my happy face on.

"That is an excellent suggestion. We have several spare bedrooms upstairs if you wish."

"Thank you for the offer, but I believe your family and I will feel more comfortable if I spend the night in the bunkhouse with Jorge and your men. *Buenas noches*, Señor."

I got up from the chair and walked toward the door. With the sound of my footsteps, Nina raised her head, saw it was me, and promptly went back to sleep with her brood. With Inca and Amigo walking beside me, Barrantes preceded me to the door, offered a *buenas noches* when he confirmed that the pilot and Jorge were waiting on the porch for me, and shut the door as soon as I stepped over the threshold. In the relatively short time I had spent with Barrantes, I obtained the confirmation that I sought for a long time about the drug route through Central Europe from South America and the return flow of European arms to the banana republics. Not a bad evening's work for a guy without a plan. Now, all I had to do was live long enough to transmit the information to PURPLE, or whatever law enforcement organization I could get to pay attention to me, and act on it.

Meanwhile, I had a head full of dangerous information, and of all the people stationed on this *ranchero*, only Isadora, and possibly her mother, trusted me to any degree. That thought wouldn't be comforting through the dark night ahead. Sleeping sitting up in the bunk, I managed to nap and stay sufficiently alert to see the extraordinary Andean sunrise the next morning with nothing worse than a stiff neck.

TESTING THE GRINGO

Before breakfast, the Shining Path graduates among the bunkhouse bunch wanted to show "*El Gringo*" their weapons skills. With their automatic rifles and abundant ammunition, they made a lot of noise and piled up a small mountain of brass casings in a short time. For the *campesinos* (peasants), this was their time to show their tricks and to judge how poorly I would perform by comparison. When my turn came, I was expected to demonstrate weapons skills or lose prestige among the ranch hands.

I had not practiced the trick I planned to demonstrate since I was a kid, but I thought if I came close, I would still make a sufficiently favorable impression on the *campesinos*. When my turn came to shoot, I spit on the tip of my index finger, touched it to the ground, and made a rough bull's-eye on the side of the barn with my muddy finger. Then, I borrowed a revolver and holster from one of the *Senderos* graduates and a knife from another *campesino*. With my back to the barn, I wheeled around quickly throwing the knife at the bull's-eye as I turned. With a smooth follow-through after releasing the knife, I drew the revolver from the holster and fired. The bullet hit inside the bull's-eye followed a split second later by the knife. I unbuckled the gunbelt and handed it back to its owner. My audience just stood there at first. Then, silently, the unbelievers went to look more closely at the bullet hole and the knife impaled in the side of the barn. By this time, I felt a familiar pain in my right shoulder similar to the pain in my left shoulder following my Indian sojourn. It felt like another visit to Dr. Scott and Jenny was in order when I returned to the States. But, the thought was erased from my brain when I heard a voice from behind me.

BREAKFAST INVITATION AND DRUG QUIZ

"Normally, I do not invite someone who seduces my daughter and dogs and then makes holes in my barn to breakfast, but today, I will make an exception," Barrantes exclaimed as he briskly approached from the main house. "Is that what Chicago cowboys do for fun?"

"No, Señor, for fun, the married Chicago cowboys generally take out the garbage, sweep the garage floor, and mow the lawn or shovel snow, depending on the season," I replied. "After that, we are too tired to fool around with knives and guns. I have been married so long, I don't remember what unmarried cowboys do. If you are really interested, I will ask around when I get back home and write you a letter."

"Come to the house for breakfast. Then, we can talk," Barrantes said without any cordiality in his voice. "I have more questions for you."

Jorge and the pilot started to come too, but Barrantes waved them off. *Uh-oh*, I thought, *this is going to be a serious conversation with El Señor*.

"Jorge tells me that you are a chemist. Is that so?"

"My career in chemistry died when the bottom fell out of a test tube of ingredients I was supposed to identify in my first year of college. Also, I never memorized the periodic table of chemical elements, but, I have enough knowledge to remember not to drink the water in Peru, India, and a lot of other places I have visited for business or pleasure."

"Then, I suppose you do not know the chemical name for LSD?" Barrantes asked while ignoring my plea of profound ignorance in chemistry.

"Do not give up on me that easily," I fought back. "LSD is lysergic acid diethylamide."

"How about Ecstasy?"

"That is a synthetic otherwise known as MDMA. If you need me to be more precise than that, it is 3,4 methylenedioxmethamphetamine."

"Now try Ice," Barrantes persisted.

"That is another synthetic out of Taiwan, South Korea, the Philippines, Japan, and Hawaii with the long name of d-methamphetamine hydrochloride. The only other one I know is CAT, which is methcathinone," I answered, trying to pre-empt a more difficult question.

"What is the most potent variety of marijuana and where is it grown?"

"THC or tetrahydrocannabinol is the hottest variety of marijuana I know, and it is grown in the States. Do not ask me any more because you are lucky I remembered that much. What is the purpose of your chemistry quiz? I thought you were interested in expanding your non-drug business. Also, I thought that Peru, Colombia, and Bolivia only deal in cocaine with maybe a little heroin for special clients. Do you need a variety of products if you want to be a full-service provider?" I continued my largely ineffectual method of evading further questions.

"I understand your point," Barrantes concurred, "but assume that I want only to specialize in cocaine. Answer one more question: Do you know how to test the purity of cocaine?"

I had achieved partial success in getting Barrantes to think business rather than chemistry, but I couldn't refuse to answer this question.

"One method is to put a sample into a glass of bleach. If the product sinks to the bottom and dissolves, the sample is not pure. The sample is high-quality cocaine if the ingredients stay on the surface and dissolve into a brown oily slick. Another method is to heat a sample. If the sample burns into black embers at about 130 degrees Fahrenheit, the cocaine has been cut. If the sample melts into a yellow oily slick, the sample is high quality."

"How did 'crack' cocaine get its name?" Barrantes persisted.

"That is two questions," I challenged him. "But, I will answer to demonstrate my goodwill so that we can have breakfast before sundown. When 'crack' is cooking, it makes a crackling sound. I think you should feed me before you try to extract anything else from my brain at this hour of the morning," I added, resolute now to bring Barrantes' questioning to a halt.

Fortunately, we had reached the porch of the main house, and Isadora was there to rescue me from further interrogation. Barrantes had his arms out to her, but she came to me first to show me her doll. Again, fortunately for me, she allowed her father to pick her up and carry her into the house. Otherwise, I would have been a corpse right there. Señora Juanita and a maid were busy setting the table and getting the girls to sit down and behave. Inca, Amigo, and Nina came flying around the corner almost taking the señora off her feet to make sure that I had not forgotten about them and the pups since last night. Before the señora recovered her balance and took a broom to all of us, I grabbed Amigo's collar and escorted him back to the game room with Inca and Nina a few steps behind us. The pups were out of the basket and exploring everything within their reach. I shut the door on them and retreated to the dining room.

Peruvian breakfast is a continental affair with rolls, butter, jams, and a choice of milk or coffee. I thought breakfast would be heartier on a working ranch, but the main meal was served at midday. Señora Juanita was the boss of the house, and she strictly enforced all the social and dining rules precisely. She also was a discrete messenger. In the bustle of the kitchen and dining room activity, she managed to slip me a note without Barrantes noticing. That was a good effort in itself because he was watching my every move around his wife and daughters as if I were a licensed kidnapper. I don't know why he was worried. I was still a million miles from any safe haven by land, sea, or air.

Halfway through breakfast, the telephone rang. Barrantes got up, and took the call in his den.

That gave me a chance to read the note the señora had handed me. It read, "Contact the U.S. Embassy as soon as you can. Jenny."

Trouble Brewing

Now I was worried. I glanced up and saw the señora looking at me. In fact, she was searching my eyes for some sign of what she should do. I thought her look and actions confirmed that she had no part in Barrantes' business, but just then he came back into the room, and we lost another opportunity to communicate. Isadora seized her chance to climb into my lap. I was glad she did because I was making my usual mess of the flaky croissant I was trying to eat. (No matter what continent I visit, when I eat a croissant, it always looks like a family of raccoons was at my place when I get up from the table.) Isadora didn't get scolded for my mess, just a swipe of a washcloth applied by her mother to clean the load of jam from her mouth. Señora tried to say something to me again as Barrantes went into the kitchen for coffee but soon recognized that the risk was too great for a conversation.

With his coffee cup in hand, Barrantes invited me into his den and closed the door. He was careful not to have any business documents lying around. He certainly had anything that might be useful to me as evidence of illegal drug trafficking locked in his safe or file cabinets. He leaned back in his desk chair and looked sternly at me.

Blaming Uncle Sam

"You know," Barrantes said, "the United States is more responsible than any other country for the proliferation of drugs around the world. If you do not think so, let me remind you of the Iran hostage crisis and the Iran-Contra scandal as two high-level examples."

I really didn't need a reminder. I had recited the Iran hostage and Iran-Contra episodes to Hassan while traveling in Russia. Between us, we declared that, in some respects, the two hostage crises contributed to the Persian Gulf War between Iraq and Kuwait. (Because of U.S. diplomatic blunders, the U.S. military fought the Iraqi Army a second time a decade later.) Now, Barrantes was using the same hostage situations to justify his drug network's expansion into the U.S. market. I accept the fact that wars have unintended consequences, but Barrantes' statement extended the concept to the breaking point. I wondered where he was going with his opening statement after what seemed to be a frank discussion between us the night before. *Was this another test to determine how loyal I was to my country, or if I would abandon my family and country when I could advance my financial self-interest?* I thought. If so, I better respond with a non-committal statement for my personal safety if nothing loftier came to mind before I opened my mouth.

TERRORISTS AND THE TERCHOVA TREASURE

"If I knew all the facts, which I do not, Señor, I might agree with you. However, I have trouble connecting U.S. diplomatic, economic, and national security interests in Iran and Nicaragua with your operations in Peru. The Iran hostage crisis occurred in the Carter administration in 1979 when 500 *Talibaners* took fifty-two U.S. Embassy employees hostage in Tehran. Then, during Reagan's administration in 1983, the Iraqi terrorist group *Al-Dawa* took thirty Western hostages to force release of members of that group imprisoned for several truck bombings. Six hostages were Americans, including a priest from my old neighborhood.[4] So far, I have a closer personal interest in the hostage situation than I can find in yours, but I am willing to listen. Allow me to think aloud a bit more," I proposed.

"To encourage release of the U.S. hostages, the U.S. shipped arms to the Iranians through Israel, then used some of the money received to fund the *Contra* rebels to oppose the *Sandinista* army of Daniel Ortega who had ousted the U.S.-backed Samoza dictatorship in Nicaragua.[5] For additional funding, the Contras also were allowed to sell drugs in the U.S. with the CIA's knowledge. If you tell me that your drug network merged with the *Contra* drug network to sell drugs in the U.S., then I understand the connection between the Iran-Contra operation and your increased business. Otherwise, I need your explanation to comprehend the connection," I concluded, discouraged by my belief that Barrantes would give me an irrelevant reply that I could not rebut.

"Earlier, you said that you did not know all the facts. Do average Americans remember all that information and additional facts you probably know and did not recite to me? I think you studied and learned much more about the *Contras* than you have told me." Barrantes broke down my assumption of his giving me a vague answer.

"I try to be modest about my skills and education. Again, I am uncertain how the hostage situations directly affected you and your colleagues without further enlightenment from you."

"From my viewpoint, any U.S. president who allows his people to be harmed because of his international policies should be tried for treason like a common criminal. Ordinary citizens would encounter that degree of justice, do you agree?" Barrantes opened forcefully.

Geez, I thought, Barrantes is sampling his own products today, and not the high-quality stuff either. I wondered if he had trouble playing with other kids when he was young. I was glad I didn't mention that the rifles shipped to the *Contras* were made in the Czech and Slovak Republics by my relatives, although the 1,000 TOW missiles that exchanged hands were home grown in the good old U.S.A. I still believed that the U.S. transfer of TOW missiles to Iran and the funding of rifle purchases from Eastern Europe for Ortega's *Contras* were more pertinent to my family than to Barrantes' cocaine operations, if Barrantes allowed me to retain my own beliefs after this discussion ended.

"You may be too harsh on President Reagan," I responded gingerly. "Americans expected him to retrieve the hostages without embarrassing the U.S. or telling average citizens the dirty details. Second, when the Lebanese magazine *Ash-Shiraa* broke the story in 1986, President Reagan's staff and National Security Council advisers who were involved stopped doing whatever they were doing and bargained the release of all but two hostages."

I had learned long ago that there is no free lunch, but now I learned that there was no free breakfast at the Barrantes' ranch either. Diplomacy is not my strong suit under those conditions, but I kept trying as I continued.

"I understand your point about applying the same legal standard to everyone and that the U.S. needs a consistent foreign policy across the globe. On a bad day, I might agree with you completely," I moved cautiously. "But, I think some of the problems in the States result from not having our national and international priorities aligned with other countries, or we fail to perceive the longer-range consequences of our actions. Then, other countries that have shrewd leaders take advantage of our lapses in foresight, diplomatic skills, and political will. For example, Islamic nations have a better way of identifying priorities. The Koran postulates the concept of 'near' and 'far' dangers, and exhorts Muslims to handle the near dangers first. By contrast, the measurement for executive and legislative priorities in the States often is what is most expedient to raise funds to get re-elected."

"Yes, I know all that, but your presidents have a long tradition of making a mess and leaving the toughest problems for their successors and other countries to resolve," Barrantes pontificated. "In fact, your presidents get advanced training in duplicity before they are elected."

I thought I would ask for whatever he had in his coffee. For a drug lord, he was making more sense than I was at that time of the morning. I had no plane reservations home, so I may as well play along. But, I was having a hard time concentrating on what Barrantes was saying when I knew his wife had something on her mind if I only could find an opportunity to talk to her.

"Perhaps, I am being too harsh on your presidents," Barrantes suddenly reversed positions. "After all, by introducing more drugs to the U.S. than I would have shipped on my own, President Reagan's administration increased my business by 25 percent. But, was Nicaragua a 'near' threat to the United States? Was Nicaragua a threat at all despite having a Communist regime in power? I do not think so. After Russia took its missiles out of Cuba, was that small island a threat to the big U.S. all these years because Castro espoused Communism? U.S. sanctions devastated Cuba without Castro being able to do anything about it. But, to protect their public images among little countries in Central America, the Reagan and G.H.W. Bush administrations allowed drugs to flood the United States."

After a short breath, Barrantes continued.

"The arms-for-drugs trade violated your Neutrality Act of 1939 that prohibits the U.S. from exporting arms to belligerent nations. That might have been excused because I am sure that the act has been prostituted many times over the years like all the rest of your *Americano* laws and foreign policies. President Clinton did so in the past, and now President G.W. Bush's administration is falsely inciting Americans and spending billions to eradicate an industry that they and their predecessors helped create. Answer that if you can. Their actions brought more drugs into the U.S. than any South American trafficker could have envisioned."

"But, again, how does all that affect you personally in Peru?" I challenged.

"Specifically, in this country, the U.S. not only opened drug traffic to the States, but it forced reductions in world coffee prices, which meant that the farmers in my country had to find other cash crops to make up the lost income. Instead of using coca leaves for legitimate purposes as we have done for centuries here, the *campesinos* expanded the drug trade to support their starving families. In Bolivia, the U.S. uncoupled its dollar from the *peso*, which caused hyperinflation there with the same result. The *campesinos* had to find other income, and they too found that growing coca for illegal purposes was more profitable than growing coffee or tea."

After a sip of coffee, Barrantes continued.

"The poor people came to me because I am educated in the United States, and they asked me to develop a market for their products so that they could survive. Now, rather than being a peaceful rancher, I must put my family in danger by fighting against the U.S. and its double-dealing

FBI and CIA. As for you, do not get super patriotic with me when I know what the U.S. did to my country and to its own citizens through your fictional war on drugs. I am a businessman selling products that the U.S. presidents invited into your country by their acts, and I do not feel at all guilty about it."

After a short pause to determine if his engine was flooded or about to restart on the same or another topic, I said flatly, "From the description you gave me of your international network, the appearance of your property, and the size of your security force, I agree that any mistakes in U.S. foreign relations or drug policy didn't hinder your operations, but, in fact, may have enhanced them. However, if you really cared about the poor *campesinos* and wanted to maximize your U.S. education on their behalf, you and your powerful colleagues could have developed other resources and industries that would not have resulted in lost lives in the U.S. and around the world through illegal drugs."

Cynically, I thought that if he aligned his drug business plan with the assumption that the U.S. would foul up its foreign policy and drug enforcement efforts in South America, he had a sure winner. More personally and patriotically, I knew I had to stop him, or, at least, damage his operation in some way while I was in the country. If I couldn't do that, I needed to escape and return with more help to put him out of business permanently. If he beat my best efforts, he wouldn't be the only foreign Ivy Leaguer who used his U.S. education against the States. That gave me sufficient incentive to try almost anything.

Having finished his oration, Barrantes was plastered to the back of his chair, surprised by the strength of his own declarations. I now knew beyond doubt that I was fighting for my life. Barrantes was a criminal, plain and simple, regardless of his diplomas and declarations of injustice. I was expendable; certainly I was dead meat to Barrantes. *How did I know?* If he trusted me and was convinced that I could deliver better merchandise safely, or provide a more efficient marketing network for his illegal products, we would be discussing detailed business plans rather than talking philosophy, social science, and world politics.

After a few agonizing seconds of silence, Barrantes found his voice again. For the moment, I would be safe because of his personal protection, or because there were too many witnesses at his main *ranchero*. To someone halfway out on the plank, the depth of the water below doesn't matter. The result is the same whether the end comes immediately or is postponed at the ship captain's pleasure.

Temporary Reprieve

"I respect the strength of your feelings," Barrantes stated. "It is good that you love your country as I love mine. Under other circumstances, we may have been close friends. I thank you for your earthquake work and for the affection and respect you have shown my family. I have regard for the safety and economic relief you seek for your European family. But, just as strongly, I believe that it will be impossible for us to be business associates now, or in the foreseeable future. Nonetheless, I want to show you the conditions under which the coca farmers live in this country. Today, we will fly to Tingo Maria so that you can see the condition of the *campesinos* for yourself. Then, I will provide transportation for you back to Lima. From there, I suggest that you leave this country promptly. I will not extend my protection indefinitely. If I learn that you are in my country in the future, or if you interfere with my operations in any way, I will not hesitate to do maximum harm to you, your family, or associates. Do you understand?"

"I hear and understand you very clearly, Señor Barrantes," I said. "But, again if you are concerned about the poverty of the farmers on your land, you are rich enough at least to help those who work for you. You are a powerful man in this country. If you wanted to do something heroic and lasting, you could persuade other landowners and politicians to make conditions better for the poor people throughout the country. By comparison, I am an ordinary man, an outsider who has no authority to speak to your government officials to aid the *campesinos*."

Now, I knew with certainty what was in store for me because I could not aggravate him any further. He had made his decision. Strangely, I was calm. Maybe my last ride would be in his jet instead of the cargo plane. That would be a more exciting and fitting finish to my illustrious clandestine career. Maybe I would not be so upset being found face down in the mud somewhere with condors circling overhead if my last ride was in Barrantes' personal jet.

I didn't get my last wish for the jet, but as I climbed aboard the aging WWII relic, Inca and Amigo jumped in and took their places near me. I gave them a hearty rubdown and stowed my gear. I had everything with me now including my useless, field-stripped .30-caliber rifle in my duffel bag. I was either going to die in Tingo Maria, or be transported to Lima where another party would conveniently dispose of me with Barrantes' blessing. Time would tell between the two options. While I was standing next to my seat, I discovered some ancient fig biscuits in my bag. I put one halfway in my mouth as I moved my stuff into place. Apparently, Inca and Amigo had not had breakfast treats, or they liked stale biscuits at any time of day. As I turned in his direction, Inca stood on his back legs, put his front paws on my shoulders including my sore left one (actually either shoulder fit that category now), and bit off the part of the fig biscuit sticking out of my mouth. I knew Inca was big, but I didn't realize he was that huge. That was the juiciest dog kiss I ever had—from ear to ear. Seizing his opportunity, Amigo didn't care how stale the other biscuits were. He wanted all of them. I gave both dogs the remaining biscuits one at a time so they would not get sick during the flight and throw up on me.

After the treats were gone, they wanted more, but that was the best I could do for them. Barrantes went into the cockpit, and took the copilot seat. Apparently, Barrantes was licensed to fly his own fleet of planes, which is a valuable skill in this country of mountains, valleys, jungles, and long distances with unpaved roads. Jorge was not invited, and I was left in the cargo area with Inca and two well-armed *Sendero gendarmes* who kept measuring me with their eyes as if they were recent embalmer school graduates. I wanted time to assemble my rifle, but the *pistoleros* watched my every move. The derringer was my only active weapon as it had been since I captured Jorge with it in Lima.

Quillabamba is on the southwestern edge of the Amazon basin and southeast of Lima. Tingo Maria is in the central highlands on the Huallaga River about the same distance northeast of Lima. This would be a long ride to Tingo Maria, or a short ride into the side of a mountain if the plane sputtered. I decided to be a well-rested corpse and napped with most of Amigo in the seat beside me and the remainder of him draped all over me. His breath smelled of fermenting fig biscuits, but I wasn't in a position to tell him that, and I didn't have any breath mints with me to remedy his problem.

THE TINGO MARIA RANCH

Tingo Maria has a population of about 15,000. Even if it welcomed tourists, which it did not, a well-equipped municipal airfield normally would not be justified by its size. But, its importance in the drug trade justified it, and the airfield was only about a mile from the center of town on the west side of the river. Amigo and I woke up on our first of several bounces onto the Tingo Maria airstrip before we came to a halt near the end of the runway. While we were taxiing to the terminal, a pickup truck with wooden benches in the back drove up in a cloud of dust to take us to Barrantes' coca plantation a short distance away. Barrantes, the pilot, and the truck driver took seats in the cab while the rest of us piled our belongings, weapons, dogs, and selves on the benches in back. The *Sendero* guards told me that we were in the area called the *ceja de la selva* the "eyebrow of the jungle." I wasn't certain of the significance, but it sounded impressive enough to remember. Two local *campesinos* jumped in the back with the *Senderos* from Quillabamba, but they didn't appear exceptionally cordial residents of the "eyebrow" area. Also, they disregarded the fact that the Rio Huallaga is a major tributary of the Rio Maranon before it becomes the Amazon River flowing eastward toward the Atlantic. My fellow travelers didn't tell me about the Temple of Kotosh either (also known as the Temple of the Crossed Hands) located in the town of Huanuco, a little south of where we were. The temple is one of the oldest archeological sites in Peru, dating from approximately 2000 BC. Inca and Amigo didn't celebrate the temple either come to think of it. With the dogs and me abstaining, the *Senderos* and the *campesinos* joyfully shared a few bottles of *aguardiente,* the local brew made from sugar cane and other unknown ingredients. With the libation celebration well under way in the rear of the truck, the driver pulled into the fence-enclosed and sentry-guarded Barrantes *ranchero* at Tingo Maria.

The main house missed Señora Juanita's supervision. The bunkhouse was bigger than the one in Quillabamba and housed more people of all descriptions. The barn was bigger and in the best shape of the three buildings. There would be no pistol shooting and knife throwing at this barn. This was the processing plant for turning raw coca leaves into coca paste, and, perhaps, the white powder end product for export through Barrantes' network. I would not be invited to tour this facility. While I took mental photographs of the *ranchero* from the back of the truck, Barrantes went into the main house and returned wearing riding pants and boots. About the same time from a smaller barn, a ranch hand was leading the most beautiful black horse I had ever seen, fully equipped with silver emblazoned saddle, bridle, and the works. This was one of the *caballos de pas* pacing horses I had heard about that was much favored by the conspicuously wealthy and fashionable folks in South America. Barrantes caught me looking with my mouth open and called me over to him.

"Do you have anything like Sancho in Chicago?" he asked while swinging into the saddle and gathering the reins from the ranch hand and patting the horse's neck.

"No, we don't have anything comparable to him even when he's taking a dump on your patio," I said. "I saw some polo ponies once that I thought looked sharp, but nothing compared to this big fellow," I responded as I came closer and reached out in admiration to touch Sancho's quivering shoulder. "I don't know how many hands high he is, or is supposed to be, but you must get a nosebleed sitting up there."

Barrantes chuckled almost in genuine good humor. "Do you ride?" he asked much too friendly following our Quillabamba discussion. "We can bring a gentler ranch horse for you. I want to show you some of the ranch and the people who work for me."

"I don't ride anything on four legs until I hand a ticket to the operator, the music starts, and we go around in a circle with a bunch of kids eating cotton candy, but thanks for the offer. After being cramped on the plane (under his dog most of the way) for so long, I don't mind walking if that's okay with you."

"As you please," Barrantes said as he put the horse into first gear and pranced down a lane leading to the coca plant area and what looked like a secluded part of the property.

I heard a church bell tolling far off in the quiet of late morning, and I thought of John Donne's famous line, "[N]ever send to know for whom the bell tolls; it tolls for thee."[6] *Would this be my finish, my last fight?* If I ever needed a *deus ex machina* (the ancient Greek playwrights' device that allowed the gods to rescue the hero of the play from an impossible situation at the last moment), I needed one now. The two armed *Senderos* who flew from Quillabamba with us were now marching in step a few yards behind me while clearing and checking their automatic rifles as if we were on a big game hunt for tonight's meal. The only escape I devised if I had any warning of the actual timing of my death was to grab Sancho's bridle to bring him down and put my derringer to Barrantes' head to force the *Senderos* not to shoot. With sore shoulders, I was not sure I had the strength to get this big horse off balance and pull Barrantes out of the saddle.

MY PERSONAL MILAGROS

As it turned out, I had another unexpected champion protecting me, none other than *El Señor de los Milagros*, the Lord of the Miracles. Peruvians celebrate the feast in October, but he came early in this Chinese Year of the Snake, and just when I needed him. Otherwise, what happened could only be attributed to *brujeria* (witchcraft or sorcery), and I had not been away from home long enough to believe in that yet. As we approached an overgrown gully leading to a grove of trees, a family of peccaries (small wild pigs who eat anything that doesn't move and most of what does) dashed out in front of Barrantes' horse shrieking and grunting while chasing something edible. Sancho was not a ranch nag but a purebred *caballo* (horse) if there ever was one. Like most purebreds in similar circumstances, Sancho freaked out immediately and went up on his hind legs pitching Barrantes off backwards. Barrantes, taken by surprise, landed heavily on his head and neck. He didn't move. In three steps, Sancho shifted into third gear, and headed for the trees.

I shouted to my *Sendero* escort, "*Caballo, caballo!*" and pointed in the direction of Barrantes' departing purebred.

At my suggestion, the *Senderos* ran after Sancho, who already had a big lead. I ran in the opposite direction toward the ranch buildings. I don't know why exactly except to put distance between the armed *Senderos* and me. *El Señor de los Milagros* was on my side momentarily. I had to exploit my temporary advantage. The first person I encountered was the pilot.

"I need help," I shouted at him while he was still a good thirty yards away. "Barrantes fell off his horse, and it looks bad."

The pilot ran toward me, and when he got close, I turned and ran back to where Barrantes lay. By the time I arrived, Sancho and the *Senderos* were nowhere in sight. Barrantes was where he landed. I checked his pulse and breathing. My Responder training was helpful, although about five minutes had elapsed since Barrantes fell (not exactly textbook emergency care) not that I believed he would crawl away. To tell the raw truth, I didn't care if he lived or died except to provide a means of escape for myself. By that time, the pilot and the dogs arrived. Despite the lower altitude of Tingo Maria, the pilot was out of breath from his run and the extra pounds he carried around his belt line. Inca and Amigo got there in good shape, excited, and ready to play.

"This isn't a good time for fun," I told Amigo as I forcefully pushed him away. "We need to get Barrantes to a hospital," I told the pilot. "The least he might have is a concussion. The worst might be a spinal injury. Is Lima the closest place for medical care?"

"We have a hospital here in town, east of the river," the pilot replied while not providing any additional information.

I had forgotten that Tingo Maria was not an ordinary town. Tingo Maria existed for drug lords who expected all the amenities. Location is as important to drug lords as it is to real estate agents.

"Get the truck, I'll stay here and try to revive him," I told the pilot.

I hadn't expected a high level of interaction with the pilot. Otherwise, I would have asked his name. Absent a formal introduction, I decided to call him Pontius (derived from Pilate and the old joke about Pontius the Pilot, of course). He ran back to the ranch as fast as his legs and the still playful dogs allowed him. Surprised that a hospital was so close, my brain follicles didn't contemplate that an ambulance also might be located nearby. Apparently, it didn't ring a bell or siren with Pontius either. He returned with the pickup quickly, but without other human help. For any earthly lord—drug or otherwise—*peons* or *campesinos* of any race or religion don't move unless instructed by the lord to do so. Like others, Barrantes' crew waited for his orders. Now that Barrantes was indisposed to give orders, his house rules played to his disadvantage. With a possible spinal injury, we shouldn't have moved him without a board and wrappings to immobilize his neck, but we skipped that part of the emergency manual. There was no time, and he would bounce around plenty in the back of the truck anyway before we got him to the hospital. Pontius and I loaded Barrantes on the truck as carefully as we could and started back up the lane toward the ranch house.

When we reached the ranch buildings, all hands were standing around curious to know what happened to Barrantes, but not skilled enough to help. The pilot kept driving down the road toward town. The *ranchero* was on the west side of the river while the town and hospital were on the east side. But the bridge across the river was not far out of our way. That was the only break Barrantes had in this exercise. Upon arrival at the small hospital, the emergency staff was on lunch or *siesta*, and didn't respond to our urgent pleas. A paramedic told us that an obstetrician was the senior physician on duty, but, presently, she was busy delivering a baby. Pontius talked to anyone who wore a white smock faster than my non-Hispanic head could translate. He finally collected two nurses to come to the truck with a board to immobilize Barrantes' neck and shoulders and to check his vital signs. We probably should have waited until word circulated the hospital that Señor Barrantes was injured and needed emergency care.

Instead, Pontius hollered at me, "Get in the truck. We will go to the airfield. We will take Barrantes to Lima!"

Consciously or unconsciously, Barrantes had one thing right. He was giving me free passage to Lima as he had promised.

Pontius drove the truck to the airfield as if witches or peccaries were after him. We loaded Barrantes onto the plane, unencumbered by proper medical procedures for handling a husky man lying on a warped board with loose straps and intended to be lifted by more than two people. Two team obstacles we overcame were member shoulder weaknesses (me), and poor member language skills (me again). For me to interpret and act on Spanish instructions from Pontius to coordinate loading Barrantes onto the plane meant that Pontius needed to pronounce each word slowly, distinctly, and in a non-emergency environment. None of those conditions existed in our present circumstances. But, we got Barrantes aboard the plane and tied down. During my free time, I transferred my stuff from the truck to the plane because I didn't expect to return here given the reception I received. With that done, Pontius started the engines and taxied to the fuel pumps. All preflight chores completed, Pontius taxied to the runway, and we took off more than an hour after Barrantes went boom off his prancing black horse.

Surprisingly, Barrantes was still breathing despite our best efforts to kill him with our ad hoc medical evacuation. Other than sitting by Barrantes and watching for signs of change, I couldn't do anything for or to him. As we got closer to Lima, I collected my belongings for a quick exit. Then, I went into the cockpit for a chat with Pontius. He had radioed ahead for emergency equipment to be waiting for us at the Lima airport. He wasn't interested in causing me trouble or preventing me from disappearing after Barrantes was in an ambulance. If Barrantes recovered, Pontius volunteered to tell Barrantes what I did for him after his accident. If Barrantes didn't recover, Pontius promised to inform Señora Juanita that I tried to help. I couldn't ask for more.

Approaching Lima, we hit the *garua* (coastal fog), and circled for a while. I could hear Pontius' steady stream of profanity informing the tower personnel that he would not be diverted to another airport under any circumstances. He had a medical emergency on board, and he was landing whether the tower liked it or not. The landing was fairly smooth considering the conditions. We were on the ground, an ambulance and emergency people were waiting as requested, and Barrantes finally was in the care of medical professionals. It seemed like ages ago when he made arrangements to eliminate me. Justice delayed is justice denied I had learned in law school. This time, however, justice was delivered right on time.

Now that Barrantes had medical attention, I didn't feel obligated to hang around for him to recover and resume his prior plan to say bye-bye to me. I waved a short wave to catch Pontius' eye, then sprinted to the terminal and out the front door to find the U.S. Embassy. I wasn't quite finished in Peru yet. I had to find out what Uncle Sam and PURPLE wanted from me, as expressed in Jenny's note that I had hidden in a container intended to look like a tube of toothpaste. In fact, it was my tube of toothpaste with a special slot for small documents.

Chapter Notes

1. Rob Rachowiecki and Charlotte Beech, *Peru*, (Melbourne: Lonely Planet Publications Pty. Ltd., 1987), p. 13 *et. seq.* By permission of Lonely Planet Publications Pty. Ltd.

2. *Ibid.*, p. 13.

3. *Ibid.*, p. 120 *et. seq.*

4. Wikipedia contributors, "Iran-Contra affair," *Wikipedia, The Free Encyclopedia*, http://en.Wikipedia.org/w/index.php?title=Iran%E2%80%93Contra_affair&oldid= 315992388 (accessed May 2, 2008). pp. 1–8.

5. Avila, *op. cit.*, p. 24.

6. John Bartlett (compiler), *Familiar Quotations 13th Edition* (Boston: Little, Brown and Company, 1955), p. 218, citing John Donne's "Devotions Upon Emergent Occasions XII."

CHAPTER 8

JENNY AND THE MISSIONARY MISSION

CHECKING WITH CHAUNCEY

For the better part of the day, people had been trying to kill me, and I was having one of those days when I was more concerned about my personal safety than almost any other thing. I needed to find the U.S. Embassy on Avenue Cuadra 17, Surco, and clear up what else needed to be done before Barrantes recovered and came after me again. Despite my appearance, I was able to hail a taxi, show the driver the address, and wave some *nuevo soles* at him to demonstrate my ability to pay. Another surge of good *karma* allowed me to be admitted to the embassy upon my arrival. Chauncey, the American charge d'affaires, who was an old friend, was pleased to see me, although he avoided shaking my grubby hand or offering me a seat. I didn't take offense. I summarized my activities with Barrantes. Chauncey was visibly shaken when I told him that I was given a note by Señora Barrantes, which I handed to him to examine personally with a generous supply of toothpaste still on it.

"Juanita?" Chauncey exclaimed. "We didn't send any note to you through Señora Barrantes."

"Good, then, I will be on my way," I said as I gathered my stuff.

"No, you don't understand. We had that message for you, but it should have been delivered to you confidentially."

"This looks like embassy stationery to me. I'm not surprised that Barrantes and other drug lords have sources in government offices, including the U.S. Embassy. Barrantes is a sharp businessman who likes to be informed about important events that may affect his activities," I speculated.

"Yes, but that doesn't explain why you received the note from Señora Barrantes," Chauncey countered. "Juanita is a fine lady and long-time friend who does many kind things for the poor children in this country. But, she is not a courier for the embassy."

"Maybe that's why she looked so distressed when she gave me the note. She seemed anxious to tell me more on several occasions, but she didn't have the opportunity. Maybe, she wanted to inform me that she was being coerced to deliver this note to me."

"That's possible. In fact, I believe you may be right in your assessment. But, why would Barrantes force her to give you a note?" Chauncey reasoned.

"Perhaps Barrantes and his embassy mole were not certain about the implications of this note or wanted to identify the sender. If Señora Barrantes pretended to secretly hand me a note, I would award it more credibility than if it came from Barrantes. Tell me what you know about the communication. Possibly, we can work backward to identify our sender or mole."

Chauncey looked more distressed than ever, if that was possible. He took a deep breath and started.

"We have communications from two, and possibly more, young missionaries in Bolivia who have run afoul of drug traffickers in La Paz. They have tried unsuccessfully over the last three weeks to cross into Peru from Bolivia for sanctuary and to get back to the States. When we first heard from them, they were near our Desaguadero border crossing on the south end of Lake Titicaca. A week later, we heard from them at Puerto Acosta about four hours away from our north shore border crossing at Tilali. In their last communication, they advised they were moving north to locate friends at a research station near Iquitos in the tri-border area in the Amazon basin. If they travel that far north, they are going directly into the Korubo tribe's sector of the jungle. A number of the tribes in that area have retained their old traditions of warfare among themselves, but especially against outsiders. They have killed government agents who were trying to help them obtain food, clothing, and other basics."

Mormons Again

"The missionaries are confused if they believe they can find sanctuary from drug traffickers in Bolivia by coming into Peru, or by heading north along the Bolivian border toward Brazil into the dense jungle at Iquitos. From my map," I continued, "Tabatinga or Benjamin Constant are comparable towns on the Brazilian side. Am I correct? The missionaries aren't Mormons by any chance, are they?" I asked, a little perturbed because I sensed I already knew the answer.

"Yes on both counts. Why do you ask?" Chauncey affirmed my suspicions.

"During my Army days, I always was treated with respect and courtesy by every Mormon I encountered without exception, young or old, man or woman. But, your missionaries are not the first Mormons I've extracted from a jungle over the years. They mistakenly identify me as the human incarnation of their Angel Moroni and assume that I have infinite resources and skills to rescue them from any situation. They never stop proselytizing, even when arrows, rocks, spears, and bullets are aimed in their direction. I don't know how many times I was down to my last round while pulling one or more of them out of trouble. I was lucky myself today and received an early miracle from *El Señor de los Milagros*. I don't want to use up all my credit, but I suspect that you've been authorized by someone to instruct me to bring the missionaries out of Bolivia, haven't you?" I asked the operative question.

"I can't keep a secret from you, can I?" Chauncey said nervously. "But, consider this. You're already grimy and somewhat familiar with the territory. There's no point muddying up another operative to do something you've executed successfully in the past. I have the utmost confidence in your ability to pull this off, old boy. Your malaria and yellow fever shots are current, I presume?" Chauncey inquired smugly.

"Yes, but I wasn't planning to test their potency when I volunteered for earthquake duty in Arequipa and the highlands. Are you planning to give jungle guide Moroni help, or do I have to walk over hill and dale for three months by myself to reach the Bolivian border?"

"I believe you know Ron from your past work. He recently arrived from another assignment and will assist you on this venture. Ron has his Aymaran guide with him to help with tracking and hauling supplies. We have a pilot at your disposal who will transport you as close as possible to the Mormons' last known position. Then, we will helicopter you to an extraction point when the missionaries are precisely located. Do you need anything else?" Chauncey asked, signifying the end of his information and available resources.

But, I needed more information that I thought highly important for actions across national borders.

"Are you in radio contact with the missionaries, and can we stop them somewhere for pickup instead of chasing them around the entire Amazon basin? Also, am I authorized to cross borders to snatch them?"

"One of the group has a college chum doing research at the Yarapa River Lodge north of Iquitos. They believe that they will find a safe haven and can be picked up there. That's why they're moving north. And, yes, a brief incursion on foot into Bolivia once they are located is authorized as long as you don't get caught in Bolivia or wander into Brazil, understand?"

"Nice. There's nothing like regular working conditions to make an assignment go smoothly. By any chance, do the missionaries know how far Iquitos is from their last reported position, what kind of terrain they face, how unfriendly the natives are toward trespassers, what supplies they need, and who is chasing them?" I asked with some heat attached.

"That would be pure speculation on my part," Chauncey replied, grateful that I asked mushy questions he could evade. "However, in their first radio transmission, they advised that they accidentally ran into a cocaine operation, and they were being pursued by drug traffickers. They did not say how many, or if they were continuing to be pursued further around the lake on the Bolivian side. They do not want to use their radio too much for fear that their communications will be intercepted, or their batteries will run low, or both, before they are rescued."

"Check my understanding of the situation, Chaunc. They have hostile Indians in front of them, and heavily armed drug enforcers are in hot pursuit behind. They don't want to use the radio for fear of being located and rescued. We don't know their physical condition and if they have food and medicines. If they're not dead or captured already, three or four of us need to cover a million square miles or equivalent hectares of jungle to bring them out. Do I have an accurate picture?"

"Yes, you have painted an accurate portrait of the situation, old bean."

"Chauncey, you crack me up. You haven't been to England in thirty years, and you still speak like a Brit. You'll never forgive your mother for giving birth to you in the States, will you?"

"Why should I? The location of my birth was pure happenstance."

"Everything about your birth was happenstance, Chaunc, but I respect your mother too much to tell her."

A knock on the door alerted us to Ron's arrival. He was my brother's friend from long ago. Ron was accompanied by his Aymaran guide and Barrantes' pilot—none other than my Pontius—formally introduced now as Bill. After greeting everyone, we addressed several more business items.

"Before you went sideways on my heritage," Chauncey started, "I intended to tell you that Bill is our mole in Barrantes' operation. He should have delivered the message from your Jenny to you, not Señora Barrantes. Apparently, someone in our office works for Barrantes, as you stated. We will find the party who intercepted the message and deal with that party expeditiously. I believe Barrantes didn't know what to do with the message, so he had it delivered to you via Señora Barrantes to test your reaction. Fortunately, you were not expecting it, and didn't react in any decipherable way. Then, totally confused about whom you were and your intentions, Barrantes decided to dispose of you to avoid any threat to his operation. I'm confident that Juanita is not involved in the drug operation. I certainly hope not anyway, but we will get to the bottom of it, and we will find the mole in our office. Fortunately, Bill did not destroy his cover to rescue you. What else do you need from me to commence this operation?" Chauncey offered, hoping that Bill, Ron, and I had no requests to cause him grief.

I spoke first.

"If possible, contact the missionaries to determine their location, resources, and intentions. If the drug thugs intercept your communications, that doesn't mean they're in the immediate area of the missionaries, or that they'll spend unlimited time chasing the choir boys, especially if the missionaries pose no threat or are likely to die in the jungle. The druggies don't want to engage an armed rescue party if they can avoid it. The Bolivian government protects the drug lords anyway, so why should they worry about God's people? Will the Mormons retaliate if the missionaries don't return home? I don't think so. The druggies might chase the missionaries a while hoping they will panic and make a deadly mistake. The missionaries are crazy to think they can reach Iquitos without help. If they can get to Iquitos by themselves, they don't need us. The best approach is to make contact and intercept them close to where they are now. Show us on the map their location when you received their last transmission, Chaunc."

"Two days ago, they were on the north shore of the lake, here," Chauncey pointed. I tried to hold them there, but they insisted on continuing north to Iquitos or Tabatinga. I'm sure they don't realize how far that is and what kind of terrain they will encounter."

"I guess not," Ron interjected. "They have been on the road three weeks, and they only traveled to the north side of the lake. Haven't they ever heard of a boat?"

Chauncey redirected the conversation to the pilot rather than answer Ron directly. "Bill, what do you think? You know the territory."

Bill thought a minute, then replied, "We could phone the Yarapa lodge to confirm if the missionaries have or haven't been there or made contact. Then, we could contact the *sertanista* (backlands expert) and Indian agent in Tabatinga to alert them to notify the tribes in their sectors to bring the missionaries in unharmed for a reward if they find them in the deep jungle. Then, we could call river ports along the Rio Heath to advise the lodges and boat captains to ask their cooperation. I don't see them getting anywhere near Iquitos and the Yarapa River Lodge. Another research station where college students stay is the Tambopata Reserve south of Puerto Maldonado here in Peru. I recommend we fly into Maldonado and use it as our base. It has a good airfield, and we can go north or south from there when we know or anticipate where the group is."

"That's excellent advice, Bill," Chauncey announced. "I will have my staff start calling while the four of you prepare to travel. Hopefully, we can make contact and tell you precisely where to collect the missionaries."

The initial planning of the search and rescue mission completed, I made my second mistake while in Peru. It was a double-pronged mistake in not correctly recognizing a problem, and then diving into the worst part of it. While we properly identified our opponents, we didn't prevent them from causing irreversible trouble for PURPLE and Jenny, but mostly to Jenny, as I learned later.

"Do you have a minute, Chauncey?" I asked. "I have something you should know on a separate, but related topic."

"Let me get my staff busy on the calls, and I will return directly," he said.

I should have recognized my error in that interlude, but I didn't. I simply wasn't viewing the larger picture of Jenny and PURPLE's security. I had no one to blame but myself. Instead of thinking, I assembled my rifle, and got reacquainted with my big revolver. In a few minutes, Chauncey returned.

"What can I do for you?" he asked.

"Before Barrantes' accident, he told me in no uncertain terms to leave the country, or he wouldn't be responsible for my safety or anyone associated with me. Now, I'm taking an assignment without leaving the country. I don't know if doing good deeds unrelated to his operation counts with Barrantes, or if his condition is such that his threat no longer matters to us. Can you contact the hospital to determine his status for me?"

"Certainly, I'll call immediately, but the doctors may not have had time to fully assess his injuries. If I don't have an answer for you by the time you leave, I'll contact you in Maldonado. Is that agreeable with you?"

Chauncey sounded almost too obliging, but I had been in a cage, been unexpectedly redeemed by Barrantes' accident, and now found myself being led toward another cage. I wasn't thinking clearly about how hostile the environment around me really was, and how I should react. The only thing in my favor was that I knew I wasn't thinking clearly. But, that realization activated my recollection of Sun Tzu's principles for selecting a place of battle and the appropriate frame of mind to go with it.[1] Sun Tzu instructed that when entering another's land, but not deeply—which he described as "light ground"—penetration shouldn't stop.

"Yes, fine. It will have to be satisfactory," I answered Chauncey not really listening to what he said as I collected my thoughts and energy for the ordeal ahead.

"Look, we have a shower on the floor below," Chauncey offered. "Take a few minutes to clean up, and some of your troubles may disappear with the dirt. Oh, I almost forgot. PURPLE forwarded another passport and visa for you in case you need to cross the border into Bolivia on this operation."

I should have shot Chauncey and anybody else I saw in the embassy at that moment, but I didn't. I missed seeing both the near and far dangers until it was much too late.

Puerto Maldonado and the Missionaries

The flight from Lima southeast across the country to Puerto Maldonado would be made in style—in Señor Barrantes' jet. We would use the drug lord's plane on the first leg of our trip to rescue missionaries who were trying to escape from Barrantes' Bolivian counterparts. Ironically, we would fly near Barrantes' Quillabamba ranch on our way to Puerto Maldonado. We were too far north to see the geoglyphs of condors and other animals made in the desert near Nazca by the predecessors of the Incas almost 900 years before Julius Caesar threw his dice across the Rubicon. I was told that 300 figures stretched out over 500 square miles of desert. They only take comprehensible shape when observed from the air. The archeological significance of the figures or their use by their makers remains uncertain.

Although archeology is interesting to me, it isn't my field of expertise, and I wouldn't have been able to solve the riddle of the figures even if I had seen them. As I noted earlier, reliable information on the location of the missionaries was absent for one reason or another on our flight across Peru toward the Bolivian border. Coming events would leave me with no desire to return to Peru to see the ancient figures in the desert, or any other Peruvian tourist attraction—ancient or otherwise.

We arrived about dark at the airport in Puerto Maldonado. The town is a logging, mining, and oil center close to the Bolivian border on the Madre de Dios River. The river is about 1,100 feet across at this point as it flows southeastward and eventually into the Amazon River basin, which makes Maldonado an important, if not scenic, stop on the inland waterway through the jungle. During the flight, I checked and cleaned my equipment and renewed my friendship with Ron. He was a former U.S. Army Ranger who reenlisted after Vietnam to claim his thirty years of active service.

My brother first met Ron in basic training, and they stayed close until Joe's death. Generally, they were assigned to the same units, which was unusual. I never had sufficient courage to ask Ron why he and Joe were not on the same assignment when Joe was killed. After his retirement, Ron became a civilian employee at the Pentagon for a few years before chucking that to return to the field as a special operations advisor for PURPLE. I had worked with him a few times, and he was solid from the ground up. The only place on earth he didn't know well was his own parlor in Chicago. Getting him to talk was a major undertaking. I achieved some success by doing or saying something that made him ask a question. After a conversation started, he reacted like a normal human being. I pulled out my three passports and paged through them as if I were on the Orient Express anticipating a document check at the Turkish border.

"How many passports do you need in this country, boy?" Ron asked on cue.

"I only needed two until you arrived," I chuckled. "How have you been?"

"Good, my life is okay. You look as ugly as ever though. Soap and water don't improve your looks much," Ron continued as he began to feel comfortable about controlling the conversation.

"In my short but eventful experience in this country, I found that looks are not as important as how fast I can run, how straight I can shoot, or how lucky I am. So far, I'm holding my own in those departments."

Then, I related the events surrounding the Barrantes' household and me over the past few days.

"That's weird about the message delivery," Ron agreed. "As you know, I hung around the embassy for a few days waiting for this assignment to develop. I saw Señora Barrantes and Bill go into Chauncey's office together. Bill may be more polecat than mole, so be careful. Your buddy Chauncey probably is on someone else's payroll in addition to Uncle Sam's too. So, don't rely on him to always decide in your favor if he has to choose between you and his adopted patrons. According to my Indian friend here, Juanita was a cabaret dancer in Pisco before becoming a lady of society. Barrantes' money made her a legitimate socialite, not her family's social standing in Lima or Madrid. The three of them appeared very interested in your clandestine employer and job description," Ron advised.

"If Juanita, Bill, and Chauncey are involved, that explains Barrantes' quick reversal of his interest in me as a potential promoter for his products. On the first night at his *ranchero*, I was invited to dinner and stroked as a potential partner in his operations. After dinner, he received a number of phone calls. Any one of them could have been Chauncey or another colleague reporting that I wasn't a playmate on the Barrantes' side of the equator. That's too bad. Chaunc was a straight shooter at one time. Maybe, the government pension isn't enough to keep him straight," I tried to excuse his behavior.

"Well, put that aside now. What else have you accomplished since the last time we worked together? Are you still dropping people off stretchers?" Ron asked mercilessly.

"You still remember that? That incident was years ago. Other than you, there was only one other time, and the guy lived to become the father of nine kids. I couldn't have done much damage to him," I testified strongly in my defense.

"At least now you admit dropping him on his head. Anybody who fathers nine kids can't be mentally sound. You're responsible for his family's situation."

"I think his Irish-Catholic heritage had more to do with his family's explosion than me dropping my end of the stretcher. Besides, I was new to special operations then. One officer yelled at me to lay down suppressing fire to cover the evacuation, while another waved at me to help with the stretcher," I continued defensively.

"Say what you want, but if I need help some day, find somebody else to carry my stretcher. (All too soon, Ron and I would wish he hadn't said that.)

"I will if I can find anyone who will come within fifty yards of you when you get a little scratch and start moaning. But, seriously, while you were rambling, it occurred to me that we're not dealing with the most reputable crowd in Peru. I agree with you. Watch my back, and I'll watch yours," I bargained.

"My heart flutters to hear you say that after all the lectures I gave you on the same subject."

"I know at least three PURPLE clients who can attest to your lack of communication and teaching skills," I jabbed back.

"Haven't you learned about teaching by example?"

"Yes, but I've tried hard to ignore you. I credit my long life to being successful at it."

"Okay, if you don't want to learn, I'll take a nap," Ron said as he rolled over and fell asleep in seconds.

On Light Ground

Pilot Bill knew the town of Maldonado and found us rooms in the Hostal Cabana Quinta that were better than Ron and I expected. After we settled and ate, Bill called Chauncey in Lima. It was late, but Bill reached Chauncey at home. Ron and I looked at each other to register that vignette as confirmation that Bill and Chauncey were closer to each other than they would testify to in court. Chauncey advised that preliminary hospital reports showed Barrantes had a serious spinal injury. He would never ride his big black horse again, and, very possibly, never walk unaided again. Señora Barrantes was publicly blaming me—as if the Barrantes family needed to accuse anyone. Bill recited that, in her rage, the señora intended revenge. That was strange talk from a woman who earlier was eager to pass on a message to me despite her husband's watchful eyes. Of course, if she really was following her husband's orders to smoke me out as a threat to the family business by passing along a message from Jenny that had gone astray, she also could have been an accessory to murder in Tingo Maria—if the wild pigs and *El Señor de los Milagros* hadn't intervened on my behalf.

After that jolt of information, Bill brought better news. Our wayward missionaries were approaching the south bank of the Rio Heath, a little east of the Peru-Bolivian border. He did not tell us the source of his information. An incursion across the border into Bolivia was the only way for Ron and me to confirm its accuracy. Bill said that the missionaries would hide at the edge of the jungle until we extracted them by helicopter early the next morning. We would chopper over their position once, confirm that they were ready for evacuation, and land at the nearest clearing to pick them up.

I thought they should hire a *peki-peki* boat (a small boat with a two-cycle engine), or take the ferry to the Peruvian side of the river. We would not violate international borders with that approach. Ron reminded me that my option might require the missionaries and us to show our passports on both sides of the border, which might not be optimal for anyone. That didn't bother me. I could produce at least three passports at a moment's notice. Or, I could place a U.S. Treasury photo of Thomas Jefferson in the photo page of any passport I presented to either country's border officers to guarantee a favorable outcome. But, a helicopter pickup had been arranged, and that's how we would conduct the extraction. I assumed that Bill would play it straight as far as the rescue was concerned. If nothing else, helping Ron and me would be to Bill's advantage in maintaining his cover as a mole for Barrantes if he was working both sides of the fencerow. He might gain points in saving his immortal soul too, but no one put money on that part of the incursion agenda.

We were up before first light, had a hearty breakfast in a restaurant frequented by gold miners in the area, and then headed to the airport. Bill wasn't licensed as a rotary wing pilot. The embassy hired a helicopter and pilot to take Ron and me the remaining seventy kilometers along the Rio Heath into Bolivia to the pickup point. One look at this chopper made me yearn for reconsideration of my *peki-peki* boat option, or the safety of the mechanically challenged helicopter in Bhuj. Bill went into the cockpit with the pilot. Ron and his Indian guide loaded their stuff in the port side cargo area. I loaded my gear on the starboard side as usual. The pilot started the engine; we climbed aboard, and buckled up. The rotors sounded rough at first, but ran more smoothly when we were airborne and moving toward the rising sun. Actually, we aimed a little northeast of the rising sun to avoid crossing too close to the border stations at the port town of Puerto Pardo on the Peruvian side, and its sister city of Puerto Heath on the Bolivian side. Trying to explain to border guards on both sides of the river our intentions for only a short illegal incursion to rescue a group of missionaries appeared to be a burdensome overemphasis on the word "illegal."

As we approached the pickup zone, we opened the side doors and readied our weapons in case any enforcers had pursued the missionaries and intended to cause trouble at the last minute. When we flew over the area, we didn't locate the group, nor did anyone try to signal us from the edge of the jungle. As I feared, now we didn't know if the missionaries were there, or if they were hiding because enforcers were in the area too. At this critical time, we all realized that the initial plan was too simple to guarantee success. More than minimal effort would be necessary to complete the rescue. The pilot made another pass over the area. This time, he approached as if we were coming directly from Peru. Coming in from the northwest, we saw a quick flash of light from a belt buckle or mirror blinking from the edge of the tree line. The pilot executed a neat pirouette to acknowledge contact. Then, he zipped to a clearing about one hundred yards to the north where enough clearance was available to set the chopper down. Ron, his Indian guide, and I climbed out on the chopper's skids, jumped off, then fanned out in three directions with our weapons ready to protect the missionaries and ourselves if we encountered hostile fire. We saw three figures emerge from the trees and run in our direction.

"Hustle up!" Ron yelled while waving to the trio, which automatically caused them to drop their belongings and stalled our efforts to get them aboard the chopper quickly.

The missionaries were about thirty-five yards from the copter when the first shot rang out near where they exited the trees. Ron and the Indian returned fire immediately. The galloping missionaries were in my line of fire, and I froze momentarily trying to decide if I should move to a new firing position, or stay put to help the trio climb aboard the chopper. When I determined that only one rifleman appeared to be firing at us, I selected option two, and helped the threesome climb aboard. Ron and the Indian had sufficient experience to keep one gunman occupied, and they did, for the most part. I heard two metallic clicks hit high on the chopper near the rotor, but I couldn't see any damage. With the missionaries on board, I fired a few suppressing rounds at the trees to give Ron and the Indian time to retreat and board the chopper on the left side. I was sitting on the starboard side floor with my feet dangling outside while firing at the trees when the pilot lifted the chopper a short distance off the ground. The missionaries grabbed my shoulders to pull me back into the tilted chopper when I heard a few more metallic clicks ricochet off the chopper's hull. Again, I observed no apparent damage, and we moved steadily out of the rifleman's range. We were returning to Peru.

FIRE!

As planned, we took a semicircular route back to Puerto Maldonado. Upon our approach with the chopper about five feet off the ground, the Indian and I opened the side doors, and had one foot on the skids as we prepared to jump down from each side. For some reason, the pilot rotated the craft back to the east when we all heard a klunk. Hanging halfway out the side doors, the Indian and I saw a flash in the cockpit, and then a large fireball engulfed the entire front of the aircraft. The chopper dropped the remaining distance to the ground knocking the Indian and me off the skids onto the concrete landing pad. The wind direction shielded the Indian and me long enough for us to quickly roll away from the craft and flames. The missionaries were temporarily protected inside the chopper's cargo area. But, as the pilot inexplicably lifted and rotated the chopper again, the flames were sucked into the open cockpit windows grilling the pilot and Bill badly. Also, with that maneuver, Ron, who was hanging halfway out the left side door, was caught in the circling flames from the rotating chopper.

Within an instant, what should have been a celebration turned into a disaster. After an eternity, Ron jumped clear; the Indian began beating on Ron's flaming clothes, then rolled Ron on the ground to finally put the flames out. Meanwhile, I pulled the three missionaries out of the copter on the starboard side. Ron had some nasty burns on his hands and face, but six of us were relatively okay. To our horror, we turned our attention to the cockpit to discover it was completely engulfed in flames. Bill and the pilot were still in there! Other flight and ground crews and bystanders from the airport were now around us with fire extinguishers and whatever else they had in their hands to help. Another eternity later, all the flames were doused. With help, we carefully moved Bill and the chopper pilot onto stretchers, and then lifted them into a converted van that served as the airport ambulance. Puerto Maldonado had two hospitals, which was remarkable for a town of 44,000 people in this part of the world. The closest hospital was Santa Rosa.

Unfortunately, Santa Rosa was not equipped to handle severe burn cases like these. Social Seguro Hospital was three kilometers outside of town on the road to Cuzco and was better equipped. We didn't have much choice. We put Ron on blankets on the floor of the van between the chopper pilot and Bill. The ambulance driver started as smoothly as he could off the landing pad for the hospital. The Indian spoke to a mine supervisor, who volunteered to take the rest of us to the hospital in the back of his truck. Ron had the old stretcher story wrong. I carried one corner of his stretcher this time, and I didn't let him fall.

Ron, Bill, and the helicopter pilot had been wheeled into the emergency room by the time we arrived at the hospital in the truck. I was on the phone to Chauncey in Lima *pronto*. With three men seriously injured, any involvement Chauncey had with Barrantes' drug operation was irrelevant for now. In an unfamiliar country, I needed a charge d'affaires to make authoritative medical arrangements. I told Chauncey that we required emergency airlift to Lima (and possibly beyond) for proper care after the men received whatever initial treatment was available here. He would arrange medical evacuation immediately. I also advised that the three missionaries were safe with me, but they had lost everything in the blaze except the clothes they wore.

Immigration officers would show up soon if they weren't in the neighborhood already after all the commotion in town. Chauncey agreed to deal with that too. Suddenly, I had nothing to do but be anxious for Ron, Bill, and the helicopter pilot's safety. Not unusual in times like these, I realized that the pilot had risked his life for us on a dangerous mission, and I didn't know his name, if he was married, if he had kids—nothing.

I walked over to where the three missionaries sat in the waiting room and introduced myself to Jim, Steve, and Scott. We had omitted social formalities with them too in our rush to leave Bolivia.

"Thanks for helping us," they voiced in unison as I approached. "We are really sorry about the accident. Will they be all right?"

"Nobody knows yet according to what I gathered from medical staff conversations. I called the U.S. Embassy in Lima to arrange medical evacuation for them and transportation for you three. I explained that you probably need special processing to the States if you lost your passports along with your other belongings. The embassy is both pleased that you are in Peru and anxious that you leave as soon as possible given all the noise we raised getting you here."

I didn't tell the missionaries that I needed to disappear quickly too before Barrantes learned that I was still in the country, especially when we appeared destined to check our injured into the same hospital in Lima where he resided. If Barrantes was too incapacitated to care immediately,

I still didn't want to deal with an angry señora intent on revenge. I chatted with the missionaries a bit longer until we all found a place to doze off either standing up, leaning against a corner wall, or lying on the floor.

I heard my name called twice before my eyes focused on Chauncey coming down the hall. The first light of dawn was breaking over the surrounding mountains.

"What's their status?" Chauncey asked me anxiously.

"Let's find out together," I responded as I stood up and reorganized my body parts to walk upright.

Ron had bandages on his face and arms, but he could travel to Lima (and beyond) I hoped. Bill and the copter pilot were in worse shape, but they were declared stable enough to be airlifted to the capital. As I anticipated, the hospital here had done all it could for them. Chauncey gave the Indian money to go home or wherever the money would take him. We shook hands, and I thanked him for his help. In his Aymaran dialect, he expressed his concern for all the injured, at least that is what I deciphered from his facial expressions and body language more than from his speech. Ambulances were ready to take our injured to the airport and a van was available for Chauncey, the missionaries, and me. The plane Chauncey commandeered for the injured was big enough for everyone. Chauncey appeared to have thought of everything—almost.

The doctors at the Hospital del Niño in Lima advised that, for the best care, Ron should be airlifted directly to the States to prevent infection in his open wounds and blistered skin. As nationals, Bill and the helicopter pilot were acclimated to the local environment, and the physicians decided that they would receive adequate treatment in Lima.

Chauncey arranged a military evacuation to the States for Ron and me. The only thing he missed was replacing Ron's passport that was lost in the fire. I improvised a remedy. Medical staff helped me wind more gauze around Ron's face. The mummified Ron now could use one of the three unburned passports that I fortunately had stored in my thigh pocket. No living immigration officer would unwind Ron's bandages to view ugly-looking burns to verify his passport photo. Ron was three years older than me, but we had the same general build. Any of my passports would be a close match. Chauncey arranged a medical escort as an extra precaution for Ron on the flight to the States. As another precaution against intruders and would-be assassins, Chauncey advised that he had spread the word through the underground grapevine that our destination was a hospital in Houston rather than our true target destination of the Brooke Army

Medical Center in San Antonio. Depending on the political environment and Ron's medical needs as we approached the States, I would accompany him to a hospital in Houston, the Brooke Medical Center in San Antonio, or to any other secure, first-class, burns unit that accepted me as Ron's sidekick with my big pistol and bigger attitude.

At the airport, I shook Chauncey's hand for what I thought would be the last time.

"Thanks for your help, Chaunc," was all I could say at first.

"Take care, but don't hurry back, my friend. I need time to put the country back in order after your visit," he responded, equally moved.

"I don't intend a return until you get Barrantes off my back. Keep me informed if you need help to stabilize the situation. I'll make sure they send someone reliable. Meanwhile, do yourself a favor and decide what side of the law you prefer. I don't want to read that they found your body under a pile of garbage some day. You may have broken some diplomatic vases that can't be easily glued back together, but I will always remember our friendship, what you did for me in the past, and for your efforts in the last few days."

"Good-bye, I'm sorry that life doesn't always lead to where one intends to go. I will do what I can to repair the damage, and take responsibility for my actions. If they let me, I'll retire and take care of my mother."

"Good, just don't tell her I was in town. She will want to send me some of her chili pepper sauce again, and I'll have to find a nuclear waste disposal site to get rid of it. *Adios, amigo.*"

RETURNING STATESIDE

Chauncey still had sufficient connections to get the missionaries on the same military flight with Ron and me. They were a fairly somber trio with Ron on board. They could see and reflect upon what damage their actions caused. The medics had Ron so heavily sedated that he could have flown back without a plane. When Ron was awake, I told him our approximate location and that I would stay with him until he received top-flight care in the States for his burns. Walking back to my seat after one short visit, I recalled my flight with Alice Bright Feather long ago. *Some ghosts never disappear.* In this case as in many others, the good guys would have the continuing nightmares. To keep myself from getting depressed, I got up and went further back to where the missionaries sat.

Helping Angel Moroni

"How is it for you gentlemen in the first class section?" I asked trying to ignite a fuse under them without being super harsh. "Without any cargo, you have plenty of legroom back here."

"We're fine. We were discussing the events of the last few days, and how fortunate we were to have God's protection and yours," Jim replied with wisdom.

"How long have you been doing this?" Scott asked.

"You mean being an International Responder? I've been at it only about six months. Why do you ask?"

"You seem, ah, rather 'mature' for this kind of thing," Scott responded diplomatically.

"But you appear confident and really competent at what you do," Steve added, trying to bail out his missionary companion.

"If you read your field manual, you'd know the answer to that," I instructed.

"Field manual?" they all chorused.

"Yes, your Bible; that's your field manual isn't it? Somewhere in there, didn't Jesus tell his disciples that he had chosen them? They hadn't chosen him."

"Were you chosen?" Jim interjected perceptively.

"Perhaps a more appropriate description is that I was 'summoned' rather than 'chosen.' I was standing in line one day when my name was called. You may not equate a sergeant major with God, but at the time, he was the closest thing to the Almighty that I had encountered, and with the decorations to prove it. He had to be a god because he was no angel. He certainly changed my life forever. How about you guys? What inspiration or calling did you receive?" I asked, although I had heard standard answers several times before from my prior Mormon clients.

"As practicing Mormons, we are expected to devote a year or more in a missionary role away from home," Steve acknowledged. "In this way, we test our commitment and ability to serve God among those who need both temporal and spiritual help."

"That describes the Bolivian drug lords nicely. How did you tangle with them?" I sparred with what would become an unwelcome lifetime memory for them.

"We were stationed in Cochabamba and Santa Cruz in the central highlands of Bolivia," Scott started. "After our official mission ended, we decided to see more of the country. First, we went south to Sucre."

"I know a little about Sucre," I interrupted. "It's in the south central highlands and named after Antonio Jose de Sucre, a freedom fighter and colleague of Simon Bolivar. Some Catholic competitors of yours send an annual delegation to help the residents improve the infrastructure there, meaning they build latrines and other basic facilities."

"Yes, we heard about their work, and we wanted to see what improvements they made over the years to report back to our supervisor," Steve acknowledged. "The information will give our project director an idea of what services are needed most and what a missionary team can do to be most helpful to the indigenous people in a relatively short time."

"A little religious spying is a useful way to determine how to allocate funds and missionaries, I suppose. But Sucre wasn't where you got into trouble, was it?"

"No," Jim admitted. "From Sucre, we decided to visit the capital city of La Paz."

"And you found that the 'City of the Peace' wasn't as peaceful as you expected, right?"

"We generally knew that the cocaine fields were in the Amazon basin further north, so we didn't anticipate any problems in the capital," Jim asserted.

"But, you found that the drug lords don't live in the lowlands with the mosquitoes, do they?"

"No, they don't, and neither do their daughters," Jim admitted. "We were in the marketplace when we learned about a *fiesta* starting that night and lasting for several days. We saw some nice girls buying vegetables in the marketplace. Scott decided to ask them if we could escort them to the dances and other festivities later that night."

"We meant no harm," Scott said in his defense. "We thought that all of us could have a good time, make friends, and learn more about the Bolivian people and their culture. We didn't know their families were connected to the drug trade."

"Your education started quickly after that, no doubt," I interrupted again as I perceived the trio being dragged further into a swamp of their own making.

"At first, we thought that the girls didn't understand our Spanish. Then, they called their bodyguards, who contacted their fathers. The race to the border started shortly after that, and they were serious about it!" Steve added. "The only thing we could think of was to find Jim's friend from college at the jungle research station to help us."

"How did you get involved in our rescue?" Jim inquired for all of them.

"Without being sacrilegious about it, my party was ready to leave Peru after helping with earthquake relief when we were told that Angel Moroni needed help getting you people out of harm's way. I must be honest and tell you that we weren't thrilled about the change in our travel plans. The information we received about you initially suggested that you were trying to reach a friend near Iquitos, which was insane. Then, more realistically, but still highly improbable, we hypothesized that you might try for Tabatinga in the tri-border area of Peru, Brazil, and Colombia. Unless you had someone fly you out of Bolivia, you had absolutely no chance of survival in the jungle, and we had no chance of reaching you anytime in the twenty-first century if you kept moving around. If you reached Tabatinga, we felt that the Americans at the research center could get you home without our help. The more we learned about your movements, the more we judged that you would be lucky to reach the Rio Heath near the Tambopata Reservation where some American students serve as guides in the area. We decided that if we set up our base at Puerto Maldonado, we could intercept you somewhere along the shore of Lake Titicaca or a little further north. Our plan was to intercept and bring you back alive, not fried from the jungle heat, or with poison arrows in your bodies."

"Yes, we appreciate your help very much, and we are very concerned about your friend Ron and the other two who stayed in Peru. We will pray for their recovery," Scott affirmed once again. "We are sorry that we caused problems for them."

"The doctors say that Ron will be okay if we can get him to a good burns unit in the States before infection sets in. He's so ugly that a few more scars won't make any difference. Fortunately, he has my passport. Otherwise, customs might never let him back into the States, burns or no burns. And neither God nor the devil want him in his present condition."

"You talk as if you have been friends for a long time," Steve observed accurately.

"Ron and my brother joined the Army about the same time and served in the same units for a number of years. They were a different kind of missionary, but the bond between them was iron-tight, probably like your friendship. They let me hang around with them from time to time."

"And now you all do rescue work for some government agency?" Scott inquired.

"Not exactly. My meeting Ron here was a coincidence. We don't work together usually, and I certainly don't work for a government agency. My brother was killed years ago. I was never told the details."

"What organization do you work for?" Jim asked eagerly as if he expected a truthful answer from me.

"I have a regular job in healthcare stateside, or I did have before I came to Peru. When the need arises, I work for my own corporation, or for a color."

"A color?" Steve echoed, highly puzzled by my statement.

"Yeah, it was set up that way from the start. If somebody asks me if I ever worked for a foreign government or for Uncle Sam, I can honestly say that outside of my military service, I never worked for either. Somebody can beat the daylights out of me, and my answer will still be the same. Someday, when I write my memoirs, I'll explain it more clearly. But, it looks like we are landing somewhere. I'll talk to you gentlemen later."

Lightening the Load

We landed in San Jose, Costa Rica, for refueling. Ordinarily, that presented no problem. On this trip, someone had alerted Costa Rican officials to expect us. Customs was very interested in the civilian passengers, even though nobody planned to deplane here. I showed an officer one of my passports, but he hardly glanced at it. I showed another officer a different edition of my passport for Ron and received the same lack of interest. For some reason, the officers were highly interested in the more recently minted passports and visa documents of the three missionaries.

The customs officers announced that the plane would not be allowed to depart for the States until the missionaries' documents were confirmed. The military pilot had orders to deliver Ron to medical care in the States as his primary assignment. The missionaries were an afterthought. In the middle of the night, the U.S. Embassy was closed, and everyone (except me for some reason) believed that the missionaries were out of danger from Bolivian drug lords. To fulfill his orders, the pilot decided to leave the missionaries with Costa Rican Customs and resume our flight to the States to deliver Ron to a hospital. I didn't have the authority to make the call, and I would really have been conflicted in choosing between Ron and the missionaries if I did.

As we unloaded the missionaries and took off, I recalled that Barrantes impressed me with his considerable influence over government officials both within and outside Peru. I wondered if the Bolivian drug lords had similar influence and a long reach into Costa Rican Customs and beyond. I also pondered if the three missionaries had told me the entire story. Asking a drug lord's daughter to a *fiesta* was not a capital offense punishable by drug lord revenge, Central American government interference, or involvement by PURPLE. At this point, the missionaries were the only people who knew for certain what had transpired in La Paz, and they were no longer on board to explain the situation.

Under the revised circumstances, I made Ron's delivery to safety in the States my primary focus, consistent with the pilot's priority. I could wonder all I wanted, but until someone changed the current plan, the missionaries were on their own again. I sat down and buckled up for continuation of our flight north.

Dos

We landed in Mexico City for another refueling stop. This time, two Mexican federales officers were interested in any civilian passengers, excluding Ron and me. The second officer held my passports in the light of his flashlight to get a better view. The photos were slightly different, but the personal information was the same. I felt certain I was going to jail, but any effort to avoid a sojourn in a Mexican slammer was worthwhile.

"Twins," I told the officer. "*Dos*," I said to clarify as I pointed back and forth between Ron and myself.

My officer said something to the official in charge, who waved him off. With a quick look at Ron's mummified head and face, he handed the passports back to me without a word. As they departed the aircraft, I heard the word "*tres*" and concluded that they were looking for the three missionaries, or they were confirming that the three missionaries were no longer on the plane. Their actions confirmed my suspicion that we were not beyond Peruvian or Bolivian drug lord reach yet. Nonetheless, we were relatively close to the States now, and my interest in getting Ron tucked in somewhere for medical attention took center stage in my mind. I was determined that nobody was going to undermine my responsibility to him on that front.

When we finally arrived in San Antonio, the action intensified. With a military police escort, Ron and I were transported by ambulance to the medical center. Other than for general security reasons, I didn't know why we were playing hide-and-seek in our own country. Although Ron could not see his hospital accommodations, he was wheeled into the celebrity suite with a military guard posted at the door. Once again on this trip, my actual location was somewhere other than shown on the duty roster.

Texas Two-Step

During a short lull in getting Ron connected to monitors and intravenous drips, Ron recognized my close presence and whispered with facial agony attached, "Where are we?"

"I am standing next to your bed in the executive suite of the University of Texas Hospital in Houston, or we are at the Brooke Medical Center in San Antonio, or we aren't at either of those hospitals. Take your pick. At least, we are somewhere in the States," I responded confidently. "But, don't call home yet if you catch my meaning. It must be important to someone to have us appear to be in several locations at the same time. Remember that when you communicate with the staff, especially when I'm not around. Remember that and keep cool. Everything will be okay, I think."

I found a seat in the hallway across from Ron's room to allow the medical staff to complete Ron's preliminary examination and hookups, when an Army colonel approached, stuck his head halfway into Ron's doorway, took a quick look at the activity, and came over to where I was sitting.

"Are you from PURPLE?" the colonel asked.

"I'm from Illinois unless someone hands me a different passport," I answered with maximum sarcasm to capitalize on my civilian status that didn't require me to salute Army brass.

"That won't be necessary," Colonel X replied not enjoying the richness of my attitude. "Your people need you to return to Costa Rica and escort the three missionaries back to the States. I'm here to deliver you to military transport for the flight. Are you ready?"

"Do I look and smell ready enough for you, Colonel?" I asked with a double dose of sarcasm.

"I realize that you've had a bad time getting here, but I am following priority orders."

My first response was to ask myself where Jenny was in all these activities. Her job as my Scout was to prepare me for new assignments, or for changes in a current one. Nonetheless, the colonel was nervous, and the situation appeared urgent, so I decided to take the high road in building a working relationship with him.

"I understand," I said not really understanding a thing Colonel X had said so far. "I'll be ready in one second."

I went into Ron's room and stood off to the side for a few moments while the medical staff completed their work and some left the room.

When I found a space at his bedside, I gently touched Ron's shoulder and told him, "If you are settled for the night, I have a pickup run back south. I'll return in a while. Do you need anything?"

"Bring me a PURPLE teddy bear," Ron mumbled painfully as he looked into my eyes for a signal to confirm his understanding that I was going out again.

While Ron watched me intently, I blinked deliberately three times, and gave a little flying motion with my two crossed index fingers followed by a head bob toward the door. Ron closed his eyes once, and tucked his chin in to approximate the best non-verbal "I understand" that he could manage. With Ron now informed that I had orders from PURPLE to fly back and pick up the three missionaries, I turned and left the room. Ron knew I would be back as soon as I could, but I need not hurry. From the flow of medication going into him, he would have a brain buzz for quite a while.

Out in the hallway again, I walked to where Colonel X stood.

"Okay, I'm ready, lead the way," I said as I picked up my bag of toys and dirty clothes while discreetly wiggling my derringer into a more favorable position up my sleeve. While we waited for the elevator, I reached into my bag, pulled out my big revolver and shoulder holster, and buckled that on in plain view of the colonel and anyone passing by. Once again, my sitting on the outboard starboard seat of the chopper in Puerto Maldonado not only saved my life, but saved my toys too. From the serious look on Colonel X's face, I might need them soon.

I followed the colonel to his military vehicle. He told me that I was flying military for the second time that night. I didn't care. I was tired, really tired now. Another flight south was not what my body needed. I gave myself a pep talk that I would do my duty no matter what, and then promptly dozed off.

I woke up when the colonel abruptly stopped at a guard station. The colonel showed his identification, and I waved one of my passports at the guard. The colonel did not give the guard much opportunity to review my identification or to see my face. As we continued toward an outlying hangar and its associated airstrip, the door on my cranial closet opened, and my brain started to function again. Suddenly, the questions began.

"Colonel, why me for this assignment?" I asked. "Certainly, a U.S. Ranger or special operations unit is available somewhere to take care of this assignment as part of a training exercise, if nothing else?"

"I agree, but your organization specifically requested you for the assignment and objected to any alternative," he answered while continuing to watch the road ahead. "If you have any objections, take it up with your superiors."

"Do you know who or what PURPLE is?" I asked, not quite ready to give up my pursuit for more information.

"If you don't know, I certainly don't, and I have no orders to provide that information to you."

"Do you know where the three missionaries are being held in Costa Rica?"

"I have no information about missionaries or any other aspect of what you will be required to do. I was informed to deliver you to the airfield, and that you will receive further information during the flight to your destination. That is all I know and can tell you."

"Should I convey any documents to someone for the missionaries' release, or has that been handled?" I asked, still not giving up on my quest for information.

"I have no word on that. Again, I presume that information will be relayed to you at the appropriate time by the person or parties in charge of this operation."

"Do I have backup, or am I solo on this assignment?" I continued, partly for information, but mostly to aggravate the colonel now.

"How many people do you see in this vehicle, mister?" the colonel snapped back angrily.

"Are you accompanying me?" I asked, unable to resist raising the colonel's temperature to the boiling point.

The colonel stopped the vehicle and turned toward me with frustration written all over him, but too exasperated to speak. I knew he was not authorized to tell me anything, but our verbal exchanges cleared my sleepy skull, which I considered a positive development given the hour and the time since my last hot meal.

Before the colonel downloaded any unsavory dialogue, I said, "I know. I will receive that information at the appropriate time."

He snickered, started the vehicle, drove a short distance, and then pulled alongside a small jet being readied for takeoff. My question and answer game was over. The colonel made no move to get out of the vehicle. I took that as my cue to gather my stuff and bail out.

"Thanks for the information, Colonel," I said. "Have a lovely evening, and say hello to your mom for me."

He gave me an abbreviated smile and an absent-minded half salute as I got out and trotted to the plane about seven giant steps away. When I reached the bottom step of the drop-down door of the sleek jet, I glanced at the night sky. Every star in the heavens was shining that night, just like they were on the weekend at the Navajo reservation eons ago. *What have I gotten myself into now*, I wondered, *and would the Great Spirit take care of me as he had so many times in the past?*

More Help for Moroni

The small jet was faster and quieter than the lumbering cargo plane but still not fast enough for me. I should have been home by now. I wanted to be home by now. The missionaries should have been home now too. I cared and didn't care about them at the same time. Self-pity and negative thoughts at a critical time are self-destructive and get other people hurt. I had to change my attitude fast. I allowed myself the luxury of wallowing and whining internally for a few more minutes, and then went to work cleaning and oiling my firearms and sharpening my bladed weapons—every last one of them. As I finished, the copilot came out of the cockpit and handed me a large envelope.

"I was instructed to give this to you when we reached the halfway point to Costa Rica," he said.

"This is getting too complicated. Tell me more if you can," I declared.

"Sorry, I don't know any more, and I probably couldn't tell you if I did. You look like you are ready for anything though with that arsenal," he said as he surveyed my assortment of weapons.

"Thanks. One never knows what one will encounter when one leaves the house these days. Let me try another question on you before you go. Are you guys going to wait for me in San Jose, or do I have to find another way home?"

"Don't know for sure, Mac. Maybe the answer is in there," the copilot suggested, pointing to the envelope.

With that non-informative exchange completed, the copilot returned to the cockpit. I tore the envelope open and out fell three passports and a short note from PURPLE. It read, "Passports are enclosed for the three lost souls. You will find them at the Costa Rican Immigration Office. You will encounter an old friend. It is imperative that you negotiate their release through your mutual efforts if at all possible. Allow your colleague to take the lead if discussions stall. Plane will wait for your return flight with subjects. If immediate release cannot be implemented, think creatively. Think broader than two cowboys. No weapons unless absolutely necessary. Good luck."

Well, that was informative and cheery. Now, I had two tasks. I needed to negotiate the release of the trio through an unknown third party, plus interpret what cowboys PURPLE had in mind. As I re-packed my weapons and changed into my least ratty civilian clothes, I kept rereading and pondering PURPLE's note, and looking at the trio's travel documents. *Think broader?* I was so tired I couldn't think in any direction. I went forward to the cockpit.

"Do you folks have a computer I can borrow for a while?" I asked.

"Sure, Mac, help yourself," the copilot said, pointing to a laptop sticking out of his travel bag. "If you don't mind sitting on the floor, I'll plug you in right here."

(Early in my civilian job, I had been paid to formulate and interpret company policies, make decisions, and interact with people to make their lives better. A new breed of managers was evolving across U.S. businesses. These folks believed that a computer was the answer to all problems large and small. If the screen didn't resolve a particular problem, they would hide behind their computers all day until the problem or the employee went somewhere else. That didn't fit my definition of problem solving. To me, a computer was merely a tool, and I intended to use one that way on the problem facing me without fretting if others considered me a computer illiterate or whiz. I definitely would interact with somebody one way or another later.) When the plane landed in San Jose, I still didn't have a firm fix on how to arrange the missionaries' release, but I had more information than I did earlier. The situation didn't improve by the time the taxi dropped me off at the immigration office. In the lobby, I didn't know whom to see or what I needed to do let alone request help. A security guard looked at me with increasing hostility as I shifted from one foot to another. Then, I felt someone touch my forearm. I turned around to recognize a familiar, but misplaced face. It was Hassan.

TERRORISTS AND THE TERCHOVA TREASURE

"What are you doing here?" I asked, taken by surprise. "You're on the wrong continent."

"Come with me to the immigration director's office. We can talk about your lost souls there," Hassan said, smiling while shaking my hand.

That was strange, I thought. *Hassan is using the same language contained in PURPLE's message.*

"I see you have new sunglasses," I told him in the elevator, not knowing what else to say with other people there. "Don't the old ones work this far away from home?"

"I see new scars on your face. You have not been home either," Hassan answered more pleasantly than I deserved.

"How many more will I get before I leave here?" I asked, hoping for a clue about what was ahead for the missionaries and me.

"You don't have room for many more scars," Hassan responded briskly. "We will try to have you and your missionary friends on a northbound flight very soon."

By that time, we were out of the elevator and entering the immigration director's suite. It was too late to press Hassan for additional information.

Hassan introduced me to Director Brujas who pointed us toward his office. I could hear the missionaries talking in an adjoining conference room, but I couldn't see them. I followed the director into his office and went toward a chair near his desk. Nope, wrong move; he wanted us in his conversation area decorated with leather chairs, fine lamps, carpets, and other conversation-enhancing appliances.

Director Brujas spoke first. "I understand that you know each other, so I only need to say that Hassan represents the interests of Señor Calderon in Bolivia, among others. I understand that you (looking at me) are here to assist the three persons in question to return to their homes in the United States as soon as possible."

UNDIPLOMATIC NEGOTIATIONS

That was diplomatically well put, I thought. The director's icebreaker stated my purpose for being in his office without recognizing any authorization from the US for my role. He was probably right. Now if he would advise me who Señor Calderon was, I may enjoy being the least informed person in the room.

"I am sure that all parties wish a prompt and reasonable resolution to the matter of the three individuals in provisional custody," Director

Brujas continued. "I perceive my role as a facilitator in this matter, and I will act in the best interests of all parties, and for my country too, of course."

Of course, I agreed silently. *Costa Rica is a refueling stop for drug traffickers from Bolivia and neighboring countries on their way to the States with cocaine. Why wouldn't he act in the best interests of his country—and himself—and not necessarily in the priority order he stated?*

"If possible," the director went on, cutting short my daydreaming, "I would like to resolve this difficulty through joint conversations, but I will have unilateral discussions if I believe they will help move the matter forward. Is that agreeable with you gentlemen?" he asked, turning his gaze between Hassan and me.

Hassan nodded as I sat there frog-like, unsure what hymnal I should have let alone what song to sing.

"Do I take that as a yes, gentlemen?" the director inquired giving me time to nod too.

Thanks, Hassan, I silently applauded him for giving me guarded notice that our conversation was being recorded. Head shaking does not record well in any language.

Abruptly, I decided that I had my quota of diplomacy and asked bluntly, "What exactly is the problem? If it involves travel documents, I can present official U.S. passports for the three missionaries to return with me to the States immediately."

"The situation is more complex than that," Director Brujas responded. "A crime has been committed. We have a question of property stolen from Señor Calderon while the individuals were in Bolivia. The señor wants his property returned and the individuals responsible punished under Bolivian law."

"What kind of property are we talking about and what are the official charges?" I asked for clarification. "I'm sorry to bore you with these basic questions, but I haven't kept up with my legal reading during the last few weeks."

If groveling will help, that statement should solve everyone's problem, I concluded.

"I see that you are a very direct person, so I will answer in the same light," the director prefaced what I expected to be a diplomatic dressing-down.

"Certain business documents were confiscated from Señor Calderon's house," Hassan interjected. "He believes that the three individuals in the adjoining room are responsible. The official charge is commercial espionage."

"Has anyone informed them directly to give the documents back?" I asked as naively as possible to conceal my growing impatience with this exercise. "After a few weeks on the run in unknown territory, and now being detained in a third country, I believe they will cooperate in almost anything, including dancing the fox trot with each other to return home without further delay," I reasoned aloud.

"We asked American authorities for your presence here with the distinct hope that you could persuade the missionaries to do just that in your fascinating Midwestern way of getting things done expeditiously," Hassan hijacked the conversation again before Director Brujas had a chance to speak.

"Have they had an opportunity to talk to legal counsel, the U.S. Ambassador, or any other U.S. representative?" I asked politely. "That might be more expeditious than me trying to guess what their international legal rights and obligations might be."

"I believe Hassan stated our position and that of Señor Calderon correctly to them," the director recited, which refreshed my memory about PURPLE's instructions to let Hassan lead the negotiations if necessary. "We wish to resolve the matter with the least amount of legal and other entanglements possible. We believe that you are particularly suited to explain the matter to them in simple terms so that they understand and fully appreciate the perilous position in which they have placed themselves," the director droned.

From that statement, I had the impression that no one intended to award the trio any rights to counsel or sanctuary as long as the missionaries were outside the U.S. and held documents that Calderon wanted returned to him. I should have started snapping the neck of everyone in sight for that obvious violation of international law. However, that approach might get innocent people killed including the trio and me. I needed to confirm that my impression was correct.

"If we can achieve the perfect remedy for all parties concerned, what would that be?" I asked diplomatically.

"As in most cases of theft, the owner would like his property restored and the perpetrators held accountable by the proper authorities as we have already stated," Director Brujas confirmed. "Otherwise, the owner will take whatever measures he believes necessary to obtain return of his property."

"I suppose some of the remedies could be life-threatening to the trio, correct?" I asked to confirm my belief that the trio and I were a long way from the protection of U.S. law.

"We are here to resolve these issues before the situation comes to that," Hassan jumped in before Director Brujas could add his complexities to the dialogue.

"If return of the property and the temporary transfer of the three people to Bolivian authorities to do so are all that you require to resolve this matter, that seems like a reasonable thing to do," I stated to reinforce Hassan's remarks and to keep the situation from escalating into physical threats against the missionaries. Then, I added a kicker.

"I can tell you though that the United States doesn't look favorably upon having its citizens subjected to legal proceedings in other countries without their being afforded legal counsel and due process of law. More emphatically, Uncle Sugar doesn't like his citizens subjected to any private punishment that individuals in other countries may wish to impose on them. With that understanding, I would like to speak privately with the missionaries to determine if I can encourage them to cooperate with respect to any Bolivian property they may wittingly or unwittingly have in their possession. And by the way, 'privately' is the important word here, no recorded conversations, please," I announced forcefully to alert Hassan and the director to turn off any recording equipment in the room where the missionaries were being held.

My litany jolted the director, but I felt I made up for my previous groveling and unfruitful waiting for Hassan to carry a strong message to Director Brujas on behalf of the missionaries. But, my lack of complete information and this weird conversation still made me nervous.

"I appreciate your spirit of cooperation and inclination to resolve this matter promptly," the director stated regaining his diplomatic podium. "Indeed, you have a valid point. I will give you an opportunity to talk with the three men. I hope that you can convince them to do the right thing in this situation."

I didn't know for certain what the "right thing" was. But, nobody was going to play hardball with people relying on me when I was under orders to protect them. Again, I wasn't impressed with Hassan's weak-kneed support thus far. I may as well play my own dice in this crapshoot. A conversation with the missionaries couldn't hurt. Further, I might discover how to break the apparent impasse that detained the missionaries and me from flying home. First, I needed to find out what Hassan's role was in Costa Rican diplomatic circles and why he was involved in the missionaries' case.

"Director, before I speak with the trio, I would like a brief conversation with Hassan," I proposed.

"Certainly, I will leave you two alone here for a few minutes," the director agreed.

"If it's all the same to you, Director, you stay here, and we'll take a short walk in your garden," I countered to eliminate the possibility of our conversation being overheard or recorded.

If that signaled Director Brujas that I had more functional brain follicles than I had displayed thus far, he covered his reaction well.

"Certainly, whatever you wish," the director said as he got up and escorted us to the office door.

"Do you know what you are doing?" I asked Hassan when we were outside the building.

"Certainly, why do you ask?"

"Okay, then, do you know what I'm doing?"

"Your purpose is not obvious from your conversation, if that's what you mean."

"Good, because I don't know what transpired before I arrived and what should happen now. I want to improve my information base before we go back inside. By the way, I thought you worked for an oil company in Kuwait. What are you doing in Costa Rica, and don't tell me you brought your grandmother to some spa here?"

"I was exploring some marketing networks to expand our business in South America when I was summoned to help resolve this difficulty."

"Swell for you, but how did you get involved with my three choir boys?"

"I happened to be discussing business with Señor Calderon when your trio appeared in his house with his daughter and her friends. Shortly after, the young men disappeared with some of Calderon's documents. When I learned that you and your associates picked up the missionaries at the border, I assured Señor Calderon as part of our proposed business relationship that if you and I discussed the matter calmly, we could get his property back without involving any law enforcement agencies or bureaucrats to complicate his life. I hope you appreciate the delicacy of this matter after your experience with Señor Barrantes."

"Oh great, you know about him too, do you? Is he a party to your marketing plans?"

"Coincidentally, yes. Does that help you understand the situation better?" Hassan nearly hissed at me.

"At least, some things are clearer to me now. I think you're telling me that the CIA has a sting operation going which we will compromise if normal U.S. State Department procedures are invoked here. Moreover, from your perspective, Calderon's documents shouldn't be divulged to any law enforcement officials in either the Northern or Southern Hemispheres. Is that a fair statement?"

"Exactly, we agree on that," Hassan answered calmly.

"Fine, I can work with that too. The part about their return to Bolivia is sticky though. I'm sure they would prefer to go home and rejoin their families after three weeks on the run. Thus far, no one has guaranteed their safe return to the States following their conveyance of the documents to Calderon. How do we solve that part of the problem?"

"Their return to Bolivia doesn't necessarily mean they will be confined there forever," Hassan explained obliquely.

"Your brain train just fell off my track," I objected. First, all that was required was the trio's return to Bolivia and their conveyance of the documents to Calderon with appropriate apologies in English or Spanish. How did we get to jail time? Or worse, are you suggesting that private confinement with the term determined by Calderon become a real possibility? How do you propose I obtain Uncle Sam's and the missionaries' parents' authorization to make that commitment for them?"

"Your Uncle Sam's authorization for much of the proposal has already been granted, my friend. You should know that by now," Hassan admonished. "Why do you think you and I are here instead of U.S. State Department brass and other people who normally handle these matters? We are here because, for some unknown reason, the state department's negotiating team has been recalled to the U.S. in a hurry. Under the circumstances, the missionaries are expendable. I will let you use my cell phone to call whomever you like to verify that. Nonetheless, when we go back inside I will argue strongly with the director against any personal confinement of the trio by Calderon. Hopefully, by that time, you will understand and support my position because the missionaries' initial confinement by Bolivian authorities may be the only way we can secure the bargain and ultimately save them from Calderon. It may also help you to remember your cowboy history."

"What cowboys would authorize us to throw away the rights of three U.S. citizens? Or, am I supposed to return here with superior firepower and blast their way to freedom?" I demanded.

"Remember, people get hurt in those kinds of incursions," Hassan warned.

"Yes, and if I am involved, I'll do my best to ensure that Director Brujas, Calderon, and you incur as much direct and collateral damage as possible if you are with them."

"Before you do that, consider the possibility that overriding U.S. security issues may extend beyond the foreign confinement of three individuals. That does not mean that we need to abandon them. I know that you are an excellent history student. Remember your Western American history, follow its trail and expand on it, and the answer will come to you. But now, we should go inside before the director goes into a frenzy and will not agree to anything."

As we came in from our walk along the garden path, my dome lights lit, and I knew what I was doing. Hassan had been helpful after all.

"Okay, I'm ready," I told him. "Is there anything else I need to know?" I asked Hassan to ensure I was on solid ground.

"Yes, my maternal grandmother likes to come to South America. My paternal grandmother is the one enamored of the Piestany spa," Hassan explained. "You can obtain the missionaries' ultimate release by observing both my grandmothers' advice and example to take life and the negotiation process as they come."

"That's helpful," I suppose. "I hope you have abundant spa time with them and rust from all the minerals in the water."

"By the way, how is your family in Slovakia?" Hassan vectored in another direction.

"Thanks for asking. We plan to visit our relatives shortly if I can return home before then to change my clothes, report to my regular job, and pick up a paycheck. Will we see you there?"

"Life is full of surprises, but I hope that my family and I will be there, yes," Hassan confirmed.

We returned to Director Brujas' office. After another round of assurances that our conversation would not be recorded, I went into the director's conference room to talk to the three sons of Mormon. They were glad to see me, but I think they would have preferred a lightening bolt to strike the director as a divine signal of their immediate release.

Moroni, Butch, and Sundance

"Are you here to help us, or are you a captive too?" Jim asked.

"I know you all have endured more than you expected from your missionary tour, but, hopefully, I am the poor man's reincarnation of Angel Moroni ordered here to help you. I need to caution you that on first blush, what I tell you will not appear positive. That said, come closer. The director gave his word that any listening devices in here are turned off, but we shouldn't put temptation in his path."

"We will appreciate anything you can do for us," Scott exclaimed.

"Okay, first, what documents allegedly belonging to Señor Calderon do you have?"

"We have lists of people in a drug network in Bolivia, South and Central America, Europe, and North Africa. We found—"

"Geez, don't tell me how or where you found anything. If they're listening, you will have me on the rack with you as a co-conspirator. I can't help you then."

"We're sorry," they all confessed crestfallen by my negative reaction.

"Okay, just answer the questions I ask. If I need further clarification, I'll keep asking questions. Got it?"

"Yes, we understand," they all agreed.

"Now, here's the deal, and it's pretty much non-negotiable if you want to see your families again. And, don't get overheated about the details because I don't have a lot of artillery with me, as you can see. The director here will hand you over to the Bolivian police because he doesn't want to be publicly identified as a major stockholder in Calderon's drug network. Also, he could easily return you to Calderon directly, and you would never be heard from again. Hopefully, all the police and judges in Bolivia are not on the network's payroll. If Calderon were a straight arrow and a man of his word who doesn't want publicity about his legitimate business affairs, he would arrange for your prompt departure home in exchange for the documents. But, because Calderon probably is a cold-hearted criminal, he believes that jail is a good way to scare you into giving back his property without his direct involvement. Furthermore, he is counting on his network of officials to find ways to avoid the terms of the formal extradition treaty between Bolivia and the United States. Without extradition, he can have his corrupt police buddies hold you indefinitely without U.S. intervention. Worse yet, he can stage your unsuccessful 'escape' from jail, or he could hide you in the jungle indefinitely as his personal guests."

"O Lord, what can we do to get away? We could give the lists back and promise never to say anything to anyone about them," they all recited.

"I think everyone believes that your case has gone beyond a simple solution like that now. But, everyone is trying to remind me about two outlaws who allegedly were in Bolivia a while back who, they tell me, may bring about your proximate relief and eventual release."

"What do you mean?" they all chorused again.

"I don't know if you remember or ever knew, but when the law got too close for them in the States, Butch Cassidy and the Sundance Kid allegedly escaped to Bolivia among other places in Central and South America to hide out or to rob banks down here. Some sources state that a special treaty was enacted to extradite the pair back to the States if they were caught by Bolivian officials. Depending on whose version of the story you believe, they were never caught or sent back to the States if they were ever in Bolivia in the first place. The special treaty may still be on Bolivian law books, although nobody in Bolivia remembers Butch and Sundance as we do in the States. In any event, any special treaty has been superseded by a formal extradition treaty signed by President Clinton on June 27, 1995.[2] Based on my computer research, it replaced an extradition treaty enacted on April 21, 1900. So, in my reckoning, a special treaty wasn't necessary for U.S. authorities to haul Butch and Sundance back to the States when they were reportedly in Bolivia in 1908, unless bank robbery was not an enumerated no-no under the 1900 treaty. I believe that Calderon is unaware of, or is conveniently trying to deny, the existence of the 1995 treaty in holding you."

"Regardless," I continued, "the bottom line is that as you hit the front door of the La Paz jail on your way in, the U.S. Ambassador in Bolivia should be demanding through Bolivian diplomatic channels that you all be extradited back to the U.S. '*muy pronto*' under the Clinton treaty. The applicable provision is that commercial espionage is a crime in both the U.S. and Bolivia, and carries a minimum one-year jail term. That provision fits the requirement for your extradition. And that's giving the broadest definition of commercial espionage possible to your swiping a drug lord's client lists. In addition to direct diplomatic actions in Bolivia, Chauncey, the charge d'affaires at the U.S. Embassy in Peru is a personal friend of mine, and is a second line of defense. I will contact him to monitor your progress. He has some explaining to do about his own recent activities, so he won't ignore you and cause more trouble for himself. Got it? Any questions? Yeah, Scott?"

"How did you learn about the Butch and Sundance treaty?"

"I read an erroneous CIA agent's report about it a while ago, and it struck me as curious that in this day and age of heavy drug trafficking that a more formal treaty of some sort didn't exist. So, I cured my computer illiteracy and researched that topic on the way down here. Hopefully, I'm not mistaken or 'fingering the *ricasso*' on the subject at a time like this. Next question, Steve?"

"We don't know what that means, but while we were waiting for the director or somebody to talk to us, we asked his secretary if we could use the photocopy machine. What do we do with a copy of the lists?"

"Angel Moroni may have a problem, but Butch and Sundance would be proud of you. Did you know that Butch was born in Beaver, Utah, and that his grandfather was a Mormon bishop? Never mind that now. Give me the copied lists. If I'm unable to sneak them out of here, I hope the extradition treaty works for the four of us. If it comes down to giving back the original lists or your life, give them the bloody originals that you have. Anything else?"

"What if Calderon and the Bolivians don't honor the treaty?"

"Then, our next option is to notify the U.S. Army Southern Command in Florida to activate a special operations team to extract you. A second option might be to have an unmarked CIA plane fly over Calderon's fields with Agent Orange or some other defoliant and accidentally release a load on his crop of coca plants to remind him to send you home promptly. A more remote option is for my wife to come here and ask me where I put my life insurance policy if I intend to stay a while. If I tell her that I don't remember, she'll tear the country and Calderon's network apart by herself. But, after a quick glance at these lists, I don't think your problem will go far. I feel more encouraged now because the lists identify many high-placed conspirators in drug trafficking in both hemispheres. I'm certain they don't want adverse publicity. What else?"

"How long do you think this will take?"

"Since you are being detained in an unscheduled landing while in transit, the treaty specifies that your provisional detention cannot be longer than ninety-six hours. So, the U.S. and Costa Rican officials need to do something with you before then, assuming they play it straight. Last chance before I go, anybody else?"

"Can we say a prayer together before you leave?" Steve persisted.

"Yes, I thought you'd never ask. Moroni should know your exact location too. We probably need his help as much as anyone's right now."

After a short prayer and handshakes all around, I left the room with a copy of the lists folded into my shorts and with considerable apprehension about the trio's safety. At the same time, I knew I had done all that I could with the cards I had been dealt. Moroni, Butch, Sundance, the 1995 treaty, and the respective diplomatic corps would have to do the rest. I went back to the director's office. Hassan was there and stood up as if ready to leave when I entered. I tried to convince myself that he had made the case against any personal confinement or punishment by Calderon.

"The missionaries understand what they need to do," I stated to confirm that the bargain was established on my side. "The people who sent me and I expect that you will keep your part of the bargain and deliver the trio safely to Bolivian authorities. If that is not your understanding, let me know now. If you do not keep your part of the bargain, there will be consequences, I assure you. Otherwise, I'd like to return home unless you want to deal with my negative attitude and lack of sleep."

"I'll walk out with you," Hassan offered.

I shook hands with Director Brujas, and Hassan and I left the director's office.

As we walked down the hallway toward the elevator, I told Hassan, "I'm always glad to see you, my friend, but I don't care much for the company you keep. Thanks for your help though."

"These are strange and difficult times," he said. "They can easily engulf people like you and me who are restless and away from home helping others. I fear that more trouble is brewing, and with the recall of state department staff and CIA operatives, nobody is in the kitchen to shut off the stove or to clean up the mess. Your country should be able to get these three people back home safely, but do not count on the United States always being as invincible as it has been in the past. A growing number of people in the world hate your country deeply. The warning flags are out, but nobody in your government is watching or changing policies to match the changing times. Be careful, *amigo*. I need to stay here a few more days. Then, I will return home myself. If this arrangement does not resolve itself while I am here, I will contact you. *Adios*."

I hailed a taxi, threw my stuff in, and rode to the airport. If I were on my own, I would have called ahead to alert someone I was coming. Under these circumstances, I believed someone was already informing the plane's crew to be ready for my arrival and a quick departure. I was right. As soon as the plane's bulkhead door was locked, we took off. On the trip north, I reflected on Hassan's warning. It was unlike him to be overly serious. I told him the truth. I didn't like his business associates. This was a different Hassan. But, as we both knew, this was a different world too.

Events definitely would confirm my belief on my return home. But, I wouldn't go directly home on this flight as I had planned. Somewhere over Mexico, the copilot came back and advised that Colonel X wanted to talk to me. I followed the copilot back to the cockpit and waited for him to inform the colonel that I was available to talk.

When I acknowledged that I had a headset on, the colonel started, "PURPLE informed me that a slight change in itinerary is contemplated for you. Rather than fly through to Chicago, PURPLE wants you to stop in Texas and escort your friend back to Chicago with you. He is stable for travel, and you have excellent facilities for his burns in the Chicago area where he can be closer to his family. Do you copy?"

That was charming of PURPLE to be considerate of Ron, but I had been in the field a long time too. Some medical evacuation unit could fly him to Chicago without my participation. *More important, where was Jenny? She should be relaying these changes to me, not some jerky colonel who I had met for only a few minutes.*

But, this was business, not whining time, so I answered, "I understand the change, and I assume that the flight crew already has its instructions. Do I look for you or someone else to connect with Ron when we arrive?"

"Thanks for reminding me. I will pick you up at the airfield."

The colonel had to be reminded to pick me up? Somebody was playing games. But, who was it, and why? It was time to start whining again.

"Colonel, if Ron can't have separate medical flight assistance back to Chicago, have him ready for a touch-and-go landing at the airfield. That will be more efficient than me deplaning and fetching him at the hospital. It's not like I need to give him a bath, change his shorts, and sign discharge papers for him when I arrive, is it? Also, I assume medical staff will accompany the flight north. Can it happen that way?"

My request caused a flurry of chatter at the other end; some of it sounded like the colonel was receiving telephone instructions from another party in addition to hospital staff conversations. Finally, the colonel got back on the line to me.

"That's affirmative on your request to have Ron available at the airfield for a quick pickup and fly through. PURPLE warned me that you are obsessive-compulsive when it comes to time and travel arrangements, but we can accommodate that request. I will confirm with the flight crew if you have nothing further."

"While you're in an accommodating mood, I have one more request, Colonel."

"Yes, go ahead."

"Can you or someone else patch me through to my Scout?"

"I'm afraid I'm not authorized to grant that request at this time," the colonel responded much too rapidly. "I need to talk to the crew now to confirm your flight change for Ron's pickup. I will contact you later if I have any additional information for you."

Something was wrong—definitely and desperately wrong for me not to be able to contact my Scout. I definitely would climb all over PURPLE when I got back home for delaying my return as well as abandoning the missionaries because of some clandestine CIA operation that had nothing to do with their safe return. For now, I had no choice but to meet Ron in Texas and complete the flight to Chicago with him on board.

The landing in Texas was not exactly touch-and-go, but the colonel had Ron in an ambulance waiting for us at the airfield. While the maintenance and medical crews removed a few rows of seats and clamped Ron's bed and surrounding equipment to the floor, the ground crew refueled the plane and performed whatever maintenance was necessary to keep us in the air for a few more hours. An hour later, we were airborne flying home. Ron had the luxury of an Army doctor who was traveling north to take a new post. I waited until we reached cruising altitude and the doctor had completed her monitoring of Ron's status before I went forward to talk to her. I needed to visit Ron first.

Scout Down

"Hey trooper, the meds informed me that you are fit for travel. You look like an overdone chicken," I told Ron.

"Thanks, you don't look so good yourself. Tough news, I hear. I'm sorry."

"Tough news about what? Nobody told me anything."

"Maybe I'm not the one to tell you either. Let's leave it at that."

"Cut the waltzing. We've known each other too long for that stuff. Tell me what you know."

"I overheard the colonel informing the flight crew while we were waiting at the airport that Jenny was killed. I thought you knew."

"How killed? Accidental? What? When?"

"Take it easy, man. Sit down before you need a doctor yourself."

"Tell me all of it, Ron, everything you know," I exploded.

The doctor looked back from her seat as if she would intervene in our conversation, so I cooled my jets as much as I could under the circumstances.

"The story is that the Barrantes guy you encountered in Peru died of some kind of seizure or stroke. His wife went crazy and ordered a hit on you through network enforcers. Nobody could find you because of our detour to retrieve the missionaries and our trip to the hospital after the copter fire. Apparently, that made her even more determined to get you. Through her connections in the Peruvian government and probably a mole in the U.S. Embassy, she was able to locate Jenny, who had contacted you several times during your earthquake relief exercise. The story goes that the black widow ordered a hit on your Scout. I'm sorry, man, that's all I know."

"Was it clean?" I blazed like a furnace.

"Oh geez, don't ask me that!" Ron pleaded.

"Was it clean?" I demanded.

"No, not with a vengeful woman involved. You know how that works. Remember the line from Molière that we all laughed about in high school, 'A woman always has her revenge ready.'"[3]

"That's why I'm asking. Tell me!"

"It wasn't a very professional hit. Put it that way. That's all I know."

"They killed my Scout, and the chicken colonel didn't have the guts to tell me. One of my people goes down, they don't defend her, and then they don't tell me they fouled up. Then, they send us on another jaunt through the jungle looking for missionaries who aren't savvy enough to stay out of a country they shouldn't be anywhere near in the first place!"

I wanted to rage more, but Ron's doctor intervened. Ron's monitoring machines were going nuts. I thought the doctor would give Ron a shot to quiet him down, but she stuck the needle in my arm. Under ordinary circumstances and being as tired as I was, I should have been totally mellow, but my adrenalin had a head start on whatever the doctor plugged into me. I took a seat to avoid collapsing on Ron if I blacked out. But, I was awake and planning retaliation. Then, I sat a few more minutes, just staring ahead at nothing. The tranquilizer was taking effect.

I recall seeing the copilot come out of the cockpit. He looked like he was approaching in slow motion. He stopped in front of my seat.

"The pilot instructed me to bring all your weapons into the cockpit," he stated firmly.

"Absolutely not. They are cleaned, oiled, and put away," I answered.

"Yeah, I know, pal. You guys had a tough time out there, but the pilot is the captain of this craft. I'm obeying orders and you should too. Do yourself a favor and hand them over peacefully. I'll take good care of them up front."

The tranquilizer was really working now, and I shuffled my weapons toward the copilot as fast as I could. Ron had the advantage over me in mental clarity now.

"What's going on?" he asked. "Nobody takes our weapons. Hey, come back here, nobody takes our weapons!"

Halfway to the cockpit with my weapons bag in his arms, the copilot turned around and looked at both of us. "Sorry, guys," he said, "you have every right to be upset, but the pilot doesn't want any holes in his plane before we land in Chicago. We just received word on the radio that your missionaries were gunned down trying to escape from being handed over to the Bolivian police."

I looked at Ron, and he looked at me. We didn't have to say anything. The pilot was right in taking my weapons away. Missionaries don't know how to be prisoners, or how to escape from a prison. Under the agreement, they should have had no need to escape from prison. The extradition treaty should have bailed them out and pointed them in the direction of their families almost immediately. With U.S. Embassy action in Bolivia and with Chauncey monitoring the situation from Lima, the whole thing should have been handled quickly and diplomatically in La Paz if not Costa Rica. *What really happened between San Jose and La Paz?* Ron and I hadn't gotten home yet. *How could disaster strike so fast unless Hassan and the director lied to me about their adherence to the extradition treaty?* Either that, or somebody besides me was totally misinformed or unscrupulous, or the CIA had one heck of an operation going to supersede and intersect so many lives. If so, we would never know the whole truth, or even a small part of it. The only thing I knew with certainty is that I should tell no one, including my Guiding Hand, that I had a copy of those lists.

Were the colonel and Ron equally misinformed about Jenny too? Or, had I really lost my Scout? No, she wasn't a Scout. She was an innocent young lady who was trying to help her country. Instead, she was tortured and killed without knowing why. After that news, the tranquilizer had no chance of putting me to sleep.

I stayed in my seat for the remainder of the flight, but somewhere in the air between Texas and Chicago, I declared total war on the Barrantes and Calderon drug networks and Vasily's weapons operation wherever I found them. I also needed to know what connection Hassan had to these networks. *Was he really my friend, or not?* It was July 14, 2001, and for me a personal war of vengeance against terrorists and their suppliers commenced then and there. I didn't need to wait until September 11 or anytime thereafter for President Bush and Congress to act. Yes, I knew the words of St. Paul's letter to the Romans from my youth: "To no man render evil for evil . . . Vengeance is mine; I will repay, says the Lord." (Rom. 12:17,19)[4] But, this time, the Lord would have help whether he wanted it or not.

When I returned home, I was in the worst physical and mental shape of my life. Beth didn't say anything, which was her coping mechanism to deal with me in these situations. Returning from Peru, I was the only one to have escaped visible physical damage. But, like Ron, I had acquired emotional wounds that would never heal.

With months of treatment and plastic surgery ahead, Ron wouldn't travel on another PURPLE assignment, although I always sought his advice before I went anywhere. Medically for me, MRIs weren't necessary to disclose a torn biceps tendon in my left arm. The tendon was coiled around the inside of my elbow. My right shoulder was missing pieces of tendon that should have held the rotator cuff in place. I scheduled surgery with Dr. Scott. He was a busy surgeon. His next open surgery date was in several weeks. I tried to return to my civilian job as soon as I could get Dr. Scott to release me, but the job wasn't the same from either side.

Before I departed for Peru what seemed like ages ago, Jenny and I had discussed therapy options for several women colleagues of mine who had contracted multiple sclerosis. I wanted to determine if a common cause was responsible, if their condition was work-related, and what kind of physical therapy they might need. My brief investigation revealed that the women appeared to have different symptoms and no common source for their illness, particularly as it might apply to their jobs. That made my employer happy, but didn't solve their medical problems. Some appeared to recover steadily with diminishing symptoms. Others had rapidly progressing symptoms that required them to take disability leave, or to quit work entirely. With Jenny gone, I never would be able to put all the pieces of that puzzle together. Nobody else seemed to care that much about the group, and without my active pursuit, they disappeared from company radar within a short time.

I knew Jenny was from Iowa, but I didn't know exactly where. Until a new Scout was found, I dealt with PURPLE through a secure post office box. I returned from Costa Rica too late for Jenny's funeral, but I flooded PURPLE's mailbox with requests for her burial site. I didn't direct my anger at Iowa residents. I would leave my weapons home. I simply wanted to pay my last respects to my Scout who had served her country as well as she knew how. I demanded that PURPLE change its name too, unless it wanted to deal directly with me. PURPLE didn't want direct confrontation with me, especially now. In the Peru and Costa Rican operations, too many people learned about the name PURPLE. It or they agreed with my reasoning. PURPLE changed the logo to MAGENTA. (The new name took somebody a second and a half of hard thought to change.) I demanded that, starting then, I would interview the finalist candidates for my Scout position. Surprisingly, MAGENTA agreed. I continued to demand to know Dick's (my former Army partner) and Jenny's final resting places. MAGENTA finally relented and gave me the locations. Ron argued against my going, but I was determined to go anyway.

Paying My Respects

Dick's grave was located in an old part of the cemetery in Muscatine. Alice Bright Feather had been right all along. His real name wasn't Dick. The cemetery custodian knew the family, but didn't remember Dick's given name. Everyone in town had known him as "Peanut," he said. After forty years, a fine oak had grown nearby to give his grave shelter from the sun and wind. The custodian left me alone with my thoughts. In the solitude, I had time to thank Dick properly for sacrificing his life for mine so many years ago.

Jenny's grave was easier to find in the only cemetery in her small Iowa hometown. The newly laid sod was turning brown in the mid-summer sun. As I stood there, an elderly couple approached.

"Did you know our Jenny?" the lady asked.

"Not long and not well," I answered respectfully. "But, she helped me when I needed help, which is more than I did for her," I answered politely and truthfully.

"She was that way with everyone. I'm her grandmother," she sobbed with the grief of her lost granddaughter still fresh in her mind.

"What is your name, if I may ask, sir?" Jenny's grandfather inquired softly.

"Legion," I answered, "Joe Legion. But, I go by many names."

"Are you from around here?" her grandmother asked not quite ready to let me go.

"Gerasa," I replied.

"We don't know where that is," Jenny's grandfather remarked somewhat bewildered by the unfamiliar place I had named.

"It's a long way from here no matter which way I go. Sometimes, I still lose my way," I admitted.

"Thank you for coming," the elderly couple said in unison. "Please visit again whenever you are in this area, Mr. Legion."

"Thank you. I may never come back here, but I will always remember Jenny and your kindness. I am very pleased to have met you both, but I need to leave now. I still have a long journey ahead of me. I promise one thing, though, I will find those responsible for her death before my journey is over."

On the way home, I played a game of mental tag with myself to determine who exactly was responsible for Jenny's murder. *Was it General Vasily, Señora Barrantes, Calderon, or someone else?*

On the beach at Chennai with General Vasily, I had told him that I would kill his wife and daughter if he ever harmed Roberto and his family. That was a stupid mistake on my part. Vasily knew that I couldn't and wouldn't enforce my threat against his family. But, by having my Scout killed, Vasily would confirm that he had no such scruples and that he had the resources to find her and me anytime, anywhere. He could arrange Jenny's death as easily as he could make restaurant reservations. But, if Vasily was responsible for Jenny's death, he would have made it a signature murder that would have left no doubt about its author.

On the other hand, if Señora Barrantes or Calderon had sent a bunch of former guerrilla fighters to kill Jenny, they would either have had to clear U.S. Customs to enter the U.S. at a border crossing or at an airline terminal, enter the country illegally, or already be here. I didn't know enough about the Barrantes and Calderon networks to determine if they could reach into the U.S. Midwest on their own, or if they would simply contract with a local group to do their dirty work. I would have to learn more about the Barrantes and Calderon operations to protect future Scouts and myself. Consistent with Ron's story, guerrilla fighters or career hit men in the U.S. would not worry about how the hit was planned and executed. They would simply do it. The autopsy report I would see later verified how cruelly Jenny died for a cause she barely understood. That would tend to exonerate Vasily. One thing was certain. If future events ran true to form in my life, someone and I would arrive at a showdown relatively soon. I would need to be ready for whatever form the showdown took.

When I returned home, I looked up Gerasa in the maps in the back of my Bible. Gerasa was located on the east side of the Sea of Galilee, and was founded around 175 BC. It was about thirty miles north of the present city of Amman, Jordan.[5] It may as well have been on Mars as far as I was concerned. I had told Jenny's grandparents the truth. I had a long way to go, and I wasn't making the journey easy on myself. *But then, why should I?* I held myself responsible for Jenny's death.

The next day, I visited the gravesites of Joe and my parents. For the first time, I noticed that the marble stone for Joe's grave showed only his birth date, not his date of death. My sister was usually efficient about handling details like that. As I stood there, Sam, the old custodian came down the road to talk. I had not visited the cemetery in a while, but Sam still recognized me. I mentioned Joe's missing date of death, and my guilt for not having visited more often.

"Does it really matter?" Sam said. "They are not here. They are with you wherever you go. The markers are for people like me who need to keep records. We'll get the stone engraved in due time. In case you're interested, your family plot has room for one more grave."

"I'm not ready yet, Sam," I said. "I still have work to do."

Chapter Notes

1. Thomas Cleary (translator), Sun Tzu, *The Art of War*, (Boston: Shambhala Publications, Inc., 2003), p. 156 of 369.

2. United States of America Department of State, *Treaty Between the Government of the United States of America and the Government of the Republic of Bolivia on Extradition* (Treaty Document 104-22 signed at La Paz on June 27, 1995, Washington, D.C.: U.S. Government Printing Office, 1995), pp. 1–22.

3. Bartlett (compiler), *op. cit.*, p. 27 citing Jean Baptiste Molière's, *Tartuffe Act II Scene 2.*
4. *The Holy Bible, New American Catholic Edition*, p. 171.
5. *Ibid.*, Index to Practical Bible Atlas, p. 1.

CHAPTER 9

REPAIRS AND RECRUITS

TIME OUT FOR REPAIRS

Dr. Scott performed his usual miracles in rearranging parts in my right shoulder and reattaching my left biceps tendon, while Dr. Chris reengineered tendons in the middle finger of my shooting hand. The procedures stung for a few days, but surgery was better than having non-functional appendages if I wanted to continue as an International Responder and a MAGENTA Operative. After the bandages, slings, and splints came off, it was time for physical therapy. My medical release allowed my employer's new management team to inquire about my interest in the way it intended to conduct future business versus my professional objectives. These discussions included components of the Kali Yuga cycle of life that Sujaya failed to inform me about during our walk on the beach in India. However, my Guiding Hand came to my rescue (or to the management team's rescue) by informing me that this major life change would be governed by the "no avenger" clause of my Jeremiah contract. Except for the three people who died during this period of my career instability without my being able to help them, I eventually came to terms with the personal aspects of my career change despite my continuing concern for the safety of my extended family on two continents. In any event, my foreign travels hadn't interfered with my inclusion in the vanguard of a growing nationwide trend for top management to eliminate, outsource, and export positions of every description. In their growing arrogance, ignorance, and greed, the U.S. executive corps forgot King Henry IV's admonition to Falstaff that "[T]hou owest God a death."[1] Did U.S. chief executive and chief operating officers think that they were exempt from the laws of nature and society, and from the consequences of their actions on their organizations and their employees? When I was ready to listen again, my Guiding Hand advised that I should prepare for more critical agenda items to fill my calendar soon. The first item was to find a new physical therapist because I couldn't force myself to go back to the same place where Jenny had worked.

Before I went to my first therapy session, I visited Ron to check out a few thoughts with him that had been rambling through my head. Ron's wife answered the door. With two battered and scarred men on her hands, she decided to leave us and go shopping.

"How have you been?" Ron asked. "If you feel as bad as you look, we should call the undertaker and florist now to get the best rates on your funeral."

"Sometimes, I ask myself why I don't visit you more often. Now I know. Besides your pleasant disposition and your crispy suntan, you still have time to criticize my looks. Despite that, I hope you're feeling better yourself because neither of us will get any Hollywood invitations based on our looks now."

"I hope you don't expect me to get you anything to drink when you bring that attitude into my house," Ron sparred verbally.

"No, your exhilarating company and a little conversation about something that's bugging me are all I need today," I prefaced my agenda as I moved a chair close to Ron's recliner.

"What's on your mind?" Ron asked as he switched channels to a more serious mode.

"The three missionaries I left behind and who killed them, if, in fact, they're dead, still trouble me," I confessed.

"Strange you mentioned that, because the same topic doesn't fit in my 'closed' file either," Ron confirmed.

DEFINING WHAT WE KNEW

"I'm glad you said that. All we know is what we heard from the copilot on our flight back here. None of it was officially confirmed by anyone credible on either side. The media picked up the same story we were told. The families requested that the bodies be returned to the States, assuming the three are dead. So far, nobody, including the La Paz police or the U.S. Embassy in Bolivia confirmed that they know anything about them, let alone help the families recover the bodies. I can understand the La Paz police stonewalling the U.S. Embassy and the families, but a downtown killing of three people is hard to cover up. Somebody usually sees something and is willing to talk for a price."

"Have you considered the possibility that the missionaries weren't held in a downtown La Paz jail or any Bolivian jail? Given the short time that elapsed when the copilot told us about them, they couldn't have made it to La Paz riding a rocket. We were only halfway home ourselves when we heard about them. If they were gunned down outside San Jose or La Paz, three shallow graves in the jungle will keep them hidden permanently," Ron posited. "You're right though. We have no confirmation that they made it alive anywhere in the musical chairs diplomacy game you concocted with Hassan. Sorry, I meant to say Hassan and Calderon concocted and pasted on you with the immigration director's assistance."

"How could things go so wrong?" I questioned. "The trio knew that they were to be surrendered by Costa Rican Immigration to the Bolivian police for provisional custody under the watchful diplomatic eyes of the U.S. Embassy in Bolivia, Chauncey in Peru, and some component of the U.S. Army or CIA. I still haven't identified the extent of the Army's connection. The trio were to be under provisional custody until they returned Calderon's lists and the U.S. processed their extradition papers with Bolivian authorities under the 1995 treaty. Other drug lords certainly don't want uncontrolled activity and publicity in their territory, and Calderon doesn't want his lists to surface among either friends or foes. Disclosure of the lists would damage his standing in South American society and his status in the drug community. The only way he could guarantee the documents' security would be to have the trio under his control in Bolivia. Gunning them down in Costa Rica wouldn't help him if the lists surfaced later. In exchange for currency, the Bolivian police wouldn't object to housing them for Calderon. The exchange of the lists and missionaries should have been transacted without a hitch. The prospects of death or long-term confinement without the protection of international and U.S. laws should have been sufficient incentive for the missionaries to return the lists and to keep their mouths shut about Calderon. Given what happened to Jenny, he has the resources to reach them wherever they go if they talk. The Costa Rican and Bolivian police were mere custodians of the trio. They should have had no further interest in the missionaries after Calderon finished with them. The entire process should have taken four days at most."

"Have you considered the possibility that other players might be involved?" Ron questioned my conclusions. "Our pilot and copilot had to be CIA to have their story available that early in the game. We obviously interrupted a covert CIA operation that involved Barrantes and/or Calderon without them or us knowing about it."

"Anything is possible, but the only tangible connection I see is between the trio and Calderon. Until he recovered his lists, Calderon, if nobody else, would protect the missionaries. After that, he probably would have liked to erase them, but he had to know that too many eyes were watching at the time. So, if they disappeared, he would need to ensure that any unfavorable evidence wouldn't surface then, or later. Killing the missionaries in or around San Jose or La Paz doesn't fit Calderon's business model for seamless and hidden operations."

"You mentioned U.S. military involvement," Ron reminded me. "I'll bet your Colonel X was more CIA than Army too," Ron said, shifting the conversation to another aspect of the case I had not fully explored.

"You could be right," I concurred. "We know this wouldn't be the first time the CIA protected drug lords for its purposes while the FBI, police, the military, and everybody else are fighting to put the kingpins out of business. If I find any evidence that the CIA protected Calderon to the detriment of the missionaries or Jenny, my first stop will be at the colonel's front door. In my view, he's the committed, non-thinking, troglodyte type who would protect Calderon even if he knew Calderon was Jenny's killer if that suited CIA purposes and he could hide behind someone else's orders. If we can find evidence to exclude Vasily and Señora Barrantes, the colonel may be our man with respect to Jenny's murder, not just a bystander or order-taker in that event. Even if we exonerate Vasily as Jenny's killer, Vasily has given me multiple reasons to bring him down. I may find good reason to bring others down with him."

"When you think about it," Ron postulated, "other possibilities exist that don't involve Jenny. What if an escape was staged as an excuse to kill the missionaries in downtown San Jose, or to let them escape 'a little bit' to erase them in private? Or, what if they actually escaped from somebody's custody and are on the run again. Under those circumstances, Calderon couldn't release the missionaries as part of an extradition proceeding—treaty or no treaty—if they were no longer in his or a proxy's custody."

"If your theory is correct, that would be a wild tale," I responded. "And the trio would hold the lists as a wild card again. Calderon would turn the countryside upside down looking for them for sure. Assuming your scenario happened, where would the trio go this time?" I asked as I rolled the "possibility of possibilities" dice around in my brain bin. "Would they head for the deep jungle at Tabatinga again to find their college chums? Could they make it to Chauncey in Lima? Would they try something totally different after the lecture I gave them about how close they came to testing their belief in eternity? Or, would they use the same escape route now that they know the terrain better and our potential ability to extract them along that route? Do you feel up to another incursion into Bolivia to confirm my hypotheses?"

"I think I've completed my last Bolivian raid, thank you," Ron stated emphatically, "especially with you and that bunch."

"Hey, don't bruise my ego. Just tell me you don't want to go, or that you're not physically up to it yet. That's sufficient. You still can be very valuable though. Are you able to contact your Aymaran Indian friend? Where does he call home?"

"I usually contact him along the Rio Heath, or along the north shore of Lake Titicaca. Hold it; are you seriously thinking about another rendition? Remember, in addition to all the other logistics, Señora Barrantes apparently has a price on your knot head," Ron rolled out another compelling reason against a second incursion.

"I was merely surveying what resources we have to verify their status, what action we can take if the trio are alive, and how we can extract them if they're running around loose in the tall grass again," I rephrased the discussion, trying to cool Ron's afterburners a bit.

"You were correct earlier to ask what country," Ron continued his strategic thinking. "The last time, we knew definitively that they were in Bolivia. Now, they could be in Bolivia, Peru, or Brazil. Take your pick, Angel Moroni."

I pursued Ron's scenario. "If they hired a small boat and a plane, they could be in Brazil floating down the Amazon toward the Atlantic. No, that's no good. They don't have any money."

"They could be singing in the choir in Salt Lake City for all we know," Ron offered, presenting a strong reason not to pursue the debate or my thoughts of another incursion any further with him at that moment.

"I concede your point. I just don't want to surrender if they're still alive. If I stop now, they'll be the first Mormon bunch I didn't bring back in my long illustrious career."

END OF DEBATE, ALMOST THE START OF ACTION

"Now we hit the heart of the hunt. This is all about your reputation, not the trio's safety. Good, that's something I can deal with. Let's see if you're big enough to pull yourself out of the cesspool of compassion you dug for yourself, Mr. Rescuer. I'll contact Manco while you phone Chauncey.

Then, we'll know if we have anything further to discuss," Ron found a way to break the deadlock and challenge me by attacking my smaller self as he had artfully done as a PURPLE adviser over the years.

"Is that his name? Manco?" I asked quickly before Ron attributed additional selfish motives to my already battered ego. "After sharing a helicopter fire with him, I'm pleased that I now officially know his name," I mocked Ron's social graces to inform him, in our convoluted way of dealing with each other, that I appreciated his efforts to break our mental logjam on what to do about the missionaries. By not baby-talking Ron in my response, I acknowledged my concern for his physical and mental pain following our unsuccessful rescue attempt without making him a psychological cripple who would be unable to help me think, plan, and resolve this and future problems.

"If your Aymaran dialect isn't any better than your Spanish, Manco will glare at you for a few minutes, then start walking home shaking his head at another stupid *gringo* in his life," Ron rebuked my criticism of his manners to let me know he took no personal offense at my remarks.

"Okay, I'll let you win on all issues this time because this is your house, and frankly, your idea of contacting a few people to determine the true status of things down south makes infinite sense. I need to go to my physical therapy séance now. Let's check back with each other by the end of the day and compare what we have on our missionaries. *Kamisaraki,* Señor."

"You just said hello in Aymaran, you lunatic, not good-bye," Ron laughed heartily despite the impact it had on his inflamed facial muscles.

"Well Mr. Languages and Dialects, I assume that Manco is sufficiently intelligent to know when the occasion requires a hello or good-bye. Why should I learn extraneous words?"

"When you get that way, I know that something we haven't discussed is bugging you. What's your problem this time?"

"Whatever could it be, pray tell?" I mimicked Beth's best imitation of a Southern belle's accent.

"Hey, it's your stupid fantasy or hang-up," Ron verbally pinned my shoulders to the floor. "You tell me."

"Okay, suppose the missionaries are in Peru or near the Bolivian border, how would you feel about combining their pickup with a pre-emptive strike against Barrantes' or Calderon's operations?"

"Please don't make me laugh again. It makes my scars really hurt. But, since you asked, let me tell you. What you proposed is an ideal way to make your wife a widow or your little friend Isadora an orphan in a hurry. Which do you prefer?" Ron responded strongly and probably correctly. "But, I can see that you've made up your mind about part or all of it already, so tell me how you reached your normally weird conclusion."

"In my view, I'd be attacking the Barrantes' drug infrastructure, not the señora and her kids. You're right in one respect, though. That's one reason why wives aren't permitted to be Scouts. We'd never have homes to return to following an assignment. We'd recognize where we used to live by the smoke and flames rising in the air and the sound of emergency vehicles on their way to our neighborhoods."

"Add to that all the Peruvian *pistoleros* you described on Barrantes' ranch. Are they hired to stand there and let you torch their mistress' property? Do you think Calderon will allow you to wipe out his business partners in Peru or get anywhere near his Bolivian assets?"

"I was thinking in terms of a night raid when the *pistoleros* are drunk or sleeping. Why do you make planning a raid so complicated? If I move fast enough, I can hold Calderon out of the action and attack him some other time," I added, trying to justify my emerging plan to Ron. "But you raise another good point. Whose cartel is it now, Calderon's or Señora Barrantes'?"

"Before I answer that question, answer this one," Ron proceeded. "Are you calling Manco and yourself a 'night raiding party' now against two drug lords and forty or fifty hired guns? You'd better sharpen up your admission speech before you meet St. Peter. He won't allow that kind of suicidal planning in heaven regardless of the unselfish intentions you profess. And, to answer your other question, it doesn't matter whose cartel it is when the shooting starts, dummy."

"Well, yes and no again. Let me explain. If Calderon controls the former Barrantes operation, it means that Juanita doesn't have the ranch, and she isn't involved in the drug network. Then, Jenny's assassination isn't by a woman's hand, particularly the señora's. I believe she's too good a person for that. Until I have proof otherwise, I now believe that her husband or Calderon ordered Jenny's death as retaliation and as a warning for me to stop further actions against them. It also signifies that their networks can reach into our neighborhoods, if necessary. Do we let them come to us, or do we pre-empt them before they reach our turf? But, going back for a minute, even assuming Juanita is in control, I can understand that she might retaliate against me, but not against Jenny who had no means or motive to cause trouble for her. I don't know Juanita well, but I believe that she's not in control. Maybe she needs rescuing as much as our trio. Any words of wisdom on that, *maestro?*"

"Granted, it was early in your outstanding military career, but I recall the fine rescue job you pulled in the prisoner swap at Freedom Bridge in Potsdam. Remember that? Everybody else showed up with regulation sidearms. You arrived with two *samurai* swords and a rocket launcher. Seeing you, our general wouldn't get out of his car. He kept asking his driver who the lunatic was out there. Both sets of prisoners were afraid to cross the bridge. Now, you're asking me to help you orchestrate a rescue of three missionaries in addition to the widow and children of a powerful drug lord because his daughter reminds you of your grandkids. Is that basically the plan you want me to bless?" Ron started to laugh again until his facial pain made him wince.

"I wouldn't describe my plan in those terms," I faltered. "But, you must admit that once the Potsdam prisoner exchange started, it was the fastest prisoner trade in history. Everybody was running, including the French officer refereeing the proceedings from the middle of the bridge."

"The only thing faster than that prisoner exchange was your transfer out of my unit," Ron refreshed my memory.

"Oh, c'mon, Ron, you were upset because you got latrine duty for a month as my accomplice when you didn't know anything about my activities. If I knew the brass would cause you that much grief, I would have played it straight," I finally confessed my culpability in that incident after almost forty years. "But, look at it this way, if we had stayed in the same outfit, life would have been very hard for the survivor if either of us saw the other one go down. Splitting us up was one of the Army's better ideas."

"I thought your brother and I did some crazy things when we were together, but he was never as reckless as you are. You and I took different routes after Potsdam, but here we are in another crazy situation. We could have been a trio too. But now one of us is dead, one of us is grounded, and one of us is a lunatic, and it's not me, mister. Yeah, what the heck, go do what you feel is best. I'll be here to guide you if you need me. That's all I can do for you now," Ron recited dejectedly.

"You and my brother probably saved the universe several times before his death," I said, trying to perk him up.

Ron gave a short laugh and nodded. "But, none of it was recorded, and we can't tell anyone about it, so, to the world, half of our lives either never happened or disappeared. That should save our obituary writers a lot of time. They can hand in a blank page and still have all the facts. It's hard for me to forget some things. My wife catches me either smiling or looking glum when I recall some events. She thinks I'm responding to something she did or said when my mind is light years away."

"I don't want to intrude on your nostalgia, but this operation appears less dramatic than some others we did successfully, *mon ami*. On this operation, all I need is your technical advice, Manco's knowledge of the terrain and people, and a good Scout to coordinate with MAGENTA. You'll see. I assume Manco can handle a bow if we need it because I won't have sufficient arm strength for a long time yet even with Dr. Scott's expertise and, hopefully, the services of a good therapist. I'm planning to interact differently with MAGENTA and my new Scout in the future—when I find one. If MAGENTA wants performance, it better protect my Scout while I'm scratching my way through the bushes and swamps. I'm not visiting another cemetery to pay my respects to another fallen Scout because of any MAGENTA security foul-ups, especially any cemetery in Iowa."

"When you go for therapy," Ron said calmly, "ask for a brain massage while you're there. That will do you the most good."

"I'm going, but you made me late already. If I get a speeding ticket, consider it yours. *Ciao!*"

GETTING TO KNOW AMY

I didn't get a speeding ticket, but I was late for my appointment. Amy, the therapist assigned to me had given me a different time than she had recorded in her appointment book. Because we set up the appointment by phone, I had no written proof of the correct appointment time. I took the blame and received a short, but earnest, lecture from her about punctuality. If she only knew that she was talking to the Grand Poobah of Promptness, she could have dispensed with the lecture. Despite all that, she gave me a cordial greeting, which immediately put us on a first name basis and set me at ease. Then, she gave me the usual insurance and medical history forms to complete. The moment of truth arrived when she began to measure the range of motion of my arms and shoulders. I was reduced to about half my normal range with absolutely no strength or stamina in my dominant arm. Fortunately, most of the surgical pain was gone, and I was able to suppress the remainder. Having prior surgical experience, my limitations did not surprise me, but that would not do for "raiding party" purposes in the next week or so. I would need another "Indian" if I planned to return to Peru anytime soon under these conditions.

Amy and I maintained a pleasant conversation as she demonstrated the initial exercises for me to do then, and prior to the next session. Ordinarily, the standard eight-week rehabilitation program would be no problem for me. Amy was certified and appeared to be a competent therapist with about a year of experience in a hospital setting. I quickly got the impression that she knew the procedures, how to encourage and motivate her patients, and how to maintain control of the rehab process. My prior rehab experience told me that I had some hard work ahead as my part of the deal. I was also motivated by the need to be as ready as I could be for another kind of exercise regimen in Peru.

"Some people believe that I have magical hands," Amy said matter-of-factly as she began to maneuver my arm in multiple directions.

"I don't doubt it," I concurred. "On an earlier rehab, my therapist and I discussed two other magical features that exceptional therapists have," I told her. "The therapist also needs the right head to know what to do, and the right heart to know how to apply the appropriate techniques, strategies, and empathy to the individual patient."

"But, sometimes patients assume that the therapist should do all the healing work without any effort by them. Some patients don't do anything to help themselves at home or after their professional therapy ends," Amy continued.

"Then, I propose that you apply the fourth 'H' in the form of your 'heel' to jump-start them into action."

"My roommate always teases me about being in the 4-H club back home in Iowa. Now, you put me back in the 4-H again," Amy laughed.

"I have many cousins in Michigan who were in 4-H, and now their kids are members. Both girls and boys learned many practical skills that serve them well in their daily lives. Also, none of them turned out like me."

"Thank God for that!" Amy mumbled purposely.

"What was that?" I asked, clearly hearing what she said, but daring her to repeat it.

"It's good that they could do that," Amy clarified as she hid behind my left shoulder where I couldn't see her.

"I'm not sure that's what you said the first time, but I'll let it go for the sake of therapeutic peace. Speaking of peace, I suppose that you and your roommate you mentioned earlier have no disagreements, and that you do nothing to aggravate her."

"Absolutely nothing," Amy replied. "I have been the perfect roommate and her best friend throughout college and now in our professional lives."

"I'm certain your last statement isn't the biggest Iowa fib I've heard in my lifetime, but your continuing to be roomies after college is rare. That tells me you are either very compatible, hard of hearing, or both. Could it be that your roommate also is bigger than you?"

The last comment was an unfortunate slip on my part. Amy was trim, energetic, and naturally attractive, but on the short side. Her absence of a north-south dimension was not noticeable to a patient lying on the exercise table. But, for a person of average size like myself, she tended to disappear when I stood up for vertical exercises. Having been friends for only thirty seconds, I didn't know how she would respond to my bold comment about her inability to cast a long shadow in any kind of sunlight.

"I am vertically challenged, as you can see, but I can handle myself and others pretty well. Nobody messes with me, and nothing gets past me around here, if you haven't noticed that for yourself already," Amy staked out her turf emphatically.

By then, I had prepared myself for a tougher rebuttal. Her statement was strong, but not too far from my observations. I believed that she could handle herself in most situations. I began to congratulate myself for dodging her heaviest barrage until she subconsciously began to yank on my arm with increased enthusiasm as if to further prove her point. I had to capitulate in a hurry to defend myself. I intended to save my arm in case I needed it in Peru—and during the remainder of my life.

"I got your message," I said too quietly for her to hear.

"What?" Amy asked from somewhere behind me over the drone of the air conditioning unit overhead.

"I agree that nobody messes with you. I really believe it!" I affirmed with sufficient volume this time for her to hear.

Her tension on my arm relaxed to a more normal level. A few more exercises at the relaxed pace, and the first session ended with all my limbs intact and operational. With peace restored between Amy and me, I didn't take Ron's suggestion to ask for a brain massage. Some ice on my shoulder was sufficient.

"Thanks for your help," I said as I sat up on the exercise table. "I will do a few of those on my own before our next séance."

"Just because you have been cooperative this time doesn't mean that I'm going to go easy on you during the remainder of your program," Amy affirmed.

"My life wouldn't be the delight that it is if I thought otherwise," I replied as I eyed her cautiously in case she wanted to add a last minute bit of torture to my program. "As the old military slogan goes, 'the easiest day of this program was yesterday,' right?"

Other patients were lining up, and we ended the session on that happy note to make room for them.

My prior rehab approach was to do three times the exercises on my own that I was given during any professional therapy session. The Peru situation gave me additional motivation to raise my activity level even higher. Hopefully, my shoulder sutures and titanium parts would hold together and execute what my brain told them to do in Peru. The only immediate problem I foresaw with Amy was that she was from Iowa. But, that was my problem. Based on my prior experience with Dick and Jenny, I hoped it wouldn't become hers.

RECRUITING AND LOGISTICS FOR MY SECOND COMING

After the rehab session, I went home and phoned Lisbon without caring what the local time was there. I needed another "Indian" even if I had to requisition one from another continent. Fortunately, Paolo was in bed where he should be at that hour of the night in Portugal.

"*Ola*, Paolo, I'm calling from the States. Now that you are awake, you can go back to sleep as long as you remember to send Advari to me in the morning. Has anyone taught him how to shoot?"

"No, we are teaching him how to read, write, compute, and conduct himself properly among people until the school year begins."

"That is excellent news. Thank you for taking him off the streets in India for me. But now I need him to help me for a few days. Put him on the first available flight to Chicago. Tell him not to bring any stones. We have plenty of stones where we're going. Okay, *adeus, obrigado*."

With my second "Indian" on order, I did two more sets of arm exercises and fell asleep. The ringing phone next to my bed woke me earlier than I would have gotten up if I were on my own agenda. I also noted how long it took my arm to stretch for the receiver. It was Ron.

"I contacted Manco," Ron said. "He will be available for you whenever you need him. Also, Manco can bring his wife and uncle to cook and track if you go into the deep jungle for more than a few days. My visiting nurse is here for my medical review; is that all you need from me now?"

"Yes, terrific, Ron," I replied, "take care of your medical problems. I will call you when I have more information. I recruited some additional help to come with me. We should be able to manage the situation even though none of us speak the same first language."

Before I made my next call, the phone rang again. It was Chauncey in Lima.

"I don't know what kind of shape you are in given your condition when you left here, but I have some important news I thought you should hear. It's about the three missionaries."

"You are absolutely correct in calling me. In fact, I was about to dial your number on the same topic. They are a hot news item with Ron and me. What information do you have?"

"As you know, the missionaries were to be transferred from provisional custody in San Jose to La Paz pending extradition to the States that you arranged. The story goes that they were shot attempting to escape along the way, or actually escaped and both Calderon and the Bolivian and Peruvian *policia* are looking for them. Earlier today, the foreman of the Quillabamba ranch was on his regular trip to Lima for supplies, and he stopped by the hospital to see Bill who is still in the burns unit with the other pilot. According to Bill, the foreman told him that Calderon is holding the missionaries prisoner at the Quillabamba ranch. He does not know if Calderon intends to hold them hostage, or dispose of them in another way if they do not prove useful to him. As you are fully aware by now, Señor Barrantes had many friends in high places, and the same can now be said of Calderon. I have no one I can trust to rescue the missionaries for you."

"That is good information about the missionaries. Thanks for your prompt call. I will get to the missionaries in a minute. First, tell me if Calderon is at Quillabamba, where are Señora Barrantes and the children?"

"Calderon took control and combined the Barrantes operation with his own cartel. But, he allowed Juanita and the children to have the *casa* in Lima and the villa in Miraflores plus whatever considerable assets she and her husband had together before his death. She will be fine in that regard."

"From that information, I assume that the señora had nothing to do with the drug operation. Further, I assume she's not holding me responsible for her husband's death. Am I correct?"

"Right you are, old man. In fact, she planned to get word to you that she had nothing to do with any of it. Calderon put out the hit on your Scout and a bounty on your head under Juanita's name so that you would believe your return to either Peru or Bolivia would be very unhealthy for you, or anyone associated with you."

"Chaunc, you have given me an extraordinary present today. I couldn't decide if Jenny's murder was Calderon's work or retaliation from a Russian general I met on several occasions. Are you absolutely certain that Calderon put out the order on my Scout?"

"Absolutely, Joe. You know I would not fabricate something like that which obviously means a great deal to you."

"That's good to hear, Chaunc, believe me. That doesn't change what happened, but it certifies who was responsible. I have a weak shoulder, but two Indians and I will come in your direction to land on top of Calderon's operation. We assume that you'll help us."

"I'd like to help, but I don't know if you can count on me for much these days because of my past involvement with the Barrantes network. I am scheduled to leave this post shortly as you likely have ascertained by now."

"What if the U.S. State Department is informed through a reliable source that you're needed there to personally negotiate a lucrative trade contract with a Portuguese shipping firm in addition to helping me during my 'second coming' rescue party for the missionaries? Would that stabilize your career and absolve some of your past sins?"

"It certainly would, Joe. But how would you accomplish it?"

"While in India, I met three Portuguese brothers who operate an international shipping fleet. Two brothers actually operate the business from Lisbon and Goa while the third is a nuclear scientist in Mumbai. I'm sure you recognize the corporate name of Southern Cross International. The brothers could be helpful to you and Peru in creating new trade opportunities. After we finish here, I'll contact one of the brothers to notify the U.S. State Department that the firm wishes to discuss legitimate trade opportunities with you exclusively. Do you think that will help you retain your position?"

"No question, old man. That will resurrect my career. What is your *quid pro quo*? And don't tell me you don't have one or more '*quids*' in mind. We have known each other far too long for me to expect charity from you."

"I think you can arrange the *quids* I need easily enough. I need military or private transport from the States into Lima for one companion and myself. Then, I need you to have Manco, Ron's Aymaran Indian guide and however many family members he wants to bring with him available to meet us in Lima. I need a plane to get my Indian army from Lima to Tingo Maria, and then on to Quillabamba without any information leaks from your office to Calderon or to the CIA. Can you guarantee that?"

"Yes, I follow you, especially the CIA part. Okay, what's next?"

"I need a plane to stand by at or near the Quillabamba ranch for our quick return to Lima and military or private transport ready at Jorge Chàvez Airport for a return flight to the States in a hurry and with a fuel range farther than Guatemala. Hopefully, the missionaries will be with us. Can you arrange all that?"

"No problem, Joe. Consider it done. When do you need it?"

"Have it ready a week from today. Normally, I would act sooner, but I know you need a few days for the arrangements, the Portuguese business letter needs to hit the right desk at the U.S. State Department, and I need to provide some skills training to Advari when he arrives here. Oh, yes, tell Manco that I won't need his wife or uncle for deep jungle work, but they may be helpful in other ways. I don't have a Scout now, so I'm making all these arrangements myself."

"Are you sure you are physically up to all this?"

"No, I'm not sure, Chauncey, but nobody else is available to uncork the missionaries from their captivity, and we may not have much time. I feel responsible for leaving them behind for Calderon's enjoyment. I don't need any Mormon martyrs on my conscience. Confirm in the usual way when you have everything ready, okay?"

"Will do, Joe. Talk to you soon. Thank you for thinking of me and for any help you can be in rehabilitating my career."

With those arrangements made, my day was off to a good beginning. I began to feel that recovering the missionaries was a real possibility, and I might not have to turn Isadora and her sisters into orphans to cause problems for the combined drug cartel now operated by Calderon. I placed my second call of the day to Paolo in Lisbon. This time he was awake and at work.

"Yes, it is good to talk to you again, Señor, but Advari is already on the plane to you as you requested earlier," Paolo answered before I had a chance to place an additional order.

"That's very good to hear, Paolo," I said, aiming to calm him, "but I need one more thing today. Then, I'll leave you alone to run your business."

Paolo was nervous about my "one more thing" until I explained Chauncey's need for a letter from the shipping company to the U.S. State Department. Paolo didn't calm down, but he shifted his excitement to the prospect of additional business in South America.

Then, my good day hit a speed bump. I went to the post office to see if I had any messages from MAGENTA in my secure mailbox. MAGENTA left a note that I was scheduled to interview two candidates for my Scout position. One interview was scheduled for the next afternoon. The second was set for the following evening. I had demanded to interview the candidates before MAGENTA made the final selection. Now that I faced actual interviews, my first reaction was to change my demand, especially if my recommendation led to the candidate's harm from one or more of my adversaries. The second consideration was the Scout's ability to terminate my MAGENTA career if the assignment demanded it.

In my civilian activities, these two items had taken on a more theoretical quality than I faced in a military setting with Alice Bright Feather. In the Army, Alice's ability to defend or eliminate me was a basic provision of her job description. The attack on Jenny erased any theoretical considerations about my relationship with a new Scout. *But, could a civilian Scout pull the trigger when the situation demanded?* I decided that my Scout had to be prepared for the full range of possibilities. I had asked, no, demanded of MAGENTA that I be allowed to interview the finalists. Now, I had no one to blame but myself for intruding into the recruiting process. Beginning now, I needed to think about the kind of person I wanted for the job. The candidates should be adults who could make important decisions for themselves, I reasoned. I wouldn't force anyone to be my Scout. Thus reassured about the legitimacy of my request to interview the finalists and the range of skills I required of the one selected, I sat down in my "thinking" chair and promptly fell asleep.

THE FIRST SCOUT CANDIDATE

The next afternoon, I met my first candidate at the appointed time and place in the back booth of a restaurant on Ogden Avenue. Jeff was a surprise candidate. Potentially, he could be my first male Scout. He was entering his fourth year as an engineering student at the University of Illinois. He was in the ROTC program, knew weapons, had studied military history and tactics, and had a family history of military service. He was clean-cut, polite, and intelligent. The sealed envelope he handed me contained his psychological profile that he completed with MAGENTA as part of the recruitment process. At least on paper, he was compatible with the job and my personality. (Matching Jeff's personality with my emotional range caused Jeff's evaluator to write several cryptic notes to me in the margin.) With all the favorable data, I asked myself what could I discover about Jeff in a short time that would be persuasive to me of his ability to be my Scout.

"From what you know about this job, why do you want it?" I asked Jeff without intending to be officious or threatening.

"I am interested in intelligence work, and my ROTC instructors tell me that I have an aptitude for it, sir. This position could test my aptitude before I make an actual commitment in my military career," Jeff answered readily and politely.

That was a good reply. It was a better reply than I would have given him if our roles were reversed. Fortunately or unfortunately for Jeff, that wasn't the answer I wanted. I didn't see myself as his career counselor when I had unfinished business in Peru. He could decide what he wanted to be on somebody else's time. *Okay,* I thought, *that may be more me than him babbling.* To be fair, I would try something else.

"Jeff, if the occasion arises, how strongly do you believe you can defend yourself if I am not available? How positive are you that you can terminate me if ordered to do so by MAGENTA's rulebook? Take your time and think about it. To me, your answer to these questions is more important than your ability to make travel arrangements and create new and exciting identities for me."

Jeff was silent for a while. Then, he whispered, "I believe that I can do what is necessary under the circumstances. I can't say for sure until the situation arises. But, my family upbringing and my ROTC training have taught me to always be prepared for difficult situations."

That was another powerful answer. And that was the end of my inquisition. I didn't believe MAGENTA would be able to find a stronger Scout candidate than Jeff.

While Jeff finished his meal, we talked about a number of subjects both related and unrelated to the Scout position. He had a wide range of interests and information. He would be valuable as a Scout with that knowledge. *Should I strongly recommend him to MAGENTA,* I asked myself, *or should I merely comment favorably and acquiesce in the decision?* As we continued our discussion, some negative blips appeared on my radar screen as they do in hiring anybody. The maximum time Jeff could give me was one school year. Then, Uncle Sam would require his services. He would just begin to be comfortable as a Scout, and he would be gone. His interest was in becoming an intelligence officer. *Would he really commit himself to do the dirty work of a Scout for an aging civilian who had lost the rulebook on intelligence protocols years ago?* I concluded those were pale blips. Before the end of my next Peru trip, I could be a tenant in a sarcophagus. Rather than torture myself, I decided to determine what the other candidate had to offer before I responded to MAGENTA regarding Jeff.

I heard myself say to him, "Jeff, thanks for pursuing this job and jumping all the hurdles to reach this point. MAGENTA has the final word on your hire, and I will present my input by tomorrow night at latest. In my opinion, you are a strong candidate. I expect to interview one other candidate tomorrow. I'm not aware of any other candidates in the pipeline. I am sure you will hear from MAGENTA by the end of the week. Good luck to you."

We shook hands, and Jeff left the restaurant. As I lingered to pay the bill, I noticed that he drove away in a new vehicle. I have nothing against rich kids who have nice cars. I could enjoy being rich myself some day. I would not exclude Jeff from consideration based on the car he drove or the size of his dad's bank account. My bias with family wealth in relation to MAGENTA work was that, for some rich people, wealth becomes the basis for determining the value of less fortunate people. If I evaluated my MAGENTA clients on that criterion, the three missionaries wouldn't have a chance. They put themselves in a mess. In their current situation, they weren't economically worth risking other lives to rescue them. Personally, I'd gain nothing from whatever happened to them one way or another. But, my job was to get them home. Someone else could evaluate their economic value or other worth by whatever yardstick they wanted to apply when the trio was safely in the States.

My first stop on Monday morning was Amy's rehab salon. This time, I was plenty early. Amy was with another patient, and I started exercising on my own. I sensed her checking me out from time to time. *Get used to it, girl.* This is the kind of guy I am even when I don't have a hot project percolating. My need to rehab my shoulder as fast as possible for my Peru trip made me even more determined to heal. *You can coach and teach me techniques, young lady, but getting well is my responsibility, thank you.*

"I'll finish with my patient and be with you soon," Amy said courteously and professionally. "Continue to exercise on your own until then, okay?"

"That's fine with me," I responded even though my arm felt heavy enough to yank the exercise pulley off its wall bracket.

After that, I entertained myself with the "ball on the wall" and pulling on elastic bands before my official turn on the exercise table.

"How have you been since your last visit?" Amy asked as she started to move my arm in several directions it did not intend to go yet.

"Okay, I can do a few more repetitions than the last time on each exercise you showed me."

"Any pain?"

"Only on my wallet side."

"I don't understand that," Amy said with concern, "it's perfectly normal for you to feel shoulder pain or soreness, but I don't understand the pain in your hip."

"It hurts when I sit on my wallet," I clarified, as I adjusted my caboose. "But, if you keep pulling on my arm, I'm sure you will reset my soreness priorities quickly."

I had to change the subject to keep thoughts of real pain from entering my cranial closet. I began staring at Amy's elbow.

"What?" she asked self-consciously. "Are you looking at my elbow?"

"Yeah, on my last visit, you said you were going sidewalk skating with your friends. I was checking for damage. It's not good business for a therapist to have bruises."

"The weather was so ugly, we didn't go. We did a lot of nothing for the entire weekend. Move over to the other side of the table now."

"Is your leverage better with me on that side of the table, or are you hoping I fall off and extend my rehab billing period?"

"Better leverage, of course. That way, when I break your arm, there is a crisp snap to the bone."

"Excellent. Now that we have that settled, tell me how I became your patient and if I can request a transfer?"

"Just the luck of the draw. You came in, and I had available time. That's the way we select patients here. As for a transfer, you're too late. The manager just left the building."

"Then, you don't believe in destiny or a greater purpose in life? Does everything in your life happen by chance? Are you just a victim of the luck of the draw in everything that happens to you? Or, do you have some control over the kind of life you want to live?"

"I don't know why you are interrogating me, but, when you put it that way, I guess I have to change my answer. Certainly I believe in a purpose in life. Otherwise, I wouldn't be here trying to help people regain their health. Why do you ask?"

"I don't know the answer to that myself. In my advanced years, I certainly believe in a purpose in life. But, I'm still searching for the Higher Authority who sets the purpose and helps me start in the right direction to accomplish it. But, we can save the theological and philosophical discussions for another time. On my last visit, you told me the name of your Iowa town. I looked it up, and in 1948, the population was slightly over 260 Iowans."

"The town hasn't grown or changed much over the years. Perhaps that's why so many young people like me move to Chicago to find jobs. Your next job, mister, is to put ice on that shoulder for ten minutes. Then you can leave. See you next time. I enjoyed our séance, as you call it."

I didn't tell Amy, but her Iowa hometown was close to Jenny's hometown and final resting place. I had told Amy the truth. I didn't have the total answer to my purpose in life. But, instinctively, I knew I wasn't assigned to her by mere chance. Our meeting was not by the luck of the draw by any means. *Okay, Higher Authority, what lofty purpose do you have planned for me in my otherwise drab existence now that you made Amy a part of my current life equation?*

I went home and did my exercise routines a few more times. I felt okay, but I simply didn't have strength and stamina in my right arm. I began to collect the equipment I thought I would need for Peru. I picked up my .30-caliber rifle. It weighed only eight pounds, but it was more than my right arm could bear comfortably. I began to practice dry firing using my left hand with the rifle resting on the back of a chair. I could do it, but awkwardly. I was not pleased. I needed to shoot better in Peru if necessary—a lot better. I kept practicing. Before long, it was time to go to the restaurant to meet the second candidate for my Scout position.

THE SECOND SCOUT CANDIDATE

I took my place in the rear booth of the Ogden Avenue restaurant again. It was shortly after 7:00 p.m. and only a few people were there. I noted Wednesday night was not a big night for this restaurant. I also noted that my candidate was late. A few minutes later, the door opened and Amy entered. She was still in her work clothes. After a quick glance around, she came straight for my booth. She was not here "by chance" just to have dinner. *What kind of discussion would her arrival precipitate, the luck of the draw or a higher purpose in life?* With Amy as the apparent second Scout candidate, I would observe what Higher Authority had in mind sooner than I expected.

"I'm sorry I'm late," Amy said, sitting down, "we were really busy today."

"I can appreciate that people are sometimes unintentionally late for important events in their lives. What brings you to my table tonight—destiny, purpose, or the luck of the draw?"

"I thought we already had that conversation?"

"Do you always answer a question with a question?"

"Why do you ask?" she continued as we both laughed.

"You better order so that the cook can go home at a reasonable hour."

The cook would not go home early that night. After a hard day of physical activity, Amy ordered everything on the right side of the menu. It would be a while before all that was delivered to the table, so I started our conversation.

"At least, we know a little about each other already. If you want to drop out now, you still get a free meal tonight," I offered the option, assuming correctly that she wouldn't take it.

"No, your personality and what I know about the Scout job so far don't scare me. I need more information about the job though."

"The object is not for me to frighten you, but some of my clients and adversaries might. First, tell me how and when you were contacted."

"I was contacted the night of your first appointment. I was really shocked, but interested too. Obviously, I have never done anything like this. I haven't voted in an election yet, so I'm not politically oriented."

"Fortunately, the job doesn't require political affiliation. Otherwise, you'd be talking to someone else. For the Scout position, the further away from political activism you are, the better. But, embracing the best of the American character and the ideals that the United States represents, or should represent to the rest of the world, are always helpful in this kind of work. Several other skills may be important too. Dependability, the ability to think clearly under pressure, and attention to details are always important. Skills learned in every facet of life can be important over time."

"In Iowa, we have a large lawn. I certainly know how to use a lawn mower."

"That's a good outdoor skill to have. We may take advantage of your arm strength and determination to complete a job. How good are you at a skill you can use both indoors and outdoors such as knowing how to shoot?"

"A gun? Yikes, I haven't been introduced to firearms yet. My dad is not a hunter, so we have no guns around the house. Is that important for the job?"

"Only when someone is shooting at you or me. The need hadn't surfaced in a long time until recently."

"Is that why this position is available?" Amy asked perceptively.

"Indirectly, I would say. The last project was expanded beyond available resources to cover all the options, but not the risks. All parties should have known better, but other lives were at stake. A decision was made to proceed despite, or without knowledge of, certain risks involved."

"Does that happen often?"

"Not on my watch. This recent event was the first time my Scout was exposed to imminent danger. I have doubled my resolve to ensure that no one working with me in the future will ever be put in that position again. I don't know if that makes you feel more comfortable because I can't completely guarantee your safety any more than I can absolutely protect myself. The primary purpose of a Scout is to ensure that an Operative has all the resources necessary to complete an assignment without having direct contact with MAGENTA."

"Mostly, your duties consist of having briefing papers, travel documents, and any weapons needed available for me in sufficient time to have maximum effectiveness on the assignment. When I'm in the field, my Scout needs to be available through secure communications, particularly when circumstances arise which may change my effectiveness or ability to complete the assignment. Difficulty arises if our interaction allows the adversary to gain access or interrupt our communications, or to discover our identities and location. Then, we all have problems. I have proposed changes to MAGENTA's operating procedures to minimize communication breaches when I'm in the field. If adopted, the changes should eliminate or substantially reduce your risk exposure. That's about as detailed as I can be on that subject. Hopefully, that is sufficient information for you at this point."

"I guess it will have to be okay until I become more familiar with the job. But, if I accept this job, don't be surprised if I ask questions about this subject and a lot more."

"I already believe you will surprise me in infinite ways if you are selected for this position. You don't strike me as a fragile person. If you aren't comfortable with firearms now, you can learn other defenses that will work in a variety of situations. If you decide to become more knowledgeable about weapons at a later date, doing so might be helpful for your personal protection and my peace of mind."

Our conversation was interrupted by the arrival of Amy's food, personally supervised by the cook who wanted to see for himself how many people were seated in the rear booth and if a responsible person was available to pay for his culinary efforts. The non-gourmet me marveled at the selections destined to be consumed by one undersized Scout candidate.

"I usually don't eat this much. But I'm really hungry tonight," Amy advised, hoping to pre-empt any comment from me.

"It doesn't bother me. Enjoy your meal. Therapy work is both physically and mentally challenging. I certainly understand that you need to refuel by this time of the night. Besides, being able to use a knife and fork properly is a big part of this job."

"Really?"

"No, I was just testing your credibility reflexes. I remember you telling me that you have only ten minutes to eat lunch. If you didn't know how to use a knife and fork properly, you would have marks all over your arms and face trying to eat that fast. I guess the healthcare industry isn't any better at setting good examples for healthy eating than any other industry. Executives take two-hour lunches to discuss one item of business while worker bees must finish in ten minutes to take care of ninety problems the executives should have addressed several lunches earlier."

I could have vented more about quaint executive luncheon customs, but that debate had to be deferred for another time. Right now, I needed a Scout. I attacked the near problem first. I asked Amy for the sealed envelope containing her psychological profile for me to survey while she dug into her food pyramids.

Now, it was my turn to say yikes. Through my rehab sessions, I already picked up some notion of Amy's qualities of intelligence, self-reliance, independence, strong work ethic, athleticism, and attachment to her family. I wasn't particularly disturbed by the reviewer's comment about her dislike of criticism of her work. I never met anyone worth her or his salt who enjoyed criticism, particularly when the reviewer wasn't qualified to comment based on that person's aptitude or experience. I never enjoyed criticism (especially the self-administered kind) even when I knew it would enable me to perform better in the future. But, the profile went further to conclude that Amy and I were not compatible in stressful environments. *Either MAGENTA's psychologist or Amy was pulling my chain on the evaluation, but which one? And, why was I concerned about it?* Only twenty-four hours earlier, I would have bet Barrantes' ranch that Jeff would be my next Scout. Then, I reminded myself that I was an Angry Dragon personality type. No one in his or her right mind was compatible with my personality type for an extended period of time, stress or no stress. At that point, I realized I had talked myself into keeping Amy in the competition for the Scout position.

Amy came up for air somewhere late in the main course. Apparently, the food energy had a positive impact by traveling straight to her head. Either that, or she chose to ignore my pained expression from having reviewed the profile documents.

"Why do you do this kind of work?" Amy asked in earnest.

"Now that I'm retired, my wife thinks I should socialize more, continue to be active, help friends, and see the world. Before that, I assumed my activity would lead to a better world for my grandkids and their generation. Somewhere between those poles live a million more reasons and motives for and against continuing this kind of work, I suppose."

"What can I do as a Scout that will be most helpful to you in your role?" Amy asked as she moved plates around.

If Jeff had asked that question, I would have knighted him on the spot. That was the essence of the Scout position. Amy identified what I felt was the missing element in my conversation with Jeff. He concentrated on what the job could do for him and his military career. Amy asked how her efforts and input could be most valuable to MAGENTA and me. Before I answered, I made sure I had recovered all my mental marbles that she had scattered.

The Real Job Requirements

"Assuming you are offered and accept the Scout position, MAGENTA will show you all its administrative procedures and systems for launching and retrieving me on a project. Obviously, MAGENTA places a high value on your knowing and performing these functions without constant referral to your supervisor. However, you become more valuable to me when you learn how and when to beat or evade those systems, and get me what I need quickly without getting yourself fired by MAGENTA or targeted by an adversary. After a while, the value of your services increases exponentially when you anticipate my needs before I recognize them myself. When you reach that level, you don't need to worry about being dismissed if you miscalculate. Your only concern then is to bring me and my associates back home alive. The job is that simple and that difficult all at the same time. *Capiche?*"

"Yes, I get it. And I have to do everything quickly, accurately, and confidentially, right?"

"Absolutely. That's the whole ball game. It's not that I'll enjoy harassing you for some wild things you never encountered just to see you squirm. It's all about completing the assignment, and, in some cases, moving people out of harm's way. Generally, the best way for me to do that is through some unorthodox or unexpected action that keeps the adversary off balance. But, *Madre de Dios*, my watch and the haggard look of the cashier tell me it's past my bedtime. Unless you have other questions, I have enough information to submit my comments to MAGENTA on your candidacy."

"There is one more thing. I need to be perfectly honest with you. If I do work at home, I don't believe I can keep my roommate from knowing what I'm doing. Does that create a problem?"

"Ordinarily it might. If you two have been together through school, that may lessen the risk. Apparently, MAGENTA has decided that question already. If your roommate's name is Heidi, MAGENTA states here that she's not a security risk, and may, in fact, be helpful in certain situations that are not identified further. That should resolve your concern for the moment. I have a question for you though. Are either of you dating anyone who we should know about?"

"Have you seen my work schedule lately?"

"Do I take that as a 'no,' a 'yes,' or a 'none of the above' question-answer?"

"I did it again, didn't I?"

"I think the only way to break you of that habit is for you to pay the bill. Do you have any money?"

"If I had money, would I be here discussing this job?"

"You're absolutely hopeless in avoiding straight answers and declarative sentences. Let's get out of here."

This time, as I stayed behind to pay the bill, I noticed that Amy drove away in a middle-aged, manual-shift beater. Apparently, she bought or inherited it the way most of us do—she earned it, or did without. A lot of character gets built that way. This was going to be a tougher decision than I expected. In my mind, Jeff had strong competition now. I was glad I held up my comments to MAGENTA until I interviewed both candidates.

ONE LITTLE INDIAN

When I arrived home, Advari was there. I purposely hadn't given him instructions about how to get from O'Hare Airport to my home to determine how he would react to a big city in a strange country. Most of us trust that the simplest way to find an unknown location other than GPS is to jump in a cab and let the driver find the place for us. Problems with that approach might surface if the driver is new and doesn't know the way, a language barrier exists, the driver is restricted to a certain area, or the driver wants to increase the fare by taking the long way. Once again, Advari demonstrated that he could surmount all obstacles in getting where he needed to be on time. Both of us had a tiring day. To Beth, Advari was one more in a regular stream of international guests over the years. Her welcoming format was the same for everyone—a brief hello, a shower, something to eat, and a crash landing in the guest room. More formal introductions and discussions could wait until the next day.

The next morning, I didn't waste time with Advari. He shoveled down the food we put in front of him, and we were off to the indoor pistol range. His eyes at half-mast told me that he was suffering a massive case of jet lag. I sympathized privately with his suffering, but we didn't have the luxury of recovery time. Chauncey confirmed that everything would be in place for our arrival in Lima in four days. I handed an unloaded .38-caliber revolver to Advari, showed him how to breathe, demonstrated how to maintain a good sight picture, and let him dry fire a few times while squeezing rather than pulling the trigger. Then, I loaded the pistol for him, spun him around a few times, and told him to shoot at the target some thirty-five meters downrange. I wasn't foolhardy. I loaded a blank round in the first chamber. BAM! As I expected, even with ear protection, the recoil of the revolver and the crack of the first shot startled Advari. Instantly, the jet lag in his bleary eyes was replaced by wide-eyed terror.

"Pull the target up, and see what you hit," I told him.

"I do not see a hole anywhere," Advari admitted as he looked at the target.

"How can you be in an enclosed space and not hit anything?" I admonished. "You managed to miss the target, four walls, the ceiling, the floor, and me."

"I had my eyes closed too, I'm pretty sure," he confessed.

"That's not unusual for the first shot. I think you jerked the trigger too. But guess what, I am positive you will do better on your next shot and the ones after that if you remember what I told you. Go through the steps mentally before you fire again. Take your time and relax."

While Advari was doing that, I retreated to a safe place just in case he forgot a step or didn't relax. BAM! BAM! In his excitement, Advari, the novice postman, rang twice hitting the lower right edge of the target both times. At least, he was consistent. I stepped out of hiding and applauded. Some of the wildness exited his eyes when he saw that he actually hit something.

"Not bad," I cheered. "Go through the routine again, and fire the remaining three shots."

BAM! BAM! BAM! This time, the last two shots caught the outer ring of the target. Advari smiled weakly, then bent over and threw up. I understood. Guns were not his thing and never would be no matter how long he practiced. We went out in the field next to the range for fresh air. After he rested a few minutes, Advari pulled out his leather slingshot, found a stone he liked, and fired at a squirrel running along the top of the fence. Fortunately, Advari did not intend to hit it. Nonetheless, he came close enough so that the squirrel would not have to shave for the next three days.

"Okay, Mr. Marksman," I told him. "See if you can find any more stones you like in the field, and then we'll go home. It looks like you as David may surprise our enforcer Goliaths in Peru with your natural intelligence and low-tech weapons skills."

When we returned to my house, an urgent message was waiting from Chauncey. Advari followed me into my den where I dialed Chauncey immediately. Events were about to accelerate.

Chapter Notes

1. "King Henry the Fourth Act V Scene I," *William Shakespeare The Complete Works*" (New York: Barnes & Noble Books, 1994), p. 443.

CHAPTER 10

UNFINISHED BUSINESS

RESCHEDULING THE RAID

"What's up Chaunc, do we have problems?" I inquired when he answered his secure line.

"We need to move the schedule up because of developments here that will take me too long to explain. Your flight is waiting for you whenever you reach the airfield. I will monitor its location and will be at Jorge Chàvez Airport when you arrive. Do you have any problems with that? We are ready at this end."

"Fine, I should be at O'Hare in about an hour, depending on traffic. You can brief me on developments when we're in the air. Do one more thing. Collect as many grenades as you can before our arrival—concussion, smoke, anything you can get your hands on. *Adios*."

The last comment was my reaction to watching Advari toss the dummy hand grenade I had as a paperweight on my desk. Maybe we would not need to be totally low tech on this trip after all.

Advari and I were out the door in ten minutes leaving Beth spinning in the vortex of our rapid departure. Before we left, I sent a message to MAGENTA on our revised departure to Peru. I also included a message concerning my choice for a Scout. MAGENTA might not feel the same way I did, but the shift to a hurry-up schedule made the decision obvious to me. *Who did I recommend, you ask? Who would you pick if you were in my position?* I had two capable candidates who could handle the job using different skills and approaches.

Advari and I arrived at O'Hare in fifty-nine minutes, and we were in the air headed south in less than fifteen. This was no lumbering military cargo plane. Chauncey had chartered a private jet. I assumed he wanted us in Peru as fast as we could get there. Shortly after the plane leveled off, I went forward to have the crew connect me with Chauncey at the embassy. Due to sunspots or other technical difficulties, we couldn't make the connection then or at any time during our flight. I wouldn't learn why the sudden change in schedule was necessary until we arrived. Also, I wouldn't be able to determine what alterations were necessary in my plans to recover the missionaries and to cripple Calderon's operations.

Based on my previous experience with Jenny, I wouldn't contact MAGENTA during the flight and expose the organization to any intercepts by Calderon or an embassy mole. *Would Peru be a constant jinx for me?* At least, I wouldn't get a Scout killed on this trip, but I needed to protect Manco and Advari to varying degrees. I went back to the passenger cabin and found Advari curled up in a blanket, sleeping off the jet lag from his flight to the States. While he slept, I did all the arm exercises I could execute in the space available. This was not fun. I was seriously impaired while lives depended on me. This was not the way I worked.

Señora's Surprise

Military transport or fast jet, the flight somehow still took the better part of twenty-four hours. We arrived and taxied to the non-commercial area of the airport in Lima. I hoped that the weather wouldn't be a factor in this *soiree*. We had enough problems facing us. The dry season still envelops Peru in August with temperatures averaging between fifty and sixty degrees Fahrenheit in Lima and a little or lot cooler at the higher elevations, as I expected. Also, as I expected, Chauncey and Manco greeted us at the airport along with a totally unexpected third party in the person of Señora Barrantes. Santa Fortunata was indeed a lady, and she had just dealt me three aces along with the fourth I brought with me. Advari didn't look much like an ace as he reluctantly crawled out of his blanket to put on his shoes. He managed to haul all his stuff and mine and dump it into the trunk of the car before we drove to Juanita's villa in Miraflores, which Chauncey informed me would be our base. I couldn't have been happier to find a location away from the prying eyes and ears of the embassy yet close enough to maintain communications with the outside world if we needed reinforcements.

I was glad that I didn't devote much time to planning strategy and tactics during the flight. Señora Barrantes' participation changed my entire action plan. Initially, I intended to attack the Tingo Maria cocaine processing facilities as a diversion, and then hit the Quillabamba *ranchero* to spring the missionaries from their captivity. Juanita's contribution allowed us to reverse my initial plan with better odds for successful recovery of the missionaries. She knew secrets about the *ranchero* that would help us bypass the armed guards or allow us to attack them from unexpected directions. She also believed that some of the guards were still loyal to her after having tasted Calderon's harsh regime for several weeks. Indeed, as we learned from her at the Miraflores villa, the señora had useful intelligence no one else had.

"First of all, I learned that Calderon is in Europe or North Africa for an unknown period," Juanita started. "I advised Chauncey that you may have a better chance of rescuing the missionaries while he's gone. That's why we hoped you would expedite your travel here. The missionaries are being held in the tool barn in the tea orchard," Juanita stated as she pointed to the location on a hand-drawn schematic of the Quillabamba ranch.

"The barn's location will require us to fight our way past all the guards unless we swing around the main buildings and come in from the rear while creating a diversion elsewhere," I thought out loud. "I'm not happy with that. Someone in our party is guaranteed to get hurt."

"Circling the main ranch building may be a good idea though," Juanita offered. "Only one or two guards are posted outside the tool barn. If you can overpower them quietly and release the missionaries, you may find the tunnel from the tool barn to the main house useful," Juanita said, adding another surprise piece of information.

"Tunnel? Useful? I guess! Do the guards know about it?" I asked her.

"No. My husband was a careful man. The tunnels were intended to provide for our escape from the main house to the orchard during the early revolutionary days. We hired former *Sendero Luminoso,* the Shining Path revolutionaries as guards, but my husband would not have disclosed the tunnels to any of them in case a counter-revolution started."

"Señora, I heard you say 'tunnels.' Are there more than one?" I asked, hoping against hope.

"*Si*, one tunnel leads from the main house to the tool barn, as I said. Another leads from the main house to the bunkhouse, and a third goes from the main house to the bank of the small river beyond the tea orchard. They are all interconnected, but the connections are not obvious if a person does not know how to activate the disguised doors and gates."

"I understand that they were intended to be escape routes from the main house and are interconnected. But, please confirm that we can gain access from the outside toward the main house too. Having a two-way connection is very important."

I wanted to be certain that we had full and accurate information about what appeared to be a substantial advantage for my small invasion party.

"*Si*, but again, only if you know where the exits are, and if you have keys to the hidden locks. I can show you the exits, and here are the keys," Juanita said as she took the keys from her pocket and waved them in front of us.

"Terrific, now please show us on the drawing approximately where the entrances and exits are. That information is extremely helpful."

"The entrances and exits are too well hidden for you to find them from anything I draw on this schematic and too hidden for you to find them on the ranch in the dark. Because we have not used them, some are hidden in the undergrowth. I will go with you to show you where they are."

"Oh, no, you don't," I reacted. "If bullets start flying, you need to think of your three girls."

"He's right," Chauncey seconded. "Juanita, you must think of your children first."

"I am a Spanish woman of noble birth, *amigos*, and when I say that I am going, you cannot stop me. I was not a dance hall girl as the vicious rumors suggest. I am the mistress of that *ranchero*, and I will take it back from Calderon with your help," Juanita proclaimed with authority.

"If you are going, so am I," Chauncey exclaimed defiantly.

"*Madre de Dios*," I intoned. "First, I am Zorro with two Indian companions, and now I have a battalion of diplomats and nobles. Is there room for all of us on the plane, Chaunc?"

"Yes, and space for the three missionaries on the return flight too," Chauncey declared.

Juanita spoke again.

"I know how to shoot. Alfredo taught me how to protect the children, myself, and the *ranchero* during the revolution—especially when he was absent," Juanita affirmed.

Manco's wife and uncle, who had been listening silently to the conversation while leaning against the far wall suddenly spoke in hurried Quechua, the language of the indigenous Aymara Indians, which was totally new to me. Manco translated as well as he could.

"We all can shoot," he said. "We have guns, and we will show you."

"I believe you, Manco. Ron told me that you and your family are versatile in both jungle and urban survival skills. Okay, I can use all of you. Chaunc, did you get the supplies I requested? That will make a difference in our individual itineraries when we get to the ranch."

"I was able to get two boxes for you, old boy," Chauncey responded proudly. "Will that do? We appear to have sufficient grenade 'chuckers' now too."

"We should be able to capture Ecuador and Chile in addition to the *ranchero* with that many grenades and people to 'chuck' them. Thanks. I knew I could count on you, Chaunc. But, if I get out of this alive, there's one more thing I need to do. So help me, Chauncey, I'm going to force you to speak American English even if I need to put you on an accelerated curriculum to do it," I threatened him jokingly.

MORE LITTLE INDIANS AND SOME BIG DOGS

I now had six people with untested guerrilla skills plus my less-than-full-strength self to attack four strongholds against an unknown number of more heavily armed guards of uncertain loyalty to the señora. I needed to be alone to think about how to deploy my "army."

"Give me a few minutes to process the information I just acquired and work out a game plan," I told the group as I went outside to walk around the yard for a while to collect my thoughts.

Three steps outside the door, I heard a vicious growl and the movement of unseen animals coming toward me. As I turned to defend myself or rush back into the house, I heard a friendlier yelp and found myself overwhelmed by Amigo, Inca, Nina, and four rambunctious pups. In the commotion, I didn't hear Juanita come out the door until she snapped her fingers. The commotion stopped instantly as all the dogs, including the pups, not only obeyed her command, but all waited for further instructions before moving again.

"The dogs could be useful to us if you want them," she said. "My husband trained them to protect the children and me."

"Now I have ten soldiers, which is a reinforced rifle squad or an understrength platoon, if not an army. But, it does open additional possibilities. We will be innovative if nothing else."

"Or dead," Juanita observed.

"Or dead," I concurred as a plan simmered and took shape in my cranial crockery. Señora Barrantes was an astute woman. She sensed that I needed time alone and herded the dogs inside the house with her.

I let my brain scroll back to the beginning. We had several objectives, not necessarily in the order of importance that I identified them. Some actions needed to be simultaneous. Our primary objective remained to rescue the missionaries. The second objective was to return the *ranchero* to Juanita's control. To be successful at both objectives, we needed to first put the machine gunner on top of the barn out of action early in the raid; second, overcome the guards watching the missionaries; third, overcome any guards on duty around the main buildings; and fourth, neutralize the guards in the bunkhouse. Equally important, we needed to stay alive. *Matka Bozia*, I prayed in Slovak, please guide my thoughts now.

A half hour later, I walked back into the house. In 375 BC, the Chinese warrior and philosopher Sun-Tzu recorded that, "A military operation involves deception. Even though you are competent, appear to be incompetent. Though effective, appear to be ineffective."[1] I thought my army could hold its own in the incompetence and ineffectiveness parts of Sun-Tzu's philosophy. Similarly, in 1832, Carl von Clausewitz in his book *On War* advocated bold strategic offensives generated by the massing and momentum of quickly concentrated forces that were not averse to taking risks.[2] Again, my small army should excel at Clausewitz's risk-taking component. The initial plan was not pretty, but it was a decent plan nonetheless. I tried to dismiss Voltaire's comment in a letter to M. le Riche that *"Dieu est toujours pour les plus gros bataillons."*[3] But, in my experience, it was hard to refute that God is always on the side with the largest battalions. We were not a full complement of two rifle squads, let alone a battalion. God would need to send us a few armed angels.

When I went back inside, I assigned Juanita and Chauncey the task of infiltrating the tunnel to the tool barn and releasing the missionaries. I told them they must execute quickly and quietly to avoid prematurely arousing the guards outside. Then, with the help of the freed missionaries and using the dogs, if necessary, they were to overcome the outside guards by surprise, taking them as quickly as possible. Hopefully, successful in that endeavor, they were to continue through the tunnel to the main house and stand ready to assist in any action to subdue guards around the primary ranch buildings. Manco and his wife would approach the main barn across the fields from the west maintaining cover as much as possible. Concurrently, with Juanita and Chauncey's commencement of action from the east, Manco and his wife would use their bows to quietly eliminate the machine gunner on the barn roof. When successful in that, they could join the fight against the perimeter guards and anyone in the bunkhouse. Manco's uncle, Advari, and I would attack any perimeter guards and the bunkhouse using grenades, slingshots, rocks, and whatever else we had that appeared sufficiently incompetent, ineffective, and foolhardy, but nonetheless deadly enough to deceive and subdue our adversaries. General Patton would have loved the plan for its sheer audacity if not for its chances of success. Lt. Col. Custer would have been thrilled by the absence of any advanced scouting to determine the actual location and movements of the guards. The group liked the plan because I didn't tell them about the million contingencies that we might encounter—most of which were not in our favor.

Grenade Party

As I concluded my strategy briefing, I noticed Advari inspecting the smoke and concussion grenades. He had never seen either variety in active form. He had the safety pin halfway out of one before I calmly took the grenade away from him and reinserted it.

"I do not know how to use these," Advari admitted. "If you want me to use them, you should teach me now."

"You are absolutely right, little soldier. Take these two, and we will go outside to practice throwing them. Do not pull on anything or try to adjust any handles. Just hold them like you have them now. Does anyone else need a demonstration or refresher course on throwing grenades?"

My group wasn't shy. Everyone except Manco volunteered for grenade practice. Manco coached his wife and uncle on the fine art of "chucking" grenades while I supervised the remainder of the group. Fortunately, the villa had a large yard because my crew launched grenades in all directions depending on their arm strength. Grenades are deceptively heavy for their size, particularly to the novice. Experienced grenadiers will flip the safety handles off to gain throwing accuracy while feeling confident about releasing the grenade within the ten seconds (more or less) before detonation. I advised my group to throw the grenades with the safety pins and handles still attached, please, for my peace of mind, and to keep the yard intact and neighborhood quiet. Within twenty minutes, we damaged enough shrubbery and flowerbeds to confirm my belief that grenades were not our strongest offensive weapons. But, we demonstrated to my satisfaction that we could intimidate any perimeter guards within the sixteen-yard effective range of where a grenade might land.

After our grenade party, I instructed the group to turn in for as much rest as they could get before our pre-dawn departure. Although I didn't particularly need company, Juanita and Chauncey lingered with me on the porch. I looked up at the night sky, trying to identify the Southern Cross that should be directly overhead. I was surprised to see gathering clouds in the midst of Peru's dry season. In a few moments, I identified the four stars of varying brilliance that made up the Crux constellation. Having performed that simple task, I didn't feel completely incompetent and alone. However, I couldn't dismiss the feeling of uneasiness about this venture with so many unknowns and my untested strike force fighting against people with automatic rifles who were paid to use them effectively.

COMMAND JITTERS, NOTHING SERIOUS

"What's troubling you, old boy?" Chauncey asked. "You look unusually apprehensive."

"Apprehensive? Chaunc, when I went on military assignments with others, I used to call what I'm now going through pre-action jitters. I never felt them when I worked alone in the service because I was always confident about my invincibility as a twenty-something-year-old. On this exercise, I'm forgetting or not addressing things that may cause my amateur army real trouble."

"Such as?" Chauncey inquired as if he were an experienced field marshal.

"Such as, we cannot fly into the Quillabamba airfield even though it's far enough away from the ranch for us not to be seen from there. Calderon isn't the kind of person to neglect being informed about who comes and goes from the town airfield."

"I see what you mean, yes," Chauncey replied with his head down too for missing a fairly obvious piece of battlefield intelligence.

HELPING HAND FROM THE NEIGHBORS

"I have a lady friend who lives two ranches east of us. Our children go to school together, or did before Calderon forced me off the ranch. She has an airstrip on her ranch similar to ours. I could contact her now to tell her we are coming," Juanita offered.

"Is her family involved in the drug trade?" I asked.

"Certainly her husband is because she and I always had to meet or talk secretly to keep Alfredo and her husband from learning about our friendship."

"If your friendship is that strong, I'm sure she won't mind us flying in unannounced, assuming her husband isn't home to quash that possibility. It solves one problem and generates others. How far away is your friend's place? Is it within walking distance from your ranch? What kind of terrain and roads will we encounter? Can we get to your ranch from your neighbor's airstrip with all of our equipment without being spotted by a routine road patrol of Calderon's guards? Lastly, are we able to retreat safely if necessary?" I verbally itemized the unknowns as smoothly as if I were teaching a philosophy class using the Socratic method of asking questions until the students' cranial candles lit up.

"Oh dear, the distance is not far, but some hills are steep for us to climb with equipment. We need a truck from the neighbor's ranch. You certainly are thorough in your work," Juanita commented.

"Over the years, I've had good assistants who kept reminding me of similar details which otherwise would have shortened my career substantially. I learned from them. I don't have an assistant at the moment to keep me focused on the big picture while he or she takes care of the dangerous details."

"Are you canceling the exercise?" Chauncey inquired, afraid of whatever answer he might receive. "It would be a shame to come all this way without rescuing the missionaries."

"No, I'm only asking Juanita to arrange to borrow the neighbor's truck for a while after we land at her airstrip. After that phone call, I recommend we all turn in for as much sleep as possible."

Señora's phone call took longer than anticipated because her neighbor wanted to know Juanita's status after Calderon's people took up residence at the Quillabamba ranch. But, when Juanita finished, we had assurances that the neighbor's husband was traveling with Calderon. He would not be home to meddle with our plans or to inform Calderon about them. Second, we had permission to use the airstrip, and third, we could use the neighbor's truck for the next day's activities.

After that, we each went to our rooms, but I couldn't sleep. I amused myself for a while by dry firing my rifle out the window. My shoulder was stiff—very stiff, too stiff for the job. I'd take my rifle with me, but I'd depend on my handguns if I needed accuracy in my shooting. I had operated in this business too long to believe that our adversaries would give up their prisoners without a fight. I spent the remainder of the night oiling and checking the action of my revolver. Just holding it out in front of me in firing position was a challenge for my shoulder.

TERRORISTS AND THE TERCHOVA TREASURE

The gathering clouds of the night accumulated into an overcast and storm-threatening early morning. At 0400, everyone (including Advari) was awake and making final preparations. He circled his backpack in the middle of the floor several times trying to determine what he forgot to pack. Then, he decided that all he needed was to put his shoes on. Breakfast was a stand-up affair with people coming and going from the table as they snatched bits of food and went away to make last-minute preparations. Nobody questioned my decision for a pre-dawn flight to Quillabamba even though earlier we had planned a night raid. I needed to get my army into position, inspect the tunnels, and decide what changes to make depending on the disposition of our adversaries. I didn't want travel delays to cause us to miss our opportunity to free the missionary trio and recover the ranch for Juanita. Our preparations woke the girls. Isadora came flying in my direction. I gave her a big hug, whirled her around several times to make her dizzy, and handed her to her mother who gave all three girls hugs and kisses. It reminded me again that Juanita was taking a huge risk in coming with us. The girls would be in big trouble if she did not return to them. I made a mental note to take special precautions for Juanita to be away from the rough action after she showed us the location of the tunnels.

Chauncey had done some thinking too. Preparations completed, we left the house and drove to the airport at varying intervals in private cars, taxis, and a pickup truck so that we wouldn't look like an armed caravan and draw undue attention if Calderon had someone watching the villa. I rode in the car with Chauncey, Juanita, and Advari. The car was old and needed some body work. A hole in the floor alongside the gas pedal allowed the driver a clear view of the road underneath.

"Nice choice of vehicles, Chaunc," I said. "If the car stalls, we can keep going if you put your foot through the hole and push like a kid on a scooter. My wife had one of these before we were married. It was a great car and had excellent mileage downhill, but it was tough on her shoes, especially her right foot."

"Anything to give you the feeling of a full life, old boy," Chauncey responded cheerily over his shoulder.

At 0530, the last bag was on board the vintage aircraft we had for local flights, and everyone was buckled up, including the dogs. As we took off, we could see a light drizzle hitting the windows. This was unusual at the height of the dry season in Lima or anywhere outside the Amazon basin. Later, as we approached Quillabamba, the rain came down harder with no sign of letting up anytime soon. Juanita went forward to assist the pilot in locating the neighbor's airfield. Even with Juanita's help, we circled the field three times before the flight crew felt confident enough to attempt a landing. Juanita's neighbor must have heard our rumbling engines overhead because she turned on landing lights to outline the field as we made our last pass. We landed on a tarmac strip, but the wheels kicked up enough water to bring us to an abrupt stop at midfield. The crew did a nice job in keeping us from flipping over. An ancient U.S. Army deuce and a half (2.5 ton) truck driven by Juanita's friend came surfing out to meet us. The canvas top had only a few leaks, but by the time we transferred our equipment from the plane and climbed inside, everyone was soaked and shivering in the continuing downpour. The neighbor lady asked if she could do anything more for us. Juanita turned to me for guidance.

"Anything you can do to have the plane refueled and the flight crew ready for a quick getaway would be very helpful," I replied. "Initially, we planned a night attack on the ranch, but this weather may be better for us. We appreciate what you have done already. Pray that we are successful. Otherwise, Calderon and his men may visit your ranch soon. We'll have your truck back to you as soon as we can."

With that, I turned around to find Chauncey already behind the wheel. I motioned Juanita to take the middle seat in order to show us the way, and I squeezed in next to her on the starboard side. My other "raiders" were in back under the haphazard protection of the leaky canvas top. By the look in their eyes, the reality of the situation was beginning to register. Except for Manco, none of them had any previous experience at this kind of adventure. Chauncey did an admirable job staying on the winding gravel road and shifting gears up and down the slippery hills through the downpour with little help from the erratic windshield wipers and fogged windshield.

THE FIRST ASSAULT

After nearly thirty minutes of this craziness, Juanita announced, "Stop here, the tunnel entrance is across the river over the next hill."

"If you can, Chaunc, pull the truck into those bushes without getting stuck in case Calderon's men are patrolling the road in this weather. But, stay on the east side of the river to keep the truck from drowning if the rain continues like this throughout the day," I instructed. "Then, turn the truck facing the road if we need to make a quick departure."

By the time I jumped down and got around the back of the truck, my army was in the rain, unloading equipment. When I saw Manco and his wife with their bows, I was about to tell them to leave them behind in this kind of weather. But, when I saw his uncle shoulder three rifles, I decided not to say anything. We needed the gunner on top of the barn out of action, quietly if possible, with noise if necessary.

Another ten minutes elapsed before we marched across the road bridge and approached the last hill marking the beginning of Barrantes' ranch property. The tunnel entrance itself was in the base of a rectangular stone sentry post similar to three others at the corners of the property. They reminded me of the stone structures at the Inca ruins of Machu Picchu. The stones blended into the terrain so well that travelers passed by without noticing them or the high berms strategically placed to further disguise the tunnel entrances. Juanita pushed on a stone about knee high to open the trap door leading into the tunnel. The space below was large enough to accommodate my entire army. We were now surrounded by what looked and felt like four solid stone walls. Juanita moved a stone to reveal a lock in which she inserted her key. A section of the disguised steel wall slid sideways like an elevator door. The dank tunnel air that enveloped us confirmed that the passageway to the tool barn and other buildings was now open for our invasion. We were also out of the rain, which was small comfort with our wet clothes clinging to us.

I called a strategy meeting now that I had a better idea of the terrain and ranch buildings in relation to the tunnel system. If confession was good for the soul, this was my way of confessing that I was changing my entire plan of attack.

"Juanita," I asked, "where does the tunnel exit into the tool barn?"

"A section of the stone wall on the east side opens similar to the door we came through here, but it is only half as high."

"What are the chances for something to be piled in front of the tunnel entrance which would block our access to the barn?"

"We always parked a tractor there which partially hides the tunnel entrance while giving us access if we crawl under the tractor. If Calderon's people put something there, the entrance may be blocked. I did not think of that."

"Too late to worry about that until we try it. Where might the missionaries be in the barn in relation to the tunnel entrance?"

"Really anywhere. The large barn door for equipment is on the west side with a small door close to it. The farm tools and supplies are hung or stacked along the walls. The middle of the barn is empty space unless Calderon put something there."

"On a day like this, the guards are probably inside with the missionaries. From what you said, the guards are not separated by any barn structure from the prisoners. What are the chances that they could be slow to react to our actions for other reasons?"

"Drunk, you mean? The chances should be very good even this early in the day. We have an excellent local *chicha*, which is a fermented maize beer."

"Will the dogs attack on your command?"

"Yes, the problem is that the dogs will not know whom to attack if neither the guards nor the missionaries threaten them."

"Maybe a few dog bites will teach the missionaries to preach further north, or at least, not become friendly with the daughters of drug lords at *fiesta* time. In any event, I'm inclined to use the dogs for the initial thrust with Manco and me following. I expect that the reaction of the guards will present enough action for the dogs to identify their targets. Juanita, you stay by the entrance to instruct the dogs. The rest of you should be ready to back us up depending on what happens. Chauncey, you make the decisions for any backup actions if I am occupied elsewhere. Advari, bring the dogs up to the front. Let's go—quickly and as quietly as possible."

Advari distributed the flashlights he carried in his backpack, and my army marched single file through the tunnel. When we arrived at the barn end of the tunnel, I halted my army temporarily to permit Juanita to squeeze by to unlock the tunnel door to the barn. While the tunnel itself was high enough for the members of my army to walk upright, the small entrance would require each of us to bend over to enter the barn one at a time. Our invasion would look more like the single-file assault of the Second Rangers on Nazi gun emplacements above the cliffs of Pointe du Hoc at Normandy rather than an encirclement of the barn guards with a massed formation. *Divine intervention of any kind would be helpful now*, I thought to myself as I readied my pistol.

We paused a moment, Juanita inserted her key, and a bottom section of the stone wall silently moved sideways. Juanita gave the dogs the command to attack. As I hoped, the startled movement of the guards was all the dogs needed to identify the enemy. It was not much of an attack. It did not need to be. The effects of the *chicha* on the guards decided the outcome. We surrounded the two dazed guards as fast as we could get out of the tunnel with no exchange of gunfire, no noise that escaped the barn, and no time for the guards to alert the main house. The three missionaries, Steve, Scott, and Jim were chained in a semicircle to the wood floor of the barn. They had been trying to free themselves while their guards were occupied with their *chichas*. The missionaries' hands were bloody and blistered from using nails as small chisels to gouge at the floorboards holding the steel anchors of their chains. Otherwise, they were in good shape. We found the keys to the chain locks on the guards and promptly ordered the guards to exchange places with their former prisoners.

First Assault Success

"Are we glad to see you!" the missionaries all chimed in mid-level monotone. "We thought that everyone had abandoned us."

"We are overjoyed ourselves, but save any celebrations for later. We still have work to do for our mutual safety and your escape. As of now, you are recruits in my army that doesn't recognize conscientious objectors," I instructed them.

"What are your plans, old boy?" Chauncey asked. "We have the missionaries. We could leave now while everyone is safe?"

"While we're in the neighborhood and ahead of schedule, we should try to reclaim the ranch for Juanita. A short time ago, I made a graveside promise I intend to keep. Any objections?"

"Not from me," Chauncey consented. "But, can we do it without losing anyone from our party?"

"I have no answer to that. Anybody else? Good. Wait, Advari, what are you doing?"

"I could not find anything to use as gags, so I thought the guards might like to finish their drinks and take a long nap," he answered as he forced their mouths open and poured more *chicha* down their throats.

"That appears to be a variation of 'waterboarding' prisoners with alcohol, although I don't hear any objections. But the next time we take prisoners, use the duct tape I brought to maintain prisoner silence. Since they are already well on their inebriated way, get them drunk without drowning them if you can. Search them again and take anything that may be used as a weapon, a signal, or means of escape. Terrific.

Everyone keep thinking innovatively like Advari until we are on the plane homeward bound."

Next Objective

"Okay, listen up. The next objective is to take the main house. Juanita, can the guard on the top of the main barn see into the house?"

"No, but he has a clear view of the front porch and almost everything outside. What do you have in mind?"

"I'll tell you when we get to the tunnel entrance to the main house. Stay close to me, and Advari, you stay close to us with the dogs. Manco, you and your people come next. Chauncey, follow them and keep your eye on the trio behind you to ensure they are able to stay with the group after being restrained for so long. Better yet, you three stay here to ensure that the guards don't notify anyone of our arrival. Use the guards' weapons only if absolutely necessary to defend yourselves. Otherwise, knock the guards out to keep them quiet. Am I asking anything you can't do as Mormons?"

"Maybe, but we are defending ourselves and supporting you to help others, so we are okay with your instructions," Scott declared.

"Good, keep the faith. The rest of you, follow me," I ordered.

We retraced our steps to the barn tunnel, reconnected with the main tunnel, and aimed for the ranch house.

"Where does the tunnel exit in the main house, Juanita?" I asked along the way.

"In the pantry. The dish cabinet in the pantry swings inward. We were working on an entry into the game room, but that is not completed."

That information was good and bad. Calderon's *conserje* (foreman), Alva probably was in the game room, or in Alfredo's former office on a rainy day like this with some *chicha* of his own for company. He would immediately see us coming out of a tunnel opening into the game room and give the alarm before we had a chance to subdue him. Equally probable, we would be noisy entering the house from the pantry opening, and give *Conserje* Alva sufficient time to call for help from the bunkhouse. I could still cancel this part of the expedition, but I had traveled a long way to damage Calderon on behalf of Juanita and Jenny. It was worth a try to me, even if I had to do it alone. So far, my amateur army had performed well enough to give me confidence in their skills to continue this phase of the operation.

SECOND SUCCESS

When we arrived at the tunnel entry to the main house, Juanita put her key in the lock, and the pantry cabinet silently swung open. Destiny took over before we had a chance to reconnoiter or invade further. The dogs smelled familiar territory, burst through the tunnel opening before Juanita or Advari could stop them, and headed straight for the game room. Manco and I ran after them past the speechless cooks and arrived at the game room in time to see the dogs leap across the desk onto *Conserje* Alva. They didn't need any command from Juanita. They were attacking a trespasser on their home turf. By the time Juanita arrived and called them off, they had drawn blood. But, the dogs prevented any alarm or call for help by the *conserje*. Our luck and *karma* held. By this time, the remainder of my army arrived along with the cooks, who were overjoyed to see their mistress back in the house. My army took control of the prisoner from the dogs while the cooks all began talking at once and tried to touch and kiss Juanita in their excitement.

"Juanita, tell everyone to quiet down before a passing guard hears them," I commanded.

"Please, everyone, no noise, please," she repeated several times putting her finger to her lips.

With order restored, I asked Juanita, "How many of your trusted men are still here on the ranch?"

Juanita repeated my question in Spanish and Quechua-Aymaran to the cooks. Both their verbal answers and the fingers they held up confirmed that there were seven trustworthy guards.

"Okay, now how many total men are there on the ranch not counting *Conserje* Alva, the two guards we captured in the tool barn, and the barn gunner? Particularly, how many are in the bunkhouse?"

Juanita translated my question to the cooks. The verbal and finger count came back as thirteen. All the other *campesinos* had been transferred to the Tingo Maria ranch.

"How do you contact the bunkhouse from here, Juanita?" I inquired beginning to get the hang of what level of opposition we faced.

"Alfredo used the intercom on the credenza there," she pointed.

"Okay Juanita, tell the *conserje* the names of your seven trusted men who we want to come to the main house. We need to separate them from the others in the bunkhouse. He will call their names on the intercom to report to the main house for a work detail. They should bring their *panchos* and pistols. If he messes up, make him understand that he is dog food. *Comprehendo,* Señor *Conserje?*"

"*Si, si*, I call, okay. You see, I call okay," *Conserje* Alva repeated needing no more instruction to behave as prompted, especially with the dogs still growling and hungry for his hide.

I cocked the hammer of my revolver and put the muzzle under his chin to ensure that he had instant recall as he repeated the names of the men Juanita recited to him. Five minutes later, we counted seven *campesinos* in *panchos* making a mad dash in the rain from the bunkhouse toward the front porch. Under cover of the porch roof, they took off their *sombreros* and waited patiently for someone to give them orders. In the deluge, no other guards were walking the perimeter of the main buildings.

Organizing the Third Assault

"What do you intend to do?" Chauncey asked for everyone present.

"Hopefully, we have all the loyal workers on the porch. They will help us with the six remaining hands in the bunkhouse and the barn gunner. Initially, I thought we would take both places by force, but this heavy rain should allow us to accomplish both objectives without a fight or bloodshed. I don't believe we can reach the barn gunner from here with either arrows or slingshot, and a gun will alert the bunkhouse bunch."

"How will you get the barn gunner down then—fly up there like Angel Moroni?" Chauncey irreverently inquired for everyone again.

"It's a fine time to invoke Moroni. In the future, I'll be more careful about what comes out of my mouth concerning other peoples' religions. We will hold Angel Moroni in reserve for now. We will use the principle of asking Mohammed to come to the mountain if the mountain is unable to travel to Mohammed. Observe innovative audacity in action. Does anyone have a dark handkerchief or rag to stuff in Señor *Conserje's* mouth?"

One of the cooks found an abandoned, non-sterile, dark towel that promptly went into our prisoner's mouth with help from many hands.

When that task was completed, I instructed my army, "When I open the door, *Conserje* Alva will stand in the doorway so that he appears to be giving instructions to the men on the porch. From that angle, he won't be visible to the guard on the barn roof, nor to anyone watching from the bunkhouse. Juanita, when I open the door, I want you and the dogs off to the side so that your men hear but do not see you. You will be the one actually giving them instructions. Everyone else should be silent and have your weapons ready in case all of the men on the porch are not as loyal as we presume. Advari, slip out the back door, run around the east side of the house, but stay hidden. Use your slingshot on anyone running back toward the bunkhouse. Lives are at stake if you miss, so do not miss, little soldier."

"What do I say to the men?" Juanita asked anxiously.

"First, tell them to stand perfectly still. They should not talk, act surprised, or turn around. Then, tell them that you have returned to reclaim the ranch, but to do so, you need their help. Pick the one you trust most and instruct him to take the place of the barn gunner. Instruct him to inform the gunner to come to the house to supervise a work detail. The remainder should stay where they are on the porch for the moment and put their *sombreros* back on their heads again. That will make it harder for anyone watching from the bunkhouse to see what is going on and who is talking. When the barn gunner comes on the porch, the men should step aside briefly, then surround him, and take any weapons he has. We will see how well all that goes, and then improvise from there. Is that clear?"

"Yes, I am very nervous, but I understand," Juanita explained as she summoned her courage for the task at hand.

Activating the Plan

"Okay, Manco, open the door. But keep out of the line of sight with your pistol ready."

Manco opened the door as instructed and stepped back. The men on the porch let out a collective gasp as they saw their *conserje* with a gag in his mouth. Then, Juanita started speaking to the men quickly as only Hispanics can do in their native tongue. They immediately recognized her voice and could barely contain themselves. Fortunately, they held their places, and one of the older ones stepped off the porch and ran to the barn. Those who stayed on the porch put their hats back on. While the *sombreros* interfered with any view of us by the remaining men in the bunkhouse, the wide hats also interfered with my view of the gunner coming from the barn. But, as it turned out, my disrupted line of sight didn't matter.

Ranch Justice

The gunner never made it to the porch. Later, I learned that, in his off-duty time, the barn gunner enjoyed aggravating and molesting the kitchen help. Now, the teenage cook's helper took her revenge without checking with us first. Armed with one of Barrantes' shotguns from the game room, we later deciphered that she sped around the west side of the house to avoid Advari posted on the east side. As the barn gunner approached the porch, she stepped away from the back of the house, called his name, and fired both barrels at her oppressor. He caught the full charge and crumpled into the mud without taking another step. She stood over him in the pouring rain watching for any sign of life on which she could vent any remaining rage, but she had vanquished her tormentor with the first volley. Reacting to the noise and shock of what we had witnessed, the *conserje* threw his elbow and shoulder at my chin. With my weak arm, I couldn't prevent him from forcing my revolver up and away from him. But, reacting quickly, Manco calmly whacked the *conserje* on the back of the head with the barrel of his pistol and deposited him on the ornate Indian rug in the doorway. He would eventually regain consciousness with more than a sinus headache for his untimely and adversarial efforts.

I intended to use the seven loyal guards to help us against the six Caldcron gunmen in the bunkhouse after the barn gunner had been subdued. That plan was now useless because upon hearing the shotgun blast, the bunkhouse bunch grabbed their automatic weapons and came running toward the main house. The new arrangement turned out better than my planned actions, strengthening my rationale against over-planning any future adventures—as if I needed any additional incentives for improvisation.

The gunfire also brought the three missionaries with two automatic rifles running from the orchard tool barn. They may have improvised a cross using the two weapons, but, beyond that, I wasn't sure what they intended to do with the rifles. As the six *campesinos* approached the porch from the bunkhouse, I saw Advari slip behind them from the east. My army in the house, and the six loyal *campesinos* on the porch were directly in front of the late arrivals. With our loyal barn gunner replacement above and to the west of them, and the missionaries advancing from the tool barn merging with Advari from the south and east, the bunkhouse bunch was effectively surrounded. Our six porch loyalists drew back their *panchos* to display their covered pistols. The bunkhouse *campesinos* now recognized their predicament and stopped in their tracks as the rain beat down on them.

"What will you do with these men?" Juanita asked. "If they have a chance, they will kill us."

"That question needs a prompt reply, any suggestions?" I asked because my plan didn't include capturing so many guards.

"They cannot stay here. They will attack us as soon as you and Chauncey leave the ranch," Juanita cautioned again. "With these men around, I was always afraid for my girls and myself when Alfredo was not here."

"Okay, tell them to put their rifles down in front of them, step back four paces, and lay face down on the ground with their hands on the back of their heads. If they do not do it quickly, instruct your men to shoot them all where they stand. Advari, move off to the side so you don't catch a stray bullet. When they all get down, collect their weapons, but do not get trapped between them and us. If anyone tries to grab you, kick him in the head, very hard."

The six gunmen got down in the mud as ordered. Advari picked up their rifles without any problem and brought them to the porch. The question about what to do with them still remained now that they were unarmed and lying in the mud.

Samurai Showdown

"Chauncey, these men will drown if we leave them face down in the rain much longer," I said, trying to gather my thoughts. Do you know any trustworthy police force in the area who will take these six, the *conserje*, and the two in the tool barn into custody?"

"I'm afraid I'm not acquainted with the local police, but they allowed the *Senderos* to operate unhindered for years, and looked the other way when Barrantes and his neighbors expanded cocaine factories as much as they wanted. Charging these men with kidnapping and attempted murder will not mean much to the local police. Do you agree, Juanita?" Chauncey asked her for confirmation.

"Yes, we cannot rely on local police assistance. Even if the police were to take these men into custody, Calderon would have them released within a short time."

"How about the men themselves. Do they have farms and families?" I asked Juanita.

"Some do, others do not, I suppose. Alfredo managed the ranch with the help of the *conserje* without my involvement. I didn't have time to interview these men concerning their personal lives before Calderon forced me off the ranch. I believe at one time, they were all poor, illiterate farmers with few prospects for achieving anything in life beyond basic survival. Unfortunately, over the years they learned to hate, kill, and steal as a way of life. Otherwise, I would give them jobs here to help me hold and operate the ranch."

"You don't give me much hope of rehabilitating them. I chided Advari several times lately to be innovative. I guess now it's my turn," I said as I looked to the horizon. "I may have to adapt something from the Musashi School of Swordsmanship."[4]

Both Juanita and Chauncey looked puzzled as I expected they would.

"Juanita, please invite the men to stand up but tell them not to move from where they are standing. Manco, collect the pistols from the men on the porch. Take out all the bullets except one in each gun. Then, spin the cylinders so that the bullets are located randomly in the cylinders of the six pistols. While he is doing that, Advari, get my duffel bag will you?"

The men on the porch surrendered their pistols to Manco while his wife and uncle covered the six *campesinos* with their weapons. I glanced quickly over my shoulder at the horizon again. The heavy clouds were breaking up in the distance, and the late afternoon sun would be shining soon, I hoped. When Advari brought my bag, I took out my old .44 pistol with its holster, buckled it on, tied the leg strap, and unhooked the safety loop. For me, this gun had better balance for a fast draw than my .44 Magnum. The men on the porch who had seen my knife and gun show on my earlier trip murmured to their *compadres* about the crazy *gringo* and his gun tricks. I certainly had everyone's attention—including *Conserje* Alva who regained consciousness and was sitting upright on the porch floor.

"Manco, have the six men line up in a row facing me with an arm's length space between them. Then, put a revolver on the ground in front of each of them. If a puddle is there, get a flat rock or something to put the gun on to keep it out of the water. Keep the chamber of the guns pointed toward me so that the men do not see what chamber the bullet is in."

As I waited for Manco to complete his task, I could see a faint shadow behind each of the six men. Hopefully, the sun would break through the clouds completely and be in their eyes as they looked toward me.

"Juanita, now tell the men to feel free to reach for the gun on the ground and try to shoot me whenever they are ready within the next two minutes. If they take one step back and walk away within two minutes, they are free to go home. I will shoot to kill any of them who reach for the gun in front of them, or anyone standing there after two minutes."

The sunlight now was strong enough for me to see that the fourth man on my left had a bullet in the next chamber to fire. The fifth man had a bullet two chambers from the firing position. These two were my near danger and my most immediate targets. The bullets in the other four pistols were three or more chambers away from firing. This gambit as taught to me by the three sergeants decades ago was not about fast-draw skills. Ten against one was a Zen exercise to free a *samurai's* thoughts to look into the opponent's mind, determine what he was about to do, and force him to decide in your favor, or else. If the opponent tried to determine what was in the *samurai's* mind (mine in this case), he would only see a reflection of himself. He would not be able to deduce the *samurai's* (my) thoughts to adjust his actions or reflexes accordingly. Anyway, that was the theory. Within the next two minutes, I would see if the theory really worked against my six opponents. It needed to work because my right shoulder and arm did not have the range of motion or strength to overcome all six men if they decided individually or collectively to take their chances against me. In fact, I wasn't sure that I could draw and shoot accurately under the most favorable conditions. If the men rejected the mutual benefits of Master Musashi's Theory of Swordsmanship, I hoped that Amy's exercises would give me sufficient shoulder strength and range of motion to perform.

A few seconds later, I determined that I had achieved as much "oneness" within my being as I was likely to acquire in the present environment. My mind was not sufficiently disciplined to penetrate the skulls of my adversaries. While my mind dallied with the pointless thought that my holster had been handmade in Argentina, my eyes watched for any tensing of a muscle, a flicker of an eye, a change in facial expression, or actual body movement among the group I faced. At least my mind and body were not giving them anything that would disclose my intentions or next move. As Master Musashi taught, I looked straight ahead at the space between the third and fourth man, and let my peripheral vision observe the others.

Now, the sun was directly in my opponents' eyes, causing them the discomfort I intended. I remained relaxed but prepared. Then, the number two man stepped backwards. Number one quickly followed. I did not let my mind dwell on their surrender. I had the four most dangerous opponents still in front of me. Everyone heard the grandfather clock in the hallway of the ranch house chime the quarter-hour. Number three and five stepped back in response to the clock's warning of the fleeting time.

Number four and six went for the guns in front of them. They did not make it. An instant earlier, I saw number four shift his weight from his heels to his toes. My old .44 was clearing the holster, but my hand and arm were so slow in aiming that I would have had to shoot to kill rather than merely wound him.

Fortunately, Advari saw the same weight shift, and matched it by releasing a stone from his slingshot. The stone bounced off the back of number four's head, and deposited him face down in the mud before his outstretched hand could reach the pistol. That was the reason I had invited Advari on this trip—to be innovative, and to save lives—principally mine. I had learned a long time ago that at least one idiot in every crowd insists on challenging the official program. Now, we had only one challenger. Number six saw what happened, realized that if I didn't get him, the barn gunner or Manco would. He quickly converted to a non-belligerent. He realized that the official program was not to have a shootout. The idea was to give the men a chance to back away from an unfair fight (at least, I thought I had an unfair advantage), and to save face and their lives if Calderon confronted them about the details of their losing control of the ranch. Calderon might kill them in any event, but their blood would not be on my hands. I motioned with my gun for the five gunmen to pick up *campesino* number four, take him back to the bunkhouse with them, gather their belongings, and clear out. They had just resigned as ranch guards, and they knew it. They had wisely escaped the severance package they would have received if their terminations were involuntary. I hoped that when number four regained consciousness, the ridicule he received from his bunkhouse colleagues would sting more than Advari's slingshot stone.

The guards' departure would give Calderon something to think about when he learned of Juanita's return to the *ranchero*. As it stood, Juanita regained control of the ranch with only one extemporaneous shotgun blast by the cook's helper against the main barn gunner, Advari's non-lethal slingshot hit on one overly assertive *campesino* in the lineup, two orchard barn guards disabled by self-inflicted *chicha*, and one *conserje* overcome by the dogs. The ranch dynamics had changed sufficiently for the men loyal to Juanita and the neighbors to help her hold onto the ranch against Calderon or anyone else if the need arose in the future. Even neighboring ranchers who continued in the drug cartel did not want this kind of skirmishing on their properties. The neighborhood had good reason now to help keep Calderon away from the Barrantes ranch and theirs.

After briefly congratulating myself on the outcome of the "duel that wasn't," my Zen feeling of "oneness" departed. If I had been killed, no one else in my group had the experience and command authority to ensure that Juanita's return could be sustained against Calderon in the future. The Zen concept of "oneness" is great within one's personal sphere of action. Individually, I could face a life-threatening situation without flinching under Zen methods. But the concept doesn't consider the consequences of one's actions on others. I had learned that the Zen perspective is too narrow for joint action in my kind of work. If I had failed, the three missionaries would have been recaptured, and Juanita would not have regained her ranch in addition to incurring fatalities among the men loyal to her. Calderon would have retaliated against any or all involved in Juanita's defense, assuming he needed additional justification for more cruelty.

Fortunately, a middle reality settled in to mitigate both excessive jubilation and faulty philosophy.

"What will you do with this one?" Chauncey said as he pointed to the *conserje*, who was now standing up.

"Manco and his family, Advari, and I will take the *conserje* with us to Tingo Maria tonight. Before you and Juanita return to Lima, stay here overnight to officially reclaim the property, and set things straight with the cooks and the loyal *campesinos* who remain."

"What will you do with these three?" Chauncey asked smiling as he pointed to the missionaries.

"I think they suffered enough in this hemisphere. If you arrange their return to the States through the embassy, I believe that will be the best way to get them home. You can sort out their visa violations or any other administrative problems they may encounter. I need to say good-bye to them in a special way now though," I said as I walked them a short distance away, gathered them in a tight circle, and bowed our heads in prayer.

Before breaking the huddle, I asked them quietly, "Where are the lists?"

"We gave them to the immigration officer in Costa Rica," Jim answered.

"We didn't know what to do with them," Steve said. "After Calderon had his lists back, he had no further use for us. Our lives were worthless to Calderon after that, but we didn't know how else to defend ourselves."

"You had that right. The only reason you're alive is that too many eyes were on Calderon at the time from both sides of the fence. Be careful whom you trust now until you are safely home. Good luck. We'd better break this up. I have more traveling to do today."

As we rejoined the others on the porch, Juanita asked, "Do you need help returning to my neighbor's airfield?"

"If the river hasn't washed out the bridge or moved the truck downstream, we should be able to return to our plane. Thanks for your offer though. You have enough work here, and a little effort from your neighbors will keep you secure between here and your villa in Miraflores. We need to be on our way to Tingo Maria."

"*Muchas gracias* to all of you. I have my ranch back and trustworthy people to work with me again. You are welcome at this ranch any time," Juanita said to me softly. "Meanwhile, *vaya con Dios*, Joe Legion, or whatever your real name is."

"Thank you. I may be back sometime. Remind me not to visit during Peru's alleged 'dry' season. I'm still not sure what stars make up the Southern Cross. Teach Isadora and her sisters about astronomy so they can show me where the four stars of the Crux are located on my next visit."

"Yes, that is a good idea. I will. Good-bye, *adios*."

"Good-bye, old boy, once again," Chauncey seconded as he shook my hand.

"Easy on pumping my hand, my friend. The therapist up north will climb all over me for not doing my exercises as it is. I can't go back with a broken arm."

"I'm glad I didn't know how tender your arm was when you were playing gunfighter with Calderon's men earlier. Otherwise, I would have told them to shoot you. Take care of yourself in Tingo. Signal me when you are finished there. I will have a fast plane waiting to take you back to the States. You will have to make do with the old hulk between here and Tingo though. That is all the help I can give you now. I really appreciate what you have done for me, and I am eager to meet the Portuguese brothers you arranged to work with me," Chauncey added enthusiastically.

"Steve, Jim, Scott," I said apologetically, "I'm sorry I didn't deposit you at your homes the first time. Chauncey will manage your safe return from here. When you arrive at the Temple in Salt Lake, salute Angel Moroni for me, will you? I meant no disrespect, and I hope no offense was taken. More importantly, say a prayer for us too. We have serious work to do in Tingo and the Rio Huallaga area before I send Advari back to the Jesuits in Lisbon."

"Good-bye and good luck," they replied. "We are glad we have another chance to return to the States, although we will arrive later than we expected."

CROSSING THE RIVER

With the tethered *conserje* preceding him, Manco and his family, followed by Advari and me, retraced our steps to the neighbor's truck we had hidden by the river what seemed like a double eternity ago. The rain had stopped, but the river was much higher than when we crossed it earlier on our way to the ranch. The bridge was under an unknown level of rushing water. As we crossed while holding onto the handrail, we could feel the floor boards groan and complain as they tried to hold steady against the force of the current. With his rope collar and hands bound firmly behind him, Conserje Alva struggled against the treacherous current. Halfway across the bridge, the *conserje* foundered behind Manco instead of being in front of him. Manco was fully occupied keeping his wife and uncle on their feet in the turbulent water. I shuffled up to the *conserje* as quickly as I could, and cut the rope binding his hands. Three steps later, Advari tripped on floating debris and went down. He was losing his grip on the handrail when the *conserje* grabbed him and put him back on his feet as if he were a chess piece. The *conserje* turned to me, and I nodded in understanding. I had helped him, and he had saved Advari. I didn't need a philosopher to tell me what had occurred.

When we got to it, the truck was in water, but not floating. Manco's uncle started it up, and we slipped and slid our way onto the road and slithered toward the neighbor's airfield. With Manco and his wife also in the cab, Advari and I were alone in the back with the *conserje*. He did not speak, but our eyes met several times. This time under the Musashi methodology, I was reading his mind and heart easily—they were no longer with Calderon. I untied his neck rope. When we slowed down for a curve, *Conserje* Alva jumped out of the truck. He stood by the side of the road for a minute watching us as we continued on our way. Then, he went south across a soggy field. I didn't know for certain where he was going, but I knew he was no longer Calderon's *conserie* at the Quillabamba ranch. Equally important, he was no longer a threat to us.

"Thanks for your shooting skills back there, little soldier," I told Advari. "Our next stop will be harder, and we'll be performing with little or no sleep, with no extra help, and in the dark. I'd like to tell you that

I'll be watching you every minute, but you know that wouldn't be truthful. So, before we land there, get as much rest as you can, and prepare yourself mentally for whatever happens."

"My growing up in the streets of India taught me to be tough. You know that I am not afraid of anyone," Advari proclaimed.

"Yes, but your street companions in Chennai didn't teach you how to avoid being dead if we run into gunfire. If you see me go down, find Manco right away. If he goes down, run away as fast as you can. Get yourself back to Chauncey in Lima even if you have to walk all the way. He will help you return to Lisbon. Do not go back to Chennai—ever. You are destined to be more than a street urchin sleeping in the marketplace whether I'm around to see the person you become or not. *Comprendo?*"

"*Si*, Señor," Advari replied as I held him close for the brief moment he allowed me to do so.

The truck gouged deep furrows in the muddy road as we approached the neighbor's airstrip. I was selectively glad that the neighbor's drug trafficking income had been lucrative enough for him to pave his airstrip. Otherwise, we would never have been able to take off from a dirt or grass runway in this weather. The pilot and copilot came running from the house when they saw and heard us coming. The neighbor lady wasn't far behind them.

"Is Juanita all right?" she asked while still running toward us with a shotgun in her hand.

"Juanita is fine. She has control of the ranch, and Calderon's men are leaving. If you can do anything to help her keep the situation that way, I'm sure she will be very grateful. The five of us are leaving for Tingo Maria now to visit the cocaine ranch. We will not see you again, but I certainly will not forget the help you gave to Juanita and us," I explained while helping load whatever I could onto the plane. "You are a very brave woman to help us. I hope we have not created a problem for you when your husband returns."

"The other neighbors and I will take care of Juanita now that we are fully aware of what happened between her and Calderon. My husband will cooperate to keep Calderon and the corrupt *policia* out of our lives, or he will get this," she proclaimed while raising the shotgun menacingly. We will make sure that they do not cause any more problems for Juanita and us. *Muchas gracias*, Señor *Pistolero*, for helping us to start a neighborhood rebellion against the cartel. Good luck, and *vaya con Dios* on your way to Tingo Maria. If you cannot beat Calderon's men, at least, send as many of those heathens to hell as you can," she instructed me as we shook hands vigorously.

"Good-bye to you. I haven't heard a motivational speech quite like yours in my travels, but it's very effective. I wish you were going with us. Then, I would be certain of the outcome," I said as I released her hand and turned to my army. "If everyone is ready, let's get on with it. My shoulder is not getting any younger standing here."

Getting airborne even with the help of a paved airstrip was almost more than the ancient plane could manage. We used the entire strip before we lifted above the puddles and gained airspeed. After we were on a steady course northwestward, I paid the flight crew a visit.

"Thanks for waiting for us back there. I understand from Chauncey that you will deliver us to Tingo but not wait around. Is that your understanding?"

"Yes, we take you in, but not out," the pilot replied. "Inform Chauncey or whomever you need to get you when you're ready to come out."

"Tell your colonel thanks for getting it right this time. He and some other CIA yo-yos left us hanging last time with three missionaries in Bolivia. Oh, sorry, Chauncey told me I'm not supposed to know you're CIA," I said with false contrition.

"Assuming that we are CIA for the sake of discussion, how did you know?"

"By the odor. You guys hang around the scum of the earth so long before you shut down an illegal operation that you begin to smell like the scum you're chasing. Tell your bosses to get better operating procedures and a spine. Innocent people are hurt long before you have enough of whatever evidence you need to close down an illegal operation. Nonetheless, I understand your need for standard operating procedures in a large organization. Don't mind me. It's been a long day with a potentially longer night. So, pardon my manners, and don't take it personally as your colonel told me the last time we spoke."

My speech over, I went back to join my group. Manco and his family were checking their weapons. Advari was curled up under his blanket. I sat down, began checking and rearranging my equipment, and inserted my now mud-free derringer up my sleeve. Take care of your weapons, and your weapons will take care of you. I first heard that in basic training and never forgot it. The one thing I could have used was an ice pack for my shoulder. I hoped my shoulder wouldn't take my inattention to it personally. We had completed only half of the assignment with possibly the roughest half still to come. I decided to talk to Manco before I started feeling sorry for myself.

Manco's Intelligence Briefing

"Manco, if Calderon has thirty to forty *pistoleros* at the Tingo Maria ranch, we need to talk about how to cause maximum damage to his buildings and equipment without getting ourselves killed. Calderon will have perimeter guards out in any kind of weather at that location. At first, I thought about using fire arrows to set the buildings on fire, but that approach might not be possible if it's raining hard. Because we will be closer to the rain forest, we are more likely to have rain there than in Quillabamba. Can we get near enough and past the perimeter guards to use arrows, grenades, and smoke without getting ourselves trapped?"

"I say yes we go on ranch, but we have big trouble to get close to cause hurt or to run from guards when they see us. If Ron is here, he surely says no we need more people to fight this *ranchero*. So, I ask you, Señor, do you know this *ranchero* okay to fight? How do you bring us close to fight?" Manco both confirmed the legitimacy of and repeated the same question I had asked him.

Manco's recitation of my question in his partial English and Quechua-Aymaran dialect fired my brain jets sufficiently to recognize that if I didn't design the strategy and tactics for this operation myself despite my skimpy knowledge of my enemy or the terrain, nobody else was available who could. I opened my mouth, and words came out unaided by any brain synapses.

"Manco, when I was at the *ranchero* my first time, Barrantes took me down a lane from the barn until we reached a swale coming from the woods at the back of the ranch," I began as I drew a sketch of the *ranchero's* layout from my foggy memory. Peccaries use the swale as their personal racetrack. I believe that we need to circle the property, and come in from the back through this swale. I don't know how much time we will need to walk to the ranch in the dark from the airport if the fields are muddy. If Calderon's guards see us, we are dead ducks before we get near the place. If we complete our assignment at the ranch, we still need to come back to the airport. We might be able to retrace the same route coming out unless you know a better way. But, if they are smart, any remaining guards will block our return to the airport regardless of how successful we are in attacking the ranch."

"We take hostages, yes?" Manco asked astutely (at least that's what emerged from my translation) with both his uncle and wife nodding vigorously in support of his idea.

"Good, but hostages can either help or slow us down. Let me think a minute."

Manco ignored my need to think and continued, "Ron says you have big trouble to do much by self. You ask no help from no people then. Ron says I must tell you this truth when we come here in trouble."

"I can imagine the words Ron used to inform you of my alleged strategic planning prowess. But, I am sad that you and Ron identified my ability to deviate from an initial plan as a weakness. I believe I have a unique skill that many corporate executives don't possess. But, the Lord knows, and so does Ron, that I'm always willing to listen to rational input from experienced people such as Ron and you. So, tell me again what thoughts you and Ron have on this operation?" I asked, attempting to excavate any helpful, Andean-style, guerrilla strategy or tactics from Manco's skull.

"You listen for sure to me?" Manco asked in mid-level disbelief.

"Certainly, otherwise I'd be taking a nap with Advari. But, speak clearly and slowly. My slow Spanish with your rapid-fire Aymaran dialect is another problem Ron should have explained in greater detail to you. But, we have no time for language classes now."

"Okay, Manco says true, but you may say no good. But, it is so. You and señora not only people hurt by Calderon," Manco continued. "One night, Calderon and his people push me from family land by Titicaca. Sometimes, my people die, some hurt. Now, my people and I go here and back, but have no home. So, Calderon and his people must die for Manco to have land for family one time again. You understand Manco?"

"Yes, I couldn't have said it more eloquently. You have personal reasons to destroy Calderon's operation. We are brothers in our work tonight. Thank you."

"We more big than brothers. All we here family, yes? I tell Ron we go with you to Tingo Maria. He says I bring my people to help at ranch, yes. Seven days now, your Chauncey friend brings my people to Pucallpa close by Tingo Maria. Then, they walk in jungle to come near to *ranchero*, hide in jungle, and wait when we come there."

"How many people do you have waiting, Manco?"

"Ten people Manco has," he said holding up ten fingers to confirm the number. "People know guns, arrows, spears, have hands too, good enough, yes?"

"I could have used this information sooner, but it is good enough, yes," I confirmed while nodding my head vigorously.

"Ron says no tell you early because you better when you not know what you do," Manco said, not quite knowing whether I would accept his statement with a laugh or frown.

"That sounds different than what you told me a few minutes ago, but never mind that now." I laughed to deliver Manco from his uncertainty. "You said your men know 'how to use guns,' but do they have guns?" I pressed Manco to ensure my future serenity if guns became the preferred implements of all-out war at the *ranchero*.

"Not all people now; some my people have bows. But, we take guns from *campesinos* when we come close," Manco announced confidently.

"How do you arrange that? Do you ask the guards politely to borrow their weapons for a while? That sounds like the Russian Army strategy in the winter offensive against the Nazis in World War II at Stalingrad. Are you sure, Manco?"

"I do not know all you say to me, but on guns, Manco says yes. My people and I learn much from Korubo tribe in deep jungle to kill good. Korubo have blowguns and darts with *curare*."

"Hello," I exclaimed as the thought of a potential new weapon entered our discussion. "Manco, do you know about *curare* and how to use it?"

"We know *curare*, yes," he answered. "See black paste here in jar? This is *curare*. Makes monkey body stiff, and monkey no can breathe, so fall down from trees when we hunt."

"Manco, *curare* is great on monkeys and other small game, but is it good for *campesinos* to go to sleep, but not dead?" I asked a little surprised that I was adapting to his speech pattern after only a few minutes. "Manco, how do you administer, ah, sorry, how do we give *curare* to ranch guards?" I asked with rising skepticism because we had gotten off the subject of guns and were now discussing monkey poison.

"We mix other poison name of *barbasco* from roots in deep jungle. We have *rotenone* roots to make more strong, yes, you know them?"

"I know *rotenone* is used to kill fish here. I think we use it or a derivative as an insecticide in the States. *Barbasco* is new to me. Have you ever used venom from the Brazilian wandering spider or the Australian taipan snake? I understand that those are permanent solutions to all problems with many species, including humans."

"What you want from poor Manco? I do not understand what you tell me?"

"No, Manco, snake and spider poisons are too potent for us to use on *campesinos*. I should not have mentioned them. I have something more important for you to listen to me. Will you and your people use poison arrows on *campesinos* who have guns?"

"Yes, we hide to shoot arrows. *Pistoleros* no see us, good, yes?" Manco announced defiantly.

"What happens if the *pistoleros* shoot all of you with their automatic rifles before you have a chance to use your bows?" I objected rhetorically. "Never mind, set that aside too. I will think of something."

"Manco, going back to the hostage idea you proposed a few minutes ago, I recalled seeing a customs office at the airport on my earlier trip there with Barrantes. A customs office makes financial sense for the government to have a source of income from all the outbound packages from the Tingo Maria drug factories to Leticia in Colombia, Tabatinga in Brazil, or Macara in Ecuador. A customs officer could retire early and live comfortably after being posted here for only a few years if his eyesight and hearing are poor at the appropriate times to satisfy the cartel's shipping needs."

"What do you say to me again?" Manco interrupted after getting a taste of my obfuscation skills, developed over many years of night school after working full days trying to solve other people's problems. "I think some time Ron is hard for Manco to know, but you more hard still. I have much trouble with you to listen good."

"Let me simplify for you if I can, Manco. I say we take the customs officer at the Tingo airport as a hostage when we arrive. Then, we use him and his car or truck to take us to the ranch and back. If your people watch from the jungle, we can shoot a fire arrow into the air or set a barn on fire to alert them to join us. Well, Manco, that is my first and final plan, because we are approaching the Tingo airport now."

"Where do you want us to let you off," the pilot shouted from the cockpit as we taxied from the runway following a smooth landing in a light mist and gathering dusk.

"At the front door, if possible," I shouted back.

"Are you nuts?" the pilot responded. "Customs will see everything we have on board."

"No, I'm Caucasian, not nuts. Well, maybe both. Can't you tell? If you noticed, we didn't make a surprise landing, so we may as well introduce ourselves to the airport officials. You are welcome to stay and hide whatever contraband you have stashed on the plane, you can watch, or you can join us inside if you want." I added options for the cockpit crew now that I had some options myself for waging war on Calderon's Tingo *ranchero* thanks to Manco's mangled English but helpful thinking.

"No thanks. Uncle Sugar doesn't pay us jungle pilots enough to watch or participate at parties like you're planning."

"Well, thanks for the ride anyway," I said as I threw a jacket at the lump under Advari's blanket to wake him up. "Before you folks fly off, let me use your radio to call Chauncey for another air cab to replace you guys, unless you really beg to hang around for our return flight. One way or another, this operation will be quicker than I initially anticipated. Do you mind hanging around long enough for me to introduce myself inside and arrange local transportation? That way, my team won't need to stand in the rain outside while I get acquainted."

"Okay, but make it quick. If you're not back by the time we refuel, we'll throw all your stuff off and leave. We want to be back in Lima in one piece before daybreak," the pilot notified me with no room for negotiation.

Chapter Notes

1. Cleary (translator), *op. cit.*, p. 48.

2. Colonel J.J. Graham (translator), Carl Von Clausewitz *On War*, (New York: Barnes & Noble Publishing Co., 2004), p. 145 *et. seq.* By permission of Barnes & Noble.

3. Harold Whitehall (editor), *Webster's New Twentieth Century Dictionary of the English Language Unabridged* (New York: Standard Reference Works Publishing Company, Inc., 1956), p. 212. Also, Bartlett (compiler), *op. cit.*, p. 325 citing Voltaire's letter to M. le Riche.

4. King, *op. cit.*, p. 119.

CHAPTER 11

TANGO AT TINGO

CUSTOM-MADE HOSTAGE

Manco released the plane door with its built-in steps, and he and I stepped down followed quickly by Manco's wife. I was about to object, but I decided that her presence could disguise our initial move on the local customs office. Besides, she had a sawed-off shotgun concealed under her brightly colored *pancho*.

"If your wife is riding shotgun for us, Manco, I think I should know her name, don't you?"

"Maya," Manco said tersely as he opened the door to the terminal lobby.

Maya had long dark hair in double braids, and the features, clothes, and demeanor of an Andean Indian woman, but that's where the resemblance ended. She was pure soldier beyond that: slim, tough, quiet, and deadly—an Aymaran Alice Bright Feather.

"Can I help you?" Customs Agent Tambos inquired of Manco and me as we presented ourselves in front of his desk after reading his nameplate on the door and squeezing into his snug office.

"We need to talk to the customs director immediately," I replied in a level voice.

"I'm afraid that will not be possib—" Agent Tambos started to say before he saw my Responder badge and one of my doctored identification cards flash briefly in my hand.

"We are authorized by our superiors in Lima to be forceful if necessary to resolve a serious health problem in Tingo Maria and elsewhere," I stated authoritatively.

Manco and his wife looked confused and surprised when they heard me change the script as the curtain went up on our play. I could hardly wait to hear what would escape from my mouth next.

"Follow me, please," Agent Tambos adjusted his answer and started toward the customs director's office.

Customs Director Pevas looked upset as we and Agent Tambos burst into his office. At that hour of the evening, he probably was completing some minor chores before leaving for home. Our interruption minutes before he closed his office had to be irritating at best. That was fine with me if he gave us what we needed without being particular about the details of my authority to hijack him and his staff for my personal war against Calderon's drug operation. He received more of an upset from my ambiguous introduction as a health inspector who represented certain cartel lords in Lima and buyers in the States. I couldn't help it if officials reached uninformed conclusions without thoroughly examining the badges and ID cards that I presented for their cursory review.

"We need to borrow you and your vehicle for a little while," I explained. "You have a serious health problem at the former Barrantes ranch, which is adversely affecting certain shipments to the States. The receivers of those shipments are concerned, and they want the situation resolved immediately. They sent me here to resolve the problem quietly and expeditiously. But, do not be anxious. If things go well, you should be home for breakfast sometime."

"What vehicle do you want?" Director Pevas asked, dumbfounded at my request and the authoritative tone in which I delivered it.

"We need your car for you, me, and one of my associates. Agent Tambos can ride in the van with my other associates. We're not going far, but we may as well be comfortable and practical as possible, don't you agree?"

"My agent and I cannot leave the airport unattended," the director objected like a seasoned bureaucrat.

"Allow me to provide additional information that may help you understand the situation. If necessary, I have authority to close the airport until we resolve the problem. Besides, you do not have another scheduled flight before noon tomorrow, according to the arrival sheet posted in the lobby. Do I need to know about any unscheduled flights before then?"

"Very well, but you better know what you are doing. Otherwise, I will alert Señor Calderon or my superiors in Lima immediately."

"Alert whomever you like, especially Calderon—after we finish. Calderon or your customs superiors will not be pleased with you if word of this problem leaks prematurely and to the wrong people. That will hurt Calderon's and the cartel's sales in the States, and neither of us want to be responsible for that kind of career-ending and life-threatening mistake," I assured the director.

Director Pevas certainly didn't delay in informing us what payroll was more important to him when he mentioned Calderon's name before identifying his customs superiors in Lima. Calderon would not have appreciated top billing if my army and I were genuine anti-crime agents. Being outnumbered at the moment, the director got up from his desk, and led Maya and me to where the customs vehicles were parked at the rear of the terminal. Meanwhile, Manco went back to the plane to alert the crew and to collect his uncle, Advari, and our equipment. Maya did an excellent job of getting into the back seat of the car without exposing the shotgun still hidden under her *pancho*.

When we were comfortably seated in the car, Director Pevas asked, "Where are we going?"

"We need medical equipment from our plane, so drive there first. Then, we can drive directly to the ranch. We need to act without attracting attention," I cautioned.

The director drove around the terminal building to the plane and waved Agent Tambos in the van to drive closer for us to load our equipment. Fortunately, Manco had the presence of mind to camouflage the guns, grenades, and ammunition boxes with other stuff before our new hosts saw what kind of "medical" equipment we were unloading from the plane. So far, my revised plan was effective in requisitioning a ride instead of hiking to the ranch, and in giving us some "official" status without gunfire on either side.

"When we arrive at the ranch," I told the director as we waited for the last of the equipment to be loaded into the van, "please introduce us to the *conserje* as inspectors representing U.S. buyers. We examined other cartel facilities, and we strongly believe that a bacterial problem in the product is coming from the Barrantes, sorry, the Calderon facilities here in Tingo Maria."

OFFICIAL ARRIVAL

I was alert for any trickery as we neared the ranch, but I perceived no misfires in the director's actions. The rain had passed, but the lingering clouds brought on darkness early as we drove up to the front entrance of the *ranchero*. Two armed guards with hostile dogs blocked our way at the front gate. Maya confirmed for me that Director Pevas accurately informed the guards that we were here to see *Conserje* Cerro in an official capacity as medical inspectors. I flashed my unnumbered Responder badge at the guards to corroborate the director's description of our identity. The guard dogs remained skeptical. Fortunately, we did not have to deal with them. In short order, the gate was opened, and our car and the van were waved through. Director Pevas drove to the front patio and stopped, but I motioned for him to turn the car around to face the front gate. Manco, as driver of the van, replicated our movements.

While Agent Tambos and my army stayed in the van, Director Pevas, Maya, and I got out of the car and walked toward the front door of the main house. I suspected that Director Pevas followed my instructions hoping that I would inadvertently disclose my fraud, inciting the ranch crew to deal with me directly and harshly if my story did not check out with *Conserje* Cerro. Maya found a clipboard and some official-looking documents in the back seat of the car to lend credibility to her presence.

Lights were on in the house and surrounding it. Two guards embracing their assault rifles were positioned on the patio. Undoubtedly, the guards at the front gate had alerted the main house and possibly the bunkhouse of our arrival. A hulking shadow, which I presumed outlined the *conserje*, was located slightly behind the guards and out of the direct light so that he could see us without being observed himself.

As we approached the tall shadow on the porch, I instructed the director, "Repeat to the *conserje* the same information you told the guards at the front gate. That should be sufficiently convincing."

When we were within a few steps of the porch, the hulking shadow moved into the light to reveal the meanest critter I had seen outside of the deep jungle. This wasn't going to be easy. As Director Pevas repeated the script for *Conserje* Cerro, I flashed my Responder badge and ID card more quickly than usual. But, *Conserje* Cerro was acquainted with all the local customs officers, and Pevas and Tambos added more credibility to our party than any of my badges or documents. *Conserje* Cerro temporarily bought the story, but the automatic pistol in his waist holster reminded me not to become overconfident or careless.

"What do you want from us?" the *conserje* asked in Quechua so harsh that I could have struck a match on his lips.

Director Pevas and Maya translated the *conserje's* response into Spanish for my benefit. Then, they waited, looking at me for further instructions. Out of the corner of my eye, I saw Manco looking at me too with

TERRORISTS AND THE TERCHOVA TREASURE 325

a slight smile of amusement on his face. *Okay, don't help,* I thought. *I'll come up with something by myself. You'll see,* I mentally pouted.

"Señor *Conserje*, the product that the buyers are receiving in the States is contaminated," I started. "We believe that the contamination is carried by bacteria from the fields or the workers who handle the product on this ranch. We inspected other facilities and have good reason to believe that the contamination comes from this facility. We need you to assemble your workers—including cooks, guards, processing people, everyone on the ranch—so that we can conduct a brief medical test that will determine if they are sources of the bacteria. I am sorry that we came at an inconvenient time, but we have been checking other processing facilities across the region as quickly as we can to stop the contamination before the cartel loses customers in the States. When we finish identifying the source and eradicate the contaminant, we will report to the buyers that they can receive shipments again. I understand that Señor Calderon is away, and we want to eliminate this problem before he learns about it and becomes anxious concerning operations at the *ranchero*."

That completed my speech. It was the best presentation of my career. I almost believed it myself. I hoped *Conserje* Cerro and Director Pevas believed it long enough for us to cause damage and escape from the ranch. I glanced at Manco. He appeared interested in what I would do next so that he could report any gaffes to Ron if we survived long enough to relate them to anyone. Maya had her hands under her *pancho*. I was relieved that she was alert and on guard with her shotgun, although I assumed I wouldn't be the first person on her list that she would defend.

FIRST CAMPESINO DRUG TEST

"What tests will you do?" our *conserje*-hulk asked.

"Excellent question, Señor *Conserje*; let me explain," I replied, really into my role now. "First, we swab a liquid in the mouth of each worker. If the worker does not taste anything, that worker is not contaminated. If the worker tastes something, we will swab his or her mouth again with another liquid. If the worker feels a numbing sensation in his mouth within a short time, that person has been exposed to the contaminating bacteria. The greater the degree of numbness the worker feels, the greater the degree of contamination. If some are really sick, we should have vehicles ready to take those workers to the hospital immediately. If the contamination is widespread, we may need several vehicles to get everyone to the hospital quickly. So, Señor *Conserje*, while you gather your workers, we will prepare the test liquid and equipment. Please do not overlook anyone, including yourself, because that person may be the very one who is contaminated. Director, please help explain it again to *Conserje* Cerro, and let me know if he has further questions. If not, I will help my people set up the tests while the *conserje* tells the workers what needs to be done. We should be able to complete our examination in a short time with your cooperation and consent of *Conserje* Cerro."

I thought that if Director Pevas repeated my instructions to the *conserje*, the director would establish a greater level of credibility than I could as a stranger. The director again would appear to be part of our program rather than a hostage of it.

Manco looked at me as if I had really overplayed my hand this time and deserved to be buried up to my neck in an anthill. I probably did, but the plan was better than a gunfight, which we had a significant chance of losing. I motioned for Maya and Manco to accompany me to the van where his uncle and Advari were standing with Agent Tambos.

"Manco, ask Agent Tambos to help the director and the *conserje* assemble the workers. Then, have him check all the buildings to ensure that everyone is present for the testing, especially the gate and perimeter guards."

"I wish Ron was here," Manco whined.

"I do too," I responded. "I'm sure he'd be enjoying himself. But, what we don't need now are attitude problems that may cause these people to kill us all where we stand. Got it?" I instructed Manco, quietly though sternly.

Manco was surprised by my quick change in demeanor and promptly aligned his head with the official program.

"What do you want us to do?" Manco inquired for himself and the others of my team.

"We need swabs from the medical kit, and a bottle of the *pisco* sour brandy your uncle has been hoarding. That will be our first test, which will make everyone taste something and require them to be retested. Manco, for the second test, dilute a small amount of *curare* or *barbasco* with water, *chicha*, *cerveza*, or something—anything. We need it strong enough to tingle or temporarily paralyze their tongue and throat muscles to make them think they are contaminated with the bacteria. Hopefully, we will be able to send all of them to the hospital and have unhindered access to the ranch. Maya, please stand guard to ensure nobody interrupts Manco while he mixes this stuff."

"What if I make too strong?" Manco objected. "Some people die bad hurt."

"Understand this, Manco. Señora Barrantes told me that these men are killers. They are not to be trusted. You told me that Calderon's men ran your family off its land. Some of these men probably come from poor families and are only trying to stay alive. But they chose to join Calderon when they could have stayed with Señora Barrantes, returned to their family farms, or tried another line of work. I'm not God or a chemist, Manco, and neither are you. We're trying to save their lives, our lives, and the lives of addicts in the States from the poison that comes from this ranch. We are doing the best we can to shut down this drug farm, if only for a little while. So, mix the *curare*, *barbasco*, or *rotenone* with whatever ingredients we have, and let's do our job before we are discovered."

"I make soft drink with *chicha morada* to give different taste from *pisco*," Manco asserted.

"Good thinking, Manco, that's better," I cheered him on, "because the *morada* is not a carbonated drink, they won't belch as their throats tighten up. That is very good thinking. Do it as quickly as you can, Manco. Advari, you and Uncle here (I still didn't know his name) come with me. Uncle, you stand guard over the *campesinos*. Be ready to shoot if something goes wrong. Advari, collect any guns from the men after I give you the signal. Meanwhile, find some stones for your slingshot and watch my back, please."

With my team busy, I went back to the porch as men filtered into the yard from all directions. No women resided on this ranch, which I hoped would lighten Manco's conscience if he blended his *curare* formula with too much octane.

"Director Pevas," I addressed my hostage, who acted more like a member of my team every minute, "I would appreciate your help in telling *Conserje* Cerro of something very important. At some of our other locations, we had reactions to the tests. Some of the men became anxious when they began to feel a mild tightening in their throats. For this reason, we strongly advise that all weapons be collected on the porch until the tests are completed. Will you do that?"

"Yes, certainly. I will do so immediately," he responded as he turned toward the *conserje* who had moved back onto the porch.

"Good, but before you do that, I need you to understand and help me with one other thing. We are certain that we will obtain a number of reactions from this group. All the evidence we have points to this place as being the source of the contamination. I expect that some of these men will require medical care. I would like you to inform the *conserje* to have two other trucks brought here in case we discover major contamination. If you and Agent Tambos can be available to drive the trucks to the hospital, we will have maximum protection in an emergency. Would you agree to help us?"

"Yes, you can count on our cooperation. I will inform *Conserje* Cerro immediately unless you have something else."

"Thank you. If you remind him once more to have the men bring any weapons to the porch that will be helpful. I believe that we have everything else in order now."

As I stood on the porch with the director and the *conserje*, thirty-five men shuffled to the porch to stack their guns and formed into three rows in the yard. I watched Agent Tambos go from building to building to confirm that everyone inside had assembled in the yard. The gate guards arrived in a truck while leaving the dogs to guard the entrance. *Conserje* Cerro instructed the gate guards to drive around the property to pick up the perimeter guards. When they returned, we assembled the men into four rows with ten men in each row. The men we believed were directly involved in cocaine processing were in the first two rows. This was a sizable staff for a ranch I calculated as about two-thirds the size of the Quillabamba property. But then, one was a working tea ranch while the other was a labor-intensive cocaine factory with heavy emphasis on security and night operations.

Manco signaled that he was ready to administer the first "test" dosages. I nodded to the *conserje* to inform the workers about the nature of the tests again and the reactions they might experience. I had the director explain the importance of containing the contamination before the product was shipped internationally. Otherwise, international buyers would demand that the operation be shut down and all of them would lose their jobs, or worse. I could tell from the reaction of the workers that they understood the consequences of our tests on their livelihoods. Then, I nodded to Manco and Maya to start the first test by swabbing the *campesinos'* mouths with the *pisco* sour brandy.

Maya began in the first row while Manco started in the third. Each would administer the test to half the men. We had overlooked how attractive Maya was especially to men who had not been around women for a while. The third man in line reached out and grabbed Maya around the waist and pulled her toward him. That was the wrong reaction to the test.

Maya spit in the aggressor's face, stomped on his foot to make him bend over, raised up to hit him in the jaw with the top of her head, and finished with a knee lift to his groin—all simple, but effective maneuvers that I had taught all my Scouts too. As Maya backed away from her attacker, Uncle moved in, drew his pistol, and shot the dazed man. That stopped all conversations and movement of any kind among the test group. Now, they had actual confirmation that our testing was serious business. The fact that none of the men cared about their fallen *compadre* indicated to me the men were hardened killers. The sight of death no longer awed them.

When Maya finished with her two lines, she came to the porch and administered a dose to the *conserje*. He tasted it as if it were something familiar, but he couldn't recall what it was at the moment. I nodded for *Conserje* Cerro to ask the men to raise their hands if they had tasted anything. Thirty-nine hands went into the air with the dead man abstaining. The *conserje* hesitated, then, he raised his hand too.

SECOND CAMPESINO DRUG TEST

"That is incredible," Director Pevas exclaimed. "Can it really be true? Everybody is contaminated!"

"We will find out for certain in the next test," I said. "I warned you that this might happen. I am positive that this ranch is the primary source of the contamination," I reiterated. "You probably should get the vehicles ready for a quick evacuation to the hospital."

Both the director and the *conserje* now had worried looks on their faces. News of this certainly would get out, and neither of them wanted to be the recipient of Calderon's or the cartel's angry responses. I left the porch and walked over to Manco, who looked more than a little shaken. Uncle and Maya joined us.

"Manco," I hissed at him, "get a grip on yourself. We are almost finished," I instructed. "Does your diluted two-poison combination react as quickly as uncut *curare*?"

"No," Maya answered for him, "it is slower by a little bit, but more potent."

"Okay, mix a stronger batch to give to the men in the first two rows. Doing so will make it appear that the workers most involved in cocaine processing are the most contaminated. Hopefully, you will have time to swab everyone before the reactions start. With luck, we will have a majority of the group eligible for the hospital. If you are calm now, I will go back to the porch. Maya, after you finish with your last person, remember to come to the porch and swab the *conserje*. Give him a heavy dose. We want an especially strong reaction from the big gorilla because he will influence what the others do. Uncle, thank you for your watchfulness. You may have saved our lives in that situation as well as Maya's dignity, although she looked like she had the situation under control."

I slowly walked back to the porch to give Manco time to blend the diluted poison doses. When I arrived, Director Pevas was pacing back and forth with obvious nervousness. *Conserje* Cerro was more controlled but kept swallowing every few seconds to rid himself of the taste of the *pisco* sour brandy (white grapes, lemon juice, sugar, and bitters) that he probably drank on many occasions without hesitation. Agent Tambos joined the group on the porch and tried to contain any emotion or reaction by tightly crossing his arms over his chest. I looked at Manco, who nodded that he was ready.

"Gentlemen, if you are ready, we are. Director, please inform Señor *Conserje* that the men should go to the trucks immediately if they feel a reaction. My team will make an initial assessment, but anyone who has a reaction of any kind should go to the hospital without delay to have prompt medical attention. Agreed?"

Each confirmed his agreement by vigorously shaking his head. *Conserje* Cerro restated my instructions that the men should go to the trucks right away if they had a reaction. He ridiculed the men who might be alarmed about a little tickle in their throats. We would see how much of a tickle he could tolerate soon enough.

Maya and Manco started the second round of swabbing. They quickly swabbed the first two rows without any immediate reaction among the nineteen recipients with the dead man abstaining again. Halfway through their rounds in the third and fourth rows, several men in the first and second rows began to cough. The *conserje* swore at them for being babies and giving in to a little throat irritation. Maya and Manco finished at about the same time. Maya came to the porch to swab *Conserje* Cerro's throat. He clenched his fists hard and opened his mouth. Maya administered a hardy dose. The *conserje* blinked and held his ground, but only for a minute. He grabbed his throat, threw up, and ran for the nearest truck. With that example, all the men broke ranks and ran for the trucks with the dead man abstaining for the third time.

"Director," I said calmly, "I was afraid of this. You and Agent Tambos better get these men to the hospital. My people will stay here and test the buildings for sources of the contamination. If contamination is widespread, we have no choice but to torch the buildings immediately."

I said the last sentence more softly than the previous ones. There was no need for my verbal caution since Director Pevas and Agent Tambos had run toward the trucks with the ranch hands. Some of the men tried to help the weaker ones get aboard so that the trucks could start for the hospital while others were concerned only about themselves. Within minutes, everyone was seated, bent over, or leaning over the side believing that they were going to die instantly. Maybe they were. At that point, we had no way of telling how potent the dosages were. The trucks sped up the driveway. We could hear the dogs barking as the trucks reached the main gate and turned onto the road toward the hospital.

My army assembled near the porch. We heard the rumble of the trucks, the barking of the guard dogs, and the sounds of the sick men become more distant in the calm night air.

"Okay, we must hurry," I told them. "Uncle, do your best to clear out any animals that may be in the stable before we torch it. Make sure no flammables, explosives, or ammunition are stored there before you set anything on fire. Advari, carry all these weapons on the porch to the van. Manco, see if anything useful to us is in the processing buildings. If not, set them on fire. Maya, shoot a fire arrow into the sky to alert any of your family members in the area, and then come with me to check the house for any important documents we may find. You all did great. Now all we need to do is level this place and go home."

As I finished giving instructions and Maya launched her lighted arrow into the dark sky, we heard a shout from the swale. Sure enough, Manco's family had been waiting for a signal to come out of hiding.

"Manco, have them help you destroy buildings and the processing equipment. That will move things along more quickly," I instructed.

As other members of my army scattered to complete their tasks, Uncle had already reached the stable and began releasing the animals. Among them was Sancho, Señor Barrantes' big black horse. Released from his stall, he raced defiantly around the corral several times until the smoke from the burning straw engulfed him. Using every ounce of his mighty strength, he thrust himself into the air and cleared the top rail of the corral fence by plenty. Like before, he raced toward the tree line and freedom. This time, no one would follow to bring him back. Maya and I went into the house and concentrated on searching for incriminating documents about the Calderon operation and its network. Nothing appeared relevant or important on the desk or among the folders piled on an adjoining table. I moved a sliding door in the bookcase to reveal a medium-size safe. Any important items plus cash to pay the workers must be there, if anywhere. The smell and sounds of burning buildings permeated the house. I raced into the yard, hoping the tool shed had not been lit yet. With a heavy hammer and a pry bar, maybe I could open the safe. I was too late. The tool shed was burning briskly. Manco and some of his family stood nearby watching their handiwork light up the night sky as they distributed Calderons' arsenal of weapons among family members before Advari had a chance to carry them to the van as I previously had instructed him.

"What you need?" Manco asked as he saw me approach.

"I wanted tools to open the safe. I guess I am too late for that."

"Too late for tools, but we have cousin Felipe. He open safe for you."

Manco spoke to one of his younger relatives who smiled broadly as if he had won the lottery.

"I am Felipe," he said. "I will open safe."

I started back toward the house, but Felipe raced ahead of me. He was turning the combination knob when I got back inside. Manco and his family gathered to watch the young master perform. Five minutes later, Felipe smiled, grabbed the handle, and we all heard the familiar klunk of the safe door unlocking. Inside was a pile of documents and a cash box. Time was pressing now. We couldn't linger because someone surely would see the smoke and flames of the ranch illuminating the area. And, if our potions had not killed or severely impaired all of Calderon's men, they would come back looking for us. Maya found a pillowcase, and helped me put the documents in it. I would have time to review them on my flight back to the States.

One set of documents looked familiar and required special treatment. It was Calderon's lists of network members and clients that the missionaries had almost lost their lives to acquire. I struck a match and lit the lists from the bottom letting them burn until only the letterhead and a few names remained readable. I returned the remains of the lists to the safe with some ashes and other half-burned papers, and spun the dial. With luck, Calderon would find the remnants, think that the lists had been virtually destroyed in the fire, and not chase the missionaries or me around the globe trying to recover his incriminating lists. I certainly wouldn't tell him that I still had the photocopies that the missionaries gave me in Costa Rica safely tucked away in a safety deposit box in the States.

I gave the cash box to Manco. "Distribute the contents of the box to your family after you drive Advari and me back to the airport," I told him. "The contents and the weapons may help them regain their homes and property. Before I forget to ask you again, what is your uncle's name?"

"Santiago, of course, what better name for an uncle, yes?"

"Don't start me on name games now. Get me to the airport or the sound of my name may be less thrilling to you in the future."

"You are no longer Jose Legion then?"

"I am Joe Legion to you and everyone else while I am here. Never forget that, Manco, never. We have no time to chat. Get your people into the jungle or somewhere safe, Manco. Our work is done here. You were magnificent, but clear out while the victory is clearly ours. I will tell Ron when I get back how talented and helpful Maya, Uncle Santiago, and you were in this project. If we ever meet again, I will bring my own beverages with me. Advari, where are you? It's time to return you to Lisbon and school and to let the Jesuits polish you like a fine gem."

Fortunately, we didn't meet any of Calderon's men on the road into town before we turned in the opposite direction toward the airfield. Equally fortunate, Chauncey had a military plane waiting at the airport for us as he had promised. This allowed me just time enough to thank Manco, Maya, and Uncle Santiago once more and to admonish them to leave the customs vehicles at the airport where they belonged.

After we loaded our gear onto the plane, I expected Advari to crawl under his blanket and sleep his way north. But, on this trip, he wanted to talk.

DEBRIEFING WITH ADVARI

"We did not need grenades and my slingshot on this project as I expected," Advari declared.

"Are you disappointed?" I responded.

"No, I like winning, but I do not like the killing."

"On jobs like this, you should not define winning or losing in terms of killing or not killing. You saved my life at Quillabamba by hitting the number four gunman with your slingshot. Now you can say that you saved my life on two continents: first against Vasily in Chennai, and now against Calderon in Quillabamba. Unfortunately, they remain my two most powerful opponents. But, my confidence in your slingshot expertise allowed me to confront them or their gunmen in situations in which killing was not my first or only option. So, you and your expertise were important elements in this enterprise although we used your slingshot skills only once on this trip. If that bonehead had not grabbed Maya, we would have avoided bloodshed entirely tonight. If any winning occurred on this project, it included rescuing the missionaries and keeping some cocaine paste from reaching the market where it can kill people and ruin the lives of others around them. Do you see now how important your slingshot skills were to our assignment?"

"You accomplished your goals although you changed your plan several times. Is that still winning?" Advari continued to press his case.

"The Chinese warrior and military writer Sun-Tzu would not call my approach winning. He wrote that victorious warriors win first and then go to war, while defeated warriors go to war first and then seek to win.[1] He would have choked at the way I did business back there, making changes as I went and never being sure of the outcome until I am on the plane going home with you."

"In the Chennai marketplace, my friends and I allowed everybody to win. We took the tourists' money but allowed them to go back to work to earn more money for us if they visited the marketplace again," Advari proclaimed.

"In Chennai, you limited your practice to snatching wallets and purses. That was very wrong, but thoughtful of you at your age. But, how long do you think it would be before your practice expanded to include bicycles, motor scooters, and ultimately to cars? Somewhere along the way somebody would introduce you to drugs and people who carry guns because you would want nicer clothes and a better place to live. You would not be satisfied hanging around the marketplace stealing purses. You would start packing a gun because you would want respect and fear from your playmates. Sometime after that, you might get angry with a client or colleague and use your gun. You might still hate killing, but now you would have a reputation to maintain unless the police put you in jail or kill you first. So, your dislike for killing is not absolute salvation for you. But, you demonstrated more than a dislike for killing at the pistol range before we came to Peru, so I understand what you mean. You do not like instruments of death, such as guns. That is why I wanted you out of the marketplace in Chennai. Maybe now you will have a chance to develop other skills, live longer, and contribute something important to people around the world."

"But, other kids I know are still there. What chance do they have for a better life?"

"Do I look like St. Thomas or Mother Teresa to you? If I could arrange for all your friends to be sent to Lisbon, don't you think I would have sent them with you? You are a handful for Paolo and his wife by yourself. He would have cardiac arrest with more than one Advari under his roof."

"We get along fine."

"I'm glad to hear that because school will not be easy for you. At the same time, you can tell your classmates what life is like on the streets. If that does not inspire them to study, nothing will."

"I will also tell them about what we did here in Peru."

"That may not be the best idea you ever had. I don't know what the European end of the Calderon network looks like yet. Who knows? One of your Lisbon classmates may be Calderon's nephew. Some day after you brag about your adventures in Peru, Calderon's nephew writes a letter to his dear uncle in Bolivia, telling him about a kid in his class who claims he burned down a drug barn in Tingo Maria. A few days after that, on your way home from school, a car pulls up and some gorilla with hairy arms picks you up by the collar and flings you into the back seat. Probably, the gorilla and his friends will want some information from you before they kill you. They will pound on you until you sing like a canary. Do you understand where I am going with this conversation, or do I have to recite the entire lesson plan for you?"

"I will forget I was ever in Peru," Advari pledged.

"Better yet, remember what you learned and saw in Peru. Just don't tell anyone about it."

As I reflected on what happened, we really didn't win anything. We temporarily slowed the flow of coca paste from Tingo Maria, but we didn't put Calderon out of business. True, we gave him a reason to search for whomever burned his ranch and disabled his men. He would not enjoy being humiliated among his peers. He would make an effort to meet me someday on his terms. I hoped he would wait long enough for my shoulders to heal.

As Advari and I chatted, I noticed that the needle of my compass that I had set on the seat beside me was wandering more to the east than I thought was appropriate for a refueling stop in Mexico. I went forward to the flight deck.

"Captain, we aren't stopping in Costa Rica for fuel this time. I already met your CIA colonel, or whoever he is, in the States. I have nothing more to discuss with him about this trip."

The pilot and copilot looked startled. They didn't know what to do. I thought I would help them to decide.

"Get on the radio, and tell the colonel that you are taking the most direct route back to the States and that you decided to go elsewhere for fuel. I will stay here and confirm that is what we will do if you feel uneasy about telling the colonel yourselves. While you are doing that, please resume your old heading so that we do not waste more time and fuel."

The copilot turned the radio to a different frequency and connected with the colonel. A few minutes later, he handed me his headset. As I put one earpiece to my ear, I heard the pilot relate what I told him. Then, the familiar voice of Colonel X responded angrily. He demanded that we land in Costa Rica. That meant I had to enter the conversation personally.

"*Buenos dias*, Colonel. *Lo siento mucho*. I am very sorry to bother you at this early hour, but we decided to take the direct route home this time. I thought you should know."

"The pilot is the captain of the plane; he will decide what route to take. He has his orders. You will obey him."

"*Por favor, no se enfade*, please do not be angry, Colonel. Ordinarily, I would do as you request, but the captain is on a coffee break, and we need to decide this matter quickly. The copilot agreed to defer to my instructions because he also wants to get back to his family as soon as possible. Actually, you have been outvoted two to one."

"What are you talking about?" the colonel's voice crackled angrily over the radio.

"The vote, Colonel, I am talking about the vote. We have a democracy on this plane. My pistol and I voted not to land in Costa Rica this time. The pilot and copilot recognize the business end of a democratic election when they see it. The captain is back now. I will let you talk to him, but I think we covered what we wanted to say. *Muchas gracias* to you, Colonel. *Adios!*"

I thought our business was concluded. I patted the pilot on the back and started back to my seat.

WHILE YOU'RE IN THE NEIGHBORHOOD

"Wait!" the pilot shouted before I made two steps out of the cockpit. "The colonel will allow us to proceed past Costa Rica if we stop in Guatemala and pick up a wounded CIA agent. He is waiting at an airfield near Quezaltenango. We can refuel and complete the pickup in one landing. Hopefully, all parties can agree on not leaving one of our people behind."

"Our democratic election has been overturned—there's nothing new in South America about a rapid change in government. Undoubtedly, the stated purpose of the change has wider implications than our personal needs or wants. Proceed as the colonel instructed. I hope the airfield is at least as long as the town name."

"Is everything okay?" Advari asked as I rejoined him in the cabin.

"I think so, but we're refueling in Guatemala rather than Mexico. Do me a favor and pull my rifle out of my bag, will you?"

"Do you get paid enough to do all this?" Advari asked without disclosing the motive for his question.

"What specific 'this' do you mean?" I stalled for more information before I answered his ambiguous question.

"Everything you do."

"Yes, very handsomely too, I might add. When I first started, my compensation included the first-born child of any family I rescued. With kids being what they are these days, now I work only for cash. Believe me, my outlook for the future is brighter when I'm paid in cash."

"You are joking, of course."

"A little bit, but I am rewarded handsomely when I'm able to fix a situation, right an injustice, or return people to where they belong. In my opinion, kids are better than adults. They would be far superior if adults taught them what they need to know to flourish and then allowed them to perform. As far as my actual compensation is concerned, it barely covers my clothing, food, equipment, repairs, ammunition, travel expenses—and incidentals like you. If you needed another stone for your slingshot back there, I would have had to file for bankruptcy."

"You must feel good about helping people, but you create enemies too," Advari stated accurately for a young mind.

"Yes, and sometimes very powerful ones. General Vasily and now Calderon are at the top of my list. I have an uneasy feeling that something very bad is brewing in the world and they are connected to it. I will meet them again soon. I hope my shoulders are healed before they strike. Which reminds me that I need to restart therapy when I get home. Then, my wife and I will go on our annual pilgrimage to visit our European family."

"If you are in trouble, you can always send for me. I will be ready whenever you need me."

"I have no doubt that you will be extra ready when school is in session. Sorry, my young friend, the Jesuits will have priority on your time in a few days. But, I certainly will come to see you when I am in the neighborhood. And when you learn how to write, you'd better write to me. Your world will be much different than mine, and you need to prepare for it. Other kids your age are ahead of you in their studies. You are intelligent and will catch up over time, but you have hard work ahead of you. Your classmates will not always be kind to you while you learn what they already know, but you have experience in dealing with people that they will not learn for years. Hopefully, in a short time, they will come to respect and like you. If some are not happy with you, do not waste your time with them because you have more important things to do."

"Like being an international businessman?"

"Exactly, if that's what you want to do in life. If you want to be an artist, then be the best painter or sculptor you can be."

"What if I want to be like you?"

"You'd better not, little soldier. Remember, I saw how you shoot a gun before we came down here. You are not wired for a career in this kind of work, believe me."

Our conversation drifted to a number of topics as the plane maintained its northeasterly course. I talked about everything other than my rising angst about being diverted by Colonel X a second time. While Advari and I talked, I casually loaded my rifle. I don't know why exactly. I could barely hold it steady, let alone hit anything with it. I would need a lot of adrenalin to overcome that handicap. After what seemed an infernal eternity, the pilot reduced power and landed at Quezaltenango. From the cabin, everything at the airport looked calm, if not inviting. The pilot taxied to the fuel depot and cut the engines. While the copilot supervised the refueling, the pilot, Advari, and I walked into the terminal to locate our passenger.

If I could have extended my arms away from my sides with my normal range of motion, I would have been able to touch both the north and south walls of the terminal compared to O'Hare. Under those conditions, we easily found our passenger surrounded by what appeared to be a Guatemalan family—all talking at the same time. I gauged that Agent Turner was in his thirties, tall and wiry, with a deep suntan, and his left arm in a sling. He was not the problem. The problem was the Guatemalan family who had found him injured and took him into their house. *How could that be a problem?* On his departure, they wanted to give him a crate of chickens. With the worldwide threat of the avian virus, I wouldn't let those chickens on any flight that I was taking back to the States! Besides, the chickens probably were the only property the family owned. *I had to break this up,* I thought. *Otherwise, we will never get home.* The copilot came into the terminal.

A Chicken's Way Out

"The plane is refueled and ready to go whenever you are," the copilot announced.

"We have a situation here," the pilot replied. "These people won't let our new passenger go until he accepts this crate of chickens. We can't take them into the States because they might be diseased or have parasites. If we don't take them, the family will be insulted. How do we resolve this dilemma?"

"Advari has the answer," I assured him.

"I do?" Advari asked in surprise.

"I will show you. Let's all head for the plane. Advari, you carry the crate of chickens and lag behind the rest of us. When we are ready to take off, the pilot will holler at you to hurry up. Then, you start running for the plane and pretend to stumble, or stumble without pretending. I don't care how you do it, but as you fall, open the hatch on the crate and let the chickens escape. By that time, the pilot will be taxiing the plane, so you have no choice but to run and let the chickens go. You hop aboard, and we will be long gone before the family captures the chickens. The family saves face, and we don't die or go to jail for bringing sick chickens into the States. Any problems with that?"

Nobody had a problem with the plan, although Advari didn't applaud playing the role of a clumsy chicken crate carrier. The plan worked perfectly except for the short time when we thought that the chickens would flutter into the engines.

"Nice job back there," I complimented Advari when he was safely aboard in the seat behind Agent Turner and directly opposite me. "For a minute, I thought we would have an engine full of feathers, but you chased them away like a professional chicken thief. I knew we could count on you."

"Thanks," Advari replied as he began to tuck himself into his blanket.

While Advari arranged his area to sleep during the remaining time into Chicago, I pulled out the pillowcase of documents Felipe had extracted from the safe in Tingo Maria. Several documents listed names and addresses throughout Europe, North Africa, and the Middle East. If these were members or clients of the Calderon network in addition to the photocopied list I already had, he had quite a business going, and he wouldn't hesitate to squash me like a ladybug for interfering with his livelihood. I wondered how much information the FBI or CIA had concerning this network, if any at all, and if I should pass these lists onto any organization outside of MAGENTA. I decided to keep the information to myself until I determined who or what agency could best use the information to put Calderon out of action permanently. I also found a list of computer codes that might be helpful when I got around to looking at Calderon's computer programs.

"You look like you're returning from serious business in the south," Agent Turner commented, opening the conversation and breaking my chain of thought.

"Nothing serious," I replied. "Before Advari starts school in Europe, he and I were visiting interesting people I had met on an earlier visit."

"You appear to be well equipped to handle any kind of meeting both in and outside the jungle," Turner commented with a movement of his chin toward our equipment bags and my rifle.

"Yes, we came prepared to meet all kinds of predators," I remarked.

"You must have been successful, you're going home without broken bones, unlike me."

"Success can be defined in a number of ways, but we're certainly taking the slow route once again by stopping at multiple airfields between here and there," I responded with a hard edge to my tired voice.

"Okay, no offense," Turner commented as he turned to face forward in his seat. "I don't always feel like talking after I complete an assignment either."

Passenger Disarmament

As he turned, I noticed a small bulge in his sling. Having had prior experience with slings myself, I knew a sling was a handy place to keep car keys, loose change, and small weapons like the bulge in his sling appeared to be.

"I apologize if I was rude," I continued. "Sometimes, my personality is quite disarming."

With my emphasis on the word "disarming," Advari stopped fussing with his blanket and looked at me for instructions. Behind the cover of the seat in front of me, I mimicked my arm in a sling, and withdrew my "index finger and thumb pistol" from it. Advari nodded his understanding and reached for his slingshot. I nearly missed his quick action as he looped the leather strap neatly over the back of the seat and around Turner's neck. As Advari pulled upward and toward himself on the ends of his slingshot to draw Turner's neck back, I caught up with his action. In one motion, I pinned Turner's bandaged arm to the armrest of the seat and snatched a 9-mm handgun from his sling.

"Excuse our inconvenient search and seizure methods of potentially dangerous equipment," I explained to Turner who was now gasping for breath. "We get nervous about armed CIA agents who may be under instructions from a certain colonel who doesn't particularly like us."

"I was instructed only to observe and report your actions," Turner explained between coughing and rubbing his chaffed neck after Advari released the tight grip he had on the ends of his slingshot.

"Good, you can observe and report our actions unobstructed by any bulges in your sling. I'm sorry if we hurt you, but while we're on the subject, you can hand over your ankle weapon too. Otherwise, we'll insist that you take your shirt and pants off for the remainder of the flight."

Turner bent forward, pulled out a .25-caliber automatic from his ankle holster and held it out toward me. Advari quickly grabbed the gun from the agent's hand and tossed it to me, which isn't the normal protocol for transferring a loaded weapon from one person to another. I unloaded both weapons and put them under the seat in front of me.

That done, Agent Turner asked, "What else do you want from me? You two play rough for us being on the same team."

"We don't need anything else from you unless you want to volunteer more information about yourself and your colonel," I suggested. "As for playing rough, we are like many other commuters who don't like to be delayed on the way home."

"You know that I can't divulge any information," he replied.

"Okay, then cool your jets for the rest of the flight and leave us alone. Otherwise, you may exit this plane in midair over the Gulf of Mexico."

We completed the remainder of the flight with Advari snoozing, Agent Turner reading or conversing with the flight crew, and me engaged in my own thoughts about my next collision with Vasily or Calderon.

When we arrived in Chicago, Turner grunted a hasty thank you as I handed his weapons back to him. He gathered his other belongings, and left the plane before I had a chance to unwrap Advari from his blanket nest.

As Turner exited the plane, he said belligerently, "The next time you get yourselves into trouble, just hope that they don't send me to rescue you."

"Based on some of the places we've been lately and the people we've encountered, we share the same hope. Say hello to your colonel for us," I responded sarcastically to end that unpleasant conversation.

DISBANDING MY ARMY

As Advari and I walked into the terminal, the early evening flights were departing for European destinations. I checked on seat availability to Lisbon. A few seats were open, and I bought a ticket for Advari without hesitation.

"Are you trying to get rid of me?" Advari asked hesitantly.

"That is precisely what I'm doing because saying good-bye now is easier than it will be tomorrow or the next day. I know you are saddle sore from the long ride here, little soldier, but this way, you will be with Paolo in Lisbon in time for lunch tomorrow."

We gave each other a monster bear hug, and I pointed him toward the gate for the Lisbon flight. Just before he turned the corner, he stopped and gave me a big wave. I waved back. Then, Advari suddenly came running toward me. *Oh no,* I thought. *This parting will be harder than either of us anticipated.*

"Advari, this is no good, you need to go now," I said as he approached.

"Yes, I know," he answered gleefully. "I only wanted to return your wallet. You may need it soon."

"Get going, you little mosquito, before I inform the Jesuits that they have a pickpocket and chicken thief on their hands," I said as I took my wallet from him.

By then, he was around the corner and out of sight. He had returned my wallet all right, but all my money was gone.

"Thanks, you little heathen," I whispered, "for making our parting as easy as possible for both of us."

The airport taxi dropped me off at home. Thankfully, Advari left my credit cards so I could pay the driver. Beth was still at work. I showered, threw my clothes in the washing machine, and looked through the stack of mail that had accumulated during my absence. I hit the button on the answering machine. The first message was from Ron confirming that the missionaries had returned safely to Salt Lake City. Finally, the missionary rescue was accomplished. The second message was from my cousin Daniela, confirming that we would be staying with her mother and her on our trip to Slovakia, which was only a few days away. The third message was from Amy, reminding me of therapy appointments that I had already missed. The last message was a coded communiqué from MAGENTA, informing me to check my post office box for further information. The washing machine needed extra time to get the "eyebrow of the jungle" grime out of my clothes, so I jumped in the car and drove to the post office. A thin brown envelope was inside my secured box. I didn't know if this was good news or not. I walked back to the car, tore open the envelope, and pulled out the single sheet of paper inside. The coded message read: "Travel reimbursement is authorized for you to visit your Scout at the QC Zone hospital." That terse message erased any travel lag, and made me reach for my code book to determine what was the civilian name of the hospital. *Who was my Scout, and what was she/he doing in the hospital?*

The Quad Cities refer to the two Illinois towns of Moline and Rock Island on the east side of the Mississippi River with the corresponding Iowa towns of Davenport and Bettendorf on the west side. All were a little north of Muscatine. *Did my old Iowa albatross return again?* I reasonably had to assume that MAGENTA had selected Amy as my Scout and that she found trouble or vice versa. I couldn't expect MAGENTA to give me precise information on my new Scout and her location following my outburst about its failure to protect Jenny before I returned from my first Peru trip.

I drove back home, and phoned hospitals in the Quad Cities area. After the third call, I confirmed that Amy indeed was a patient following an auto accident. Naturally, she was in the furthest hospital from me. I was in no shape for any further activity then, but would start out in the morning. Beth reminded me about our trip to Slovakia in three days. There's nothing like a tight schedule to bring out the best in a person.

Chapter Notes

1. Cleary (translator), *op. cit.*, p. 57.

CHAPTER 12

A DOE, A DOC, A DECLARATION

VISITING MY SCOUT

I was out of bed early the next morning, but I decided to let the rush-hour crowd have the roads before I started out. The drive toward Iowa on Interstate 88 was an efficient if not a scenic two-hour trip. I arrived at the hospital about noon, stopped at the reception desk to confirm Amy's room, and went up the stairs in that direction. I expected to see her family in or around her room, but only an intern was present reading Amy's chart and checking the various intravenous drips and monitors. He turned and nodded for me to come in as he saw me standing in the doorway.

"She's a very lucky lady," he announced politely. "No damage that won't heal. Are you a relative?"

"No, heck no. Amy may be lucky, but not lucky enough to be related to me," I teased him. "In fact, I expected to find her family here."

"They arrived two days ago. I think they went to lunch. They should be back shortly."

"Do you know what happened?" I asked the intern who was completing his charts.

"I understand that two deer tried to jump into her car along the highway. She went off the road and landed upside down in a ditch. She has a lot of bumps and bruises and a major concussion, but we expect a full recovery. We have her sedated to keep her from moving her head and neck too much before we can fully evaluate that area after the swelling subsides."

"That sounds right. She doesn't like guns, so she went deer hunting with her car—out of season too. Did she hit a buck or a doe?"

"I believe it was a doe. If she had hit the larger buck, she might not be here now."

"That sounds right too. Deer don't stand much of a chance with her on the road. Right now, she looks a mess. I'm glad that you can repair the damage."

"I'm Dr. Andrews. I didn't get your name."

"Joe," I said, "Joe Legion."

"You seem to know her fairly well. Have you known her long?"

"I've always known her to be short," I teased him again. "She'll never get any taller than she is now. Actually, we have a complicated relationship. I'm her therapy patient, and she will start working part time with me when she's ready."

I saw Dr. Andrew's eyebrows furrow at my mention of a "complicated relationship," but he brightened considerably following my explanation. Concurrently, I came to understand the underlying significance of the full-service medical attention Amy was receiving. Amy attracted this handsome dark-haired intern even when she was unconscious. That's not a bad skill to have in Iowa or anywhere else. I put that thought in my brain bin for future reference. Dr. Andrews was about to say something to me when Amy's parents and sister returned.

"I need to visit my other patients," the young doctor explained to Amy's folks.

"She's doing well. I will be back to check on her later," he stated, a little too flushed to stay longer and lose his professional cool in front of Amy's family and me.

"We are Amy's parents," her mother introduced herself as she stepped forward and offered her hand.

"I'm Joe Legion," I replied, shaking hands with her, Amy's father, and sister in turn. "I'm a friend of Amy's from Chicago," I added, explaining my presence.

"Oh, Amy never mentioned you," her mother responded inquisitively, "have you known her long?"

"I've only known her, ah, um—only a short time," I answered, taking the polite route this time.

"I'm a patient of Amy's. I had shoulder surgery a short time ago. Coincidentally, she applied for a part-time position with my organization. I was out of the country, but when I learned that she was hurt, I thought I'd see if I could help in any way."

"What is your company?" her father asked picking up the business connection immediately.

"To paraphrase Louis XIV, I am the company. I do risk management for a colorized group," I said too fast for them to catch.

"And what will Amy do for your company?" her mother asked, not satisfied with my lack of full disclosure.

"Actually, Amy is not on my payroll. She will provide liaison services that I need from the government to do my risk assessments."

"Where do you do your risk assessments?" her father asked, still fidgety about the way the conversation was going.

"I work internationally. That's why I need someone in the States to coordinate things between the government and me as I move around."

"How did Amy—?" her mother was about to ask when Amy stirred and opened her eyes, at least the eye that wasn't black and swollen shut.

Everyone turned in her direction, and her mother and sister, as nurse and nurse-in-training, respectively went to her bedside. *Thank you, Amy, for your timely rescue when I needed one badly.* Obviously, she hadn't told her family about her new career yet. *I didn't drive all this way to upset her family with information they should be hearing from their daughter (if at all) rather than from me.* After receiving hugs and kisses from her family, Amy zeroed in on me in the background.

"Hi, how was Peru?" she asked sleepily.

"I left it in the same location, but not in the same condition," I answered thankful that she had asked a question with an international ring to it.

Fuzzy-headed from painkillers, Amy was saving my caboose by saying the right thing in front of her family. I should thank her for that some day—in the distant future the way our "complicated relationship" was going.

"Are the black eyes and bruises the best Halloween costume you could find? Besides, you're a little early, aren't you?" I asked, attempting to control a part of the conversation.

"Have you looked at yourself lately? You look like you need a room here too. How is your shoulder?" Amy remarked lucidly given her condition.

"I can wait for your return. Besides, my wife and I are going to Europe in a few days."

"Will my job be there when I get back?" Amy asked in a way that answered my question about her employment status with MAGENTA.

"Sure, how many people do you know who would work with me?"

"Is that a question or an answer?" she responded quickly, demonstrating that her brain wasn't scrambled by the accident, and notifying me that any hazing period I normally might have for new Scouts would not include her.

"Now you know how it feels when you do that to me. What do you think?"

"When do we start?" Amy asked, showing that she had more skill and practice at the "question game" than I did.

"When you're ready to resume your regular career and have enough stamina to play with me, I'll be glad to have you join the team," I decided to let her win this round with her parents present.

"Will I have a code name?"

"I selected one already."

"Without telling me?"

"It's my prerogative. Besides, if I told you, you'd probably start a war to change it."

"Is it that bad? What is it?"

"Your code name henceforth will be 'Shortcake'. Do you like it?"

"The first thing I'll do when I get out of here is sue you for vertical discrimination!"

"I take that as a no on 'Shortcake'. We could try '*La Pucelle*' if you prefer French. That name sounds better, but it is not as endearing as 'Shortcake'. And, I propose a change to your agenda. The first thing you'll do when you're discharged is to rest at home for a few days, assuming your folks will have you. I'll contact your supervisor and confirm your condition. I'm sure your colleagues don't want you around them while you look like a patient yourself. It's bad for business. After you feel better, you can decide if you should pursue your claim for vertical justice. Remember that the cost of justice is expensive."

"Thanks, but you really don't have to go out of your way to notify my supervisor for me," Amy pushed her charm button.

"Maybe not, but I will. Another thing I need to do is drive home. I'm glad to see that you are mending and that you have your family with you. Your doctor is concerned about your welfare too. He will take good care of you, I'm certain of that. As for your vertical discrimination lawsuit, the biggest hurdle for you is to find a jury short enough to see eye-to-eye with your case. If somehow you win the first trial, I will take the case to a higher court where the judge won't be able to locate you from his elevated seat on the bench," I said, getting as much leverage as I could out of the play on words without her family attacking me.

"Did you come to mock me or to cheer me up?"

"Do I have to answer that in front of your parents?"

"I thought you said you were leaving?"

"I am now that I know your cranial spark plugs are firing," I capitulated again for the sake of family harmony. "I'll see you in the neighborhood when you're ready."

I shook hands with Amy's mother and father who appeared relieved about what I was doing there, although they didn't have much more information about me than when we first met. That was the best situation for all concerned. But, Amy's sister, Alexandra, followed me into the hall.

Agreement with Alexandra

After we traveled a few steps from Amy's room, Alexandra asked, "Amy told me a little about having a part-time job, but she didn't describe it very much or tell me about you. It sounded scary and weird to me, but you don't look so tough. Will she be in any danger?"

"So far, I think she's in more danger driving home than she'll be working with me. But, I admit her job is unique. As for me, I'm wearing my worn-out-and-achy look today, so don't draw any conclusions from my appearance."

"I'm sorry, but you look as old as my parents," Alexandra observed.

"Ah, geez, just when I was beginning to like you, you insult your parents. When you reach our ages, a few decades one way or another don't make much difference."

"Can we restart this conversation? I'm really worried about my sister."

"I hoped that was the direction you intended. What do you want to know?"

"What will Amy be doing?" Alexandra asked pointedly.

"I'm afraid that Amy or I can't tell you or your parents any more specifics about the job than you already know. In fact, you may have more information than is healthy for you already. The best way that you can help her is by being the good sister that you have been and, obviously, still are to her. Amy may have left home, but she hasn't left your family. Continue to share your secrets and whatever else sisters do, but don't ask her about what she's doing unless you want your hair to fall out, have red blotches all over your face, and date guys with bad breath. If you keep cool and avoid infecting Amy with your concerns, she'll be okay."

"I'll be a good sister if you promise me you'll make her quit the job if she's in trouble."

I stopped walking, and looked straight into Alexandra's eyes.

"You may be a little young to fully appreciate what I'm going to say, but, sooner or later, most people realize that other folks inhabit this planet too. Unless a person is morally depraved or financially destitute, at some point we need to fill an otherwise empty spot in our psyche by helping others. Amy is an intelligent young lady who I respect immensely despite the short time we've known each other. She may have reached the point of needing to help people earlier than most. You could argue that she should find sufficient satisfaction in helping people regain their health through her therapy work. But, her need for fulfillment may require more than that. I won't create barriers that prevent her from doing what she wants in life, but I promise you that I will intervene if she messes up or creates dangerous situations that she can't handle. I'll do my utmost to ensure that she is safe. I will put my life on the line if necessary to protect her. Does that help you?"

"She won't be involved in anything illegal, will she?" Alexandra extended the conversation.

"I can see that answering questions with another question is a family trait, but don't worry, I'm getting used to it. Amy may not always be doing God's work directly, but she'll be working for Uncle Sam one way or another. We don't deliberately and knowingly break the laws of this country or any other nation. Bending rules is a different story. I'm sure you've driven over the speed limit for a worthwhile purpose at some point in your driving career, but not fast enough for the police to turn on the siren and come after you. Is that a clear example for you? As Groucho Marx supposedly said, 'If you don't like my principles, I have others.'"

"Groucho who?" Alexandra asked, reminding me of the age chasm between us.

"Never mind, who. Do you understand my point?"

"I understand your point, although it doesn't make me any more comfortable about Amy working with you," Alexandra admitted.

"Well, let's see how this fits. In our conversations, Amy informed me that your family has no interest or experience in hunting, law enforcement, or military service. Consequently, I would be nuts to rely on Amy's judgment or expect her to perform as an expert in those fields."

"What's left for her to do?" Alexandra asked, still searching for the reassurance I hadn't given her.

"Making arrangements for resources to come together to resolve problems will be a big part of Amy's job. With her judgment, perspective, perseverance, and follow-through, Amy can help me in those areas. In fact, she has already. She understands that completing paperwork is only the media for her efforts, not the desired end in itself."

"How so?" Alexandra kept digging.

"For example, in one of my early therapy sessions, she reminded me that true friends don't cause trouble for their friends. That's a powerful statement if you think about it a while. In crucial situations, I'll ask Amy for reminders to guide my conduct, particularly when I'm in a foreign country with different values, or if I'm surrounded by people who don't subscribe to my views. At times like those, I need level-headed thinking, not documents to complete and send in by return mail."

"And you think my sister is clever enough to help you in those situations?"

"I believe she's gifted in that ability, yes, unless you have contradictory evidence. If so, I'd like to hear it."

"Just because she's older doesn't mean she always knows best. If we had more time, I'd tell you stories that would make your hair curl. Oops, that wasn't the best analogy I could have used, was it?" Alexandra testified.

"Unfortunately, I agree with you. Any hair curls come from my wavy skull these days. They follow the contours of the terrain. But, whether you realize it or not, you've told me a great deal about your family and your relationship with your sister."

"What did I say?" Alexandra asked apprehensively.

"By following me into the hallway, you told me that you're concerned about your sister in ways so private that you won't even share them with your parents. Your bond with Amy applies no matter how many times you've argued with each other over silly stuff; the times you were jealous of each other's looks, skills, clothes, attitudes, academic and sports successes, and boyfriends. How many times have you both competed for attention from your parents and family over the years? By continuing to ask me questions, you demonstrated that you want sufficient information to counsel Amy regardless of any decisions she's already made or the position your parents appear to take on a subject. That's not bad news coming from a younger sister."

"We both are independent people; do you think you can handle her?" Alexandra asked as she directed her inquiry to another dimension.

"Winning a personal argument isn't the same as successfully demonstrating to someone that they haven't considered all the pertinent facts, or that they should re-evaluate a particular aspect of a problem because of changed conditions. That's what counts. That's where Amy's judgment becomes valuable. And because of her value in guiding my thoughts and decisions, I'll do everything possible to avoid endangering your sister—ever. Similarly, I don't take it kindly when someone endangers me unnecessarily. That applies whether people I work with are independent-minded or not. But, look, we're running out of hallway. We either need to end this conversation or put on hospital gowns and go through that door to have an X-ray. What else can I do to ease your concerns while we're standing here?" I asked hoping that Alexandra had no other major concerns because I was running on empty for ways to satisfy her probing.

"Um—"

"Look, I have a younger sister too. She started out as my older sister, but when she hit age twenty-nine, she stopped counting birthdays. She didn't notify me for several years. Now, she claims that she's my younger sister, but she worries about me just the same. I think I understand how you feel. Amy will be fine, I promise. If you continue to be the sister she loves, Amy will be fine, you will be fine, and your parents will be fine. Somewhere in there, I may even be fine. Okay?"

"Okay, thanks for coming to visit her. Have a safe trip home. Good-bye!"

"Thank you, Alexandra, for being a high-caliber sister. Good luck in your studies. You picked a tough profession, but we need all the nurses we can get. With both Amy and you running loose in the world, I wish everyone in your family and the people you encounter in your life a lot of luck too!"

ANSWERS FOR ANDREWS

I was almost down the stairs following my conversation with Alexandra when Dr. Andrews intercepted me on his way up. I considered him to be a good young man who would become a fine doctor some day. He had to be a fantastic athlete already considering he visited all his other patients in world record time to be returning to Amy's room so soon.

"Are you leaving already?" Andrews asked not even out of breath from his uphill sprint. "I wanted to talk to you a little more."

"I should start for home, but don't let that stop you from stopping me, assuming you intend to stop me—especially if you intend to charge me for an office consultation. If you intend to charge me, then don't stop me. Do you want a conversation here in the stairwell, or somewhere more private?"

Dr. Andrews blinked at my rapid-fire rendition of Marx Brothers' dialog, but he recovered quickly.

"We have a chapel on the first floor. If nobody is using it, I find it's a good place to talk."

"The last time I went into a chapel with my private thoughts, I encountered a significant lifestyle change that I'm still trying to resolve. I hope you're not planning anything sacrilegious."

"No, it's just a quiet place to talk privately."

"As long as you don't take up a collection after we talk, I guess it's okay. Lead on, McDoc."

With all the suffering and death around, I believe that chapels are one of the most underutilized rooms in a hospital. The same was true of this one because we had it all to ourselves. Dr. Andrews sat in the first pew, and I semi-reclined in the one behind. I meant no disrespect to Higher Authority, but my shoulder was stiffening. Because it was Andrews' chapel and hospital, I expected him to open the conversation, and he did.

"What do you think of Amy?" he blurted out nervously.

"She's more amazing than I previously gave her credit for," I replied without allowing any judgmental brain synapses to occur.

"Why do you say that?" Dr. Andrews asked, considerably less bold than with his first question.

"Amy has been lying upstairs mostly unconscious for several days, and she's still sending messages. I'd call that pretty amazing, wouldn't you? Or do you have your receiver turned off?" I teased mercilessly.

"You get to the point quickly, don't you?" Andrews conceded.

"Is she the point of this conversation, or do you have something else on your mind?" I asked without letting up on a now thoroughly distressed young physician who was unable to hide his feelings.

"I have only met and talked to her for a few days, but I feel like I've known her all my life. I can't eat, sleep, or work without thinking about her," Andrews laid all his cards on the table.

"If you're assisting in any brain surgeries this afternoon, be prepared to say 'oops' a few times, and be sure to contact your malpractice attorney shortly after you finish. You may also want to consider changing your brand of pizzas, or have your last meal earlier in the day. That may help you sleep better."

"Now you're making fun of me!" Andrews proclaimed defensively.

"Well, maybe just a little bit, but you have some powerful symptoms. How can I help?" I asked sincerely trying to act my chronological age in providing advice to a younger mortal who was facing the same feelings almost every guy feels about a girl at his age or earlier.

"Do you know if she's dating anyone?" Andrews asked, fearful of the answer he might get from me.

"If I recall correctly, the last time that subject came up, her answer was, 'Have you seen my work schedule lately?'"

"And you interpreted that as a definite no?" Andrews prodded.

"I interpreted that as a young lady's response to a question I probably shouldn't have asked and that I shouldn't have expected a reply to given the situation."

"But, you don't think she's dating anyone seriously now, right?"

"Between her regular job and potentially working for me, Amy is carrying a full load. I have four concerns. The first is that she recovers her health and strength after this accident. The second is that she's available to rehab my shoulder. The third is that she uses her professional skills to earn a living. A distant fourth item is for her to begin helping me in a new job when she can. What she does with her free time after that is her business. To answer your question more directly, she's not dating anyone regularly, but that could change quickly. She is very personable and has many friends. So, if you intend to be a friend or more, I suggest you don't delay. How you work that out with both of you having heavy work schedules plus the distance between here and Chicago should be interesting. But, if your feelings are genuine, both of you will connect somehow. Does that answer all your questions?"

"Yes, very clearly and bluntly. I can't thank you enough," Andrews beamed as if I had handed him a winning lottery ticket.

"Well, you're wrong on that score. You can thank me by letting me know whenever you keep Amy out late at night. I don't want her pounding on my shoulder and arm without her having had a good night's sleep. I enjoyed your company, Doc, but I really need to go unless you have something else," I said while checking my watch. "I perceive you to be a fine person. You and Amy have many things in common on that score. I wouldn't hesitate to let her know how you feel about her. One way to test how she feels about you when she's physically fit again is to challenge her to an arm wrestling match."

"Arm wrestling? That sounds weird, are you sure? I should win every time because of my greater arm length and leverage," Andrews answered clinically.

"One would think so, but that's the whole point. Will you always display your macho dominance? Or, without telling her directly, will you 'signal' her that she has an equal chance of winning a wrestling match or other contests between you because you're more interested in building a relationship than you are in proving you have bigger arm muscles and a fatter head than she has?"

"And she understands an arm wrestling challenge in those terms?" Andrews continued his interrogation.

"Let's say she had some coaching on the topic, although it didn't work out as intended. I would be interested to learn how she reacts to a challenge from you, and if the 'prize' makes a difference in her response."

"Thank you very much, I think. This has been an unusual conversation, to say the least. In a strange way, you have been more helpful and supportive than I could have imagined," Andrews announced ecstatically.

"Good, I'm glad that my non-expert comments are helpful. But, understand, I'm not her father, although certain family members put me in the same age group. I'm certain her father has additional expectations for the guys his daughters date. Here's my phone number if you need another strange conversation sometime, or if her medical condition is cause for concern. I hope things work out well between you. Before I leave, I'd like a few minutes alone in the chapel to check my credit balance with the Proprietor before I drive back home. Between you two and some other things going on, I'll need prompt medical attention and spiritual intervention very soon."

We shook hands, and Dr. Andrews glided toward the back door as if on angels' wings. *There's nothing like young love to make life sparkle,* I thought. If Andrews could keep Amy unconscious for another forty or fifty years, he might have the best relationship he could possibly desire in a date or marriage partner.

Gathering Clouds

Alone in the chapel, I couldn't concentrate on a purpose for prayer other than for right thinking and God's protection in my next assignments for myself and those assisting me, particularly Amy. Instead, I recalled

Shakespeare's admonition that: "We, ignorant of ourselves, beg often our own harms, which the wise powers deny us for our good; so find we profit by losing of our prayers."[1] I decided that, at my age and life experience, I was responsible for my actions and that prayer, *karma*, and dumb luck could only cover a portion of the outcomes that might lie ahead.

On the drive home, my thoughts of young Dr. Romeo and his patient Juliet at the hospital were more pleasant. I wished both of them well if they truly had found their hearts' desire. Perhaps, I could have helped Andrews more if I had remembered Shakespeare's observation that "Love looks not with the eyes, but with the mind."[2] But, Shakespeare had a head start on me in recognizing that "The course of true love never did run smooth," whether in *A Midsummer Night's Dream*, or in the current day.[3] I also recognized that continued thoughts about their prospects for romance would either put me to sleep, into a ditch, or both. I began to pay more attention to the deer-crossing signs, but, fortunately, I didn't run into a deer or any other woodland critters.

I arrived home past my bedtime. The flashing light on the phone message machine was relentless in reminding me of calls waiting, but they could wait until tomorrow. The risk of waking the lady of the manor superseded the importance of any phone conversations.

The next morning came all too soon. The only message worth answering was from Ron. I had breakfast and returned his call early, hoping to catch him still in the sack because he considered himself an early riser despite years of evidence to the contrary.

"What's on your mind, and how have you been since my last visit?" I asked when I heard his grumpy 6:00 a.m. voice on the other end.

"I'm busy growing new skin, but I have plenty on my mind. Most of it involves you, and it's not good."

"Do you want to share the bad news on the phone, or should I come to your house?"

"The news will only take a few minutes, but you may want to brace yourself," Ron cautioned.

"Okay, I'm securely wedged against the kitchen counter, and my arm is on top of the hot toaster. What do you have?" I asked calmly.

"After you left Tingo Maria, I learned from Manco that Calderon's men returned to the ranch and saw the place on fire."

"Terrific, we did some damage without killing anybody with the *curare*. Isn't that good news?" I answered, ready to launch additional anti-irritability comments if necessary.

"Not exactly. Instead of clearing out as you instructed them, Manco's family remained in the area until Calderon's men returned. There's been bad blood between them since the revolution ten years ago, and Manco's family decided to take their revenge while they controlled all the weapons. Manco's family surrounded Calderon's men and gunned down every one of them."

"Ouch, that's incredible. Manco was cool and collected during most of my time with him. He helped me tremendously. How could he let that happen?"

"I agree that Manco is a good man, but he's not the tribal chief," Ron advised. "He was outranked and had to obey his tribal elders. When the chief orders a massacre, that's exactly what happens in that part of the world."

"It doesn't matter now, but Calderon probably will hold me responsible if he learns I was on his turf again. For me, a massacre goes beyond vengeance for Jenny's death or retaliation for Manco's family being forced off their lands by Calderon."

"Calderon can't help but find out about your return, and he already has a bounty on your scalp, remember?"

"Maybe it's timely that my wife and I are leaving for Europe tomorrow. Hopefully, Calderon won't track me to Slovakia," I answered, trying to find some relief from a steady stream of bad news.

"Don't count on it. There's more information you should have. The Calderon you know has a twin brother who spends most of his time in Europe and North Africa marketing the family's products. Not one, but both of them are looking for you. Their network will alert the Calderon boys the minute you step off a plane in any European country."

"That I don't like. A member of my family could be in the way of a hit intended for me."

"Now you're thinking my thoughts, bucko. You and your family will be hunting treasure, and the Calderons will be hunting you."

"I wondered why I was hyper about trouble closing in on me during the last few days. Thanks for the warning. How are you feeling yourself, Ron?"

"Healing is slow, darn slow, but each day when I look in the mirror, I see improvement."

"I'm glad you are healing, but your mirror can't perform miracles."

"I'm glad you're back in town to cheer me up. Watch your potatoes while you're in Europe. I don't know how much backup you have there, *amigo*. Call me when you get back, or earlier if I need to bail you out of trouble."

"Thanks, take care of yourself, trooper. *Sayonara*."

After I hung up the phone, I looked at the calendar. Tomorrow would be Tuesday, August 28, 2001. As I packed for our annual visit to our Slovak family, the big trouble that was coming in two weeks had not found the United States and me yet, but it was approaching rapidly. Although I considered myself at war with Calderon since July 14 because of Jenny's murder, I didn't connect my personal war with the larger conflict that would result in a totally changed world on September 11, 2001. In retrospect, other knowledgeable people were also plagued by the same unscratchable itch that I had about coming events. When I informed MAGENTA that Calderon had a brother somewhere in Europe, MAGENTA took it as old news, but the big "M" arranged for me to carry my .44-caliber revolver. Officially, that was the only firepower and support I would have. With that kind of response, I knew MAGENTA must be some kind of government agency. Normal people take precautions before trouble starts. As Shakespeare advised in *Richard the Third:*

> "When clouds are seen, wise men put on their cloaks;
> When great leaves fall, Then winter is at hand;
> When the sun sets, who doth not look for night?
> Untimely storms make men expect a dearth.
> All may be well; but, if God sort it so,
> "Tis more than we deserve, or I expect.
> Truly, the hearts of men are full of fear;
> You cannot reason almost with a man
> That looks not heavily and full of dread.
> Before the days of change, still is it so;
> By a divine instinct men's minds mistrust
> Ensuing danger; as by proof, we see
> The waters swell before a monstrous storm."[4]

Government agencies have no instinct for danger or for providing protection for the people they are intended to serve, particularly in times of monumental trouble. MAGENTA was no different from any other governmental agency in September 2001. All of them were equally unprepared for what befell the people of the United States.

At the beginning of my story, I related the events and people my wife and I encountered on our September 2001 trip to visit our relatives in Slovakia, our chance meeting with Hassan and his associates in Piestany, his invitation to travel with him to Morocco, his sudden disappearance in Lisbon before the announcement of the Pentagon and World Trade Center attacks, and his emergence from the shadows to help my wife and I return to the United States through Madrid.

Declaration of Total War

While we joined with all the citizens of the United States in mourning our 9/11 losses, Beth and I knew instinctively that, if we let it happen, our private war would disappear against the background of the larger conflict that reverberated after the September 11 attacks. I firmly believed that my encounters with Vasily, Barrantes, and Calderon were connected somehow to these larger events. Before MAGENTA began assigning me its own priority projects, I had to persuade MAGENTA to allow me to continue pursuing the hot trail of my opponents wherever they led me through Europe, India, North Africa, South America, Russia, and within the United States.

I not only needed to defend my extended family and friends from my personal foes, but I needed to uncover the linkages of these junior renegades and suppliers to the larger, more dangerous, terrorist networks. I had to try. In my mind, I had a duty to try. As a citizen with special skills honed over a lifetime, I needed to track the moves of Vasily, the Calderons, Hassan, and their contacts wherever I found them.

Fortunately, in my emotional state, I didn't dwell on the fact that my shoulder had not fully recovered from surgery, that my newly hired Scout was recovering from her auto accident, and that Advari's slingshot had been the principal difference between me and a corpse on my last two excursions outside the United States. Otherwise, I would have recognized that I didn't have a strong bargaining position to argue with MAGENTA for help. I would have given up. Instead, I sent my coded but emphatic demands to MAGENTA stating all the reasons why I should expand my personal war of vengeance for Jenny's murder that I began on July 14, 2001 to a declaration of total war against all enemies of the United States. Several days later, the postmaster handed me MAGENTA's unrestricted approval to pursue any and all of my identified targets, but with no additional support.

As events unfolded, I realized that MAGENTA's approval was based more on the absence of accurate intelligence on terrorist support networks than on my eloquence in describing my plans for expanding my personal war. The intelligence community would become intensely interested in any information I and others could develop about those responsible for the 9/11 attacks or any group or persons who assisted them. I was not alone now. Many others were in the field gathering information and trying to find any trails not previously explored. Diplomats were trying to build coalitions among countries to help in the search for the terrorists. Military units were preparing for combat. National and state agencies were preparing emergency plans. My private declaration of total war would not command any newspaper headlines or deploy any troops. I would use whatever resources I could find. I only had MAGENTA's authorization to travel with a concealed weapon. That was all I needed or would obtain from any official source at this stage of our national fight for survival.

CHAPTER NOTES

1. "Anthony and Cleopatra Act II Scene I," *William Shakespeare The Complete Works*, (New York: Barnes & Noble Books, 1994), p. 931.
2. "A Midsummer's Night Dream Act I Scene I," *Ibid.*, p. 281.
3. *Ibid.*, p. 280.
4. "Richard the Third Act II Scene III," *Ibid.*, p. 113.

CHAPTER 13

THE OMEN—A FIGHT ON HOME GROUND

Prologuing the Past

Up to this point, I presented a detailed description of events that occurred and the people whom Beth and I encountered prior to and on September 11, 2001. I described both the people who I perceived had already or would help me, and those who already were or would be antagonists going forward. Each added or subtracted from my private war against terrorist networks and their suppliers. Initially, I perceived MAGENTA's offer of minimum support as a liability. In fact, minimum supervision caused or allowed me to expand my creativity in dealing with people and events that MAGENTA would have frowned upon if I had engaged exclusively in MAGENTA activities. In any event, I didn't expect my expanded personal war and MAGENTA activities after 9/11 to start in my own neighborhood. But, they did.

When Beth and I returned home from Madrid late on Saturday, September 15, 2001, three phone messages were particularly important to me. The first was from Daniela confirming that she had returned home to Presov safely. The second was from Ron, and the third was from Amy. Ron wanted to know how Europe reacted to the news of the World Trade Center and Pentagon attacks. Amy informed me of her return from Iowa and my need to revive my active shoulder therapy. My responses to all three messages could wait. For now, all Beth and I needed was the comfort and security of a hot shower and a good night's sleep. Before that, my priority tasks included dumping my dirty clothes out of the luggage before dry rot set in and cleaning my weapons. The adrenalin rush of our European and North African adventures had evaporated, and neither of us required any external inducement to reach a high level of unconsciousness that night.

The next morning, Beth's internal clock woke her in sufficient time to get us to church at 7:00 a.m. My body was there, and I should have prayed for the victims of the attacks and their families, but my brain and heart were disconnected and still in bed. Aided by a poke in the ribs from Beth, I roused myself sufficiently to contribute when the collection basket was passed. Having completed that task, I believed that I fulfilled my Sunday obligation despite having no recollection of the Gospel readings, the homily, or the priest who presided that day.

Partially resuscitated by breakfast, I glanced at the newspaper headlines and noted that President Bush had escalated my private war to a national level without any intelligence briefing from me. He didn't need me to inform him that the terrorists had brought warfare to United States turf. Still, he could have profited from information I had on supplier networks and their operations that I acquired in Europe, North Africa, and South America.

"What will you do now?" Beth asked when I recited the headlines from among the newspapers that had accumulated in our absence.

"The first thing I intend to do is rehabilitate my arm. Otherwise, I won't be much use to anyone. I suppose there's no better time than the present to begin," I announced as I marched to my exercise area in the basement.

After a light workout, I recognized that Amy would not be impressed with my limited range of shoulder motion. I wasn't particularly pleased with it myself. I was fortunate that my lack of disciplined and focused exercise during my second expedition to Peru had not frozen my shoulder entirely. To recover lost time, I supplemented my therapy exercises with yard work. I conceded that the height of the grass could have hidden a regiment, not having been touched by human hands since my first trip to Peru in June. The overgrown bushes provided ample shade for me as the tall grass grudgingly succumbed to my hard-pressed mower. In the process of restoring my back yard and bushes to their normal proportions, I located three bicycles, a shovel, and a wheelbarrow that had been reported AWOL in the neighborhood for several weeks. I was proud of my success in recovering the neighbors' lost tools and pleased that no children were reported missing in my absence. I decided that was sufficient environmental achievement for one Sunday afternoon.

Ron's Early Morning Surprise

On Monday morning, I placed my 6:00 a.m. call to Ron to hear his lullaby voice at that hour.

"Hullo," the grumpy voice at the other end huffed.

I didn't respond.

"C'mon, I know it's you. Nobody else calls me at this ungodly hour of the morning. I know you're back from Europe. Say something!"

"Your cheery voice leaves me speechless as always," I snickered.

"It will take more than your being alive and back in the States to cheer me up. They tagged us good while you were away—whoever the 'they' are," Ron got right to the point.

"Yeah, I know. I caught some of the events from the European perspective. I'm just beginning to comprehend the magnitude of the strike from the U.S. viewpoint. I don't know if I should protect my European or U.S. families. Have you heard about any plans for a counterstrike? I'm sure this won't go unanswered. The American people won't let this go unanswered no matter who is behind it. This was no haphazard event. This had money and planning to support it," I spouted, not being able to stop the flow of words once they started.

"I agree with everything you say. But the leadership was caught off guard. We need time for instructions to filter down to our level. Meanwhile, get yourself in shape for whatever happens. In addition, prepare yourself for whatever the Calderons have in mind for you. Surely, Gilberto will not let the damage you caused him in Peru go unanswered. Who knows how their network might be involved? The money had to come from somewhere, and drug lords have money along with having their tentacles in all kinds of shady and legitimate businesses," Ron recited the official MAGENTA line, which slowed me down and allowed me to recover a normal pulse.

"I'm glad you mentioned Calderon. I didn't know his first name is Gilberto. Now, I perceive him as one of my prime adversaries. Reviewing the documents we lifted from the safe at the Tingo Maria ranch, a piece of his drug network runs through Chicago into Spain and Morocco."

"That's old news. The FBI and CIA already know about that," Ron said more calmly than usual for him at this early hour.

"I'll bet they don't know about the branch of the network through Central and Eastern Europe from Madrid or Tangier though. I'll go a step further. Even if they know about the entire Calderon network, the FBI, CIA, and Interpol will not attack it as a high priority item for a long time given the current situation. Maybe this is work for us. Do you have any guidance on that?" I asked, hoping Ron would agree and support any proposal that I presented to MAGENTA.

"For once, I agree with you, although you obviously don't know all the facts," Ron stated firmly as he usually did when he thought I was hip deep in quicksand and continuing to sink.

"How so this time?" I asked penitently, having been in uninformed positions many times in the past.

"Easy, knucklehead. If you didn't know Calderon's first name, I'm certain that you don't know Gilberto's twin brother, Ernesto's, habits in running the European and North African operations. I told you about the Calderon twins before you left for Europe, but I guess I didn't give you sufficient details about how they operate. Speaking as a friend, I don't know how you missed Ernesto. He runs around in plain sight all over Europe, probably as far as your native Slovakia and beyond to Afghanistan because all the local *gendarmes* are on his payroll."

"Well, I guess I missed him or saw him and didn't connect him with drug trafficking despite all the training and experience I've had over the years."

"Don't be too hard on yourself. If you saw a guy with a slight limp on his starboard side wearing a straw hat with a red hatband surrounded by some heavies carrying cannon-size heat, you have seen Ernesto. Feel better now?"

"Umh, yes and no. I saw him close enough several times to shoot. If I knew who he was, I would have. I don't feel good about missed opportunities with devils like the Calderons," I declared. "They generally don't give anyone a second chance at them. More likely, they take affirmative steps to ensure that a second opportunity doesn't occur."

"Well, good. You certainly have learned your math on that part of the equation," Ron affirmed.

BEGINNINGS OF A NEW GAME PLAN

"Don't dwell on that now. If you want to interrupt or stop the Calderons' drug and other contraband networks, you'll have to do it yourself. Maybe you can obtain additional MAGENTA support if you tie your plans into compatible MAGENTA operations," Ron advised without my begging.

"We'd better stop this discussion. We're agreeing with each other. MAGENTA should want the Calderons shut down as much as we do. Maybe Gilberto penetrated MAGENTA to get my prior Scout, Jenny.

That should give MAGENTA some incentive to help me. And if you do your usual magic getting MAGENTA to listen, that will go a long way toward approval of any proposal that I submit. Doggone it, Ron, I promised my new Scout that she would be secure, and MAGENTA knows how I feel about its lack of support and security for Jenny while I was in Peru."

"If nobody else will, the Calderons should applaud your game plan. Scouts are there to protect you, not the other way round," Ron stated uncharacteristically supportive while being his critical self.

"If the Calderons give me time to train my new Scout, we might dazzle them into a trap," I said more boldly than I felt at the moment.

"You may dazzle them with the sunlight shining through the bullet holes in you and your Scout's bodies unless you have a more substantial approach than that. After your jet lag wears off, rethink your strategy and tactics. You don't have to rush to call me about your decision either. I'll know when you're ready," Ron prophesied.

"Maybe you're right, but if the Calderons aren't cool when they plan their next move, my Scout has enough training for us to beat at least a half-baked offensive against us, don't you think?" I asked, searching for Ron's affirmation.

"Your Scout needs to be fast enough to outrun fatal bullets fired by network hired guns while you and the Calderons play mind games. Just because you wiggled out of Peru twice doesn't guarantee lifetime success. But, if they get you, at least I'll sleep in longer without you calling me in the middle of the night. Is that all you have for now?"

Ron's voice faded, giving me notice that this conversation was over as far as he was concerned.

"Thanks for your reassuring conversation. We will be extra careful. You're right though. We don't know who the real enemy is after these attacks and how they are arrayed in the international picture. The Calderons probably are small potatoes compared to the varsity team. In my rush to talk to you, I forgot to ask how you're feeling," I continued not yet ready to end the conversation without one of Ron's caustic remarks.

"I generally get a full night's sleep when you're out of the country, so I'm feeling better lately."

"Okay, I'll let you go back to bed," I conceded, having received Ron's commitment to promote my plans with MAGENTA. "I need to contact my Scout and get my rehab restarted plus learn how she's progressing in her training program. I'll keep in touch. *Sayonara*."

An Omen of What?

"Oh, wait! I just saw something unusual in my back yard!"

"What's that, your grass has an ugly fungus or something?" Ron asked, irritated by my delayed reaction and continued interruption of his sleep schedule.

"No, while we were talking, I watched a young squirrel frolicking around the base of my wild cherry tree. Then, as he climbed up into a clump of little branches, a red-tailed hawk swooped in with its talons in attack position as it tried to grab the squirrel. The hawk got one talon on the squirrel, but the clump of branches interfered just enough with the hawk's outstretched wings to make the hawk release its hold on the squirrel. That gave the squirrel sufficient time to scoot around the far side of the tree into a denser clump of limbs before the hawk made another pass at him. In frustration, the hawk glided to a branch of my oak tree while keeping an eye on the squirrel. For a young guy, the squirrel has smarts. He stayed motionless for several minutes until the hawk temporarily took his eyes off him. Then, the squirrel climbed down the back side of the cherry tree so that the hawk couldn't see him, ran flat out toward my second oak tree, and scampered up the back side of that oak into its hole. Meanwhile, the hawk sat in the first oak tree having missed the squirrel's escape. Now, the hawk flew away to the deep woods."

"What do you make of that, Mr. Woodsman Philosopher?" Ron asked.

"I was about to ask you the same question. The ancient Greeks and Romans would interpret it as a war omen, do you agree? Sun Tzu might see it as an escape from danger on home ground."

"Possibly," Ron concurred. "Now all you have to do is decipher what it means, and you have your game plan against the Calderons. Call me when you have additional news. Meanwhile, if you have woodpeckers around your place, don't go outside without a hard hat. Now let me go back to sleep."

"Thanks for your sage advice, Merlin. I'll definitely keep you informed," I said as I heard Ron's phone click.

I couldn't settle on an informed interpretation of the "omen" I had witnessed, so I scheduled a therapy session with Amy. She had an open slot later that day.

Fossil Therapy

I did my "promptness plus" early arrival. As usual, Amy was with another patient. I waved at her as I collected my rehab toys near the exercise tables in the rear. For the next fifteen minutes, I focused on the exercises that I should have been doing all along. When my official turn came, Amy came back to where I was instead of moving me up to a front table. That was good. We could talk more privately in the back. We certainly needed to talk about recent events.

"You looked as stiff as a robot from where I stood," Amy said as she approached.

"A few weeks ago, you could barely open your eyes. Now you can see around corners. That is a remarkable recovery. MAGENTA will be glad to know you acquired an unusual skill during your hospital stay."

"No, I watched you in the mirror, if you must know. That's why we have mirrors in strategic locations to keep tabs on problem patients like you."

"I'm sure the patient who you just worked on appreciated your lack of attention to her needs while you were watching me."

"I can do more than one thing at the same time. Have you heard of multi-tasking, or were you brain dead before that term was created? Besides, it's not every day I see a live dinosaur come through the front door. I thought your kind was extinct long ago."

"If I make one more trip to Peru, you may get your wish. I will have my fossilized bones delivered to your doorstep."

"Okay, Mr. Fossil, I understand you had a hallway conversation with my sister when I was in the hospital. I want to inform you of your right to counsel and that you are in big trouble with me," Amy steered the conversation to the primary item on her agenda *du jour*.

"Rudyard Kipling had the correct insight into the interactions of sisters. He wrote that one should, 'Never praise a sister to a sister in the hope of your compliments reaching the proper ears.'[1] He could have gone further and flatly state that one should never talk about a sister to her sister under any circumstances if one has plans for a long and peaceful life. The bottom line of our conversation was that she is worried about you and the MAGENTA job."

"With me hanging around you, how could she not worry about me? Is that all you have to say in your defense?"

"Not entirely, but I throw myself on the mercy of the court."

"Not entirely?"

"Yes, I probably should have told her that like the Biblical Ruth, you have signed a MAGENTA contract to go wherever I go and to lodge wherever I lodge. I could have thrown in a provision that you walk three paces behind me at all times, but that might have been overdoing it. That type of airtight agreement should have convinced her. But, based on the emerging trait of skepticism in your family about me, maybe not. I can envision MAGENTA and me being sued if you happen to skin your knees while inline skating with your friends."

"Well, what's your conclusion?"

"See what I mean?"

"Are you asking a question in response to a question, *monsieur?*"

"I'm trying to adjust to the conversational pattern common to your family. Hmm, that's an interesting thought."

"What?"

"Until now, I haven't thought of you as someone who has knees. With your work jeans on, I may never know for sure if you already have pre-existing scabby knees from skating, or if you incurred a Worker's Compensation injury while on a MAGENTA project."

"Don't plan on having a definitive demonstration of my knees anytime soon, mister," Amy answered sharply, setting up her professional fences.

"It's probably just as well," I acknowledged her prerogative to establish boundaries in her workplace without any easements for me or anyone else if she chose not to do so.

"Now that we have exchanged our opening pleasantries, we really need to talk business. First, how have you been? You certainly look better than the last time I saw you in the hospital picking deer and car parts out of your forehead," I asked in a non-threatening voice to let her know that I respected her verbal borders and defenses, but I could find ways around them if the situation demanded.

"I'm healed, and I've completed my initial MAGENTA training, so I'm ready to go. Rick took good care of me, and a few extra days at home helped a lot. Thanks for making that recommendation to him. But, you look like you need some major attention. Is anything particular bothering you?"

"My shoulder klunks when I move it like this," I said as I demonstrated the jerky arm movement to her. "Is that permanent due to the missing labrum tendon, or can I work out a smoother motion in time? And who is Rick?"

"I'm pretty sure that any klunk in your shoulder will disappear. The klunk in your head is a permanent condition. Other people function without their labrum tendon and resume their normal activities without klunking. Rick is Dr. Andrews, the doctor who took care of me in the hospital. I thought you met him?"

"I did briefly, but I didn't get his first name or pedigree. Okay, I believe you about the klunk in my shoulder. Just recall that my normal activities exceed the usual activity level of my age group by a factor of ten. At some point fairly soon, I need to recover my arm strength to handle a bow again. As for any klunk in my head, until I heal I'll let you do the thinking for us, especially when we're in a tough spot. You may get a different perspective on my klunky brain activity then."

"How big of a bow?" Amy asked quickly.

"That was an artful change of subject. I commend you. My training bow is a six-foot English longbow that helps me gain or maintain my arm strength while sending an arrow to the target in a hurry. It's taller than you. In fact, I think my arrows are taller than you. Sorry for the cheap shot about your size, but, it felt so good for me to say it after my recent experiences."

"Go ahead and have your fun if it helps you heal. After all, I'm just a Scout," Amy sniffed.

"Yes, and recent events make your input to the MAGENTA operation more important than ever."

"You're serious now, aren't you?" Amy asked and declared a truce at the same time.

No Fluff, Just the Facts

"To put it mildly, yeah, I'm serious now. Our world changed overnight when those towers went down. My encounters with my opponents, Vasily and Calderon, are small potatoes compared to what happened on the East Coast. I'm certain that a connection exists between them, however loose it might be. We need to find that connection, and, if possible, the people involved because Uncle Sam is too busy with problems on a global scale. If you want to withdraw as my Scout at any time, I'll understand."

"You can't get rid of me that easily after all my hard work to learn the MAGENTA routines and procedures. Are you asking me to quit?"

"Not at all. I want you to realize that the risk level of our jobs may have increased since your interview with MAGENTA, which seems like a million lifetimes ago."

"Yes, but I hope you remember that at our meeting I told you I would have more questions about the job if I was accepted. Turn over, please," Amy instructed.

"Okay, I'm turned over and at your mercy. Ask your questions."

"What are the priority things I should know?" my upstart Scout asked.

"Initially, we need to concentrate on practical things. If MAGENTA gives us sufficient time, we can concentrate on strategy, tactics, and philosophy later."

"Practical things such as?"

"Items such as keeping your *sangfroid*, a cool head, if you will, while continuing to be a problem-solver when the party gets rough. What I'm suggesting is an approach rather than a specific set of skills or rules. Zen masters describe it as absence of self-consciousness in which your training allows you to react appropriately without thinking about it."

I caught Amy by surprise. She anticipated a litany of dos and don'ts to improve her value to MAGENTA and to me that she could easily check off during a performance or after-action review.

Amy hesitated before she replied, "Applying concepts appears simple, and maybe it is for you because you've done this work for so long that everything comes naturally to you. I wish I were that confident and competent to handle any situation. I don't know what else to ask right now."

"If you're looking for something more specific, tell me if this helps you get your arms around your MAGENTA activities and your interactions with me. The psychological testing you did as part of your application points toward some differences we might have in dealing with stressful situations. If I thought your way of doing business under stress wasn't mature and reliable, I would've disqualified you on the spot—and that was before September 11. Now, we definitely need to understand how each of us operates during periods of intense activity and stress."

"What do I need to do?" Amy asked intently.

"Again, think in terms of an approach rather than a specific list of actions. Most frequently, MAGENTA will give you and me specific instructions, and we'll carry them out as ordered. That is the easy stuff. As time goes by, you'll find that I disagree with MAGENTA fairly regularly, or the situation changes rapidly, which requires me to modify my actions without asking MAGENTA's permission or informing you to get authorization for my next move. This will cause you immense stress because of conflicting instructions from MAGENTA and me. The solution is to follow my instructions and ignore MAGENTA after you have enough experience to evaluate situations for yourself. The worst case for you occurs when MAGENTA gives you instructions that you know I have already modified in the field, but I haven't signaled you to pass along to MAGENTA yet. When that happens, you must rely on all your life's training to decide your actions or reactions. In these situations, draw on your *zeitgeist*, your creative spirit, and do the most audacious thing that comes to mind. If you do that, you'll be close to what I'm doing in the field."

PATTON AND AMY, A FINE COMBINATION

"As an example," I continued, "General Patton allowed his staff to act audaciously in moving elements of the U.S. Third Army to relieve the 101st Airborne at Bastogne during the Battle of the Bulge in December 1944. Many thought Patton was a mean cuss. Maybe he was, but he believed in preparation, training, and audacity. Patton had his staff prepare three action plans for countering the Nazi bulge in the U.S. Army's front line before he went into Eisenhower's briefing with all the other Allied commanders about how to stop the advance of Hitler's Panzer Divisions in the Ardennes Forest.[2] Patton came out of Eisenhower's meeting in Verdun, and activated his action plan before any other U.S. general started to design one. If Patton and his staff hadn't thought audaciously, a large American military cemetery would be located near Bastogne now. You may feel uncomfortable and fearful at first about creating a mess, but strive to think audaciously, and you'll be fine. As Patton would tell you, think, "*De l'audace, encore de l'audace, et toujours de l'audace.*" That is, audacity, more audacity, and always audacity."[3]

"Where do you get all this stuff?"

"Like Patton, I read and remember—not the source as much as the idea. Also, I have *mucho* more life experience than you do. If you're interested in Patton, I can lend you an excellent biography about him."

"Getting back to what I need today, what if I use your audacity approach and really mess up?"

"Then, MAGENTA will remove you from its payroll, justifying the change with the Italian saying, '*Bis peccare in bello non licet,*' which means 'It is not permissible to blunder twice in war.'[4] But, if I'm still alive after your display of audacity, you won't hear any criticism from me, and I'll defend your actions to MAGENTA. There's another interesting part to the Bastogne story. Some war experts speculate that the Nazi objective was not only Bastogne with its eleven crossroads, but also the nearby village of St. Vith with its important road junctions.[5] Further, the daily train was still running between St. Vith and Paris. If the Nazis had captured St. Vith, they could have taken the afternoon train into Paris and split the American and British armies. War won, war done in one afternoon. We would all be speaking audacious German now. Have you thought of anything else while I've been rambling here?"

AMY'S FIRST STANDING ORDER

"Your approach is so different from the regimentation by my parents, teachers, and supervisors that I may really enjoy being able to think independently for once."

"I'll certainly give you sufficient rope to hang yourself and to tie a nice bow around your neck. While you ponder that, I'll give you a specific directive that you should set up immediately. I want you to find a place to hide. I mean deep cover—not just with friends in your neighborhood or downtown, or at your parents' or relatives' homes in Iowa or nearby. In reviewing documents we found in Peru, I'm certain that Calderon's primary networks to Europe and North Africa run through Miami and Central America the same as other drug and contraband routes. But, a sizable branch appears to run through Chicago too. I believe that's why Calderon was able to get to Jenny so fast. His gunmen were already here. If I can't stop Calderon first, he will come looking for both of us. Your best defense if I'm not around is to hide where Calderon will not intuitively think to look for you."

"Now that you've scared me to death, what kind of place would that be?"

"Some place where you feel secure and where you can resurface relatively quickly when danger passes. For example, who do you know in the Quad Cities area?"

"I have some relatives, and now Rick, umh—Dr. Andrews, of course."

"Of course, Dr. Andrews, of all people! Why didn't I think of him? Do your relatives a favor. Don't make them a target or get them involved. Calderon has the resources to check out your family too quickly."

"So you think Rick—?"

"Absolutely, if you feel comfortable with that arrangement. A hospital should have a million hiding places, and people of every kind come and go at all hours. You'd have access to food, avenues of escape, sources of information, possible disguises, and someone who is concerned about you. But, don't expect me to play chaperone or you'll cause another kind of problem for yourself at home."

"How will I know when you need me, or when the coast is clear?"

"We can use Dr. Andrews as our zealous intermediary if he doesn't kill off his other patients through neglect while he hides you."

"Your use of the word 'zealous' reminded me of something. I have a present for you. The Mormon missionaries sent you photos they took in Bolivia, including several of Calderon. You never met him did you?"

"For all the dancing I did because of him, you're right. I never met him. Photos are helpful. Not to be outdone, my wife and I took photos in Morocco, Portugal, and Spain that you should see and pass on to MAGENTA. I also have a present for you. I'll give it to you before I leave."

"We're almost finished, unless I accidentally break your arm in the remaining time. I won't get on your case about keeping up your exercise program while you're in town. You have plenty of incentive to get stronger. You're a little stiff, but you haven't injured any major shoulder parts, so you should feel better in a few days. I'll put an ice pack on now, and then you can leave, okay?"

Arming My Scout

"In that case, get my gym bag and take out the brown bag inside, but don't open it until you get home."

"What is it?"

"It's not your lunch or supper, that's certain. I found several weapons for you. You said your father didn't teach you how to handle a gun, so I found alternative weapons that you can use without intensive training."

"The package feels lumpy. What do you have in there?"

"Brass knuckles, throwing stars, and throwing darts. I got the idea for the knucks from the rings you wear. If you've thrown a Frisbee, you already know how to throw the stars. Be careful how you handle them because they're razor sharp. Grip the small end of the darts and throw them overhand like a knife. The weighted sharp end will take the dart to wherever you throw it. Go somewhere private and practice a bit. I know you can throw a softball, so you have the arm strength and accuracy to feel comfortable with all these toys in a short time. Your effective range on the stars and darts may be around fifteen yards, but you should be able to intimidate somebody beyond that distance. By the way, these items are illegal for you to carry, so don't show them around to impress your friends."

"You carry guns, but I go to jail if I'm caught with brass knuckles?"

"Life is never fair, is it? Jail wouldn't be a bad place to hide either. A convent would be an excellent place for Sister Amy Immaculate to hide. I'm sure that Calderon, your family, friends, and especially God would never look for you there. In fact, neither would I. But that's a topic for another time. Someday, if you demonstrate that you can handle firearms better than Advari, I'll teach you to shoot. Until then, be happy with the weapons you have. Hopefully, you'll never need them. Here comes a load of other patients, so I'll clear out. Thanks for the exercises, I feel better already. Until I hear from MAGENTA, my primary job is to rehab my shoulders and be alert for an attack by Calderon. I'll see you here in a few days. I'm glad Dr. Andrews—sorry, my mistake—Rick was good to you, and that you feel better yourself. I talked to him only for a few minutes, but I like him. He seems to be a genuinely good guy."

"He called me every day when I was at home and asked if he could see me the next time I go home or when he comes to Chicago."

"You received very intensive and personal care while you were in the hospital. Life may be unfair, but it can be full of good and surprising things too. Don't you think?"

"Wait a minute. Are you involved with Rick in some way? You are! I can tell by the look on your face! What are you two cooking up against me?"

"Hold it. Remember, I'm your patient, not a dating service. I don't get involved in *affaires d'amour*. Also, I was out of the country for a long time. Don't forget that I didn't know his first name was Rick! And Sister Amy Immaculate shouldn't be dating anyway. She should be on her knees—here we go with the knees again—praying night and day for my safety and salvation."

"Don't try your diversionary out-of-town tricks on me because now I know that you and Rick are guilty of some conspiracy against me. If I didn't have patients waiting, you would never leave here alive until you told me exactly what you and Rick concocted. I will get you next time for sure! Do your exercises, and come back in two days. You'd better show a lot of improvement next time! And take your ratty Bonzo the Clown towel with you!"

"Hey, no fair picking on Bonzo. As you can see, he's been with me a long time. Also, in my defense, Dr. Andrews and I happened to be sitting in the hospital chapel when he began extolling the praises of some heavenly creature whom he had met recently, or some metaphysical revelation that he had just experienced. I had nothing to do with it. In fact, I attempted to have him get a grip on reality, change his diet, and get some sleep. Lord knows I'd never connect you with anything of a divine nature like that. Bye!" I said as I pranced out of the door.

There was nothing wrong with my legs, so I made it out the door without Amy flinging a load of weights in my direction. I didn't mind what could be a budding romance between Amy and Andrews as long as it didn't interfere with any professional or MAGENTA work she needed to do. And there was plenty of the latter to occupy us. Certainly, use of the hospital could have advantages if the situation ever became ultra hot and Amy needed a place to hide. Although I kept my conversation with Amy on the light side, I could tell that the downing of the twin towers had imposed a deeper seriousness on both of us to accelerate what we needed to accomplish within a very short time. My first task would be to discipline myself to heal and stay in shape for whatever was ahead. Otherwise, neither of us would be prepared when it came time to think and act in the absence of clear instructions from MAGENTA.

They're Here!

The next morning, I got up later than usual and did my exercises. My shoulder was stiff, but my forearms were regaining definition. I hoped Amy had given me the correct exercise program for my shoulders. I went upstairs at about 11:30 a.m. for a break and noticed an unfamiliar car parked at the corner a half block away. The sky was overcast, and I couldn't make out the two occupants through the tinted car windows other than to discern two independent heads in the front seat. The dark sedan had a nondescript Illinois license plate. The neighbors, their families, and guests were always coming and going in a variety of vehicles. Consequently, the car and its passengers didn't merit additional attention other than a cursory glance and my noting its presence, make, and plate number. Mentally, I named the driver T1 and the passenger T2, short for Target One and Target Two as I routinely do for my personal use. Then, I returned to the basement to resume exercising.

When I went upstairs at about 2:15 p.m., the car and T1 were still there, but T2 wasn't. That was enough to pique my interest. I dug out my binoculars to take a closer look. The driver was huge, possibly Latin, maybe a South American Indian. He definitely was trying hard to watch my house without appearing to look at it. I now saw that he was wearing a suit or sport jacket, which was out of place in my neighborhood on a mild sunny mid-September day, especially for the time the driver was in the car with the windows shut. After watching T1 for about ten minutes without observing significant action, I decided to locate T2.

As I made the rounds of the front windows on the first floor, my wild cherry trees and the drapes in the parlor hampered my vision. After watching for activity at the neighbors' houses close to me, I still couldn't locate T2. I decided to go upstairs for a better view if I could see through the leafy canopy of the ancient oaks in my back yard. As I went into the rear bedroom that overlooked my patio, several of the neighbors' back yards, and a slice of the cul-de-sac to the west, I spotted T2 hiding behind the neighbor's woodpile directly behind my property. The trees and the slope of the hill in my back yard had prevented me from seeing him from the first floor. T2 was darker complexioned than T1. But, like his companion, he was overdressed in a dark suit and raincoat that bulged where I suspected he concealed a weapon.

Gilberto Calderon hadn't wasted time in ordering his *pistoleros* to pay me a visit. Around 2:30 p.m., the elementary school buses would unload the neighborhood kids at the corner. Unless I wanted them caught in crossfire or grabbed as hostages, I had to act fast. With weapons on every floor of my house, arming myself was less of a problem than coming up with a plan of attack or defense.

I was about to launch phase one of my hawk and squirrel offensive-defensive plan when another problem pulled into my driveway in the form of Amy's white coupe. My Scouts knew the cardinal rule from day one not to contact me at my house for both their protection and mine. Yet, apparently, Amy and I would initiate our first action on my home turf with Amy unaware of any danger to herself or anyone else. T1 hadn't moved from his car. I ran downstairs to meet Amy just as she reached for the doorbell. I opened the door, grabbed her arm, and abruptly pulled her inside. The sting in my shoulder let me know that she was sturdy, and that my action was forceful.

"What's wrong with you, girl?" I barked at her. "Do you want to get us both killed?"

I startled Amy by my reception, and she would have deposited herself on the tiled foyer floor if I hadn't held onto her arm.

"I know I'm not supposed to come to your house, but Heidi and I spotted something in your European photos that you should know right away. Today is my short day at the shop, so I came here directly from work," Amy gasped, trying to catch her breath and talk at the same time as she reached into her purse for the photos.

"Okay, what do you have that's worth catching a bullet in the head for your efforts?" I demanded.

"Look at this photo of Calderon that the missionaries took in Bolivia, and then look at the photo of the man in the hat with the red hatband you saw in Slovakia and Morocco. It's the same guy! This proves your theory that Calderon's network extends into Europe and North Africa. Isn't that important information?"

"Partly, but it's a good first try, Scout," I responded more calmly.

"Why only partly?" Amy asked with her ego bruised that I was not more excited and appreciative of her and Heidi's detective work.

"The photo is definitive about the Calderon network, but from the angle of the photo, I can't tell if this is Gilberto Calderon or his twin brother, Ernesto, except for the red hatband."

"No one told me about twin brothers. How was I supposed to know?" Amy said, crestfallen that she didn't have all the pertinent facts.

"I didn't know the full story myself until Ron told me this morning, so you get a passing grade on your first intelligence effort because I didn't inform you about it at the shop. I understand that Gilberto mostly stays in South America while Ernesto, our Mr. Red Hatband, runs the European and African operations. I didn't want to confuse you earlier with discussion of the twins until I confirmed it for myself. You and Heidi did good investigative work. There's no question about that. But, we have a more pressing problem of getting you out of here alive. I am responsible for our predicament by not telling you about the two Calderons. Consequently, I am responsible for getting you out of this current dilemma. Are you ready?"

"You aren't mad at me then?" Amy sought to confirm her status with me.

"No, not unless you get me killed in the next few minutes. Then, I'll never speak to you again no matter how much you beg me."

AUDACITY IN ACTION

"What do you want me to do?" Amy finally reacted to my call to action two sentences earlier.

"First, stay away from the windows, but keep an eye on the driver of the car parked at the corner. See there?" I said pointing to the car. "I call him T1, and he is our near danger. Yell for me if he gets out of the car and comes this way. In fact, yell for me if he does anything," I instructed.

"Where are you going? You aren't leaving me alone, are you?"

"His *compadre*, T2 is out back," I answered her two questions indirectly. "See him? Look through the kitchen window toward the north side of the neighbor's house in the back. If I can take T2 first, we may have a chance to get out of this."

"Which way is north? Never mind, yes, I see him. Oh look, the school kids are getting off the buses on the corner! I hope none of them get in your way!" Amy identified the danger correctly as she turned toward the front of the house again in response to the happy noises of the kids racing to be the first one home.

"The Catholic kids are safe. They live down the block on the opposite side from the park. The Protestant kids and the non-believers may become a problem if T1 and T2 are interested in hostages. Help me arm this crossbow. If you were a better therapist, I'd be able to use my regular bow by now."

"If you were a better patient, I'd be home getting ready to go out with my friends tonight."

"Message received and acknowledged. Next time, don't try so hard to motivate me."

"How are you going to get outside? T2 will see you as soon as you open your back door," Amy perceived the situation correctly again.

"I decided not to go out the back door. I'm going out the garage window on the north side, that way," I pointed, "and through the gate of the neighbor's stockade fence. The slope of the hill, the big oak, and the neighbor's utility shed should block T2's view of me doing all that. If Dottie's dogs aren't in the yard, I should be able to get a close shot at him."

"What if they are?" Amy blinked hard, trying to hold back tears despite my absolving her of any guilt for the current situation.

"Then, you fly solo in developing and executing your own audacious survival plan," I answered as coolly as I could manage with my personal survival instincts kicking into high gear.

"What if the driver at the corner comes toward the house while you're outside?" Amy asked, serving notice that she was more interested in a mutually beneficial survival plan than anything she could devise on her own.

"Two Jehovah Witnesses dropped off literature the other day. Have T1 read their magazines until I get back. If he can, ask him to underline the important information. I'm behind in my religious reading these days."

"What if he really gets impatient and breaks into the house?" Amy persisted in her personal concerns encompassed in our mutual survival plan.

"If T1 doesn't shoot you first, use your brass knuckles on him. Also, see that flintlock pistol on the wall rack in my den? It is both real and charged for a surprise occasion such as this. Pull back the hammer with both of your thumbs if you can't do it with one, aim the barrel at T1's belt buckle, close your eyes, and pull the trigger. If you forget everything else, remember to close your eyes. Otherwise, the ignition of the priming powder will fry your eyeballs. If you miss, do anything to stay alive. If he chases you into the kitchen, the knives are on the left side of the utensil drawer, the forks and spoons are on the right side. Take your pick. I'd like to chat with you a little more, but I really have to go. Think you can handle it, Shortcake?"

"We'll soon find out if I'm audacious enough for this job," she said with her voice wavering but her chin firmly set and resolute.

"If a squirrel can ad lib a defense against a hawk, so can we," I tried to encourage her.

"What? I don't understand," she said, reminding me that she wasn't a party to this morning's conversation about the squirrel versus hawk omen with Ron.

"Never mind. I'll tell you later, or read my memoirs if I live long enough to write them."

Determining that my survival was the best approach for our mutual survival, I ran down the hallway through the utility room and into my garage. Getting out of the garage window without making noise was a challenge with my tender shoulders impeding my progress every inch of the way. But, I finally deposited myself headfirst into the flowerbed alongside my garage. I rolled out of the flowerbed and waited a moment to determine if T2 had seen me. By the absence of gunfire, he apparently hadn't. Then, I crawled to the gate of Dottie's fence, lifted the latch, and let myself into her back yard. Dottie's dogs were not out, which was a relief because one would want me to play while the other one would try to take my leg off. I crouched low, skipped through a few flowerbeds, and made it to the back fence and the utility shed at the southwest corner of Dottie's yard. I was at about a forty-five degree angle to T2's position.

I would have a close shot from this position, but T2 would likely see me as soon as I raised my head over the fence. I couldn't allow him to signal T1 under any circumstances. Another option was to climb over the north fence, go to the outside of the northwest corner, and take a shot at T2 from there. I would have a longer though shallower uphill shot, but T2 would have less chance of seeing me before I got the arrow away. The height of the south fence and the utility shed would block T2's view of me scaling the north fence and circling to the northwest corner of Dottie's property.

I arrived at my firing position without alerting T2 and without destroying Dottie's flowerbeds beyond all recognition. I paused a minute to check my bow and gain control of my breathing. My shot wouldn't be anywhere near as spectacular as the legendary arrow shot by the early thirteenth century Tartar invader who silenced the Polish bugler stationed in the Mariacki Church bell tower in Krakow, but my shot needed to have the same deadly result.[6] I needed to be both fast and accurate without hurrying. I took two quick breaths, held the last one, put my head and crossbow around the corner of the fence, zeroed in on T2, and let the arrow fly in one continuous motion without T2 seeing me. With a slight tailwind, the arrow ran the seventy-five yards straight and true, piercing T2's throat up to the feathers before he had a chance to react. T2 went face down into the grass without uttering a sound or knowing what hit him. The Polish people continue to commemorate their bugler's demise by playing an abbreviated note that stops on the alleged last sound that the Polish bugler played when he took the Tartar's arrow in his throat. Nobody in Poland commemorates the fantastic shot made by the Tartar warrior, and his name is lost in history as mine would be on this shot with the possible exception of the Calderons' reaction when they learned that they had lost a hired gun.

I didn't need public recognition for my shot, especially from the local police department. I waited a few moments to see if a second shot was necessary, but the "one shot one kill" training that the three sergeants taught me applied to archery as well as firearms. Now, I needed to get back and see how Amy's relationship with T1 was progressing.

I ran along the back of Dottie's fence into my yard, crossed my patio in full stride, and burst through the kitchen door, scaring the daylights out of Amy as I arrived back in the house. As I closed the door, I glanced back to see two cars stopping at the end of the cul-de-sac to the west near where I initially saw T2. I not only had T1 in front to deal with, but now I had an unknown number of T reinforcements advancing into my back yard. As they progressed, they would find T2 with the unsightly arrow through his neck and conjure up something unpleasant for Amy and me.

Audacity is one thing. Being overwhelmed is another. "*Benedetto e qual male che vien solo.*"[7] Indeed, "blessed are the misfortunes that only come singly." I would need to invent a plan for a multi-front campaign or a quick escape.

"What time do you have, Scout?" I asked Amy as I ran to rejoin her in the front hallway.

"What? Oohh—3:25 p.m. precisely, why?"

"Because, the Benet Academy track teams run by here at 3:30 p.m. each day like clockwork."

"And?"

"And they always run through the park at the end of this court, take a left on Ohio Street, and go down the hill to Yackley Road. It's an important 'and' for us right now."

"I still don't follow you."

"True, you don't follow me. We mingle with the runners down the hill and keep going past Yackley, then past the public high school to the Lisle Police Headquarters on Lincoln Road, if necessary. T1 won't wipe out the entire Benet Academy track team just to get us. The Benet Alumni Association won't allow it."

"That won't prevent T1 and his friends from trying for us some other time, though, will it?" Amy accurately assessed the weak spot in my plan.

"No, it won't. But right now, the odds are definitely not in our favor. We need to run and fight another day. The Benet runners are in pretty good condition. Do you think you can keep up with them at least until they make the turn onto Ohio Street?" I stated in the form of a question to provide unequivocal advance warning to Amy of what I needed her to do.

"Do I look like a pansy?" she replied, confirming my belief that asking her questions was a fool-proof form of communicating instructions and expectations to her.

"You are hopeless in your interrogatory answers to questions even in the face of grave danger, but apparently it works consistently for you and your family. I definitely need to record that in your MAGENTA performance report if I get the opportunity."

"Will we be able to hear the team coming so that we can be ready?" Amy asked insightfully.

"Baby Bob's dog, Ruby, directly across the street, will hear the runners coming before we do, and she will start wailing. That's our signal to be ready."

"It's 3:35 p.m. now. Where are the runners?" Amy asked apprehensively confirming that under stressful circumstances she would hold me accountable for every word that escaped my mouth.

"Well, 3:30–3:35 p.m. more or less. I never needed them to be particularly precise before today. I'd better see what the other Ts are doing in my back yard."

The four new Ts in the back were gathered around T2's body. With their cell phones, they undoubtedly were calling T1 and, possibly, their boss about what to do with T2's remains. They would have to deal with a number of kids and moms in the street as witnesses now if they insisted on retaliating with a noisy raid on my house, or if they merely tried to get T2's body quietly into a car. One way or another, their decision would be important to me.

"I hear a dog whining!" Amy exclaimed.

"That's either a signal that the runners are near, or that Ruby wants to go back inside. In either case, be ready because the Benet kids really move. If for some reason I get delayed or stop, you keep running. Understand? That's weird, Ruby usually cries louder than she is now."

Then, I saw the reason for Ruby's half-hearted wail. Only the freshman Benet girls were running today. They were tall enough to hide Amy, but I would tower over them and remain a splendid target for T1. I couldn't expose the runners to that kind of danger without knowing T1's shooting skills.

"Get going," I ordered Amy. "And don't look back. If Dottie is home, we'll meet you in a black roadster convertible at the corner of Ohio and Yackley. If we don't meet you there, keep running east—straight ahead at the stoplight, and we'll meet you somewhere along Ohio Street. If not there, keep going until you get to the high school where Ohio becomes Short Street. If necessary, keep going further east toward the Police Headquarters building on the corner of Short and Lincoln. On second thought, never mind the details, you'll see the police cars parked in back of the building. Run in that direction. Tell the cops that you are turning yourself in for assaulting your fortuneteller who predicted that today would be your lucky day. Offer to buy doughnuts for the cops if they're nice to you. Let's see what else. Ah, no matter what, stay at the police building until we or someone you know comes for you."

"What if you don't?"

"We never dwell on those 'what ifs' at MAGENTA. I said that we'll pick you up somewhere along the way, and we will. Now go!"

Dialing Up More Audacity

As I watched Amy slip out the front door and churn her legs to join the runners, I dialed Dottie's number. The head movement in T1's car confirmed that he had seen Amy. But now, he faced a dilemma. He had to decide to come after me or to pursue Amy. He made the decision I anticipated he'd make. He would come for me first. The choice was rational because he had potential help from the Ts in my back yard. After he finished with me, Amy would be an easy target unless she married a policeman in the next half hour or so. My job was to negate T1's actions and set a defensive screen to protect both Amy and myself. I had a head start in activating my escape plan. I was on the phone to my neighbor before T1 made his first move.

"Hello," Dottie answered on the second ring.

"Dot, I need a short ride if you have gas in your road beast," I said in my most recognizable and neighborly voice.

"Sure, fine. What's going on? I saw you run through my yard a while ago with your bow. Are you hunting chipmunks again?"

"I'm hunting South American skunks now. But we need to pick up a friend down the hill. I'll fill in the details later. If you open the side door of your garage, I'll come out of my garage window and meet you in thirty seconds. Oh, put the top down on your 'beast,' if it's not down already."

"Should I make sandwiches for the trip too?" Dottie asked in good humor. "I hope you realize that it's not easy being your neighbor day in and day out."

"I don't see a 'For Sale' sign in your front yard if I'm that intolerable."

My neighbors were great. They had been around me long enough not to get whacked out by anything I did or asked them to do. I took a quick look to see where Amy and the Benet runners were, then ran downstairs to get two smoke canisters left over from Peru. In seconds, I was back upstairs, through my garage window again, and into the side door of Dottie's garage. She had the motor of the beast rumbling nicely, and I jumped into the cargo area in the back that was big enough to hold two sets of golf clubs comfortably as advertised, or one screwy neighbor uncomfortably.

"Where are we going, *maestro*, and will I like it when we get there?" Dottie asked cautiously though still a committed neighbor to the assignment I had yet to divulge.

"Certainly. Did I ever take advantage of our friendship before? Don't think about that now. Just back out into the street and drive toward the corner. When you get alongside the car parked there on the left, slow down a little so I can toss these smoke cans. Then, move out smartly onto Oak Hill Drive. Turn north on Yackley, and then east on Short Street. We'll pick up my friend somewhere along there."

"Are you going to get me killed this time?" Dottie asked apprehensively.

"Absolutely not, I guarantee it. They won't risk damaging your car. Trust me."

"Do you trust my Mafia relatives?"

"I trust everyone except Mario. He's a little strange. But, I trust all of them to protect you, or at least to take their revenge if something bad happens to us in the next few minutes. If we survive, I'll buy you a tank of gas."

"And you call my cousin Mario nuts. I should live so long to see you buy gas for my big black street cruiser. This adventure will make life worth living—my big Mafioso family against your little cowboy friends. I'm glad you asked me to participate in this sporting event."

"Thanks, Dot, for your help. We really need to go now," I cut the conversation short.

Dottie lost no time following my instructions. Her beast roared out of the driveway and up the hill toward the corner. T1 couldn't see me reclining in the cargo area. He was totally surprised when my first smoke canister landed on the hood of his car. The second one sailed through his open rear side window. The beast's tires squealed as Dottie punched the gas pedal, made a sharp left onto Oak Hill Drive, and headed east toward Yackley. Halfway down the block, we heard a deafening boom behind us, and saw a giant fireball rise above the trees lining the parkway. The white phosphorus smoke canister had ignited something flammable inside the car. We didn't slow down or go back to check T1's status. We had no need to do that given the pyrotechnics and the explosion.

When we reached the corner of Yackley and Oak Hill Drive, the Benet runners passed in front of us southbound on their way back to the school. Amy wasn't with them. Hopefully, she set her internal compass correctly and continued running east toward the high school and the police headquarters as I had instructed her. I realized the irony of picking up Shortcake on Short Street, but kept that distraction to myself. Dottie had serious work to do. Short Street weaves through an industrial park before it straightens at the high school and its athletic fields leading to the police headquarters. I saw Amy ahead at the stop sign just west of the school. From a distance, I could see that her ponytail was not bobbing as perkily as it had been when she started, but she maintained a steady pace.

As Dottie pulled alongside Amy, I sat up straighter to shout, "Hey, Scout, are you planning to run all the way to Chicago, or do you want a ride?"

All the energy seemed to escape from her in that instant. Amy took two more steps, grabbed the door handle of the beast, and flopped into the front passenger seat. I reached forward from the back storage compartment, and gently tugged her ponytail twice in silent salute to her effort.

"In espionage jargon, you just executed a 'minimize your limitations' exercise. Instead of your size being a limitation, it helped us avoid a dangerous situation. Remember that because we'll try to use that technique frequently in the future," I told Amy in admiration.

"Where to now?" Dottie asked as she turned toward me.

"We can go back home. The squirrel certainly escaped from the hawk today. By the way, Dottie, our red-faced squirrel here is Amy, my physical therapist."

"I don't understand a thing you're telling me as usual," Dottie announced. "But should we go back so soon? I hear emergency vehicle sirens coming."

"*Au contraire*, now is the best time for our arrival. The firemen will be witnesses that we are coming home, and that we weren't anywhere near there when the car spontaneously went boom. When we get close to the fire truck, let the beast growl a little to get the firefighters' full attention."

"You are rotten to the core, neighbor," Dottie accurately defined our relationship while relishing every moment of the beast psychology I proposed. Dottie made a U-turn, drove back to Yackley, and then made the corner onto Oak Hill Drive toward my house with the beast's engine purring. When we arrived at the corner, the firefighters were hosing down the remains of T1's car. They had responded to an emergency call quickly as usual, but almost too fast in this case. Now, several firefighters turned their heads to look at us as if they had read my script. One approached us as we pulled alongside the fire truck.

"You can't go through yet," he told Dottie while looking at Amy's crimson face to see if she needed a fire extinguisher too.

"Too bad you feel that way," Dottie replied. (When Dottie displayed her Mafia attitude, I left her alone. She could handle this conversation herself.) "My husband will be home shortly from a business trip to California. Unless you want to hang around and tell him why his supper isn't ready, I suggest you let us through. I'm not going to steal your little yellow and white fire truck or run over your hoses if that's what's bothering you."

"*Mafioso*," I said, pointing toward Dottie to reinforce her demands. "I wouldn't mess with her over a minor car fire, Lieutenant."

The lieutenant motioned for two of his crew to clear enough of the fire equipment out of the road for us to pass. Dottie gunned the engine and pulled into her driveway and garage in one fluid motion that was fine for her and Amy who were buckled securely in their seats. In Dottie's defense, I only hit my head on the top and side of the cargo area twice when we went over the curb into her driveway.

"You two stay put for a second while I see if we still have visitors in my back yard," I cautioned as I rubbed my head, squeezed myself out of the rear storage area, and jumped over the side of the car in less than poetry-in-motion moves. "The other Ts should have departed before the fire crew arrived, but *pistoleros* aren't as reliable as they could be these days," I commented over my shoulder as I went around the corner of Dottie's garage and into my back yard. As I expected, the late-arriving Ts had fled and conveniently had taken T2's body with them. Obviously, they didn't want to explain to either the police or fire department why they were keeping company with a dead body in my back yard. I returned to Dottie's garage.

The Chief, the Jasons, and the Deal

"Thanks, Dot, for the ride. Amy, you can go home safely now. Keep an eye out for anyone following you, but I think the *pistoleros* need to regroup and talk to their leader before they try anything else. If I can schedule therapy for your last appointment tomorrow, that will be the most convenient time for me."

"Okay, I'll see you then," Amy replied without looking back as she trotted to her car in my driveway and drove off a little shaky from her first encounter with the forces of darkness in her "short" though, thus far, illustrious career as my Scout.

I didn't tell Amy that I expected the next assault from our South American foes to occur at the therapy center the next evening. I anticipated that she would be the primary target, although the *pistoleros* would try to eliminate both of us if I happened to be there to interfere with their plans. I intended to do more than to interfere because I had promised Amy that I would not lose another Scout as long as I lived. More immediately, I recognized I was about to have a visit from Police Chief Franzen, who was walking toward Dottie and me from the remains of T1's car on the corner.

He was a friend to the community and fine as police chiefs go, but he always appeared aggravated by the number of unusual events that occurred in my neighborhood. Over the years, the events and his assumption that I knew more about them than I disclosed or that he could connect to me prevented the chief and me from being close buddies. My neighbors were equally oblique in responding to his questions. They knew I was involved in something unusual, but they weren't overly curious to find out what that was as long as it didn't disturb the neighborhood's tranquility. By his appearance and stride as he approached, I forecasted that Chief Franzen expected this to be another unrewarding interrogation.

"Would I be accurate in assuming that you folks know nothing about the car fire on the corner?" Franzen asked while still six paces from where Dottie and I stood.

"What car fire on what corner, Chief?" I answered, testing his resolve to pursue the issue further.

"If you check with the firefighters, they'll tell you that we just arrived home a few minutes ago," Dottie seconded, wearing her inscrutable Mafia face.

"I checked with the firefighters, and that's exactly what they told me. They also mentioned that your husband is due home for supper shortly," Franzen answered, looking at Dottie and me while scanning his cranial cavity for any possible avenues to continue this conversation on the slim chance that he might obtain a grain of information from us.

"Thanks for reminding me, Chief; if you want more information, discuss your concerns with the fire department," Dottie suggested. "I need to put dinner on the stove."

"Well, this may be a convenient time for the private chat I've been meaning to have with you for quite a while," the chief told me as Dottie disappeared into her house. "Let's walk up to the corner as we talk."

"I'm flattered, Chief," I told Franzen as I fell into step with him walking toward the smoldering remains of T1's car. "I may have misjudged you, but, I was under the impression that you, like other local politicians, only visit this neighborhood every four years at election time. And now, you want a private chat. I don't know how you find the time for all this community service. By the way, Dottie told me that our street doesn't appear on the official village map. Lucky for you that the post office, the refuse company, and the snowplow drivers don't rely on that map to find us," I said as I began taking irregular steps to build up his aggravation level as we strode along with me either a step ahead or behind him.

However, the chief seemed not to notice my clowning this time.

"Does the name JASON mean anything to you?" the chief asked calmly.

"As in Jason and the Argonauts of Greek legend?" I inquired, continuing my tomfoolery but now trying to hide the hitch in my last step as my reflexes responded to a name that I hadn't heard for many years.

Again, the chief appeared not to notice.

"Not exactly," the chief corrected me. "It's capital J-A-S-O-N" he spelled out.

I stopped in my tracks. I recalled that on one occasion during my military days long ago, I saw Alice Bright Feather put a folder into my briefcase with that name printed on it. As a rookie go-fetch-it at the time, I didn't ask questions. But, Alice knew I had seen the folder, and she immediately disappeared into the colonel's office. Within minutes, both of them reappeared. The colonel reminded me that I hadn't seen anything, and, therefore, I knew nothing, and had nothing to say to anyone about the contents of my briefcase regardless of the circumstances. I told him I understood. And I did.

If that had been my sole encounter with the name, I might not have remembered it from that long ago. But, after I completed my active military service and returned home, my father gave me Joe's duffel bag. Going through Joe's personal effects was too heavy a burden for him to bear. With my new bride and baby to occupy me, I tossed the bag in the back of a closet without inspecting its contents. Years later, at a family gathering, several family members remarked that the tenth anniversary of Joe's death was approaching. On a rainy afternoon a few days later, I dug out Joe's duffel bag to see what it contained. Except for some family photos, my exploration of the bag uncovered the usual combination of military and civilian clothing. As I removed several layers of clothes, I unearthed Joe's shaving kit, which I set aside momentarily to continue my journey to the bottom of the bag. The trip was unremarkable, so I turned my attention back to the shaving kit. On first glance, the contents appeared equally unremarkable.

As I held Joe's razor, the kitchen phone rang. I got off my knees and hurried from the bedroom to answer it, unconsciously taking the razor with me. The caller was my insurance agent who I had asked for a quote on additional homeowner's coverage. The conversation regressed into discussing coverage that I didn't want, and I began to nervously twist the razor handle while trying to find the right words to end the agent's sales pitch. After I had hung up the phone, I realized that I had unscrewed the handle from the razor head. After two unsuccessful attempts to reattach the razor parts, I decided that my problem was a piece of paper sticking out of the hollow handle. Borrowing tweezers from my wife's dresser, I dug the piece of paper out after a few stabs. After carefully unfolding the fragile paper fragment, I could still make out the faded but unmistakable letters of "JASONs" in Joe's handwriting, followed by what I believed were the Cyrillic letters "BacbIJIH" that I didn't translate. The remainder of whatever Joe had written was fatally lost to time and deterioration. I reassembled the razor, placed it in the shaving kit, returned all the contents to the duffel bag, and consigned the bag to the back of my closet for the next twenty years.

Now, I was standing in my front yard being interrogated by Chief Franzen about a name I had only seen twice in my lifetime with no connecting information other than to learn at some point in the last forty years that JASON was a group of U.S. scientists who periodically advised the U.S. President, Congress, the Pentagon, Cabinet Secretaries, and intelligence agency chiefs about classified scientific topics and studies. I decided to continue my clowning, but I listened very intently to every word the chief spoke and observed every gesture he made. *What connection did the chief have to JASON?* I struggled internally to understand the implications of his information on my operations. My good *karma* must have activated the chief's communication genes because he began to vocalize information without my priming his speech pump.

"In case you really don't know," the chief began, "JASON is a group of Nobel Prize-caliber U.S. scientists who provide classified information to the U.S. Department of Defense (DoD), and Department of Energy (DoE), among others."[8] (His definition of JASON differed from mine, but was close enough to confirm that my description and his encompassed the same group.) "I was an Army liaison to this group at one time," the chief continued. "Your recent escapades have come to the attention of JASON members, the DoD, and various intelligence agencies. They are impressed with both the extent and quality of the information you have transmitted through MAGENTA. The group also is concerned about your safety and that of your colleagues. Because of my prior experience with this group, I have been assigned to protect your sorry self with my department's resources while you're at home or in the area until further notice."

Even if nothing else happened in the next seven hours, this would be an extraordinary day for me. First, Calderon's local *pistoleros* introduced themselves, and now this surprise announcement by the chief made the day eligible for entry into my personal journal. But, recalling my years of training, I decided not to disclose or confirm any connection or knowledge that I had about MAGENTA or JASON to the chief, or anyone else. This wouldn't be the first or last recorded incident of a public official posing as a knowledgeable buddy to gain or confirm sensitive information to pass along to the wrong people. I knew the story of the Garden of Eden well enough to avoid accepting any low-hanging fruit offered by the chief without thoroughly washing it through my knowledge and intuition machines first.

"Are you sure you have the name correct, Chief?" I stalled. Maybe you mean Masons as in the Masonic Lodge. I've certainly heard of them. As for MAGENTA, I wouldn't know the color if I saw it. My red-green color deficiency gives me enough eye trouble as it is without introducing magenta for my retinal recognition."

"I'm sorry, but this time, I'm not playing games with you," the chief shot back at me. "You know that I have the name and organization correct, although you don't know much more about JASON than you did years ago, do you?"

"So, where do we go with this informational impasse, Chief?" I asked, more subdued than I had intended to be given my prior history of successful circumlocution with Franzen.

"Knowingly or unknowingly, you stumbled into an international network of military, political, scientific, and business people who are involved in drug trafficking, money laundering, document forgery, weapons sales, and most important to JASON, the transfer or sale of nuclear, biological, and chemical weapons. Ever since the DoD organized JASON in 1960, it has provided the government with technical information to defend the country against such attacks. Now, you, as an outsider, come along after September 11 and stumble across more classified intelligence than some of the top professionals have after years of experience infiltrating foreign and domestic rogue operations. These support groups or networks make weapons available to unsavory folks who have money and an interest in doing grave harm to this country. Do you have any idea of the chaos you created within the DoD, the CIA, and FBI with your activities in Peru? Both sides want and need you dead. Our people think you are a loose cannon, and they don't care about how you are eliminated or which side takes credit for it. The only thing between you and eternal damnation right now is your Scout. Fortunately for you, neither side has a sure-fire plan to dispose of your Scout without creating unwanted publicity about the second unexplained disappearance or demise of a small-town Iowa girl who comes to Chicago to be a physical therapist and who connects with a freelance nuisance like you. Do you realize that you've uncovered weapons and drug networks that the big boys don't know about? Do you realize that if your Scout disappears, her family and the media will keep her story in the headlines until they get an explanation from the local police, FBI, CIA, Congress, the president, and maybe the pope if necessary? I may be exaggerating a bit, but you get my drift, don't you? Nobody has a cover story for what you've discovered. The only option we have short of dumping you in the river is to ask you to remain calm and let the Calderons be someone else's problem to solve."

"I know I underestimate Amy's abilities on occasion, but I didn't realize that she is held in such high regard to warrant all this attention by Uncle Sugar's friends and enemies. You and I agree on one point though. The surprise visitors to this neighborhood earlier today will strike again soon with or without a plan. My guess is that they've observed Amy's work and personal schedules, and they know when she's most vulnerable. To put it succinctly, I believe they will strike tomorrow evening at her therapy shop, and I intend to be there. I'm sure Calderon's people can make Amy's departure look like anything they want to avoid unflattering national media attention."

"In that case, I'll be there with you," Franzen vowed.

"I'm sure Amy and I appreciate your offer of help, but if I recall my village boundaries correctly, her shop is outside your jurisdiction. Do you intend to attract more attention by bringing unauthorized law enforcement people into the picture?"

"Do you think that the neighboring police chief will mind if my SWAT team and I happen to be in civilian clothes and happen to be celebrating a special event at the restaurant next door to the rehab center when an attack occurs? Do you think that any lawyer for the drug network will file a legal action against us for wrongful death if we take down every member of the raiding party? They are dangerous, but they are expendable as far as the bigger picture is concerned," Franzen pronounced.

"Chief, you continue to surprise me. You sound like you have given this topic a good deal of thought. Did I hear you say that you don't want any prisoners or escapees?"

"That certainly will make any cover story simpler if we need to have one, yes."

"Okay, then there's one more thing you should know."

"What's that?"

"Stay away from the hot sauce served at that restaurant. It's a killer. We don't want your team incapacitated in the men's room when the action starts."

"Did anyone ever tell you that you have a weird sense of humor?"

"Nobody who's still living. Why do you ask?" I answered with an Amy-ism question.

"Someone who enlists his neighbors in a fight against terrorists and has them ready to do whatever he asks, including lie to the police can't be interested in a long lifespan."

"That's one way for me to overcome my high cholesterol score. Also, I'm allergic to statins. Besides, I shoveled a lot of snowy driveways, cut a lot of lawns, and trimmed a lot of bushes to build the level of trust I have in this neighborhood. Occasionally, like now, I call in some of my markers. Also, President Bush said the fight against terrorism is everybody's fight. If anybody from this neighborhood lied to the firefighters or to your people on any occasion, I certainly will admonish the perpetrators severely."

"If only I could believe just part of that, my professional life would be complete. Okay, as a test, if you intend to be perfectly honest with my people and me from now on, answer this. How many smoke canisters, grenades, and other military equipment will I find if I search your house?"

"That's easy, Chief. I can honestly say that you won't find any. Despite any intensive search that you, your ordnance people, and your canine crews undertake, you'll never find any contraband in my house."

"You select your words very carefully."

"Well for crying out loud, Chief, now that we're buddies, will you parse every word that exits my mouth as if we were in seventh grade or in a DuPage County courtroom? Oh, I have one more thing before you go. Tomorrow night, I'll concentrate on protecting Amy if your team can find and isolate the *pistoleros*. Okay?"

"Done," Chief Franzen agreed, shaking my hand. "See you then. But, if something happens prior to tomorrow night, call me whether or not the action occurs within my official jurisdiction. If not, I'll clap you in irons for the rest of your life."

CUTTING TO A DIFFERENT CHASE

Obviously, Chief Franzen learned about my activities from some source not connected with my MAGENTA contacts. Franzen had a lot more information than a local police chief normally has about federal and international operations even considering the terrorist paranoia that swept all the U.S. law enforcement agencies immediately following 9/11. This was totally screwy. Until now, MAGENTA (and PURPLE before it) never allowed this much information on its personnel and operations to be in the hands of local officials, or for data to be accessible to unknown parties interested in breaching MAGENTA security. I hadn't operated this way in all my time with the organization. Something definitely was different. I had to maintain MAGENTA's security for Amy's and my own protection. *Under the present circumstances, whom could I trust to help me? Who could help me initiate countermeasures and protect my Scout and me?* The more I thought about it, the more I decided that, for the moment, I wouldn't trust anyone until I could definitively separate friend from foe. I wouldn't depend on MAGENTA, the police, or my Scout to help me. This was a dangerous approach, but, I was fresh out of options. As the old Eastern European saying goes, "You are permitted in time of great danger to walk with the devil until you have crossed the bridge."[9] I would accept help from the chief in getting Amy and me across the dangerous Calderon bridge immediately confronting us, but no further.

Shortly after Chief Franzen departed, I came out of my cranial coma and realized that I had overlooked lessons I had learned in India and Peru. Calderon's *pistoleros* who I had seen on the cul-de-sac behind my house (T3 through T6), but who I had not engaged, didn't need to contact Calderon for further instructions. They were as expendable to Calderon as were his crews at the Quillabamba and Tingo Maria *rancheros*. They had all the instructions they would receive from Calderon. They knew that their families in Bolivia or Peru were virtual, if not actual, hostages to ensure that his instructions were carried out successfully. Calderon would leave a gap between his hired guns and himself so that their actions could not be traced back to him. If the *pistoleros* succeeded against Amy and me on the first try, terrific for them. If they didn't, they better try harder if they wanted their families to survive.

As expendables, I assumed with some certainty that the *pistoleros* themselves were not skilled strategists, tacticians, or killers. Even so, I shouldn't underestimate their ability to succeed. Somewhere, they had a local supervisor to do their strategizing for them even though he had not shown his hand yet. But, I had no doubt that he had observed Amy's habits and travel routes (and possibly mine) to determine the best time and opportunity to strike. Thus, the *pistoleros* had no reason to delay. Calderon would be impatient for success. Ergo, the next strike against Amy wouldn't wait until the next night. The strike would occur tonight at her home. Witnesses wouldn't be a problem there. In an apartment complex full of young people focused on themselves and their personal agendas, the setting was ideal. Either no one would be aware of anything unusual happening if the *pistoleros* were skillful or lucky enough, or far worse, a number of conflicting witnesses and stories would surface among the tenants. The *pistoleros* would disappear under either scenario. Law enforcement would have no leads or be caught in an endless whirlpool of conflicting leads and eyewitness accounts. Yes, Amy's apartment complex was an ideal setting for a hit. For the second time in one day, Amy and I would break MAGENTA's cardinal rule about contacting each other at our homes. Nonetheless, if I wanted a live Scout, I'd better find her without delay.

As I inventoried the "professional tools" I needed to bring with me, I called Amy's cell phone and got the "your call is important" response. Without knowing where she was, I couldn't leave instructions advising her to stay away from her home or to get out of her apartment and hide. If the *pistoleros* were in her neighborhood or apartment already, I would place her directly into their hands. I called the number that Chief Franzen had written down for me, or the number I thought he had written. His handwriting was as legible as a physician's prescription. I couldn't waste time trying all the possible combinations and permutations of the seven mystery digits. I gathered my professional tools, jumped in my car, and drove to Amy's apartment complex.

Chapter Notes

1. Bartlett (compiler), *op. cit.*, p. 813, citing Rudyard Kipling's, *False Dawn*.

2. Carlo D'Este, *Patton A Genius for War* (New York: HarperCollins, 1995), pp. 675–679. By permission of HarperCollins Publishers. Also, Wikipedia contributors, "Battle of the Bulge," *Wikipedia,The Free Encyclopedia*, http://en.wikipedia.org/w/index.php?title=Battle_of_the_Bulge&oldid=315832797 (accessed September 2, 2009). pp. 1–20.

3. Whitehall (editor), *op. cit.*, p. 212.

4. *Ibid.*, p. 211.

5. Charles B. MacDonald, *A Time for Trumpets The Untold Story of the Battle of the Bulge* (New York: Bantam Books, 1985), pp. 466–487. By permission of Brandt & Hochman Literary Agents, Inc. as representatives of the Estate of Charles B. MacDonald. Also, Wikipedia contributors, "Battle of the Bulge," *Wikipedia, The Free Encyclopedia,* http://en.wikipedia.org/w/index.php?title=Battle_of_the_Bulge&oldid=315832797 (accessed September 2, 2009). p. 12.

6. Mark Salter and Gordon McLachlan, *Poland A Rough Guide* (London: Rough Guides Ltd., 1993), p. 316.

7. Whitehall (editor), *op. cit.*, p. 211.

8. "The Commission on the Capabilities of the United States Regarding Weapons of Mass Destruction," *Report to the President of the United States* (Washington, D.C.: U.S. Government Printing Office, 2005), p. 510. Also, David Biello, "A Need for New Warheads?" *Scientific American*, Volume 297 Number 5 (November 2007), p. 83. By permission of Scientific American.

9. Shanahan (editor), *op. cit.*, p. 214.

CHAPTER 14

AMBUSH AT AMY'S PLACE

YARD WORK

I'd never been there, so I could only devise a sketchy plan of attack or defense as I drove through the gathering rush-hour traffic. Based on my knowledge of the general area, Amy's apartment complex was in a residential neighborhood with a mix of churches, schools, offices, and a busy shopping area to the west. When I arrived, I found that the layout of the apartment complex was a great recipe for cooked goose. A circle of apartment buildings formed the main administration area with spokes of other buildings radiating from it. The layout was a sure-fire theater for getting somebody killed—gunfire in any direction was bound to hit some body or some thing. I decided not to park my car in the middle of that bullring.

As I cruised Amy's parking lot on my way out, I looked for her car and the *pistoleros* but didn't see either of them. Each apartment unit had its address on the side of the building, which would have been helpful, but I couldn't locate Amy's as I drove cautiously to avoid hitting pedestrians and residents while watching for *pistoleros* at the same time. I was certain that the *pistoleros* had surveyed the area earlier to identify the correct building and apartment. Within the complex, four apartments shared a common entrance. Again, this feature enhanced the probability of disaster. I set my brain microwave on "Devise" with a sub-setting of "Effective offensive and defensive plans," but nothing percolated. That was a colossal waste considering the exorbitant fees Advari thought I collected from MAGENTA for initiating quick fixes. I drove around the corner to a strip mall and parked in a spot with easy egress.

As I sat in my car with the sun fading behind me, I decided that the only way to take effective action was to do something—anything. Vehicle and foot traffic in and out of the complex increased as residents came home from work, others left to go out for the evening, and still others were jogging, skating, or bicycling in all directions. *This won't be smooth,* I told myself. I put my .44-caliber pistol in my shoulder holster and put on my light jacket to cover it. I donned sunglasses to keep the setting sun out of my eyes and to observe people without everyone knowing where I was looking. Before I got out of my car, I tried Amy and the chief's phone numbers again with similar results—no response no matter how important my call may have been to them. I wasn't catching any breaks. I got out of my car and walked between the stores of the strip mall to the apartment complex behind them.

I completed my first assignment by locating Amy's apartment building precisely and confirming that the *pistoleros* were not in the immediate area. I walked around the complex to become familiar with the total terrain and possible lines of fire until I noticed that I was attracting more attention among some residents than I wanted. I found a bench under a clump of trees, pulled out a paperback book from my jacket pocket, and pretended to read while observing the cars and the people. As twilight settled in after 7:00 p.m., I gave up my reading and walked toward my car the long way around the complex to allow myself another look.

I raised my annoyance level by confirming that Amy and the *pistoleros* weren't in the area. *Had I misfired in my assumption that the hit would take place here?* Maintenance workers started lawn sprinklers. The summer had been hot and dry. Because of water conservation ordinances, lawn watering was permitted only during dusk and night hours. When I arrived back at my car, I traded my book and sunglasses for an old baseball cap, a small flashlight, a number of plastic strips, my Responder badge, and a snub-nosed .38-caliber pistol to replace my heavier .44-caliber. If any shooting occurred at this time or later, it would occur at close range. There was no salvation in initiating gunfire that would penetrate the walls or windows of the apartment buildings and put more lives at risk. In the last rays of the late September sunlight, the shapes of the runners, sidewalk skaters, and dog walkers who were still out became as softly indistinct as a Monet painting.

I returned to my bench in the apartment complex and was about to sit down when I saw two dark sedans turn off their headlights as they pulled into the main parking area. The drivers parked the cars in the darkest corner of the lot with an open line of sight to Amy's apartment. Through the tinted windows of the car, I could only see the outline of the occupants. But, from that distance and with their unobstructed view of Amy's entrance and windows, she would be a dead Scout if she turned on any apartment or entrance lights. I assumed the gunmen were aware that

Amy's roommate, Heidi, might also be home or arrive at any time—not that her presence would cause them to change their plans. With thoughts of all the bad outcomes possible under the current layout, I decided that a pre-emptive strike against the *pistoleros* was my best option. My first objective was to relocate them out of the direct line of sight of Amy's door and windows.

My problem was how to corral four gunmen in two cars at the same time. Cunning and audacity were the appropriate characteristics for a first strike, but sometimes under stress and the press of time, those are hard qualities to generate. I would need help.

Reluctant Runners

Two husky joggers approached on what appeared to be the final leg of their run. I stepped into the sidewalk to intercept them. They slowed to a trot about ten paces from me.

"Gentlemen," I addressed them as I flashed my Responder badge sufficiently for them to see I had a badge, but not long enough for them to identify it in the dim light. "I need your help."

"Did we do something wrong, officer," they said in unison.

"Maybe, but you can settle that with God or the local constabulary on your own time. I need you for different work."

"We're tired and sweaty, can we shower and then help you?" was their Generation X response to phase themselves out of my plan before I phased them in.

"I didn't plan to take you guys on a date, and your being sweaty and dirty for a few more minutes may save some lives. If you do it right, a cash reward could pay your bar tab for the evening."

"Really! What do you want us to do?" they asked in unison again with a spike in their interest level.

"If you casually look over my left shoulder while we continue to talk, you will see two cars waiting on the opposite side of the parking lot. The four occupants are drug enforcers. Their target is a tenant in the building behind you. If gunfire erupts in this arena, innocent people likely will get hurt. I intend to prevent that if I can count on your help."

"Can you call more cops or something?" they rang another Generation X bell, betraying their unwillingness to help despite a bounty.

"That's already in the works, but we need to act before they arrive. Are you guys building muscles to make your grandmas proud of you in the next family photo, or do you have enough spine to help me in a tough situation, yes or no?" I blatantly tried to shame them.

"What if they have guns?" the Gen X choir chorused again.

"I'm certain that they have, but don't worry. You have something more potent. You have me. We can neutralize their weapons. Once again, are you guys in or out?"

Before they responded, a third runner executed his finishing sprint and slowed down as he approached. Fortunately or not, he was a friend of my two apprehensive recruits.

"Hey, guys, what's up? I thought we were going out after our run?" the newcomer asked.

"We are," one of the original twosome replied. "But, this officer wants us to help him nab some drug dealers in the two cars over there."

"Where are the cops?" the number three runner asked.

"They were decoyed elsewhere, and we need to take care of the hostiles here before somebody gets hurt. Look, we've already lost valuable time. Do you guys want to help, or would you rather learn tomorrow at the local pub that a buddy or girlfriend was killed and you did nothing? Worse yet, what if everybody in the bar knew you could have helped but didn't? How many glamour girls will have a drink with you after I circulate that story?" I poured layers of potential lifetime shame in their direction.

"We'd like to help, but we don't want to get killed either," number three affirmed.

"Well, if you three daisies can't spare the time, I'll handle it myself. But, don't let me catch you guys in a bar somewhere telling the ladies how tough you are because I'll spoil your evening for sure." (Fortunately, they didn't know I don't spend my time in bars.)

"Okay, we'll help," they all agreed, but more passively than I desired. "What do you want us to do?"

"The first thing is to lose your negative attitude. It will get you killed, and I won't grieve about you later. More to the point, if those *pistoleros* don't get you, I'll shoot you myself for conduct unbecoming vertebrates. We can do this if you follow my lead and instructions. When it's time, move like you mean it. I'll take the risks, you just move when and where I tell you. If you want to run home to your mommies, do it now because the situation can't wait any longer. Are you really in or not?"

"Okay, we're definitely in," number three confirmed for all of them.

I wasn't totally convinced, but I had no choice. I had to move against Calderon's men now.

"Okay, children, listen up. I haven't seen the lawn maintenance men for a while, so we can move the hoses and lawn sprinklers to have the water splash on the *pistoleros* and their cars. We need them out of the cars, or, at least, have them move their cars to the east side of the parking lot. That will obstruct their view of the building behind you. If they yell at you in Spanish or whatever language they select, keep pointing toward the east side of the lot and keep the water spraying on them. If they have the car windows open, try to get as much water inside the car as possible. If they get out of the cars where they are currently parked, by all means keep the water flowing on them. If we need to muscle them out of their vehicles, I'll take the driver of the car to our left. You, Recruit Bravo take the passenger of the same car," I said pointing to the third runner. "You, Recruit Charlie take the driver of the car on our right, and you, Recruit Foxtrot take the passenger of that car," I instructed the two original runners in turn.

"Can any of you handle a gun?"

All my recruits shook their heads negatively.

"*Madre de Dios*, how can you shame your grandparents like that!" I exclaimed for maximum psychological effect. "Can you handle a garden hose?"

They either knew or now were too embarrassed to admit they didn't have a clue about anything resembling what I had in mind. Frankly, it no longer mattered to me. I committed my task force to this job whether they were ready or not. We had been standing in one spot too long for the *pistoleros* not to observe us to determine if we were potential obstacles to their night's work. They would act soon to cause us trouble if we didn't pre-empt them. It was D-Day and H-Hour with no other options.

"Okay, everybody grab a hose and sprinkler and follow me toward the cars."

As I pretended to be the supervisor and picked up a rake, my three recruits crimped the hoses to stop the flow of water until we got closer to the cars. As we moved the hoses and sprinklers within range of the cars, it became obvious to the drivers that we intended to water the grass near them. They started their engines to relocate. I really wanted them to get wet first, but this would have to do.

"*Lo siento mucho.* I'm very sorry," I kept repeating and pointing toward the empty parking places on the east side of the lot where I wanted them to go.

The drivers moved the cars eastward quickly, but my team of reluctant recruits managed to get some water on both cars and the passengers. I ran after the *pistoleros'* cars in what I wanted to appear as my attempt to catch up and apologize for my crew getting them wet. I motioned for my recruits to follow me.

I caught up with the first car as the driver reached his new parking place and shut off the engine. The second car pulled alongside and stopped. My recruits were only a few strides behind me. I motioned them to their respective places on each side of the cars.

"*Lo siento mucho. Lo siento mucho,*" I repeated, getting louder at each repetition.

The driver of the first car heard me and rolled down his window.

"*Lo siento mucho,*" I repeated again. "I'm very sorry, Señor."

"Okay, okay, please. You are okay," the driver said with his strong Spanish accent, trying to wave me away and getting more agitated with each vocalization of my Americanized Spanish apology.

(Great, I enjoy assignments in which I can use my ersatz language skills! No doubt, they would really have an impact in my résumé if I ever needed one in my current incarnation as a misplaced International Responder from suburban Chicago.)

"No, I mean I really am sorry," I said as I pulled my .38-caliber pistol from my pocket with my right hand, cocked the hammer, and put the gun to the driver's temple while using my left hand to put the rake through the open window to pin the passenger in his seat.

Those two actions didn't please my shoulders, but I was committed to that maneuver before any pain started in earnest. Besides, I was really into this drill now and felt the adrenalin rush.

"If you or any of your men twitch an eyebrow, you will be very uncomfortable and it won't be from *agua*," I warned the *pistoleros*.

Surprise! My old baseball cap and sweaty recruits had fooled the *pistoleros* more than I could have dreamed. As fictitious groundskeepers, we currently held the high ground. I had to fully exploit our temporary advantage.

"Get your men out of the cars and force them onto their bellies on the grass with their hands on the back of their heads," I shouted to my recruits. "If they give you any trouble, my *pistolero* dies first," I announced, recognizing that my prisoner had enough English in him to understand his situation.

Now, my recruits realized that with a little effort and minimum risk to themselves, they really could help capture the bad guys and have something to impress the chicks with on the next date. They tugged on their assigned *pistoleros* and wrestled them to the ground in a few minutes.

"Okay, put your knee into your guy's back while you keep one hand over his hands. If you can do it safely, search your prisoner for weapons. If you don't think you can do that, just keep your hands over his so that he can't move without you feeling it. I'll be with you shortly. If your man moves before I get to you, keep kicking him in the head until he stops moving," I instructed them.

As it turned out, I correctly assumed that my *pistolero* was the leader of the pack, and I needed to handle him differently if I wanted information from him and his colleagues. With my pistol pointed at the driver's head, I had discarded my rake hold on the passenger, opened the car door, grabbed the collar of the driver's jacket, firmly ejected him from the front seat, and spun him backwards onto the hood of the car as adroitly as I could with my sore shoulders.

"Did Calderon send you?" I asked him as I put my knee into his groin. "Did Gilberto Calderon send you? I repeated, scraping his shin with the heel of my shoe. "Calderon, Calderon. Do you work for Calderon?!" I kept up the pressure.

"I know nothing," the driver replied contemptuously and spit but missed me.

His attempted provocation was sufficient for me to get rough if that's the way he wanted it. He remained silent.

"Okay, then you're eligible for grass stains on your shirt too," I said as I pulled him onto the grass while stomping on the back of his knee to force him down.

He really didn't want to play this game, although I could feel that he was stronger than me. I whacked him on the side of the head with my pistol to get his attention. That drew blood, and he obediently went down face first on the wet grass. His *compadres* were watching, and I could tell they were impressed enough to behave themselves and allow my recruits to manage them. While my driver was still dazed, I grabbed the plastic strips from my pocket, and wrapped his hands behind his back with a strip. I quickly hobbled his legs with another strip. With my *pistolero* secure for the moment, I went to the other three in turn and repeated the procedure. *How was that for logistical planning?* I had brought the correct number of plastic strips plus a few extras.

When I finished, I told my recruits, "Good work, but watch your man closely. Now you should be able to search your man for weapons, identification, keys, anything. If you find any cash in his pockets, it's yours. Do any of you have a cell phone on you?"

Recruit Bravo did.

"Call 911, tell the dispatcher that an officer is down, and give our location. That should bring law enforcement help quickly," I declared.

As I helped my recruits disarm their individual *pistoleros*, we could hear the sirens of police and emergency vehicles converging on the apartment complex from all directions. My privateer recruits accelerated their search for cash after delivering three handguns to me. I returned to my driver, who still appeared groggy. I took his car keys and went around to the trunk of the first car. Upon opening it, I wasn't surprised to find two automatic rifles, a gym bag that felt like it contained drugs or other contraband, and a briefcase that I suspected had bundled money in it. I didn't want my fingerprints on any of that stuff, so I closed the trunk with my knuckles, and started back to my prisoner, who was becoming more active as he came out of his induced coma.

"What was in the trunk?" Recruit Charlie asked.

"The usual stuff," I replied. "Cash, drugs, and weapons."

"We only have about $75 from their pockets. That will buy us a few beers. But, how about opening the trunk again, and really giving us something to celebrate," Recruit Foxtrot proposed.

"If the police or the *pistoleros*' boss learn of any discrepancies in the money or drug package count, you guys will be sipping your beers in tin prison cups, or trying to swallow before your beer leaks out of the bullet holes in your face. I saw you guys run. You're pretty good, but this isn't bonus bucks night. You can't run long enough or fast enough to keep out of trouble from either the law or the drug cartel on this excursion. Remember how hard I had to work to convince you to help me? If you want to survive in this kind of team sport, you guys need to be a lot cooler than you think you are right now. Be happy you didn't get hurt. With all that said, thanks for helping. I couldn't have done it without you. Now before an official rescue party arrives, put the cash away, or we'll all be trying to explain how we spent our evening to the FBI, DEA, ICE, and any other law enforcement agency that shows up."

TERRORISTS AND THE TERCHOVA TREASURE

As I returned to check on my driver, who had shifted his position, the thought occurred to me that the police would be upset about my using the "officer down" call to get their undivided attention and response. I no sooner finished that thought than my driver reached up as far as he could with his legs hobbled, and stabbed me in the left thigh with a small dagger he must have had hidden up his sleeve. I should have searched him more thoroughly or felt the dagger when I bound his hands with the plastic strip. But, in the rush to ensure that my recruits were safe, I didn't spend enough time searching my own prisoner. For his part, he was savvy enough to play possum and buy himself time to cut the plastic strip binding his hands. The only thing I could do now was to smack my unruly prisoner with the butt end of my pistol, and rebind his hands with some wire I found in his car's trunk. Then, I sat on his back, grabbed my handkerchief, and tried to stop the flow of blood from my leg as the first car of the rescue party pulled into the parking lot. At least, I wouldn't have to worry about the "officer down" part of my story now.

Chief Franzen arrived first in an unmarked police car and his street clothes, both of which were helpful because he was outside the western boundary of his jurisdiction by plenty. Amy arrived next in her car closely followed by three Naperville police cars and an ambulance. Chief Franzen was the first to speak as he exited his car and surveyed the scene.

"What happened here?" Franzen asked, initially taking in the big picture then narrowing his focus to me.

"My new recruits and I were playing tag with these guys while I was waiting for my Scout to arrive, and our guests got unruly," I summarized for his benefit.

AMY'S ARRIVAL

Amy parked her car and came running in time to hear my response.

"Tonight was my volleyball night," she explained. "I thought the chief told you. It was all right for me to go, wasn't it?"

"I guess I forgot to pass that piece of information along to you," the chief admitted to me sheepishly.

"Now that we're all here, can someone help me plug this hole in my leg?" I asked to establish priority need as the paramedics arrived with their medical kits. "And yes, Amy, volleyball was fine, although your timing was a little off tonight. But your absence kept you out of harm's way, especially if the chief was with you. I was worried that if Heidi appeared before you arrived, she might become the unfortunate recipient of whatever gift these heavies intended for you."

"I don't know where she was earlier tonight, but Heidi is standing over there in the crowd now," Amy informed us while pointing and waving at her roommate to join us.

"I think she should stay where she is until we sort things out," Chief Franzen ordered. "Tell her to wait there, or go to your apartment until we come for her."

"Go back, Heidi," Amy shouted. "I'll be there as soon as I can. If you're cold, go inside. There's not much to see here now, unless you want to see an old man with torn pants and a bloody leg," Amy snickered.

"Nice, really nice. Thanks for your inspirational description of my medical condition. Besides your magic therapy hands, you certainly have the power of healing words," I commented sarcastically. "And to think I could have selected a Scout with military and weapons training who could have been here to protect my flank. Maybe both flanks."

"Are you reconsidering your 'luck of the draw' policy?" Amy inquired with eyebrows raised. "Or are you questioning your interviewing skills?"

"As a neophyte Scout, shouldn't you be drawing a schematic of the scene and taking notes on what happened, helping the paramedics bandage my leg, finding out what the police need from us before we leave for the emergency room, notifying your contact that I have prisoners, but, I am wounded—in summary, any number of things to occupy your time more profitably than harassing me?" I summarized my frustration and fulfilled my on-the-job training obligation to my Scout at the same time.

"Oh, I'm sorry. What should I do first?"

"Start anywhere, but make sure those things are done before we leave here. And, no, I'm not angry. I'm instructing you about procedures and actions that you won't find in your Scout manual. If I'm mad at anyone, I'm mad at myself for not securing my prisoner. But, if you hang your head, Amy, and begin feeling sorry for yourself, you're off the team. Understand?"

I didn't expect Amy to get moody and depressed, and, to her credit, she didn't, although helping the paramedics bandage my bloody leg turned out not to be her first priority. Meanwhile, the Naperville police milled around trying to find out who the real "officer down" was because they didn't recognize me as a member of their fraternal order of law enforcers, and I didn't prominently display my unnumbered Responder badge. Finally, one of the *gendarmes* came forward and asked me directly.

"Are you the 'officer down,' or is there someone else hurt on the premises?"

I was about to identify myself as the reincarnated J. Edgar Hoover, but Chief Franzen interjected on my behalf.

"He's my special deputy working undercover. I don't know who these other gentlemen are," Franzen said as he pointed to my Bravo, Charlie, and Foxtrot recruits.

"These three are my special deputies, Chief, and the four critters reclining on the grass are guests from south of the equator who wanted to pay their respects to Amy when she arrived. But, we convinced them to resign their Calderon jobs to spend time in your jail with cold weather approaching and all. We confiscated their wallets to look for identification, and here are their pocket toys. They have bigger poppers in their two cars there, along with some drugs and cash. You may want to take charge of this stuff before it disappears. Amy, I thought you told me you lived in a nice neighborhood?" I asked as she went by on one of her chores to confirm to my satisfaction that she really had maintained her natural spunkiness and was engaged in completing the tasks I had assigned to her.

"The neighborhood was nice until you brought your friends here," she shot back emphatically but without rancor. "How's your leg?"

"My leg is fine, but the paramedics just ripped my best pair of work pants. That will be a deduction from your paycheck, young lady."

"I suppose you'll want free leg therapy now too," Amy countered.

"It doesn't have to be free, but I certainly need a good therapist. Do you know any?"

"None that will take you as a patient, that's for sure," she answered quickly, a little touchy at my continued needling.

But she had her head on straight as I had hoped and expected.

"If you two don't mind, I'm sure the local police would like to secure the area, get initial statements from everyone involved, and restore tranquility to the neighborhood," Chief Franzen interrupted. "We should commend these three young men for stepping forward to help you tonight."

"Volunteering their services was more like everyone else in the neighborhood stepping backwards rather than my recruits stepping forward. But, I agree, they should receive some official recognition unless that gives them a spot on Calderon's hit list. Let's not do them any favors that will make their lives and ours unpleasant. Besides, they received compensation for their work tonight."

"Will the desk sergeant receive any complaints about missing items in the detainees' wallets when they are booked?" the chief inquired. "Four suspects with absolutely no cash among them certainly would be unusual."

"Don't let it bother you, Chief, unless they can recite the serial numbers of any missing items."

"I'm glad you don't work for me," the chief asserted.

"Me too, Chief. You would have way too much fun with me around," I acknowledged.

After the Naperville police took my foursome into custody, a late-arriving detective took my statement of the evening's events while the paramedics hovered over me, eager to get me off their clipboards and into the emergency room for stitches. Against the paramedics' advice, I stood up to see how much damage I had incurred. I could stand, but my thigh stung a little (interpret as it hurt a lot more than I expected), and some blood oozed out of the bandage.

"You need to get that wound stitched now," one of the paramedics urged. "It's relatively small, but deep, and the knife may have nicked a blood vessel deeper inside. We can take you or you can go with someone. But don't delay because we can't see exactly what's happening internally with the equipment we have with us."

"I'm finished with what I need to do here. I'll go with you in the ambulance," the chief offered. "You can fill me in on more of the details of what happened tonight as we ride. Fred, drive my car back to the station when you go; I'll ride in the ambulance and hitch another ride home," the chief instructed one of his crew.

Paramedic Parade

"It's such a minor cut, I hate to tie up the ambulance when someone else in town may need it more than I do," I fretted.

"Nonsense," the chief argued. "If we want to put your four friends behind bars we need to demonstrate that they inflicted serious harm to you. Ambulance records can show that your wound was serious enough for emergency care. Get in the ambulance. We're going right now," the chief ordered protectively.

"I think I need to come too," Amy said, expressing her support. "I completed all the items you wanted."

"If you really want to come, fine. But accompanying us isn't compulsory if it's past your bedtime," I noted, giving Amy a chance to reconsider if she really didn't want to come.

"It's okay. Heidi can come too. If I drive your car and Heidi drives hers, we can drive you home after you get your stitches and then come back here in her car."

"Remember, Deerslayer, I know how you drive. If Heidi comes, she can drive my car," I asserted trying to rearrange the driving assignments.

"Wait a minute. As your Scout, I have priority to protect you and your car," Amy declared as if quoting her rights from the Scout's manual.

"Your priority rights wouldn't have anything to do with my super-charged engine, would they?"

"Absolutely not. I'm trying to fulfill my responsibilities to you as you so frequently point out to me," Amy answered petulantly, marking the lateness of the hour more than anger.

"Okay, Ms. Spacewalker, but keep it below warp speed. No fair beating the ambulance to the hospital. My car is parked in the strip mall over there," I said and pointed. It's pearl white with chrome hubcaps," I added as I grudgingly handed Amy the keys.

"I know what your car looks like from your therapy sessions. As a small-town girl with an ordinary car, I'm not interested in the power boost that a super-charged engine offers anyway," Amy said over her shoulder as she trotted toward the strip mall while Heidi went toward her car parked in front of their apartment.

"Thank you Amy for reminding me not to disclose any information about my car to you ever again," I called out after her.

"Well, Chief," I said, "at least I started the night with a nice car and two good legs. Is my profession getting rougher, or am I showing my age?"

Before he could answer, I heard tires squeal in the strip mall parking lot and the sound of the power boost as my car exited the lot onto the road and turned the corner into the apartment complex.

"That didn't take long. We'd better move, Chief, my Scout may need an ambulance more than I do before the evening is over," I said. "Also, I'd like to see my car in one piece just once more before it becomes scrap metal and my insurance premiums orbit out of sight."

"You're lucky," the chief responded. "I have two teenage boys at home. I haven't seen my family car in weeks."

With help from the paramedics, I loaded myself into the back of the ambulance and sat down on the cot.

"You'd better lie down and elevate your leg," one of the paramedics instructed. "That will keep the blood from draining out of your wound. Plus, you won't get light-headed and pass out on us on the way."

That sounded reasonable, so I stretched out on the cot. The chief climbed in and sat on the jump seat on the opposite side. I saw Amy pull my car behind the ambulance, flash the headlights, and wave as the second paramedic shut the back door and ran to take his seat next to the driver. As we circled to exit the apartment parking lot, I caught a glimpse of Heidi in her car ready to take her position behind Amy in our parade. *So far, so good,* I thought to myself. But, halfway to the Aurora hospital, even further outside the chief's official jurisdiction, crazy things began happening.

I bounced around and winced when the ambulance drove over the curb as we exited the parking lot and a little bit more as the ambulance turned onto the street and picked up speed with the siren wailing and lights flashing.

"I think he should be strapped in, don't you?" the second paramedic shouted to the driver as he reached back across the front seat for the harness that was bolted to the side of the ambulance.

The chief reached over my head to help the paramedic untangle the harness.

"I don't need that, Chief," I said. "I'm solid now that we're on the street."

"Okay," the second paramedic interrupted. "But, I insist that you get an injection of procaine to make you comfortable if you bang your leg on something during the remainder of the trip."

I saw the paramedic fill a needle from a bottle containing a yellowish liquid.

As the paramedic climbed in back to administer the injection to me, the chief halted him.

"I'm certified to administer shots"—he probably had a number on his badge too—"I can administer this injection," he said as he took the needle from the paramedic and aimed it at my shoulder.

The paramedic didn't look pleased but retreated to his seat, keeping an eye on the chief and me the entire time.

Something was grossly wrong here. A few weeks earlier, when a tree trimmer fell out of one of my ancient oak trees and cut his leg, I remembered that the emergency room physician gave the workman a shot of procaine at the site of the cut before stitching him up. I recalled that procaine was a clear liquid and was intended for use as a local rather than as a general anesthetic. Also, my dentist sometimes injected procaine to numb an individual tooth before beginning major work. I had learned a few medical facts as a Responder even if I didn't have a number on my badge. Allowing the chief to administer an injection when paramedics were present equally violated medical protocol.

"I'd rather not have an injection of anything, Chief," I told him. "I'm doing well enough as I am. The pain isn't that severe."

"You heard the paramedic; we insist," the chief said as he lunged for my arm.

I fended him off with my forearm, but he lunged again and almost stuck me with the needle. I reached for my pistol in my jacket pocket but didn't have it out when the chief lunged again. I caught his chest with my right foot, and recoiled to push him toward the back door of the ambulance. His shoulder or arm must have hit the door handle, and the back door flew open. He lost his balance, tumbled out onto the road, and bounced a few times toward the curb. The tires on my car squealed as Amy, who was following the ambulance closely, swerved to avoid hitting the chief. A few seconds later, tires squealed again as Heidi replicated Amy's maneuver around the chief's body, which appeared limp and lifeless on the side of the road.

By this time, I had my pistol out and informed the paramedics in no uncertain terms to stop the ambulance immediately despite our presence in the middle of Aurora's busiest shopping area. They did. I ordered them out of the ambulance, and instructed them to lie face down on the pavement where I could see them with their hands on the top of their heads. My adventures at Amy's place with the *pistoleros* must have been a warm-up for this action. Amy and Heidi stopped their cars. Heidi came running while Amy stayed in my car.

"Heidi, call 911, and inform the dispatcher that we have an officer down and bodies all over Route 59 and New York Street."

"Are you sure?" Heidi asked, Amy-like and equally cynical of the efficacy of my order.

"We might as well. We practiced the drill only a few minutes ago at your place. Let's see who shows up this time," I answered.

This had to be a memorable night for any dispatcher who was monitoring emergency calls in Chicago's western suburbs. As I stood in the middle of the street with a bloody thigh bandage, my pant leg ripped open, the lifeless body of the chief lying in the gutter, and my pistol aimed at two paramedics who moments before I thought were helping me to the hospital, I concluded that protecting Amy was a more difficult assignment than I anticipated. Beth wouldn't believe this story, even if she read about it in the newspaper or saw it on TV news in addition to hearing my version—if I could make it home sometime tonight or tomorrow to tell her.

A few moments later, my head cleared. I started mentally searching for audacious ways out of this mess. We had totally stopped traffic on a busy commercial street, and people were encircling us from all directions.

"Sit on those two over there," I instructed nobody in particular as I hobbled toward where the chief had rolled.

I checked his pulse. I could not feel one. My next stop was to visit Amy, who was still sitting in my car, dazed by what had happened in the last few minutes.

"Are you okay, Shortcake?" I asked her as tenderly as I could under the prevailing conditions.

She shook her head affirmatively, but then confided, "I think I'm going to be sick!"

"Not in my car, you won't!" I told her as I forgot my pain, opened the door, and pulled her out. "Go over there," I told her, pointing toward some bushes near the curb.

Amy got out of the car and started running in that direction. I gave her credit for a valiant try.

She almost made it to the bushes before getting sick in the middle of the right-hand turn lane, which effectively shut down the only remaining southbound traffic exit. Heidi saw Amy's distress and ran to comfort her or to get sick with her—I couldn't determine which at the time. I glanced toward the two paramedics who were being held down by several men who had come out of a restaurant. I took out my remaining plastic strips, limped over to where the paramedics were lying, and tied their hands. Fortunately, the chief was in civilian clothes because the crowd was trying very hard to sort out what team to cheer for among us. They weren't having much luck from what they saw, or thought they saw. I definitely needed the cooperation of the crowd until professional help arrived.

Well, it worked earlier tonight, I thought to myself, as I took out my Responder badge, waved it briefly, and shouted to the befuddled crowd.

"Somebody with a cell phone, call 911 and tell the dispatcher that an officer is down, he has prisoners, and several other civilians need medical attention at this location!" I instructed as audaciously as I could to win the crowd's favor, not knowing for certain if Heidi had already placed the call before she ran to help Amy.

My next thought was to find the hypodermic needle the chief tried to use on me. It would be critical evidence, and I didn't want it to disappear. I searched the ambulance first. It wasn't there. The next place to search was the road where the back door of the ambulance opened and the chief fell out. As I walked away from the ambulance, a black sedan drove cautiously through the crowd and stopped alongside me. A black man of medium build stepped out and flashed a badge at me long enough for me to determine that it was authentic even though I had not seen or used one of those kind of badges in a while.

Scout Supremacy

"I'm Sanders, FBI," he said, as he looked me over. "Who are you, and what's happening here? I'll take your weapon too until we straighten things out," he ordered.

"I'm Joe Legion. Sorry, I can't comply with your instructions. My weapon stays with me. No shots were fired, so I have no reason to surrender it to you. The way things are going tonight, I may need it to arrange reliable transportation for myself the remainder of the way to the hospital."

"Unless you show me a badge or some authorization for you to have that weapon, I want you to put it down in front of you, and back away from it. Otherwise, I'll use whatever force is necessary to disarm you," Sanders continued.

"I don't think that's a good plan," Amy interrupted from behind him. "He's being attacked by all these men. You may be one of them yourself, so you'd better put down your gun, or you'll be in the same ambulance," she advised Sanders boldly.

Amy must have picked up the chief's revolver and now she was wobbling the business end of it in the general direction of both Sanders and me. Fortunately, Sanders couldn't see how shaky Amy was with his back turned. Unfortunately, I could. Somehow, she had gotten the hammer pulled back and was more of a danger to me, any birds sitting on nearby telephone wires, and to the gathering crowd than she was to Sanders. Nevertheless, there she was with a pistol in hand, reminiscent of Alice Bright Feather displaying her weapons skills.

"I'm telling you for the last time, mister, put down your gun or I'll shoot," Amy bravely reaffirmed to Sanders.

Not seeing any voluntary movement from Sanders to comply, Heidi stepped forward to relieve Sanders of his weapon. The streetlights were on now, and Sanders could see Heidi's shadow approaching from the right side. Instinctively, I knew what would happen, but I was powerless to prevent it without causing additional damage. As Heidi came within arm's length of Sanders, he whirled around intending to take Heidi hostage and force Amy and me to disarm. Instead, as he pivoted, Sanders caught a jaw full of brass knuckles from Amy and slumped to the pavement like a rag doll. The girls certainly had brought their audacity with them tonight if not their weapons expertise. A shout went up from the crowd, which was now solidly on our side, or at least, the girls' side. And once again tonight, wailing sirens from all points of the compass began to materialize into police cars and another ambulance.

"I contacted MAGENTA and Heidi called 911 for the local police," Amy confirmed to me as police cars encircled the scene.

"Good thinking for making the calls," I congratulated her, "and nice going because you and Heidi just decked an FBI agent. I told you not to show your brass knuckles to anyone, but I'll forgive you this time. We'll need all the outside help we can get. While I confer with the Aurora police, you and Heidi hide your weapons and look for a hypodermic needle in the road somewhere near the ambulance and where the chief is laying. We desperately need it as evidence of tonight's events."

As Aurora police officers got out of their multiple vehicles, the radios in Sanders' car and theirs crackled urgently. Hopefully, the messages would help them sort out the sheep from the goats in this menagerie because my leg was weakening. I needed medical attention in addition to finding a roost for my captives. The news was more prompt and favorable than I could have hoped, even from MAGENTA.

"I'm Sergeant Biggens. We'll take over for you now," the Aurora police sergeant informed me. "Identify your people for us."

"That body over there is the late Lisle police chief, who tried to kill me a few minutes ago by lethal injection," I began the roll call for the sergeant. "Those two paramedic types over there probably are the chief's associates and could be employees of a drug network. Those two young ladies over there, one of whom just picked up a hypodermic needle in the gutter, are my associates. The needle is evidence that the chief intended to send me to the cemetery rather than to the hospital emergency room tonight, so take good care of it."

"We heard about a ruckus at an apartment complex north of here in Naperville earlier tonight. Were any of you involved in that?" Biggens asked.

"The Naperville police have four other colleagues of these men in custody. The four in Naperville definitely are involved in a drug network that I tangled with in South America. They were assigned to silence my two associates tonight in retaliation for my disrupting their business operations in Peru. It's a little complicated, I know. Did you get enough of that to make sense?"

"I get the general picture. We'll fill in the details as we interrogate the primary players. You realize that you are in big trouble if your story doesn't check out. How did you get your leg wound?"

"One of the *pistoleros* in Naperville cut through his plastic handcuffs with a knife I believe he had hidden up his sleeve. I didn't find it until he stuck it in my leg. I was fairly busy at the time trying to corral three of his friends using some reluctant residential help that I rounded up at the scene."

"We've heard of a heavy-duty drug operation coming through here for some time, but our task force could never catch them or penetrate their network to make any arrests. Looks like you and your team did a lot of work for us tonight. That's still assuming your story is verified, of course."

"If you can determine that Agent Sanders is and Chief Franzen was involved, that should explain why you weren't successful until now."

"Not entirely. Franzen's daughter is a botanist in Bolivia. She was taken hostage several months ago by drug dealers, and the chief was playing along with the cartel until he could rescue his daughter. So, he's one of us, or was. Whatever's in the needle isn't lethal. At least, it shouldn't be," Biggens explained. "Or, if it was, Franzen may have known it was toxic and wanted to pretend to administer it to you rather than let the paramedic cause your untimely departure."

"I hope you're right. The paramedic put the stuff into the needle, not the chief. If the paramedics belong to Calderon, I'm certain that the needle doesn't contain a saline solution or a painkiller," I answered.

"Either way, we'll wait for an analysis to be certain," Biggens confirmed. "Franzen is a good man. I'd like to think he died trying to keep the paramedics from giving you a lethal injection. How did he get separated from the ambulance?"

"As I said, because of his aggressive actions, I assumed that he was unfriendly, and I couldn't be certain that he was only pretending to administer the needle. When he lunged at me with the needle, I pushed him out the back door with my foot."

"You and your ladies play rough. In addition to Franzen, you really messed up Sanders who is working undercover with our task force. What did you do to him?"

With the aid of the Aurora paramedics, Agent Sanders was now sitting up, although I was sure that his head was buzzing like a hornet's nest following an eviction notice.

"I'm not sure. One minute I was talking to him; the next minute he was on the ground like a snowplow ran over him. It happened so fast; I'm not sure what overcame him. Chief Franzen's daughter is a botanist in Bolivia, you say? That has a familiar ring to it."

"You look awfully pale. We need to get you medical attention. I think we have enough information from you and your people for now. Take Sanders too, if he wants to go to the emergency room with you."

Agent Sanders had lost all his enthusiasm to play with us tonight. He made other arrangements for medical treatment and for a way home. I understood. I lost my enthusiasm for continuing the ambulance ride myself and informed Sergeant Biggens of my interest in having the girls take me to the hospital for repairs.

"That's fine with me," Biggens agreed. "We probably should use the Aurora ambulance to transport the chief's body anyway. My team will take custody of the Naperville ambulance along with your needle evidence and start moving this traffic. We will need official statements from everyone tomorrow after you all complete your medical repairs. Good Lord, look at that! My people found assault rifles in the Naperville ambulance! We'll be busy here for a while. You'd better go."

"Fair enough," I answered, shaking his hand, "thanks for your help. I'm glad we didn't have to duke it out with your team. You may have beaten us eventually, but my girls would have inflicted a lot of damage on your people before that happened. They were just warming up when you arrived."

Sergeant Biggens acknowledged the incongruity of my force ratio assessment with a hearty laugh.

"Seeing the condition of your prisoners, and members of our task force, I don't doubt that for a minute. I'm glad the girls don't live in Aurora. We couldn't afford the medical expenses for our police force.

See you tomorrow at the police station. I strongly recommend that you be there. If you don't show up, we'll find you. One way or another, you can't outrun us with your bad leg."

Our conversation in the middle of the street ended; I skip-hopped toward my car, where Amy and Heidi were standing. Both were yawning and looked really tired.

"Is this a great night or what?" I said with false and pretentious enthusiasm as I approached them with a definite limp on my port side.

"We're having the time of our lives," Amy countered sarcastically. "How are things with you?"

"The Aurora *gendarmes* are done with us tonight. I have an invitation to recite what happened here at the Aurora police station tomorrow. Did both of you give statements?"

"Yes, the police don't need anything else from us," Amy confirmed.

"In that case, you have a choice of driving me to the emergency room or going home. Either way doesn't matter to me. I've stopped bleeding, and I'm so tired I don't feel any pain. So, I can get to the hospital from here by myself."

"What happens if you get an injection at the ER and you aren't allowed to drive? How will you get home then?" Amy questioned correctly.

"If that happens, I'll call the Aurora police station and keep the night squad up until daybreak recording my very lengthy statement."

"I think we'd better go to the hospital with you," Amy offered. "If you're allowed to drive yourself home, Heidi and I can leave your car there and take Heidi's car back to our place. I'll drive you there, though. I still have the keys to your car, remember?" Amy said as she jingled the keys in front of me.

"If those keys don't find their way into my pocket before I leave the hospital, you get to complete all my overdue paperwork that MAGENTA has requested since 1975."

"Threats, threats. All that Heidi and I get from you are threats after we save your sorry body time after time."

"Thanks for informing me of the current state of my team's morale. I'll put that report on the bottom of my 'get-to' pile. Okay, Shortcake, if you're driving, slide the driver's seat further forward than you have it already," I said as I inched my left leg into the passenger side as gingerly as I could. "You already demonstrated that you can reach the gas pedal, but I would feel tons better if one of your feet came within range of the brake pedal too. Adjust the rearview mirror so you can see Heidi behind us."

Edging Toward the ER

With those adjustments made and our seatbelts buckled, we took off for the hospital. Heidi tried her best to keep close behind us. I could tell Amy was tired. She was driving only slightly above the posted speed limit. As I turned over the events of the day in my mind, neither of us talked for a while until Amy broke the silence.

"Are you angry at me, or are you into something else?" Amy inquired, turning her head to look at me to emphasize her question.

"No, I'm not angry at you, not at all. Why should I be angry with you and Heidi for driving me to the hospital? No, I was self-administering a performance review of today's events. I'm not pleased with my performance although no one on my team was hurt except me."

"While you have your rating sheet out, how would you rate me?" Amy asked in a hopeful tone.

"Both you and Heidi handled yourselves well given the circumstances, but my appraisal is a little different than what you have in mind."

"How so?"

"Although today's events differ from the strict military definition, I am evaluating myself against the criteria for urban warfare. A commander engaged in urban warfare should consider and continue to monitor several elements before commencing or continuing action against an opponent in such a setting. I didn't do all of that today, so I'm not happy with myself, even though the outcome was favorable for us."

"Are you going boringly technical on me? Oh well, I'll take the chance and ask anyway. What kind of elements?"

"In an urban warfare battle plan, a commander must consider, among other factors, the ultimate objective, attack speed, surprise opportunities, ways to maintain the momentum of attack, resupply and replacement of resources as the fight continues, overall troop and area security from ambush or counterattack, and, lastly, an exit strategy."

"I should have kept quiet. Can I put on some music?"

"I have a pounding headache, so I'd prefer quiet, if you don't mind. Let me push this button to eject the cassette I had in there though."

"Can I change my mind about hearing a lecture on war strategy and tactics? I think I'm getting a headache too," Amy said, attempting to bail out.

"Nope, you're too late to change the agenda. Once an after-action agenda is set, I'm required to lecture you for the remainder of our way to the hospital to ensure we're maintaining our personal security and pursuing appropriate assistance."

"What? Where does it say that in the Scout's manual?"

"It's in my copy. You must have been issued a redacted paperback version. Tell MAGENTA that you need the complete hardcover text of the manual for your well-rounded education. The old version is rather nice to keep on your coffee table too. The old books are a bit heavy, but they are illuminated manuscript editions which were hand-copied in Latin by monks similar to the Book of Kells you might have seen at my house."

"We don't have too far to go to the hospital. I may as well hear the lecture and get it over with. Otherwise, I'll be up all night thinking about what you possibly could have told me."

"Spoken like a true Scout eager to assume additional duties at a moment's notice. I sincerely commend you. Okay, let's start. As far as our activities of the day were concerned, we did okay, but not perfect. I left a few holes that Calderon's men could have leveraged to their advantage if they were more coordinated. The ultimate objective of the day was to keep you safe after you broke one of MAGENTA's primary rules and came to my house to show me the Calderon photos. As it turned out, I think the information you presented was valuable and worth the risk. Regarding speed and surprise, our surprise tactics with the high school runners and the phosphorus canisters against T1's car got us away from the near danger. My putting T2 out of action early allowed us to concentrate our offense against T1. We maintained momentum by taking the fight to your neighborhood tonight rather than allowing ourselves to be attacked by Calderon's men on their schedule at your therapy center tomorrow. The element of re-supply wasn't applicable to our situation because of the short duration of the project. We had everything we needed at the time. The force security element is a problem because I tried to control four of Calderon's professionals with the help of three amateurs who happened to come along. If those three runners hadn't stopped or hadn't helped me, I would have been outgunned by the *pistoleros*. If either party or both started spraying bullets around your apartment complex, a number of innocent people might have been hurt. I tried to cover too much ground and left myself open for my leg wound. Lastly, once I engaged the *pistoleros*, I didn't provide an opportunity to safely disengage. Getting a knife stuck in me probably was not what military planners consider a good exit strategy. Using the emergency 'officer down' call for help was an effective way for me to exploit an unanticipated field advantage. The *pistoleros* gave me a way out by not pressing their attack effectively after inflicting my leg wound. I didn't have an exit strategy. The unknown collaboration of Chief Franzen with the *pistoleros*, albeit under duress in attempting to keep his daughter alive, could have been an overwhelming factor in their favor had he been required to press his advantage more forcefully."

"Wait a minute. Back up. Did I hear you correctly? You expected an attack against me tomorrow at the therapy center? When were you going to tell me about that?" Amy inquired as she pulled into the emergency driveway of the hospital while almost running over the entrance sign and a man on crutches.

"I'm positive I would have mentioned the possibility of an attack against you sometime tomorrow night, probably when I came for my therapy session. Certainly I wouldn't want you to be totally surprised about something that serious."

"Did you consider the possibility of having me hide in a situation like that?"

"The *pistoleros* never would have attacked if you weren't there. Then, Calderon's men would have buzzed around your neighborhood until they had an opportunity to hit you like they did Jenny. I wasn't sure if you had firmly arranged your hiding place with Rick, but I did think about the pleasant possibility of you hiding in a hospital closet for the remainder of your life. Unfortunately, I was misled and concurred with Chief Franzen's plan to have his SWAT team, and possibly a backup team from Downers Grove available near your shop. But, most important, I would have been there no matter what. You know I don't miss a scheduled appointment when I receive the correct time."

"If the gunmen arrived earlier than you, did you expect them to hang around the therapy center's waiting area until you arrived?"

"No, I think that level of politeness would have been asking too much of them, don't you? I wouldn't expect them to be that well mannered. You have a point about timeliness though. The chief's SWAT team could have been delayed somewhere, he and his people might have skipped the event altogether if he was taking orders from Calderon, or, worse still, he could have been there as one of Calderon's representatives without us knowing about it until it was too late to escape. With him dead now, we may never know for sure where his loyalties resided."

"I can't believe you're telling me all this so casually!"

"Before you run over that nurse and the lady in a wheelchair, now is a good time to mention that I would have guarded your apartment during the night, followed you to and from work if necessary, and sat up on the roof of your shop with a sniper rifle all day if that was required to keep you safe."

"How many days would you have done that?"

"Only one. Your safety would have been MAGENTA's problem if the attack didn't occur tomorrow night. But we don't have to worry about that now, do we? See how things work out for the best with planning and coordination? Careful, I think the old lady might attack us with her cane. Let me off here. Find a place to park at least two spaces away from any other cars so I can open the door wide if I need to when I come out. Before that, though, reach for my big pistol in the back seat, please."

"I can't believe I'm helping you after what you just told me," Amy exclaimed as she grabbed my loaded .44-caliber pistol by the barrel and handed it to me.

"Thanks, now that you have your fingerprints all over the barrel and cylinder, I'll have to clean it tonight when I get home so that it won't rust. I guess we need to teach you about guns sometime, and probably the sooner the better."

Where we had stopped, we blocked the emergency entrance to the hospital and the entry to the parking area for emergency patients. Heidi had trailed us closely all the way to the hospital, but as we entered the hospital entrance, a heavy, black SUV pulled in between Heidi and us. The driver tapped his horn twice. Instinctively, I had asked Amy for my pistol and looked in the right outside mirror to determine if I could see him.

UPHILL ALL THE WAY

"Sit tight a minute," I told Amy as I opened the passenger door, got my legs out of the car, and waved at the driver in back of us to solicit his patience until I was able to stand upright on my stiff leg. As I stood up, I quickly pointed my pistol at the driver and fired. The bullet shattered the windshield and struck him in the forehead. His head slammed back against the seat headrest, and then he fell forward on the steering wheel. With the windshield out of my way, I could see the passenger with his automatic rifle pointed at Amy, and I fired my second shot at him while the driver was still rebounding between the headrest and the steering wheel. The passenger slumped forward without getting off a shot at anyone.

"What are you doing?" Amy screamed.

"Directing traffic—what do you think I'm doing? And don't yell. This is a hospital quiet zone," I shouted back at her as my body reacted to the energy surge from having to deal with two adversaries at the hospital door. "The two valets behind us wanted to park you in a cemetery. When you finish screaming and find time to look at the missionaries' photos of Calderon that you brought me, you'll understand what I mean. In the background of one of the photos, the driver behind us is the third man from the left. I wondered all day about when and where he would appear. That should be the last of Calderon's men in the immediate neighborhood," I said as I limped toward the emergency room entrance with my pistol in hand.

I was almost to the entrance when I turned and noticed that Amy was transfixed in the same spot where she was when I exited the car. Her hands were still glued to the steering wheel. I hobbled back and opened the front passenger door.

"Hey Scout," I said in a conversational tone, "remember to park my car carefully. I don't want any scratches on it. And you can lock my pistol in the glove box. I won't need it any more tonight. Thanks for your help throughout our trials today."

By this time, uniformed and plainclothes hospital security people, emergency room staff, and fire department paramedics came running to the scene from all directions. A number of police cars of every description and jurisdiction converged around us too. Patients in the emergency waiting room forgot their ailments and rushed to the windows to see what was happening. Among all the chaos, a doctor in light blue scrubs with a badge on his white smock directed two nurse's aides to push a wheelchair through the gathering crowd toward me while he followed closely behind.

"We heard that you were on your way here," Dr. Murphy, a former MAGENTA colleague and an old friend, said when he reached me. "What took you so long?"

"It was uphill all the way, Doc," I answered, "and I have a new driver. Take care of her too. She was sick to her stomach earlier, and she's probably in shock now although she was rock solid most of the time. Her friend Heidi in the car behind the SUV also may need attention. The people in the SUV need a coroner when the police finish with them."

MEDICAL PIT STOP

After Dr. Murphy instructed the official hospital valets to drive my car and Heidi's into the parking lot and for the nurse's aides to escort Amy and Heidi inside, Dr. Murphy wheeled me into a treatment room without stopping at the patient registration station.

"Sometimes it's nice to have others make arrangements for me," I commented as I stretched out on the treatment table.

"Yes, we heard your conversation with your driver loud and clear as you were approaching. Will you tell her about activating your car's emergency GPS signal when the driver's seat is moved and about the hidden microphone in the mirror right away or should we have some fun first?"

"You already know that answer, Doc. But, I believe the girls are really upset after all they've been through tonight, so let's take it easy on them."

"Do I detect a hint of compassion from an old scoundrel like you? You'd never let up on anyone in the old days."

"I hope I'm not catching a bad case of sympathy or compassion. Do you have a vaccine for it? No, scratch that. I've had enough attempted injections for one evening."

"You know that compassion in your job comes with a premature tombstone. That's the only remedy I know for you and your colleague Ron. He was in earlier. He was concerned about events and the way they've been handled by MAGENTA for some time now."

"How is he? I've talked to him, but I haven't visited him lately. MAGENTA is okay, but we're trying to accomplish a lot while the team apparently is changing personnel similar to a hockey game."

"His burns will heal, and, in time, the plastic surgeons will have him looking ten years younger. His real pain is not being in the field with you in times like these."

"If you believe I'm a scoundrel, three sergeants taught me all the lessons I needed to be a great one."

"I think you trained each other. But, relax for a while, and don't move your leg until we get it cleaned and sewn. A good samaritan could have given you a few pins to close your pant leg tonight. Do you need the name of a good tailor? Never mind, relax—relax. We're going to be here a while."

As Dr. Murphy and his assistants finished stitching me, Amy and Heidi entered the room. The girls looked cleaner and more refreshed than the last time I saw them despite the late, or very early hour.

"How are you?" they asked with quiet concern.

"Okay, I think. The doctor won't let me look at his work," I complained. "He has a low sympathy ratio tonight. Thanks for retaining yours."

"All of you look better than when you first arrived," Dr. Murphy said as he turned to observe Amy and Heidi more closely. "I hope you're satisfied with the care you received. As for him," the doctor said pointing toward me with his scissors, "we were concerned about infection at first, but, unfortunately, this old dinosaur will survive. In fact, I believe he has something important to tell you," the doctor added mischievously as he turned his back and fussed with equipment on his treatment cart.

"Before that," Heidi declared emphatically, "Amy has something to show you!"

"I do not," Amy corrected her while pushing Heidi away and shushing her.

"Oh, yes, you do," Heidi asserted even more emphatically as she pushed back to her former position.

"This is as good a time as any to pay your bet," Heidi stated with her voice rising with authority.

"What's this all about?" I asked both of them on the premise that their conversation potentially was better than the news I had for them.

"Earlier tonight, Amy said that if you got her out of trouble and home alive tonight, she would show you her knees," Heidi asserted, this time pushing Amy toward the treatment table.

"I did no such thing," Amy flatly denied Heidi's accusation without sounding anywhere near convincing.

Even if Amy had been convincing, the subject was too good to let it die without adding fuel to a potential inferno. Dr. Murphy and a nurse who re-entered the room in time to hear Amy's rebuttal also were highly interested in the direction of the conversation. I appreciated their presence. I'd probably need witnesses and more stitches before the conversation ended.

"As senior medical staff in this room, I'm authorized to decide all controversies as the official tie-breaker," Dr. Murphy said attempting to stake out his turf.

"Not this time, Murph," I corrected him. "The subject of Amy's knees came up at my morning therapy session, and it seems to have re-surfaced without any prompting from me. Obviously, we can't consider recall of the subject as mere coincidence. Therefore, I believe that Heidi's statement is credible, and Amy is hereby ordered to fulfill the terms and conditions of her oral statements to Heidi."

"Your Honor, I agree with your ruling," Dr. Murphy affirmed, fully enjoying our contentious conversation. "In this jurisdiction, an oral contract is valid. Unfortunately, I know that all too well from some of the malpractice claims I've experienced."

"Okay, but I didn't commit to where and when I would do it," Amy pleaded in her defense. "So, I don't have to do it here and now," she stated as she tried to forestall her assumed obligation to display her knees.

"It's better to fulfill your commitments here behind closed doors, young lady, rather than in the middle of the waiting room full of strangers," the doctor counseled.

Seeing no way out of her predicament, Amy bent over and pulled first one pant leg and then the other up and down so quickly that the most observant and interested spectators could only have had a subliminal view of her knees.

"There, are you all satisfied now?" she chanted with satisfaction at having devised a way to fulfill the letter, but not the spirit, of the decree against her.

I decided not to let her skip away that easily with only minimal performance of her agreement.

"That was a skimpy performance of your obligations for someone who wants to be recognized as a person of high integrity. Nonetheless, we will accept it for what it is. However, it's a shame that the night of your performance occurred on a volleyball night. It was obvious to me, if not to all the others here, that you must have been on your knees digging the ball out of the dirt on more than one occasion during your game tonight."

"You saw that?" Amy asked incredulously.

"Certainly. Remember I'm a trained observer. I saw everything," I bald-faced lied. "What do you expect? You stated that you see everything going on in your therapy shop, so you shouldn't find it unbelievable that other people have similar powers of observation in their line of work. If I were you, I'd spend extra time using a generous amount of soap '*sur les genoux*,' that is, 'on the knees' when you shower tonight," I added, trying to mess with her head a little more and push her aggravation level as high as I could within the bounds of good humor.

With Dr. Murphy present, I had hoped not to take the full burden of aggravating Amy on myself. But then, the doctor went soft on me.

"Because you have been a good sport, young lady, your injured colleague here has an admission of his own for you," the doctor declared with a flourish and bow toward Amy.

"Well, he should," Amy retorted. "After all, I risked life and limb to get him here safely."

"If you feel that way," the doctor continued, "perhaps you should be seated while you hear what your esteemed colleague has to say. Go ahead, speak, esteemed colleague," the doctor urged, pointing his scissors toward me again.

"This better be good," Amy asserted with eyes flashing a surprising level of emotion for that time of day or night.

"Amy," I started, "I told you earlier that you and Heidi conducted yourselves very well today and tonight. I meant that sincerely."

"This sounds like a varnish job already," Amy interjected.

"Let me finish. Remember when I asked you to adjust the driver's seat and mirror in my car?"

"Yes, I couldn't believe you allowed me to touch your precious car let alone drive it."

"There's a reason for that beyond my selfish attachment to a pile of steel, plastic, and rubber that cost more than the first house my wife and I bought. If someone not my weight moves the driver's seat, an alarm is activated at MAGENTA. Also, moving the rear view mirror activates a microphone so that MAGENTA hears whatever conversation takes place in my car. Remember my running through the elements of urban warfare and telling you not to play the radio?"

"Okay, I remember all that."

"I was transmitting a summary of the day's events to MAGENTA while sending a constant signal of our location and information about where we were going and why. As we drove to the hospital, the signal alerted Dr. Murphy to expect our arrival."

"So, you see, young lady, your colleague was protecting you the entire way," the doctor interrupted.

"And you didn't tell me?" Amy glared at me.

"No, I didn't tell you," I answered. "Why should I tell you? You were scaring me to death driving my car as it was. I didn't need you to run it up a light pole. But, with all the protection we thought we had around us on our way here, the SUV with the two Calderon gunmen still was able to cut between Heidi and us at the hospital entrance. From the photos you showed me, I recognized the driver immediately and saw him clearly in the outside mirror for a moment as he cut Heidi off. I suspected that Calderon would send several teams of *pistoleros* on this errand. But, with the darkened windows of the SUV, I couldn't see the gunman on the passenger side until the light reflected off his gun barrel. For simplicity, let's just say his automatic rifle wasn't pointed at me when I took my second shot. Earlier, when I asked you to hand me my big pistol from the back seat, you bent over between the divided seats. In that position, you were hidden from the gunman's view. Equally fortunate, you handed me the heavy weapon that could penetrate the SUV's windshield without having the bullet deflected. Otherwise, the coroner would have had a room full of customers tonight. I'm sure you don't find all of that amusing, do you?"

"No, I don't. I think I'm going to be sick again," Amy said, giving an honest assessment of her condition and feelings. "Why would he want to shoot me rather than you anyway?"

"Call it a psychological message similar to what happened to Jenny. By shooting you in my presence, Calderon would be sending me a message that he's capable of hitting any of my Scouts anywhere at any time regardless of my precautions. You are entitled to be upset and sick," I agreed. "MAGENTA and I spent considerable time and effort trying to build protective systems, and they almost weren't enough again. We dealt with serious adversaries today and almost came up short—with no dig intended about the size of your shadow, Amy."

The doctor tried to put a cheery end to the conversational melody that had hit several sour notes.

"If you three are finished bashing each other, I'm finished here," he said as he took one more look at my sutures. "And, young ladies, being sick to your stomach is a residual behavior left over from the age of the dinosaurs. The reaction was intended to make the human body as light as possible to run away from grave danger. You noticed that this old dinosaur here," he said, pointing to me a third time, "didn't get sick. He would have been eaten alive."

Dr. Murphy's attempt at humor fell as flat as yesterday's opened beer, and he knew it. He tried to recover by examining his handiwork on my leg again.

"How does that feel?" he asked me as he tugged on his last stitch.

"Now I know why my father told me never to make my doctor my life insurance beneficiary," I answered, trying to regain some conversational levity myself.

My efforts didn't work either. We were all too tired. I decided on a practical approach for ending the conversation and our business at the hospital.

"I think we're finished needling each other tonight. I'm glad you enjoyed our company, Doctor. Now that I'm sewn up, I believe I can escort these young ladies to the parking lot without disrupting your other patients or requiring MAGENTA to mobilize the National Guard. Thanks for your help."

"I enjoyed your company on an otherwise aggravating day for me," the doctor volunteered. "Come anytime if that wound gives you trouble," he said, providing notice of his follow-up treatment.

"I will, but be careful about inviting us back. We're not safely out the door yet."

He gave me a hand up and a pat on the back.

"I've had worse patients than you in here. I don't know what project you three are involved in, but be careful. The outside world is a dangerous place these days."

"Amen to that," I responded as I took my first shuffling steps toward the exit. "But sometimes with luck and skill, squirrels are able to protect themselves from hawks," I stated philosophically.

"I don't know what that means," the doctor said, "but good luck to all of you."

Before I said good night to Amy and Heidi in the parking lot, I made sure that Amy had returned my car keys. In my patched-up condition, I was not equipped to walk home that night.

"Good night," I told both of the girls. "Nobody else should bother you tonight, but don't hesitate to call the police, MAGENTA, and me if anything is the least bit suspicious. I'm certain you'll have increased police presence in your neighborhood for a few days too, but keep your eyes open yourselves."

"You can count on it, good night," they echoed each other. "We hope you feel better tomorrow."

"Amy, I'll call you after I finish with the Aurora police tomorrow to confirm if you have time for a therapy session. My shoulder rehab has taken on a higher urgency again."

"Yes, and I will delight in developing extremely painful exercises for you to do after the way you made me run and generally picked on me all day. Have you ever thought about sitting under a shade tree on your patio like other people your age—at least until you heal? I don't perform miracles for people who bully me or who continue to injure themselves."

"Hey, I didn't stab myself in the leg, and tonight's performance should teach you to be careful about what kind of bets you make with your equally whacky roommate. Besides, at the rates you charge for therapy, I think some magic should be included in the price."

"Sorry, we include a hot pack or ice in the basic package, but no magic. Miracles and magic are extra. You can direct any complaints to our customer service department in Istanbul. Good night Mr. MAGENTA Man, Sir," Amy said, saluting as she pivoted toward Heidi's car.

"I'm glad you said 'sir.' See, you can be respectful with a little training. But, be careful when you designate an exotic location. It may be my next assignment, and I know people in Istanbul who can make your life more miserable than me requiring you to show your knees."

That last bit of humor was a tension reliever for all of us after a long day. But, during my drive home, I developed a more serious mood despite being aware of how ridiculous I must have looked to all the people on the street, the patients in the waiting room, and the hospital staff with my floppy pant leg. At least the nurse took pity on me and closed my torn pant leg with several safety pins. I still was an object of interest and comment among the people in the emergency waiting room as we passed by on our way out of the hospital. But now, as I drove home, I reminded myself that while most of the people in the community had gone to bed hours ago, I was still awake fighting my personal terrorist war. Ready or not, Amy as my Scout had fully participated in that war. As squirrels, we escaped two traps set by the hawks and removed a chunk of Calderon's local network. How relatively big or small a chunk we didn't know. We were novices in this kind of war against terrorists, guerrilla fighters, drug lords, warlords, their suppliers, and affiliated sympathizers.

Nonetheless, I hoped that we had sufficiently crimped Calderon's operation so that I could concentrate on other pieces of his network while Gilberto Calderon thought twice before coming after my Scout and me again on my home turf. He had lost ten men, and all the local police departments were alerted in addition to MAGENTA. At the moment, we didn't know how many local police might be on Calderon's payroll, or who, in addition to Chief Franzen, had been coerced into Calderon's service. But, no matter how angry Calderon might be at me for disrupting his Peruvian operations and undermining his followers in my neighborhood, I believed Calderon would understand how irrational he would be to risk losing additional resources and bring further attention to his Chicago connections simply to take revenge on Amy and me. At the same time, I was mortified that no matter how many barriers I built for my Scout, Calderon was able to penetrate them, at least for a while. *If Calderon wanted to pursue the fight, Amy was as vulnerable as Jenny had been.* That thought was not satisfying to me at all.

However desirable additional protection for Amy might be to me personally, I knew that MAGENTA did not view her safety as my top priority under my current contract, rules of engagement, or pending assignments. One way to change MAGENTA's priorities might be to request authorization to strike against Calderon's European and Moroccan networks as my next move. Besides taking the heat off Amy and my neighborhood, I might be able to unravel more of Calderon's connections and make everyone safer. I would instruct Amy to prepare a proposal to MAGENTA promptly. But right now, I barely had enough energy to get home and fall into bed. At that moment, I didn't care that I might be late for my appointment at the Aurora police station in a few hours.

The Morning After

The next morning, in compliance with the note I left on the kitchen counter, Beth made sufficient noise getting ready for work to gently remind me that I was running late for my interview with the Aurora police.

"I heard you come in late last night or early this morning. But, I didn't bother to look at the clock. Is anything special going on that I should know about other than to throw away your bloody pants? Where were you in those pants?" Beth asked as I slid gingerly out of bed. "Oh, I see a new gauze bandage too. How nice. The doctor did very nice stitching—as good as my grandmother's. You must have had quite a night!"

"We did, but the show isn't over yet. I need to talk to the Aurora police this morning. I know on the plane coming home from Spain that you said you were in no hurry to go back to Europe, but you can come with me on a return trip if you want."

"When and where?" Beth asked without hesitation.

"In a few weeks, I think—after I finish my therapy. Probably I'll start with Spain and Morocco and decide where else after that."

"Which therapy?" Beth needled.

"I'm still working on my shoulders. I don't need therapy for my leg scratch."

"Do I just hang around our relatives, or do I actually go with you—wherever that is?"

"Take your pick. I could use your help if you want to come with me. In the last few days, my Scout and I broke every MAGENTA rule possible. Getting you involved in this work is no longer a giant breach of MAGENTA protocol as long as I don't get you or me killed."

"How long do you expect the trip to be?"

"Maybe ten days to two weeks. If it goes longer than that, you could come home when you need to be back at work. Still interested?"

"I'll ask at work and let you know tonight. I have to run. See you tonight. Do everyone a favor, and keep your pants on today if you can. It's a long time until your birthday, so you have to make do with the clothes you have unless you plan to wear a bedsheet. You may have trouble getting on any plane only wearing a sheet."

After many years of marriage, I decoded that as Beth's admonition for me to stay out of trouble if I could, or, at least, to take it easy on my wardrobe if I couldn't. I was okay with that. After Beth left for work, I dressed, had a more leisurely breakfast than usual, and drove to the Aurora police station. Starting out late had an advantage. I didn't tangle with rush-hour traffic. The net result was that I was only ten minutes late according to my clock as I pulled into the parking lot. So, I took a few more minutes to review what had transpired the day before. *What was really going on in my neighborhood? Was Franzen the only police chief in the area who was on Calderon's payroll or under his thumb? Who else besides Franzen knew about the super-secret JASON organization and what relevance might that have? Had MAGENTA or JASON been penetrated by Calderon's people? Chief Franzen's appearance at my house led me to believe that he was well informed about my activities. He appeared to protect Amy during her volleyball game, arrived at Amy's apartment complex in time to rescue me again, but, maybe, he tried to kill me in the ambulance. Why?* The questions were coming fast with no corresponding answers in sight. Sitting in my car watching the people go by certainly wouldn't clarify anything. I got out of my car and went into the station to talk to Chief Dunbar. Sergeant Biggens was already in the chief's office.

"I see you're on your feet," Chief Dunbar announced as he came around his desk to shake hands. "Sergeant Biggens told me about your adventures last night. I didn't know someone like you was active in this area."

"I don't usually work this close to home, and someone other than Sergeant Biggens must have informed you about my history," I answered testily.

"Is that your current job title now, International Responder? I've never heard that one before either. But, as a Responder, you come directly to the point, don't you?" the chief stated.

"Yes, but I become annoyed and don't answer questions politely when someone tries to kill my assistant or me. I become more annoyed when officials put their thumb prints all over me by forcing an unnecessary interrogation when they have sufficient information already," I verbally counter-punched at the chief's remarks. "I've tried to overcome these pesky traits for years, but they still surface more often than welcome."

"You're referring to your encounter with Chief.Franzen, I assume?" Dunbar stated incorrectly.

"Partly right, Chief," I obliquely affirmed his error to determine where this conversation was going with Biggens in the room. "I really get upset when I find a law enforcement officer on the other end of an attempted murder. You knew Franzen well. What was he doing and why?" I asked directly.

While the chief squirmed uneasily in his chair, Sergeant Biggens got up and nervously began pacing behind me between the observation window and the office door.

"That's another bad habit I have, Chief," I admitted. "When I get nervous, I don't appreciate someone pacing bchind mc. When that happens, the only way to calm me down is to clear any subordinates out of the office, tell me what's going on, and why. You probably want to do a ballistics test on my pistol, so while we're talking, perhaps Sergeant Biggens can test fire my weapon in the laboratory downstairs now so that I can have it when I leave. Firearms don't help me when they're locked in your evidence room when people are shooting at me on the street. If you need it for an inquest, I'll surrender it to you then."

"That's plain enough. Jack, have his weapon tested by the lab technicians. Stay there and bring the gun back when they're finished," the chief instructed Sergeant Biggens.

"Sergeant, if the chief and I are still talking when you return with my pistol, I'd appreciate it if you wipe your fingerprints off the barrel and cylinder before rust starts. Thanks," I added.

As Biggens went past my chair toward the door, I pulled his sidearm from its holster, ejected the magazine, and handed the weapon back to him in one smooth movement that startled him and the chief. He stopped and looked at the chief as if waiting for further instructions.

"Go ahead, Jack," the chief nodded in the direction of the door. "Everything is under control here. Ask Eva to bring in some forms so that we can record his official statement concerning last night. And, please, shut the door behind you."

"Better yet, if you want a confidential séance, Chief, I prefer to walk with you outside while your staff chase whatever forms you want me to complete," I said, allowing a bit of anger to rise in my voice.

"Nervous and careful," the chief responded as he stood up. "That could be a dangerous or an effective combination. Are you certain you should be walking around with your leg wound?"

"I certainly hope so," I answered as I stood up, put the sergeant's ammo clip in my pocket, and motioned for the chief to precede me outside. "As they say, dangerous missions need dangerous men. I don't have time to collapse from a mosquito bite and fail to be ready for the next event now."

When we reached the outside door and stepped aside to let other people enter, the chief commented, "You know that ammo clip isn't the only one in the building. Jack probably has another one by now."

"I understand perfectly, Chief, but Biggens doesn't have 'this' clip. I hope a little applied psychology doesn't cloud up the rest of the day for you and him."

"As long as your demands aren't dangerous, I'm sure we can accommodate a bit of friendly psychology in today's activities."

"Good, then tell me about Chief Franzen," I proposed as we started our walk.

"We know for certain that Franzen's daughter is a botanist with a team of scientists searching the Amazon for medicinal jungle plants before the rain forests are destroyed by population growth and logging poachers. About two months ago, Franzen told me he received a letter supposedly signed by his daughter advising him that she was captured by a group of present or former paramilitary fighters working for various drug lords."

"Did any ransom demands accompany that?"

"No, the cartel wanted Franzen's cooperation in allowing drugs to flow through the suburbs to local distributors here and bigger shipments to have safe passage through O'Hare to other destinations."

"Do you have any idea where his daughter is held and if a rescue team can extract her and her colleagues?"

"We learned over time that the drug cartel has moles in the FBI and CIA, so we haven't contacted any agency other than Sanders and the local FBI office for help until we figure out who we can trust."

"Who is the 'we' you're talking about, where along the Amazon might Franzen's daughter be, and where are the drugs flowing through here ultimately directed?"

"To my knowledge, the 'we' were Franzen from Lisle, FBI Agent Sanders, and the police chiefs of Downers Grove, Naperville, and me. The letter Franzen received from his daughter was posted from Picaflor, Peru several months ago. When we contacted the research center there, we were told that a party of researchers including Franzen's daughter and her colleagues were last seen in the area with a group of well-armed guerrilla types. Franzen contacted Picaflor several times after that, but nobody saw his daughter, or will admit it. We believe the kidnappers move their prisoners regularly to make any rescue attempt or escape more difficult. Also, we're fairly certain that the drugs move from here by air to Europe and other parts unknown, but we haven't interdicted any thus far. Are you familiar with any of this?"

"If I were any more familiar, I'd either be dead or the chairman of the board for Calderon's cartel. I've been informed that the Picaflor research center is along the Rio Tambopata in the neighborhood of a large national forest preserve called the Reserva Nacional Tambopata. I haven't been there myself, but I've seen it on maps and met people from the general area. That neighborhood can hide a lot of live or dead hostages for a long time. In addition to an extraction team, you'd need local Indian trackers to help find one person or a local group that doesn't want to be found. Franzen's daughter searching in that area for medicinal herbs and plants makes sense because researchers have discovered that an extract of *chuchuhuasi* bark and rum helps relieve arthritic and other types of pain. I don't know if the key ingredient of the formula is the bark or the rum, but I've seen bottles of the stuff in Peru and in herbal medicine stores around here. One of the big men of the drug cartels in that area and Bolivia is a guy named Gilberto Calderon. I learned that his twin brother Ernesto is active in Europe and Morocco. Your belief that certain drug shipments through Chicago move eastward agrees with my working hypothesis. The Calderon operation employs many former guerrilla fighters who have no other jobs or hope for a better life. So, Calderon always has a ready supply of firepower to protect him. I came through that area recently, but while I'm chasing another assignment in his global network, maybe I can arrange to have another party help you sooner than I can. I have one condition though."

"What's that?" Dunbar asked.

"This conversation isn't repeated to Sanders, any of your police colleagues, Biggens, your wife, grandmother, parish priest, cleaning lady, or anybody else at least until I'm out from under the 800-pound Calderon gorilla."

"That's fair enough. I assume that you're okay with us keeping a lid on what happened last night and having our off-duty people run past the girls' apartment complex more frequently than usual."

"That would be great whether on an official or unofficial basis. But, I reserve the right to change my mind based on future events and information about any other police department that may have ties to the Calderons."

Following our conversation, the chief and I went inside to find Sergeant Biggens and to complete my statement forms. I handed the ammo clip back to Biggens in exchange for my pistol on the way out and drove home. Hopefully, my next phone call would confirm a therapy session with Amy. Ironically, my appointment was for the same time I initially thought Calderon's men might pay Amy a visit at her workplace. The timing was good. As the last patient of the day, we could talk freely.

CLEARING THE AIR

"I'd ask you where it hurts, but I don't want to be here all night," Amy said in greeting as I came in the door and flopped on an exercise table.

"Ah, yes, greeted in my suffering by a rhapsody of words from a candied tongue. I am a man whom Fortune hath cruelly scratcht."

"Well, Shakespeare, you wanted an appointment when I'm tired and hungry. So, you get what you deserve. Do your warm-ups, and I'll be with you in a few minutes after I complete the charts for my earlier patients."

"How many other patients do you have who can extemporaneously recite a combination of sentences from *Hamlet* and *All's Well That Ends Well?*"[1] Haven't you heard of monumental events of pure chance such as that, or alternatively, the luck of the draw?" I asked with drama attached.

"None but you, thank goodness, and your therapy will end soon if there's a god in heaven. How do you come up with this stuff? You really enjoy jabbing me with the luck of the draw line every chance you get, don't you?"

"See what I mean about chance? It's existence flows unfettered from your very lips. Actually, my Shakespeare book fell out when I opened the car door to come in here. The wind happened to open those pages of the book. Truthfully, I recall interviewing you when you were similarly tired and hungry. How could I have been so misled? I must not have been paying close attention to the job dimensions or to my usually infallible intuition."

"Good for you. Now you're blaming yourself for your troubles as you should."

"How perceptive and kind you are. You must have had an exceptional day with such an outpouring of high quality compassion for your patients. Before I leave for Europe, I must remember to inform Rick of a few more of your undisclosed virtues. I'm sure he'll appreciate the information."

"Are you going to Europe? I didn't hear about that," Amy asked as she came over to the exercise table.

"I am if you obtain MAGENTA authorization for me to continue chasing the Calderon network there and in Morocco. I think I can be more effective at that end of the network at this point. While I'm there, I might be able to observe if any contraband is moving in either direction through the Calderon pipeline. I want to finish my shoulder therapy before I leave though. So, set my departure date on the request form for a few weeks from now."

"How's your leg?"

"Stiff, but you saw me walk through the door. It should be better in a few weeks too. Something tells me that I shouldn't go as a cripple as I did on my last visit to Peru. I may run into a hornet's nest."

"Okay, what will you need?"

"Tell MAGENTA I need the full package including weapons permits and several IDs. My wife may join me too. I want Hassan and Advari if they're available, but I'll contact them myself. While we have MAGENTA's attention, we need all the background information we can obtain on our local police chiefs and FBI Agent Sanders. Somebody has far too much information about MAGENTA, secret operations such as JASON, and my individual activities. We either have a leak, a mole, or both in our system."

"Okay, I'll pass your requests along tonight. Anything else?"

"That will do for now."

"While I'm thinking of it, MAGENTA wants you to formally evaluate my performance during the last few days. Do you think you can do that before you leave for Europe?" Amy asked without revealing if she personally wanted that to happen or not.

"Sure, I can do that now. Tell MAGENTA that it's premature to evaluate your 'force-ratio effectiveness' on such a short time frame."

"What does that mean?"

"It means I haven't seen enough to determine if you're more dangerous to our opponents or to me."

"Are you serious?"

"For the most part, yeah. Your review can wait, but, if MAGENTA really needs something, I can always relate how effectively you put Agent Sanders on the pavement with one swing, plus all the other good things you did last night."

"I was so angry at losing the volleyball game by two points that I had to take it out on someone."

"Then I'm glad Sanders was available to receive your pent-up sports frustrations. If you had missed his jaw with the hardware you had, I'm sure he would have fainted from the surprise of seeing your brass knuckles. I hope you didn't mention anything about them in your police report."

"No, I remembered what you said about carrying them. We're almost done here for tonight. Stand up, and I'll measure the range of motion of your shoulder."

While Amy was taking measurements, I ventured into dangerous conversational territory. I needed to know how secure Amy would be while I was away.

"It is and isn't my business, but I'll ask anyway. How are you and Rick coming along?"

"Okay, I guess," Amy answered without much enthusiasm. "Your range of motion increased about ten degrees. That's pretty good. Keep up your exercises," she instructed as she absent-mindedly patted my shoulder.

"Okay, Shortcake, thanks for the measurements. Now, answer the question I asked. I need to know that you have a safe place to hide if necessary when I'm in Europe. Is Rick's hospital still a hideout option for you?"

Amy didn't say anything, so I turned around to see tears in her eyes.

"You may be tired and hungry, but I'm not leaving until I know that my Scout has her head on straight, so start talking."

"It's just that Rick and I are so far apart. We don't see each other often, and when we do, he has an emergency call or I'm tired from driving, so our time together is short or not as much fun as we want. So, I'm not confident about us being right for each other. Then, if my parents find out I've driven that far without stopping to see them, they are upset. I thought dating was supposed to be a happy time."

The tears were flowing freely now. Lord knows I'm no spiritual or family counselor, but I knew enough not to stop the waterworks before Amy felt their therapeutic effect. The same thing happens in every profession. Who counsels the counselors when they are victimized by their own emotions as we all are from time to time?

"Is that the entire story, or is there more?" I asked gently after a few minutes.

With her tears flowing, I didn't expect an answer until Amy calmed down. After a few more minutes, she was ready to talk again.

"My parents are terrific, and we get along really great. They see the difficulty Rick and I have, and they believe we will never be able to work it out. So, they try to push me toward other guys. Mom has her favorites, and Dad has his. I know they mean well, but it's not helping me right now. What can I do?"

"You were doing fine until you asked me for advice. I don't know if I have any direct experience related to your problem, but I may have encountered something useful for you to consider. First, I think you're right about your parents. They gave me the impression at the hospital that they are genuinely concerned about you and only want the best for you in every aspect of your life. And why shouldn't they? You reciprocate by expressing your love for them. They see you as a solid citizen with the possible exception of your hanging around me."

"They certainly know my feelings toward them, that's true. I had a hard time leaving home to take this job and move here," Amy admitted.

"The second factor is that Rick has genuine feelings for you based on what I saw in his behavior at the hospital. I may tease him and you about the nutty things you do as you grow in your relationship, but I believe your behavior is normal for young people who encounter strong feelings for a person that they may not have felt for anyone else. As the old saying goes, '*Omnis amans amens,*' or 'every lover is demented.'[2] Given that general condition, Rick certainly is sincere about his feelings for you."

"I'm glad you think Rick is sincere, but that still doesn't help me much. As for nutty behavior, everybody knows that you are totally weird, eccentric, dogmatic, demanding, and unreasonable," Amy said, trying to laugh through her tears as the adjectives flowed from her mouth.

"I'm overwhelmed that you identified all my good traits. I hope you remember to articulate them to MAGENTA when you rate my performance. I had to identify your strongest personality characteristics earlier for MAGENTA. I recall writing about your compassion, tolerance, objectivity, determination, and creativity to name a few. Between you and Rick, I've observed another characteristic that deserves explanation, and that feature is your impatience. At your age, nature has you lined up in mind and body for a life partner. You look around and don't identify anyone immediately with the same life commitment that you have. Our society isn't very helpful in this department. But, in other societies and families, the problem is worse because the parents make the marriage decision for you. And that's where my answer to your question lies."

"You want my parents to arrange a marriage for me! That will never happen, believe me!"

"Patience, Shortcake, patience. Listen, please. Let me finish. A family I know had seven children—three girls and four boys. In due time, each of the children grew up and married—all except the middle girl. She was a good person, worked hard, and was attractive enough. In her parents' minds, she had no reason to remain unmarried. She reached her thirties with no husband and no apparent prospects. To the parents, that situation was almost criminal. The parents were kind to the daughter, and they held out against pressure from the extended family and peers as long as they could. But, eventually, family honor required them to have their daughter married. Similarly, but more diabolically than your family, the mother had her list, and the father had his candidates. One day, a showdown occurred—dear daughter, select a husband, or we will select one for you."

"Did she or her parents select someone from the lists, or did she commit suicide?" Amy asked with interest.

"Neither, because, fortunately for the girl, her grandmother had listened quietly to all the ongoing family static. Equally fortunate, the daughter was close to her grandmother. In one of their private chats, the daughter revealed that she secretly loved someone for a long time. But, she knew her parents wouldn't welcome that marriage because her suitor was of another religion. In her family, such a marriage was more criminal than remaining single, if that was possible. Finally, one day the grandmother told both parents, 'You demand that your daughter answer you about this name or that name, and she tells you no. How would your daughter reply if you let her answer her heart about whom she loves?' Needless to say, the parents were astonished, but they were silent while their daughter spoke of the man she truly loved. The story may not be totally parallel to your situation from this point on, but I think the grandmother's question is relevant to you. How will you answer when your heart asks you, whom do you love?"

"You know, I hate you when you give advice without actually telling me what to do."

"Yes, I suppose you do, but it comes with my job description. I can add another thought if you're ready for it."

"Do I have a choice?"

"Certainly. We're not trying to replicate the *parousia* here. So, you can listen or not."

"You did that on purpose. What is a parasol, or whatever word you used?"

"*Parousia* means 'presence,' but in a biblical context, it refers to the second coming of Christ. You have a choice between being a heathen and not listening, or electing to listen and learn in the true spirit of a believer."

"Then, by all means, counselor, advise me as a true believer."

"It's nothing grand, but it might give you a fresh perspective. Earlier, you raised the issue of your concern about Rick's constancy when you're apart. He might have a similar concern about you. I'm sure you've heard the expression many times that, 'Absence makes the heart grow fonder.' I'm not sure that's a true statement of people's behavior. But, if it makes you feel any better, the poet Homer addressed a similar question sometime around 850 BC. In his *Iliad*, Homer wrote, 'Achilles absent was Achilles still.'[3] So, if the feelings you and Rick have for each other are genuine, being out of each other's sight doesn't change your characters or how you feel about each other. Rick is still Rick whether he's in Illinois or Iowa. Similarly, Amy is Amy wherever you are. *Capiche?*"

"Yes, I understand your point, or Homer's point. I suppose reprobates like you are exempt from this rule, so I won't ask you to embarrass yourself by telling me how the saying applied to you before you were married. Was the daughter in your story allowed to marry the man she loved?"

"By definition, a reprobate cannot be embarrassed. But, to answer your question, yes, eventually the parents allowed their daughter to marry the man she loved and who she thought loved her."

"And did the couple live happily ever after?"

"I knew you'd ask that question. If my brain worked correctly, I would have selected another example. Unfortunately, no, the marriage ended in disaster, but not because of any religious differences. The husband turned out to be an alcoholic, so the parents were right about his being unsuitable, but for the wrong reason."

"What guidance am I supposed to get from that crazy story?"

"Well, the daughter was right too because she predicted correctly to her parents that religion wouldn't be a problem for the couple. How do you start a discussion about religion with a drunk? Beyond that, the lesson to be learned is that selecting a marriage partner is harder than any other relationship. For example, you and I interact in only two dimensions, as therapist and patient and as Operative and Scout. We don't need compatibility in religion, age, intelligence, financial management, sexuality, seasonal allergies, exercise programs, or personal hygiene to name a few. Learning all the issues involved in a marriage takes more time for observation and insight into each other's character than our one interview and a few therapy sessions took to determine if I can regain strength in my shoulder, or if you can handle a Scout position. We can work together and enjoy carving each other's personality up when opportunities present themselves without taking the relationship any further. You and Rick have much more 'finding out' to do that doesn't enter into our interactions. How's that for guidance?"

"If I had my brass knuckles now, you'd be on the floor. But, for a reprobate, you probably are right."

"Well, this isn't quantum physics, but people have struggled since Homo erectus or Homo sapiens attempted to differentiate himself and herself from the apes to determine how to select a life partner. Based on the evidence, we still don't have a foolproof method. Who knows, you and Rick may solve the puzzle for yourselves and for all humans. Perhaps that's your destiny rather than punching me in my sore arm."

"Was the grandmother in your story your grandmother?"

"No, it was the great-grandmother of a girl who lived across the street from us. The old lady didn't have much formal education, if any, but she had life experience and wisdom. Actually, she probably dated Homer when they were younger, and she helped him write his book. No, I'm fibbing now. She wrote the book while Homer helped her collate the pages, but somehow he got credit as the author. Does any of that help you?"

"Strangely, yes, coming from you," Amy asserted as she wiped her eyes with her hands and attempted a laugh.

"Your constant characteristic is that you are consistently weird, so I have to believe in your concept of constancy. If ever a constant reprobate existed, you're living proof," Amy said, assessing my counseling skills.

"Don't believe it just because I make a pronouncement. I was fortunate to have an excellent English Literature professor in college. He applied our readings of the classics to everyday life. His premise was that human nature hasn't changed much over the centuries. He introduced me to the belief that in ancient times, lovers anguished over the same problems you recited to me now. I can't recall if I came across an old proverb in my high school Latin class or in his English Literature class something to the effect that, '*Caelum non animum mutant qui trans mare currunt*' which I think translates to, 'They who cross the sea change their sky, but not their feelings.'"[4] As I said before, no single solution exists, but an *affaire d'amour* generally works out if given a chance."

"And you believe in Rick."

"I haven't dated him and don't intend to, but I think he's a good guy. Whether he's the right one for you will be your call to make at the appropriate time."

"Thanks for this chat and for allowing me to have a good cry."

"Any time, Shortcake. I have an interest in keeping your generation happy because your age group will pay my Social Security benefits. I need those benefits to arrive in the mail regularly and with periodic increases for the remainder of my lifetime. That's my only concession to socialism."

"You really are incorrigible! You certainly know that by now!"

"No, I'm still Caucasian the last time I looked at my passport."

"Which one?"

"Which one indeed is a good question for our next assignment. Well, Amy, that's enough fooling around for tonight. I need to get myself home. I hope I helped you a bit."

"Good night, and thanks. You helped. I'll follow up with MAGENTA on your trip. I should have an answer when you come in for your next therapy session."

I was out the door and almost into my car when Amy opened the door and shouted after me, "Rick thinks the world of you too!"

"That statement verifies that even good people can lose their way," I shouted back. "But, now that you stopped me, I'll hang around until you lock up and are on your way home. No sense ruining what otherwise was a productive evening by ignoring a possible visit by one of Calderon's stray drones, however remote that possibility might be after yesterday's events."

"Okay, I'm ready to leave. Bye."

THE TWENTY-YEAR MYSTERY

We had no life-threatening incidents that night or any other for the next several weeks as I continued my shoulder therapy and strengthening exercises. Amy received MAGENTA's positive response to my request to undermine Calderon's European and North African operations if I could. I may be incorrigible and a reprobate in Amy's lexicon, but I judged correctly that the CIA and the FBI still had their hands full confronting more immediate threats from aggressive terrorist networks in the days and months following 9/11. My job was to stop the minor leaguers like the Calderons, Vasily, and others yet unknown from joining forces with or providing resources to well-organized and well-financed extremist groups that were active threats to our country.

I had plenty of incentive to keep myself from being bored or tired of rehabilitation during those weeks. During one of my infrequent breaks, Beth instructed me to clean out my bedroom closet and to pitch whatever was no longer useful that had accumulated since my previous venture twenty years earlier. Once again, I came upon Joe's duffel bag tucked away where I had deposited it years earlier. As I dug through the contents, I came upon his long-forgotten shaving kit. I smiled to myself as I held his can of shaving cream that should have exploded in the summer's heat of the stuffy closet years ago. Setting the can aside for a moment, I retrieved Joe's razor and unscrewed the top from the handle. The little piece of paper was still there where I had put it. Joe's writing hadn't faded much during that time. I could still read the word JASONs and BacbIJIH. Wait a minute, wait a minute!

The unknown BacbIJIH now had meaning for me given my exposure to the Cyrillic alphabet of Russia and other Eastern European countries. God Almighty, I began to shake as I translated the note as if I had discovered the Rosetta Stone of Egypt. "B" in the Cyrillic alphabet is "V" in English. The letter "a" is equivalent to ours, and the letter "c" is our "s." The Cyrillic "bI" is roughly our "i." The Cyrillic letter "JI" is our "l." Joe's letter "H" stumped me for a while until I mentally slanted the crossbar of the "H" to run from the top of the right vertical line to the bottom of the left vertical line. Then, when I put a little hat on it, the "H" converted to our letter "y." *What did I have as I arranged all the letters?* I had V-a-s-i-l-y. *Vasily? Joe knew or had connections with Vasily, or was this coincidence? Any number of Vasilys could be spies or FSB agents,* I told myself. All kinds of crazy thoughts flooded my mind. *If my Vasily and Joe's were the same person, did Vasily know about JASON? Did Vasily penetrate that organization in some way? Did Vasily kill my brother? Did Vasily know that I was Joe's brother masquerading as Joe all these years? What implications would all this have on my trip to Europe to disrupt the Calderon network and prevent Vasily from selling weapons or nuclear materials to the Calderons, or to some other terrorist network?* If I was energized for the European trip before, now I was on fire to train and to be ready for it. I went down to the basement and exercised for two additional hours before I calmed down.

When I reappeared upstairs all red-faced and sweaty, Beth took one look and asked, "What's with you, Hercules?"

"Vasily," I said. "I need to be ready to meet Vasily again."

"I thought you were chasing the Calderons on this trip?" Beth questioned my sudden change of mission objectives.

"I am, but they're connected. Sooner or later, one will lead me to the other. I'm sure of it."

"Can you take on both at the same time in the shape you're in?"

"That's a good question. I don't know. All I know is that I'll be solo because the big boys are busy searching for Osama bin Laden and his followers in the al-Qaida organization."

"And you want my help on this trip, is that it?" Beth sought to define her level of participation.

"Yeah, pretty much. Any objections?"

"Most husbands take their wives to London, Paris, Rome—those sort of places, remember?"

"You've been there under varying circumstances more than once. I thought you'd like to try new places and new faces to expand your global perspective. Or, you can stay with your relatives in Slovakia and hunt for Janosik's treasure until I need you," I offered without enthusiasm.

"Somehow, that's not infinitely better. As it is, I'm the only one to go to church in a car with bullet holes in it. But, I'll go with you if you say the magic word."

"Okay, please!"

"Fine, let me know when I should start packing but consider me retired from your work after this trip. And do one more thing for me—put your Bonzo the Clown towel in the wash already."

"Consider it done," I answered in unwavering obedience to the voice of higher authority in my house when it comes to such matters.

Chapter Notes

1. "Hamlet Act III Scene II," *William Shakespeare The Complete Works* (New York: Barnes & Noble Books, 1994), p. 690. Also, "All's Well That Ends Well Act V Scene II," *Ibid.*, p. 780.
2. Whitehall (editor), *op. cit.*, p. 216.
3. Bartlett (compiler), *op. cit.*, p. 5. citing Homer's *Iliad* Book XXII, Line 418.
4. Whitehall (editor), *op. cit.*, p. 211.

CHAPTER 15

OPERATION HERCULES

Preparing for My Personal Parousia

During the weeks of my intensive shoulder therapy and personal conditioning, I took time out to call Advari and Hassan about my anticipated *parousia* (second coming) to Spain, Portugal, and Morocco. I wanted them to be available to help me reconnoiter the Calderons' European and North African operations, if not more. I assumed that Advari would be eager to help me in Lisbon, especially if that meant an excused absence from school. To avoid contributing toward his delinquency more than I usually do when we're together, I needed to check with Paolo as his *ex officio* guardian before I talked directly to Advari. Consequently, I called Paolo in Lisbon to confirm Advari's progress as a student and citizen of the world. To provide a good example on conducting business properly, I noted the time difference and called Paolo during regular business hours when I expected Advari to be in class. I got the time difference right for a change.

"Paolo," I said in opening, "as usual, I am calling when I need a favor."

"Business is good, the sun is shining, and my wife is pregnant again," he replied cheerily. "So, you called at a good time. What can I do for you?"

"You sound very happy. Therefore, I assume you are a co-conspirator in your wife's pregnancy. That's good. Congratulations to both of you. I'm calling to advise that I'm coming in your direction sometime in the next few weeks. I will need Advari's unique skills during my time in Lisbon, provided he won't miss too much school. How is his progress with the Jesuits?"

"Advari is progressing very well. He helps me in the office when he can. He bruised his leg playing soccer the other day, but, otherwise, he is fine. He is several miracles and many prayers away from sainthood, but he could be a shrewd businessman some day. I am sure that he will be delighted that you called because sometimes he is like a wild colt and needs to run free."

"Paolo, I believe you told me politely that I am a major contributor toward any of Advari's lingering bad habits. I guess I deserved that."

"Oh no, Señor, that is not what I meant. You both get along so well together and share the same spirit—"

"For mischief?" I tried to complete Paolo's sentence intending to award myself a lighter sentence for my crimes than Paolo would if I allowed him to speak freely.

"Now you put your words into my mouth. No, I mean for life, Señor. You two stallions have the same spirit for freedom. Okay, maybe a small rebellion here and there too. I will go now before I cause trouble with you. I will tell Advari you called when he returns from school."

"Fine, Paolo, I'm pleased to hear that our mischievous cub is doing well under your guidance. I will ensure that Advari recognizes his debt to you for taking him into your house when you have a family and business to run. I appreciate what you have done for him very much. We will fly into Madrid first, and come to Lisbon a few days later. We will talk more after I arrive. If Advari meets us at the airport, that will be very helpful. I will send him instructions about what I want him to do before we arrive. *Adios* for now, Paolo—oh sorry, wrong country for *adios*. Convert my *adios* to *adeus*."

"Before you go, who is the 'we' you talk about?" Paolo asked.

"Sorry, I failed to tell you that my wife will come with me," I answered promptly.

"That is good. Our wives can shop while you attend to your business."

"Regretfully, my wife will have little time for shopping on this trip, Paolo. I need her feminine skills of observation among her other talents. But, if she can find what I need in a short time, she deserves a shopping spree. I'm sure you must return to your work, and I need to prepare for the trip, so, I will see you in a few weeks."

My call to Hassan's home in Kuwait was less successful. His wife said that he was on an extended business trip. She did not know where he was or when he would return. As a good Arab wife, she would not have told me if she knew. Over the years, Beth often did not know where I was or when I would return. So, lack of communication was not a characteristic unique to Hassan's household. Hassan's absence didn't surprise me either. Almost two months after the 9/11 attacks, I felt certain that I would encounter him somewhere in Madrid, Lisbon, or Morocco. With astute scouting by Beth and Advari, I might learn if Hassan was my friend, or if he had changed. Those were the only available choices. After 9/11, nobody I dealt with remained a neutral party.

PLANE TALK

In the last week of October, Beth and I finally were ready for our European and North African trip. The intervening time had gone as I anticipated, except for one small change. MAGENTA advised Amy that my weapons would be shipped to the U.S. Embassy in Madrid rather than accompany me. In the early days following the September attacks, no government agency was taking any chances on having a dormant homegrown terrorist on its payroll suddenly become active within the U.S. or abroad. I accepted that. For my part, I didn't need a hyperactive air marshal or flight crew to become belligerent about my armed presence on a plane. My war with the Calderons and anyone else could wait until I arrived on European or North African turf.

After an earlier than normal rush to the airport because of the new security rules and screenings, Beth and I completed all the required hurdles and found ourselves airborne on our long night flight to Madrid. Within a short time, the plane reached its cruising altitude and speed. In the same time frame, the cabin crew revealed the new industry-wide, anti-passenger, non-service attitude. Eventually, everyone settled down for the long flight which allowed Beth and me to have an extended and overdue conversation.

"I suppose it's useless for me to ask after all these years why you really need me on this trip?" Beth asked, putting her magazine aside.

"Actually, your timing is excellent, and for once my answers will be straightforward. Besides Daniela and me, you're the only one who saw the young boy and the lady in the black *burka* at the restaurant across the street from the Royal Mansour Hotel in Casablanca. I'm depending on your superior profiling skills to identify her if we see her again, especially if she has different sunglasses and is wearing a red or green *burka* this time, which will totally throw me off."

"Are you admitting that after all these years you can't identify and track a woman walking down the street? You'll never get me to believe that!"

"I'm simply maximizing use of available resources. Women are much better than men at noticing what jewelry a woman wears, if she has wrinkles on her neck, if her purse doesn't match her outfit, what kind of shoes she has, and if her hair coloring has changed—stuff like that."

"Granted, my feminine genes are better than yours for observing those types of things. But, while I'm observing those items, what do you observe when you see a woman?"

"If I can't see anything else, I look at a woman's posture, the way she walks, and any distinctive gestures or body language that can identify her. Seeing her hands up close or hearing her voice obviously helps."

"And is that all you observe?"

"That's it while I'm performing MAGENTA duties, of course."

"Of course. I won't ask about your observations during your personal time. With all the women walking around Europe and North Africa covered to their eyeballs in *burkas*, *hajibs*, shawls, or whatever, do you really expect me to identify this particular lady I saw for only a few minutes months ago?"

"Yes, I do. You do it all the time around home."

"But those observations are for pleasure and gossip purposes, not detective work. I think your attempt to find Calderon's twin brother will be hard enough, and we have photos of him. Do you think we will encounter Madame Black Burka somewhere too?"

"We'll encounter her, for two reasons. First, a major item of our business is to find her. Second, I believe she's connected to the Calderons or Hassan in some way. When we find one, we'll find the others if we are patient and observant."

"If that's what you're thinking, you're either very clever or totally loopy. I'm not sure which adjective applies."

"Then, be grateful I'm not a twin like the Calderons. Compared to whatever else is occurring in the world, you should consider my behavior as close to normal as it has ever been."

"Discussion of your personality and normalcy are not possible in the same sentence. You lost all your marbles years ago."

"You're probably right. It's been so long, I don't miss them any more. But, let me enjoy my insanity. I suffer enough when I'm in my right mind."

"You may fool other people, but, when you're sarcastic, I know you're serious or concerned about something. You're serious about this network theory, aren't you?"

"Yes, I am profoundly serious about it. All my multiple personalities and identities tell me the same story. I believe that the Calderon network is widespread, and that it's a very effective marketer, moneymaker, and murderer. Several things I don't know yet include: one, how extensive the network really is; two, if it's directly connected to major terrorist operations; three, if it has corrupted powerful politicians; four, if it deals with the likes of General Vasily on nuclear or conventional weapons trafficking; and five, God only knows what else. That's why we're on this flight. After we have sufficient information, we destroy the network, or, at least, cripple it sufficiently for the big boys to engage and destroy it later."

"I should have read my magazine and kept my mouth shut. If this project is that serious, we should have a catchy name and mission statement for obituary purposes. Do we have those items to focus our minds and activities while we wend our way through your grand adventure?"

"Consider yourself a participant in Operation Hercules. Our mission is to locate, isolate, and, if possible, obliterate our opponents. Does that satisfy your administrative needs for labels and slogans?"

"Locate, isolate, and obliterate. That's pretty good. How long did it take you to dream that up?"

"It's not difficult to label something. Doing something positive is the hard part. We'll be on both sides of the Straits of Gibraltar, which were known as the Pillars of Hercules in ancient days. Ergo, naming the operation was easy. We need to be effective against the network at our level of ability. That's why I refer to Vasily and the Calderons as the junior varsity compared to the networks that make headlines. But, those two opponents are big and ugly enough for us while the CIA, Interpol, FBI, and whoever else is involved now in anti-terrorist activities are chasing major organizations. If we cut off supplies, destroy infrastructure, or disrupt funding sources to the top tier organizations, we'll make a worthwhile contribution toward U.S. and global security."

"I realize now how much thought you've given this project. But, tell me again why we're doing all this by ourselves instead of vacationing somewhere peaceful and expensive?"

"The 'me' of 'we' is doing this because I believe our government, military, and commercial establishments fell asleep after the Cold War. Without the Soviets as our common focus, the U.S. government and corporate America lost their national identities and purpose. We fumbled Korea and Vietnam on macro levels politically and militarily. (Actually, North Korea unilaterally withdrew from the July 27, 1953 armistice on May 27, 2009. Because no treaty officially ending the war was signed, the U.S. and North Korea technically resumed the war as of that date. I hoped that nobody interested in resumption of active combat noticed. We did better on the Vietnam paperwork with both sides signing the Paris

Peace Accords on January 27, 1973 which established an immediate cease-fire status with U.S. forces, but the fighting in Vietnam proceeded between the South and North Vietnamese armies with continued U.S. military aid to the South until the North Vietnamese captured Saigon on April 30, 1975.[1]) In my opinion, we're set to fumble additional opportunities to make the world a better place for ourselves and other nations. Americans lost control of our government. We have no respected voice of opposition to make us think. Look at the poor quality of people we elect to public office. Once there, they act as if they're not accountable to anyone. I can't change or repair all that's broken in the U.S. by myself. Hopefully, I can act and shout long enough to get someone's attention to help fix something and start a chain reaction for improvement. I owe that much to our grandkids."

"Particularly pertinent to this kind of work," I continued, "the Pentagon went high tech on the assumption that our technology would overwhelm every opponent on every type of battlefield under every circumstance. The idea was sold to the American public that, under the high-tech umbrella, fewer military and civilian casualties would result with our pinpoint destruction of primary targets. The military establishment didn't envision asymmetrical conflicts with extremists defending their homelands or the lives of others joined to them by religious, family, clan, or other long-established bonds that frequently require family members to take revenge on others for real or perceived injuries."

"In addition to corruption and incompetence," I added, "our business leaders are so engrossed in acquiring personal wealth that they don't recognize that the world no longer needs or wants the U.S. as a business model, or as the supplier of all their material goods. If U.S. firms can't provide the desired goods and services at competitive prices, businesses in other nations can and will compete with us on the global stage to our financial detriment. Also, as individuals and as a nation, we forget that we have a stake in the collective welfare of all of the citizens of the world, not just our own needs and pleasures. At the same time, people in other countries want similar rights and the material goods we have, but, frequently, they fail to recognize that responsibilities as world citizens are attached to those rights, and work is required to produce personal and national wealth. Those are some of the reasons why the 'me' of 'we' is on this plane. In my small way, I'm trying to protect my piece of the world until our national intelligence and military organizations are operational to protect the larger 'us' from terrorist attacks."

"As for you and me as a married couple, nothing has changed over the years," I continued. "We both still reside in the same hand basket headed toward perdition at light speed. How much more information and inspiration can I give you during my current incarnation as a committed network buster? On a micro level, maybe you and Advari should team up to find our missing *burka* lady in Lisbon or Morocco if we don't find her in Madrid."

"What should we do if we find her, sing 'America the Beautiful' in the street until you show up with your guns?" Beth asked pointedly.

"Try singing 'Nearer My God To Thee.' I may come sooner if I know your ship has snagged an iceberg and is sinking. But, doggone, once again, I think that if we find one, the others will be in the neighborhood. We may converge and be able to sing a duet in the street."

"What do—?"

"Cool it a while," I interrupted Beth. "We'll talk later. Here comes the lunch lady."

"Why are you making a face? Airline food is very nutritious. I understand that many frequent fliers have survived eating airline food and have gone on to lead normal productive lives," Beth advised.

"Remember that box lunch we decided not to have on the flight from Riga to Moscow?" I commented.

"Yes, I remember the uncooked slab of bacon on rye very well. The Russian guard dog on the plane choked when I gave him a bite. But the lunch wasn't the only deadly thing on that flight was it? That plane had empty spaces where the oxygen masks should have been."

"Either they counted on us being so busy trying to bite through the raw bacon not to notice the trivial absence of safety equipment, or they didn't think the old plane could reach the altitude where oxygen might be needed. We had a better chance of survival if we crashed into the Baltic—then again, maybe not. We'd have had a race between the toxic effect of the lunch, or the nuclear poison leaking from sunken Soviet nuclear submarines to determine what would destroy us first. The only difference between that plane and the Titanic was that the Titanic had a gift shop."

After having finished what passed for an airline meal, Beth reintroduced the question she had started before I cut her off.

"What do you think our government will do now that the terrorists have attacked U.S. citizens and our land directly?"

"That's a good question, Beth, because now we're faced with one or more terrorist organizations with roots in several countries, and maybe our own, rather than only a distant terrorist country or group that we can subdue at our leisure. Accommodation toward past terrorist threats and actions was unsuccessful. This time, the U.S. needs to respond accurately and decisively."

"Is the president perceptive and strong enough to do it, and do it right?"

"You keep dealing hard questions. Did you have a different lunch than I did?"

"No, but I didn't eat the little tomatoes that will give the passengers a major attack of another kind shortly. Hopefully, we'll be off the plane by then."

"Their first problem is getting the tomato seeds from between their teeth. Maybe that will distract their tummies long enough for us to land in Madrid before they change the ambient cabin pressure on this plane."

"Then, I encourage you and the other passengers to make friends with your digestive systems through negotiation and accommodation rather than declaring war. Take your antacids and answer my questions before you explode."

"Talking about recent presidential successes in decision-making isn't the best way to pacify my stomach. Recent presidents have all acted as if political maneuvering will always trump good judgment and diplomacy in U.S. relationships with other countries. Of course, history has not given our presidents good mentors either."

"How so?"

"Like most major events in life and world politics, what happened on September 11 and preceding it, take their origin from an array of overt acts, unintended consequences, missed opportunities, and downright mistakes over time. Some people want to take the causes of our current conflict back to the Crusades as if those wars were the only defining moments in the history of the Western and Eastern worlds. On the ferry back to Spain, Hassan winced when I brought up the word 'Crusades.' The uncomplimentary Arabic word for 'crusader' is '*jahili*,' and fervent followers of Islam are duty bound to raise *jihad* or holy war against the forces of '*jahiliyya*,' the unbelievers."

"And right now, the U.S. represents the center of *jahiliyya* for the terrorists, I suppose."

"Not only for the terrorists, but devout followers of Islam in many countries envy us for our material goods, although they despise our lack of firm national and individual moral and ethical conduct."

"In that case, I think you should join Advari and me on any reconnaissance forays you have in mind. I get distracted from my moral and personal ethics when someone points a gun at me. All I remember then is our European relatives telling us that Slovakia manufactures the best assault rifles. I get totally lost thinking that the gun pointed at me probably was assembled by one of our Slovak uncles or cousins," Beth confessed.

"Your concerns and advice are duly noted," I conceded. "For our mutual protection and peace of mind, Advari and the two of us will act as three *caballeros* in our Operation Hercules activities whenever possible."

Both of us were silent for a while and looked straight ahead at nothing in particular as the seriousness of our mission crept into our private thoughts. After a few minutes, Beth broke the silence.

"Now what's happening in your head?"

"I was thinking that the United States isn't solely to blame for the current state in which it finds itself. Plenty of evidence points toward European colonialism before and after the World Wars and the erroneous partitioning of countries following World War II as sources of ongoing dissension in the Middle East and Africa. For example, Portugal, Spain, Britain, and France were rivals for control of India and Africa for centuries. Britain eventually gained control in India through use of the British East India Company as a proxy for Queen Victoria's imperialistic policies. British control in India reached its zenith during the Raj period of Victoria's reign. Britain also had its protectorate over Israel, Palestine, and other countries or territories in the Middle East following World War II. The British didn't resolve the question of control of Kashmir between India and Pakistan, and that continues to be a sore point today. Nor did Britain establish firm borders and resolve other conflicts between Iraq, Iran, Kuwait, or Afghanistan and some of their neighbors. France controlled North Africa, mainly Morocco and Algeria in addition to French Somaliland, and Indochina, of course. Germany had its holdings through the Boers and Afrikaners in Central and South Africa. With maybe Hong Kong as the exception that proves the rule, the various countries and territories didn't prosper as a result of European stewardship. Natives waited for opportunities for independence and economic growth in their homelands that never came. While they waited, the more aggressive groups learned how to take by force what they didn't receive voluntarily or through their hard work.

That's my quick interpretation of the European reasons for our current Middle East troubles."

"Don't forget that the U.S. bailed out the Europeans, or, at least, took over for them in Vietnam, Afghanistan, Somalia, and Yugoslavia, among other countries," Beth added.

"Lord knows the U.S. didn't always handle those problems correctly when it intervened or was the referee in those conflicts," I offered in mitigation of my previous raps against European diplomatic efforts, but Beth was not in a forgiving mood.

"Such as?" she asked.

"One relevant 'such as' is the Russian invasion of Afghanistan in 1979 in which the U.S. supported the Taliban and the Islamic *mujahedeen* to oppose the Russians. The U.S. created more problems than it solved in that intervention. U.S. support for the *mujahedeen* emboldened them to enter the already out-of-control conflict in the Balkans that split former Yugoslavian unity into its fractious Serbian, Macedonian, Croatian, Slovenian, Bosnian, Kosovar, and Albanian components with the collateral loss of countless Christian and Islamic lives in the process. A Yugoslavian partition could and should have been settled between the Europeans and Russia without any U.S. involvement."

"I thought that Russia invaded Afghanistan to gain access to Persian Gulf oil?"

"Partly, but another Russian objective was to create Middle East markets for its own products."

"Either way, the U.S. wanted similar or better access to Middle East oil and geopolitical stability in the region. I don't know how the U.S. can solve the region's stability problem and maintain our moral high ground by using our military forces to shoot first and try diplomacy later under the current administration. Have we lost our diplomatic leverage and credibility too?" Beth continued to press her view of the world order.

"Fortunately for me, I see another well-timed pause coming which will give me time to think of an answer, if there is one. Here comes the beverage wagon. Do you want anything?"

"Whatever they have in liquid form that doesn't interrupt the circadian rhythms of the geopolitical universe is fine with me," Beth identified her beverage preference.

"I'll ask for orange juice for both of us, and I won't mention global circadian rhythms. How's that?" I asked, attempting to have Beth downshift a political gear or two.

"Okay, but meanwhile, keep going with your dissertation at least until the movie starts. I've never seen you so fidgety. You're making me antsy. I can't believe it!"

"If you think I'm tense now, you should have seen me in Tingo Maria when we were feeding diluted poison to the ranch hands," I said without relieving her anxiety.

"Okay, back to my history and political lecture that you demanded. People who know more than I do about U.S.-styled diplomacy may point toward our mishandling of the Iranian hostage crisis by President Carter's crowd and the Iran-Contra affair during President Reagan's administration as well-worn examples of how the U.S. created significant flashpoints and some proximate causes for our present Middle East problems."

"I remember that you talked to Hassan at length about the hostage topic as it might have related to Iraq's invasion of Kuwait," Beth recalled. "You also told me that Barrantes tried to justify his drug network by the way the U.S. handled the Iran-Contra situation. How do U.S. foreign policies relate to the junior varsity networks you want to confront now?"

"You make a good point, as did Barrantes. Those two hostage events have many facets. Both cases demonstrated lowdown ways to treat the lives of innocent hostages as well as diplomatic nearsightedness. The U.S. was duplicitous in providing arms and support to groups we now consider enemies, and we allowed easy access of drug dealers into the U.S. while proclaiming a national war against them. The varsity networks expanded their horizons from arms and drugs to human trafficking, money laundering, murder of public officials who opposed them, and mayhem of every sort among innocent people who happened to be in their way. This allowed smaller operators such as Barrantes and the Calderons to grow, form cartels to act as suppliers to the big boys, or prosper from their independent operations."

"So, let me guess. You're saying that recent U.S. diplomacy is 'bush league' at best."

"That's clever. I wish I had thought of it. More diplomatically, if the past Carter, G.H.W. Bush, and Clinton administrations serve as prologue for what President George W. Bush and his successors intend for U.S. involvement in Iraq, Afghanistan, Pakistan, other Middle East countries, and against al-Qaida and the Taliban, you and I will have many foreign trips, or we'll have prime locations in Ascension Cemetery. Take your pick."

"I think it's time for a woman president," Beth countered in a new direction.

"Don't bet on that horse before we have a qualified jockey," I cautioned. "And, as you well know, I'm not opposed to a woman president as a matter of principle. In fact, I've identified my first woman candidate already."

"Do I know her, and would I vote for her?" Beth probed.

"Definitely, but if someone else is selected who is perceived or demonstrates that she is a bad or premature selection, that choice will set the women's rights movement back a million years in this country, to say nothing of emerging nations. And, probably, the first woman candidate for president will need to be three times better than any male opponent to get elected. That may not be fair, but that's the way I see it until the U.S. has experienced its first woman president. Because our current international troubles occur in the Middle East where women are not generally respected, I would have a hard time putting any woman in a position in which she is compromised merely because she is female. Bad diplomacy and lack of foresight can afflict any resident of the Oval Office regardless of gender, political party, religion, education, or pedigree. But, the day will come when a qualified woman can take control of the Oval Office and do a good job there. Fortunately, until then, we can count on our trusted allies to help us."

"What trusted allies?" Beth maneuvered in the direction I led her.

"You've hit another diplomatic nerve with that question. I agree. I don't see Europe or the United Nations running to get ahead of us in cleaning up the messes they left the first time around in the Middle East. Supposedly, the UN was created to correct world problems through discussion, negotiation, and sanctions, if necessary. Now it runs from fulfilling its charter whenever the world needs it most to end conflicts, fix boundaries, feed starving nations, or defend oppressed people. The way the UN operates, we can't pile all the blame on U.S. presidents."

THE TALK GETS TREASONOUS

"Nonetheless, why aren't our presidents censured or found guilty of treason when they put the United States in such perilous positions or give away our resources time after time?"

"Our Founding Fathers looked at the track record of European royalty, who determined that anything they didn't like was treason. So, our Founders drafted Article III Section 3 of our Constitution to narrowly define treason in the U.S. as: one, levying war against our country; two, adhering to our enemies; or three, giving our enemies aid and comfort as the only criminal treasonous acts. Pretty clever of them at the time, don't you think? They knew we were coming, I guess."

"It might have been nifty at the time, but now our leaders are bleeding the country of our heritage, resources, and advantages."

"Like what particularly for you? I'm sure I can develop my own list."

"For starters, why wasn't it treason when President G.H.W. Bush's administration gave away U.S. supremacy in quantum physics?"

"I know where you're going now, and my naïve, U.S.-biased, down-home, nonpolitical mind agrees with you. Maybe, Congress was on a break in November 1988 rather than providing guidance for President Bush's incoming administration. Consequently, President Bush's actions through the Department of Energy were defined in history simply as political largesse: old-fashioned, unvarnished, political pork, or sheer political ignorance—all of which are everyday occurrences in Washington. Officially, his decision to squander U.S. quantum physics leadership to please his Texas buddies didn't reach the level of a constitutional crime according to our Founding Fathers and our Supreme Court."

"Well, someone should have recognized that the Founding Fathers' gene pool would be diluted by the time our forty-first president came along. His and Congress' misguided act was not a thoughtful attempt to improve basic research facilities in this country. President Bush, his congressional cronies, and business pals deliberately squandered U.S. leadership in quantum physics by trying to build a new $4.4 billion research laboratory in Texas when world class physics laboratories were already operating in California and Illinois. President Bush's and House Speaker Jim Wright's act was not a careless mistake; it was a deliberate decision. In case you've forgotten, let me refresh your memory based on the facts as I know them, and judge for yourself if I'm not right about the Super Collider project."

Beth was in high gear now and the safety of the universe was in my hands not to allow her frustration to endanger the other passengers on board or the universe at large.

"Okay, Tiger, get it out of your system while we're safely at 37,000 feet or more above the Atlantic and far enough away from Washington, D.C. not to seriously injure anyone."

"You already know that the Fermi National Accelerator Laboratory in Batavia is a national research center about thirty-five miles west of Chicago. Fermilab operates in conjunction with the U.S. Department of Energy and the University of Chicago similar to Argonne National Laboratory southwest of Chicago near Lemont. Fermilab's big project when President Bush Sr. was in office in 1992 involved the search for subatomic particles called *quarks*, which scientists theorized as existing, but they had not yet unequivocally identified them or their properties. Many big league physicists were at Fermilab working on the project at the time. The scientists were optimistic that they could identify all the subatomic *quark* particles given sufficient resources and time. The scientists made an unfortunate mistake of telling President Bush's budget bunch that the chances for project success could improve if they had a bigger underground accelerator ring to find the elusive *Top quark* and the postulated, but equally elusive, *Higgs boson particle*. President Bush and his congressional cronies took that opportunity to reward Texas with a Super Collider construction site in Waxahachie near Dallas to replace Fermilab's Tevatron accelerator."

In those few sentences, she had my taxpayer blood pressure boiling too. That didn't dissuade Beth from pursuing scientific justice, as she perceived it.

"Texans don't have basements because the rocky soil forces groundwater through any cracks in poured concrete basements or subterranean structures. But that didn't stop the politicians from starting construction on the Super Collider there. After spending $100 million or so digging the underground tunnel, pouring the concrete, and wiring the big magnets to bend the super-fast particles to accelerate around the ring, the contractors discovered that raspberry ants were eating the insulation off the wiring faster than the electricians could install it.[2] The groundwater and ants made the Texas site totally unusable. But, the buffoonery didn't stop there," Beth paused for a moment before resuming her scientific dissertation.

"After spending another exorbitant sum to bury the Texas site with its ants and porous rocks, President Bush's crew informed U.S. scientists not to complain. Rather, they should continue their research with current equipment and collaborate with the European scientific consortium that was building its own world-class accelerator at the CERN facility near Geneva, Switzerland that is projected to be seven times more powerful than Fermilab's accelerator.[3] At that point, the U.S. was ten years ahead of anything Europe had. The Large Hadron Collider at the CERN facility is projected to fire up in 2008. By that time, the best and brightest physicists at Fermilab will scatter all over the map to work on other projects. The U.S. squandered a ten-year lead in quantum physics—all because of a stupid political decision. How many leadership positions can we throw away before the U.S. is no longer credible in scientific research?"

> The actual impact of President Bush and Congress' decision was more damaging than Beth described during our 2001 plane trip. The seventeen-mile underground circle of the Large Hadron Collider at CERN went online on September 10, 2008, and crashed after thirty-six hours of initial operation due to a bad electrical connection between two magnets that caused a liquid helium leak. Because the particle accelerator operates near absolute zero—minus 273 degrees Fahrenheit—the scientists had to gradually bring the collider up to normal temperatures over a two-week period before they could assess the damage. By that time, scientists decided to leave the collider shut down over the winter because the European electrical grid that powers the collider cannot supply sufficient energy to both the collider and to its French/Swiss neighborhood during winter months. Subsequently, examination disclosed that the collider would take until mid-2009 to repair. In short, the scientific community and the world were victimized by a very unscientific political decision a U.S. president and Congress had made years earlier. Later media reports disclosed that the Large Hadron Collider had been undergoing repairs until restarted on November 20, 2009.[4]

If the collective lives of the other passengers didn't depend on me getting Beth to cool her engines, I'd have agreed that she presented a convincing argument. But, like an uncontrolled forest fire, the best I could do was to let her burn herself out.

"As a result of the Department of Energy's decision under President Bush's administration," Beth continued, "years later the U.S. continues to lose its preeminence in quantum physics research, the U.S. scientific community was delayed in identifying the subatomic *Top quark*, and President Bush wasted $4.4 billion of taxpayer dollars that could have gone for a gold-plated Linear Accelerator tunnel at Fermilab. Instead, U.S. physicists scattered to work on pitty-pat projects, while the best that any remaining Fermilab scientists could do was to establish computer facilities to monitor the work being done by CERN.[5] All the collaborators at the CERN facility profited from disclosure of our advanced knowledge, and the U.S. is only an observer, not a member of the European Organization for Nuclear Research consortium. If that isn't treason and aiding enemies of our country, what is? It certainly aided all the other nuclear powers, including Russia and China that undoubtedly obtained inside information despite not being CERN members, to know where we were and where we were going in nuclear and particle physics research. Do you still object to the prompt election of a woman president?"

Beth had me agreeing with her more than ever, but this was my chance for appeasement that I hoped would be more fruitful than British Prime Minister Chamberlain's attempt to appease Hitler before the outbreak of World War II.

"On its face, you have a strong scientific and practical basis for your charge of treason under old European monarchy rules. Better men than President Bush lost their lives for doing less under those old forms of government. But if I were President Bush's defense attorney, I would introduce the subject of the 'string theory' of the universe, assuming you'd be willing to give him and his congressional cronies a trial."

"Like stringing them up? I like that approach," Beth proposed enthusiastically.

"No, or at least not before providing a fair trial. As I understand it, the 'string theory' postulates that our observable universe may be only one of multiple universes, and a small one at that.[6] A model of divergent universes under the 'string theory' would have multiple dimensions beyond time, space, height, length, and depth. At this point, cosmologists worldwide don't know how to test the 'string theory' for proof because the question is almost too complex for our humanoid brains to grasp. The 'string theory' through super-symmetry modeling aims to: explain why matter exists, how mass and force particles interact, why antimatter is in short supply in our universe, and interpret the impact of dark matter and its particle partners on the energy and matter particles that we know."[7]

"How does that defend Bush's treason in giving away our quantum physics research?"

"It's a stretch, but, as his defense counsel, I'd argue that while the Europeans are all gathered around the Large Hadron Collider in Switzerland looking for the subatomic particles of this universe, U.S. scientists could be working on unlocking the deeper secrets of the existence of multiple universes, which is a far greater and nobler challenge. Consequently, President Bush's act was not treasonous because the U.S. is maintaining its scientific supremacy, albeit on a totally different project with no evidence that other universes exist or why they should matter to us earthlings if they do."

"You just stated the problem I see with your defense strategy," Beth said, demonstrating that she had plenty of fight left in her. "We're still working to understand this universe, let alone conjuring up others that we can't explain or experience. We can't get funding for scientific projects that have a reasonable chance of benefiting people on this planet in the foreseeable future. We can't get potholes in the roads fixed, let alone have Congress fund pure research. How do you expect to obtain government funding and support for research on other universes that may not exist and that we cannot travel to even if they do? On a more practical level, you must admit that unless we know our universe first, we probably don't have the scientific tools and knowledge to understand multiple universes. Going back to my original premise in our present universe, all other countries large and small take considerable comfort in knowing that they can beat the U.S. in any scientific project when it involves a decision by our political leaders because they always manage to mismanage the project and make the information available to our adversaries. Our presidents and Congress continually confirm their stupid *modus operandi* time after time on critical issues. Is it just me or is our federal government a collection of all the biggest idiots in the country?"

"If I were sitting in the jury box, you would have convinced me long ago on that point."

"If you were the judge, how would you decide the verdict, smarty-shorts?"

"If I were the judge in your court, I'd vote for the first woman candidate for president, and like Dickens' *Madame Defarge* in the *Tale of Two Cities*, I'd be braiding a rope from the 'string' material while I listened to the testimony on the CERN project. But humans haven't changed much over the centuries. In 550 BC, Aesop wrote, 'We hang the petty thieves and appoint the great ones to public office.'"[8]

"So, you agree with me that our politicians have a poor record on practical, near-term, environmental issues, let alone envisioning the existence of parallel or divergent universes?"

"Sadly, I agree with you about politicians in general. But, on the positive side, the Tower Commission in its 1987 final report held President Reagan ultimately responsible for the Iran-Contra affair. That may not be the immediate bench justice you'd like, but a Greater Power may have evened the score on that item. I shudder at what lies ahead for me.

In my case, I'm praying for mercy, not justice. The second positive is that you've convinced me you're a true patriot and an advocate for free speech regarding quantum physics, although I would give you a failing grade in political chicanery, ah oops, science class. If President Bush had been convicted of treason as an opponent of U.S. science and being the hidden power behind the Waxahachie project, the Washington Beltway crowd would have pardoned him anyway. The Supreme Court would have declared that the treasonous raspberry ants were at fault and not the members of the executive or legislative branches of our government. Any rational debate on spending public funds for pure research is not a winning argument when government officials are involved. My small involvement in local politics convinced me of that. Another issue would be that if the Large Hadron Collider were located in the U.S. that would give terrorists additional motivation to attack us, or to infiltrate the scientific community to pass on nuclear information to subversive groups. But, we're building an underground laboratory in South Dakota to study dark matter where the enemies of science will find it more difficult to interrupt that research."[9]

"It would be interesting to know if your friend, Roberto is invited to CERN as a member scientist from Portugal, or as an invited guest from India," Beth raised a thought-provoking topic.

"That's a valuable idea for me to keep in mind for the future. For the present, I'd be more interested to know if Vasily hangs around the parking lot handing out his business card."

"In any event, some politicians don't quit their meddling even after they leave office," Beth noted. "Do you remember when the former Department of Education official invited you on a consulting trip to Africa to talk about the U.S. education system including the proposed 'No Child Left Behind' program?"

"I recall my response was that the program appears to be a funding mechanism rather than an educational reform program. We shouldn't peddle it to other countries when the program won't lift the quality of education for U.S. children, particularly the minorities. As evidence, I can cite the experience of minority schools in Chicago that routinely send the kids on field trips during the winter because the schools have no heat. At least some of the students are warm while they're on the bus or at a museum."

"But, what was in your orange juice, Beth? Don't drink any more of that stuff or you'll become a political outcast like me. And you can let go of my arm anytime it's convenient for you. I know that keeping America safe, healthy, and prosperous are important goals for both of us, but with you squeezing my arm in your enthusiasm, blood hasn't reached my fingers for the last three minutes."

MEETING THE MARSHAL

As I finished my comment, the man in the seat in front of me turned around, and said in a quiet voice, "Buddy, you and your wife may be on the right track, and you have the right as Americans to speak your mind, but if you keep demeaning the U.S. government, this train will run all over both of you."

"Hey, Marshal Train," I answered with fake surprise, "I wondered how long you'd sit there listening while my wife and I had our private discussion, which, theoretically at least, is protected by the First Amendment of our Constitution. We don't recall inviting you as a guest listener!"

"Don't mind him," Beth said. "He's been this way ever since a flowerpot fell out of an open window in Germany and landed on his head. Consequently, we're no longer welcome in Munich, Berlin, Dresden, Frankfurt, Cologne, Potsdam—you name it."

"Scratch Potsdam off your list. Ron and I were *personae non grata* in Potsdam on other charges long before the flowerpot incident and President Bush and Congress' decision to disembowel Fermilab and other scientific facilities in the States."

Then, Air Marshal Train interrupted our conversation again.

"How did you identify me as an air marshal," the officer asked, turning around as far as he could to look at me directly while ignoring Beth's attempt to diffuse the confrontation that her oration had initiated in the first place.

"That's easy," I answered him. "Working backwards, I noticed that you're not as relaxed as the other passengers at this point in the flight. You watch every movement of the crew and passengers. Second, I noticed earlier the pistol lump on the left side of your jacket and the ammo clip lump on the right side, so you are a right-handed air marshal, or awfully slow on the draw as a lefty in these tight seats. Both items were exposed briefly when you put your luggage in the overhead compartment. You need to be more careful about that. You need a better tailor for your jackets, and please listen to his advice about selecting better colors and avoid plaids next time. Third, you carry a small backup gun in your cowboy boots, but it rubs on your ankle, doesn't it? I noticed you favoring your right leg as you walked down the entrance ramp at the airport. You broke your cover with me before you got on the plane. If you intend to succeed in your line of work, you'd better get a lot sharper at it than you are now."

"I also thought marshals sit with a bulkhead wall to their back so that, for example, a passenger behind you can't untie a shoelace and use it as a garrote around your unskilled federal neck," I continued. "I say all this to be helpful to you, Marshal Train, because, right now, the crew and passengers of this plane need all the confidence in your skills and protection that they can get. Intimidating my wife and me is not one of your better occupational skills. I believe this information might be useful to you before you get into a difficult situation."

"Thanks, I'll keep that in mind," Marshal Train said gruffly as he faced forward again in his seat. "But I've been instructed that my protection includes you two as U.S. citizens, however ungrateful you are to receive any cover."

"In that case, tell your handlers thanks for your help and protection. I truly appreciate it," I said earnestly. "I hope you have many uneventful trips."

Marshal Train didn't bother us for the remainder of the flight. That was too bad because he had the wrong attitude about learning how to do his job better, maintain his cover, and ride shotgun for other outbound operatives. Despite his attitude, I was pleased to have him aboard this flight. His presence confirmed that MAGENTA had something to do with his seat selection in relation to Beth's and mine. I was glad that somebody in my organization was thinking and cared enough to adjust the seating arrangements. I hoped that Shortcake had something to do with it. I was glad, particularly with my wife along on this trip that my Scout was beginning to make her presence felt in the way she handled her activities and my agenda by surpassing MAGENTA's basic checklist of procedures.

No Rain in Spain, Only Advari

Weather conditions were good, and we had a smooth landing on the first try into Madrid's Aeropuerto Internacional de Barajas. The overwhelming crowd of anxious passengers had diminished considerably from our post-September 11 flight out of here two months earlier, although, in my opinion, the airport still had a larger name than the size of the building justified. In the process of clearing customs and retrieving our luggage, I recognized familiar faces among the *Policia de Securitas* group from our previous trip. Under the new security procedures, they were far too busy checking people and luggage entering the building to recognize and talk to folks like us leaving the airport. It was just as well because as we turned the corner into the main lobby, Advari saw us and finished his short sprint toward me with a leap into my arms despite my full load of luggage.

"Señor *Gringo*," Advari shouted into my ear, temporarily deafening me, "I have so much to tell you!"

"Good, but you were instructed to meet us in Lisbon. The sign says that this is Madrid. So, you can carry señora's stuff as we walk toward the taxi stand. Talk to me while we walk," I urged him while poking him in the ribs to break his hold around my neck as I shifted the straps of Beth's carry-on to his shoulders. "Where did you get the '*gringo*' term? I know you didn't pick that up from the Jesuits."

The weight of the luggage or my playful admonition didn't diminish Advari's enthusiasm or disregard for what I said.

"Señora, I am pleased to see you again," Advari said, greeting Beth to demonstrate his acquisition of manners since his departure from the marketplace in India as well as to ignore my question.

"Thank you," she replied, "you look very well. You look like you are happy in Lisbon."

"Oh yes, they treat me very well, but, sometimes I miss my old friends, and, of course, I miss *El Gringo* and the adventures I have when I am with him," he answered, pointing at me.

"With your intelligence, and God's grace, I'm sure that in time you will overcome any detrimental effects you have from your connection with my husband," Beth assured him.

"But look, Señor, there goes your friend Hassan!" Advari interrupted while pointing in the direction of the *Policia de Securitas* area we had just vacated.

That bit of news brought the polite conversation and our progress toward the exit to an abrupt halt as Beth and I pivoted in unison to look where Advari was pointing. Even with his back turned and walking quickly in the opposite direction, there was no mistaking Hassan's features and tailored suit.

"Do you want me to bring him here?" Advari asked.

"Not now, little soldier. Unless you think we won't find Hassan again, we need to talk before we contact him."

"No, I have seen him often at the airport in Lisbon and now here. While in Madrid, he stays at the Agumar Hotel near the Prado Museum and the Atocha train station. I followed him there several times."

"You are full of valuable information, my little friend. I won't ask you how many days you have been in Madrid gathering the information or what you are doing hanging around the Lisbon airport. But I definitely picked the right person for reconnaissance in advance of our arrival. Let's save any more important conversation until we get to the hotel. One never knows how many ears are listening these days."

"Are we going to the hotel now?" Advari asked.

"Not directly. First I need to pick up a package at the U.S. Embassy. Show me how much you have learned since we last saw each other and instruct the taxi driver to take us to the U.S. Embassy at 75 Calle de Serrano. Also, because you picked my pocket last time, you pay for the ride."

"But I was only joking, Señor."

"I'm sure you were. I enjoyed the joke myself. But that was then, and this is now. This is work time. When we get to the embassy, both of you stay in the taxi while I go inside. I should only be a few minutes."

Advari was a little crestfallen by my stern attitude, but his little bits of information made me realize that Operation Hercules was already in motion.

"Don't worry, little soldier," I told him as I saw his eyes moisten with the beginning of tears. "You did very well. I am proud of you. We are after powerful and very bad people. I don't want you to get hurt because I'm not caring for you properly and setting a good example. To show you my good faith, I will pay the taxi fare this time, and I won't flinch if you order an extra dessert at dinner tonight."

Advari's eyes cleared immediately, his spirit returned, and he gave the taxi driver authoritative instructions to take us to the embassy. On the way, we talked about his schooling and life in Lisbon with Paolo and his family. He was progressing nicely in his new environment.

Diplomatic Detour

Upon our arrival, I went into the embassy, gave the receptionist my name, and asked if a package was awaiting my arrival. The sudden tensing of the receptionist's shoulder and neck muscles informed me that she recognized my name. She asked me to wait in the reception area and disappeared into one of the larger offices. Before I had time to look closely at some

TERRORISTS AND THE TERCHOVA TREASURE

of the original paintings done by Domenikos Theotokopoulos (better known worldwide as El Greco), the receptionist returned, followed by the ambassador.

"Welcome to Madrid, Señor," the ambassador said while extending his hand in greeting. "Will you be staying in Madrid very long?"

"Thank you for taking time from your busy schedule to meet me. I probably will be staying longer than you want me in your neighborhood, but a few days at most should be sufficient. Hopefully, a prompt departure will mean that I have completed the business I came for and I will not trouble you or your staff further."

"In that case, I will not delay you," the ambassador replied, looking greatly relieved. "Jacinta, ask Miguel to bring the gentleman's packages from the storeroom and help bring them to his car without delay," the ambassador instructed the receptionist.

"Taxi," I corrected him.

"Very well. Taxi it is, Señor," the ambassador corrected himself nervously. Meanwhile, Jacinta was in motion to find Miguel in order to eject me from her reception area as quickly as humanly possible.

"I'm sorry I clouded up your day, Ambassador," I commented, "but these are tense times for all of us. If you have a minute, I'd like to ask you a question in private."

"Yes, certainly, come into my office," the ambassador replied as a heavily burdened Miguel rounded the corner with my "toys" under both arms.

"Good thing for Miguel I'm traveling light on this trip, isn't it?" I commented to the ambassador.

"I hope you do not have anything dangerous in there," the ambassador inquired, hoping against hope that I would answer in the negative but almost certain that was not the answer he would receive.

I tried to soften my response. No, on second thought, I really tried increasing rather than diminishing the ambassador's anxiety.

"If Miguel stands too close to the fireplace with my cases as he is now, we'll all have a free ride to the monument of *Santa Cruz del Valle de los Caidos*—the Holy Cross of the Valley of the Fallen—a fair distance outside of town if I recall correctly," I replied for maximum effect on the ambassador.

"Miguel, get those things downstairs to the taxi immediately," the ambassador instructed his hapless employee.

"If you have all your luggage, I only need to give you this," the ambassador said reaching into the inside pocket of his suit coat for an envelope he handed to me. "I have other matters to attend to now, but be sure to contact me immediately if you need anything while you are in Madrid," the ambassador stated without rancor but without hospitality either.

"*Muchas gracias* for your hospitality, but I still need to ask you a question in private, if you don't mind?"

"Oh, yes, I forgot you wanted a private conversation," the ambassador replied nervously with a few beads of perspiration appearing on his brow. "Come this way," he said, gesturing toward his office. I counter-gestured for him to lead the way—which he did. A few steps into the office, he turned to close the door behind me and pointed toward a chair as he prepared to take his seat behind his desk.

"Thank you, no, I won't stay long enough to have a seat. I will be direct. Do you know a Kuwaiti gentleman named Hassan who seems to travel a lot between the Middle East, Eastern Europe, your country, Portugal, and North Africa?"

"No, I do not think so," the ambassador responded without convincing me. "Should I?"

"You probably should to determine if he has terrorist connections, and, if so, how willing and able he is to identify some of his playmates. If he is a friend, he possibly can save lives and valuable time in identifying people we need to know about *pronto*. Now, if I ask you the question again, will you give me the same answer?"

"Hassan has worked for the embassy in the past, yes. Is that all you need?" the ambassador asked as he got up from his chair.

"But he has worked both sides of the Pillars of Hercules between Spain and Morocco, right? Is that what you're telling me? So, whose agent is he really?"

"That is hard to say. He is a capitalist at heart."

"That means he works for the highest bidder, I suppose?"

"Yes, I believe that is a correct statement."

"*Habra tempestad.* Ambassador, a storm is coming in this direction, and all you know is suppositions. I'm glad I didn't apply for a State Department position."

"I am sure that the diplomatic corps shares your delight in that you did not select State Department service as your career. Now, I really must attend to other matters. Is there anything else you need?"

"Not this minute, but if I do, I'll contact you in the middle of the night so that I can haul you and your crew out of bed to lend me a hand. *Adios!*"

"*Adios* to you too, Señor. At my earliest opportunity, I will confirm to your superiors that you have the charming personality we have heard so much about from several sources."

"Because I work for myself, I don't have any superiors unless my wife is around. But the people I report to on these projects already know about the extent of my diplomatic skills—especially when I'm dealing with uncooperative and incompetent people who are in my way or who are not helpful when American lives are at stake. I'd have copies of my past performance appraisals sent to you for your enlightenment if I thought they would do any good. In case you missed the news lately, terrorists attacked the U.S. a short time ago. I don't have the resources to pursue the people engaged in the main event, but I can neutralize smaller operators who helped them. If you don't support me when the time comes, I'll count you as one of them."

With my *faux* tantrum finished, I left the office and passed the receptionist who was startled by my undiplomatic voice echoing out of the ambassador's office followed by my quick exit past her desk. Before I left the embassy, I took the envelope that the ambassador gave me out of my pocket and read the short message in Shortcake's handwriting. It was helpful and timely information, no doubt about that. Outside at last, I located the taxi where Beth and Advari were waiting less patiently than they were twenty minutes earlier.

"You were longer than the driver and we expected," Beth scolded. "Buying the taxi is cheaper than paying the fare for waiting here. Do you have everything you need now?"

"Not everything, but I have information I didn't have when I went into the embassy. Surprisingly and ironically, I received more information from the ambassador indirectly than from what he said."

"Like what, pray tell?"

"According to a note Shortcake sent, the ambassador recently paid cash for a new villa in Ceuta with a Mediterranean view fully equipped with a spa and masseuse, stables, armed security guards, servants' quarters, and a yacht and crew when he needs to get away from it all."

"I'm so glad that the U.S. pays its top diplomatic officers so well, aren't you? You must tell me more, such as where Ceuta is and how do we get invited there."

"Jackpot, you recognized the key factor. As well paid as U.S. diplomats might be, an ocean-view villa and whatever goes with it is still beyond the reach of our honest senior diplomats. I'll tell you more about Ceuta later, which may diminish your zeal to visit the place. For now, let's go to our hotel."

"What hotel?" Advari asked.

"I thought you'd never ask. Instruct the driver to go to the Agumar Hotel near the Prado Museum and the Atocha train station, of course. I like to be close to my work."

As Advari took charge of ensuring that the driver took the shortest route to our hotel, I made certain that I put Shortcake's message safely into a deep pocket. The message confirmed my earlier suspicions and intuition that the foxes in the neighborhood controlled the local henhouse and its surroundings. If I lived long enough, I was certain that I would confirm many of my thoughts and suspicions before I concluded Operation Hercules.

As the taxi pulled away from the curb, a black limousine with diplomatic flags flying turned into the embassy driveway, drove up to the closed gate, received a salute from the Marine sentry, and disappeared into the embassy complex.

"Add one more mystery to Operation Hercules," I commented.

"What now?" Beth asked.

"If the ambassador is in that limo, who was I talking to inside the embassy?" I questioned myself.

"Do you want to go back?" Beth asked apprehensively.

"With all the people looking out the window at us, it's too late for that now. I'm sure the ambassador or his impersonator and colleagues will contact us sooner or later. At least I have my weapons. Let's go to the hotel and prepare for further developments."

Hunting for the Real Hassan

When we arrived at the Agumar, finding Hassan was no problem. He was at the front desk transacting business with the cashier. For a few moments, I didn't know if I should greet him. Then, I realized that whoever might be watching already knew we were more than casual acquaintances from our previous trips to Russia, Europe, and Morocco.

"*Assalamu alaykum*, Hassan," I said in greeting.

"Hello to you," he replied rattled a bit at hearing my voice speak his name behind him. But, he recovered quickly, turned, and shook my outstretched hand. "You startled me for a moment."

"I've had the same effect on other people lately too. I'm glad I startled you out of kissing me on both cheeks. I respect your Arab customs, but I have my wife with me. Also, you look like you need a shave, and I don't know where your face has been lately."

"What brings you back to Europe so soon?" Hassan asked without his usual smile. "I thought Beth was eager to leave Europe and Africa a while ago and never return."

"You know the remedy for falling off a horse or bicycle—get back on as soon as you are released from the hospital—that's what she's doing. In addition, we came back to see how you were coping with the new environment in Europe and if your government had given any more thought to providing voting rights to Kuwaiti women."

"You always manage a jab, don't you?" Hassan replied sharply and still with no hint of a smile.

"Beth would call it a friendly nudge and less stressful than voting for a woman president in our next election. Still, Kuwaiti women have waited for equality for only 2,000 years or so. I thought I'd give you a friendly reminder if the topic is still near the bottom of your country's political agenda."

"I will spar with you on that topic another time as if I can do anything about it. But you are correct that life has changed for me and many other people since I saw you last. Europe is worried that the U.S. will involve the European Union or NATO in searching for the New York and Pentagon attackers. The Arab nations are worried that the U.S. will retaliate against all Islamic countries in trying to find the individuals who are responsible for the attacks."

"Europe and the Middle East shouldn't worry if a response will come. Some form of U.S. response is a sure thing. Call it our Pearl Harbor syndrome. An attack on American people and on our home ground doesn't go unanswered. I'm sure that al-Qaida or whatever organizations are involved recognize that."

"Is that why you're here?"

"Mostly, but we can talk about the details at dinner if you'll join us tonight."

"Yes, I certainly will," Hassan replied with his usual smile as Beth and Advari approached after making our room arrangements. "I suggest a place where we can talk freely."

"Make sure the food is good," Beth instructed. "Whenever we go somewhere with you, we find that you are the only one who can read the menu. You men can talk all night as long as you feed Advari and me while we sit and listen to your endless conversation."

"I agree with Señora Beth," Advari exclaimed. "I have not eaten since early this morning, and it was airline food."

"I see that schooling and cultural exposure have taken their toll on your former disciplined eating habits, little soldier," I remarked. "When you were on the street in India, I'm sure you had many hungry days. Now you want a feeding tube attached to you directly from a stove or refrigerator. What have I done to spoil you so badly?"

"Nothing, but now I must study and keep myself clean all day. It has not been easy for me to adopt Western habits and culture, you know."

"Hassan, allow me to go to our room and put a leash and muzzle on these two grizzlies. We can meet in the lobby here in two hours. Is that acceptable to you?"

"Excellent, I will see you then," Hassan consented.

"You won't disappear on us this time, will you?" Beth asked adroitly.

"See there, Hassan," I whined for sympathy. "I'm not the only one who recalls past sins and breaches of etiquette," I stated philosophically. "Maybe the Kuwaiti view of gender inequality is the correct answer after all."

With a quick smile, Hassan started for the elevator while we found a baggage cart and loaded our luggage on it. A porter suddenly appeared and reminded us in his best Castilian Spanish (I assumed) that he, and he alone was responsible for luggage in this hotel. I took my gun cases off the cart and agreed to the porter's request to handle the remainder. He smiled weakly in my direction as the business part of his cranium realized what might be in my cases while the diplomatic part of his brain told him to keep his thoughts fenced inside his job description if he wanted to earn a tip from me.

At Advari's urging, and to Beth's relief, we stepped out of the elevator into the lobby exactly two hours later to find Hassan showered, shaved, and hospitable.

"Did I do all that to you with just a few words?" I asked.

"If you did, I will never admit it. But, I feel refreshed and ready for a good meal now. How about you?" Hassan asked politely.

"We all feel and look better, thank you," Beth answered for all of us. "And yes, Advari is hungrier than ever. Where are you taking us?"

"I know a good restaurant on the Calle de Ventura de la Vega in the Huertas district," Hassan began. "We have a short taxi ride, but it is far enough from the tourists and noise of central Madrid. Is that agreeable?"

"I'm sure we'll be delighted as always with your choice of restaurants, Hassan," Beth responded, casting ballots for Advari and me. "Please lead the way."

As usual, Hassan selected an excellent restaurant and helped us make our choices from the menu, not that it meant anything to Advari, who dove into anything put in front of him—even one of my plates. I mentally noted to bring a trough and a shovel for the next time. During the course of the meal, our conversation was light and animated. As the coffee or tea cups replaced empty dessert plates and Advari's second dessert, I noticed Hassan becoming more subdued. Something definitely was on his mind. I decided to let him introduce his thoughts to us when he was ready. After the waiter left the coffee and tea pots on the table and went to care for other diners, Hassan signaled his readiness to talk business.

Personal Connections

"Why are you here?" Hassan asked so abruptly that it startled me even though I was expecting a serious conversation.

"Besides my overwhelming desire to put a permanent tea stain on the tablecloth when you surprise me like that, I mentioned earlier that U.S. law enforcement and intelligence agencies need time to accelerate their operations to full speed to determine exactly who is responsible for the aircraft hijackings and attacks on the World Trade Center and Pentagon buildings. The White House and Congress need time to contact other countries, to set policies and strategies, and to build alliances for dealing with the situation. The military needs time to assemble its resources. As a lone wolf, I go wherever I can help in a short time and without the fanfare and political posturing needed by other law enforcement agencies. I believe the drug network I sparred with recently in South America and in my back yard may provide funding, and, possibly, other resources to terrorist networks in this neighborhood. A terrorist operation such as the one that hit New York needs international connections and cash. Even a small drug or weapons network can provide cash or contraband items while not actually engaging in terrorist activities. So, I'm following the bread crumbs to determine if the South American drug network I encountered has connections here with any terrorist or extremist group involved in attacking or seeking to attack my country."

"You are talking about the Calderon network, correct?" Hassan asked, although he must have known the answer I would give.

"Yes, what more have you learned about it since we negotiated for the lives of the missionaries against your friend Gilberto's wishes for their disappearance in Costa Rica?"

"I should know something useful about the network for you. I work for it now—almost full time."

"Do I shoot you now or give you a chance to explain? I don't connect you with that kind of organization. You are more professionally discriminating, if that is the correct term to use."

"I do not connect you with the Calderons either, but you have spent a great deal of time with them lately," Hassan counter-punched to my surprise.

"That was an unfortunate choice of words. If you check my position with the Calderons, you will find that I have not been cordial toward their operation in any way. That includes keeping them out of my house."

"You do not consider orchestrating ties between the Calderon network and U.S officials who look the other way as strengthening their network?"

"Now you've lost me entirely. Back up, and explain what you are talking about," I asked politely, but urgently.

"Very simply, I'm talking about your connecting an official in the U.S. Embassy in Peru with owners of SCI Shipping Company in Europe, Africa, and India. That should be simple enough for you to comprehend."

"Please back up further because I'm more confused than ever."

"I have reliable information that your friend in the U.S. Embassy in Peru and another friend operating SCI out of Lisbon are heavily involved in drug and other contraband trafficking."

"My friend Chauncey is the charge d'affaires at the Lima Embassy, as you know, and Paolo, Advari's guardian here, co-manages Southern Cross International from its Lisbon office. I admit that freely. I learned that Chauncey was involved on the fringe of the Barrantes operations in Bolivia and Peru. His relationship there surfaced quickly. I chalked it up to traditional political graft. In his defense, he saved me from premature arrival at the cemetery on several occasions in dealing with both Barrantes and Calderon. Paolo is one of three brothers who own SCI. I put Chauncey and Paolo together to initiate legitimate business between Peru and Europe to keep them out of trouble. Now, you're telling me that their activities are more subversive than occasionally skimming profits from

Calderon and his colleagues. That is a dangerous game in itself. I know Chauncey is weak in resisting opportunities for prestige and money, but establishing him as a catalyst for additional Peruvian trade was his last chance with me to save his U.S. State Department position and pension. As for SCI, Paolo and his wife are expecting a baby shortly. I can't believe that either Chauncey or Paolo would jeopardize their professional or family security under these circumstances."

"My friend," Hassan whispered, "do you realize how much money is involved in a drug network of this size, efficiency, and power? You describe it as junior varsity, but with only a slight risk of local or international police action against it, even your pope would not be immune to the temptation of active participation in that network."

"I've recently seen a demonstration of Calderon's reach into my neighborhood that killed my former Scout and nearly trapped my new Scout and me. Which reminds me, if you have increasing influence with the Calderons, please arrange the release of Police Chief Franzen's daughter. She is a botanist looking for medicinal herbs in the jungle with no connection to law enforcement or anything remotely hostile to the network. Her status as a hostage led to her father's death. I believe that she is being held by the Calderons somewhere in Peru, Bolivia, or Brazil."

"That information certainly pinpoints her location for me. I heard you were responsible for her father's death."

"Your information is partially accurate. Chief Franzen was impersonating a Calderon gunslinger to obtain his daughter's release from captivity. He was such a good actor that I believed he was on Calderon's payroll. Maybe he was. In any event, he died at my hand trying to give me an injection of a lethal substance, or, at least, pretending to inject me with something harmful. But, the basic question remains. Do you have sufficient influence with Calderon to obtain the daughter's release? Corollary questions are: one, what is your connection to the network now, and two, what is the basis of your influence?"

"I do not know what it would take to secure the daughter's release at the moment. With her father dead, she is of no use to the Calderons. To the Calderons, killing her would be more efficient than releasing her to tell tales of her captivity. But, I will try. As for my story, you know that I take my family, particularly my grandmother, to the spa in Slovakia annually. Initially, I did not know that the Calderon network ran drugs through Slovakia and other locations in Central and Eastern Europe. I did not know that my son, who saved my life when Saddam's Iraqi army invaded Kuwait in 1990 would succumb to cocaine introduced to him by someone in Calderon's network only a few years later," Hassan related as he choked back the tears and pain of his family's experience. "Despite the prohibitions of the Koran and with Allah's blessing, I want revenge in my personal *jihad* against the Calderons and anyone associated with them for my son's addiction. My allegiance to you may not be apparent at all times. In fact, it serves my purposes not to display my allegiance to you or any law enforcement agency. At times, I must act counter to your purposes to maintain my cover with the Calderons and others."

"You hid your true allegiance very well when we were negotiating for the lives of the three missionaries. Yet, I know you are especially devoted to your son. I can only imagine how difficult it must be for you, my friend. With heroin being so accessible in your part of the world through Afghanistan, I'm sure you were devastated when your efforts to guard him against that danger led to his exposure to cocaine from the Western world."

"I still hope to save him, but if I cannot, I certainly want to avenge his addiction and virtual imprisonment by the Calderons," Hassan stated fiercely as he tried to compose himself. "I had hoped you could help me, but now you are an enemy too."

"Not so fast, *mon ami*," I countered. "I am motivated to unravel the Calderon network from my own recent experience. You just reinforced that motivation with your high impact reasons. Chauncey is a long-time friend. Despite his weaknesses, I wanted to give him another chance. Paolo and his brothers come from a good family. I thought his heart was true, especially when he took Advari here into his house. Through my actions to help them and perhaps bring some additional international trade to the people of Peru through them, I now understand that I also have opened additional avenues for the Calderon network to prosper. If we share our information and collaborate to bring the network down, we still may be able to eliminate a funding source for terrorists, cut off at least one source of drug trafficking on four continents, and avenge the murder of my Scout, Jenny as well as the addiction of your son."

"You would help me even if I identify your friends as part of the network?"

"You introduced entirely new thoughts for me tonight that I haven't fully analyzed. My experience with Chief Franzen in the States resulting from his daughter's capture by the Calderon network in South America, our experience with the missionaries, and your son's addiction and captivity here, all demonstrate a pattern by the Calderons of creating drug addicts and hostages to do their bidding, or to cause others to do their bidding in high-risk situations. But, if we can destroy the Calderons while legally making it possible for my two friends and your son to escape the worst of their deserved punishment by aiding us in opposing the network, I will accept your approach. Both men are adults, and they are responsible for their actions. If the house collapses with them inside, ultimately, they are responsible for what they have done. As far as I am concerned, there's no better time to start than now, so tell me what you know about the network, and I'll tell you how your information squares with mine."

Hassan recharged his batteries for a few minutes, and then described his current association with the Calderon network in a rambling, but informative way.

"From what I have seen, drug shipments start in South America, probably from Peru, Bolivia, and Brazil. Most certainly, the Calderons have connections with Colombian drug cartels, but I was never foolhardy enough to ask questions about those possible relationships. My primary contact is with Ernesto Calderon, who generally travels between Portugal, Spain, and Morocco. From time to time, his brother, Gilberto, comes from South America, but they only talk to each other, and they do not share their plans with anyone else."

"Before you go further, tell me how you got involved."

"I knew you would ask that, and I am very ashamed. Before the Iraqi invasion, Kuwaiti citizens did not pay income taxes. In fact, the government provided subsidies to each family from oil revenues. We became accustomed to living well and paying foreigners to do the work we no longer wanted to do ourselves."

"The last part sounds familiar from immigration issues in the United States. Sorry, I interrupted you. Please go on."

"As time passed, the subsidies became smaller as oil revenues did not keep pace with governmental and our personal spending. But, by that time, my family was accustomed to the good life. As a husband and father, I enjoyed spoiling my wife and son with expensive gifts. One day in Piestany, I met Ernesto, and, shortly thereafter, I became his lieutenant to ensure that shipments and members of the network made it through customs at the Madrid and Lisbon airports without interference. Initially, I was sufficiently removed from the actual buyers and sellers not to become personally moved by the damage drugs do to individuals, families, and communities. Soon, most of the security and luggage people at the airports were on the Calderon payroll. Everything was fine until the United States demanded tightened security on all cargo and passenger flights moving in or out of the States. The Calderons put intense pressure on everyone to keep the network operating at full capacity despite the increased international surveillance."

HITCHING HASSAN TO HERCULES

"Let me stop you a moment, my friend, before the thought escapes me. It may be painful for you, but I need to ask a tough question. I think it's reasonable for me to presume it took a while for you to become a trusted member of the Calderons' organization."

"Yes, that is correct."

"Then, your son's introduction to cocaine wasn't a chance event through an unscheduled encounter with someone in the network, was it?"

"Your question is like a dagger in my heart," Hassan blurted. "Every day I must live with the thought that my actions directly led to my son's addiction. Somehow, I must stop these evil people from destroying other lives and other families although my family has been ruined. I want them all punished or killed. I need someone to help me because I am not a violent man. I know nothing about killing—even a mouse. I thought about asking for your help when you were here in September. But then, the attacks occurred in the United States, and I knew that your only thought was to get your wife home safely. When I heard about some of the things you did to the network when you were in Peru and in the States, I took heart again that you possibly could help me. But when I learned that your friends at the embassy in Peru and the SCI firm improved the ability of the Calderon network to function without government interference, I lost all hope of finding someone to help me until now."

"How did you learn that I do this stuff? My military records are sealed or destroyed, and I certainly don't advertise my services as a civilian counterpart of my former military self. My civilian employers didn't know about this part of my life. In fact, you probably know more about what I do than Beth. What is your source of information?"

"The best library for clandestine operations around the world is the former KGB archives. The KGB and now the FSB have interesting information on you. Do you remember General Vasily, who we met in Moscow in 1993? Secretly, he is an admirer of yours if you are the Napokon he always talks about, and he keeps records of every operation in which

Napokon may have participated. Lately, I lost track of him, and now I miss his ability to obtain information for me that I cannot get from other sources."

"Yes, I remember General Vasily. Please don't yearn for him on my account. We have enough problems without his arrival in Madrid. It's strange how the same names keep resurfacing in my life. They always re-appear accompanied by new faces who are equally intent on mischief. But, let's get back to the task in front of us, which Beth and I have named Operation Hercules."

"I hope the name is not indicative of what lies ahead of us. In Greek mythology, Hercules killed his wife and son while he was temporarily insane. Hera, the jealous wife of Zeus sentenced Hercules to perform twelve difficult tasks to redeem himself."

"Oh brother," Beth sighed. "Now we're reliving mythology. I knew I should have stayed home."

"Don't look now, folks," I advised, covering Beth's verbal retreat, "but the proprietor appears eager to close for the evening. Before we are evicted, let's leave and continue our discussion while we walk back to the hotel. It's not that far," I suggested. "Your information is extremely helpful, Hassan, but I need more facts about the network and your intentions before I can solidify Operation Hercules into an actual plan. Advari, do you prefer to be carried or dragged back to our room? I knew the second dessert would overwhelm you."

"Why do you all keep talking when I want to sleep?" Advari inquired with both eyes shut as he tried to stand.

"It's our job as caring adults to inspire you day and night with intellectual and philosophical conversation whether you are conscious or not," Beth answered definitively, but not convincingly to Advari.

"Don't fret, little soldier," I told Advari, "when Señora Beth sounds as cynical as me, I know she is tired too. We'll get you into bed shortly, but right now, some people's lives, including our own, may depend on what additional information Hassan has about the Calderon network."

After we paid our bill and left the restaurant, Hassan asked, "What further information would be helpful to you?"

"You could start by telling me what you knew about the New York and Pentagon attacks before they happened, but I know you won't divulge that information now no matter how much I beat on you. Be ready to tell me at some future date though if you really want me to go out on a limb to rescue your son and yourself. To start on an easier note, you mentioned drug shipments originating in South America and arriving at the Madrid airport. I can't argue with that, but alternative routes must be available in case of trouble. Where are they, and who or what determines the route for a particular shipment?"

"At first, I thought all the shipments were routed to Spain through Central America, Mexico, or Miami. More recently, several air shipments were routed through Chicago."

"How about bulk shipments that would set off alarms if routed by air?"

"That is where your SCI brothers are involved. Drugs are put into shipping containers with legitimate goods coming from South America."

"Okay, but how do people on this side of the Atlantic know what containers the drugs and other contraband are in? They can't open every freight container without arousing suspicion from law enforcement agencies or slowing down their operations?"

"I do not know all the technology involved, but computer chips are imbedded in the packaging to identify Calderon merchandise. Then, routers use a scanner during transit and upon arrival to locate and tally the Calderon packages."

"So far, so good. But there's a dark cloud on everybody's horizon. How does the network adjust if a change in dock or airport personnel occurs while a package is in transit?"

"I do not know the answer to that question. That situation has never come up while I have been involved with the network."

"Don't take what I'm going to say badly, but the situation probably has not arisen because the network must be capable of adjusting and re-routing packages and containers before the shipment arrives and falls into law enforcement hands. Can you think of any place where adjustments or re-routing of shipments can occur before the goods reach a Spanish or Portuguese harbor or airport?"

"No, not offhand. Wait, the Canary Islands are an autonomous part of Spain offshore from Morocco, and they are about a three-hour flight from Madrid. Container shipments or cargo re-routing could occur there," Hassan affirmed.

"Good, but let's investigate that potential further," I urged. "The Canaries were great starting places for Columbus' voyages to America because of the prevailing easterly winds and supplies of port wine, but, in my opinion, they aren't a suitable transfer point for the Calderon network. Too many European tourists and law enforcement agents come from the north and converge on the illegal immigrants coming by boat from sub-Saharan Africa to ultimately enter Portugal and Spain. That human traffic makes the Canary Islands an unsuitable location for a Calderon offshore transfer point. Also, commercial activity in the Canaries is insufficient to conceal the Calderons' operations unless they pay local officials very well. Bribery sometimes is an uncertain venture, and I don't characterize either of the Calderons as trusting souls who leave crucial matters to others. Both Calderons are very careful, deliberate, and efficient about what they do. Is there any other favorable offshore location for diverting or re-packaging drug and arms shipments before European or North African authorities can intercept them?"

"Yes, yes, yes! I should have thought of it myself. The Cape Verde islands are further south off the African coast of Senegal. Travel time by air from Tenerife Island in the Canaries to one of the nine Cape Verde islands is about one-and-a-half hours. Porto Grande on Mindelo Island has a deep-water harbor and is an increasingly busy trans-shipment point for merchandise of all kinds moving in either direction across the Atlantic. Porto Grande is expected to surpass the Cape Verde capital's harbor of Praia on Sao Tiago Island because Porto Grande has a greater capacity to handle container ships. Its port fees are only half those of the closest deep-water port of Dakar, Senegal. That would be an ideal place for Calderon to transfer drugs to other containers or ships to confuse European or North African inspection teams. The Cape Verde islands were Portuguese until they became independent in 1975."

"Theoretically," Hassan continued, "the islands are heavily patrolled for drug trafficking, terrorism, and money laundering under a joint agreement between them, the Netherlands, Spain, and Portugal. That should create no problems for the Calderon organization with its contacts in high places in those European countries. The islands also have a program called Registre Commercial that permits businesses to register as commercial enterprises online in one day. Following registration, companies have access to several continental and island banks. The islands have a stock exchange, which, along with the banks, I am certain the Calderon network uses to launder its excess funds. The Cape Verde islands are also actively pursuing stronger economic ties with Brazil, which is compatible with Calderon operations. You may have solved the puzzle that has been troubling me for a long time!"

"Fine on that part, now tell me how drugs, money, and other contraband travel from North Africa to Spain or Portugal, and vice versa. Do you know about that?"

"Yes, I am certain about that part of the network because I have seen it often enough with my own eyes."

"Excellent, maybe our Operation Hercules has a chance for success after all."

"First, Tangier, and Casablanca are always available to receive whatever goods arrive by boat, plane, or camel. Illicit trade has been a way of life there for centuries. However, authorities periodically clamp down, especially as elections approach. For those occasions, drug lords in Spain re-route their traffic through two towns on the Mediterranean coast east of Tangier named Ceuta and Melilla. Over time, the drug lords conveniently expanded traffic through these towns as part of normal business. The towns are really Spanish enclaves left over from Moorish rule in the tenth century. France and Spain periodically argue over them, but the Berber people in the Rif Mountains a short distance to the south strongly resist change, and the towns remain under firm Spanish control. In addition, Spanish people receive tax breaks for living there. Consequently, Ernesto Calderon has a palatial estate on the cliffs overlooking the Mediterranean which allows him to operate his illegal drug trade plus receive tax credits for being an enterprising Spanish citizen and outlaw."

"So, Ernesto is our man with the red hatband on his straw hat, am I right?" I asked to confirm with Hassan what Shortcake and Heidi had almost paid the ultimate price to learn and tell me about following their review of Beth's and Daniela's photos from our September trip.

"Yes, Ernesto is a fancy dresser which shows how little he fears identification and arrest by the authorities wherever he goes," Hassan confirmed.

"I understand that the U.S. Ambassador to Spain now has a villa in that area too. Is that true?" I continued.

"Your information is correct. Ernesto's villa is higher up the hill, and the ambassador has a smaller villa in the same gated compound about halfway up the cliff. Supposedly, the ambassador's villa was a gift from Ernesto in appreciation for services rendered by the *Americano* Ambassador."

"So, every morning that he's in Ceuta, the U.S. Ambassador looks out his window to remind himself who is the king of the hill in that neighborhood when he sees Ernesto's house higher up the hill than his own."

"That is true. If the ambassador forgets, he can listen as Ernesto's executive jet or helicopter comes and goes between Ceuta, Madrid, Lisbon or his other villa in La Montagne, which is an exclusive area about fourteen kilometers west of Tangier."

"I think that covers the housing issues. But the Calderons must have other places for actual receipt and storage of shipments. Surely, he doesn't park his cars outside while his garage is full of cocaine, fake passports, cash bundles, weapons, prostitutes, and anything else moving through the network."

"No, that would not look professional for a powerful person who flies from the European Pillar of Hercules at Gibraltar to the Moroccan Pillar at Monte Hacho or Jebel Musa depending on who is arguing the point. That is why most of the bulk Mediterranean drug shipments are directed through Tangier west of Ceuta or through Melilla, which is a hellhole of illegal activity east of Ceuta along the Mediterranean coast and near the Algerian border. Typical of any businessman in Europe, Ernesto keeps his business life separate from his family life. For that reason, he has offices in Tangier, Casablanca, and Marrakesh. Only special business partners or powerful government officials ever see his homes and family."

"His business approach makes more sense than the business practices of U.S. executives or executive wannabes. They are so confused. They are always at work when they are at home and vice versa. That wouldn't be bad, except they want everybody else in the company to be available to them twenty-four hours a day."

"Don't crusaders behave in a similar manner?"

"Hey, ease up on the crusader case. Europe hasn't had a Crusade to the Middle East since the year 1291 or thereabouts, and the States were born too late to participate in any of them. But, after the New York and Pentagon attacks, I understand more clearly now the negative connotation the term 'crusader' has among Muslims. I'm after small-to-medium-size killers, drug dealers, their suppliers, and associates. I don't check out my opponents' religious beliefs unless they run into a church and declare sanctuary, if such a concept still exists. Then, if services are in progress and the collection has been taken, I send Advari in to chase the *banditos* out quietly with his slingshot. So far, I haven't met an Arab other than you with any connection to the Calderon network. So, if you need a descriptive title for me, call me a *paladin* or *ronin*. A *paladin* was one of Charlemagne's knights, and a *ronin* was a self-employed *samurai*. Probably, the last title is more descriptive of my current U.S. and international status."

"Okay, Mr. Ronin, how do we cripple the Calderon empire, save my son, and other mothers' sons without outside help?"

Just then, Hassan's cell phone buzzed. He reached into his inside pocket and came up with what looked like an enlarged garage door opener or TV remote control. That didn't stop the buzz, so he reached inside his jacket again and pulled out a cell phone. He mouthed the word "wife" as he dropped a few steps behind us to gain privacy while we continued our walk back to the hotel. We put a few more steps between Hassan and us to give him more privacy, but we continued to hear everything he said in the quiet evening. From the conversation, Hassan clearly regarded his wife as a partner in his household. His son's addiction undoubtedly brought them closer together despite the stereotypical Islamic public separation of the sexes and his long absences from home. After a few minutes, Hassan finished his conversation and quickened his pace to rejoin us.

"I am sorry for the interruption. That was my wife. She worries about me, especially when I do not call her at my usual time."

"You don't have to apologize for anything," Beth affirmed. "You should be glad that your wife is concerned about you."

"Thank you. I am concerned about her being home alone most of the time now. We have friends and relatives in our neighborhood, but she cannot stay with them all the time whenever I travel. What were we discussing? Oh yes, we were talking about how to put the Calderons out of business?"

"You told me that the network has business locations in Tangier, Casablanca, and Marrakesh, but you didn't tell me where they stay or their habits. Do you know anything more about them?" I asked to re-ignite the business conversation.

"Ernesto operates out of the Royal Mansour Hotel when he is in Casablanca. The incident you wrote to me about with the black *burka* woman and little boy was a demonstration of his disdain for the police. Probably, the event was staged to impress a potential client at the hotel. Calderon certainly is bold enough to swap cash for a package of counterfeit passports in broad daylight in the middle of the street. The *burka* lady is the prime supplier of false travel documents to the network. I do not know anything else about her."

"Does Calderon do stupid things like that often to exercise his ego muscles?"

"No, Ernesto usually is in total control of himself and his environment."

"Okay, I'm sorry I interrupted you. Where else does he do business?"

"In Tangier, he has an office close to the docks. In Marrakesh, he has two adjoining shops in the marketplace. One is a carpet shop, and the adjoining shop makes coffins as a front business."

"Unknowingly, we may have been in his carpet shop when we were in Marrakesh in September. Is the shop a two-story building a short distance into the medina with carpets hung all over the store from top to bottom so that nobody can see anything but carpets when they walk into the shop?"

"Yes, and you can be certain that plenty of eyes are watching you from behind those carpets."

"Is his shop equipped with a little donkey for hauling the rugs that the tourists buy to their cars or buses?"

"Yes, indeed. That little donkey has hauled a lot of drugs hidden among the carpets in his day."

"I guess! We saw the little guy leaning against the wall of the store in the hot sun when he was not delivering packages. If we can't pin drug charges on Calderon, maybe we can get him for cruelty to animals."

"Try it and the next morning you will wake up with a nest of cobras in your bed," Hassan warned.

"My friend, you have unique ways of articulating thoughts that are dancing around in my head without a firm place to land."

"Why, what do you intend to do?"

"For now, I have dismissed any thoughts about animal protection as part of Operation Hercules, but cobras have a certain attraction that may be worth pursuing at the right moment. Let me ask you one more question before I answer your question."

"Okay, I am listening," Hassan stated intently.

"The carpet shop is a fairly busy place. How do the Calderons separate the human mules carrying drugs and other contraband from the tourists who are interested only in buying a rug?"

"That is easy. I told you earlier that the freight containers with drugs inside have an imbedded computer chip that responds to a scanner like I have here," Hassan answered as he pulled out the device that looked like a TV remote control from his pocket again. "The network is very high tech. The 'mules,' as you call them, have a computer chip embedded in their left shoulder. A quick wave of the scanner by someone standing behind the wall of carpets separates the mules from the tourists."

"How do we get a scanner?"

"Not very easily," Hassan responded quickly. "The scanners are closely guarded and given only to trusted members of the network who need them. I was very careless in pulling mine out of my pocket a few minutes ago. If one of Calderon's associates saw me do that, I would be dead now."

"In that case, one of the first actions under Operation Hercules will be to get our hands on a scanner. Is the carpet shop in Marrakesh the best place to grab one?"

"When I said the scanners are hard to get, I really meant to say they are impossible to get unless Calderon personally gives one to you. I would loan you mine, but tomorrow I fly to Ceuta for a meeting with Ernesto. I cannot meet him unless I have the scanner with me. I cannot postpone the meeting either. I know those conditions would stop a normal person from trying to get a scanner, but from previous experience, I know that you—"

"Let me stop you before you say I'm not a normal person again. Let's leave it as me being a motivated member of a select group of people who don't let an opponent's usual business practices hinder me from achieving my primary objectives."

"I could not have said it better or agree more. I certainly do not have it in my power to dissuade you from anything you intend to do. So, if you go to Marrakesh, what do you need from me?"

"If you fly off in a corporate plane, we could use your car to drive to Algeciras to catch the ferry to Tangier, then drive to Marrakesh."

"That is not a good idea. My car is too recognizable by network people."

"Alternatively, I was about to suggest that we use your car to get to the ferry, and then rent another car in Morocco, but I see your point. We will rent a car to drive to Algeciras, and then rent another one in Tangier to drive to Marrakesh. How reliable are rental cars in Tangier?"

"As reliable as the buses or train. Have you ever ridden a camel?"

"No, and I won't consider it a missed opportunity in my life if I never ride one."

"Okay, that is settled. You can find a decent car in Tangier. Bargain hard with the rental agent to get a good car. More important, should I be prepared to say anything to Ernesto when he receives a call from his Marrakesh operation informing him of whatever you do to his shops and people there?"

"Nothing in particular, just be as surprised as I will be by whatever happens. If you contact me later to warn me about how Calderon intends to retaliate, that will be helpful."

"Where will you be staying?"

"Probably at the same place under the name of Joe Cannon."

"The name is descriptive and easy to remember. We are only about a block away from our hotel now. We should split up here in case Calderon has someone staying at the hotel or watching the lobby. Good luck tomorrow."

"Thanks, and the same to you. We may not be able to act tomorrow or for several days. Will you be with Calderon in Ceuta for a while?"

"Yes, I stay at his villa frequently. I can stay several days without calling attention to myself."

"Good, because we may need you to help us exit Morocco when the time comes. Having you near will be helpful. We'll see you then."

Hassan walked ahead to the hotel lobby while Beth, Advari, and I lingered in the street for a few minutes. Our precautions were unnecessary. No Calderon guests were there, and none of the hotel staff were particularly interested in our activities as long as we didn't bother them. When we got to our room, I pulled Advari's clothes off his limp body, handed him a loaded toothbrush, put him in the shower, stayed with him to ensure he wouldn't drown, and dumped his damp body into bed. In his unconscious state, I didn't read a bedtime story or help him recite his nightly prayers. He automatically curled up in the blankets like I'd seen him do so many times during our plane trips in South and Central America.

By the time I finished with Advari, Beth completed her toilette. I met her in the hallway as I commenced my pre-sleep brush and flush activities.

"What should I do while we're touring the carpet and coffin shops tomorrow?" Beth asked.

"You have the very important task of buying a rug and entertaining Ernesto's troops."

"What kind of rug?"

"Preferably, whatever kind they don't have in the shop, or, at least one that will allow you to see what's behind the big carpets on display."

"Meanwhile, what will you be doing?"

"While you bargain for a rug that doesn't exist, or one with an absolutely ridiculous price, I'll search for a scanner and locate an exit before bullets find our backsides. We may have a hectic few days because I keep thinking of additional questions I should have asked Hassan. Hopefully, Calderon's is the same carpet shop we visited on our last trip. Otherwise, I may need extra time to think about how to get the job done."

"What did you forget to ask Hassan?"

"First, I don't know if the rug shop and the coffin shop are connected. Second, I don't know how many of Calderon's people will be there. I won't bother you about other unimportant stuff that could have enlightened us about the environment."

"You always took care of yourself in the past with or without full information. What's different about this situation?"

"On past projects, I was concerned only about my activities. This international terrorism thing has dimensions far beyond any projects I've encountered. We may gripe about the way our government does business as if our elected officials are comatose, but I think the attacks have everyone's attention now. This is a big deal. People died on U.S. turf. Now, it's up to the U.S. to collect itself and go on the offensive against the masterminds behind the attacks. We need to keep our country safe. We're trying to buy time for our intelligence and law enforcement people to determine who the enemy is and how to prevent further attacks. If I can't be involved in the main event, at least, I want to handle my share of the covering action until the big guns are ready to return fire."

"Then we both better get some sleep. You shouldn't expect to make the world safe in one day all by yourself."

Chapter Notes

1. Wikipedia contributors, "Korean War," *Wikipedia, The Free Encyclopedia*, http://en.wikipedia.org/w/index.php?title=Korean_War&oldid=319148601 (accessed August 9, 2009), pp. 1–22. Also, Wikipedia contributors, "Vietnam War," *Wikipedia, The Free Encyclopedia*, http://en.wikipedia.org/w/index.php?title=Vietnam_War&oldid=319260093 (accessed October 11, 2009), pp. 1–33.

2. Associated Press Article "Crazy Raspberry Ants Leave Sour Taste in Texas," *Chicago Tribune*, May 15, 2008, p. 3.

3. Wikipedia contributors, "CERN," *Wikipedia, The Free Encyclopedia*, http://en.wikipedia.org/w/index.php?title=CERN&oldid=319278216 (accessed October 11, 2009). pp. 1–12.

4. Alexander G. Higgins, "Winter, Repairs Stall Atom Smasher Until Spring," *Associated Press*, September 23, 2008, pp. 1–3. Also, Frank Jordans, "Big Particle Collider Repairs to Cost $21 Million," *Associated Press*, November 17, 2008, p. 1. Also, Bradley S. Klapper, Frank Jordans, and Deborah Seward, "French Arrest Physicist Suspected of al-Qaida Link," *Associated Press*, October 9, 2009, pp. 1–3. Also, "Europe: Proton Beams Circulate in Big Bang Machine," *Associated Press*, November 21, 2009, pp. 1–3.

5. Jeremy Manier and Jo Napolitano, "Fermilab Gears Up for New Project," *Chicago Tribune*, September 5, 2008, p. 2. Also, Julia Keller, "Fermilab's All-Night Pajama Party," *Chicago Tribune*, Metro Section, September 11, 2008, p. 1. By permission of Chicago Tribune Company.

6. George Musser, *The Complete Idiot's Guide to String Theory* (Indianapolis: Alpha Books, 2008), pp. 1–9. By permission of Penguin Group (USA).

7. *Ibid.*, pp. 220–222.

8. Shanahan (editor), *op. cit.*, p. 277.

9. Jeremy Manier and Jo Napolitano, *op. cit.* pp. 1–3. Also, "Work Begins on the World's Deepest Underground Lab," *Associated Press*, June 22, 2009, pp. 1–3.

CHAPTER 16

MARKETPLACE MADNESS

First Target

The next morning, the hotel concierge helped us get an early start by renting a decent car for our drive to the ferry at Algeciras. I deposited my equipment in the trunk and Advari on the back seat in the same position I had dumped him into bed the night before, but, at least, he was dry now. Replicating what we did in September helped us arrive at the harbor on time to catch the 0700 ferry. Several of the rougher-looking crew members glanced questioningly at my gear. Fortunately, Advari was awake, and I off-loaded my most menacing cases on him.

We found seats in a secluded spot on the middle deck of the ferry. I hid my equipment among our regular luggage as well as one can hide implements of war. We gave Advari some Moroccan *dirhams* with instructions to find food somewhere on the boat. Giving Advari money was not really necessary because he could always pick someone's pocket or break into an ATM machine, but it was early in the day, we were among strangers, we wanted to be nice, and we made an effort not to draw undue attention to ourselves. About fifteen minutes later, we saw an armload of food approaching us from starboard, and we assumed Advari was somewhere behind it.

"Guess what?" Advari said as he unloaded his food cache onto the table and into our laps. "The name of this ship is the *Banasa*. Do you know what that means?"

"We're probably on the wrong boat?" Beth responded quickly.

"We're about to sink?" was the best I could do. "Do you know?"

None of us knew the significance of the ship's name and continue to remain uninformed to the present day. We hoped we were not disrespectful to some renowned Arab or Moroccan person, event, or place. However, Advari assured me that he paid full price for our food and did not cheat the steward in any way. We photographed the ship's nameplate in the event we needed to verify its existence and our presence on the vessel sometime in the future. But, as those thoughts and Gibraltar faded into the morning haze and the ferry churned through the calm Mediterranean on a steady southwesterly course toward Tangier, my thoughts focused on the task ahead in our second coming to Morocco. *Should I treat our assault on the carpet and coffin shops as a siege against a stronghold, or as a pre-emptive strike?* The battle elements were nearly the same: define clear objectives, gather intelligence, dominate the surrounding area, and have an endgame. I decided that something entirely different would happen anyway, and I shouldn't crank up Operation Hercules to the level of a clandestine assault.

While I pondered possible Herculean outcomes, we unraveled our previous good manners by not sharing our food with our fellow travelers according to Moroccan custom. But, we didn't have enough *dirhams* to buy breakfast for all the ferry's passengers and crew, so we limited our poor manners to our immediate Arab or Berber neighbors by acknowledging their presence and left it at that. They did not seem terribly upset based on what they saw us put in our mouths. A piece of my breakfast had two humps in it, so I could have eaten a baby camel for all I knew.

The ferry docked at the designated spot in Tangier harbor on time. We slipped by the customs officials without incident despite my collection of weaponry on our baggage carts. Our next task was to rent a car for our 600-kilometer drive (about 400 miles) to Marrakesh. We did not identify a rental agency dockside, so we flagged down a *petit taxi*, one licensed to drive only within Tangier city limits, or anywhere in the Sahara with the meter running if passengers were inattentive. Sometime before lunch, we tired of driving past the same mosque from different directions, and the driver deposited us in front of an auto rental office. The taxi driver quoted the meter price while we pointed to the location of the sun and counter-offered a substantially lower rate. With the driver now under the watchful gaze of a passing police officer, we settled on a fare somewhat less than the average American household monthly mortgage payment.

We gathered our stuff and went into the car rental office eager to find out what kind of scam we would encounter there. The only option available to us was to rent a mid-size car, which when compared to a donkey, we hoped was a reasonable upgrade. The car turned out to be a grander touring vehicle than we imagined—and the price was right. Surprisingly, with a few rest stops and no mechanical problems, we arrived at the outskirts of Marrakesh in central Morocco at twilight. We located the hotel, which was close to the *medina*, and dropped our baggage in our room. After a quick shower, we walked to the main square, the *Djemaa el-Fna*, for food and to confirm the location of Calderon's carpet and coffin *souks*.

We were not concerned about the approaching darkness. The main square was crowded and well lit. The open-air food stalls were grilling beef, lamb, *m'choui*—roasted lamb on a spit, in fact, anything that could be hoisted onto the large grills. The smoke, flames, and the sizzling sounds of cooking meat guaranteed that the meat was well done regardless of any personal culinary preference. The aroma was not bad, just a little overpowering because of the sheer number of flaming grills. On our way toward the food stalls, we made the obligatory stop at the snake handlers, watched the acrobats, and observed the colorful outfit and antics of the Water Man. Before the availability of a municipal water supply, the Water Man was a person of great importance to thirsty souls in the marketplace. Traditions associated with water men of the past were continued for the benefit of tourists by the current performer in his full regalia. A photo or two with the Water Man, and a few *dirhams* in one of his many cups was all that was required unless one wanted to take a chance on the quality of water he carried. We were hungry so Beth and I left Advari watching the snake charmers and acrobats while we continued to the food stalls.

Halfway through her meat and vegetable kabob, Beth noticed Advari's prolonged absence.

"Where is Advari?" she asked me.

"I suspect he's still among the cobras and acrobats," I answered. "That's where I'd be at his age."

"You'd think he had plenty of those performers in his own country, wouldn't you?"

"That's why he's probably renewing his attachment to India and the life he left behind."

"Should we go find him?"

"Yeah, but not because he's in trouble. It's getting late if we want to locate the carpet and coffin shops tonight. We should buy a kabob for him and go toward the main square. Hopefully, we'll find him along the way because I think the carpet *souks* are on the north side of the square."

"The marketplace is such a jumble, how do you recall where the shops are?"

"Actually, the jumble has logic. If the shops were all lined up along a straight road, every shop would be exposed to the sun and be unbearably hot. In the jumble of awnings, shutters, and whatever bits of wood or cloth the shop owners patch together, the shade they generate creates a cross current of air among the *souks* to relieve some of the heat. Give the Moroccans credit for an ingenious air conditioning system that doesn't use electrical energy. I recall when we went through there last month, the sun was off my right shoulder and the top of my unprotected head, so the carpet *souk* should be over that way," I explained and pointed northeast from our current location.

"I think they could use more air conditioning among the fish stalls," Beth commented.

"I'll mention that to King Mohammed VI next time I see him. Meanwhile, let's go exploring for our carpet shop before Advari falls asleep in a corner somewhere."

"The cobras on display look sleepy too," Beth noted.

"You'd be sleepy if you had your tummy on the hot asphalt while tourists took your photo all day. That's hard work for any snake."

"You were right. There's Advari watching the acrobats make a human pyramid with a small boy perched on the top. They are daring, aren't they?"

"If that was the only way we could earn a living, we'd be daring too. Most of these people will never have a solid education, a professional career, or a steady income. In the States, the majority of us have decent homes, families, education, and earnings, and we still don't know what we're doing. We still sell ourselves to employers as the current incarnation of slave masters who rule our lives. We haven't progressed much further than the people in the square. The only difference is we get paid a little more for our slavery. Hey, Advari, time to go carpet hunting," I hollered.

"I'm coming," he answered. "No thanks, I'm not hungry," he told Beth, but then devoured the *kefta brochette* (lamb kabob) she offered him. "The acrobats are really great, aren't they? I made friends with Omar already."

"Which one is he?" I asked.

"The boy on the top, naturally," Advari exclaimed as he pointed to the top of the human pyramid. "I wish I could do that," he continued.

"Maybe you will be on the top of a pyramid someday. Life is full of surprises," I responded, unknowingly prophetic as it turned out.

My guess on the location of the carpet *souk* in the *medina* was accurate. From the north end of the *Djemaa el Fna*, we passed through the *Place Bab Fteuh* (gate), made a right turn off the *Rue Souk Smarrine* through *Place Rahba Qedima*, and continued a short distance further north to the *Criee Berbere* where the carpet shops were located.

"Nice guess for a guy who can't find his way through downtown Naperville," Beth teased.

"Downtown Naperville is too easy, and I lose my concentration," I answered in rebuttal.

"But, after twenty years, you should be able to drive through Naperville blindfolded," Beth countered.

"The Naperville traffic police think I do that now. I have a drawer full of traffic documents to prove it. Besides, it was snowing heavily the last time I was temporarily disoriented," I counter-argued knowing that I didn't have a winning case.

"It was during summer in bright sunlight," I heard Beth whisper to Advari.

Advari tried everything to keep from laughing by putting his hand over his mouth, but a giggle escaped from between his fingers. By that time, Operation Hercules occupied my mind. I needed to get my two hecklers to focus on the mission as we stood in front of the shops.

Ernesto's carpet shop was the largest *souk* in that area of the marketplace. His adjacent coffin shop was about half that size and out of place in the carpet *souk* area at any size. Both were stucco or cinder block rectangles with no distinguishing characteristics other than their painted signs in Arabic and French. I didn't expect the carpet and coffin shops to be open for business at that hour, and they weren't. But we could see lights through several windows on the second floor and a beam of light aimed skyward from the roof of the carpet shop. As we stood there, I tried to grasp why Calderon had selected these shops in this location at the edge of the marketplace.

Just then, as a private plane flew low over the marketplace, someone on the carpet shop's roof aimed a light beam at the plane and flashed the light on and off—once, twice. The plane wagged its wings—once, twice and continued on its northeasterly course. For a high-tech operation, somebody remembered that radio signals could be intercepted. In a crowded medina and marketplace, nobody paid attention to momentary signals to and from a small plane flying overhead. Nobody, that is, but me. The light signals were too precise to be coincidental. I noted the plane's azimuth on my compass. The flight path was consistent with a plane flying northeast from the Cape Verde islands with a destination of Ceuta on the Mediterranean coast. Or, the flight path could have its origin and destination to and from a thousand and one other places. I couldn't be absolutely sure. All I could do was store that piece of information in my brain closet for future reference. More immediately, I needed to get my little group out of the middle of the street. We were not ready to meet Ernesto Calderon and his associates that night.

"Okay, we found our *souk*. Let's go to the hotel and get some sleep. Tomorrow might be a busy day," I again spoke prophetically without fully appreciating my talent for understating the impact of future events.

"Shouldn't we stay to see who comes out?" Beth asked as the lights went out in both shops.

"Good thought," I answered. "But, we should use the shadows by the wall as our observation place instead of standing in the middle of the street," I suggested only to find that the three of us were moving instinctively in that direction already.

We waited a few moments before the door opened and two men in Arab robes emerged, hurried around the corner, and disappeared in the jumble of the jewelers' *souks*.

"All I got as a description is that the one on the left had fat ankles," I whispered. "Did either of you observe anything else?"

"Both had beards," Beth added. "I didn't see their faces enough to identify them."

"I saw both of them earlier in the square watching the *fantasias*, the horsemanship contests," Advari added. "The one on the right loads the carpets onto the donkey and brings the load to the tourist buses in the square. I don't know what the other man with the fat ankles does, or who he is, but I saw them together handing a package to a police officer."

"*Brigade Touristique* police or a regular one?" I inquired.

"Regular one, I'm certain," Advari testified. "Believe me, I know my police."

"Good detective work, little soldier. I don't know what all that means, but we have something to think about overnight. We'd better start back to the hotel."

It was indeed time to turn in. As we returned to the *Djemaa el-Fna*, the *fantasias* horsemen in their traditional Berber costumes galloped toward us on their spirited Arabian horses in the final cavalry charge of the evening. To the delight of the remaining tourists in the square, all the riders pulled up their steeds at the same time and simultaneously fired their muskets in the air with a deafening roar. Now, each rider smiled and accepted the applause of the crowd. But, I could imagine the frightening impact their ancestors might have had in light cavalry tactics against heavily armored, eleventh century, Christian crusaders, or Queen Victoria's, nineteenth century, British redcoats.

After several hours of unsuccessfully trying to sleep, I gave up, got dressed, and walked to the now quiet square and the carpet *souk*. Lights were on again upstairs in the carpet shop. Keeping to the shadows, I walked slowly between the front and back of the shop several times. I couldn't detect any movement within or around the shop. Then, someone on the roof flashed a strong beam of light to the southwest, and signaled once and then again as we had seen earlier that evening with the small plane. The signal was returned twice almost instantly from a building a short distance southwest of the *Djemaa el-Fna*. I confirmed my bearings on the building in the distance and walked in that direction while stopping frequently to look back toward Calderon's carpet shop to check for any other signals or movement. There were none. As I approached the large building, many lights were on, which provided me a clear beacon toward it. The streets were silent except for the sound of occasional snoring from homeless men sleeping in doorways, tentative growls from dogs awakened by my footsteps, and the rustle of rats scurrying to find a hiding place as I approached. The air was mild compared to the heat of the day, and my walk was only about a half mile, maybe a kilometer at most. As I rounded a corner, the building I sought was to my right. I couldn't read the Arabic sign, but I didn't need any signage to recognize the building as the Police Prefecture.

As I stood and watched for several minutes, police officers entered and exited the building, congregated in small groups to talk to their colleagues, or walked from or toward the parking lot for their vehicles. I looked back toward the square in the general direction of the carpet *souk*. The slope of the land and other buildings in between made a view of the ground floor of the prefecture impossible to see from Calderon's carpet shop. Consequently, the signal back to Calderon's *souk* had to come from one of the higher floors of the prefecture.

Upper floors in businesses, military bases, and prefectures are reserved for officers, not rank and file workers. Following that line of reasoning, I was fairly certain that Calderon's network had extended its reach into the upper ranks of the Marrakesh police. Although I didn't know the purpose of the exchanged signals, I felt comfortable in establishing a working hypothesis that I shouldn't expect help from the local police if I tangled with Calderon's network in Marrakesh. That was valuable information to me, certainly enough for that night. Now I could sleep. I made my way back to the hotel and crawled into bed to await the events of the next day.

"Time for breakfast," Beth announced in my ear all too early the next morning.

"What day and time is it?"

"It's 0800 Tuesday in African *Maghreb* time, which corresponds to Greenwich Mean Time. It's 3:00 a.m. in Chicago. Do you want the weather forecast too?"

"Hopefully, it'll be warm because I didn't bring any heavy shirts."

"How about sweltering?"

"Sweltering is good as long as my weapons don't rust," I proclaimed as I adjusted my shoulder and boot holsters.

"Are you going to wear those to breakfast?"

"Maybe you're right," I agreed as I dropped both pistols on the bed and inserted my derringer in my left pocket. "My baby gun should be good enough if the cook serves watery scrambled eggs."

"Is that all it takes for you to shoot a cook?"

"I can forgive watery eggs, but Calderon probably doesn't if he stays at this hotel when he's in town. As proof, the last time we passed the kitchen, did you see any old cooks?"

"Now that you mention it, no, I didn't."

"Short-term employees also might help his coffin business."

"Why are you talking about eggs and coffins so early in the morning?" Advari interrupted as he tried to stand with a pile of blankets in disarray around him.

"It's a nonviolent way to get you out of bed, soldier," I advised as I launched my pillow in his direction, closely followed by Beth's pillow from her side of the room. The only easy day in this program was yesterday as the drill instructors used to tell us. Rise and shine, trooper!"

"What happened to the Islamic greeting '*Assalamu alaykum*' as a nonviolent way to start the morning?" Advari protested.

"Nonviolence is fine. But, peace will not be upon you until you are dressed, fed, and ready for the day's activities. Move, move, move, soldier. Go, go, go," I chanted, which generated sufficient forward movement to get Advari into the bathroom. He emerged clean and fully dressed more quickly than usual.

At the breakfast buffet for Western infidels such as us, the scrambled eggs and other dishes were well prepared. After we found a private place to sit, Beth was the first to speak.

Getting the Details Right

"Because this is my first time officially playing den mother to you two, tell me again what I'm supposed to do today."

"This may be difficult for you to comprehend at first, but pretend you are an experienced carpet shopper. Specifically, you're interested in buying a rug of some kind that is not in the front displays. Start by asking for their *shedwi* carpets. They are flat-woven carpets with black and white stripes. Most likely, they will be in front. Then, keep asking to see other rugs such as *hanbels*, *kilims*, *zanafi*, and *glaoua* that are not in the front display for tourists. We need to find out what, if anything, or who, if anybody, important hides behind the large rugs in the front."

"When did you become such a carpet expert?"

"When I decided to keep my wife alive on this project so that we could grow old together in a world safe for our grandkids and us. Otherwise, I don't know dink about carpets other than that quality rugs have more knots per given area than lesser quality ones. So, I'm relying on you to keep the carpet staff showing you more and more samples while you dally and absorb every detail you can about where the offices and other things are behind the large carpet barriers in front."

"Wouldn't it be easier if you came with me and explored the things that are important to you while I pretend to shop? Where will you be while I'm in there?"

"I'll stay outside and watch for any foot traffic coming and going into both the carpet and coffin shops. I suppose it would be too convenient if the *burka* lady paid a visit while we're here, but I can hope. Also, I'm interested in what kind of packages are delivered to or leave the shops, especially if heavy coffins are moved in and out, and who is allowed to enter the shops. Lastly, I'm concerned that someone inside was alerted by Calderon and is watching for me. We could send Advari in with you if you want companionship."

"Do you think they are stupid enough to engage in drug trafficking during the day?"

"I don't think they're stupid at all. I think they have their business environment under tight control, which allows them to move drugs and other contraband anytime they choose without interference from the police or anyone else."

"Besides watching for anything unusual, what can I do inside?" Advari asked lightly.

I suspected what he wanted to do, and, like a good genie, I was ready to grant his first wish.

"If you can sneak into the offices, look for any customer lists, maps, billings, or other documents that confirm operation of the network through the U.S., South America, or Europe, what the cargo is, how it's shipped, and how the shipments evade inspections. That would be great evidence to hand over to the CIA, FBI, or Interpol."

"What if I find documents on the store clerks rather than in their offices?"

The genie was willing to grant Advari's second wish.

"I authorize you to use your judgment and skills to take possession of any relevant documents you believe are carried by the shop workers or guests as long as your actions don't endanger Beth and you."

"Do you consider money a document?"

The genie was working overtime now, but he was still agreeable.

"If you lift documents from a worker or supervisor, I don't expect you to stand there and separate the good from the bad documents. If some *dirhams* stick to other documents you acquire, consider them as a contribution to your education fund—but don't get caught at it. If the situation looks risky, pass it up so that you and Beth can leave the shop in one piece. Got it?"

"Yes, I understand. I may be a little rusty. I haven't practiced in several weeks. Here comes the waiter with the bill. Do you want your wallet back?"

"Yeah, that may be handier than turning you over to the police. By the way, when did you lift it?"

"On your second trip to the buffet, I blocked the big man's path in front of you, and made him distract you long enough to snatch your wallet. But I did it for practice only."

"So you're the one who keeps ripping the pocket buttons off his pants. I must have sewn three dozen buttons on those pants in the last few months," Beth voiced her complaint. "Advari, I appreciate your need to practice to maintain your skills, but pick on someone besides my husband as a practice dummy for a while, will you? I didn't bring my sewing kit with me."

Recovering my wallet, I paid the bill and gave final instructions to my assault team.

"This has been a charming meal and conversation. Now it's time for work. I want to go to our room to pick up my toys before we go to the marketplace. You can come or wait for me in the lobby."

"No, we're coming," both echoed. We have other things we want to take with us too."

"Advari, you apparently can have my wallet any time you want, what else do you need?" I inquired.

As Advari charged ahead toward the elevator without the benefit of my chastisement, I hung back for a last minute conversation with my wife.

"Beth, if you don't feel up to doing this, tell me now because I probably am sending you into harm's way."

"No, I'm okay. You'll be nearby, so what can happen to me, right?"

Plenty can happen in a short time and space, I thought to myself, but I let her rhetorical question go unanswered. Teeth brushed and appropriately armed, we left the hotel for the marketplace.

We walked the short distance to the *medina* and passed through the open gate. Most of the *souks* were open, but the crowd was sparse in the early morning.

As we turned to the right to go to the carpet shop, a voice behind us chanted, "*Ssalamu 'lekum.*" (Peace be upon you.) We turned to find Advari's new friend, Omar, of the acrobat team, walking behind us.

"*Wa 'lekum salam*" (And upon you), we all returned his greeting.

"*Labas?* (How are you?)" Omar continued the traditional Moroccan greeting.

"*Labas, hamdullah, shukran*" (Okay, praise Allah, thank you)," we guessed as close as we could get to the appropriate response to Omar's continued greeting in his Moroccan dialect.[1]

Other than the two Spanish enclaves of Ceuta and Melilla, this part of *Maghreb* (Western) Africa was a former French colony until Morocco gained independence on March 2, 1956. Most Moroccans understand and speak French in addition to Moroccan Arabic or the Berber *Riffi*, *Tahelheit*, *Tamazight* or *Soussi* dialects. In his short schooling or as a delinquent in the Chennai marketplace in India, Advari apparently had acquired basic French in addition to his pickpocket skills.

With that and recognizable sign language between them, the two boys were quickly engaged in their own conversation as we continued the remaining distance to the carpet shop. I wasn't pleased with having a distracted Advari backing up my wife in the shop. On the other hand, he might gain useful information from Omar, so I let their conversation continue. At the moment, I was more interested in Beth's performance and safety anyway.

"Here I go," Beth declared, appearing outwardly calm as we reached the carpet *souk*.

"I won't be far away. If nothing else works until I get to you, shout as loudly as you can and swing your 400-pound purse at anyone who threatens you. I'll be walking around the side and rear to see if any traffic enters or exits the shop from there. If you're in the shop more than a half hour, I'll come get you. When you're behind the rugs, speak louder than usual so I can find you. If things get messy, get out of there fast. Okay?"

"I'll be fine. See you later. Don't get sunstroke out here."

Five seconds after Beth entered the shop with the two boys trailing her I began my shoulda-woulda-coulda litany of better approaches than the plan I had concocted. Pushing those thoughts aside, I walked around the side of the shop and saw the donkey tethered there with no shade, no food, and no water. I warned myself that I couldn't let thoughts of his comfort crowd into my already overstretched brain. The plain décor on the outside of the Arab buildings and stalls of the *souks* were not much to look at after five minutes. Any decoration was on the inside, and the principal means for relief from the heat might be an inner courtyard with a splashing fountain. I couldn't detect anything that pleasant from the street or the rear passageway. I decided to return to the front of the store. As I rounded the corner of the shop, Advari and Omar came running hard from the opposite direction almost knocking me off my feet.

THE PLAN GOES AWRY

"They locked us out," Advari gasped.

"What happened?" I asked with quickly building fury at the boys for deserting Beth.

"Señora went with two men behind the first row of carpets. We were by the front door because the store is hot, and another man came and pushed us out. We tried the door, but now it is locked. Señora is still in there!" Advari sobbed while Omar nodded and gestured in unison with him. By the time Advari finished his message, I had my derringer in my hand, and the three of us were running to the front door. After a few strides, I adjusted the plan.

"Advari, go back and watch the rear. Yell loudly if anyone comes out that way. Anybody at all!"

Upon reaching the front door, I put my shoulder into it firmly. It didn't give—solid steel disguised as wood. I tried again with the same outcome. Omar tugged on my arm.

"No, *monsieur*, no. Wait, I come back," he said in his best French-English as he ran like a scalded rabbit toward the main square.

I didn't understand his actions. My only response was several more worthless kicks to the door handle. As I stepped back from the door to determine what other options I had for entry, I saw Omar running toward me followed by a bunch of men dressed in loose-fitting white shirts and pants. They were not just any men. Omar's acrobat team members came running as fast as they could. As soon as they arrived, they formed their human pyramid high enough to put Omar on the flat roof of the carpet shop. I could hear glass shatter as he kicked in what may have been a skylight or window we could not see from ground level. *C'est magnifique, mais ce n'est pas la guerre,* I thought to myself in French.[2] *This is magnificent, but it is not war*, I thought as my overloaded brain recalled the words of a French officer who observed the Charge of the Light Brigade at Balaklava in the Crimean War. As I watched the acrobats, I couldn't believe what was happening! This certainly was not the traditional way to fight a war, but it was audaciously close to my way, and it would have to do for now.

While we waited for Omar to report his findings or to open the front door, the Water Man came along to observe the unusual activity in his marketplace and to determine if he wanted to participate. The acrobats told him what they knew about my problem. Omar put his head over the side of the roof and advised everyone who could understand him that he could see nothing in the carpet shop from the broken skylight, and the door on the roof was locked. Advari, who had returned to my side translated for me.

"Advari, get up there," I ordered, pulling him roughly by the shirtsleeve toward the bottom men of the human pyramid, which was still in place. Find a way for you or Omar to climb down into the shop on one of the rugs or something and open the door. If someone grabs you, shoot him and start hollering at the top of your voice," I ordered, handing him my derringer, forgetting that a gun was not Advari's weapon of choice in a fight. But this was a desperate time.

My sharp instructions to Advari prompted the Water Man to come over to me.

"No good to send boy inside if bad mans there," he said in his best English, "and too late. Tunnel go under to leather *souk* that way," he pointed a half dozen or more *souks* to the northeast. No mans in carpet *souk* now for sure."

"The coffin shop?" I spoke slowly. "Are bad people hiding in the coffin shop?" I asked and pointed to the adjoining shop to the right.

"Yes or not," he answered. "Hard to know. We have try. You have *dirhams*?"

"Yes, here," I said as I took out my wallet and handed him all the *dirhams* that Advari had not confiscated.

The Water Man grunted disapprovingly but spoke in what might have been one of the Berber dialects to the chief acrobat who immediately took the *dirhams* and ran off toward the main square.

"We wait little time," the Water Man said. "We have good way to find bad mans if they in shop. I have man watch tunnel," he said as he instructed a bystander to go to the leather *souk* about four hundred meters north of the carpet *souk*.

In less than five minutes, the chief acrobat came running back from the main square followed closely by two other turbaned men, each carrying a wicker basket. As they approached, they looked familiar, but in my mounting anxiety, I didn't identify them as the snake handlers in the main square until they were directly in front of me.

MOROCCAN STYLE AUDACITY

The acrobats lost no time in rebuilding another human pyramid for one of the snake men to climb up high enough to hand Omar a basket. Omar accepted the basket as if it were full of snakes. It was—cobras, to be precise. This might be the kind of warfare *dirhams* buy, but this definitely was not regulation warfare, even with audacity. Before I could tell Advari again to climb down inside and unlock a door, Omar emptied the contents of the basket down the skylight. The Water Man smiled and put his hand on my shoulder.

"In little time, we know if bad mans in shop," he declared with certainty as if this activity was as familiar to him as pouring a cup of water for a customer.

"We will know if my wife is there too," I said. "If she sees snakes, she will bust right through the wall or roof, even if she is tied up."

"No worry," the Water Man said diplomatically. "I think mans go in tunnel with your woman long time now. They are not in shop still. Yet, we are certain in small time now."

"If you already saw the bad men leave with my wife through the tunnel, why are we putting snakes in the shop now?" I asked what I thought was a valid question.

"You know where mans took wife? Maybe some mans hide in shop yet. We find and ask them where your woman is," the Water Man answered wisely.

"Will the snakes bring them out for certain?"

"First basket, not so much," the Water Man said. "Those snakes have no teeth or mouth is sewn tight. They are only for tourists in square. With them, we ask mans to come out nice. Next basket, snakes have teeth, so mans come out fast, yes? No more play then. You understand?"

I nodded my understanding as the second basket was handed to Omar who wasted no time in depositing its contents down the skylight.

Five minutes went by without any sound from within the shop. Ten minutes went by. I lifted my pant leg, and pulled my boot gun out, and put the gun in my side pocket. The Water Man was impressed with my hidden firepower. So were the acrobats. A few minutes later, we heard a scream from the shop and the sound of running feet followed by banging as someone tried to open the front door. A few more minutes elapsed until we heard the security bar removed and the door swung open to reveal two visibly shaken men. One favored his right leg. I grabbed him by the collar and threw him down in the dusty street. The Water Man did the same with the second man. The snake handlers rushed by us into the shop to collect their pets while the acrobats got Omar and Advari off the roof. The Water Man stood over the two prisoners while looking at me to observe what I would do next. Right now, I needed information, not two dead prisoners.

The prisoner with the cobra bite had sufficient incentive to talk if he wanted prompt medical attention. I grabbed the bitten man by the collar again, and jabbed the barrel of my boot gun into his neck. The Water Man shook his head, and gently pushed me away as he drew a curved dagger from inside his wide shirt. I had to admit that the Water Man's *kris* was the weapon of choice in interrogating the frightened pair. Men were more familiar with bladed weapons than handguns in this part of the world. The Water Man sat on the prisoner's stomach, grabbed a handful of the man's hair, and calmly carved an Arabic symbol under the man's chin. The cut was not deep, but sufficient to draw blood. Then, the Water Man spoke firmly to the prisoner as the acrobats dragged the other prisoner closer so that he could participate in the conversation. After both prisoners responded to the Water Man's questions, he smiled broadly and stood up.

"They say maybe more mans hide in coffin shop. Other mans take your wife into coffin shop, then later to chief man at ocean house. You know about chief man?"

"Calderon?" I asked intently. "Yes, I know the chief man Calderon with a big house by the ocean north of here."

"Calderon, good, yes. You know chief man. You go there soon. Now, we find any mans with wife in coffin shop to talk," the Water Man said, pointing to the coffin shop with his dagger.

Leaving the two prisoners in the custody of the acrobats and the snake charmers who applied a salve to the snakebite and gave the man some dark-colored potion, the Water Man confidently led Advari and me into the carpet shop. Speaking for Advari and myself, I hoped that the snake handlers were good at math and could account for all their pets, especially those with active fangs. We didn't have time to inventory the shop because the Water Man quickly led us past several rows of carpets to a side door leading to the coffin shop. Without hesitation, the Water Man opened the door. Except for a few scraps of wood against the far wall and several partially assembled Arab coffins, the furnishings in the shop were insufficient to hide a spider. Nonetheless, the Water Man went over to what appeared to be a heavy stone sarcophagus in the middle of the room. He touched a trigger somewhere, and the sarcophagus rotated to reveal a stairway leading to a small chamber below which was just large enough to contain one or two people standing upright. At the moment, the chamber was the hiding place of a very frightened lady in a black *burka*. She was not "our lady in the black *burka*." All the women seemed to be wearing black around the marketplace that day.

Pointing to himself and unsheathing his curved dagger again, the Water Man asked, "You okay? I ask her about your woman, yes?"

"Advari, come with me," I commanded as I started back up the stairs. "We have other business outside. The Water Man has everything under control here."

I didn't stop until I was outside on the street in front of the carpet shop.

Restructuring the Plan

"What will we do?" Advari anxiously wanted to know.

"Whatever it is, our next plan better be superior to the one we had until now," I answered Advari as I realized how calm I had become. "A short time ago, one of my Scouts was killed. More recently, I almost lost another one, and now my wife is in jeopardy. I couldn't protect any of them although I have an arsenal of weapons. But I'm standing here with you in the street as calmly as if you and I were eating a bunch of grapes and watching the sights in the square."

"Yeah, *sangfroid* is good at a time like this, but I am abusing the privilege," I continued. "To make matters worse, Beth was snatched quickly, which meant Calderon was aware of our presence in Marrakesh and knew we would come to the carpet shop. Other than Beth, you, and me, the only person who knew we were coming here was Hassan. *Did Hassan rat on us, or did Calderon have another way of learning about our plans?*" I wondered. "If Calderon knows more about us than we know about his intentions and moves, we are at a distinct disadvantage in this war. He can manipulate us any way he wants. As the old Latin saying goes, '*Bis peccare in bello non licet*,' meaning, 'It is not permissible to blunder twice in war,'"[3] I declared to Advari.

"You say that a lot lately," Advari observed.

"If so, it still isn't enough to remind myself that I've been fumbling many things recently and getting away with most of them until now. But I can't be wrong or merely guess on our next move."

"Here comes the Water Man," Advari advised. "Maybe he has information that will help."

The Water Man approached at a deliberate pace that made me confident I shouldn't be too hasty in my despair.

"I have good story, no, good sayings for you, yes?" The Water Man started. "Woman there," he continued as he pointed to the coffin shop, "she say other mans take your wife through tunnel under *souks* to boss man's house. She no can open tunnel door after they go, and she cannot follow them. She hide there but is now good prisoner for us, you think?"

"Yes, she would be a good hostage if Calderon cares about her, but I don't think he does. She is expendable, not important," I answered truthfully, which did not please the Water Man. While I deflated his ego, *I may as well go all the way,* I thought, so I asked, "How do you know about these shops and tunnel? Do you work for Calderon too?"

"No, I no work for boss man. Water Man job very important here. Very respectable is Water Man. My father has shops before he die. He dig tunnel to fight French before Maroc independence. When my father die, I sell shops to boss man because I do not want that life. Boss man cheat me, so I no work for boss man. You happy now? I help you now?"

"Yes, you and the acrobats have been very helpful. I thank you very much. But I must go to Ceuta to rescue my wife from Calderon. I must find fighting men to help me."

"Mans here all help you," the Water Man said, smiling from ear to ear and waving for the acrobats to gather closer. Mans all help you," he said again. We have family and friends who work in boss man's house and land. You have plan, we help," he roared for everyone to hear.

The acrobats applauded and jumped in agreement with the Water Man to do something bold in their otherwise repressed lives. They wanted to help. All I needed was a plan for them to follow. The embryo of a plan to attack Calderon's Mediterranean villa had been percolating in the back of my skull since getting off the plane in Madrid. But, I didn't expect an army of marketplace performers to be my strike force. I couldn't agree to let all of them come with me. All of them couldn't be away from the marketplace and the tourist income they depended on to support their families. The city fathers would be highly distressed if their primary tourist attraction took a sabbatical for my private war. Also, I could imagine MAGENTA's reaction when I submitted a voucher to reimburse one Water Man, nine acrobats, and two snake handlers for services rendered on this assignment. I could use the Water Man and five acrobats, including Omar. I needed to contact Shortcake for additional resources. But first, I wanted to see the tunnel under the *souks*.

"Water Man, show me the tunnel," I declared. "I want to see if my wife left any clues. Then, I will decide who comes with me to Ceuta."

"You need much light. Very dark is tunnel," the Water Man instructed as he went into the carpet shop momentarily and returned with two flashlights as if he were in his own house and knew exactly where all the tools were located.

"I go now," he advised, which I interpreted correctly to mean that he would lead the way.

CONFISCATING A SCANNER

Despite two flashlights, the tunnel remained dark and dank. I kept stumbling on the planks that had been put down as flooring to keep "the mans" from stepping in the mud. *What was mud doing in the middle of the desert?* I thought, *unless the shop owners were using the tunnel as a sewer.* I decided to walk on the planks at all costs. If Beth left a clue in the tunnel, it needed to be larger than a refrigerator for me to see it until we approached the daylight of the north exit. The leather workers paid little attention to us as we raised the trap door and climbed out of the tunnel in the back of their stall. I identified no evidence that my wife had been through the tunnel, but I did discover something useful. As I looked back down the hole, I noticed a black plastic object near the bottom of the ladder we had just climbed (fortunately it was not in the water). I went down the ladder to retrieve it while the Water Man conversed with the leather workers. As soon as I touched the object, I knew from having seen Hassan's that I had found a scanner that someone in Calderon's network had lost—perhaps in his haste to get Beth out of the tunnel unnoticed and away from the *souks* and tourists. Calderon would slit someone's throat for carelessness for sure if he learned a scanner was now in the hands of his opponent. I put the scanner in my pocket and climbed the ladder to rejoin the Water Man, who was still chatting with his friends.

"Friends say two mans come through tunnel not long ago with heavy rug. They pull hard to bring rug up from tunnel. Mans ask for help, but friends no help them. They say too busy working to help. Mans put carpet in car and go away. Friends do not ask where they go. Friends no help, no bother. I think mans have wife in carpet. All the time, same happens with womans and girls here, so friends blind, do nothing, no want police. You understand?"

"Yes, Water Man, say *shukran bezzef* (thank you very much) to your friends for their information. Calderon wants me to come to the trap he undoubtedly has waiting for me in Ceuta. I must go there. He's using my wife as bait. Water Man, if you and some acrobats will come to Ceuta to help me fight boss man, I could use your help. But first, I need to go back to the carpet shop, and then to my hotel. Help me find the best way through the *souks* back to the carpet shop. I've had enough of this tunnel."

The Water Man jogged south at a brisk pace, and we reached Calderon's carpet shop in a short time through the gathering crowd of tourists and shoppers. Advari, the acrobats, and the snake charmers milled around waiting for instructions about what to do next. They all looked relieved to see the Water Man and me return.

"You did not find her?" Advari asked dejectedly.

"No, but I suspect where she is. At least she will be safe until we come close. We will go there soon. First, you can help me get ready. Can you find your way back to the hotel from here later?"

"Of course, why do you ask?"

"Because I need to go back to the hotel now and contact people to help us. You and Omar select four acrobats to come with us. The other four should stay here and perform for the crowd as usual while we are gone so that the tourists do not complain to the police or other town officials that no acrobats are performing in the square."

"Can Omar be one of the five performers to come with us?" Advari asked, apprehensive of the negative answer I might give him for adding one more performer.

"Believe it or not, yes. We can use him. We also need one of the snake handlers plus an assortment of sleepy and active cobras and the Water Man. Find out if they have a truck or van that can make the long drive to Ceuta without falling apart in the desert."

"When do we leave? They might want to go home and pack some clothes."

"This will sound weird, but we aren't in a hurry to drive to Ceuta. The acrobats can leave after the last performance tomorrow night. Others might leave at different times."

"Why are we waiting so long? They could kill Señora Beth before then!" Advari argued.

"Yes, they could. They could easily have killed her here, but they didn't. Her life doesn't matter one way or another to Calderon except as a means to entrap me. She will live at least until we arrive in Ceuta for Calderon to ensure my coming there. After that, though, our friends and both of us need to do our jobs very well for her to stay alive. That's why we can't rush into Calderon's trap without a plan and extra help that I need to arrange. Are you with me?"

"Of course. Have I ever failed you?"

"You came close a few times. Okay, you're in charge of recruiting our army here. When you finish all the arrangements you can possibly make, join me at the hotel. Oh, one other thing. Come outside with me for a moment. I'll give you something."

We stepped away from the carpet and coffin *souks* and walked to the *medina* wall across the street.

"This is a scanner I found in the tunnel. According to Hassan, microchips are embedded in packages of contraband and in the left shoulder of people working for Calderon. The presence of a microchip should generate a signal on the scanner. If you can do it discretely, wave the scanner at the left shoulder of everyone here, and especially the Water Man and the woman in the black *burka*. If they catch you doing it, just run as fast as you can back to the hotel, but don't let anyone take the scanner away from you. If you can do that, I'll never make a wisecrack about your way of doing business again—ever. The results of the scan are that important. If you can pick pockets, you should be able to scan people without getting caught. I'm counting on you in a big way to do this important task."

"I can do it," Advari replied confidently, "if the scanner shows a display without making any sound."

"You may be technologically correct on that," I praised Advari as we played with the buttons for a while to dial up a silent display—we hoped.

As I ran back to the hotel, the misgivings about taking my time to rescue Beth in Ceuta, and my nearly total dependence on Advari almost got the best of me. But, I reminded myself of the "nine grounds" tactics of the Chinese warlord Sun Tzu in choosing the field of battle. I assumed that my army was weaker than Calderon's because he had well-trained armed guards around him and his villas while I had marketplace performers and a few snakes. If I chose to fight on the well-defended heavy ground of my opponent, as Sun Tzu described it, I'd better have some reliable resources at my disposal to keep Calderon's turf from becoming my "dying ground."

The hotel lobby was deserted except for the clerk standing behind the front desk and the porter helping a traveler with his baggage. I had the strange feeling that the porter was looking at me, but when I turned in his direction, he appeared totally engrossed with his immediate client.

I took the stairs two at a time to our room on the third floor, opened the door, and found the room in total disarray. I knew we hadn't left the room in that condition. The only thing that was left untouched was a used bar of soap. When I climbed over the mattress I made a more devastating discovery. My guns and other toys were gone. I was about to place an energetic kick to my *derriere* for being so careless about my equipment in enemy territory when a maid and the porter appeared at the door. I was about to make exculpatory remarks about finding the room in this shape rather than being a slob of a guest, but all they did was wave for me to come with them. They stopped two doors down the hallway, opened the door with a plastic key card, and motioned for me to come into the room. As I did, I recognized our clothes, luggage, and my equipment cases all neatly in place. I reached for my wallet to give each of them a tip, and then realized that I previously had given all of my *dirhams* to the Water Man at the carpet shop.

FULL EMPLOYMENT

"That is not necessary," the porter said in his best English. "My name is Ahmed. We have already been hired by another party to help you."

"Who is 'we,' and does your employer have a name?" I asked.

"This is my wife, Cala," the porter explained, pointing to the maid. "As for our 'employer' as you call her, we have never met her, and we do not know her real name, but she referred to herself as 'Shortcake,'" the maid advised. "She was very generous in compensating us," the maid continued.

"Her generosity," I stated, "is news to me, but I'm willing to take your word for it. But there goes my operating budget for sure," I exclaimed with false pathos. "First, acrobats and snake handlers, now porters and maids. I had a nice second career going as a Responder while it lasted."

"We would help you without receiving such a generous sum," Ahmed continued. "You see, our son is under Calderon's influence, and we plead with you to help us bring him home for us to care for him."

"What's his problem?" I asked reflexively. "We have a growing number of family members under Calderon's influence—Hassan's son, my wife, and now your son. That is an unwelcome trend which needs prompt attention."

"Calderon promised that he would teach our son to operate an international business. Instead, he made him a drug addict. *Kif*, the name of the local marijuana, is grown widely in the Rif Mountains northeast of here. Calderon started our son in that business. Then, our son, Ali, found it very easy to upgrade his drug habit to heroin and cocaine. We want him back with us while he still has a chance to recover from his addiction. More urgently, we believe he is involved in Calderon's illegal immigrant and sex trade in Tangier and Melilla. Authorities here and in Europe may look the other way or silently take their bribes from drug operations, but human trafficking is more serious and authorities could put Ali in jail for a very long time if they arrest him."

"Where is your son now?" I asked, thinking that we possibly could extract Ali and Beth if both were at Calderon's villa in Ceuta.

"The last we heard, Ali is working at Calderon's La Montagne villa, which is a very exclusive area between Tangier and Cap Spartel less than fourteen kilometers northwest of Tangier."

"I must be truthful," I told them. "I wasn't planning to go anywhere near Tangier except to catch a ferry back to Spain when I finish my business in Morocco. If I can reclaim my wife and damage Calderon's operations in Ceuta, I will consider my trip to Morocco a success."

"If you consider going to La Montagne to rescue our son, we can help you enlist enough fighting men to go with you to Calderon's villa in Ceuta and his warehouse in Melilla to finally rid us of that devil."

"A diversion on dying ground," I mused aloud. "That is an interesting twist to Sun Tzu's war strategies."

"We do not understand what you are saying," Cala responded apprehensively.

"Don't worry," I answered. "That's my way of classifying my workload. If I'm able to rescue your son, I'll do it. But understand that I may use unorthodox methods you may not appreciate at the time."

"Then, how can we help you?" both exclaimed with their eyes glistening.

"Foremost, we need reliable transportation for my army of nine to go north to the coast, a place to stay, and a photo to identify your son. I'm sure I'll think of more, but that's sufficient to activate my brain train for now."

"Consider it done," Ahmed said with determination. "Tell us where you want to go and when. We will take care of the details for you."

Just then, I saw Advari pass by the door on his way to our former room. He had the same reaction as I did when he saw the mess.

"Who did this?" he asked no one in particular.

"Never mind the condition of that room," I called to him as I stepped into the hall. "We live over here now," I announced as he turned toward me totally confused.

"Mind your manners, and meet our new friends," I informed him when he came toward me.

"They are so new that all I know about them are their names, Ahmed and Cala, and that they were recruited to help us with the Calderons if we can rescue their son too. Is your army capable of multi-tasking on heavy ground?"

"What?" Advari asked with his mind still locked on the appearance of our former room.

"They came along just in time, didn't they?" Advari noted wisely as the appropriate brain synapse fired to return his mind to the present tense.

"The only thing more timely is for you to return the *dirhams* I gave you earlier so that I can conduct business and buy something to eat when you're not around," I said with my hand outstretched to receive my rebate. "I know you didn't spend all of it hiring the acrobats and snake handlers. In all my conversations with them, they never mentioned generosity as one of your crowning attributes."

"You know I would return your money as soon as I could," Advari said, trying to deflect my mild criticism with a sly smile as he dug *dirhams* out of various pockets in his shirt and pants.

"Yeah, I know, little soldier. I just need relief from what looks like an ever-growing pile of problems. Let's help our new friends put the heavy pieces of furniture in our old room back in place, and then we'll plan our strategy for coming events with dinner attached."

"Could we eat first? No, I guess we can't. Forget I mentioned it."

"Consider it forgotten. Let's get to work. The way it's going, Operation Hercules will be our contribution to full employment in Morocco if nothing else," I declared my frustration.

After we put the furniture in place and left Ahmed and Cala to finish the lighter chores, Advari and I went to our new room to think and plan strategy. At least, I went there to think and plan strategy while Advari napped. I thought this would be an opportune time to contact Shortcake about additional resources I could use now that my army needed to visit both of the Calderons' Mediterranean villas.

LINING UP A LIFELINE

"Shortcake," I started our conversation on a secure line. "I need you to recruit some unusual help for me. I know you can do it because you landed Ahmed and Cala for me in the nick of time."

"Thanks, I'm always glad when you appreciate my services, but who are Ahmed and Cala?"

"They are the porter and maid at the hotel here who helped us after our room was ransacked. They said you hired them to look after our things while we were away from the hotel. Are you having an amnesia attack, is Rick in town, both, or do I have an enemy infiltration problem in this project?"

"Rick is in town, but we didn't stay out late enough for me to forget something that I didn't do. Your friend Marika came into the shop a while ago asking about you and where you were. After she identified herself I told her your general location. Then, she began making phone calls and ran out the door to her car. What should I do now?"

"First, forget I mentioned Ahmed and Cala. I'll take care of that situation myself. I'm sure Marika intervened in some way if she believed that Beth and I were in trouble. I need you to find a team of experts to meet me in Ceuta in three days. A Spanish military base is in the area; so don't trip over the Spanish military, U.S. diplomatic corps imposters, or the Calderons to fill my requisition, if you understand my meaning. If you can't find Ceuta on your Moroccan map, the Arab name for the town is Sebta, but because it's under Spanish jurisdiction, I'll use the Spanish name. When the Romans were in town, they called the place Septem, if you want to drive yourself totally crazy. In any event, I don't care where the experts I need come from, although at least one Moroccan team may have more credibility with Calderon's guards. Hopefully, the language skills of the people you get and mine will allow us to communicate. If you have paper and pencil handy, take down these specifications. The closer you come to the specs, the handier it'll be for me."

After I gave Shortcake the details of my needs, she complimented my ideas in her normal insightful way.

"That sounds awfully weird to me. Are you sure your plan will work? If I were your wife, I wouldn't let you risk my life on a scheme like that."

"Thanks for your vote of confidence. Hopefully, we'll witness another example of my Guiding Hand knowing what needs doing when I'm uncertain or lost."

"Accept my 'no comment' as my best response to your relationship with your Guiding Hand. Do you need anything else?"

"Yes, listen carefully because you have no other option. If Marika didn't intervene, we have a different problem associated with Ahmed and Cala citing your code name when I asked them how they arrived on my doorstep. When you finish rounding up the team of experts, execute Plan R. If I need anything, I'll use 'Snowflake' as backup. Got that?"

"Yes, I understand. Will do. Bye."

If MAGENTA's communication system was breached to the point of revealing the meaning of Plan R as: one, Shortcake hides with Rick's help; and two, Amy's roommate, Heidi, acts as Amy's replacement under the code name "Snowflake," we'd all be dead, and nothing else would matter. As bad as conditions appeared, I had to believe that Marika intervened in some way, or that the communications breach didn't extend that far. Or, if it did, I still needed to recover Beth despite any breach in MAGENTA's security.

Rather than fuss about my adversaries possibly knowing more about MAGENTA than I did, I decided my immediate task was to put food into Advari, who had just regained a vertical position following his nap. As weird as it might seem, feeding Advari was my first step in fighting back against Calderon to rescue my wife.

"I'm sorry, I forgot to tell you," Advari began while yawning. "This will not make you happy."

"What, somebody picked your pocket and all our money you didn't return to me is gone?"

"No, it's what happened when I used the scanner after you left the carpet shop."

"You're going to tell me that either everybody rang the buzzer, nobody set off the buzzer, or you used the scanner incorrectly. Let me have the scanner. We'll find another time to wave the magic wand at our group."

"Here's the scanner, but I'm sure I used it correctly."

"What makes you so certain?"

"The scanner did not register when I went past the *burka* lady, the acrobats, and the snake handlers."

"What's bad about that?"

"Nothing, but when I scanned the Water Man, the number 1035 appeared on the screen."

"Ouch, you're right, Advari, there goes my appetite."

"What does it mean?" Advari searched my face for an answer.

"On the positive side, I'd say this *burka* lady obviously isn't the '*burka* lady' we want, and the acrobats and snake people aren't on the Calderons' payroll. On the negative side, it means I need to watch the Water Man carefully. Did I forget anyone?"

"When I scanned the porter and the maid, the numbers 1101 and 1102 came up."

"The Calderons deserve credit. They use their people to 'protect' our belongings to gain our confidence, and tell them what our plans are. Porters and maids are invisible people like taxi drivers. They hear and see everything because nobody pays any attention to them."

"We could be wrong about them, you know," Advari counseled.

"We could be wrong, but they probably worked for the Calderons at some point. Everyone else in Morocco seems to have worked for Calderon at some time. You did good work today with your scanner, little soldier. I'd say that we're not wrong about Ahmed and Cala because, if we were tourists and found our room ransacked like ours was, the police, hotel security, and the hotel manager would be very active trying to make us happy. Did you see anybody around besides the porter and maid trying to make us happy?"

"No, no one."

"Then, the scanner correctly identified them as 'unfriendlies,' and we must treat them as such until proven otherwise. Or, if they're our friends, they and their son are in grave danger if they try to escape the Calderons. Let's eat before I get a tummy ache trying to determine who to shoot or shake hands with tonight."

"Should we hide your equipment first?"

"Good thought, but, my equipment has been fully inventoried and is under Calderon's personal protection. Nobody will mess with it and cause us to think we're surrounded by Calderon *camarades*. Although why he didn't confiscate the stuff when his people had the chance is a mystery to me. Possibly, they want us to feel overconfident and become our own worst enemies."

"Maybe this room is bugged, and they are listening to us now."

"Trashing our first room that might not have been bugged to get us to move here would make sense. That's a good reason to go outside the hotel to eat. But, I brought my 'bug jammer'. If the Calderons are listening, all they hear is a high-pitched squeal that'll give them a pounding headache for days. If you're ready, let's go. I'll tell you what I'm planning, which may not make you happy. Otherwise, you'll scan me and think I've gone totally wacko."

"You forget. I've been with you on other expeditions. You wacko? Absolutely not, *Mon Capitan*," Advari accented the end of our conversation with a hearty salute.

Chapter Notes

1. Paula Hardy, Mara Vorhees, and others. *Morocco*, 7th Edition (Melbourne: Lonely Planet Publications Pty Ltd., 2005), p. 37 *et. seq.* By permission of Lonely Planet Publications Pty. Ltd.

2. Whitehall (editor), *op. cit.*, p. 211.

3. *Ibid.*, p. 211.

CHAPTER 17

WESTERN WAR

DINNER CONVERSATION AND WET PANTS

On our walk to the Cafe Argana overlooking the *Djemaa el-Fna*, we doubled back several times to determine if we were being followed. I wouldn't have been surprised if we were. I simply wanted to know the Calderon method for obtaining information.

Finally seated at the rooftop restaurant, I ordered *pastilla* while Advari selected *tajine*, both specialties of the Marrakesh region. (*Pastilla* is a hyped-up chicken pot pie with a nice blend of almonds, spices, and lemon-flavored eggs in a pastry crust. *Tajine* is an excellent stew.) My descriptions don't do justice to the flavor and preparation involved in these dishes. Advari was disappointed when he discovered what he had ordered, but dove in heartily after the first few bites. Eating Moroccan-style using only our right hands guaranteed we would make a mess of our table and its surroundings. Advari always had stomach space for dessert and selected *kaab el-ghzal*, which are crescent rolls stuffed with almonds and covered with icing. We lingered over our mint *atay* (tea) while the restaurant staff confiscated the desecrated tablecloth. I needed to discuss our plans and strategies before Advari fell asleep. The diners at the tables closest to us left. The vacant space around us coupled with the din from the main square below would ensure a confidential conversation.

"I mentioned before that you may not like the strategy I've selected for our opening salvo against Calderon," I told Advari quietly to initiate the conversation.

"In what way?"

"Our usual approach is a direct attack, but Morocco is the Calderons' home turf. They're too strong for us to barge in on them anywhere. Without having seen the villas, I assume that they have fences, dogs, cameras, and armed guards at each of the sites. Two sources told me they have storage and transfer facilities in Melilla about 300 kilometers along the Mediterranean coast east of Ceuta. If that information is correct, we can attack Calderon's facilities at Melilla and leave the trans-shipment locations in the Cape Verde islands for another time. Returning to my main theme, other than Hassan and possibly Chauncey, nobody remotely reliable has been inside the Calderon villas. We need to take a different approach if we want to rescue Beth and live long enough to get you back to school and Beth and me back to the States."

"How about tunnels? Have you forgotten the tunnels in Peru? Barrantes and the Calderons like tunnels," Advari questioned.

"Good point, little soldier, especially if someone dug the tunnels prior to the Calderons taking possession of the property. Although the presence of tunnels won't change my basic strategy, we certainly can try to locate some when we scout the La Montagne and Ceuta villas. On my map, I noticed that along the beach between Cap Spartel and Ceuta is a place called the Grottes d'Hercules. In mythology, that was the place Hercules stayed when he allegedly separated Europe from Africa. More recently, I understand that the grotto is used for private parties and weddings because it's close to the Le Mirage Hotel near the Cap. Thanks for refreshing my memory about tunnels. If an ancient grotto exists, chances are good for an ancient or more recent Calderon cave and tunnel system," I asserted.

"So what are your plans?" Advari asked between mouthfuls of dessert.

"I'm on a Sun Tzu kick lately. One strategy used by successful Chinese warlords to confuse their opponents was to disguise their strength and capabilities. Where their forces were strong, they wanted to appear weak. When they were capable and efficient, they portrayed themselves as incompetent and disorganized."

"As you said before, all we have is each other, a few acrobats, and a few snakes. We can't fully trust the Water Man, the porter, and the maid if the scanner is correct. We are a sad army as it is without additional effort to appear incompetent," Advari argued.

"In terms of the La Montagne villa, other than rescuing Ahmed and Cala's son and watching a romantic sunset from the lighthouse at Cap Spartel, we don't have any immediate interest in the Calderon villa there. I'm not sure Ali actually exists. The tale of Ali's addiction may have been concocted by Calderon and recited for our benefit by Ahmed and Cala as a diversion to get us trapped and killed in La Montagne. If we escape or succeed in La Montagne but are killed in Ceuta, I've lost money on the return leg of my round-trip airline ticket. We have only one chance in Ceuta, and we need to be very sharp and successful there."

"So, why are we wasting time in Cap Spartel? Why not attack the Ceuta villa with all we have?" Advari counter-argued.

"The Chinese warlords knew they should never attack an enemy before they were ready. Also, the warlords liked to have their enemies wear themselves out before they attacked them," I attempted to clarify my plan.

"How so?" Advari continued his questioning.

"The Calderons know our primary target is Ceuta. They engineered it that way by kidnapping Beth. What they don't know is when and under what circumstances we will attack. I'm sure they have all the men and dogs waiting for us. You never stood military guard duty like I have, but imagine being on guard during a hot day or on a cold dark night—day after day, night after night. After a few days of constant vigilance, the Calderons' hotshot security guards will get bored or over-hyped watching for us. Every day, they burn up energy and strength standing or walking their post because they know the Calderons will cut their tongues out if our attack starts in their sector and they aren't alert to stop it. That's why we won't rush directly to Ceuta to rescue Beth, although, emotionally, I want to do that very much. We need the Calderons' security people to become tired, bored, or careless before we make our move," I explained.

"Okay, I understand that better now. For a while, I thought you were interested in collecting on Señora Beth's life insurance."

"Her insurance isn't sufficient for me to risk spending the rest of my life in a Moroccan prison, or as buzzard bait tied to an ant hill in the Sahara. In addition, her return airline ticket is prepaid like mine, so rescuing her is financially worthwhile to me. On a theoretical basis, our success in her rescue will confirm the validity of ancient Chinese war strategies and tactics if nothing else. If we crimp the Calderons' operations, we will have achieved all that I expect from this venture. But now, we should clear out of here and get some sleep before you get hungry again. Before you get up though, turn your head slowly to the right and look at our waiter standing near the kitchen door. He is a perfect example of what I've been telling you. He's waited for a half hour for a signal from us that we're ready to leave. He's so bored and traumatized by waiting for us that he can barely stand upright," I set the stage.

As Advari turned to look at the waiter, I reached over and poured his half-filled glass of water into his lap.

"Hey, what was that for?" Advari responded angrily.

"That was a demonstration of the diversion and surprise attack you and the Calderons' *pistoleros* should expect. See what I mean? With the right strategy, troops, attitude, and luck, we have a chance against Calderon," I prophesied as I waved to the waiter to bring our check.

"Okay, I see your point, but now everyone in Marrakesh will see my wet pants on our way back to the hotel."

"Take it as a badge of advanced education and walk proudly. That should confuse most onlookers. Besides, it's dark now."

"Can we take a taxi back to the hotel?"

"Okay, just this once. But I don't want you going soft on me when we launch Operation Hercules."

"Some general you would have made. You make getting my pants wet sound patriotic."

"Think of it as one of the many services I provide. Here is a scarf some lady left behind. If you hold it in front of you while we find a taxi, nobody will see your patriotic pants. If you think I did that out of malice, you're absolutely wrong. I want you and your head with me completely when the action begins."

Upon our return to the hotel, Ahmed was waiting for us in the lobby.

Moroccan Magic

"*Aseedee*, I have three superb sedans available for our drive north tomorrow," Ahmed advised, very pleased with himself for making what he assumed were excellent arrangements.

"Sedans are no good," I informed him despite his polite greeting. "They will attract too much attention along the way. Get something else, please."

"But those cars will not be noticed in La Montagne. Everyone there has luxury cars."

"I understand, Ahmed, but find something else."

"I could rent three desert vehicles. They would not attract attention on the road, but they would be noticed in town."

"Find us a vehicle that will hold all of us and our equipment. I understand and appreciate the advantage of several vehicles to make us more versatile and maneuverable, but humor me and get one large vehicle, please."

"You mean a bus? That would be noticeable and heard everywhere. Are you sure that is what you want?"

"Strangely, a bus demonstrates our incompetence much better than a luxury vehicle. Find a bus that has some wear on it, but reliable enough to get us there. Have it ready to go at 0300."

"That early?"

"Sure, I want the group assembled in the parking lot at 0245. We'll have everyone drink a lot of water before going to bed. While they're up early taking care of their excess fluids, they may as well dress and be ready to travel. While I think about it, find a professional bus driver who listens, does not talk out of turn, and wants to be paid in cash. Otherwise, you and the Water Man are designated drivers."

"The Water Man and I have never driven a bus in our lives," Ahmed conceded.

"Fine, that should be sufficient incentive for both of you to find a competent professional driver. Is there anything else you can think of to help us reclaim your son?"

"You are a very difficult man to deal with, but I think you already know that," Ahmed proclaimed.

"Maybe so, but you asked me to help you. Under the extraordinary circumstances you imposed on me and my companions who I need to safely return to their families after this adventure, this is as good as I get. Sometime, we need to discuss the circumstances surrounding you and your wife's employment with Calderon. I won't change my mind about helping you and your son, but I may not send you a Christmas card unless I know for certain that you're not secretly working for Calderon and transmitting information to him about our plans and travel arrangements. The other people you've seen with me have volunteered to risk their lives to fight the Calderons. I have an obligation to protect them any way I can."

"You know about Calderon and us?" Ahmed asked in surprise.

"Not as much as you will tell me in the next few minutes, *Aseedee* Ahmed, but enough to start the discussion," I responded, returning his polite form of Arabic address with a sharp edge on it.

"If your son was in trouble, would you be willing to die for him if necessary?"

"I wouldn't before he explained why he was in trouble, if the problem was of his own making, and his personal plans to remedy the situation if I weren't around to bail him out. Then, if his explanation were satisfactory, I would apply maximum effort to help him. But my military training taught me to let my opponent die for his cause while I live for mine.

Perhaps I'm not being fair applying my relationship with my son to your situation. But, I understand what you're telling me."

"Calderon always promised to free our son after I did one more thing for him, then another, then one more, and the next one. Always, I knew Calderon's promises were no good, but what could I do? He is a powerful man here."

"I understand. You cannot go to the police or to any other public official he owns. Find a bus and driver for us. If we don't retrieve your son from La Montagne, it won't be because we didn't exert maximum effort."

"Thank you, that is all I ask, *thellah f'rassek* (take care of your head)," Ahmed stated almost reverently in wishing me good fortune in the Arabic idiom.

Ahmed could have asked for more, but, with my wife held hostage, I wasn't prepared to provide additional guarantees of assistance to him that might jeopardize Beth's safety. Secondly, I didn't know what my patchwork strike force was capable of doing—if anything at all.

Our departure was only a few hours away. I needed sleep. I went to my room, threw a blanket over Advari, and moved him to his side of the bed. I discovered too late that he had the only blankets available. I unwound him from a small corner of the blanket he had wrapped around himself in his sleep and fell into the deepest coma I had experienced on this trip. Despite that, I awoke at 0200 without external help, collected my stuff plus Beth's luggage, and carried it all to the lobby in one trip. When I returned to the room, Advari was dressed, talking to himself with random questions meant for me that went unanswered, and, within minutes, he was ready to move out. I couldn't believe Advari's newly minted motivation until we went to the lobby to find Omar, the acrobats, snake handlers, the Water Man, Ahmed, and a professional bus driver waiting for us.

As we walked into the darkness outside, I faintly discerned the outline of a sparkling twelve-meter European bus parked in the farthest corner of the hotel lot. Its appearance didn't square with the look of incompetence, but we couldn't afford the time to find a less appealing replacement. My strike force began loading their luggage and equipment into the luggage bins below until I stopped them. At our destination, we might not have the luxury of standing around waiting for baggage to be unloaded. Besides, a bus that size could hold forty or more passengers. We had plenty of space inside for our gear.

As the men quietly entered the front and side doors of the bus with their equipment, I noticed that I had more acrobats than I had requisitioned.

I had eight adult acrobats, one Omar, two snake handlers, one Water Man, and one Ahmed. I also noticed that the acrobats traded their white costumes for darker traditional Berber garb. The next item that fluttered past my brain was what Berber dialect did they speak—*Riffi, Tamazight, Tahelheit,* or *Soussi* (or some combination)? Or, did it really matter since I couldn't speak any of those dialects? I would have to rely on English, French, Spanish, Portuguese, or smoke signals unless they could catch onto Czech or Slovak in a hurry. When they noticed me observing them file onto the bus without taking adverse action against the surplus ones, they each chanted softly in my direction, *"Allahu akbar, Allahu akbar. Ashahadu an la Ilah ila Allah. Ashahadu an Mohammedan rasul Allah."* I understood that part of their Muslim chant. I didn't know if it was Modern Standard Arabic or the Moroccan Arabic *darija* dialect, but I had heard it five times a day as the *muezzin* (or a recorded message) in the mosque tower called the Islamic faithful to prayer, "Allah is great. Allah is great. There is no God but Allah. Mohammed is His Prophet." Also, I didn't know if my Berber commandos were true believers of Islam, or if they privately held to their Berber traditions dating back to Neolithic days. I decided not to care because I was distracted by another revelation.

As the third acrobat boarded the bus, his scarf loosened from around his shoulders. Even in the darkness, I would have been blind not to recognize the outline of a fine-looking Russian automatic rifle and accompanying ammunition belts crisscrossing the acrobat's shoulders. I stepped forward and reached out my hand in an unmistakable sign that I wanted to inspect the man's rifle. He looked furtively for help from his comrades, but they froze in their places waiting for my next move. He unslung his rifle from his shoulder and handed it to me. I pulled out my small flashlight, focused the beam by cupping my hand, and aimed the light at the rifle's breach. Etched in the blackened steel was the gunsmith's mark. The weapon had been made in Slovakia (perhaps by one of my relatives) and probably borrowed from the Calderons' contraband arsenal at some prior date. Now, it was being carried on the bus to be used, if necessary, against its previous owner. The irony was not lost on me.

With an approving nod, I handed the weapon back to the acrobat. With a look of relief, he continued up the bus stairs to join his fellow warriors. They all sat on the left side of the bus with their gear piled in the right-hand seats. The acrobats' seating arrangement was a small item, but demonstrated that they were seasoned travelers, if not seasoned warriors. We would be driving generally north toward Tangier with the rising sun shining on the right side of the bus making it the hottest side in the morning. I expected that I would find the opposite seating arrangement in the afternoon. My troops were accustomed to non-functional air conditioning in their local buses. This finely crafted bus was built for international travel, and fully operational air conditioning would be a new experience for my army.

Motoring to La Montagne

Our route would take us from Marrakesh near the center of Morocco northwest toward the coastal highway through Casablanca to the capital city of Rabat, and then continue northeast on the coastal highway toward Tangier and suburban La Montagne. The 600 kilometers would be quite a haul in this country despite the relatively luxurious transportation we had. Underway long before daybreak, I walked forward to ask Ahmed to inform the bus driver to stop at the next Moroccan equivalent of a gas station so that the men could stretch their legs and do whatever else needed doing. U.S.-styled service stations were few and far between in this part of Africa, so I had trouble identifying good places to stop unless they had the words "Gas" or "Toilettes," (or their Arabic equivalents) hand painted on the side of the mud brick or concrete block building, or if an obvious gas pump was visible.

Ahmed interpreted the driver's answer that we weren't close to such a place and inquired if I wanted to stop in the desolate area we presently were traversing. I agreed on the premise that the men would welcome the chance to walk around and test fire their weapons that they had been disassembling and cleaning during the first leg of our trip. Certainly, they would appreciate the relative coolness of the bus for the remainder of the trip compared to the scorched earth and rapidly rising temperature outside. I wanted to shoot a few arrows to loosen up my shoulders and confirm to the men that archery might be a part of my battle plan of demonstrated incompetence at La Montagne, if necessary. I also wanted to test fire my sniper rifle with its new and untried laser sight.

I didn't need an audience to observe my archery skills, but I had one anyway. I found a discarded bucket half buried in the sand for my target and set it on a rock about seventy-five yards away. I strung my bow, selected an arrow, took aim, and knocked the pail off the rock like magic. I intended to shoot a few more arrows, but when I heard the applause behind me, I decided to stop there and retrieve my arrow before the shifting sands buried it completely. The arrow had dug itself into the ground several yards beyond the target. As I bent over to pull it out of the ground, I noticed that it was imbedded in the bleached rib cage of a partially exposed human skeleton. I didn't linger to collect any more information about the skeleton. I grabbed my arrow, put it in my quiver, and ordered everyone back onto the bus. Shooting my sniper rifle could wait for another time because I didn't want to risk disclosure of any possible skeletal bad omens to my amateur army.

While most of the acrobats immediately lined up to pile onto the bus, three lingered long enough to fire short bursts of their rifles toward my former target, making the bucket dance across the parched earth. That was too much fun for the others who had climbed on the bus to ignore.

Immediately, they evacuated the bus and lined up to fire their rifles with great success to the detriment of the flattened bucket. Fortunately, none went forward to examine the pail more closely, which would have put them on the path of discovering the partially buried skeleton. That was a close call. I needed to regain control of my warriors immediately. I stepped forward into the line of fire to prevent any more shooting unless someone wanted to permanently ventilate my body. I began applauding with a big grin on my face.

"Excellent shooting; very good shooting!" I exclaimed. "I know you are Berber warriors and excellent shots. That is why I selected you. But save your ammunition for the work ahead of us tonight."

Whatever they understood from what I said seemed to work. They cheered themselves as they filed back onto the bus and continued jabbering as they took their seats. Applause was a dialect they understood. I would keep that in mind.

In my activity to corral the Berber riflemen, I didn't immediately notice Advari off to the side teaching Omar how to get more range and accuracy from his slingshot. Whatever Advari's teaching technique was, it worked because Omar hit his target area drawn in the sand on his last two shots. I shouted for Advari and Omar to get on the bus, and the two boys came running very pleased with themselves. Assembling everyone on the bus should have resolved my concerns about my leadership and control of the group, and observing their rifle skills should have demonstrated their fighting potential to me. That much was accomplished, but I now had a larger problem.

My plan to launch an inept attack against the Calderons' La Montagne villa to deceive them into thinking we were no match for his security forces there or in Ceuta disintegrated. I could see now that the Berbers would fight hard at La Montagne. They wouldn't understand the nuances of my strategy of half measures and apparent incompetence. Equally important, I didn't want Calderon to move Beth to another location where I couldn't find her. Between now and the time the bus reached Tangier, I had to decide what level of competence I wanted my group to display at La Montagne. I knew that news of any attack on La Montagne would be reported to Ceuta immediately, and I had better make the correct guess for Beth's sake and for the lives of my fighters. Unfortunately, I didn't have sufficient information about what my group would face at the La Montagne villa to relieve my concerns.

I went forward and brought Ahmed and the Water Man to the rear of the bus with me for a strategy conference.

"What do you know about the tunnels at the La Montagne villa?" I asked the Water Man, who blanched immediately and looked at Ahmed for inspiration in formulating an answer. Help from Ahmed was not forthcoming. The Water Man gave the best non-answer he could.

"I know only little, nothing to help."

"In Marrakesh, you said you'd help me," I scolded him. "I accept the word of an honest man, a man of character and distinction, an *Aseedee*. I know that you are or were a member of the Calderon operation at one time. You must decide now if you are still a Calderon man or the distinguished Water Man. The first is a man who does bad things. The second is an honorable man who helps people in trouble. I have very little time to decide what kind of man you are. I can shoot you now or throw you off the bus to starve in the desert, but I will do neither. I want you to make up your mind about what kind of man you are or want to be. Think about it, then tell me if I can trust the Water Man or not. Earlier, you said that Ernesto cheated you. Besides stealing the *souks* from you, how did he cheat you?"

"Calderon say I would be his number one man. Then, he has another man number one."

"Who is this other man?"

"Man named Hassan."

"Very interesting. Tell me about him."

"I only know he is Kuwaiti."

"Are you sure?"

"Yes, this man is with Calderon much time always. He is number one with Calderon."

"I think I know this Hassan—slender build, moustache, always wears sunglasses. If he is the man you identified, he is a very smart man. He is smart enough to fool the U.S. and Spanish governments and probably others. If I help remove Hassan from his number one job, would you return to Calderon?"

"No, no more work for Calderon. I no trust Calderon no more."

INTERMISSION FOR ADMONITIONS

"If I remove both Hassan and Calderon, would you work for me, Water Man?"

"You make difficulty for me, but you are okay man. You no sell drugs, people, or guns. I no work for you that way. Maybe you buy carpet shop. Then, I work for you. I send people to the shop," he said, trying to make me smile.

"I appreciate that, but I have no immediate interest in selling flying or non-flying carpets. Tell me all you can about the tunnels at La Montagne."

"I know nothing to help with tunnels."

"You spoke the truth for a while, Water Man. You are no use to me when you do not speak the truth. Go up front to your seat. Here is some paper and a pencil. Draw me a layout of the Calderon buildings, yards, entrances, security systems, walls, fences, guard stations—everything you know about La Montagne and Ceuta. Be as accurate as you can. After I see what you have, I will decide if you are truly an *Aseedee* Water Man who will help me as he said, or only a thief and a liar who should be disgraced among his own people."

That was tough talk, and I wasn't sure how he would receive it. The Water Man dejectedly got up from his seat next to me and walked toward the front of the bus. When he was out of earshot, I turned to Ahmed who had been sitting silently in a seat opposite me on the hot side of the bus.

"Was he telling me the truth about the tunnels?" I asked.

"I do not know for certain. I have heard about tunnels, but I have never seen them. If we can rescue my son, perhaps he knows where they are."

"More likely, your son is a prisoner in one of the tunnels. Hopefully, if we find one or the other, we will find both of them. Do you see my problem? Now, I can appreciate Hercules's difficulty in his second task to kill Hydra, the seven-headed snake. When Hercules cut one head off, two grew back. The more information I obtain, the less certain I am about its accuracy. Okay, Ahmed, go back to your seat too and draw me layouts of the Calderon villas from what you know. Then, I will compare the Water Man's drawings with yours to get as complete and accurate a picture as possible of the layout of the Calderon property. Lives are at stake here. I will plan some way to deal with our access to the villas and the location of any tunnels. Pray that Allah favors us in this venture."

As Ahmed went forward to his seat, I decided that when we arrived in La Montagne, a short look at the Grottes d'Hercules might be helpful to determine if I could make a connection between them and the Calderon property. If I couldn't find any connecting tunnels from the grotto to the Calderon villa, I could make or fake an above-ground attack on the villa and assess what impact that had, if any, and if I could control and maneuver my Berber militia in the attack. I might not be able to spring Ahmed's son using this approach, but I didn't force him to become one of Calderon's henchmen. Rescuing Beth and damaging Calderon operations were my primary objectives. As far as the reliability of the Water Man and Ahmed were concerned, I would use the principle of trust I had heard in an Arabic saying: "Trust in Allah, but keep your camels tied."

We stopped several times along the way and again around dusk at a real gas station between Rabat and Tangier. As the sun set in a splash of brilliant colors, I understood why this land, this Morocco was called *al-Maghreb al Aqsa*—the Farthest Land of the Setting Sun. Unromantically, the sunset reminded me that I had one more task before we boarded the bus for the final leg of our journey. I needed to teach my army some simple hand and whistle signals so I could direct their actions against the Calderon villa.

"We will arrive in the middle of the night," Advari reminded me. "How will we see your hand signals? Maybe, we will be too far away to hear the whistle because of gunfire too."

Advari was correct on both counts, but I had to salvage something to make the men think as a unit and to look to me for leadership and direction.

"Do you think Calderon's house and surrounding property will remain dark when his security guards are alerted, little soldier? We should consider ourselves lucky if lights don't go on around the entire outside perimeter of the property."

I demonstrated several hand and whistle signals and had Ahmed recite their meaning to the group. Then, I had them demonstrate the signals back to me as I pointed randomly to individuals in the group. The responses weren't perfect, but the sun had disappeared over the horizon, and it was time to return to the bus. The signal training would have to do. While the men slept or stared out into the darkness, I turned on a reading light and examined the drawings the Water Man and Ahmed had given me of the La Montagne villa. Both drawings were good. The Water Man's drawings were detailed, but I would have to see the place for myself before I engaged my army in what could be the battle of their lives. I went forward to where the Water Man and Ahmed were sitting.

"Thank you both for your drawings. They are helpful in giving me an idea of the layout. I want both of you to stay close to me when we arrive in La Montagne. Your knowledge of the place and what you recall when you are actually there should be helpful in rescuing Ahmed's son when the time comes. After we unload, I want the bus to move a short distance away to prevent any damage to it. You two can also help direct the men back to the bus after we finish whatever we do to the house. Rest now, if you can. We have a long night ahead."

Tangier Terrain

Upon our arrival in Tangier, I instructed the driver to take us to the grotto first. No one had told me that the place was a major tourist attraction. For the off-season and with the time approaching 2010, a sizeable crowd was still on hand. We parked in the lot of the Le Mirage Hotel on the cliffs overlooking the cave. As my army unloaded from the bus to walk down the terraced steps toward the cave and the beach, I saw why tourists lingered around the shore despite the chilly sea breeze. On the beach were twenty riders in traditional Berber garb who lined up their Arabian ponies for their last *fantasias* cavalry charge of the evening. It was a splendid and noisy show when the riders shot off their long muskets as they pulled up their horses just before they reached the crowd of tourists.

"Where is the villa from here?" I asked the Water Man.

"Short way there," he replied, pointing east. "No good to see from here. We go to top of cliff. I show you. See big stone wall and lights there between trees?" he said, pointing east again after we retraced our steps to the top of the terraced lawn of the hotel. "That is Calderon villa."

"Then, why are we standing here?" I asked the Water Man to his utter surprise.

"I do not know what you mean," he answered in his befuddlement.

"Go hire the horsemen to help us," I instructed him as if it were the most natural thing to do on a moment's notice.

"All of them?" the Water Man gulped.

"Certainly, all of them. They perform as a team, right? How will you separate the good riders from the average ones at this time of night? Conduct auditions? If you have trouble, bring the leader to me, and together we will ask him to help us for another hour or so if the horses aren't too tired."

As the Water Man started down toward the beach, Ahmed exclaimed to me, "Please do not get angry, but I am as confused as the Water Man about your interest in the *fantasias* riders. Why are you hiring them?"

"If they agree, they'll be our diversion. From the touristy looks of the grotto and the distance from the villa, a tunnel might not exit from the villa, and the area is too busy to be a reliable entrance or exit for the villa anyway. We'll make a ground-level attack. The Berber light cavalry will be a better diversion than us stumbling around in a dark cave or tunnel when we don't know where we're going. Do you agree?"

"When did you conceive this idea?"

"When I saw the cave, the riders, and the distance to the villa from here, why? This is no big deal for me. Some people go bowling. Some people sew and knit. Others commit suicide. This is what I do. This is what Uncle Sam pays me well over the minimum wage to deliver. At least, I believe I'm working for Uncle Sam and he's happy with my performance."

"Allah gave you an unusual gift," Ahmed proclaimed.

"Don't be too quick to blame my planning skills on Allah. He may object vigorously. Ah, good, here comes the Water Man and hopefully an agreeable leader of the horsemen. Stay close. I may need you to translate if the Water Man does not understand and cannot convey the reason why I want the horsemen."

FARID AND THE FANTASIAS

"Farid is leader of the *fantasias* horsemen," the Water Man said in introduction. "He likes our project, but he wants more talk about it. So please, you tell him about what you want as our leader, yes?"

"*Wash kat'ref negleezeeya, Aseedee Farid?* (Do you speak English, Mr. Farid?)" I asked and received a negative shake of his head.

"That's okay. We are equal because I don't speak Arabic, let alone a Berber dialect."

"I will translate," Ahmed volunteered. "He speaks in the *Soussi* dialect."

"*Soussi*," Farid affirmed, pointing to himself and the semicircle of his riders.

"A bit far from home, isn't he?" I inquired of Ahmed while nodding toward Farid.

"One goes wherever the road leads to support a man's family in this country," Ahmed clarified.

"Your point is well taken. The need to travel for work is not limited to Morocco. Very well, Ahmed, tell Farid we want to hire him and his troupe for several cavalry charges toward the front and back gates of the Calderon villa tonight. We will pay the same rate the hotel pays him to entertain the tourists."

Ahmed conveyed my message to Farid, which set off an energetic round of comments from his men near enough to hear Ahmed recite my proposal.

"The men want to know how long they need to perform because they usually do a cavalry charge every fifteen minutes for the hotel. The hour is late, and the horses and men are tired."

"We need four charges alternating between the front and back gates of the Calderon estate. That should take fifteen to thirty minutes at most."

Ahmed's exchange with Farid and his pointing to the Calderon villa set off another round of discussion among the horsemen.

"What now?" I asked Ahmed.

"They did not know that was the Calderons' property. They want more money."

"Remind them that the Calderons kidnap their women and children and sell them into slavery, or make them prostitutes or prisoners of drugs like your son. Are they Berber warriors or desert scorpions without stingers to allow the Calderons' shame to continue unanswered?"

This time, Ahmed's translation received heated comments from the men and snorting and prancing from their mounts before Ahmed was halfway finished. I either had hired some horsemen, or I was about to lose my head. I couldn't determine which option until Ahmed translated what they said.

"They want to know if you will allow them to use live ammunition in their muskets to defend themselves, and if they can enter Calderon property. If you let them break through the gates, they will accept the pay you offered if they can claim whatever they want from the house," Ahmed repeated for my benefit.

"Having Calderon pay part of the bill for our trespassing on his property is a fair price based on the reaction you received from the troupe. What was that all about?"

"The story has been the same for many years. Some of their family or friends worked for Calderon from time to time. Sooner or later, they were all embarrassed, beaten, or disappeared when Calderon was displeased with them. Sometimes, they were beaten or intimidated for no apparent reason. Now they can take their revenge. They are eager as true Berber warriors."

"That sounds more hostile than forming a union and negotiating a collaborative collective bargaining contract with Calderon. But, I agree to let them pillage the place because I don't think I can stop them after they are inside the gates. Nonetheless, tell Farid that his people must follow my orders and coordinate their actions with ours. Otherwise, someone will get hurt if everyone is shooting at the same time while we are attacking from different directions. They must promise not to harm anyone who is a non-combatant or who clearly surrenders. Make sure that they understand that, Ahmed," I instructed. "Also, ask them how they intend to get through the gates—attach ropes and pull them down using the horses? Their saddles don't have saddle horns like the Western American saddle."

Ahmed conveyed my thoughts to Farid, and then turned to me with a faint smile on his face.

"Farid says they perform *fantasias* all over Morocco, so they have trucks and horse carts. After the first charge at the gates with the horses to see how strong the gates are, the trucks will precede the second charge and punch through the gates with the horsemen following closely behind—if that is acceptable to you, of course. All the trucks have steel frame bumpers in front to avoid damage to the trucks because they often drive through herds of animals in the desert or cattle and sheep herds in the farm country."

"That tactic might be useful on Chicago expressways too. Tell Farid that I accept his plan. His approach will reduce the number of cavalry charges by half, and the diversion will be an integral part of the attack. Hey, everybody, gather around! I will give you your assignments now because when Calderon's people hear an army of this size coming in their direction, we will need to act as soon as we arrive."

"Could we split up in small groups and have the horsemen come last? That way, we could be in position before the horsemen arrive," Advari suggested.

"Good, very good thinking, little soldier. The thought came to me too, but if you look around the stone wall, some places are very dark and others are in the shadows. I can't believe that the Calderons have haphazard security around the perimeter of the property. If they have motion sensors to turn on additional perimeter lights, we'll be caught in the light before the horsemen are in position. Without the horsemen as a diversion or element of the initial attack, we are dead ducks before we get close to the property, either over the wall or through the gates. *Comprendo?*"

"Yes, but what would we have done if we did not have the horsemen? You did not know about them until we arrived."

"If the horsemen weren't here, I would have prayed a lot longer and a lot harder than I am now. And, stumbling through dark caves or tunnels is highly dangerous. Unless anyone else has any suggestions, we'll use my plan because we need to start before the horses die of old age."

"I think you are right," Ahmed concurred. "We need to start before the hotel staff become alarmed at this large group standing here and notify the police."

"Okay, for better or worse, here's my plan," I started as I looked directly at Advari and Omar.

"You two collect beach stones for your slingshots. Your job is to knock out any perimeter lights, particularly along the east and west walls. You two stay outside the walls until any gunfire stops. If Calderon has guards outside the walls, use your slingshots on them, or run to safety, understand?"

"What if we need the lights later?" Advari asked, giving me the impression that he wasn't thrilled with his assignment that he correctly perceived was removed from the main action.

"If there's gunfire, the neighbors will provide us with all the lights we need. Does that satisfy you for now, little soldier?"

"Okay, we will do it your way," Advari answered for Omar and himself.

With Advari appeased, I continued my instructions to my army.

"I need four acrobats on the east wall and four acrobats and one snake handler on the west wall. Stay behind, on top of, or drop down inside the wall depending on what position is safest for you and the person next to you. Watch your line of fire to avoid hitting the team on the opposite side and the horsemen when they come through the north and south gates. After the horsemen are inside the compound, Farid and his men should ride down any of Calderon's men on the grounds while the acrobats converge with me on the house to silence any gunfire from there and the outlying buildings."

"What should I do?" the remaining snake charmer asked, unsure whether to speak up or not.

"Stay close to me along with Ahmed and Water Man," I answered, patting him on the shoulder.

"We may need you and your friends inside the house. Does anyone else have comments or questions?" I added as I observed Farid talking to Ahmed.

Ahmed translated their discussion.

"Farid said he would like to avoid bloodshed, if possible, by riding slowly up to the gates and asking the guards if they will allow his troupe to stage a practice cavalry charge or two to give his men experience in what cavalry charges against walled fortifications were really like in the old days. This will help him make the troupe's future performances more authentic. The subterfuge may also draw guards from the grounds and house into exposed positions where we can surround or overcome them more easily. What do you think?"

I thought a moment, and replied, "If the guards become suspicious, we may have more bloodshed while we're still outside the walls. But I gave Farid's troupe permission to pillage the house if we take it. He needs sufficient incentive to be a credible actor in talking to the guards. I like it. His idea is audacious enough to work at this time of night. Okay everyone, let's go to the villa."

The clomping of the horses' hooves on the pavement and the droning bus engine at that hour of the night in this upscale neighborhood were as subtle as a *sirocco* wind off the Sahara in our short march toward the Calderon villa. In any other neighborhood, the houses would be considered palaces. But, big houses with huge yards and servants were the norm here. A few lights went on in the other estates as we passed. Whatever else my small army may have going for it, the element of surprise was not included in the package. Farid's idea of diplomacy at the gates might have a fair chance of success.

An Audacious Cavalry Trot

We stopped our bus and horse trucks about a quarter mile from Ernesto's stone wall, which encompassed his expansive yard. The horsemen went forward at a slow walk on the respective roads and paths toward the north and south gates while the remainder of my army started toward their positions along the east and west walls. Advari went with the acrobat group that headed for the east wall, and Omar went with the west wall group. After about ten paces, both groups were engulfed in darkness. From a distance, I thought the planned positioning of my army would have the property virtually surrounded. Closer, as we were now, we had a better chance of surrounding the Great Wall of China than we did the estate. At this point, cranial and intestinal feedback gave me the first inklings that this venture wouldn't go even remotely as planned.

Farid rode his horse to the sentry box adjacent to the south gate while the remainder of his group formed a semicircle in the shadows a short distance behind him. Nobody appeared to have any offensive or defensive weapons ready for action. In the dim light, I could see the faint image of a guard come out of the sentry box and stand in front of Farid's horse. After a few minutes of conversation, the guard went inside the gate while Farid motioned for his group to come closer. Their approach simultaneously caused additional lights to go on in the immediate area of the south gate and its guard station, but nowhere else along the south wall.

From my ground-level vantage point, I couldn't see what was happening at the north gate, or if Advari and Omar with their respective acrobat groups were in position along the east and west walls. I had the Water Man and Ahmed hoist me through the air vent on top of the bus to give me an elevated view. I was not foolhardy enough for the acrobats to elevate me by forming a pyramid if they had been in the area to do so. However, once on the bus roof, I could see ten horsemen astride their mounts in a semicircle at the north gate leisurely chatting with the guard. Additional lights went on near the north gate, but not along the perimeter of the north wall.

The absence of additional perimeter lights had advantages and disadvantages for us. I could not see any guards who might be stationed along the east and west walls where they could be targets for Omar and Advari's slingshots or the acrobats' rifles. Similarly, in the darkness, guards couldn't see Advari, Omar, or the acrobats. More distressing, without perimeter lights, I could not locate Advari, Omar, or their accompanying acrobats. This was weird beyond belief. My militia and mercenary horsemen had either disappeared or were consorting with the enemy.

I couldn't tolerate the suspense of inaction. After instructing the snake handler and the Water Man to stay with the bus driver, I took my two pistols and set out with Ahmed on foot toward the south gate to find out why an apparent armistice was in effect before war was declared. Coinciding with my arrival at the south gate, a guard came out carrying a large green flag and reverently presented it to Farid. Farid accepted it with great solemnity and grace.

"What's going on?" I asked Ahmed impatiently.

"Muhammed is said to have worn green clothes. Thus, the color green is highly revered by Muslims and is the color of Morocco's flag. The guard is giving Farid a flag that was allegedly taken some time ago by an unknown party from the Zwiya of Sidi Abdallah ibn Hassoun Shrine near the Grande Mosquee in the town of Sale. Sidi Abdallah ibn Hassoun was a very important seventeenth century Muslim saint and patron of travelers similar to Saint Christopher for Christians. Farid will be highly rewarded when he returns the flag to the shrine with no questions asked."

"I accept what you say with reverence and respect for Muslim religious articles, but how does that fit into our situation with Calderon?"

"Other than demonstrating that Farid has some influence with the guards, I do not see any connection at the moment."

I was about to explode all over that part of the *Maghreb* peninsula when another guard emerged from the house guiding a young man who definitely needed medical attention by the way he walked and the vacant expression on his face when he came into the lights of the south gate.

"My son," Ahmed shouted with glee as he ran to the gate to embrace Ali again and again.

As I jogged toward the gate trying to determine if I was having a bad dream or if this was the usual way the Moroccan army conducted warfare, Farid backed his horse out of the pack of riders and met me as I came alongside Ahmed and his son.

"This is a night of great joy for us," Farid stated solemnly as Ahmed interpreted his words for me. "A holy war trophy of the Grande Mosquee is reclaimed, and Ali has been returned to his father. The guards said that your wife is not here. Most likely, she is at the villa in Ceuta. My riders and I will go now. We have no more reason to fight. Allah be with you in your future travels," Farid said as he motioned for his riders to follow him to their trucks and horse trailers parked down the road. They, in turn, shouted to the members of their troupe at the north gate to join them.

As the horsemen departed, the acrobats, Advari, and Omar appeared out of the shadows of the east and west walls and circled around me, waiting for information about who called a truce and what I intended to do about it. Ahmed and the Water Man stood near me supporting Ali between them.

"We will not fight tonight, but my war against the Calderons is not finished," I told my army, using my best Sun Tzu war propaganda. "I will go to Ceuta to find my wife since she is not here. I can understand if any of you do not want to come with me. Step forward and tell me now if you want to return home instead of going to Ceuta. If you come to Ceuta with me, I promise you a fight, but I cannot guarantee the outcome or your safety. I have arranged for additional help to meet us there, which will give us advantages we did not have tonight. If we are victorious, whatever the Calderons have in Ceuta that is not illegal, or that we do not destroy, is yours."

"For those who stay with me only through tonight, unload your weapons and get on the bus with those who will go to Ceuta with me. We will drive to the Cap lighthouse now and sleep on the bus. When we arrive there, I need three volunteers to stand guard for two-hour shifts during the remainder of the night. If any of you do not want to go to Ceuta or to the Cap, you can leave for Marrakesh at any time. I will pay your bus fare back to Marrakesh for having stood with me tonight."

As Ahmed translated my message to my army to ensure that everyone understood, I turned and started walking toward the bus. Everyone followed.

Unbridled Success

"What happened?" Advari asked, trying to catch up with me while Omar tagged along.

"Farid recovered a holy Muslim battle flag that probably Calderon or one of his men previously confiscated from its rightful owner. Ahmed recovered his son, who is so drugged that he barely recognizes his father and cannot stand unaided. The rest of us demonstrated the ultimate level of incompetence I could have imagined. The spirit of Sun Tzu would be extremely proud tonight of our ability to disguise our true intentions and capabilities to harm the Calderons' drug, weapons, and human trafficking networks. We achieved all that incompetence in less than a half hour without firing a shot or unnecessarily disturbing the tranquility of the neighborhood. Not bad for one night's work. Thank you all."

"What do you intend to do now?" Omar queried, a little out of breath as he tried to keep up with my fast and frustrated pace.

"I intend to let Ahmed and his son go wherever they need to go for medical care in Tangier or Marrakesh. I need the Water Man to trade this bus for three vans to take us to Ceuta. Maybe we can do some real harm to the Calderons there and recover Beth alive."

"We will go with you—my family of acrobats," Omar declared. "We have not yet had our revenge on the Calderons as we promised ourselves and you. We will go with you to fight."

I slowed my pace and turned to look at Omar and Advari. They were tired, dirty, and confused, but they were with me. I smiled within myself. I recalled the caption on one of my daughter-in-law's slides for her consulting practice, "Attitudes are contagious. Mine might kill you." The Calderons only thought they had the advantage in my personal war against them. I was frustrated, but not defeated. I still had a surprise to deliver to Ernesto and Gilberto Calderon in Ceuta.

Accounting for Casualties

As the men settled in their seats on the bus, I went where Ahmed and his son were seated.

"Ahmed, maybe we should take your son to a hospital in Tangier and have you stay with him instead of you going to Ceuta. I will miss you, but I believe that is best for both of you. The next best option is to start you back toward Marrakesh tonight. What do you think?"

"If I can hire a car tonight, I will start back to Marrakesh. I am sure Ali will need time to recover in a hospital. If he is in Marrakesh, my wife and I will be close to him. If Ali was able to care for himself, I certainly would go to Ceuta with you for what Calderon has done to my son."

"Your son's recovery is most important, but, perhaps, you can remain connected to our war effort from Marrakesh. First, ask the bus driver to call for a taxi to take you to the airport. At the same time, the driver can arrange a charter flight for both of you directly to Marrakesh tonight."

"I really appreciate that, but a private plane is very expensive. I could never repay you," Ahmed said dejectedly.

"I looked at a rate chart on the wall at the ferry terminal. The rate per hour for a four-seat private plane is less than 4,700 *dirhams*. I would have paid more than that for the horsemens' services tonight. Besides, you will be working for me when you return to Marrakesh."

"I will?" Ahmed said, perking up considerably at his prospects for continuing the war from his home. "But that could be an old rate sheet," Ahmed deflated almost immediately at the cost of a chartered flight.

"First, you will continue in the war by delivering a package to Calderon's carpet shop for me. Second, if the airline hasn't posted its most current rates, the posted rates apply, in Tangier or anywhere else."

"Delivering a package is not close to 4,700 *dirhams* worth of work. How big is the package?" Ahmed asked.

"The package is relatively small, but the time of the delivery is important. Come with me. We will ask the driver to make your travel arrangements, and I will tell you more about how to deliver the package while you wait for your taxi."

Ahmed and I went forward to inform the driver about our need for prompt transportation to the airport and a flight to Marrakesh. While we waited for the taxi to arrive and for the bus driver to arrange a private flight, I showed Ahmed how to operate the package. After the driver finished his calls, he sat watching my demonstration with interest.

Ahmed had returned to his seat in the middle of the bus when the driver asked me a question I couldn't interpret. I waved at Ahmed to come to the front of the bus to translate what the driver said, thinking it concerned Ahmed's travel arrangements. Ahmed returned, listened to the driver repeat the question, and interpreted it for me.

"The driver wants to know if you have other packages to deliver to the Calderons," Ahmed informed me.

"I have a few in the back of the bus, why?" I inquired cautiously.

With Ahmed serving as the language link between the driver and me, the driver added another dimension to our war.

"I operate a small delivery business in addition to driving a bus. Perhaps, I can deliver another package to the villa here in La Montagne so that Calderon is sure to receive your message wherever he is. I could arrange such a delivery for a reasonable price."

"What is a reasonable price for delivering two packages—one at the south gate and the other at the north gate?" I asked, opening the bargaining.

"You were willing to pay Ahmed 4,700 *dirhams* for delivery of one package in Marrakesh. My reasonable fee will be 9,400 *dirhams* for two packages delivered in La Montagne," the driver proposed.

"You are breaking my heart and my budget at that amount. Besides, Ahmed will deliver his package inside the shop rather than at the gate," I counter-proposed remembering that, in Morocco, failure to negotiate the terms and price of any transaction is highly impolite.

"Then I will personally deliver two packages—one at the front, and the other at the back door of the house without any disturbance or injury to the guards or house staff. But, my price will be 9,500 *dirhams*," the driver countered.

"Agreed," I stated without enthusiasm, according to the Moroccan rules of negotiation.

"But the timing must coincide with Ahmed's delivery of his package at the carpet *souk* in Marrakesh. Further, the packages must be delivered with the same care as I demonstrated to Ahmed a few minutes ago," I added the additional terms to the delight of both parties.

"Done." The driver concluded the bargaining with a handshake.

"Do you need another demonstration of how the packages work?" I asked the driver.

"If Ahmed writes the instructions for me, I will deliver the packages as you desire," the driver assured me.

"Package delivery can be risky. May I ask what your motivation is for helping me other than the sizable amount of *dirhams* involved?"

"Ahmed is my cousin," the driver said, smiling. "I am glad to see him happy again, and you have made that possible. Delivering the packages will be a family celebration."

"Then I should know your name, *Aseedee* Driver."

"My name is Tabriz," the driver replied.

"Thank you, *Aseedee* Tabriz for your help to all of us tonight."

Still somewhat awed by Tabriz's cooperation, I repeated the package instructions for Ahmed to write down in Arabic for Tabriz's reference.

When the taxi arrived, we all helped Ahmed get his son and their belongings into the car.

"Allah bless you for rescuing my son," Ahmed said in parting. "Will I meet you again?"

"I did very little to return your son to you, as you saw. Take care of him and Cala. I hope to see you sometime in the future, Ahmed, but if I rescue my wife, we will leave Morocco in a hurry."

"Then, Allah be with you until we meet again."

"*Wa 'lekum salam* (and with you), my friend," I replied as Ahmed got into the taxi. As the taxi disappeared into the darkness, I thought to myself, *By whatever name we call our Supreme Being, may Allah or God be with all people of good hearts and help us put an end to these dark days and endless nights.*

With Tabriz's help, the Water Man requisitioned three vans the next morning. We arrived at the rental agency before the manager was ready for customers. He was not overjoyed about the kind of luggage we were toting, but additional *dirhams* brought a smile to his face and silence to his lips. We started for Ceuta early. Besides enlisting three acrobats as *kamikaze* drivers of our vans, the coastal highway east from Tangier curves and bounces most of the way to Ceuta.[1] We stopped for breakfast at Ksar es-Seghir, a former Portuguese fishing village about twenty-five kilometers east of Tangier.[2]

While my army was finishing its breakfast, I assembled my new sniper rifle with scope and silencer and walked to a deserted spot on the beach. I noticed that a stiff breeze was common to the entire coastal area. The accuracy of a bow would be doubtful at best under those conditions. I needed to zero in my rifle before we arrived in Ceuta. This quiet beach was as good a place as any to get acquainted with this custom-made weapon. My target was a piece of driftwood on the beach about 250 yards away. My first three shots were scattered but definitely to the right and low. I adjusted the elevation and windage settings. The next three shots were clustered but still slightly to the right. The next three shots hit the base of two forked branches exactly where I aimed. I turned around to discover that my army had finished its breakfast and had come out to observe my shooting. Most had never seen a silencer. They were amazed to hear only a muffled sound. The others were justly curious about my rifle skills. They might be important to any one or all the troops in a firefight in Ceuta.

Chapter Notes

1. Dorothy Stannard, *Morocco Insight Pocket Guide* (New York: Langenscheidt Publishers, Inc., 2001), p. 19 *et. seq.*

2. Paula Hardy, *op. cit.*, p. 169 *et. seq.*

CHAPTER 18

EASTERN EXTRACTION

SURVEYING THE LANDSCAPE

From my map, I determined that Ceuta was located on a peninsula jutting out into the Mediterranean with a fishermen's port to the east for the workers and a yacht harbor to the west for those who did not labor under the blazing sun for a living. Monte Hacho, called by some the southern pillar of Hercules (with the northern pillar of Gibraltar across the straits visible on clear days) overlooked the town with the Spanish, formerly Portuguese, Fortaleza de Hacho military base at the top and the mission of Ermita de San Antonio about halfway down the slope. Slightly below the mission on the northern slope sat the immense villa of Ernesto Calderon enclosed in a walled enclave along the main road. A smaller villa gifted by Ernesto to the U.S. Ambassador to Spain for the latter's use when he was in town, and villas of local luminaries who were of no interest to Operation Hercules rested in the same compound, but were much lower on the slope than Ernesto's villa.

Our three-vehicle caravan stopped about two kilometers northwest of the Calderon compound to connect with the other resources I had requested from Shortcake a few days earlier. The resources were unobtrusively waiting for us.

Before she went into hiding, I had requested Amy to send a team of seismologists for my use as cover for the *entrée* of my army into the Calderon compound. I wished I were clever enough to have invented the idea myself. But, I borrowed from a ruse used in World War II by two GIs in their escape from a Nazi stockade. The GIs found a length of rope that they used as a substitute for a measuring tape. They collected a number of wooden pegs that they used to stake out what appeared to the guards to be a wider road leading out of the main prison gate. When the GIs reached the prison gate with their crude measuring tape and pegs, they officiously waved their arms and shouted for the guards to open the gate so that they could continue their road layout. The Nazi guards opened the gate and allowed the presumptive road-building measurements to proceed over the hill and out of sight. By the time the guards thought to look for their road-surveying prisoners, the GIs were on their way to freedom. In that case, the Trojan GIs wanted out of the stockade. In my case, as in the original story, I wanted my Trojan horse with its Berber warriors and myself inside the Calderon compound.

I had instructed Shortcake to construct redundancy in case one team of seismologists was delayed, lost in travel, or hijacked, and to ensure that I could communicate with the team leaders. If any shooting started, I wanted the valuable scientists out of harm's way. Amy had outdone herself and conscripted a Spanish seismology team from Salamanca, a Moroccan seismology crew from the capital city of Rabat, and a seismology professor and his two graduate assistants from Iowa. Getting my Trojan group inside the Calderon compound was not assured, but scientific presence at the site exceeded redundancy. Awed by the sheer number of scientists available, I was convinced that the excess number of seismologists would work to our advantage.

Through the Water Man, Omar, Advari, and my own efforts, I instructed the Rabat crew that its assignment was to take measurements and observations of any ground movement and geological faults running between Monte Hacho to the coastal town of Al-Hoceima almost 250 kilometers to the southeast of Ceuta. I assigned the Salamancan team to perform similar scientific measurements from Monte Hacho about the same distance due south from Ceuta to the Rif mountain town of Quezzane. I explained that the Iowa team would extend the North African triangulations from Monte Hacho to Gibraltar across the straits as a basis for future scientific reference from the European continent. With that distribution of assignments, I hoped to spend most of my time conferring with the Iowa seismic team.

"Why not put the American team on Gibraltar and do a triangulation from there?" the leader of the Rabat team asked. "Doing so will guarantee greater accuracy of all our observations and calculations."

"I agree and thank you for your input," I responded. "But British Gibraltar is surrounded by Spanish Andalusia. How many lifetimes will it take me to obtain permission from all the various government bureaucracies for us to gain access and set up our equipment there?" I answered his question with an Amy-like response. "Besides, can you guarantee accurate observations and calculations when Gibraltar's Barbary apes are crawling all over you? How about at night when you leave your sensors and other equipment out to detect any earth movements? Will the apes leave the equipment alone? Will the scientific community be satisfied with haphazard calculations that may put hundreds of Moroccan lives at stake when you cannot predict any time horizon for an earthquake in this region?"

I threw down my scientific gauntlet harder than I intended and much more forcefully than the Rabat team leader appreciated, but I succeeded. I had no time to fool around with scientists other than to use them as delicately as I could to get my wife back from the Calderons and damage the brothers' business in any way possible. I could always apologize or rationalize my lack of ethics to all parties later if anyone was still interested or alive. If they found any scientific data worth informing the authorities or students about in their respective countries, I authorized them to use the data in whatever way it benefited the most people as long as they didn't obstruct my work or movements now. After the Moroccan and Salamancan team leaders told their groups what I required, the Rabat crew almost choked on my imprecise geometry and geography in establishing the three reference points, but they said nothing as they accepted prepayment for their services, got into their respective vehicles, and drove to their first work stations in the Calderons' back yard. The Salamancan crew looked especially perplexed as if their leader had misinterpreted my instructions. At one point, the Spaniards turned their map in a complete circle before they surrendered and followed the Moroccan scientists up the hill in their vehicle to also obtain their initial bearings in Ernesto's back yard.

The Iowa crew thought this was a nice place and wondered where they would eat lunch. They had the right idea. *Go easy on the science, people. Just rely on me to tell you what you need to know and do it without question.* Professor Palmer wasn't upset that his team hadn't received detailed instructions about his crew's assignment to survey the coastal area between Monte Hacho and Gibraltar. His attitude led to my decision to closely coordinate the activities of the Iowa team and my acrobat army. The Iowa team followed my army's vehicles to the Calderon compound without question. Fortunately, no Moroccan or Spanish official of stature was in town to inquire what we were doing there or require us to produce authorization papers for our activities. Any such official would have received multiple answers, but no documents. As we drove the short distance to the villa, I prayed silently that I could safely rescue my wife and that Hassan would be there to help me in addition to the Berber bunch I already had around me.

The Calderons' Ceuta villa was larger and more majestic than I could have imagined. The La Montagne estate looked like a playpen by comparison. By the time my acrobat army vehicles arrived, the Moroccan seismic team had reached the ornate iron front gate and was arguing with the Calderon security guards. I could tell by the shouting and gesturing that the guards were demanding to talk to *numero uno* about this operation. I took my time walking from the van toward the front gate with Advari, Omar, and the Water Man beside me and the acrobats following closely behind holding their weapons non-threateningly at their sides for the moment.

"What is the trouble here?" I asked both innocently and authoritatively as I approached the villa entrance.

"Are you the *commandante* of this group?" the senior guard asked when I arrived at the gate.

His speech confirmed our presence in one of the few remaining Spanish enclaves in North Africa.

"*Si*," I replied sternly. "Open the gate, and allow us to begin our work. We have no time to waste before a damaging earthquake occurs. Or, would you rather be buried under that mountain?" I asked while pointing to Monte Hacho.

Advari and the Water Man did their best to translate my words into Spanish, Moroccan Arabic, and Berber dialects to determine which language the guards could understand best.

"We have no earthquakes here," the second guard objected in Spanish.

"True, but you will soon," I rebutted. "Open the gate, and let us begin our scientific measurements," I said as I pushed my way forward through the Rabat seismic team toward the gate.

Actually, I didn't lie in my projections of catastrophe. I was unknowingly premature by only a few years—a mere heartbeat in seismic terms. On February 24, 2004, the region within my unscientific triangulation experienced a magnitude 6.4 earthquake centered in the mountain village of Ait-Kamara near Al-Hoceima.[1] The quake killed more than 500 people and left thousands of Berber farmers and their families homeless as their mud brick huts collapsed on top of them. I had been around earthquakes in India and Peru for so long that I now was able to forecast them in Africa. Later, I was mortified when I heard the news about the actual earthquakes. I didn't intend to add earthquake predictions to my skill set. I never learned if the Rabat team ever made any useful predictions from their calculations while they were in the area, or if they appropriately recorded them for future use in the disaster to come.

The guards shifted their weapons from their shoulders into firing position. But the noise of operating levers on automatic rifles from behind me confirmed that my acrobats beat the Calderon guards to the draw. The guards conceded to our superior firepower, surrendered their weapons, and opened the gate for our vehicles to enter the compound. Fortunately, with the official Moroccan seal on the Rabat team vehicle, the guards didn't object further to our entry, or call their supervisors for instructions.

While the three crews of seismologists set up their base camps and equipment in Ernesto's yard, I directed my army to return to the vehicles and surround the primary house. I sent Advari and four acrobats to cover the east side with Omar and the other four acrobats and one snake handler to circle around the west side. The Water Man and I set a course for the south entrance. When we reached the south door without opposition, I knew that our quarry had escaped. To be certain, we raced through the house and converged at the north door. From there, we could see the yacht harbor a short distance away. We didn't see anyone running toward the boats or any yacht leaving the harbor. If Calderon had been there, he and his staff had escaped through a passageway of some kind.

I instructed my army to search the house and immediate grounds more thoroughly for any traces of Beth's presence. In the gardener's shack, Advari found a small stool with a "B" traced in the dirt floor behind it. With Beth's love of flowers, it was ironic that she would be held prisoner among Ernesto's potted plants. Obviously, Ernesto had taken her with him. Where they went wasn't obvious. I took some comfort knowing that the Calderons still valued Beth as a hostage. Hopefully, I could reclaim her before her trade-in value depreciated.

I was contemplating the possibility of the Calderons' next move to their warehouses and other facilities in Melilla further east along the coast near the Algerian border when Professor Palmer approached.

"Now that I've seen the place and the action of your people, why are my team and I here?" Palmer asked emphatically. "And, I insist that you tell me immediately if we are in any danger."

"I'm sure when you were first contacted about this expedition, you recognized that this assignment wasn't designed to win a Nobel Prize in seismology for you and your team. Am I right? And, as for immediate danger, the buzzards have flown elsewhere. But, you can be useful if you agree to help. I don't have time for a lengthy discussion, but I'll tell you enough to bring your blood pressure back within normal limits. Are you interested?"

"I'll listen and make up my mind after that," the professor asserted with academic rancor.

"That's fair enough. Based on what I know so far, Ernesto Calderon, the owner of this executive compound and his brother, Gilberto from South America provide guns, drugs, cash, and people to support and fund terrorist networks. They're relative small fry compared to the dealers and suppliers you might learn about in the media at home, but big enough for me to engage while Uncle Sam and professional counter-terrorists take on the varsity players. Currently, Ernesto is holding my wife hostage. I'm here to rescue her, and to inflict as much damage on the Calderon network as possible with the amateur army that you see around me. You and the other seismology teams were requisitioned to help me gain access to this compound. That's all I asked at the time. We gained entry to the estate, so you completed your job, although I'm not prepared to inform the Rabat and Salamancan teams about that yet. You can either go home or help me a bit more. You need to decide your comfort level and how much risk is involved in playing with the Calderons and other vipers we face. The more vipers we dispose of here, the less we need to reckon with on U.S. soil. Take my word for it, my neighborhood is infested with them already."

"Calderon loaned or gifted the villa down the slope to the U.S. Ambassador to Spain to ensure his cooperation, or, at least, his non-interference with any Calderon operations," I continued. "While my army and I check out the ambassador's place for signs of my wife and other evidence, you can decide if you want to help us or go back home. Come find me if you want to help further, or you can return to Tangier and home any time you want without any ill will from me. But, you may hear voices of discontent from fellow Americans and your own gut if the news ever circulates in the future that you had a chance to help secure U.S. territory and citizens and didn't bother."

My speech concluded, I turned and led my troops down the hill toward the ambassador's *mucho* big *casa*. I didn't expect to find anyone there, and I wasn't disappointed. Even the normal skeleton crew of servants was absent. The doors were locked, but a second floor window was partially open. Getting inside wasn't much of a challenge for Omar and his acrobat relatives. I did a quick tour of the upstairs. Later, when

I was strolling through the basement wine cellar, which my army was quickly liberating of its contents for Berber medicinal purposes, Professor Palmer came down the stairs followed by his team.

"After discussing the situation with my team, we decided to help you in Ceuta if we can, but we are not trained soldiers, so don't expect too much from us."

"Actually, I'm not interested in your combat skills. Take a look at this stone foundation and tell me what you see."

"It looks similar to the cellar of the other house," Palmer acknowledged superficially.

"That's a decent start. Take a minute, and tell me what else strikes you. I'll give you a clue. Lift that large flagstone in front of the wine rack."

The professor and his team members moved the stone and scratched around for a few minutes, then he stated somewhat tentatively, "I'm not an archeologist, but it appears that this house was built on top of another layer of much older construction."

"Have you ever been to the Coliseum in Rome and examined some of the original stone and brick work?" I asked, leading him toward the conclusion I wanted him to draw.

"No, I haven't," Palmer replied. "Are you suggesting that Roman ruins are under this foundation?"

"I'm not suggesting anything. Move the stone a little more and tell me what you see."

The professor grunted as he gave the stone a hearty shove and knelt, looking at the opening he made in the floor. In the dim light, he reached into the hole to touch what he couldn't see clearly.

Bath Water and the Baby

"The pipes feel like metal. Are they metal pipes?"

"What kind of metal pipes?" I pursued his partially correct answer.

"I don't know. They look old, but they appear to be in very good condition. Do you know what they are?"

"I'm not an archeologist either, but I've traveled a bit. Putting bits and pieces of information together, I've made some conclusions I believe are valid. To me, it's no secret that the Romans were here. The Romans were everywhere, so that's not a big revelation. But, look how the stones and especially the bricks fit together perfectly. A good guide at the Coliseum in Rome will show you an entrance where the old and newer brickwork is exposed. The bricks here are nearly identical to the old Coliseum bricks before the contractors and later restorers began cutting corners in their reconstruction work. Do you want another guess at the metal pipes now? Think water."

"No, I'm sorry. I don't have a clue," Palmer conceded.

"Everywhere the Romans went water was sure to follow if it wasn't there already. The Romans moved water by . . . on the surface, and by . . . underground? Fill in the blanks," I continued to lead the professor.

"Aqueducts on the surface, and by underground pipes, but I still don't know what kind of metal they used. It looks like steel or aluminum, but I know that can't be. Steel would have rusted by now, it's too heavy to be aluminum, but the pipe is crimped on one side. So, what is it?" Palmer asked, giving up his side of the quiz.

"I believe the metal is lead. If you go to the Roman spa in Bath, England, you'll see similar construction. Lead is heavy, but pliable and durable. The Romans were able to crimp it into a watertight pipe that is still used in Bath today. The pipes are interesting historically, but the stonework remains the most important aspect of this construction to me. Notice what look like curbstones along each side of the stonework," I continued giving Palmer clues.

"Yes, I see that."

"Pipes were okay for moving water into rooms or small pools, but, for public baths and fountains, a lot more water needed to flow a lot faster along aqueducts or underground waterways such as this."

"We have a waterway. All we need is the water. Is that it?" Palmer asked, still not seeing the picture I was painting for him.

"I was leading you into that trap, but I'm glad you went into the cage by yourself. My first guess is that some sort of reservoir lies uphill on the south side of Monte Hacho. My second thought is that the Ermita de San Antonio Mission just below it taps into that water supply, and that the water is cut off somewhere below the mission on the north face of the mountain. If you really want to help us after my army and I leave for Melilla without exposing your team to any danger, go up the hill, pull the plug on the water source if you can find it, count to twenty, and put the plug back in again."

"But, judging from the size of the waterways under this house and Calderon's, won't that volume of water be too much for—? Oh, I understand now. The house should float all the way down the hill to the yacht harbor. That's rather a unique way to flush out your antagonist," Palmer smiled with his arrival at the purpose of our conversation.

"Good. That's my Herculean project for you," I applauded his delayed arrival at my intended purpose. "However, I suggest you don't linger to enjoy your handiwork, or Hercules might get tossed into deep Mediterranean water. If the waterfall works its magic, even the most disinterested town officials will be looking for whomever washed this compound and other homes downhill into the harbor. I thought about a charge of C-4 explosives to redistribute the compound over the landscape, but that approach may draw a crowd before we depart. And with these stiff ocean breezes, I don't want to ignite the entire town. Considering my Chicago connections, I can see the local headlines: 'Mrs. O'Leary's cow kicks C-4 explosive lantern and destroys Ceuta.'"

"That would generate undesirable international headlines. So, flushing the Calderon property and a minimum number of other houses into the Mediterranean appears to be a humane and less newsworthy approach. Now that you know the plan, do you want to participate? If you participate, you have a unique story to tell your grandchildren. If not, you can go home and prepare seismological charts that nobody will read until after a catastrophic event occurs," I added, trying to seduce a positive answer from Palmer.

"You present a very attractive offer, but what if we're caught in the act by the local police? We could spend the rest of our lives in prison here."

"You could, but your lives would be relatively short anyway. So, I wouldn't worry about a long prison term or your cholesterol score. If you're detained and still alive when I finish my chores in Melilla, I'll come back and put in a good word for you with the police. How does that strike you?" I gave a non-answer to Palmer's earnest question.

"And you guarantee that your good word will be sufficient to obtain our release?" Palmer hesitated in his commitment again.

"Based on my experience, *dirhams* trump the value of my word. But, if I don't have enough *dirhams* to spring you initially, I can send my young colleague to tour the marketplace and obtain more. My army needs to start for Melilla now; will you handle things for us here?"

"What about the other two teams of seismologists?" Palmer quibbled again.

"Let them do their thing. Their survey work may be useful to Morocco or Spain in some way. When they get tired or run out of money, they'll go home. My employer has already paid for their time and services the same as you have been compensated."

"And who do you work for?"

"My chief could be your university's dean, for all I know. I stopped asking questions on that topic long ago. I assume that I'm working for a color that Uncle Sam likes and leave it at that. By the way, is that an international cell phone you have?"

"Yes, it's very handy."

"Do you mind if I use it? I would use my own, but the people I'm phoning have caller identification, and I want my call to be a surprise."

"Do you reimburse for your calls?" Palmer asked another non-committal question.

"Certainly, put the charges on your bill," I assured him.

No More Nice Guy

My first call was to Hassan. He didn't answer. My second call was to Paolo in Portugal. He answered.

"Paolo, it's me," I said, expecting him to recognize my voice, which he did. "Where are they holding her? If you know, you'd better tell me now. Otherwise, this will be the last day you spend on earth without ankle chains. I'm extremely disappointed that you joined the Calderon network. You are doing an excellent job with Advari, and you have a baby on the way. I opened up new legitimate business for you and your firm in South America, and you threw it away. What's wrong with your head? Your family has all the money it needs for the next seven generations," I rambled without giving Paolo a chance to respond.

"I know I did wrong, but it was easy money, and other shippers do it," Paolo confessed. "But you must believe me, I know nothing else about the Calderons' business. Who is the woman you talk about?"

"My wife, Paolo," I answered with rising anger. "Calderon had Beth in Ceuta for a while. Now, I believe he has moved her eastward to Melilla. Do you know any place around Melilla where he would likely hide her?"

"I know he has property and buildings there, but I am only involved in shipments to or from Portugal. I do not know what he does in Morocco. Will you report me to the Portuguese Policia or Interpol?"

"I might if I can find a law enforcement agency less corrupt than the Calderon network. Reporting you will only get you killed, and you need to live for your family and Advari. I'll think of an extremely unpleasant penance for you. Meanwhile, if I call for help, or you learn that both Beth and I are in trouble, you'd better help in any way you can. In your situation, I'm the only hope you have of seeing your grandchildren," I told Paolo angrily.

"I am so ashamed. Yes, I will help you if you need me," Paolo conceded as I had hoped.

My next call was to Chauncey in Peru. I didn't worry about what time it was in Lima.

"Chauncey, don't say anything, just listen. I don't care if you are overworked, sick, drunk, or overweight. I know you're a weak person, but I tried to help you many times as a friend. Now, you fouled up almost beyond repair. Your redemption or death is at hand, depending on how you respond to me."

"I don't know what you mean, old boy. What do you want from me?" he asked vaguely.

"You sold your soul to the Calderons by skimming off part of their illegal shipments. Then, you corrupted a good man like Paolo to move drugs on your own. Do I need to add other charges to the list, or is that sufficient material for your arrest by the police, or worse, becoming a prisoner of the Calderons? Beyond that, I'll scald what's left of your miserable hide if you don't tell me what I need to know. Where is Ernesto holding my wife?"

"I'm afraid I don't understand," Chauncey answered coolly again.

"If I have to repeat the question, Chauncey, you will die the most horrible death that I can arrange. We were close friends, but you betrayed my trust once too often. Even worse, you betrayed thousands who suffer from the drugs you aided the Calderons to ship out of Peru unimpeded. I chased Ernesto out of Ceuta, and I'm certain he ran for Melilla with my wife as a hostage. I want two things from you in exchange for your freedom and, perhaps, your life. First, I want to know where Ernesto is hiding my wife. Second, I want you and Gilberto to be in Melilla in two days."

"You know that Gilberto rarely travels outside of South America. I don't know what I'd say to induce him to come to Morocco on short notice."

"If he isn't with Ernesto in Morocco already based on what Juanita told me about his extended trip to Europe or North Africa, you could tell him that his brother is dead, and that you can identify his killer. Hopefully, that will be true by the time you arrive."

"Yes, that might work, but he is very cautious. What if he refuses to come?" Chauncey tried to weasel out of my tightening noose.

"You could add that rivals will take over his European and African operations if he doesn't come to take charge immediately. That may infiltrate his black soul more than his brother's death. As a bonus incentive for you, if you and Gilberto don't arrive in Melilla in two days, I will call Ron to send someone to Lima to find you. You remember Ron's Aymaran Indian guide, Manco, don't you? Ron has wanted you to disappear for a long time, even after I told him that you helped me. I'm listening very hard, Chauncey. You'd better say something I want to hear," I stated my final proposal.

"All I know is that Ernesto has your wife hidden in a cave somewhere outside Melilla, possibly near one of his hashish factories close to the Algerian border."

"If Ernesto has her in a cave with bats, I'll let her kill you, Ernesto, and Gilberto herself. She hates bats more than getting her slacks dirty sitting in a tool shed or cave somewhere. She will invent a death for each of you more horrible than anything I can invent. I'll sell tickets and applaud when you die. One way or another, Chauncey, you've run out of options to avoid an immediate career change. The fact that you take care of your ailing mother will not save you this time," I stated my terms emphatically.

"Is it that bad between us now?" Chauncey tried to negotiate better treatment from me.

"If anything, I understated your precarious position, and it'll only get worse if you foul this up because I won't help you. To confirm your situation, don't ask Paolo for help. He's on notice for his complicity with Calderon and you, and he has a baby coming soon. I made it clear to him that he has no choice but to inform me if you contact him or try to intimidate him in any way."

"What assurances do I have if I help you?" Chauncey persisted in his negotiations.

"I'm glad to hear you say that because when you start to bargain and whine, I know the gravity of your situation is finally making an impact on you. The only thing I'll promise is to kill you quickly rather than hand you over to Manco or to my Berber warriors who will practice their ancient art of slow torture and painful death. So, full cooperation with me is your only option. I hope you have no other questions?"

"No, I understand completely now. Can I ask your forgiveness? I never intended that your wife should be harmed in any way."

"Unintended consequences for someone of your intelligence and experience don't move me, Chauncey. You know very well what kind of people the Calderons are and how they operate. Forgiveness from me doesn't buy you cooler accommodations in hell. You're going there in any event. So, get busy on Gilberto. You don't have much time. If he's already in the neighborhood here, you'd better discover ways to keep him where I can deal with him."

Finished with my conversation, I handed the phone back to Professor Palmer.

"You play rough. You have a disarmingly different personality than one gets on first impression," the professor declared as if he were a psychology major instead of an earth scientist. Let me know in advance if you're getting angry with me. I'll leave town immediately."

"I only behave that way around old friends. Don't let it bother you. I need to start my army on the road east. Are you clear on what you need to do here?"

"Yes, and be assured that I'll make every effort to accomplish it. I don't want you or the police after me. But, understand that neither of us knows for certain if the old Roman waterway is still connected all the way down the mountainside."

"You have a point. In that case, I will leave a few emergency flares with you. If nothing else works, light a flare, and toss it into something flammable in or near the house. I recommend that you or your team throw the flares from a running start. Thanks for your help. Good luck. Take the ferry from Tangier to Algeciras, and fly out from Spain when you go home. That is the quickest way, and you don't want to linger after your work is finished here. Anything else?"

"Do you know how my team and I were selected for this junket?"

"Do any of you have family in the Turkey River area in Iowa?"

"Why, yes, I grew up there before I accepted the position at the university and moved to Iowa City. My assistants come from the Quad Cities area."

"There's your answer to the selection process," I replied obliquely. "I'd like to chat more, but I really need to go."

We shook hands, and that was the last time I saw Professor Palmer. Ten minutes later, my army was on the road toward Melilla. Later, I learned from Professor Palmer's letter to me when I returned to the States that although the old Roman underground waterway had not been used for centuries, it worked fine, but not for our purposes. When Professor Palmer's team unplugged the old waterway on the mountain above the compound, the rushing water tore a trench six feet deep and three feet wide between Calderon's villa and the ambassador's house, but the rushing water did no other damage. However, the flares worked as expected for Palmer to torch the Calderon and ambassador's villas.

We were on the road to Melilla (or Russadir, as it was known to the founding Phoenicians) about a half hour when I poked Advari to exchange seats with the Water Man so that I could interrogate the Water Man about the general and specific layout of the villa, warehouses, and surrounding terrain of Melilla.

"Water Man, what do you know about the tunnels and caves around Melilla?" I asked specifically so that he couldn't deny that caves and tunnels existed in that area.

"Yes, caves and tunnels are in Melilla. But, south in mountains has many more mines and tunnels. Biggest cave is in Atlas Mountains little way from Taza called Gouffre du Friouato. Here is said we have biggest cave in North Africa. Cave goes further than people want to go. Nobody knows how big. Past 300 meters, nobody goes there."

"Taza is a long way from Melilla on my map. What caves or tunnels are closer?"

"Near Midelt also in Atlas, we have Gorges d'Aouli, which had many mines for copper, silver, and lead."

"Do people go there?" I asked.

"In past, people go there. Now barricades, so people no go so much."

"That is still too far south. What is around Melilla itself? Anything?"

"Closer is Berkane, which has La Grotte de Chameau and very big caves all around. Most closed now. What else you want?" he asked as he detected the exasperated look on my face mixed with the firm belief that I knew he was playing with me.

"Thanks for the geography lesson, but what caves or tunnels are in or close to the town of Melilla itself?" I asked, continuing to narrow the boundaries for a more precise answer.

"In Melilla town, there is Las Cuevas del Conventico, many caves and tunnels."

"Who goes there?" I asked as I continued to fine-tune the answer I wanted.

"Everybody goes there. Tourists like you. Good to see and museum too."

"The caves are open to tourists, you say?"

"Yes, many guides take people around to see caves."

"Does Calderon have tunnels or caves on his land that tourists do not see?" I finally asked the jackpot question I had been leading up to for the last twenty minutes.

"Water Man does not know that," he said slipping away from my trap again.

"Well, if we find any caves or tunnels on Calderon's property, I will send you in first so that you will remember where they are in the future," I admonished while confirming to him once again that I didn't buy his lack of knowledge about Calderon's possible hiding places for Beth.

"Do not look for big Calderon place like Ceuta," the Water Man volunteered. "Melilla is small town only."

"That's good information. Where is Calderon's place from the ocean? Old town? New town?" I asked, hoping for more information now that he let slip some worthwhile intelligence.

"New town west of harbor is place of Calderon villa. Old town called Melilla la Vieja is big fort and harbor."

I had another question ready for the Water Man about the layout of the Calderon villa when a helicopter thundered directly over our three-vehicle caravan from the east, then turned sharply north out over the Mediterranean toward Spain. We were near the town of El-Jebha at the time. The Water Man was instantly transformed into a panicky plate of mush.

"That is very bad happening," was all the Water Man could articulate.

"Why, what was that all about?" I asked him eagerly, almost threateningly.

"That was Calderon helicopter. Now, he knows certain that we come to Melilla to meet our death. Allah protect me!" he wailed.

"Was Calderon in that helicopter?" I asked loudly, hoping to keep the Water Man from going catatonic on me.

"No can say for certain," the Water Man babbled. "Calderon has many planes. But, surely that helicopter will send message to him that we come."

"You're probably right about that," I replied more softly now, trying to calm the Water Man as I took a quick look at my map.

"Advari, tell the driver to take the next road southeast toward Ketama," I ordered, but discovered that my army wasn't ready for a briskly executed right turn within a few meters after Advari relayed my instructions to the driver.

Fortunately, we were in the lead van. I heard the tires squeal on the two vans behind us as they replicated our sharp change of direction with the added difficulty of having absolutely no warning and the dust of our vehicle in their faces. I felt comfortable thinking that our change of direction would cause Calderon to wonder where my army went if he sent other search planes to determine our proximity to Melilla. Then, the Water Man, the driver, Omar, and the two acrobats riding with us all began talking in low tones, and all at the same time. I caught only a word or two, and I was not totally sure about those.

"Advari, what's going on with the crew? What are they talking about?" I asked more than a little perplexed.

"They say you made a good decision to confuse Calderon by turning off the road to Melilla. But the Ketama region, especially the town of Issaguen, where we are going now, is the center of the hashish smuggling area. We cannot stay there tonight because we barely have enough guns to protect ourselves if we pass through the town driving very fast. They hope that you lead us somewhere else, please."

I grabbed my map quickly to determine another line of advance for my army. The absence of alternative coastal and east-west roads in this area didn't help our progress toward Melilla, although the absence of options certainly reduced my decision-processing time.

"Advari, tell the driver to continue toward Ketama. When we get there, he should turn northeast toward the coast and Al-Hoceima. We cannot get there tonight, so we'll turn off the road, and sleep somewhere in the woods. That's the best I can do. If anyone has a better plan, I'm willing to hear it."

After a few minutes of buzzing, I detected a lighter tone of agreement, which was confirmed when Advari said, "They say okay to your plan. They want to stop soon to tell the plan to our people in the other vans so that they do not become frightened and desert us. They also want you to tell everyone to have their weapons ready. They can find a quiet place in the forest to turn off the road to eat and sleep."

"Good, Advari, tell them if they do that, I will stand guard with my silent rifle tonight."

When Advari related that information to them, they all applauded and cheered, including the driver who took his hands off the wheel and his eyes off the curving road a lot longer than was safe or comfortable for the passengers (especially me). When the road widened enough for us to pull off, we stopped and informed the passengers of the other vans of our plan. Agreement was unanimous. Nature calls completed, the men readied their weapons, and we drove toward Ketama. We exceeded any safe speed long before we reached the outskirts of town. We arrived at Issaguen after dark, drove through without causing anyone to pay undue attention to us, and headed northeast through the pine forest and the foothills of the Rif Mountains without paying attention to the single-engine plane circling high overhead.

About twenty kilometers northeast of Ketama, we pulled off the road into a particularly dense pine grove that hid our campfires from the road. The men wasted no time warming leftovers from our restaurant stop in the morning, or cooking whatever food they had brought with them or scavenged somewhere along the way. Within an hour, the men had eaten, found comfortable places under the trees, and were in their blankets for the night. As promised, I removed my sniper rifle from its case, attached a night scope, put on a heavier jacket against the light mist and fog that began to envelop the forest and surrounding hills, and prepared myself mentally to spend the night guarding my flock from any nocturnal predators.

Night Fight

As the mist grew heavier, I zipped my jacket higher and kept walking to keep myself from sitting down or falling asleep. As I made my rounds of the camp about 0200, I began hearing rodents and other small animals scurrying past me from the south. That was strange because small critters usually hole up on a damp chilly night. Something coming from the south through the woods had disturbed them. I decided to circle our camp in that direction and see what was causing the mini-mammal migration. By that time, the flames of the campfires had burned down to glowing embers aided by the steady mist. The fires didn't provide enough light to see beyond the perimeter of the camp. On the plus side, I wasn't concerned about casting a shadow.

About fifty yards south of the camp, I stopped, knelt down on one knee behind a tree, and listened intently. At first, I heard nothing but the light wind through the trees, but imagined that I heard all sorts of threatening sounds. I was about to stand up and continue walking when I definitely heard a twig snap a short distance to my right. I stayed motionless for an eternity without hearing any following sound except the rising wind through the trees. Then, I heard a distinct footstep on pine needles directly in front of me. I raised my rifle slowly, and peered through the night scope to see a man in dark clothing carrying an automatic rifle walking directly toward me.

One breath in and out, a second breath in and hold, and my first silent shot was on its way. Through the night scope, I saw the man crumple where he stood without uttering a sound. I didn't hear his body hit the ground because I was busy working the bolt action to put another round in the chamber. That done, I looked to my right to see if I could locate the invader who had stepped on the twig earlier. By the time I located him, he was only twenty yards away. At that range, I could have slid the bullet down the barrel and dropped it on his head. But there was no point in allowing myself to have careless thoughts at a time like this. Two breaths, hold, and my second shot sped on its way with the same lethal result.

Now was decision time. If Calderon had sent these night invaders, more than two had to be in the area because, at a minimum, he knew our general, if not our actual, numbers from his plane spotters and ground spies in the towns that we drove through on our way toward Melilla. Two gunmen were not an overwhelming force for a night attack even with the element of surprise. *Should I wake the camp and create chaos without knowing the number and location of other invaders, or should I continue my silent hunt?* A burst of automatic rifle fire from the camp, then another and another, gave me my answer. The acrobats were skilled Berber warriors first, and acrobats second. They were awake and defending themselves. I dodged around the far side of a tree before I became a shadowy target for my riflemen.

The activity of taking cover jogged my brain to realize that the invaders must have transportation waiting somewhere. Unless the gunfire had chased off any waiting vehicles, they had to be parked along the road south of me. I was on my feet and running like a rabbit through the trees, hoping that I wouldn't catch friendly fire in the back before I was over the hill and out of range. Forests in the States typically have underbrush growing that makes a sprint through the woods impossible. Europeans clear their forests of underbrush to encourage faster growth of desirable trees and to reduce the danger of forest fires. Fortunately, this was a European-style forest in Morocco, and I made good time through it, aiming to come out near a bend in the road about a hundred yards southwest of our camp. I couldn't have run that hundred yards any faster than if I were a thief running from the police with a stolen computer.

My instincts were good. Before I reached the edge of the woods, I saw the outline of two, dark-colored, pickup trucks on the far side of the road facing southwest for a quick retreat. One driver was in his truck while the other stood alongside talking to him. The waiting drivers had heard the gunfire from the camp and probably were debating what to do. I thought I could speed their decision process. I knew I could not calm my breathing quickly enough after my hundred-yard dash, so I leaned my rifle and myself against a tree for support. The more I tried to relax, the closer I came to exploding. But, I aimed as carefully as I could under adverse conditions and pulled the trigger. My aim and the results were satisfactory to bring down the standing driver, but my judgment was poor. Had I been thinking more clearly, my first target would have been the driver in the truck. Before I could load another round, the driver left his fallen buddy in the road and took off around the curve and out of sight. Within a short time, Calderon surely would receive complete information about that night's events.

As I walked down to the driver lying in the road, I told myself that if none of his raiders returned, Calderon would know conclusively that his night attack hadn't succeeded. Under the current circumstances, Calderon wouldn't know the extent of his success or failure until he debriefed the escaped driver or the driver called in the information. In either case, that would buy time for my army to regroup and clear the area. Searching the fallen driver for identification took my mind off thinking that a few minutes earlier this corpse had been a living, breathing, human being with hopes, plans, and maybe family responsibilities. I tried to alibi my shot selection of this driver with thoughts that I was displaying my strike force's incompetence to Calderon as envisioned in Sun Tzu's principles of warfare. Setting that distraction aside, I found no documents other than maps of northern Morocco that were inconclusive in directly linking the forest invaders to the Calderons. I put the maps in my jacket pocket, loaded the driver into the back of the pickup truck, and drove toward camp too tired to feel any emotion for him or myself.

As I neared the camp, I sounded the horn repeatedly to ensure that absolutely nobody mistook me for another invader. Advari and Omar came running toward me as I crunched to a stop twenty yards before I had intended. The truck was out of gas, diesel, petrol, camel grease, or whatever fuel it ran on. My army and I were not the only ones in this war displaying intentional or unintentional incompetence.

"We thought you were dead or captured," Advari sobbed as his tears overwhelmed him and he grabbed me tightly around the waist.

"Certainly, we thought you were killed in the forest," Omar said, adding details to Advari's admission of concern.

"We happy you are here," the Water Man said a few steps ahead of the others in my army as he strode up to shake my hand. "We count ten dead," he demonstrated, holding up the correct number of fingers and thumbs.

"Make that thirteen with one escapee," I adjusted the Water Man's body count. "Did any invader escape from here? Is anyone hurt?" I asked quickly, but not soon enough to avoid some frowns among the senior members of the group, who recognized the downside of my escapee statistic.

"We okay that nobody escape from us," the Water Man declared. "We okay that with our mans nobody is shot. What to do with bodies here?"

"I'm glad that all of you are okay," I told my army, now grouped in a semicircle around me. "Calderon knows or soon will know that we are here and that he has combat losses. We will go to Al-Hoceima to eat breakfast as soon as all the equipment is loaded. Then, we will continue directly to Melilla because we no longer have the element of surprise, if we ever had it. We have no shovels with us, so put the bodies in the back of the pickup truck, and cover them with a tarp. Hopefully, the local police or someone will find them soon, but not too soon. Make sure that the campfires are totally out and that nothing gets left behind, including any expended rifle shell casings. After everyone and everything is in the vans, we will wait for Advari and Omar to sweep the campsite toward the road with pine branches to erase as many footprints as they can. Let's all move quickly so we can leave before sunrise and before traffic picks up along this road."

While the men were breaking camp, I studied the maps I had found on the driver and in the pickup more closely. We would go directly to Melilla from Al-Hoceima as I had told the men, but that didn't mean we all had to arrive in Melilla at the same time. Splitting my forces held some risk, as Lt. Colonel Custer learned at the Battle of the Little Bighorn. But, I could hold that decision until later.

Al-Hoceima was a Spanish-styled town of over 100,000 people with a decent range of hotels and restaurants for my army to bathe and have breakfast. The more important attractions for me were its airport and the presence of military personnel from the Spanish bases on the islands of Penon de Velez de la Gomera in the bay to the west, and Penon de Alhucemas to the northeast. Of immense interest to me was a guest I encountered in the lobby of the Hotel al-Khhouzama. He appeared to be in a hurry to check out until I accosted him at the cashier's desk.

"Hassan, I had hoped to meet you in Ceuta, but I'm even more delighted to meet you here," I announced, approaching him from behind and carefully blocking any escape route for him.

"I also am glad to see you, my friend," Hassan replied turning halfway around to acknowledge his recognition of my voice.

"But, as you can see, I am in a hurry now."

"That doesn't matter. We're always in a hurry going here and there. But, I won't detain you long because I'm in a rush myself. All I need is air transportation that I believe you can arrange for me on short notice."

"Señor," the cashier intervened. "The hotel is glad to help our guests and their associates with all their transportation needs."

"Gracias, Señor," I replied. "But I'm sure my friend here has contacts in the neighborhood who can fulfill my transportation needs and possibly help resolve a problem in his family at the same time. Don't you think so, Hassan?"

"What do you want from me?" Hassan asked, trying to smile but not quite getting there.

"I need to reach Melilla *pronto*. I need military or private aircraft to fly us to Nador and ground transportation from there the remaining thirteen kilometers north across the Spanish border to Melilla if I can't fly directly into Melilla from here. See, that's not a difficult request for you."

"For how many people?" Hassan asked conceding he understood I wouldn't leave him alone until he consented to my request.

"Ten, if possible, but not less than seven," I replied quickly not disclosing the real count was thirteen, including me. "A large helicopter could carry seven to ten. A fixed-wing plane could carry ten or more if we have additional passengers returning with us."

By this time, the colonel standing patiently behind us in line to check out of the hotel failed completely in his attempt to remain disinterested in our conversation. Relief came when Hassan turned and addressed the colonel, "Excuse me, *Commandante*, I know many of the Spanish military officers in the area, but I have not met you. Is this a new command for you?"

"I am Colonel Sebastian," the officer introduced himself. "I am the new Commander of Spanish Military Operations in North Africa. I could not help but overhear part of your conversation with your friend about his need for military transportation. Perhaps I can be of service if I have more information about what is needed, why, and when."

"We need not bother you with our problems, Colonel," Hassan replied.

"On the contrary, Hassan, don't turn down an offer of help to rescue my wife and your son from criminals as minor problems," I interjected. "That's not only poor manners, but dreadful combat strategy and conduct for a friend."

"What is this, your wife is a hostage of criminals in this area? You are American, am I correct?" the colonel asked me as he became fully engaged in the conversation.

"My language skills are too poor to deny it," I admitted. "However, your English is surprisingly good," I noted.

"My son is a student in America. My wife and I enjoy visiting him and your country very much. Tell me more about how I might help you, Señor—actually both of you," the colonel stated with apparent concern, much to Hassan's chagrin.

In a few sentences, I outlined the salient points for my need to get to Melilla to recover Beth from wherever she was being held by Calderon, and possibly extract Hassan's son as a bonus. I told the colonel of the proposed plan for my acrobat army, which brought a hint of a smile to the corners of his mouth.

"You developed a difficult strategy for your small group, Señor," Colonel Sebastian remarked. "May I suggest that you consider very carefully my offer to replace your small army with my troops to ensure positive results for both captives, and to prevent any mishaps along the way to them or any other innocent parties?"

"I accept whatever help you can provide with one change," I said after deliberating about five nanoseconds. "I accept your military help as a supplement rather than as a replacement for my paramilitary forces. See, Hassan, it pays to be polite to strangers."

"You do not understand fully, my friend," Hassan retorted. "You continue to forget that your wife is not the only hostage of the Calderons. They have my son, and Ernesto threatened to kill him if I assist you in any way. Also, your plan treats my son as secondary to rescuing your wife. Our priorities differ."

"Then we have even more reason to accept the colonel's offer to cover the full range of our needs. With Gilberto on his way toward Melilla from South America, or already there, with the colonel's help we can bag both Calderon brothers, shut down their operations in North Africa, and rescue our family members. I have confidence in the fighting spirit of my Berber acrobats, but remember the old French saying, '*Dieu est toujours pour les plus gros bataillons,*' that 'God is always on the side with the most battalions.'"[2]

"Colonel, how can we integrate our activities to accomplish our combined objectives?" I asked while turning away from Hassan. "I won't allow you to do everything yourself, but I look forward to your assistance," I added to ensure the colonel understood that his was only a supporting, diversionary, or transportation role when it came to rescuing Beth and Hassan's son.

TOO GOOD TO BE TRUE

"If you wish to drive to Nador or to the Spanish border with your men, you will be in position to receive your wife and any other hostages without your people being in harm's way while my men overcome the smugglers. For that reason, I must insist that you do not cross the border and come into Spanish territory at Melilla or anywhere else. Is that understood?"

"I have no choice but to accept your terms," I acquiesced and lied at the same time catching his use of the word "smugglers" when he allegedly had no detailed information about the Calderons' job descriptions. But, I wasn't about to discourage an offer of help at a critical time. So, I continued the charade by asking "How soon will you be able to assemble and move your people into Melilla?"

"By the time you and your people drive to Nador in your vans, my men should be in position to arrest the smugglers," the colonel stated confidently. (Colonel Sebastian had to be psychic, intoxicated, or thoroughly informed to know our mode of transportation. If the conversation continued, he might recite our license plate numbers too.) "To do that, I must start now," the colonel said as he finished checking out of the hotel.

"Good, unless you have anything else, I'll collect my army and start for Nador *pronto*," I recited a partial truth to the colonel as he started to walk away.

"Hassan, do you want to come with us? We can find room for you somewhere."

"No, I believe I should stay with the colonel and help him identify the Calderons and members of their network in addition to my son who probably is now in more danger than your wife if Ernesto has influence with Colonel Sebastian. You didn't think of that, did you?"

"What if something unravels and Calderon and his men attempt to escape into Moroccan territory through Nador? You'd be helpful in identifying the Calderon henchmen who we should corral," I proposed while I slowly became aware of the possible severe consequences to Hassan and his son if I had exposed them as disloyal to Calderon through my statements to Sebastian.

"I think you are less concerned about henchmen escaping than you are about rescuing your wife, as you should be," Hassan rebutted. "Your Water Man certainly can identify the Calderon people for you. Consequently, I repeat my belief that I am more valuable with the colonel."

"Okay, I definitely see your point. Play it your way," I agreed without changing my mind about who should have the lead and supporting roles in this program. I was the only one I could trust to rescue my wife. Hassan was right. Rescuing his son was a distant second on my to-do list.

For my purposes, leaving Hassan with Colonel Sebastian was a bigger miscue than I anticipated, as I would discover shortly. But, to maintain the pace of the chase at that moment, I trotted out of the lobby and assembled my army on the front sidewalk. I explained that we now had military help for an assault on the Calderons' facilities in Melilla. Our first action would be to drive to Nador to block the Calderons from escaping the colonel's troops by crossing the border from Spanish into Moroccan territory. My army received that news more soberly than I expected, but we started for Nador without anyone verbally raising objections. With the absence of a coastal highway in this area of Morocco, we drove southeast through the Rif Mountains from Al-Hoceima to Midar, then east to Driouch, and finally northeast to Nador, which is located thirteen kilometers directly south on the main road and border crossing from the Spanish enclave of Melilla. The drive through the twisting mountain roads ate up most of the morning. We arrived in Nador early in the afternoon. We wolfed down some food at a restaurant there, and then drove the thirteen kilometers to be as close as possible to Melilla.

My doubt pangs had increased as we approached Nador. As we waited in the vans at Melilla, I realized that I had missed key signals in Al-Hoceima. I re-ran a mental tape of Hassan's and the colonel's conversations. I remembered Hassan telling me that his son had accepted the life of a drug addict and voluntarily worked for Calderon to maintain his drug supply. If so, Calderon had no reason to hold Hassan's son hostage if Hassan and his son were accomplices. Second, I recalled the detailed information the colonel apparently had about my army's numbers and mode of transportation. Third, Hassan possibly stayed with the colonel so that we couldn't use him as a hostage, not that Ernesto was concerned about ransoming anyone working for him if that meant inconveniencing himself. Fourth, I realized that Hassan needed to stay with Sebastian to protect his son from becoming a victim of any agreement or relationship between the colonel and the Calderons. Finally, I fully appreciated the extent of the Calderons' reach into all facets of civilian and military organizations on multiple continents. Indeed, the brothers had constructed an extensive network, and I shouldn't consider them as junior varsity players under any circumstances.

CRASHING THE BORDER

With my cranial cubicle cleared, I jumped out of the van and shouted to the drivers and passengers of the other two vehicles to hide their weapons. We were going across the Spanish-Moroccan border into Melilla. Then, I jumped back into the lead van and instructed the driver to floor the gas pedal and drive north, accompanied by cheers echoing from the entire convoy.

"What we do?" the Water Man asked in absolute confusion.

"Once past the border guards, we are going directly to the Calderon villa. I am counting on you to guide us there."

"I am not there many times, but I find it surely," the Water Man declared.

"I definitely hope so, Water Man, because my wife's continued existence depends on it. I'm sorry to pressure you, but sometimes I need time to overcome my own deficiencies when everyone I meet is an enemy in disguise."

After our passports, accompanied by effectively positioned *euros* or *dirhams* between the pages were accepted by the border guards on both sides of the crossing, the Water Man directed the drivers on the route to the Calderon villa. After a few missed turns, we arrived at the villa to find that the Spanish Army had arrived earlier and seemingly had taken charge of the area.

Momentarily, I felt relieved when I saw the colonel and Hassan near the front entrance of the villa as we drove up.

"We anticipated that you would not be satisfied sitting at the border very long, and we expected your arrival. In fact, you are a few minutes late," Hassan stated bluntly.

"Have you located my wife?" was my only comment.

"The Calderons and their enforcers are in military custody," the colonel explained. "They informed us that your wife and other hostages were released in the desert yesterday," he continued. "That is all we know at this point. Now that you are here, we can organize a search party to find them."

"Do you know the whereabouts of an American diplomat named Chauncey? He should have arrived here from Peru with or shortly after Gilberto Calderon. If so, I want to speak to him," I replied forcefully.

Colonel Sebastian and Hassan looked at each other hesitantly before the colonel answered.

"I believe the man you want is being interrogated at our La Vieja headquarters as we speak. We can escort you there."

"No thanks, we will find our way there if you inform your men not to interfere with my companions and me while we conduct business on your base. I assume you are holding the Calderons there too."

"The Calderons are being detained elsewhere, and Hassan's son is under protective custody at another location," the colonel stated slyly.

"You might have more control if you detain the Calderons somewhere outside their stronghold. I agree with your statement that they are not here," I barked angrily as I turned and ran toward the vans.

Before I reached them, my army fully recognized by my behavior that Hassan and the colonel had reasons of their own not to help us. They would not allow the Calderons to become our prisoners under any circumstances. Once again, it was our war to finish.

"What we to do now?" the Water Man asked as he correctly gauged the situation.

"First, we need to talk to a man at Spanish Army Headquarters in La Vieja, the Old Town. Do you know how to get there?" I demanded of the Water Man without directly answering his question.

"We find it," the Water Man declared, shaken by my building rage.

"We'd better, my wife's life is at stake."

"Then, we go fast," the Water Man promised as he urged the driver into action.

We arrived at the Spanish Army Headquarters in a few minutes and parked our vans in the "No Parking" area in front of the building.

"Bring your weapons," I ordered my army in the absence of any signs that prohibited carrying loaded firearms into the headquarters building.

For the first time that day, the acrobats looked convincingly happy as if they subconsciously remembered their Berber heritage as warriors despite possibly being outnumbered three or four to one by Spanish soldiers in the area.

"Advari, tell the officer in charge that we want to see Chauncey, and, if that request is honored promptly, we will present no problem for anyone here. Then, have the men collect all the weapons in the building that they can find. We will return them as soon as I finish talking to Chauncey and we are ready to leave."

After Advari relayed my message to the officer in charge, a soldier opened a door leading to the holding cells in the basement. The colonel had efficiently notified his staff of my intentions. I handed my rifle to Advari, instructed him and my army to stay alert, and followed the soldier down the stairs to Chauncey's cell.

A Friend Left Behind

"Have you come to my rescue?" Chauncey asked hopefully as he saw me approach down the corridor.

"I have no miracles for you unless you tell me what happened to Beth. To demonstrate my good faith, I left all my weapons upstairs so that I wouldn't kill you on the spot. Start talking, Chauncey," I ordered as ferociously as I could while maintaining a firm grip on my earnest desire to blast Chauncey where he stood.

"You have to understand," Chauncey started. "My life is no longer my own. Once the Calderons have you, they have you for life. I was foolish to start with them to acquire easy money that wouldn't harm anyone. Now look at me. I am a disgraced diplomat of the United States sitting in a Spanish Army jail not knowing what will happen to me."

"I might feel sympathetic if you answer my one question with extreme accuracy. Where is Beth?"

"I don't know how reliable my information is, but yesterday I overheard Ernesto tell Gilberto that your wife was taken to a grotto south of here. Then, the soldiers put me in here."

"That doesn't help much. My people told me that the hills south of here have many caves, tunnels, and hiding places for smugglers. Think harder because you know how I get when I need information and it doesn't arrive on time," I insisted.

"They also talked about a town near the Algerian border with a name something like Sadie. I am sorry. I am so upset I cannot think straight," Chauncey pleaded.

"If you're dead, you won't be able to think at all. The map shows a small town called Saidia near the Algerian border, or a cave called La Grotte de Chameau southeast of Berkane. Which is it?"

"The Grotte sounds familiar to me, but the town was different than the one you mentioned," Chauncey continued to bargain for his life with bits of information.

"Okay, how about Taforalt or the Zegzel Gorge?"

"That could be it. Taforalt sounds right!" Chauncey jumped at the chance to save his worthless hide.

"It better be, or I will let my Berber tribesmen skin you alive and roast you over an open fire. And that will be the closest you will ever come to being Saint Joan of Arc."

"I truly hope you find your wife. If you can forgive me, please take me with you, or at least, come back and get me out of here."

"Count on it, Chauncey. If I can't find Beth, I'll come back for you. Meanwhile, stay put, and pray that I do the right thing. If I have to hunt for you, you'll regret asking me to help you. Then, you'll become an unforgettable example of Berber justice."

I ran upstairs to where I had left my army. A stalemate existed in a siege between the Spanish soldiers and my army. Apparently, they had not gained control of all the weapons in the building as I had instructed. The acrobats had some soldiers cornered, while several Spanish soldiers had the snake handlers surrounded.

"We are done here for now, let's go," I announced to all parties.

"Where are we going?" Advari asked for all.

"If you're done with your playmates, I'll tell you when we are on the road. Take the ammo clips out of your rifles and move back toward the door," I suggested as a way of disengaging the potential combatants while preserving the option for reopening hostilities quickly if necessary. Fortunately for all participants, my exit plan worked.

When we were safely on the road past the Spanish border and Nador and heading southeast toward Berkane, I asked the Water Man, "In one of our conversations, which seems like years ago, you told me about a grotto near Berkane. Hopefully, that is where my wife is."

"Yes, I told you about the Grotte de Chameau, but no public can go there."

"Okay, but you natives must know another way into the cave. Am I right?"

"Sure, we look for wife through other passage."

"If she's not there, we'll have few chances to find her anywhere else."

"We go southwest from Berkane to Taforalt to big entrance one time, then we see around side way," the Water Man suggested giving me options to consider.

The Water Man's mention of Taforalt coincided with Chauncey's story, so either both were telling the truth, or both weren't. I would find out soon enough. I was anxious because we would waste a lot of time if Beth wasn't there. Time was our enemy in our search for Beth as well as in allowing the Calderons and their cohort to devise other troubles for us.

About ten kilometers east of Taforalt, we arrived at the main entrance to the cave. We couldn't miss it. It was huge. I instructed everyone except Advari and the Water Man to stay in the vans. I wanted to check for recent footprints, if I could find any, without having them obliterated by my army. I didn't find anything resembling Beth's petite shoe size around the front entrance.

"Okay, Water Man, show me the side entrance. I can't find anything definitive here," I informed him.

"Path is up and down," he advised. "Must watch good or fall down. I go first?"

"No, I'll lead to look for footprints, but you two stay close to catch me if I stumble. If you fall and land on me, I don't guarantee absolute success in being able to catch you."

From the main entrance to the cave and along the path, I noticed two recent sets of booted male footprints, judging by their size, with one set overlapping part of the other set. Both sets maintained regular spacing and made deep impressions in the sand, or dislocated a sizeable amount of gravel and small stones when those were underfoot. At first, I didn't know how to interpret the tracks other than to surmise that they were made by two husky men with one following the other. Because of irregularities in the gait, one or both of them could have been drunk. I couldn't find evidence of Beth's track until we reached the side entrance to the cave.

"Water Man, look at this!" I shouted at the Water Man, who was standing behind me as I saw Beth's footprints suddenly appear out of nowhere at the hidden side entrance to the cave.

Now, I could interpret the trail of footprints. Finding her footprints at the cave entrance meant that she was alive, able to stand, and her feet were not shackled. Those were better conditions than I had expected.

CATCHING UP WITH BETH

"I see, but I no understand," the Water Man admitted.

"Look," I explained to him. "Two men carried her to the cave because their boots made deep impressions in the sand, and they maintained a consistent interval. The man in back stepped on the tracks of the first man. Their weaving back and forth tells me that Beth was conscious, maybe wrapped in a carpet or bound, and fighting all the way. Sure enough, look here. They brought her to the cave entrance, but they didn't get her inside. If she thought bats were in the cave, they would never get her in there alive. Look, she broke free, and she went that way," I said, pointing to a trail that was obvious to me for at least twenty yards.

"How do you know is wife for certain?"

"Over forty years of experience with the way she does business—that's how I know, Water Man," I answered. "She ran toward that field of wildflowers. She loves flowers as much as she hates bats. So, she was drawn toward a place of comfort after her ordeal. Her second priority was to find something to eat. So, she aimed for the orchard over there. This broken piece of prickly pear is more confirmation. We spent a day with a Berber family on a previous trip, and the grandmother served us tea and slices of prickly pear as an afternoon treat. Most women who are unacquainted with the taste of prickly pear would pass it up as just another desert cactus. Beth is scavenging for food as she goes and leaving a trail for me to follow at the same time. That's not bad for a city girl. I don't understand why the men aren't pursuing her though."

"Not to offend, but one camel in this country is worth more than ten foreign women," the Water Man suggested.

"I'll be sure to inform Beth of your estimate of her relative value sometime when you're within range of her left fist. Then, you can judge her personal value for yourself."

"You make joke for me, but I tell you true that Calderon mans have no need to follow her path because she can leave Zegzel valley only one way. Mans drive truck around and wait for her on other side of valley. That way, they no work much. When she comes out on road again, they cut her throat and tell Calderon snake bit her and she die. Nobody cares different, yes?"

"Thank you. I understand her situation completely now. She's still in danger, we have more work to do, and we need to be quick and accurate about it. Advari, go back to our men. Tell one van to follow the road to the other side of this gorge. They should attack any Calderon men who are there. If fighting isn't necessary, have our men remain alert and watch for Beth, for us, and for anybody else who comes that way. Have our other men follow you back this way, but tell them not to step on Beth's tracks. I'll continue following Beth's trail now, but if I lose it, I will need to go back where it disappears and start again. So, our men should not step on her footprints, do you understand? I am counting on you once again, Advari. Señora's life may be in your hands more than mine right now, so don't disappoint me."

"You know I will not fail Señora Beth," Advari affirmed. "Then, I will come back here to you quickly."

"Advari, have the men bring all their weapons. Water Man, go back with Advari. Bring all my weapons too. We don't know if the Calderons have men searching for her in the lower valley and also waiting for her and us on the other side."

"Yes, I go fast and tell mans to come," the Water Man said in earnest as he sprinted with Advari back toward the cave and parking area.

While the Water Man and Advari were engaged in deploying my acrobat army, I continued to follow Beth's trail across the valley, or what appeared to be a series of valleys or broad terraces leading deeper and deeper into the gorge with the road the Water Man mentioned somewhere out of sight beyond the tree line. At times, Beth's trail was hard to follow, especially over rocky or gravely ground. When she encountered hard ground, I always found a prickly pear that had been stepped on or broken off, so my girl was thinking, although she might not have any destination in mind beyond the flower field and fruit orchard ahead.

I was halfway through the field of wildflowers when I saw Beth sitting rigidly on the ground at the edge of a tangerine orchard. I called her name, but she didn't move. I called her name again, and started running toward her. As I got closer, I could see that she had her eyes shut tight. I sensed that she had her eyes voluntarily shut tight as opposed to being dead tight or hurt tight, so I stopped running and began walking slowly and carefully toward her on the assumption that she was booby trapped in some way to discourage rescuers.

Cobra Convention

When she judged by my footsteps that I was close, Beth opened her eyes, and asked softly, "Is it gone?"

"Whatever 'it' is that you want me to see, I don't see 'it.' What is 'it' that I'm not seeing?" I questioned her.

"The 'it' is a black snake a little toward the clump of grass to your left. See there? 'It' looks like a tree branch until 'it' raises its head. 'It' is looking at your left leg as if you are lunch. Do you see 'it' now?"

"Yes, now that you identified 'it' and 'its' location. If you spotted 'it,' I'm sure you already know 'it' might have brought 'its' family with 'it.' If you slowly glance off your right shoulder, you will see another one. This isn't a marketplace where the snakes are defanged or have their mouths sewn shut. Have you been bitten?"

"I don't think so," Beth demurred, knowing full well under less stressful circumstances that both she and the snake would know unequivocally if she had been bitten.

"Good," I told her without being critical. "I suppose from your actions that keeping your eyes closed is an effective way to prevent snakebites. What do you think we should do?" I asked, trying to relax myself with conversation while thinking of ways to get her out of danger.

"You could shoot them before they get closer," Beth recommended strongly.

"Yeah, I could shoot them with my index finger and thumb, but they may not be amused. I sent Advari and the Water Man back to bring my weapons."

"I thought you always carry your little gun in your sleeve."

"I do, except when I'm trying to protect my men from being slaughtered at the Spanish Army Headquarters in La Vieja."

"That was careless of you not to put the gun back in your sleeve, wasn't it?" Beth critiqued my emergency preparedness.

"Well, you have me there. I promise I'll never be caught without my derringer again if you promise never to wander into another snake pit again. Advari and the men should be here shortly if you can hold on a bit longer," I tried to comfort her.

"I can hold on, but will the snakes hold on? Oh good, I see Advari coming across the field."

"Excellent. Meanwhile, if I circle around to the rear of these snakes, maybe I can draw them away from you. Can you get up and run if they become interested in me? Stop. Forget what I said. I see another one in the grass behind your original 'it.' Don't move. Let me see what you attracted on the other side. Congratulations, you're the main attraction at a cobra convention. That's why they're so interested in you. You aren't wearing your name tag. They want to know who you are. Sit tight for a few more seconds until the cavalry arrives. I'm looking for a stick if any of your friends move closer to you before the army arrives."

"Didn't you go through some kind of snake school when you were in the army?"

"Yes, but I had my nails done on cobra day and I missed that lecture. Just when you think you never need a course, bingo, it becomes the most important information you need at some point in your life. Wait until I tell the kids in the neighborhood to study their math and science or the snakes will get them. Your friends haven't moved. How close is my army? I don't want to shift my position."

"Almost here. I think the sound of your voice is putting the snakes to sleep. You would have made a horrible professor."

"Why? Studies show that college students don't get enough sleep. I'd be performing an important service. If I lectured early in the morning, the students would be rested for their other classes, get better grades, and make their parents and country proud of them."

My army sensed that something was wrong because Beth and I were as motionless as stalactites the entire time it took them to reach us. When they were within effective range, I put my arm out behind me with my hand open to stop them from approaching too near and disturbing the snakes as I had done earlier.

"Advari, load and hand me my shotgun," I instructed him as nonchalantly as possible. "We have hungry cobras around us."

"I can load your gun, but did you forget Zaki, our snake handler?"

"Thank you for reminding me in a senior moment of forgetfulness. Yes, I forgot about Zaki and his uncle because I haven't seen them with their snake baskets for so long that they blend in with the acrobats. If Zaki and anyone else feels comfortable collecting these snakes, I will not interfere with someone's livelihood or hobby."

"Advari, what did he say just now?" I asked as I was distracted momentarily by the movement of one of the snakes.

"Zaki asked if he can go back to the van and get his snake basket while his uncle stays here. He says that the snakes are curious about you and they will not harm you and Señora Beth if you do not move toward them."

"Tell Zaki that he'd better run faster than he has ever run in his life to bring his snake baskets back here. I'm more concerned about the cobras moving toward us than I am about our infringing on their territory. If he hears a shotgun blast before he returns, he'll know that he can stop running and put the baskets back where they were. By the way, where on the bus and in the vans did he have his snake baskets?"

"Under your seat because you were always in the back where there was less activity and you keep your area orderly. That reduced the chance of someone accidentally bumping into the baskets, especially those holding the snakes that do not have their mouths sewn shut," Advari advised, giving me more information on the snake logistics of this trip than I needed.

That revelation brought a roar of laughter from my army, which caused the cobras to rise higher and spread their hoods wider. But, otherwise, the snakes didn't advance. Nonetheless, I motioned for Advari to hand me my shotgun as I held out my arm in back of me to receive it.

Meanwhile, other members of my army saw Zaki round the hill at full speed on his return trip toward us with a basket in each hand. Each of my soldiers thought it was his personal duty to periodically report Zaki's progress to me. When he arrived, Zaki took a few moments to catch his breath. Then, he went about gathering the snakes as if he were gathering firewood. With all the snakes safely stored in Zaki's baskets, Beth's rescue was complete except to determine if any Calderon men waited for us in the lower valley. After we returned to the vans, I needed no reminder to inform Zaki to relocate his friends somewhere nearer to him than under my seat. If I happened to forget, Beth was now available to jog my memory, or she would take the issue up with Zaki directly.

In the late afternoon, I didn't relish the idea of taking a reconnaissance squad across the fields, especially if we encountered more snakes. I decided to have my army return to the vans and drive around to the lower valley for a quick look, reunite with the men in the third van, and call it a day. Our walk back to the vans gave me a chance to get re-acquainted with Beth, and find out how the Calderon people had treated her.

"I know you didn't get a chance to select a carpet of your choice. But, otherwise, are you okay? Did they harm you in any way?" I started the conversation somewhere between lighthearted and fearful of the answers I might receive.

"I have rug burns over most of my body from when they grabbed me and rolled me up in a carpet in the store. I remember being bounced around as we went through some place cool and damp before coming out into the heat again. After that, I was in the back of a vehicle, and we drove for a long time. Then, I was locked in a cellar for a day or more. Lastly, some other men came and drove me to another place. Sometime during the night, they tried to put me in the cave. I went in a little way, and I thought I saw bats. I decided that they could kill me, but I wasn't going any further. We were still close to the entrance, and the men started arguing among themselves, probably trying to decide what to do with me. While they argued, our *burka* lady arrived. That resulted in another argument. Then, the *burka* lady received a call on her cell phone. I couldn't hear the conversation. Suddenly, she said something to the men, who grabbed me again and forced me through the field where you found me. I don't know where the *burka* lady went, but she didn't come with us. The men didn't tie me very well this time, so I was able to get loose from the ropes. I was about to stand and run toward the road when I spotted the snakes, or they saw me. I read somewhere not to look a snake in the eye, so I shut my eyes and stayed quiet hoping they would go away and you would find me."

"How long were you sitting there?" I asked her.

"Actual time, I probably sat there about ten or more hours. Psychological time, I was there three centuries. That sums up my last few days except to declare that I am dirty, hungry, and I want to go home."

"I don't blame you. We'll go home as soon as we can. Doggone, look here; I had my derringer with me all the time. I guess I couldn't feel it up my sleeve with all the excitement."

"I was surrounded by snakes, and you were excited? How could that be?!" Beth asked incredulously while punching me in the arm.

"Derringers aren't the weapon of choice against cobras. If I had missed, I'd have to kill two cobras with my one remaining shot without causing a ricochet that might bounce off you. My humble skills don't approach that level of accuracy and confidence."

"You could have tried."

"If we were out of other options, I would have. I wouldn't have missed in either case if you wonder about it sometime in the future."

Debriefing

"But, causing your captors trouble when they wanted to put you in the cave was the premier life-saving event of your adventures," I said, advancing a different line of discussion. "You wouldn't have had anything to eat in the cave, finding you would have been extremely difficult, if not impossible, and I don't particularly enjoy bats myself and the rabies they carry. I don't know enough about cobras to understand why you attracted so many except that you may have stumbled across a den of them. For all that we've encountered in Morocco, our home may be the best place for both of us until I rethink other ways to damage the Calderon network and determine if Hassan is our friend or enemy. I certainly didn't dent the Calderon organization, and I could have gotten you killed. I'm sorry I dragged you into danger."

"Thanks for finally acknowledging that you're not invincible. I don't know whether to smack you hard on the back of your head with a stick or to be grateful that you found me. I admit you were right about the Calderons, the *burka* lady, and all the others being connected. By the way, who are all these people with you?" Beth asked as she became more aware of her surroundings.

"We have a great group. Besides Advari, who you know, I have an assortment of people from the marketplace in Marrakesh—Omar and his family of acrobats, the Water Man, and Zaki the snake handler who you just saw in action and his uncle. All are volunteers and have their own reasons to bring down the Calderons for past injustices to them or family members. In La Montagne, we had *fantasias* horsemen as our cavalry, but we sent them home because we didn't want to take unfair advantage of the Calderons. How about you? Did you meet any interesting characters in your travels that you haven't told me about?"

"I didn't meet him, but I'm sure I heard Hassan's voice through a vent in the first house I was in. He was talking to a 'Sebastian' in Spanish. That's all I recall at the moment. Is it worth anything to you?"

"It's worth a lot. Hassan operates on both sides of the fence. Furthermore, I can't determine if the Calderons are holding his son hostage, or if he works for them voluntarily when he isn't overwhelmed by his drug habit. Hassan pops up before or after the heaviest action, and on the opposite side too often for my comfort. But, he'll identify his true stripes shortly, I'm sure. Your 'Sebastian' probably is my 'Colonel Sebastian,' who claimed he had or would arrest the Calderons and their men while we hunted for you. He's probably on the Calderons' payroll like so many others in this area. His diverting me from hunting the Calderons to search for you could have produced a double benefit for himself. He may have thought that if I found you, I would be so grateful that I wouldn't renew my efforts against the Calderons. If I stopped pursuing the Calderons, they might be grateful (using their definition of gratitude) to him in some way. His superiors in Madrid would be pleased with him for keeping the neighborhood peaceful. The unhappy ones are all the people the Calderon network damaged and us. I'm not sure MAGENTA cares one way or another because it believes it has bigger fish flopping around its boat. I still need to prove that the Calderons and others are suppliers for the bigger operators."

Penetrating Questions

"Are you giving up?" Beth asked with all the insight she had acquired from being married to me and surrounded by my environment for so long.

"I'll discontinue this operation, send my acrobat army back to Marrakesh, deliver Advari to school in Lisbon, take you home, and find my Scout, wherever she's hiding."

"You didn't answer my question with a simple yes or no which means your war isn't over. Why isn't the war over for you?"

"In tracking you down, I confirmed that Chauncey and Paolo are involved with the Calderons, or, at least, starting a side business using Calderon assets. Either way, they will get fitted for jail cells or coffins if that continues. They may be too involved for me to salvage, but I need to try, or, at least, determine how deeply they're involved. They're aware that I know what they're doing. I'm interested in learning if they have a soul left in them."

"Then, why are you sending Advari back to Lisbon to live with Paolo? Paolo could hold Advari hostage to trap you again. Then what would you do?"

"With a baby on the way, I'm counting on whatever backbone Paolo has left to do the right thing for Advari. Perhaps, I need to persuade Paolo to send Advari to a boarding school on the premise that Paolo's wife won't be able to tend both her children and Advari. I'm also counting on Advari to influence Paolo to be the man he should be in his position."

"Why not bring Advari to the States? Let him live with us, or attend a boarding school in the Chicago area."

"I thought about that, but Advari's renegade spirit must remain alive. I would spoil him. He needs an Indian or European environment to give him the freedom to do something different from all the other boys his age while exposing him to different cultures, languages, and people. Our environment in the States is too homogeneous for him. Second, if he learns that I changed his home base because Paolo is part of the Calderon network, Advari will lose faith in everyone trying to help him, including us. I can pressure Paolo to behave by informing his brothers that he put the family business in jeopardy by his actions. I'm sure they will straighten his backbone under those circumstances. Third, if Advari and I hang around each other all the time, I'd have to buy a new wallet every week."

"You seem to have given Advari's future a lot of thought."

"I've considered his future as much as the other young people in our near and extended family, certainly."

"That's good, but sometime you'll confront the Calderons again, right? How many armies will that take?"

"An army of two."

"That's a quick answer. You must have given that some thought too. You and who else?"

"Knowing what I know now about the Calderons and what she knows plus her European connections, Marika and I should be a big enough army to take on the Calderons and General Vasily from another direction, don't you think?"

"So now you've returned Vasily to the equation along with the Calderons, as if they aren't enough for you by themselves."

"I don't have the connection fully diagnosed yet, but an affiliation, possibly through another European network wouldn't surprise me. That conflict will be bigger than I originally projected."

"Our tanks and air power put people out of business in the Persian desert fairly quickly in 1991. What's different about what you want to do now?"

"In 1991, as Hassan told us, we forced the Iraqis out of Kuwait with tanks and technology. That war had a territorial dimension. The people responsible for the World Trade Center and Pentagon attacks don't have territorial ambitions like Saddam Hussein. The new crowd fights what's known as asymmetrical warfare for primarily ideological reasons. In Vietnam, we called it guerrilla warfare. The Vietcong had the Communist ideology to bind them in a common cause. We didn't stop its spread by being there. Asymmetrical or guerrilla warfare is intended to neutralize and wear down superior firepower and technology. It comes down to a handful of men with small arms against a force with superior equipment and numbers. So far, the U.S. hasn't demonstrated it can successfully handle guerrilla warfare. The terrorists can look to Vietnam and Somalia for examples of how to effectively overcome U.S. war technology. The Vietcong were supplied through the Ho Chi Minh Trail. Today, terrorists use international networks like the Calderons' for money and supplies. Nothing has really changed since cavemen began throwing rocks at each other."[3]

"I'll grant you that Marika is tough, but she and you aren't enough to take on terrorists single-handed. Have you thought about something more relaxing like going to Slovakia and organizing another family hunt for Janosik's treasure?"

"Believe it or not, I have. The problem is that I'll keep running into Vasily and Hassan on their way from one network or terrorist group to another. Do I stop hunting treasure and chase them while the family waits for me to identify the next place to search, or hhmm . . . ."

"What hhmm now?"

"Hhmm what if I stop chasing the Calderons, Vasily, and Hassan, and let them come to my lair for a change by waving Janosik's treasure at them? Why just be satisfied with hit-and-run attacks against that bunch when I can put them all out of business entirely?"

"Okay, Mr. Hhmm, but no matter what you do or where you travel, I'm still your life insurance beneficiary, right?"

"I keep requesting change forms, but I never receive any. Have you been intercepting my insurance mail lately?"

"You won't live long enough to sign the change forms anyway after what I've been through."

"Hey, did you know that the cave has a stalagmite shaped like a camel?" I asked Beth as we passed the entrance to the cave on our way back to the vans. "At least, that's what the Water Man told me."

"All I saw were bats looking and acting like bats hanging from the cave ceiling. Just so you know, changing the subject won't get you anywhere the way I feel."

"Then we better get you cleaned up, fed, and headed homeward. After we pick up the remainder of my army and our third van down the valley, I'll have my army drive us to Tangier. We can catch the ferry to Algeciras, rent a car, drive to Madrid, send Advari to Lisbon, and fly home tomorrow or the next day. If my soldiers go back to their regular jobs in Marrakesh, hopefully Calderon will leave them alone. They're a brave bunch trusting a stranger like me to join with them against the likes of the Calderons."

"The real question is will your army leave the Calderons alone? You may not have succeeded in your objectives on this trip, but you showed these people the possibility of engaging the Calderon network by themselves. Your Moroccan army doesn't need you anymore as its leader. With tensions high and escalating further, another leader, patriot, or fanatic will arrive soon enough to lead most of them to their deaths before all this is over. Mark my words and your calendar on that," Beth prophesied.

We rounded up the crews in our two vans and set off down the road to pick up the third van in the lower valley. No one said much. For now, we were beaten, and we knew it. I was very fortunate to have my wife back in one piece. The men in the third van hadn't seen any Calderon people come their way, either on the road or across the valley.

All that was left was to retrace our route to Tangier. The ferry and the Spanish airlines would repatriate Beth and me to the United States and Advari to Lisbon. *Then, why was I still studying the map of the area?*

ONE MORE ENCOUNTER

"This won't work," I told Beth and my army. "If we go back the same way we came, the Calderons can ambush us anywhere along the way. We have to find a different way back. We can't assume that they realize we have no capacity or will to continue this fight under the current circumstances. As if they don't have sufficient manpower themselves, now they have the protection of Colonel Sebastian and his garrison of Spanish troops."

"What to do?" the Water Man inquired with more anxiety in his voice than comfortable for the other men to hear and maintain their survival instincts.

"Water Man, do you know where this road goes?" I asked him to keep his jitters from infecting the other members of my army.

"This road leads to Oujda," the Water Man proclaimed. "There in Oujda, you find main road southwest to Taza, then Fez. But then, you are far from Tangier. No good to go there for you."

"Actually, that is precisely where we're going because, from Fez, Beth and I can catch a flight to Paris and avoid Tangier and the ferry altogether. Advari can come with us, or take a Moroccan flight to Madrid, then on to Lisbon from there. Everyone else certainly can return to Marrakesh from Fez in the vans."

"Why you think that way?" the Water Man pressed his concerns about my change in travel plans.

"We need to reduce our exposure to attacks from the Calderons. If they see our vulnerability now, we are dead camels. So, we reduce or eliminate ambushes on the road by not going directly west from Melilla to Tangier as they expect, and we eliminate possible attack against my wife and me on the ferry to Algeciras. The further southwest we drive, the further and quicker we move out of range of Calderon's surveillance planes for the first leg of everyone's return home."

The positive murmurs and nods among my army overruled any objections from the Water Man, although his negative response allowed my brain to concentrate on my last thought longer than I ordinarily would have.

"The Water Man has a good point," I told my army, surprising both the Water Man and myself by giving him credit for my thoughts.

Even Advari looked askance at me before translating that sentence.

"Calderon will likely send a plane or helicopter to look for us so that he can alert any men he has waiting in ambush, especially if he doesn't receive information that we're on the road to Tangier. If we see a plane or helicopter approaching our caravan while we're still in range of Melilla, the three drivers should pull off the road immediately, but stay in the vans to find a place to conceal and protect them, if possible. All others should keep their eyes open and their weapons ready, particularly when we are away from any towns or villages where we are more vulnerable to attack in the open. Get out of the vans if the plane is low enough, and fire at it with short bursts to conserve our ammunition. Perhaps Allah will grant us the benefit of a lucky shot and allow us to do some damage to the Calderons yet."

If anyone had called me the biggest doofus in North Africa anywhere east of Taourirt for proposing this plan, I would have agreed with him. But, we had a plan, and my army started southwest toward our ultimate destination of Fez. In the quiet mountainous area west of Taourirt, and not far from Oujda, we heard the unmistakable rotor noise of a helicopter reverberating off the canyons and valleys definitely coming our way, although still out of sight on the far side of the hills. The lead driver of our caravan pulled off the left side of the road, terrorizing an oncoming truck, to hide under an overhanging cliff large enough to cover all three vans. My army piled out and waited with rifles ready as the approaching throb of the helicopter grew louder. The copter definitely was following the mountain road and taking its time searching the twists and turns looking for any sign of us.

Then, like a whale breaching the surface of the water, the two-seat copter erupted over the top of the hill that we had traversed only minutes before. We had seen this helicopter on our way to Melilla. Recognizing it as a Calderon copter, my army opened fire with their rifles long before it was within the effective range of their weapons. I couldn't worry about that now. I inhaled my second breath and aimed my sniper rifle at the pilot. A few more seconds and the copter would be directly over us.

Simultaneously with the pilot and passenger looking in our direction, my shot pierced the clear plastic windshield within the frame of the pilot's head or throat. The chopper's nose dipped sharply, then recovered as it continued on course directly toward us. Now definitely within range of all our weapons, a hailstorm of rifle rounds pierced the plastic bubble while several others hit the bulkhead behind the pilot. The passenger appeared unharmed, and was frantically trying to gain control of the aircraft. But he was too late. The pilot's body slumped forward across the controls, and the copter veered right and downward into the valley below. A fireball and a black oily cloud shot upward from the place of impact.

We didn't celebrate or examine the wreckage. A second helicopter appeared over the hill and was upon us almost before I had time to reload—almost. My army was surprised by the appearance of the second chopper, but their fighting spirit was up now. My shot missed the pilot, but a hail of gunfire from my army peppered the open cockpit and the left side of the aircraft. The pilot steered hard right to avoid the gunfire, but fuel poured from behind the bubble as the pilot took the craft out over the same valley as the first chopper. For a few moments, the copter appeared able to clear the hills on the opposite side of the valley. But then the engine spasmed at a critical moment, and the copter's skids snagged the tops of tall pines that rotated the aircraft on its right side. The rotors tangled in the trees, the copter stopped abruptly, turned upside down, and dropped heavily to the valley floor.

"Go! Go!" I yelled. "Let's get out of here before another one comes! Go! Keep moving, people! Let's get out of here!" I kept yelling with no translation needed to activate my soldiers.

Everyone ran at full speed back to the vans. We piled in on top of one another, and the drivers roared off with people still getting in and doors not closed. Beth grabbed my rifle to keep it from being damaged while I tumbled between the seats and the van floor. Fortunately, I didn't disturb Zaki's snake basket. No one else was injured. My army was together, and we had drawn Calderon blood. Like the battle of Midway Island in World War II, the tide of battle turned in our favor within a matter of minutes.[4]

With adrenaline pumping full blast for countless kilometers after that encounter, I didn't need to remind anyone to be vigilant for another assault. None came. Had we known the extent of the damage we had caused the Calderon empire in our final encounter, we all could have relaxed.

Contrary to Master Sun Tzu's principles, the Calderons made the war between them and me personal by attempting to destroy my retreating army that was no longer a threat. Their pursuit cost the Calderons dearly, as we would learn later, and as Sun Tzu predicted of all warlords who are ruled by their passions and poor judgment.

At the Fez airport the next afternoon, Beth and I said our good-byes to my acrobat army before dispatching them back to their civilian lives and families in Marrakesh. As I shook the Water Man's hand, I told him that trying to earn a living on both sides of the law was a dangerous game and that some day circumstances would require him to choose between them. He understood, but did not commit himself to either option.

Another Good-bye

With my army dispatched, the time came for us to say good-bye to Advari again. As before, we had no words of comfort to offer each other. A big hug and a fast grab for my wallet were all we initially could muster between us.

"Write to us often," Beth told Advari.

"I will, I promise," he replied earnestly.

"When will we be together on an adventure again?" Advari asked me after we both regained our voices.

"The day after you pass your exams for advancement to the next grade," I told him. "And, if your grades are exceptional, I'll call you to go treasure hunting with us next summer."

"But that will be a hundred years from now. What if someone else finds the treasure before we do?"

"Then I'd better call you the next time I'm in Europe."

"When will that be?"

"As soon as I get Señora Beth home, clean my weapons, wash my clothes, talk to some people, and devise a plan to attack the Calderon network from a different angle. Is that fast enough for you?"

"Don't waste time planning. You always change the plan anyway."

"Terrorist attacks have made our lives more complicated, little soldier. I'll need to do more studying and planning in the future."

"Maybe you will study more and develop a better initial plan, but you will change it anyway. You are a better fighter when nobody knows what you will do next. Your way allowed you to become the old, old, old, old man that you are. Why change your approach now?"

"I got your point after the first 'old.' I've used Master Sun Tzu's war principles against the Calderons for too long. I need to reinvent myself, or they will become accustomed to my style. That's enough war talk for now. Give me my wallet back, and go catch your plane. Be good to Paolo and his wife. Paolo has a big decision to make very soon, and his wife will be busy with the new baby. Help them when you can. Get going, the second boarding call was just announced."

On our flight to Paris from Fez, Beth read her magazine while my retro-brain locked onto a comment she had made the previous day at the cave about the growing animosity and intolerance between Islamic radicals and Americans. Once the thoughts were there, I couldn't get them out of my head. Beth's thoughts were not frivolous.

> Similar to Mexicans crossing the southern U.S. border to find jobs in the States, Moroccans and other Africans immigrated or seasonally migrated to Spain and other European countries to find work. Most of the time, seasonal migration went well for everyone. However, when Europeans perceived that the immigrants were overstaying their welcome or visa dates and were taking jobs away from them, the process broke down with various displays of mutual aggression. Speculation about the real level of animosity between Islamic extremists and Spaniards became clearer on March 11, 2004, when twenty-nine extremists launched a series of bomb attacks at or near Madrid's Atocha commuter train station, killing over 190 and injuring 1,800 people. The extremist cell responsible for the bombing included Moroccans and other nationals who had lived in Spain for extended periods.[5]
>
> For unknown reasons, the cell members hadn't connected with the Spanish culture even after spending substantial time in the country. Probably of more importance, the train bombings led Spanish voters to elect a liberal government that did not favor U.S. war policies and Spanish participation in any U.S.-led coalition in Iraq, or anywhere else in the Middle East.[6] The Calderons had taught me long before the Madrid attack that if a small group of radicals could change government policies and alliances that dramatically, I needed to escalate my efforts against terrorists and their suppliers above the junior varsity level I had grown accustomed to in my civilian role as Joe Legion.

I didn't fully comprehend all of this while flying home with Beth in November 2001. But I wasn't alone. The top levels of U.S. government struggled for a long time after September 11, 2001, to define "the enemy" let alone develop appropriate strategies and tactics. The one thing I knew for certain was that Joe Legion had to stay active, at least until Uncle Sam was ready to meet his foes on effective terms. With the 2004 Madrid train bombings occurring at the Atocha station close to the hotel in which we stayed in November 2001 exactly 911 days after the 9/11/01 attacks in the U.S., the connection or symbolism would be too great for me to disengage from my personal war against terrorists on any continent.

Meanwhile, I comforted myself with the thought that I now had two pieces of information that I didn't have on my arrival in Morocco. One, I had a scanner that could identify people and things that had an embedded Calderon chip in them. Two, I was convinced that the war philosophy espoused by the Chinese war strategist Sun Tzu somewhere between the fifth and third centuries BCE (before the common era) required modification if I were to be effective in any future actions against the Calderon and other networks. Patton-like, I would need to be more agile and audacious in conducting any future business with the Calderon organization, General Vasily, Hassan, Chauncey, Paolo and anyone affiliated with them.

CHAPTER NOTES

1. Wikipedia contributors, "2004 Morocco earthquake," *Wikipedia, The Free Encyclopedia*, http://en.wikipedia.org/w/index.php?title=2004_Morocco_earthquake&oldid=305540601 (accessed September 28, 2009). p. 1.

2. Whitehall (editor), *op. cit.*, p. 212.

3. Stanley Karnow, "*Vietnam A History*," (New York: Penguin Books, 1984), pp. 15–24. By permission of Mr. Karnow and WGBH Enterprises. Also, Wikipedia contributors, "Vietnam War," *Wikipedia, The Free Encyclopedia*, http://en.wikipedia.org/w/index.php?title=Vietnam_War&oldid=319260093 (accessed October 11, 2009). pp. 1–33.

4. Wikipedia contributors, "Battle of Midway," *Wikipedia, The Free Encyclopedia*, http://en.wikipedia.org/w/index.php?title=Battle_of_Midway&oldid=316181067 (accessed September 25, 2009). pp. 1–19. Also, John Costello, "The Pacific War 1941–1945," (New York: William Morrow and Company, Inc.,1982), pp. 294–304.

5. Todd Richissin, "Rush-Hour Blasts Kill 192 on Madrid Trains," *Chicago Tribune*, March 12, 2004, p. 1. Also, Michael Martinez and Tom Hundley, "Moroccans Fear Spain's Crackdown," *Chicago Tribune*, March 17, 2004, p. 3. Both articles by permission of Chicago Tribune Company.

6. Marlise Simons, "Spain's New Premier Orders Pullout in Iraq," *Chicago Tribune*," April 19, 2004, p. 7. By permission of Chicago Tribune Company.

CHAPTER 19

GHOSTS AND REGRETS

Ron's News Coup

After a late night arrival in Chicago following our flight from Paris, my first order of business early the next morning was to call Ron. I hoped to find healing for my less than stellar performance in Operation Hercules by hearing his grumpy early morning voice. This time, I was the tired, grumpy, and unprepared one for the surprises he had for me.

"Terrific, Ron, you answered the phone on the first ring! I couldn't have disturbed your sleep. Are you sick or just getting in?" I announced myself.

"Neither, because I've been up for an hour or more expecting your call," was Ron's surprise response.

"That bad, huh? I know I really messed up the operation, but I didn't think it was bad enough to give you insomnia," I responded penitently.

"What are you talking about?" Ron replied sharply.

"My attempted take-down of the Calderon network in Morocco, of course. Beth and I named it Operation Hercules. What do you think I'm talking about?"

"We're talking about the same thing, lame brain. Maybe you should be the one to go back to bed this time," Ron recommended.

"We're not getting anywhere in this conversation," I exclaimed. "Tell me your story, and when you finish, I'll tell you mine. Then, we'll compare notes to determine if there are any similarities. How does that sound?"

"I accept your proposal. I agree that Operation Hercules was going absolutely nowhere until you shot down Gilberto in the helicopter."

"What? Say that again. We must have a bad connection. Start all over."

"At first, I thought you were joking, but I can tell by your voice that you really don't know."

"Know what? Are we on the same story? Start again."

"Gilberto Calderon was in one of the helicopters you and your *compadres* shot down in the Rif Mountains."

"Wait. Are you sure? Did MAGENTA confirm that?"

"He's dead, my friend—stone, cold dead. It's a confirmed kill. Do I need to keep repeating it until your micro brain explodes, or do you understand now?"

"I got it, I got it—no, I don't have it. I can't wrap my mind around it for some reason. My Moroccan army and I were breaking off contact with the Calderons. I was conceding defeat, or, at least, executing a strategic retreat. I was satisfied to have my wife back."

"Don't tell that to MAGENTA in your after-action report. MAGENTA wants to canonize you."

"I don't need sainthood. Your information is fine. In fact, it's better than fine."

"That's the most humility you've displayed since I've been around you, but there's more."

"More? What more could there be?" I continued, demanding information from Ron.

"The word in Tangier, Marrakesh, Ceuta, and Melilla is approximately what you just told me. The Calderons out-maneuvered or beat you at every turn. But, the street story adds that while you distracted the Calderons with your meddling and fumbling, a rival drug lord capitalized on your mess and took Gilberto out. You not only erased Gilberto, but also shifted the blame to a rival. I don't know what possessed you to adopt the strategy and tactics you used, but the results were astonishing to everybody up and down the ranks at MAGENTA."

"I followed the war principles of Sun Tzu in presenting my acrobat army to the Calderons as formlessly and incompetently as possible to deceive their superior force," I replied. "I had some casual thoughts about shifting blame to another organization for any damage my army created, but I never specifically acted on that line of thought. I was busy enough positioning myself to exploit any opening the Calderons might give me through a mistake or carelessness. But, after what you just told me, I realize that I shouldn't describe Operation Hercules in those terms to MAGENTA. Now that I reflect on your version, I did cause the Calderons to violate two of Sun Tzu's cardinal rules of warfare."

"I may as well ask what they are because you'll tell me anyway," Ron confirmed my thoughts.

"First, never stop an army on its way home, and two, don't press a desperate enemy. That certainly describes the status of our retreat toward Fez."

"I never studied Sun Tzu's theories, and I don't know if they apply in your case," Ron admitted. "But, I have studied the Battle of Midway in World War II, which has similarities to your situation. The Japanese Imperial Navy had everything going its way after Pearl Harbor, Wake Island, and across the Pacific. They had us ducking for cover at Midway until a few of our fighter-bomber pilots fortuitously caught the Japanese refueling their planes on their carriers' decks. Within minutes, three Japanese aircraft carriers were hit and sinking, and a fourth one was sunk the following day with the loss of many of the highly trained, irreplaceable, Japanese pilots. The Japanese troop ships carrying the invasion force scheduled to land on Midway and the Hawaiian Islands returned to Japan.[1] I'm sure the American admirals were pleasantly surprised and totally grateful that the Japanese defeated themselves on that occasion, but that didn't stop the Navy brass from taking credit for the U.S. victory. Maybe you were bailed out in the same way with a lucky shot at the helicopter. If that's what happened, shut up, take the credit, and get ready for your next assignments that will pit you against every insurgent on the planet. Next time, try something planned rather than accidental. Now that I said my piece, I'm going back to bed. By the way, your Scout is in town. I suggest that you thank her for sending the Iowa seismology team to rescue your pitiful posterior."

"Thanks for the information on the Calderons. Funny, when we knocked the helicopters down, I thought of the turn-around at Midway too, but from the humble perspective of my army being saved from disaster rather than me leading the men to victory."

"Geez, don't use the word 'humble' more than once in a conversation. I'm stressed enough going back to bed without breakfast."

"Before you go, thanks for letting me know that Amy returned. I'll wait until after daybreak to call her. You didn't have anything to do with keeping her safe while I was away, did you?"

"Not me, bucko, I had no idea where she was. Besides, you picked her, so you should know that she's as hard-headed as you are. I stay far away from her when you're in the field. Otherwise, she's a savvy young lady. I don't know how you two ever got together."

"When I discovered she was a big fan of Sun Tzu's war theories in addition to her physical therapy skills, we connected right away," I said, trying not to laugh out loud. "Formlessness as a battle tactic draws gifted people together no matter what," I shot another round at Ron.

"If I knew you'd regress to your smart-aleck attitude, I wouldn't have given you any information. I'll give you some advice, though. You'd better prepare your Scout for bad times ahead."

"I appreciate your advice anytime, but particularly after what occurred in Morocco. As for Amy, you just said she's a savvy lady. She has good survival instincts. Wait a minute, now what are you trying to tell me? Or, did you spill hot coffee in your lap?"

Followed by a Lecture

"You know what I mean. People don't know what we go through to complete an operation. The U.S. will be at war with somebody very soon. The advance people are already in the field. One day your Scout will discover that she doesn't like the business you're in, how you conduct yourself, and what kind of person she's become through dealing with you. If you need more evidence, remember that, until your Moroccan adventure, your wife really didn't know what you do or did, what impact it has, if any, and what you might be called upon to do in the future. That's a lot of years gone by without knowing who the guy she married really is. All that my wife knows is how many times I woke her up during the night through the last quarter century from bouncing around in bed or pacing the floor. Unlike your Scout, our wives have seen us before and after a lot of ugly situations, but never during one."

"Well, Beth now knows what it feels like to be a prisoner and hostage. Are you suggesting that we use our wives as Scouts in the future?"

"Don't tempt me. I might loan you my wife for your next venture without any thought of compensation. But, I need to tell you something that will scorch your shorts. I hope you're sitting down. Again, you know darn well what I mean. Everybody has this notion that we play games like movie stars. You know what my face looks like after the helicopter fire. Could I get a movie contract with my appearance? How many scars do you have on your body? Are you the rage of all the chicks on the beach? So, don't wait too long to tell your Scout that the party will likely get rougher from now on. She either should prepare herself to be a controlled hellcat like Alice Bright Feather was for you, or you should find yourself another Scout who is."

Followed by a Death Notice

"I haven't heard Alice's name mentioned in a long time, and I didn't expect to hear it from you. What brings her to your mind now?"

"She died a few days ago."

"I'm truly sorry to hear that. Do you have any more information about her?"

"I have more information about her than you're equipped to handle. Are you sitting down?"

"I'm in a lotus position on the kitchen floor. Tell me already."

"Alice was ordered to give you a permanent discharge from PURPLE before or during your flight back to San Francisco many moons ago. Did you know that? Do you want to hear more?"

"I know what her standing orders were when either an assignment or PURPLE security was jeopardized. What else do you have?" I asked with my blood pressure rising rapidly.

"You were scheduled for an accident for some prior transgression when she took you to the reservation too, although what transgression occurred remains unclear to me unless it was the JASON folder you saw in the security briefcase. She didn't go through with her part of PURPLE's orders to turn off your lights. I'll bet you didn't know that, did you?"

"No, I didn't know that. How could I? She and everyone else on the reservation treated me very well. She stayed away from me most of the time I was there. I didn't have any weapons. The tribe could have dragged me into the desert where no one would find me. Why does the JASON name ring a bell with you?"

"There you go always asking the wrong questions. Knowing about the group back then could have been your ticket to a premature departure to another planet. But, we'll never get at the truth now with the principals gone."

"What other more current blockbuster news do you have for me? Should I be watching my back for someone from MAGENTA coming after me, or an attack from Amy despite her lack of apparent weapons skills?"

"Before we get to anything like that, the story on Alice didn't end where you interrupted me."

"Okay, I'm listening, Ron. Go ahead."

Alice's father banished her for disgracing the tribe by not doing her duty in dispatching you to immortality. He tried to persuade her or help her finish you off, but she refused to participate. That's why her attitude toward you changed, and PURPLE stopped giving you assignments toward the end of your enlistment. She saved your life and lost her family and roots, and you didn't acknowledge any of it except maybe with a measly thank you once in a great while."

"Hold on a minute, Ron. Alice was a very special person to me. I would have put my life on the line for her any time. However, under PURPLE's rules of engagement, we both knew that we were expendable if our continued existence posed a danger to an assignment or to PURPLE's security. That's as far as it went. I had Beth waiting for me at home, and Alice knew it."

"Sometimes knowing facts and getting our emotions under control don't coincide, buddy boy. How many times have we fought our private battles to get our demons under control?"

"I agree with you, but Alice never indicated to me that she was the least bit interested in me outside of PURPLE assignments."

"That was the Navajo in her. You had to make the first move before she could express her feelings. That didn't happen, did it?"

"So, what has she been doing all this time?" I asked trying to replace emotional conjecturing for something more tangible that I could comprehend.

"She taught school on the reservation most of the time. After you left the neighborhood, Alice's father relented enough to allow her to return to the reservation to teach the kids because the tribe couldn't find another teacher. But, she still was an outsider on almost everything else in her life related to her tribe and family because of you."

"Did she ever leave the reservation, marry, or have a family of her own?"

"Her family and friends were her memories and the kids she taught over the years."

"That was a criminal waste of her life and talents. She could have been whatever she wanted to be with a little help and encouragement. To my knowledge, her father wasn't part of PURPLE. What business was it of his to treat her like that? Didn't he see what he was doing to her?"

"All I know is that her father didn't 'forgive' her disgrace to him or to the tribe until he was on his deathbed. Then, he gave her his ceremonial dagger as a sign that she was once again a full member of the tribe and his family. She kept it all these years. She sent it to me about a week before she died to give to you."

"I hope I don't offend anyone, but I can't accept the dagger under those circumstances. It belongs to the tribe as part of its history, if nothing else. You should send it back."

"I'm glad to hear you say that because I already did."

"Good, I'm glad this is the end of that terrible story, or is it?"

"There's more, but even I don't want to torture you after what you've just been through."

"Why, did Alice die of some horrible disease?" I continued, fighting to hear the full story, although a large portion of me didn't want to hear any of it.

"I wouldn't describe it as a disease, but it's a fatal condition nonetheless. If anyone can die of a broken heart, she did. Her life totally unraveled because you asked her to help you get back to the States alive. That's the end of my story about Alice Bright Feather because you need a clear head to get ready for your next trip. What do you have planned?"

"I know you're stone-headed enough not to tell me more about Alice no matter how much I beg. I'll say one last thing, and then let the subject drop until another time. Your story about Alice is particularly important to me now because I'm trying to decide if I should or shouldn't have a Scout on my next *sortie*. I should be able to decide that despite how depressed and angry I feel about what happened to Alice."

BACK TO THE LECTURE

"In your mental condition, I predict you will have more trouble making a decision about Amy than you think. Scouts aren't supposed to be family, or lovers, or friends, or people who need your protection. Both of us know that you treat Amy the same way as you did your other Scouts. But Amy is someone who gets into your bloodstream like some of my former Scouts did to me. Fortunately, I had the sense to pick men for my Scouts. Even so, after two people share danger and risk their lives for each other, I believe that an indestructible bond is formed between them that our civilian society doesn't recognize or have a name for, but the bond definitely exists. Don't kid yourself, my friend, your decision to include or exclude your Scout from your next venture will give you a first-class headache. The only possible relief is that she'll recognize the bond is there, she'll understand your mutual agony, and she'll do something to put distance between the two of you to make your decision easier. Mark my words on that."

"I accept your wisdom on how to perceive my relationship with my Scout without further argument. Before you totally turn my backbone and brain into mush, let me ask you about a different topic. You said earlier that the Calderon story is going up and down the ranks of MAGENTA. Obviously, you have information about MAGENTA and PURPLE that I don't have after all these years. So, tell me who or what PURPLE was or what MAGENTA is, and I'll let you go back to bed."

"Not in a million years, bucko, not in a million years. Up and down the ranks is an expression I used, not a description of MAGENTA's organization chart. Look, my burns are healing nicely, and I'm beginning to enjoy life again. I'm even beginning to like you again—just a little. You have to appreciate how hard it was for me to compliment you without you whining for praise and attention. But, your lack of knowledge about MAGENTA saved your life more than once in the past and is likely to save your posterior in the future. So, do not, I repeat, DO NOT in capital letters ask me about MAGENTA again. Go have your sugar fix for breakfast, call your Scout and make her cry by telling her about your bum decision for your next outing, and let me get some rest. I will say this. Whether you believe that you deserve accolades or not, you did a good job in Morocco. You weren't just lucky. You and the people you recruited stuck with you and the assignment until it generated positive results in interfering with the Calderon network. That was your objective, and you did it. That was a nice touch having Professor Palmer and his team torch Calderon's and the ambassador's houses for you when washing them down the hill didn't work. Yeah, your MAGENTA job isn't finished, and it probably never will be completed to your satisfaction. That's why they select bone-heads like us to do this kind of stuff. Rational people want answers. We pretend it doesn't matter. Say hello to your wife for me. I'm glad you're both safely home. Call me when you define your next assignment. Operation Hercules? Geez, was that your classically schooled brain spasm, or someone else's? Never mind. Bye."

I was definitely upset and skipped breakfast—something I rarely do. I shouldn't have let Ron's lecture infiltrate my defenses like that, but after he hung up, Ron's information generated all kinds of misfiring neurological synapses. Under those conditions, I forgot to wait until after daybreak to call Amy.

Scout's Honor

"Hi, Shortcake, I'm just checking in to find out if everything went okay with you during my absence," I started.

"Everything was fine until you called," she said sleepily. "I usually don't get up for another hour, even when I start work early like today."

"Then, I'm sorry I bothered you. Forgive me if my brain is still on North African time. I wanted to thank you for sending the Iowa seismology team to assist me. Professor Palmer enjoyed the diversion from his academic routine. Is he related to you?"

"No, he's an old neighbor. He still has relatives living in my hometown. When you rush me, I do whatever pops into my head."

"Your head popping was on target this time. Professor Palmer really helped. How did your disappearance go with Rick?"

"I hid out with a friend in Minneapolis."

I was good to Amy and myself. I didn't ask her if her Minnesota friend was male or female.

"I take that to mean you didn't contact Rick to hide you in the hospital. Action like that might earn you an audacity badge from me, but how did that go with Rick? I presume I haven't heard the entire story on that subject."

"To be honest, first, my boss was really upset about my sudden disappearance. We're pretty busy at work at this time of year. But, somebody from MAGENTA must have contacted him because he calmed down a few days later. (I found out later that Ron had a discussion with Amy's supervisor, but never learned what was said. So, I never apologized to Amy's supervisor, or informed Amy.) Second, Rick and I decided that our relationship for lack of a better description is going absolutely nowhere given our careers, the distance between us, and what we want from life."

"Was that a Rick and Amy decision, or an Amy solo verdict?"

"Well, either way, the results are the same. Do you need something from me?"

"Because you're determined to avoid any conversation about Rick before it starts, I'm armed with other agenda items on the shaky assumption that you're awake now. The first question is: Do you have any information that I should know?"

"You probably should be aware that my boss is sending me to several of our other therapy centers to learn how they operate. If everything goes well, I hope to be promoted soon."

"That's terrific for you. I believe you have potential to move even further into management ranks."

"You also should be aware that, if I get promoted, I can't be disappearing without notice again. More important, I probably can't be both a facility manager and a Scout. I hope you realize that! Remember, you asked me to tell you what's happening in my life. I'm being totally honest with you."

(Within a few sentences, Amy introduced the probable end of her Scouting career, or at least recasting the Scout relationship between us in different terms, as Ron predicted. Ron was insightful, but not that insightful if he had prior knowledge of Amy's intentions. Further discussion between Ron and me could wait. Right now, I needed to determine if I had a Scout or not.)

"I'd hate to lose you, but I understand that you need to follow your professional career first," I continued probing politely.

"I'm not quitting yet, but if I need to, will you consider Heidi as a Scout replacement for me?"

"I appreciate your suggestion. I definitely will keep her in mind, although you mentioned that she travels a lot. To be totally honest with you in return, I envision my next assignment as being off-the-books. If I survive that, I'll consider her for future assignments if you're no longer available."

"What do you mean by off-the-books?"

"If something goes wrong, MAGENTA disavows any knowledge of its Operatives and Scouts. You already know that. And, if my corpse washes up on a beach somewhere, nobody at MAGENTA publicly knows or cares about how it got there. Certainly, nobody at MAGENTA will hurry to a police station or hospital to inquire about my welfare, request a search for me, or provide information to any law enforcement or media personnel about my activities."

"The FBI or CIA may already be watching some of your playmates such as Calderon or General Vasily for their own purposes, don't you think?" Amy re-directed the conversation.

"That's a strong possibility. I'm beginning to learn that the characters we're playing with may be more of a threat to the U.S. than I previously believed. Given current conditions, a national security agency won't appreciate exposure of its covert operations through my MAGENTA-level activities. Until recently, I was certain that our national security agencies had higher value targets than a Calderon or a Vasily to occupy their time. In the past, we generally had sufficient space to operate without interfering with each other. Now, we may have to collaborate or operate jointly. In any case, I don't want Calderon's goons chasing you or my wife around the local landscape while I'm playing tag with their associates elsewhere."

"So then, are you sacking me or telling me to resign now? What exactly are you saying?"

"Absolutely don't quit MAGENTA unless you are jeopardizing your professional career, or if you want to resign for other reasons. My convenience shouldn't be a factor in your decision either way. Decide who you want to be, and pay the price to achieve it because everything comes with a price tag attached. To begin with, the off-the-books operation I'm talking about relates only to my next *sortie* against Calderon, not to longer-term operations. I'm doing this to minimize the possibility of you or my wife becoming hostages or targets, which—believe it or not—will distract me from focusing on disrupting or eliminating Calderon's or other networks. In Morocco, the network demonstrated that it's larger, more insidious, and more dangerous than I initially believed. I probably will ask another MAGENTA Operative for information and advice, but otherwise, I plan to be the only one in the field against the Calderon network on my next trip. Does that clear things up for you?"

Ron had predicted accurately that this conversation was not going to be as smooth as I wanted.

"Are you sure that you know what you're doing attacking Calderon again without a Scout or MAGENTA's support?"

"That's a strange question after what we've been through already. Of course I don't know what I'm doing unless you think your running around my neighborhood with the Benet Academy track team was a scheduled sporting event. You know that I improvise as I go along."

"So, I should continue to interact with MAGENTA, but I won't have specific duties or instructions from you on your next assignment. Is that what you're saying?"

"I couldn't have stated the plan more concisely. Yes, please continue to interact with MAGENTA unless it interferes with your professional life. If you need to quit MAGENTA, tell your contacts that you can't get along with me. They'll believe you without asking any other questions. They might give you a separation bonus or trophy for working with me as well as you have."

"And that's all you need from me now?"

"If you order some blocks of C-4 and about 800 feet of wire to be delivered to Paolo in Lisbon identified as landscaping supplies, that would be helpful."

"How much cyclonite is 'some' in case somebody asks?" Amy questioned for clarity.

"Twenty blocks is enough to move Europe closer to North America, or possibly send a shipping container into orbit. I don't know how I'll use it yet, if at all. I probably forgot something, but that's all I need from you now. Do you have anything else for me?"

"Just to confirm once again before you disappear on me and I don't have anyone to speak on my behalf to MAGENTA, if my Scout position changes permanently from your perspective, can we talk about it again before you propose changes?"

"Yes, definitely. I can't predict what MAGENTA, your career, or my needs will be in the future. But, if I believe that your Scout job needs to change in any way, I'll discuss it with you fully before I take any action with MAGENTA, I promise, Scout's honor," I told her truthfully.

"Meanwhile, if you have any concerns, I wouldn't take them to Ron before we have our own séance. Ron has high regard for you, as he should, but until otherwise notified, you're my Scout, not his. We should be able to construct our relationship the way it works best for us rather than what may appear to be a better arrangement negotiated by third parties. Okay?"

Despite our *"entente cordial,"* i.e., our mutually amicable agreement, somewhere in the last few sentences I thought I heard a muffled sob at the other end of the line. There was more going on with Amy than the conversation we were having. Between getting involved in Amy's emotional state or avoiding trouble for myself, I exercised the first option as Ron predicted I would.

CALLING MR. RIGHT

"Okay, Shortcake, what else is going on?" I asked as calmly as I could without displaying my increasing agitation at my inability to control this simple conversation with my Scout, let alone tend to our mutual needs or begin to plan any future actions against any adversaries.

"Oh, I'm okay. It's just the whole thing with Rick, your asking for emergency help when I was extra busy at work, me trying to hide other than with Rick, my chances for promotion, which probably means I see my family less, and me trying to have a life of my own with my friends—sometimes it is just too much tugging and pulling for me to handle at one time."

"Welcome to adulthood, *mademoiselle*. If you can juggle all those concerns, then what Ron told me about you a short time ago is true—you're a savvy lady. If Rick isn't your Mr. Right, you'll find your life partner somewhere else when time and circumstances are better for you. Your guy will have to be mature to deal with you, as I told you before. Also, your relationship might prosper if your Mr. Right is deaf, dumb, and blind," I added softly but apparently not softly enough to keep Amy from hearing.

"What did you say? I didn't hear the last part. My alarm went off."

"I said it would help your relationship if your Mr. Right has a quick and clear mind," I re-phrased liberally with added emphasis on the last word.

"I don't think that's what you said the first time. My alarm isn't that loud. You just made that up. Now you're teasing me!"

"No, I'm not making fun of you in the mood we're in—well, maybe a little. I have this mental image of you as the mother of five kids—two sets of twins and a spare. All of them are screaming their heads off at the same time. And there you stand in the kitchen trying to decide which of your brood receives your attention first. In that moment of confusion and chaos, you'll recall this conversation and think to yourself how challenging and worthwhile the Scout position was in preparing you for your future."

"I think you're over-selling the Scout job, don't you? Are we back to another 'luck of the draw' conversation?"

"No, I think we squeezed as much as we can from that topic. Let me pass along something more sublime. This old Italian saying might help you. It goes, '*Sempre il mai non vien per nuocere.*'"[2]

"What does that mean, get my butt out of bed and go to work?"

"No, hopefully it's something more helpful to you. It means, 'Misfortune does not always come to injure.' Take the lessons that the present seemingly hard times give you to be stronger when more difficult times visit you in the future. That's the best counsel I can offer you now. And, as you say, it's time to get your butt out of bed and go to work. I need to do some work myself."

PROMISES

"Thanks truckloads for waking me up and putting me in the right frame of mind to see me through the day, or a least the next ten minutes. We'll talk before you make any final decision about me being your Scout, won't we? Promise me again at least that much. Besides, you never introduced me to firearms yet, so you'd better make good on your promises."

"I promise, Shortcake, because sometimes I need your words of wisdom when I get stuck on a problem. Just because I'm the ancient member of our team doesn't mean I have a monopoly on smarts as I have so amply demonstrated to you on numerous occasions. I thought I introduced you to firearms when I instructed you to use my flintlock pistol against T1 if necessary while I slipped out the back way to take care of T2 in my yard?"

"Yes, those were helpful instructions—pull the hammer back with my thumbs, point the gun at T1, close my eyes, and pull the trigger. That was truly a great introduction!"

"Sure, but even now, you remember what I told you, which is important. Also, remember that you had the drop on Agent Sanders in the middle of the street and added insult to injury by clobbering him with your knucks. Beyond that, I didn't think you needed an *'affaire d'amour'* with firearms. Against T1, the double ignition of the priming and projectile powder of the flintlock pistol with its noise, flames, and smoke would have been sufficient to alert me that you needed immediate help. I would have come running instantly. Talk about running, both of us better do some of that now. Talk to you soon. Bye."

After I hung up, I realized that circumstances would likely increase the distance between Amy and me. A part of me didn't like the thought of being out in the cold without her competent backup. To make matters worse, the thought struck me that if a similar relationship of open conversation and exchange of feelings and ideas had time to develop between Jenny and me, Jenny might still be alive. Amy's current state of mind reminded me of what had likely been Alice Bright Feather's struggle with her personal and tribal demons. *It was weird how promises and unresolved issues kept popping up in different formats and with different names attached, but without resolution.*

Being a MAGENTA Operative often is tough and thankless, but not unlike the jobs one-third of the world's population faces every day. The other two-thirds of the earth's inhabitants have it rougher. They are unemployed with no prospects for a better future. I could tell I would have a rough day if I didn't dismiss those thoughts and concentrate on the task in front of me. I promised myself that my next move was to have breakfast. Then, I would call Marika for her input about what I might need for my next action against the Calderon network in Europe. I had learned not to call Marika on an empty stomach. She could be brutally frank in her assessment of situations and people, how they should be treated, and how incompetent she believed I was in handling them. After breakfast, I decided not to call Marika. I would go to her office and deal with her directly.

Chapter Notes

1. Prange, Gordon W., Donald M. Goldstein, and Katherine V. Dillon, *Miracle at Midway* (New York: McGraw-Hill, 1982), pp. 269–276. Also, Wikipedia contributors, "Battle of Midway," *Wikipedia, The Free Encyclopedia*, http://en.wikipedia.org/w/index.php?title=Battle_of_Midway&oldid=316181067 (accessed September 7, 2009). pp. 1–19.

2. Whitehall (editor), *op. cit.*, p. 219.

CHAPTER 20

MARIKA AND ST. GEORGE

Mending Fences

At about 10:00 a.m., I walked into Marika's tastefully decorated ground floor suite in a medium-sized professional building. As I opened the door, I heard voices from the back office. Marika was "counseling" her assistant concerning some transgression. Because of her management style, Marika was always training and counseling new assistants. As I pushed the door all the way open, it announced my presence by generating a series of creaks and groans. Although the door could have been oiled or re-hung for silent operation with minimum effort, I was convinced that Marika purposely left it in its present condition so that she was forewarned about the arrival of any visitors. I couldn't argue with her rationale. In its present state, the door was as effective as any alarm system and substantially less expensive. Not that she needed more security. Nobody who knew Marika would dare infringe on her space at any time of day or night. She kept a .357 Magnum in the drawer with her medical tools and knew how to use it.

"Who's there?" Marika called out from her office a little on the testy side at having her counseling session interrupted.

"*Svaty Juraj* (St. George in Slovak)," I answered promptly. "I'm here to fix your dragon problem unless you're the dragon problem."

Oops, I almost blew my cover, alluding to my real first name. Fortunately, Marika knew me only as Joe, and my linguistic slip skidded under her radar. Under either name, she certainly wouldn't connect me with sainthood, nor to my Angry Dragon birth sign in Chinese astrology. Nonetheless, that kind of loose talk was dangerous around Marika, who generally saw, heard, knew, and responded sharply to everything large or small. I got away with it this time because she decided to ignore both my words and my sarcasm. However, with a new assignment brewing, I instructed myself to be more careful about everything as I made the transition away from my Joe Legion identity.

"Saint George has been in his Orthodox tomb for centuries, and today is not anywhere near *Jurjevo* in my country (St. George's Day in her native Serbia). Did anyone see you come in?"

"Not that I noticed. Whatever remains of your reputation is still safe with me from the outside world, or, at least, your immediate neighbors," I answered, annoyed that she had indeed heard my introductory greeting.

"I'm busy now, what do you want?" she announced more sharply than I thought possible with an exchange of only a few short sentences.

"For starters, you could stop tormenting your employee and either let me come in your office, or you come out here to have a business discussion. Is that sufficient, or do you need additional details to grant me an audience?"

"Have a seat, and I'll be with you in a few minutes."

"That's not a good idea. If I overhear any more conversation along the lines of what I just heard, I'll need to be a witness for your employee in any harassment action against you. I might enjoy that, but I don't think you will."

"Okay, come in before you disrupt my staff and my entire appointment schedule," Marika capitulated.

"Now that wasn't so bad, was it?" I commented as the red-faced assistant whizzed past me on her way out of Marika's office.

"I don't appreciate being embarrassed in front of my people," Marika declared as I entered her domain and shut the door behind me.

"Then, stop embarrassing yourself in the way you supervise them. Remember, you're in America now. This is where you wanted to be. This is why you left your family and whatever went with it in Serbia. You risked your life to be here. Lighten up on the natives and let them enjoy their human rights and the softer side of your personality."

"Then, all my tension will build up, and I'll splatter all over you when you come to see me. How would you like that?"

"Look," I verbally retaliated, "both of us are from the same generation, both of us grew up under similar house rules, and both of us didn't thrive very well in our younger days under a kick-everybody-in-the-butt environment. So why pass our grief and faults onto the next generation, for Pete's sake?"

"Yes, but our generation is still physically and mentally tough, disciplined in our thinking, and we know how to do things besides play computer games all day."

"Maybe so, but the larger problem is that we have to remain all those mean-spirited things because for all of our toughness, we haven't made a better or safer world for future generations. We're still stuck in the same unforgiving time warp in which we were born. I'd continue my sermon, but I need your help in attacking the Calderon network in Europe," I petitioned, hoping that she'd appreciate my mental agility in transitioning from my dissertation on the difficulties of our childhood to the main topic of my visit.

"Maybe you're not as tough as I've given you credit for in the past," Marika sputtered. "You waste your time on small fish like Calderon while the larger problems go unchecked. At least, I have my team going after bigger fish. Did you know that?"

"Okay, I'm interested, especially about working with a team when I may not have a Scout for backup this time. By the way, thanks for engaging Ahmed and Cala in Shortcake's name for me. Both were very helpful in the La Montagne part of my Moroccan madness."

"I thought you could use additional resources the way I heard things were going for you. I quit MAGENTA entirely myself. I play with a larger organization that has professional teams, expert support, current intelligence, resources, and federal money."

"I didn't know you changed employers. What unsavory stuff is on your agenda as a federal *ouvrier*?"

"A what?"

"*Ouvrier*—that's French for operative. Sorry if I derailed your thought train."

"I was about to say that while you dally with minor networks, which I admit are bad enough, I've been following a global slave, prostitution, weapons, and drug trafficking network that primarily runs between Southeast Asia through Europe and North Africa into South America. If you're such a hotshot human rights advocate, why don't you join me to stop the human trafficking around the globe?"

"Maybe I should. Tell me more about your target network, especially the human trafficking component. Your playmates may be connected to Calderon's operation. They all seem to know each other if they're not engaged in business directly."

"You are closer to the truth in your last statement than you know. You and your three missionaries interrupted my team's covert operation in South America that could have cost some lives. We left you and them to hang out to dry to save our assignment. I still don't know how you managed not only to escape, but also to bring the missionaries back with you. I was about to call Beth to go on a shopping spree with her when I heard that you were back in town. I was so stressed out that I had to go shopping by myself."

"I noticed your new car in the parking lot. I'm disappointed. I thought I could stress you out for a more expensive model than that. But, these are not fun times. Tell me what's happening in human trafficking circles these days."

"When I speak of human trafficking, most people think only about prostitution. But the problem is bigger than that. It's a modern-day slave trade of men, women, and children," Marika explained.

"I agree with you. I think the problem stems from unrelenting poverty around the world. Have you found that to be true in your work?"

"Mostly, and we've followed the flow of human traffic all over the planet to confirm it. Sometimes, the slave traders snatch somebody off the street when the opportunity presents itself. In such a case, the background of the individual doesn't matter in the least. The victim winds up being somebody's toy. As bad as that is, I think the more vicious schemes are when a slave recruiter approaches a poor family and offers to find jobs for the parents, or proposes to find educational opportunities for the children in another country. Of course, the trader has expenses and fees for these services that the family can never hope to repay from their nonexistent savings. No problem, says the trader, he will loan the family the money which they can pay back when they find the good jobs or better schools in a country of the trader's choosing. The details may vary from case to case, but the bottom line is that the promised jobs and schools never materialize," Marika continued, becoming more aggravated with each sentence she uttered.

"The adults and kids become servants, guerrilla fighters, camel jockeys, prostitutes, drug dealers, or enforcers for the trader or his clients for as long as it takes to repay the loan, or until they wind up in a garbage pile somewhere when they're no longer useful," Marika added. "Nobody escapes the slave network because the families have no money to search for the victims, who usually are hidden or moved from country to country. The international police don't have the time or resources to track missing people around the globe, and the trader's clients don't ask questions as long as they have their 'playthings.' The families can't complain to anyone because they don't know where the children have been taken, and they certainly don't want the bodies of their loved ones deposited on their doorstep during the night. That's horrible, and we must stop it. You think that I'm hard on my employees, but when I see these things in the world and I cannot stop them or get help to stop them, every cell of my body is filled with anger," Marika ended her summary description of the slave trade and displayed her emotions by pounding on her desk.

"Good, stay angry, Marika. I won't argue about the global problem you've described. In my wanderings, I've identified the Calderon drug network as running between Peru and Bolivia into the States and then on to Europe and North Africa through Portugal or Spain. Alternatively, shipments go directly from South America through the Cape Verde islands into Europe or North Africa. Once a drug network is established, I don't doubt that other commodities flow along the same routes. While I was in Morocco, I heard that a sizable group of sub-Saharan refugees pay exorbitant fees or take loans with local coyotes to transport them to Senegal in small boats just to have a shot at reaching Spain, Portugal, or across the Atlantic to the States if they don't capsize and drown first. I have more than I can handle with just the drug routes I mentioned, so I haven't studied the weapons or human traffic routes as you have. You mentioned large multi-purpose networks, but, in your experience, are most set up that way, or are the majority smaller and specialized?"

"Some of both," Marika replied. "For example, an open source identified the top fifty-six countries with the heaviest volume of human trafficking. I have a list here that is shocking and probably includes your Peruvian and Bolivian networks. Other countries on the list may surprise you such as: Algeria, Argentina, Armenia, Bahrain, Brazil, Cambodia, the Central African Republic, China, Cyprus, Djibouti, Ecuador, Egypt, Equatorial Guinea, France, Germany, India, Indonesia, Israel, Italy, Jamaica, Kenya, Kuwait, Libya, Lithuania, Macau, Malaysia, Mauritania, Mexico, Oman, Qatar, Russia, South Africa, Taiwan, Togo, and the United Arab Emirates," she read in one breath. "Particularly heavy trafficking occurs in Albania, Belarus, Belize, Burma (Myanmar), Cuba, Iran, North Korea, Romania, Saudi Arabia, Sudan, Syria, Ukraine, Uzbekistan, Venezuela, and Zimbabwe," Marika continued on breath two.[1] "So, if you think the United States and its supposed allies are exempt from trafficking or are devoting enough resources to stopping it, you're absolutely wrong. I forgot to mention Thailand and Laos. Lord knows we wouldn't want to omit any country on the list. Yes, you're absolutely and terribly wrong if you think that the world community has these networks under control. As I said, as bad as they are in themselves, they also provide funding for international terrorist groups. You won't be able to stop them by yourself.

I'm not confident that my team can stop the trafficking without additional resources and international cooperation," Marika emphasized the overwhelming scope of this human tragedy in our present world.

"What country or area in the world is free from illegal trafficking? You named every place or organization on earth except the St. Chrysogonus Glee Club and Knitting Society as a haven for human trafficking. Have you had any success in stopping or penetrating the networks?"

"Last week, I unfortunately found the body of one of my *ouvriers*, as you call them, in an abandoned warehouse in Southeast Asia. Does that count as penetration?"

"That's a discouraging picture you've painted."

"Speaking of painting," Marika continued as she dug in her desk drawer, pulled out a piece of paper, and handed it to me, "this was found alongside the body of my operative. Apparently, he used his finger and his own blood to paint this page as he was dying. Can you make any sense of what he wrote?"

"The lettering appears fairly clear at the start," I stated after looking at the page for a few minutes. "It looks like he wrote 'Do Spi' with the last letters trailing off as if he didn't have enough blood or life left in him to finish the message."

"That's what we concluded," Marika said as she took the paper back from me. "But, we don't know who or what it means. We investigated all the shops, restaurants, and other merchants in the immediate area, but we couldn't locate a 'Do Spi' connection. We used all sorts of variations such as 'Pi SDo,' 'S pi Do' and so forth, but we still can't decipher the message."

"In what country did you say the agent was killed?"

"I didn't say, but it was Thailand."

"Do you know the town or village?"

"It was on an island actually, Ko Pha Ngan if I pronounced it correctly. Do you know this place?"[2]

I almost said no before a favorable brain synapse activated my recall button on a case from years ago.

DOUBLE DEALING

Instead, I said, "Yes, but that information comes at a price."

"I have a generous budget, but it's not ethical for you to extort money from a federal agency. But, I'll let you handle that problem when I report you. Name your price."

"I won't cripple your budget or violate CIA or FBI ethics—if one of those agencies pays your expenses. If I give you the information, my price includes two non-cash items."

"Okay, I am listening, Mr. *Ouvrier Svaty Juraj* (Operative St. George)."

"My first item is a request that you lighten up on your employees. If you don't like their performance, train them to work more efficiently rather than hollering and beating them up. Do you agree?"

"You're totally nuts to blackmail me concerning my business practices, do you know that? I know you jumped from airplanes. Did you ever fall on your head? But, yes I agree," Marika closed quickly before I added additional provisions or sanctions.

"Remember, there's no limit to what you can accomplish if you do things my way. Okay, my second item requires that you help me bring down the Calderon network. If you agree, I'll help you with your problem because you gave me real-life examples that any network can be interchangeably linked for drugs, prostitution, money laundering, human trafficking, gun-running, you name it."

"Now that I know what you want, I should have given you cash and kept my mouth shut," Marika fidgeted. "We are independent people with two different management methods. Are you sure we can work together?"

"I didn't say 'work together,' I said 'collaborate'—keep each other informed and lend a hand or resources when the other is in trouble. I don't want to give up my freedom to operate as I think best any more than you do."

"Okay, it's a deal, but your information better be good or there's no deal," Marika challenged as I knew she would.

"Agreed," I said. "Here's my first installment of useful information. Although drugs are strictly prohibited in Thailand, it's no secret that drugs are as readily available as candy on Ko Pha Ngan where some big money types like to take their vacations accompanied by their playthings. The island has nice beaches, waterfalls, and other attractions to bring in enough tourists for the Calderon or other networks to make a nice living off drugs, even after compensating the local *gendarmes*, if necessary. Call it coincidence, but that island has a Moroccan restaurant through which Calderon associates or other networks can conveniently conduct business. For instance, Calderon's henchmen from Tangier or Ceuta could blend in among the restaurant's North African guests very nicely. On the other hand, a naïve, non-network tourist could be arrested for possession of a small amount of drugs, and be forced to pay the police *beaucoup bahts* (the Thai currency) to get out of jail in time to attend his grandkids' college graduation."

"That's informative, but what about Do Spi? Is he the local police chief or network boss?" Marika asked urgently.

"You're not even close. Remember that Ko Pha Ngan is an island. To get to an island without a helicopter you need a boat, and a boat needs a dock or pier on both shores. The island is about a hundred-kilometer trip from the Thai mainland port of Surat Thani. Surat Thani has three piers in the neighborhood. The Ban Don pier is in the town itself. The Tha Thong pier is about five kilometers outside of town. A third pier located about sixty kilometers from Surat Thani is named—ta dah—Don Sak pi__!"

"Don Sak pier, yes!" Marika shouted gleefully to accompany my vocal drum roll. "It's so obvious now! Why couldn't we get it?"

"Why, indeed? Don Sak pier has ferries to handle cars and buses. It's not a mental stretch to assume that the Calderon and other networks use the Don Sak pier as the supply point for drugs and other contraband going to or from Ko Pha Ngan. The same may be true of other resort islands in the Gulf of Thailand. If a messenger or dealer wants to go first class, or if he's being pursued by the police or competitors, the area has express, charter, and private boats. Your operative may have made the connection between the island's receiving point and the mainland's shipping point for contraband and paid for his education with his life. Do you still want to operate alone, or shall we collaborate to get these people?" I asked, ending my interpretation of the data Marika presented to me.

"How did you connect the dots on Don Sak pier when you were never near the place?"

"One miracle after another, they just keep coming," I taunted her. "The question remains. Do you want to collaborate or not?"

"Before I answer that question, I also have information that you might find valuable. As you say, my information has a price tag on it too."

"Before you tell me anything else, what is your price? I don't have a lot of cash behind my activities. Second, I will not negotiate further on the two conditions I proposed and that you accepted before I gave you my information on Don Sak pier."

"Agreed. I will work hard not to harass my employees again, although I may slip into my old habits when you're not around. But, if we collaborate, I want you to promise that I get the first chance to bring down a person who I believe is connected to the Calderon network and to the network that I'm following. That's my price."

"Okay, I agree to your price."

"You're not going to ask who it is, or why I want credit for his capture?"

"No, I'm only one person and I have my hands loaded already with the remaining Calderon brother. Apparently, you have a nice budget and capable people working with you. If you have the resources to bring down somebody connected to Calderon, that's fine with me. Just let me know who it is and what I need to do to assist you, or to stay out of your way."

"I hate negotiating with you. You collapse without any effort to bargain. You don't have a clue about who my target is," Marika shifted to her aggressive persona as I had anticipated she would.

"Your target is General Vasily. He's a veteran with many years of military service devoted to the sale of stolen and contraband goods. Further, I'll venture that he's peddling conventional weapons or nuclear, biological, or chemical devices that he's stolen from bases in the Ukraine. He recognizes that the Calderon network may be useful for his purposes. How do I know about Vasily, you ask? He's done everything except take out advertising in the major international newspapers on the commodities he has for sale. Your target network boss and Calderon are big enough to consider enhancing their reputations by acquiring or trading weapons to some well-heeled client—either a terrorist group or rogue country. So, Vasily is an important player. Can you confirm if he's working with a Kuwaiti named Hassan?"

"First, tell me why you are so interested in Vasily's and your man Hassan's activities since the last time we talked."

"My cousin Daniela in Slovakia has good ears, bright eyes, and her own connections to keep tabs on Vasily for me while he's in or passing through Slovakia. Hassan generally surfaces in a country about the same time as Vasily shows up. I'm glad you haven't forgotten our brief conversation about him when you were still a Scout. Now that I know more about his travels and interests, I believe he is big and dangerous enough for CIA or FBI attention. So, are you ready to collaborate on our operations, or do I have to bribe you with pastries from your favorite bakery?"

"You continue to surprise me with the extent of your information about seemingly unrelated things. So, yes, we can act independently, keep each other informed, and help each other if needed. I agree to that. Oh, one more thing. Is your wife going on this trip?"

"I'll leave that to her. Initially, I thought not. But, she could stay in Slovakia with Daniela and observe Vasily and Hassan, or watch for a lady in a black *burka* who we believe is connected to the Calderon network. We also have a family project she could amuse herself with in her spare time."

"Okay, we agree to the working arrangement, let's shake on it," Marika said as she extended her hand.

Scheming

"Good, I have my first collaborative request," I answered while putting my right hand at risk to shake hands with her.

"I should have given you more credit for being a sneaky negotiator after all. What do you want now?"

"Ron told me that Ernesto Calderon believes a rival gang is responsible for killing his brother, Gilberto, in a helicopter crash. I'd like to capitalize on his misinformation, possibly start a gang war, and let the rival groups destroy each other."

"To catch fish in that pond, you need attractive bait. For big fish, you need very attractive bait. Do you have the right bait to catch these fish?" Marika interrogated and scolded me simultaneously.

"A few minutes ago, you chided me that I'm wasting time with small fry. Now you want to know what size bait I use. If we hadn't agreed to collaborate with each other, I might be upset with you. But in the spirit of mutual cooperation, I'll give you a forthright answer."

"Don't strain yourself trying something entirely new like being forthright," Marika smirked.

"Calm yourself, and mark the words of a master strategist. I contemplated diverting several Calderon containers from South America to a rival gang relatively close to Calderon's locations in Europe or North Africa. You said that the network you're tracking is extensive. Does it have seaport connections in the western Mediterranean to receive some wayward shipping containers that might trigger a gang war if Calderon believes another network is angling to take over his business?"

"Where do you want the shipping containers to go? I can arrange shipment to my brother's house in Belgrade," Marika responded sarcastically.

"That might be a good start. How big is his garage and what is the nearest seaport that might mishandle a few Calderon containers of contraband goods originally intended to dock in Tangier or Ceuta?"

"Not big enough to hold a shipload of containers certainly, but you show some genius in your ramblings. The Sandzak network that I'm tracking—"

"You're tracking Sancak?! Is it the same or a descendant network of the Turkish paramilitary organization dating back to the Ottoman feudal system when Turkey controlled the Balkans?[3] That Sancak? Why don't we try something easy like starting a war with Russia and China simultaneously? Sorry, I should have listened closer when you said that you were tailing an extensive network. Sancak—wow, that is huge!"

"Before you interrupted me, I wanted to tell you that the SANDZAK network as we know it in Serbia has its headquarters in Belgrade. It is not connected to the Turkish Sancak organization of the banner that you're wowing about. But, it is big and well organized."

"Belgrade is in the middle of Serbia. I need a seaport to make my plan work. How can a Muslim organization have a base of operations in Belgrade of all places after the Yugoslav wars in the early 1990s? I thought that Slobodan Milosevic and the Serbian Army killed or evicted most of the Muslims from Bosnia, Kosovo, and the other former Yugoslavian republics long before the United Nations sent in NATO's reluctant 'Rapid Response' peacekeepers?"

DEADLY DETAILS

"Listen to me a minute before you start whining about the information I'm giving you at no cost. First, which Mediterranean, Aegean, or Adriatic seaport under Sandzak's control do you prefer? Naples? Tunis? Venice? Dubrovnik? Trieste? I can set you up in any port city that you want. Second, the Sandzak network is operated exclusively by Serbians. The name no longer has anything to do with Ottoman, medieval, or paramilitary units. The current Sandzak network has an Arabic-sounding name because it has its tentacles and clients throughout Turkey, the Middle East, and North Africa as well as Europe. The Serbian bosses use the old name to make the network palatable to their Arab clients who think that they're dealing with a Turkish-controlled operation. More important, because certain post-Milosevic Serbian officials have 'shares' in the organization, these illustrious politicians can publicly denounce and disengage more easily from 'a despicable Muslim network' than one with a Serbian name. That way, they can have their blood money while publicly maintaining Serbia's centuries-long feud with Islam and the more recently inserted Muslim *mujahedeen* fighters of the 1990s' Yugoslav wars. So, the network's name is set up for Muslims to get a black eye if the United States, the United Nations, Interpol, or the European

Union close down the network. Clever of the Serbian network bosses, don't you think?"

"Okay, I get the picture. Trieste might do for my purposes if it has container facilities and trucks that can transport containers inland from there."

"My dear, lost soul, Italy and the Balkan countries were trading with the Turks, Egyptians, Greeks, and other Islamic countries as far back as Roman times. Do you think that the Balkan countries have not established the necessary ocean and land infrastructure for trade of any kind—including containers—ages ago? Do you believe that General Vasily is the first one to think of shipping weapons or nuclear materials from Russia or the Ukraine through any of these European ports?"

"I'd guess the answer you're looking for is no."

"You have excellent perception. To continue your geography lesson, the Balkan coastline is dotted with *karst* areas and innumerable caves and valleys to hide people, goods, and shipping containers. You have a point, though. Vasily could be interested in or be persuaded to have an interest in a port like Trieste to get his weapons from Europe to North Africa if he has a buyer there. But, you forgot one thing."

"Are you asking how do we get Vasily to climb into a container with Calderon and a nuclear warhead for a Mediterranean cruise to Ceuta?" I tried an all-encompassing, but unlikely, vision of Vasily's destruction.

"No, but unless the Sandzak and Calderon networks are totally stupid, they send containers with legitimate goods in addition to their contraband shipments. We don't have a way to separate contraband containers from legitimate ones to start a network war between them."

"You're almost right," I reassured Marika to regain my former stature as a can-do wizard in her eyes. "I fortuitously came upon a Calderon scanner in the marketplace in Marrakesh when I was trying to rescue a carpet containing my wife. If Calderon hasn't changed codes, we can identify his illegal containers and his hired help too by scanning them for embedded microchips."

"That's a high-powered answer for a small time *ouvrier* like you. I like it. But, have you considered the implications of my group helping you divert Calderon's containers at the Cape Verde shipyards past the Gibraltar Straits through the Mediterranean and into the Adriatic Sea to a safe haven in Italy or Slovenia with all the tensions remaining between the Albanians, Serbs, Kosovars, Croats, Bosnians, and others?" Marika reminded me.

"Yes, that sums up my proposal nicely, if it isn't too much trouble for you. I don't care if you need to divert a few containers to locations other than Trieste if we can get Calderon and Sandzak to notice that their formerly smooth-running networks suddenly have unexplained glitches caused by rivals interdicting their shipments."

"And you don't think Calderon will look for his containers soon after his ship captains report them missing from the Cape Verde docks?"

"I can minimize that risk through my contacts in Portugal and Peru."

"You're sure about that?"

"If one of my contacts wants to go to jail, dishonor his family, and miss seeing his new baby, he might disappoint me and refuse to cooperate, but I don't think so. I can use him to maneuver my contact in Peru into our web. Now that I think about it, both are in excellent positions to divert Calderon shipments on their own authority. Then, all you and your team need do is find an empty warehouse or cave somewhere to hide the containers and wait for Calderon or Sandzak to show up after they receive an anonymous tip concerning the location of their diverted property. How does that strike you?" I asked pleasantly.

"Why don't we interdict the containers at a resort along the Dalmatian Coast? Then, I can work on my tan while we wait for network representatives to arrive," Marika suggested with accompanying sarcasm.

"You know that area better than I do. Whatever works for you is fine with me," I played it uncharacteristically straight to determine if Marika would wobble.

"You really have a diabolical mind, do you know that? Let me think about it, and I'll get back to you."

"Make it soon, and don't tell the people you report to about it yet. Calderon has half of Africa and South America on his payroll, and your Sandzak network probably has Europe plus several other continents under its control. I wouldn't be surprised if they have a few payrollees in your organization too. Any loose lips on this voyage will sink both of our ships," I admonished.

"What if someone I report to asks why I put through vouchers funding this project without prior explanation or justification?"

"Tell them the charges are for preservation of watershed refuges for wild cranes migrating between Europe and Africa. I don't know. I'm sure you can invent something. I already semi-solved the container diversion problem for you plus interdicted a scanner. What else do you want from me this morning?"

"Container diversion was your problem when you came in here, not mine, remember?"

"Details, details. Set your mind on the big picture for now, Marika, and I'll help you through the details as they become important. I need to run home now. *Do videnja*—(good-bye)."

As I left Marika's office, I went past her assistant's desk where the young lady was facing the wall as she worked at her computer.

NO HARASSMENT, JUST FAMILY FUN

"Hopefully, life will get better for you around here very soon," I told her as she turned in her chair to face me. "I talked to Marika about her business manners and reminded her to treat her employees with respect."

"Oh, that's okay," the receptionist said. "Aunt Marika has always been a little gruff, but I don't mind. She shouts a lot, but she's always been good to me and to a lot of other troubled people who come to her. She's paying my college tuition for the little part-time work I do here. I'm her niece, Anna. And you are?"

"Apparently, I'm a dead duck," I responded, laughing mostly at myself. "I was attempting to rescue you when you don't need rescuing. But, as far as your Aunt Marika is concerned, the old Latin saying '*Varium et mutabile semper foemina*' still holds true. 'Woman is ever a changeful and capricious thing.'"[4]

"I don't understand," Anna sought an explanation.

"Good, leave it that way for now," I told her as I grabbed a mint from the candy jar on my way out.

But, capricious or not, the fact remained that I needed Marika's help and whatever resources she had to assist me on this project. An illegal network with political connections would be a real challenge to disrupt or close down in any country.

The next person I wanted to talk to was Beth. I needed a favorable outcome in that discussion too. I drove home surprised at how much time had elapsed despite my early start in the morning. As I gathered my equipment for the trip, I decided to contact Advari by e-mail. I temporarily abandoned my equipment piles at various locations throughout the house while I engaged in cyber-conversation with Advari. My timing for abandoning my equipment couldn't have been worse as Beth discovered when she returned from grocery shopping.

"Do you have any particular reason for making a pigsty out of our house with all your stuff laying around?" Beth inquired somewhat upset.

"I was in the equipment assembly stage of packing, if that's not obvious to you," I protested. "I sent an e-mail to Advari, then started playing with Calderon's computer code sheets that Felipe pulled out of the Tingo Maria safe to see if they worked. Don't worry, I'll straighten out the equipment mess," I submitted obediently to give her hope of recovering living space within her lifetime. "But that's not your real question, is it? You're really asking where am I going, and if you can come. Did I interpret your real question correctly?"

"Close. But, I would have phrased it as, 'Do I have to come with you on this trip?'"

"If you haven't recovered from being a carpet hostage yet, I understand, and you can stay home. But Daniela and you can watch the back door in Slovakia for Vasily, Hassan, the *burka* lady, and anyone else who may be traveling with them while I collaborate with Marika in Serbia."

"In her last letter, Daniela said she and her observers haven't seen any of them around Piestany for an unusually long time."

BETH'S PROPOSED ITINERARY

"Yes, I read her letter. That's why I hope Daniela and you can visit some of the other spas in Slovakia and the Czech Republic to determine if Calderon moved his central operations elsewhere."

"We could search for them around Hradcany Castle, the Charles Bridge, or the Opera House in Prague. If they aren't there, we could extend our surveillance to the spa and shops of Karlovy Vary, the beer caves in Plzen, the breweries of Ceske Budejovice, or the old town of Cesky Krumlov with a stop on the way from Slovakia at Brno in Moravia on the outside chance that they might be there." Beth checked off her proposed travel itinerary.

"I compliment your efforts to design touristy trips for Daniela and yourself, but you're arranging an itinerary with more practical applications than you might intend. Calderon and other related or competitive networks have more tentacles than an octopus roundup. If they're entertaining potential customers from North Africa, Europe, the Middle East, and Asia, they might bring their guests to the places you named."

"How about the ski lodges, mountain trails, and kayaking centers in the Tatra Mountains? Shouldn't we cover them too?" Beth pursued her itinerary further.

"They're possibilities." I decided not to challenge her directly. "If you girls cover the towns you mentioned, maybe Marek the Magnificent and his park rangers can cover the natural attractions."

"Do you seriously want Daniela and me to do this?"

"I wasn't certain a few minutes ago, but I'm warming to the idea. This is a good way for both of you to help me in surroundings that are familiar to you. At least, you should be able to hunt around without getting yourselves rolled up in carpets and dropped off in the middle of a desert."

"And among all the people in Central Europe, you want us to locate Vasily, Hassan, and the *burka* lady, correct?"

"You ask as if that's an impossible task for motivated tourists like Daniela and you. I'll grant you that Vasily is a wildcard. But you know that Hassan always travels first class. So, automatically you can eliminate any other level of hotels and shops to find him. *Burka* lady is a puzzle too. Who knows? While in Europe, she may convert to a skirt or slacks and not wear her *burka* at all. Then, how would you know her? We've never seen her face."

"Then, Daniela and I will observe her accessories, her voice, how she stands, and how she walks to identify her as you coached me on our last trip."

"Okay, good. You remember our discussions about what we look for when we have no face or hair to observe. Since then, I've rerun my mental tape on her walking around that restaurant across the street from the Royal Mansour Hotel a million times. I've come down to one characteristic that is out of place."

"She walks funny, doesn't she?" Beth pre-empted me. I mean her stride appears longer than someone accustomed to being confined by a *burka*."

"Good, and what kind of person might that be?"

"Like you said, perhaps a woman who normally doesn't wear a *burka*."

"Okay, stretch your cranial muscles a little further. What other possibilities are there?"

"A man doesn't wear a *burka* either."

"You've taken a giant leap, but that's a good answer. Why?"

"You're rushing me, and I don't know where you're going with this."

"Okay, I'll help you because my evidence is circumstantial. We assume that the *burka* lady isn't Ernesto Calderon because Ernesto wears a straw hat with a red hatband. A man wearing a hat with a red hatband exchanged packages with the *burka* lady. But, what if Ernesto was the *burka* lady that day, and another person wore the hat on that occasion to impress potential buyers as Hassan suggested. Since then, we've never seen Ernesto Calderon, a red hatband, and the *burka* lady in the same place at the same time, have we? We need to know if the *burka* lady is Ernesto or different people as the occasion requires."

"You may be right, but, do you think macho Spanish *conquistadors* such as Gilberto and Ernesto Calderon would dress as a woman? I think that would be impossible for their masculine minds to contemplate."

"That's a good observation. Nonetheless, if you find the *burka* lady you probably have found Calderon too. At worst, Calderon isn't the *burka* lady, but he's somewhere nearby."

My Proposed Itinerary

"And where will you be while Daniela and I are working hard for you?" Beth inquired to ensure a balanced workload between us.

"My first stop will be at Paolo's in Lisbon. Marika confirmed my belief that both Chauncey and Paolo are involved up to their shirt collars in the Calderon network. I know that Chauncey is weak, and I don't know what Paolo's problem is, but their participation in illegal shipments for Calderon or themselves must stop. From what Marika told me, I don't think I'll shield either one from arrest now, even if I can."

"What becomes of Advari if Paolo is arrested or gunned down?"

"I admit that's another unknown. I hope the networks I'm fighting haven't swallowed Advari too. I only have Paolo's word for it that Advari is applying himself properly in school. About the only person who I can trust besides you is Amy, and she's barely keeping her boat afloat doing her therapy job."

"That's not uncommon these days. Everybody is being pulled in forty directions at once," Beth remarked.

"Another way of stating it is that nobody's problems are being resolved in our society. We've created a world we can't live in, and we don't have any good alternatives. The world is like a carnival run by morons. Many people have less than we have, so I don't have any idea of how to solve their problems except to get rid of scum like Calderon who prey upon them."

"And I thought you retired to a period of blissful leisure, silly me. Before we pack to chase the bad guys, I want you to know that I bought your apples. I forgot what kind you wanted that the store never has anyway, so I bought three varieties including your favorite Grandma, see? Are these okay?" Beth asked, pulling an apple out of her shopping bag for my inspection.

ERRANT APPLE

I had looked away from Beth and returned to inputting Calderon's codes to infiltrate the firewalls and security systems protecting his tracking system for contraband shipments. As I was about to press the Enter key, the apple slipped out of Beth's hand and landed on the computer keyboard. Taken by surprise, the monitor generated solar flares while displaying multiple screens loaded with an array of cargo ship names, sailing dates, ports of exit and entry, shipping container numbers, and money amounts. After the computer settled on one screen, I needed several minutes to interpret what I saw and to express thanks to my Guiding Hand that I had not been electrocuted.

"Oops, I'm sorry. Did I destroy your computer? The apple was slippery," Beth explained and apologized. "Will that cost me a lot of money to replace?" she asked apprehensively.

"Actually, the collision of fruit and mechanical apples was fortuitous. Look at this."

"I'm looking, but I don't know what it is. Do you know what those numbers are?"

"The numbers on the left are mundane shipping data. If my interpretation is correct, the numbers in the columns on the right are the fun factors."

"Like what kind of fun?"

"The shipping information on the far left identifies ships coming out of the Mediterranean, Portugal, or Spain destined for the U.S. or South America. Paolo monitors those ships in Lisbon. That's my working hypothesis, but I think I'm on target because the next column to the right identifies ships coming out of South American ports that Chauncey monitors, see?"

"Why do some have money amounts listed while others don't?"

"I think the ships shown with money amounts represent those with Calderon's contraband cargo on board. The numbers in parentheses probably identify the containers and the value of the illegal part of the cargo. You may have recreated the cosmic 'Big Bang' of the shipping universe the more I look at this. See here. The money amounts shown for cargo coming out of Europe are in *euros*, while the money figures for containers coming out of South America are in *pesos*. Sure enough, tracing down the list verifies my premise in every case. Good job, Beth!"

"You have three more columns of smaller numbers on the right side to go. What are they?"

"I knew you'd question numbers I'm less confident about as soon as I complimented you. Mirror, mirror, on the wall, what do I the three columns call?"

"Commissions or payoffs, maybe?" Beth suggested.

"Uhmm, commissions on illegal cargo, I don't think so. The numbers are too small to be bribes. The data confirm unequivocally that Hassan was correct in suspecting that Paolo and Chauncey are skimming off some of Calderon's cargo and profits. Look, the numbers always reduce the total cargo values by either odd-numbered *pesos* or *euros*. I challenged Chauncey and Paolo on alleged skimming based on what Hassan had told me, and now I have proof."

"Then, what does the last column of numbers represent?"

"Those small numbers, my dear Pirate Queen—and now I'm certain—represent the impact of a brief, but productive, Jesuit education on a street urchin from Chennai, alias Advari. I was worried that he'd be sucked into the Calderon network. On the contrary, the little thief is taking his cut from cargo going in both directions. They're small, but always in odd-numbered amounts, like Paolo and Chauncey's numbers. This has to be Advari's chart. No wonder Paolo said that Advari was interested in the shipping business and that he was helpful around the office. A little larceny over time will make him a rich man—or a dead student if Calderon catches him at it."

"What do you intend to do?" Beth asked with growing concern.

"I didn't plan to involve Advari in this next trip. I just sent him an e-mail to let him know that. Now, I don't know if that was wise because I don't want my e-mail to go astray and bring premature attention to him or his innovative enterprise. Calderon won't leave enough of him to bury if he finds out what Advari is doing."

"Will Calderon do the same thing to Chauncey and Paolo?"

"Almost certainly, and I can envision them dying slow deaths too. Advari is just playing, but the other two are deeply involved in illegal trafficking. Maybe I can use this information to force cooperation from them in dismantling Calderon's network. If worse comes to worse, I can have them arrested for smuggling. At least, that could spare their lives.

Scratch that; no it won't. Calderon probably has prison guards on his payroll too. He can reach anyone in jail just as easily as he can on the street. I'll think of something. Well, all this information has potential value one way or another."

"Whatever you decide, it looks like your computer took a couple of chunks out of Granny on her way to the floor," Beth said as she retrieved the apple from under my chair. "You may as well wipe the carpet fuzzies off and finish her while you think about how to rescue your friends. They always seem to get themselves and you into trouble no matter what you do for them."

"I agree with you. Having them as friends is becoming hard work. I hope they remain alive long enough for me to extract them from harm one more time. In any event, I should make paper copies of these lists while I have them available. Bouncing apples off the keyboard may not be a sure-fire way of retrieving future data if Calderon changes codes regularly."

"When do you propose we leave, after Christmas church services or after the New Year's football games?"

"Unless you want a houseful of family and guests walking over my equipment in the middle of the hall, I plan to leave before Christmas. An early departure date is more imperative and complicated now that I know about Advari's computer lists."

"Do you think your family will understand why we're not inviting them for Christmas dinner this year?"

"They will if you send them nice cards and presents from Prague. Think of it—Christmas in Prague."

"Okay, you made your point. I'll start packing."

A few minutes of intense packing took place before the phone rang. It was Marika.

Marika Invites Herself

"I thought about our conversation and decided to join you," she said calmly. "You won't survive in Serbia as a tourist let alone as a terrorist hunter."

"By going with me, I hope you don't mean on the same plane because I intend to fly to Lisbon first, plus ensure that Beth connects with my cousin in Prague or Bratislava before I go anywhere near Serbia."

"That's fine with me. I can visit my brother in Belgrade and wait for you there."

"If you're worried about my survival in your homeland and are at a loss about what to do with yourself, you and your colleagues could eliminate some of the local terrorists before I arrive. That would tie in nicely with your intent to receive credit for this entire Calderon-Sandzak joint venture."

"Tell me the truth. Are you afraid to engage them by yourself?" Marika cajoled.

"Actually, I am more afraid of you than any terrorist network. I have absolutely no idea how you'll act or react in any given situation."

"That's good. We will keep it that way. Contact me when you arrive in Belgrade. Good-bye."

A few more minutes of intense packing occurred after I hung up the phone. I placed a call to Chauncey at the embassy in Peru. He was not there, so I left a message stating, in no uncertain terms, that it was urgent for him to meet Paolo and me in Lisbon in two days. After leaving him behind in the Melilla military prison, I wasn't sure if Chauncey would ever travel at my insistence again. But, he knew Beth's rescue was my first priority. And, Calderon may have put him in prison for appearance's sake and protective custody against my wrath for his involvement in illegal activities. Somehow, he had managed his release or escape. So, this was as good a way as any to test his loyalties once more.

"Who was that?" Beth asked as she returned to the room with an armload of clothes, having missed my phone message to Chauncey.

"My Serbian tour guide, Marika," I answered.

"What did she want?"

"She was checking to see if I needed hotel reservations while I'm in Belgrade. You know, she really is a thoughtful person under her tough exterior. She also wanted my measurements to give to the undertaker. Serbia lacks cemetery space so she wants to ensure room is available if I need it."

"You have perceptive and helpful friends. You should invite them over sometime when we need work done around the house."

"Although I didn't invite Amy, her tour of our house really didn't go well, if you recall. She and others aren't in a hurry to be invited here regardless of what's on the menu. Plus, matching my schedule with theirs is too complicated for a few hours of fun on the patio, especially in winter. Besides, if I invite only a few, those left out would feel, well, left out, and you know how that goes."

"Yes, believe me, I understand how that goes. For forty years, I've understood how that goes."

"Yeah, I suppose you do, but you have a chance to spend Christmas in Prague. How many other wives in the neighborhood have that opportunity?"

"The other wives in the neighborhood are Irish, Italian, German, Indian, or Oriental. They don't care about Christmas in Prague."

"They would if they knew a set of crystal glassware comes with it."

"Does that mean I finally can buy crystal glassware while I'm in Prague?"

"Certainly, why not? You've waited long enough."

Itinerary Change Payoff

Two days later, Beth and I flew into London's Heathrow Airport. From there, Beth went to meet Daniela in Bratislava while I flew to Lisbon. I wasn't looking forward to visiting either Paolo or Chauncey. At the last minute, I responded to an unsolicited, but useful warning from my Guiding Hand and changed my flight to Madrid. Then, I chartered a private flight to Lisbon with help from Marika. The extra cost and time difference was worth the effort. When I arrived at the Lisbon airport, the gates usually reserved for flights directly from the U.S. or the capital cities of Europe appeared especially active with security police milling about. Nobody noticed my arrival at one of the quieter gates on the far side of the terminal. From my position behind a handy sign, I scanned the crowd for my two derelict friends, who I firmly believed were responsible for the extra police presence. Within a few minutes, I spotted Paolo and Chauncey at a rear table in a coffee shop. My Guiding Hand was especially generous to me that night in providing an incoming flight that attracted the full attention of waiting relatives and the *Policia de Securitas*. With everyone distracted and looking in the opposite direction, I walked into the coffee shop unnoticed until it was too late for Chauncey or Paolo to announce my arrival to any Calderon representatives or security personnel.

"*Bom dia*, gentlemen, *fala Ingles*?" I said as I approached their table taking them totally by surprise.

"*Ola* to you," Paolo replied weakly. "We did not know when to expect you."

"Yes, I understand you need extra *vigilantes* to watch for me," I said as I swept my hand to encompass the crowd of police at the gates on the opposite side of the concourse. But, I'm here now and tired from my travels. Paolo, could we leave as soon as possible for your *casa*? I have my luggage with me. No, it's okay, Chauncey, I can handle it comfortably by myself. How have you two been since I saw you last?"

"I hope you are not upset if we go to my *casa* in Cascais," Paolo explained, not bothering to answer my question or to give Chauncey a chance to talk. My wife is close to her birthing time, and she needs all the rest and quiet she can get at our Lisbon home."

"Paolo, I understand and apologize for coming at this busy and anxious time for you and your wife, but sometimes events cannot wait for our comfort, can they?"

Having raised their level of discomfort by alluding to pressing matters, I decided not to talk more than absolutely necessary during our drive to Paolo's seaside home. I let my silence chip away at their respective psyches. Neither Paolo nor Chauncey spoke during the trip, but, under the pressure of my nonverbal engagement, their brain magma must have been percolating close to the surface. When we arrived at Paolo's house, the presence of the maid and valet allowed me to slip away to the shower and sheets without disclosing the purpose of my visit. The next morning, I took my time with flush and brush activities to ensure that I would be the last one to arrive downstairs for breakfast. Paolo and Chauncey were still at the breakfast table. The time of their reckoning had arrived.

Sermon by the Sea

"Good morning, I hope you slept well," Paolo said cordially.

"Yes, very well, thank you. I was really wiped out last night. I hope you will pardon my manners. I try to avoid important conversations when I'm that tired," I answered as I went to the sideboard to find something familiar to eat.

"Oh," Chauncey spoke up as he came to the sideboard to refill his coffee cup, "do we have something important to discuss? I thought this was merely a holiday gathering."

"Without being melodramatic, our families could celebrate the anniversaries of our respective deaths in addition to Christmas in future years. I leave it to you whether that has any importance to you or not," I advised Chauncey sharply as I sat down at the table.

"You do have a flair for drama. What's this all about?"

"It's about you two skimming both products and profits from Calderon's shipments of illegal goods. If I can find the evidence, so can Calderon. And, if he finds out, you won't be able to talk fast enough for him to let you live. Is that sufficient drama for both of you?"

"How did you find out?" Paolo asked, not even attempting to deny my charges against him.

"A grandma's timely interaction with my computer helped me dial up the correct computer program," I answered coyly.

"An old lady?" Chauncey rebutted. "How on earth did an old lady breach Calderon's computer firewalls?"

"I felt the same way when I learned about it, but there it was. I've learned never to underestimate the talents of the Smith family. My question to both of you is why did you start dipping into Calderon's cash and illegal inventory? Chauncey, I know you can't control yourself when faced with prospects of an easy profit. But Paolo, I'm really surprised at you, given your family's wealth and prospects for a new baby. What were you two thinking?"

"You should realize, my friend, that here in Portugal, the authorities have decriminalized drugs," Paolo proclaimed as if I was torturing the truth out of him. "I did nothing wrong."

"If you look at the small print of the Portuguese law as I have, you'll find that drug possession is no longer a crime in Portugal, as you say, but selling drugs still is. Besides, the answer you give to the police will not necessarily satisfy Calderon. Have you thought about that?"

"So what will you do about it, turn us over to the police or Calderon?" Chauncey asked belligerently.

"Neither if you enroll in my rehabilitation program. If you graduate, you might avoid the stiffest punishment under international law and resume normal law-abiding lives."

"What will you require for our redemption?" Chauncey intoned with continued arrogance.

"I perceive that one rehab recruit has an attitude problem," I stated as I trolled for sliced peaches in a large bowl at the sideboard. "Remember when our elementary school teachers punished the entire class because one student misbehaved and didn't own up to it? The attitude displayed in this room reminds me of that situation. Chauncey, you're a diplomat who should search for problem resolution through civilized discussions, not belligerent pronouncements. Keep your present attitude, and you'll bring down Paolo with you. When that happens, I'll give Paolo's wife a gun and amuse myself watching who gets you first, Paolo's wife or Calderon."

"Please, Señor," Paolo begged, "do not listen to him, and do not tell my wife. What do you want from us to save ourselves from Calderon? I have been totally stupid in getting involved in this scheme. No more, no more will I do this ever again," Paolo confessed contritely.

"Now that speech was dramatic and effective, don't you think so, Chauncey? I don't mean to add to Paolo's distress, but his family could lose everything if Calderon discovers what both of you are doing. Have you become so jaded by government service that you can't admit when you're wrong?"

"You and your high-and-mighty crusader code have belittled me for years. I'm sick of it. I want you to leave me alone," Chauncey struck out verbally, still not admitting his guilt.

"I wish I could, Chauncey. But, you and Paolo are or were my friends. My crusader code, as you call it, won't let me abandon you even when you foul up this badly. Don't think your safety is assured by my intended protection. Remember what happened to you in Melilla? You'll have to tell me sometime how you talked yourself out of the military prison there while I was absorbed in rescuing Beth. The Fates don't guarantee your survival despite my best efforts this time either. I don't have the resources to watch you and Paolo every minute. I may not be able to defend myself when the time comes. You've heard that speech from me several times in the past. You know it almost came true more frequently than desirable for either of us. So decide now what destiny you choose."

I ended my sermon by slipping my derringer out of my sleeve, placing it on the table in front of me, and spinning it like a wheel of fortune. Ironically, the pistol stopped spinning with its barrel pointing directly at Chauncey.

RECRUITING ACCOMPLICES

"All right, all right. I admit I did an absurdly stupid thing and got Paolo deeply involved too. What do you want us to do now?" Chauncey inquired with his hands in his pockets, which suggested in body language code that he would try to modify any agreement if he detected ambiguity in its terms or softness in my enforcement.

"Have either of you heard about the Sandzak network?"

"We heard about Sandzak before we learned about Father Christmas," Paolo answered. "More recently, we heard that Sandzak wants to take over the Calderon network, and it killed Gilberto Calderon as its overture."

"Good, that's helpful."

"What do you mean that's helpful? On what basis is that helpful to you? What are you saying?" Paolo asked.

"He means that our perception of the Sandzak network's attempted takeover is not correct, but that our perception—if Calderon shares the same perception—is exactly what he wants it to be. Good grief, Paolo, can't you see he's playing with us?" Chauncey whined.

"Easy, Chaunc," I interjected. "Take another minute to decide again how long you want to live. Then, we'll use my approach, or your soul will find itself in a parallel universe of dark matter that scientists haven't fully defined yet. Pardon my jet lag, but I'm out of patience with you, Chauncey. Events can't wait until both of you catch onto the accelerated curriculum here."

"Okay, we know about the Sandzak network," Chauncey confessed. "We know that Sandzak is more powerful and is involved in a broader range of activities than the Calderon network, including the transfer of people. Are you happy now?"

"Transfer of people, Chauncey? Is that what you've become to casually talk about slavery and the destruction of innocent lives and families as the 'transfer of people'? I will fulfill the promise I just made to help both of you survive this mess of your own making, but you should no longer consider me your close friend. One false move from either of you to notify Calderon about my plans, or if you don't cooperate fully with me when I need help, and one of you will return to Peru in a plain wooden wrapper while the other will float through the sewer system into Lisbon's harbor face down. Do you understand?"

"They understand very well," Advari proclaimed as he came into the room twirling his new leather slingshot, "and they will do everything you ask them."

"And so will you, my larcenous computer *bandito*," I responded, getting out of my chair to give him a hug. "Why aren't you in school?"

"I'm doing a special project for school in which I interview people from a number of occupations and backgrounds and give my recommendations about how the government can help these people do better in life and contribute to society. Or, if they can live without government assistance, how they can volunteer to help the community by using their own resources. I was selected because I know a number of languages and know what it means to be without a family."

"That is a heavy-duty assignment even for us grown-ups. Give it your best effort. Meanwhile, I'm glad to see you, little soldier. Maybe you should start by interviewing these two heterozygotes to determine why they need help in accepting the rules of society given all their advantages. Genetics didn't work very well in passing down favorable genes in their families."

GAUGING THE PENALTIES

"Apparently, you know a great deal more about what we have done than you are telling us," Paolo declared with his eyes searching mine for clues about what I knew and what I really intended to do with Chauncey and him. "Second, because of this knowledge, I am sure you intend that we help you substantially, either with the Sandzak or Calderon networks. Am I correct? If we cooperate with you, will you turn us over to the police or tell my wife?"

"This is a fine time to be concerned about consequences, Paolo. One thing I won't do is name a star after you or Chauncey. A star named 'Melon Head' won't be very popular anyway. To clarify what I said earlier for the benefit of any slow learners in the audience, I intend to do my best to extract you from the clutches of Calderon's network and any police who aren't on Calderon's payroll. If I succeed in that and find myself alive, I'll let you decide if you have additional obligations to your families, the laws of your respective countries, and any collateral damage to other people you may have harmed by your actions."

"I understand and accept your terms," Paolo affirmed sincerely.

"Before I commit myself, I want to know specifically what help you intend for us to give you," Chauncey challenged.

"That's fair enough. Here are my terms. First, the money equivalent you shaved from Calderon's shipments—including your share Advari—will go into an escrow fund in a Swiss bank under an account number I will select. Obviously, the account will be under my sole control."

"I only took a little," Advari objected.

"Yes, but the principle, not the amount, is the most important factor here," I explained. "Even if you stole from thieves, innocent people may have been harmed."

"But, you break the law all the time. It's not fair to punish us!" Advari continued to complain along with Chauncey.

"I bend the law on occasion, but not for my personal gain, little soldier. Are you with me or against me? Decide now. I don't have time or the energy to engage in a philosophical debate with you. Do you want to go back to your previous life on the streets in Chennai? Is that what you want for yourself?"

"No, but I really learned a lot about the shipping business and how to track cargo. Now, that is all wasted effort. Perhaps I should go back to India. My friends and I can get by a long time on that money."

"Actually, your acquired computer skills will be very valuable to your two co-conspirators and me now. I will tell you more about that shortly. If you want to send the money to your friends in Chennai rather than to the Swiss bank, I consider that a worthwhile alternative—provided they use it to help their families or enroll in school."

At least I had one penitent embezzler who now thought of how to help others with his ill-gotten gains. I turned back to Paolo and Chauncey to determine if I could obtain similar support from them.

"My second term requires you to divert a few shipments of Calderon's illegal goods that you are channeling into Portugal through the Cape Verde islands. Calderon should "accidentally" receive shipping documents indicating that the goods were diverted to Sandzak in Trieste or Belgrade. Conversely, Sandzak must receive bogus documents indicating shipments of Sandzak goods were diverted to Calderon in Ceuta, Melilla, or wherever they normally go. In reality, the containers will go to a warehouse in Venice that I will specify for you. Doing so will cause both parties to believe that their goods are being hijacked by the other network. Both of you may lose some sleep during this period if the networks even remotely suspect that you are involved in diverting cargo. Don't expect me to stand guard at your door during this period. Advari, I will need your computer skills to identify and divert contraband containers from the Calderon and Sandzak systems without implicating Chauncey or Paolo if you can. Is that possible?"

"Now I understand what you want. Yes, I will enjoy diverting the containers, and Cape Verde is the best place to break up bulk cargo and trans-ship smaller cargo to various destinations. The Calderon people on the docks in Mindelo, Porto Grande will be surprised. Can I divert a container to my old friends in Chennai?"

"At best, I will agree to misdirecting only one container that will be useful to the people there. But, I will tell you when it's safe to ship anything. Do you all agree to my second term?"

"Yes, we will do it, especially if Calderon cannot track the diversion of containers back to us," they all consented.

"My third term concerns an event that may or may not happen. A tough Russian general named Vasily has access to nuclear devices that he stole in the Ukraine. He's trying to sell them to either rogue nations or terrorist groups, whomever has money. Under no circumstances should he be allowed to succeed even if we all die in attempting to prevent it. Obviously, a shipment of that nature will bring status and power to the network that can handle such a transaction. From your contacts within the Calderon network, I need to know if Vasily and Calderon have reached any agreement on shipments of nuclear devices and the details of any other weapons shipments."

"We can do that for the Calderon network, but we have no similar contacts with Sandzak if your Vasily goes there," Chauncey clarified.

"Concentrate on the Calderon network first then. Hopefully, another party will help me if Vasily contacts Sandzak. Once again, do you agree to this term?"

"Yes, we have no problem with this item, but you should not expect us to know everything that happens in the Calderon network. We only monitor the shipments between South America and Europe," Paolo answered for Chauncey and himself.

"I understand that Calderon doesn't discuss his business with everyone he employs. But, I want you to be aware that I'm deeply interested in General Vasily and any contacts he has with Calderon that you can discover without risking harm to yourselves. A second component of the last item is to determine what connection, if any, a Kuwaiti by the name of Hassan has with Calderon. He appears to have influence with the *Policia de Securitas* at the Madrid airport, but I need more information about his whereabouts, activities, and connections other than his appearances in Europe with Calderon or a lady in a black *burka*. Do any of you know him and what he does for Calderon?"

"Yes, we know about him as you described, but nothing more. Sometimes, I do not see him for a long time. Then, he appears when something unusual happens," Paolo acknowledged.

"What kind of unusual things happen?" I asked.

"Sometimes, the police appear to take instructions from him. At other times, Interpol or the national police arrest people or confiscate baggage when he is present. I do not know if he has business connections with

Calderon. But, in my opinion, too many unexplainable things happen to be mere coincidence when he is around."

"Chauncey, do you have anything to add?" I asked as I turned toward him.

"Only to affirm what Paolo said. I've known about Hassan's presence from time to time in Peru and Bolivia in addition to his and your involvement in the missionaries' rescue. But, I'm not confident about the reliability of any other information I have about him except that people know not to cross him in whatever he does."

"Have either of you seen a lady in a black *burka* traveling with or otherwise in the company of Calderon, Hassan, or Vasily?"

"We frequently see women in *burkas* in airports and on the street, but we have not noticed any particular Arab lady closely connected to Calderon," Paolo asserted strongly for both himself and Chauncey.

"Okay, those are my conditions for not reporting you to any police or military authorities that may be interested in you in the foreseeable future."

"Really, that is all you want us to do?" Advari asked hopefully.

"Yes, those are my requirements. But, you should understand that Calderon has people watching and listening too. If anything you do raises Calderon's suspicions about you, I may not be able to help you. That is the one, but very large, penalty that you may encounter for helping me."

"When do you want us to begin diverting containers?" Paolo asked.

"If it's possible for Advari or either of you to reprogram the shipping instructions on containers coming from South America, you should start before Chauncey returns to Peru. That way, if Calderon challenges Chauncey, Chaunc can say he was traveling, and the diversion must be some sort of computer mistake. Similarly, when you're ready, Paolo, you can travel to India to visit your brothers while the shipments go astray, your wife and baby's health permitting, of course. That may be good cover for you."

"Where will you be while all this is going on?" Chauncey inquired more heatedly than I wanted after our lengthy discussion.

"Truthfully, I don't know where I'll be. We should communicate through Advari using a contact he has developed."

"What is the emergency code word for the contact?" Chauncey asked. "I know you always use some code word when you work."

"Remind me not to share so much information about my methods with you in the future, not that I'll work with you on sensitive projects again after the mess you created," I shot back angrily before I regained control of myself. "But, actually, Chauncey, you're correct. For purposes of this operation, our emergency code word will be *sabadilla*. It's a Spanish lily that has seeds used to make insect poison in case you wondered. That should fit our Hispanic connection on this project."

Actually, I had given the genuine code word of "mosquito" to Advari earlier. I didn't mind taking chances when required. But, I wouldn't confide in Chauncey and Paolo until they had proven themselves worthy to me again.

"You never stop, do you?" Chauncey responded with an irritated tone. "By the way, this is Portugal, you know. Portuguese is spoken here."

"I don't have as much exposure to Portuguese in Chicago as I do to Spanish, Chaunc, and even then my Spanish won't win me any language prizes. I'm doing the best I can with the brain, tools, time, and help I have available. I just thought of that word as one we can all pronounce and remember under stress. Have a nice flight back to Peru, Chaunc. Paolo, good luck to you here. Anytime you want to pull out of this project and go to jail or need protective custody, contact me or go straight to the FBI, CIA, or Interpol. That way, I won't have to look for you or your corpse. Now, I need to get acquainted with some unfriendly people."

Chapter Notes

1. Ethan B. Kapstein, "The New Global Slave Trade," *Foreign Affairs*, Volume 85, Number 6 (November/December, 2006), p. 109. By permission of Foreign Affairs.

2. China Williams and others, *Southeast Asia on a Shoestring*, 13th Edition (Melbourne: Lonely Planet Publications Pty. Ltd., 2006), pp. 780–791. By permission of Lonely Planet Publications Pty. Ltd.

3. Noel Malcolm, *op. cit.* p. 47.

4. Whitehall (ed.), *op. cit.*, p. 212.

CHAPTER 21

UNFAMILIAR KIND OF WAR

Belgrade Beginnings

Advari followed me upstairs to my bedroom and sat on the bed while I rearranged a few things in my luggage.

"Who is the special contact you told them about downstairs that I have developed?"

"Your contact is the headmaster of your school. He was with the MI-6 branch of British Intelligence before he became a Jesuit. How's that for on-the-job training to become a school teacher?"

"Can you tell me where you will be?" Advari probed.

"Until now, I thought we could trust each other with anything. Is that still true?" I responded gently.

"At one time, you thought you could trust Paolo and Chauncey with anything, but now look how different they are."

"Underneath, they are still good people, just confused right now. Paolo is treating you well, isn't he?" I asked, assuming a favorable response.

"Yes, he is good to me," Advari admitted.

"In fact, he is so good to you that he gave you the opportunity to do some creative accounting and banking with Calderon's shipping documents. See what I mean about them being confused between right and wrong while still being good people? We all go through that kind of stuff in our lives and seldom get it right on the first attempt," I counseled Advari without letting him off the hook entirely.

"How were you able to find my computer lists," Advari proceeded without acknowledging culpability for his computer larceny. "First, the Calderon system itself is buried under many layers of firewalls. Then, I had additional codes to protect my lists. Besides, you're not that great at Spanish, let alone computers. How did you do it?"

"I didn't need to be a hyper cyber jockey. I used the code documents that we found in the safe at Tingo Maria to penetrate the overall Calderon system. Then, my Grandma showed me how to penetrate your firewalls from an entirely different direction, top down, in fact."

"Your grandmother helped you break through my security codes?" Advari continued as a non-believer.

"Yep, don't ever underestimate us old folks and our low-tech drilling and detection methods."

"I don't suppose you'll tell me how she did it?"

"Nope, that's her secret and mine—swallowed up inside of me forever," I toyed with Advari.

"Is it a secret where you are going? You still haven't told me," Advari re-routed his thoughts to a potentially more prosperous avenue of information.

"It's not a secret from you. I'm going to Belgrade to meet a friend who may be able to get me close enough to the Sandzak group to do some damage."

"But you won't tell me her name?"

"How do you know it's a her?" I stalled a bit more, testing my own thoughts about how much information Advari should have for his own safety.

"Because I know all the men you deal with, so it must be a woman. Is she pretty like the picture of Amy I saw?"

"Her name is Marika, and she is far too tough and busy for you to be interested in her to say nothing of the substantial age difference between you. But, if your headmaster mentions her name to you, come find me and bring your slingshot because I will need your help *pronto*. And when did you start noticing girls?"

"How did you get to know my headmaster?" Advari asked, not ready to volunteer an answer to my last question.

"Marika told me about him. I don't know much else about him except what Marika told me. But, I suppose he is an old man like me who will sneak up behind you and do this," I said as I grabbed him and flipped him over onto the bed. "The rule for you on girls at your age is to make friends if you can, but don't touch, especially my Scout. Got it?"

"I wish I could go with you now," Advari said, changing the subject again without externally acknowledging my instructions, questions, and sage advice—although I was sure that he took internal notice of all of them.

To maximize my influence with Advari in the short time we had together, I needed to stop framing my conversation in the form of questions and start responding more directly to his concerns.

"Yeah, me too, little soldier. But the school will have Christmas holidays soon whether you understand and accept the Christian faith in your life or not. When, and not if, I need you, I will send for you and whatever supplies we might need. Meanwhile, keep your head in your schoolbooks rather than the Calderon books. You will find your future in your schoolbooks if old folks like me can make the world safe for your generation again. Now, it's time for me to go. Carry this case downstairs for me, please."

"What's in here, bricks?" Advari gasped as he tried to recover from his surprise at the weight of the flight bag.

"Yes, they're bricks all right. They're not good for building, but they do a bang-up job taking things apart."

"C-4 *plastiques*?"

"Yes, C-4."

"How did you get them through airport security?"

"You just committed a '*post hoc ergo propter hoc*.'"

"What's that?"

"That's the sound of your headmaster putting you on academic probation during the holidays for not knowing your Latin and Logic."

"Hey, I am studying French now, and I am getting good grades in my other subjects too!"

"I know, I asked your headmaster. I'm proud of you for what you have accomplished in a short time. Keep at it. You are naturally intelligent, but absorb all the lessons you can from your books and the events around you. As a reward, I'll tell you what '*post hoc ergo propter hoc*' means because it's more a question of logic than semantics anyway. The translation means 'after this, therefore because of this.' In your case, because the C-4 blocks are in my flight bag and I arrived by plane, you assumed incorrectly that I carried the explosives on a commercial airplane with me. Don't fret about it. Adults frequently make false assumptions, including me."

"How did you get them here then?"

"Ask your headmaster sometime when you're not on scholastic probation. Remember, I said I talked to him?"

"I already told you that my grades are good. If you don't believe me, ask the headmaster."

"I'd believe you even if I hadn't checked with the headmaster. But, because I happened to check your grades with the headmaster, I believe you even more. Does that satisfy you?"

"Not really. It gives me a headache interpreting what you say sometimes."

"Then, I must work harder to confuse you all the time. I would like to hang around and chat, but I have a plane to catch. Recite your Ave Marias and Pater Nosters or their equivalents in the Hindu, Buddhist, or Islamic faiths for me because this exercise may be more demanding than I can handle without your prayers and good *karma* to protect me."

After a formal handshake and a giant informal hug, I left Advari at the front door and got into the waiting taxi to take me to the airport and to Belgrade in the private jet Marika had arranged for me.

Despite the age and differences in life experiences between Advari, Amy, Marika, and me, we were basically doing the same stuff—trying to sift the wheat and chaff of life and attempting to make it through another day. If we were lucky, we would help somebody and make the sun shine a little brighter. But, to keep the sun shining in the future for the people I cared about, I would have to isolate or destroy people like Calderon and organizations like the Sandzak network. Sometimes, from my actions, I would create unintended consequences among innocent family members, bystanders, or people helping me like my former Scout, Jenny. I found little consolation in those thoughts.

The private jet ride was pleasant enough, but I decided to arrive at Surcin Airport about eighteen kilometers west of Belgrade in a foul mood. I was aided in achieving that temperament during the flight by finding a Langley, Virginia luggage tag carelessly left under my seat by a previous passenger or crewmember, maybe by Marika herself. The CIA and FBI couldn't have advertised the arrival or departure of an agent in the local newspaper any better than that. *If the varsity team could mess up its security, why couldn't I?* Memories of complete breakdowns of my own alleged well-thought-out security or operational plans were not helping my disposition.

That changed when I saw the car Marika had arranged to pick me up and deposit me at her brother's house. I wasn't expecting a black limousine with diplomatic flags attached, but the ancient red wreck with the passenger door that wouldn't close unless I slammed it with every ounce of my strength, and the muffler that clung to the underside of the car with the aid of the last available coat hanger in town guaranteed that my driver and I would absorb a full load of attention from the holiday shoppers who we passed on the street.

In due time, we turned toward the "old money" residential district. There were no "teardowns" in this part of Belgrade. The stone houses were early nineteenth century and, externally, suffered from city grime, but they were large enough to house the wealthiest of families and their domestic staff. Not surprising, after this description of the neighborhood, my driver deposited my belongings and me at the back entrance of a house befitting the neighborhood. Marika stood in the covered doorway watching as I unloaded my gear in the driving rain and ice storm that commenced with greater intensity as soon as I stepped out of the car. I was about to shut the servants' door behind me on my last trip inside when Marika announced my further obligations to the driver.

"Certainly, you will tip the driver, won't you?" Marika inquired and commanded at the same time to christen our collaborative European relationship.

"How much?" I mumbled in my chilled mind and body.

"What do you think? Five U.S. dollars is a modest tip for the time the driver waited for your plane to arrive."

"I flew the plane as fast as I could from my passenger seat. For five bucks, I could buy the driver and that car. Also, if he really waited a long time for my arrival, I'm sure he was well fed, given the appearance of the upholstery. But, assuming you're right, what is five bucks in *dinars*, *euros*, or whatever money is in vogue in Belgrade now? I didn't bring my Scout or the local currency."

"Give me your five dollars, and I'll pay the driver myself," Marika exclaimed, feinting indignation at my lack of knowledge and manners as she grabbed the five-dollar bill out of my hand and went to the door.

"Knock yourself out, or lock yourself out—whatever grabs you," I called out too late for her to hear.

For some reason, that little exchange with Marika made me notice the kind of lock on the door. My Guiding Hand gave me a message that I couldn't decipher at the time. I stored the information in the miscellaneous folder of my brain bin. When Marika returned, I could see that she was chilled to the bone in just that short time, but if she didn't admit her discomfort, I would play by her house rules and not aggravate her.

OLD SCHOOL CHUMS

"We have a change in plans that I need to tell you about," Marika said sharply as she moved to a warm place by the kitchen stove. I'm leaving for Budapest in the next day or so to follow Kabrinovic, one of the three men who operate the Sandzak network. I will give you information about

Milovan; the Sandzak partner who I know is in Belgrade now. You can chase him while I'm away."

"I appreciate the confidence you place in me to wander around Belgrade by myself in an ice storm. But, I thought this would be one of our collaborative moments to unravel the Sandzak operation and hunt down General Vasily during my quickly dwindling life span."

"I will give you Milovan's address," Marika stated as if she hadn't heard me. "When you go there, you will meet someone who will help you in whatever you need. Before we hunt your General Vasily, who may come to Belgrade anyway if he has weapons to sell, we need to remove Zandar, the third leader of the Sandzak network too. Currently, I don't know where Zandar is, but do you agree with my approach?"

"And you have Milovan's home address because . . . ?" I inquired before I committed to her strategic initiative.

"Because he and I went to the university together," Marika nearly shouted. "What other information do you need? Stop looking at me that way! Yes, we dated for a while before I left for the United States. Yes, I gave my first child up for adoption because of him. Yes, at the time, he was the best and smartest, though cruelest, man I had ever met. Is that enough background for you to find him? Does it matter that I dated the others too?"

"I would have settled for less information, but that confession should suffice for both your local Orthodox priest and my memoirs. I'll start now unless you have anything else you want to confess such as what Milovan and the others look like, and if they have any guardians around their residences who will not be pleased to greet me."

"The guide you will meet on your way to Milovan's house will give you all those details. Do you fool around with all this superfluous information on every project, or are you simply trying to upset me?"

"I attempt to inform myself as much as possible about my adversaries before I launch any action. But, I usually proceed without information on my subject's college dating habits and partners," I confirmed. "As a dedicated disciple of the Chinese war strategist, Sun Tzu, I believe that battles are won through pre-planning rather than in the execution of an ill-conceived attack. As for aggravating you, the idea crossed my mind, but I'm gaining more control over myself in that respect. Don't you think?"

"Everyone knows your planning and strategies are haphazard. You better be careful this time. Milovan knows his business and will surprise you if you are not ready."

"Thanks for sharing with me CIA or FBI gossip about me. But that doesn't negate my appreciation of Sun Tzu's strategy to appear unprepared to confuse the opponent, especially if my formidable staff of one is outnumbered. I try to acquire sufficient information about my adversaries so that I can shake hands if we are formally introduced before we try to kill each other."

"You may not be so fortunate if you use that approach on this project," Marika intoned ominously.

"Then, I'll be particularly cautious in dealing with Milovan, his associates, and you. If I'm successful against Milovan, do you want me to come to Budapest to help you with Kabrinovic, or should I track Zandar if the contact you identified can guide me to both of them?" I asked intent on the business at hand.

"Whatever you want," Marika responded, surprisingly nonchalant compared to the seriousness she had exhibited a few moments earlier as she took a sheet of paper from the kitchen desk and began writing.

I obviously was missing one or more important ingredients in our information exchange. Perhaps, her youthful feelings for Milovan after all these years were not totally dead. But she was supposed to be a highly trained intelligence professional who knew better than to stumble over her emotions when engaged in a crucial situation. I couldn't let her frame of mind interfere with my job. I left most of my professional trinkets except my derringer and some pocket tools to dry in the kitchen and went outside into the teeth of the still-raging ice storm with no thoughts of Christmas or sugarplums in my head.

Out on the street with Marika's instructions to find the guide to take me to Milovan's residence, I oriented myself as Marika had suggested by observing the remains of the Kalemegdan Citadel that stood on a hill overlooking the Sava River. I kept it to my right, and marched south along Tadeusa Kosaiuszka Street, which turned southwest into Pariska Street. As I hunted for Kneza Mihailova Street, I recalled that allegedly, Belgrade had been sacked and rebuilt forty or more times in its twenty-three-century history.[1] So, the citadel was not exactly a good luck charm for the city and its inhabitants over the years. If nothing else, I hoped it would satisfy my personal global positioning needs. Strangely though, Marika's directions took me through the heart of town along Kneza Mihailova to Terazije then southeast to Kralja Milana Street. From there, I went southwest along Kneza Milosa Street into the heart of foreign embassy territory. *This couldn't be right,* I told myself. Marika was retaliating for my non-verbal criticism of her university dating habits.

As I stood momentarily perplexed and totally drenched in front of the U.S. Embassy compound on the corner of Kneza Milosa and Vojvode Milenka Tirsova, an elderly man in a somewhat tattered coat came out of the crowd of wind-whipped umbrellas toward me. Instinctively, I reached into my pocket for a few coins and recalled that I hadn't been in the city long enough to have acquired *euros*. As he came closer, I took a subliminal opportunity to look at him. Yes, he wore a tattered coat, but he did not have the hunched and desolate look of a man down on his luck. His hair had been cut within the past week or so, and his shoes, though wet, were of recent vintage and in good repair. This had to be the contact Marika had told me about. I let the old man approach me.

"You must be Josip Legion," he asked and declared in five words. "Josip is my name too," he added in English with a heavy European accent.

"I have been called worse names," I replied. "Call me Joe if that is easier for you. What can I do for you besides get you out of the rain somewhere?"

"That is very considerate of you. But, I am here to help you find someone and to teach you how business is conducted in Belgrade these days."

"I will thank you now while reserving the right to change my mind later. Are we going somewhere close?"

"The place is less than a kilometer from here near Marshal Tito's mausoleum," Josip pointed southwest down Tirsova Street. "I hope you do not mind walking a bit further since we are already drenched, and it is impossible to find a taxi in this weather."

"I am sure that pneumonia already has taken hold in my lungs too, so another kilometer in the cold rain will not make much difference," I confessed my present mental and physical condition.

"I enjoy Americans," Josip admitted, flavoring his comment with a slight smile and nod. "You always go directly to the target. Europeans take an indirect approach, you know. Europeans get acquainted before we conduct important business."

"You identified me from among a crowd of people and umbrellas, so obviously you are more acquainted with me than I am with you. Will that suffice to expedite business on a miserable day like today?"

"You are correct, sir, absolutely correct," Josip agreed as we started walking. "I will not trouble you further about getting to know each other better before we discuss business. Indeed, Marika told me much about you. Conversely, I am unimportant for your purposes."

The brief conversation over, Josip didn't utter another word as we hurried along Tirsova Street while dodging umbrellas and people in our path. We did not go into Marshal Tito's mausoleum as I had hoped, but toward the adjacent Historical Museum of Yugoslavia which appeared to be officially and unofficially closed.

"Oh dear, this is dreadful," Josip exclaimed as we stood outside the locked entrance. "I am afraid I cannot find my key."

"Are you a member or officer of the museum? Perhaps we can find someone to let us in through another door," I suggested.

"Perhaps, but then they will ask why I do not have my key, and I surely will be in trouble. I am sorry to put you through this. Oh, this is dreadful!" Josip repeated, shaking his head while pulling on the door handle one more time in a futile attempt to have the door magically open for us.

"Turn your back to me for a minute, will you Josip? Maybe I have a solution to your problem. Does this door have an alarm on it?"

As he turned his back, Josip shook his head no, then declared, "An alarm? I really do not remember, Joe. I have never heard an alarm for this door. Oh my, how silly of me not to know if the door has an alarm. No, I do not think the door has an alarm."

With Josip's back turned to shield both him and me from the spiraling slashing ice, I took a little case of lock picks out of my pocket that Manco's cousin, Felipe had presented to me at the Tingo Maria *ranchero* after our work was completed there. I carried them almost everywhere but had never used them until now. My skills were as rusty as the lock. But, after only three attempts the lock that was a close cousin to the one I had seen in Marika's family house clicked. The door opened easily to my slight pull without setting off an alarm. Now I knew why my Guiding Hand had me notice the kitchen door lock earlier.

"Okay, Josip, where do we go from here?" I asked to let him know that he could turn around. The rush of musty air from the open museum door also informed him that I had successfully gained entrance, although I wasn't certain that I wanted to go into that moldy environment.

"Down the stairs to the right," Josip instructed looking highly relieved.

He still had to deal with the problem of his missing key, but he could find it or confess its loss another day. Apparently, I had people to meet and things to do downstairs.

After taking a few steps inside, I tried the light switch, but no lights went on in the stairwell or the gloomy hallway below. I knew Russians and Serbians operate with the same mindset about many things, but I didn't think they needed to be similarly averse to turning on a few lights for their own safety. As I reached the bottom of the stairs without breaking my neck and with Josip a few steps behind me, a big fist came out of the darkness and kissed me just below my left eye. As I dropped to the floor like the wet rag that I was, my last conscious thought before total darkness enveloped me was that I had been completely suckered. Josip and Marika's chums, whoever they were, obviously were professionals to be able to overcome my natural and trained instincts for self-preservation.

When I regained consciousness, I slowly became aware that I was sitting and that my hands and feet were tied to a heavy wooden chair. A single light bulb generated the only light in the musty room with no windows. *This was as dumb as a low-grade movie,* my brain waves laughed at me menacingly. Then, my scattered thoughts collected themselves sufficiently to tell me that I was still somewhere in the museum. A few minutes later, I felt the presence of several people in the room with me, but they kept themselves outside the circle of the dim light projected by the bulb overhead. The musty smell of the museum prevented me from picking up any perfume scents or body odors, if they were present. In my semi-stupor, I recalled the dim lighting and dark hallway leading to the uniformed customs officers and police dogs at Sheremetyevo Airport in Moscow. Everything there was designed for its maximum psychological effect on travelers to behave unless they wanted accommodations in Lubyanka Prison. I wasn't in prison here, not yet anyway, but my pounding brain was on notice to be careful about anything I did or said if I wanted to survive whatever ugliness was scheduled next.

Although I tried to remain motionless until my head cleared, or a reasonable facsimile thereof, someone must have detected an involuntary muscle tightening or other subtle movement of my body and declared, "He is coming around now. Be careful." That was followed by a slap across my mouth by a hand the size of a toilet seat. I was fully awake now, and I could taste my own AB-positive blood. My dentist would not like this. *Fortunately, I did not feel the need to spit out or swallow any teeth, so I still must be alive,* I thought.

"What are you doing in Serbia?" an unfamiliar voice asked followed by another face slap, a little harder this time, but still administered with an open hand. *That was unusual,* my scrambled brain thought. *Why not use a fist or brass knuckles,* I inquired internally, *unless someone cared about how I looked after this exercise was over.* That thought process took only a nanosecond, but it wasn't fast enough for my interrogator.

"I ask you again, what are you doing in Serbia?" he said and followed up with another slap to the right side of my face this time. I thought it was my turn to say something if I could get my mouth to work.

"Christmas shopping," I answered.

"You could do that in America," the gruff and breathy voice said. "Why are you here?" That was followed by a slap to the left side of my face again.

"We can't find pond scum where I live in America at this time of year, so I came here," I mocked with painful sarcasm. "I think I found some."

I hoped my interrogator would become bored with slapping me, or at least stick to one side of my face.

"Not a good reason? Okay, let's see how delightful this sounds to you. I am looking for a special gift for my wife," I said somewhat proud of myself for still being able to frame and articulate a complete sentence.

"And what is that?" the voice asked.

"A right-handed skunk like you," I replied expecting another slap or worse.

It never came. Instead, I heard a woman's familiar voice say, "That's enough. When he becomes sarcastic like this, he will not tell you anything. And he had enough training to determine what your dominant hand is by the way you hit him. He was well coached, as I told you."

Additional lights came on in the room. Although blinded by the sudden brightness, I recognized Marika's form to match her voice and Josip standing quietly in the corner. The three Neanderthals surrounding me were newcomers, but I would never forget them after this. One began to untie me, then stepped aside as Marika and Josip approached.

"I am sorry we had to do this to you," Marika said solicitously while untying my legs as Josip worked on the ropes binding my arms. "But, my people needed to be certain that you can resist interrogation if you are taken by Sandzak guards. You look terrible. Quickly, Skaric, get a wet towel for him. Joe, do you need to lie down or anything?" she asked.

"No, I'm fine, really," I answered more angry than hurt at not picking up Josip's signals and her indirect warnings to me before I left her brother's house. To prove it, when Skaric left himself open as he handed me the towel, I administered a head butt to his chest and a kick to his groin that sent him reeling into the wall. He wouldn't do a Serbian limbo dance for a while. "Here," I said as I threw the towel back to him as he groaned on the floor, "you might need this more than I do. I must say that I'm not profoundly impressed with the European custom of getting acquainted before conducting serious business."

Josip chuckled softly.

The two other Neanderthals grabbed me by the arms and lifted me out of the chair, but Marika called them off.

"The war is over, you two. When Joe is ready, we will go back to my brother's place, and I will inform him about what we know about Sandzak. From now on, we will cooperate fully with him. Do you understand?"

They must have understood because after resting for ten minutes, Skaric and I were ready to travel—as long as we didn't share the same vehicle. Somebody from MAGENTA must have gotten to Marika. Even on a good day, she was never this solicitous to me back in the States. Nonetheless, she, her CIA or FBI buddies, and her Paleolithic pals didn't need to put me through this meat grinder. We had enough enemies around the world to deal with without banging on each other to establish the local pecking order for this project.

I rode back to Marika's brother's house in a black limousine minus any diplomatic flags. Once again, if I were patient enough and gave my *karma* a chance to respond, my every wish in life would come true. But, on a treacherous assignment like this, I'd better think twice about my wishes. Marika and Josip didn't appear interested in any *karmic* conversation as they stared out of the car windows. I decided not to waste the available interlude on business and initiated a lighter conversation even though my jaw was still feeling the effects of the roughing up I had received.

"Josip," I started, "how did you get involved with Marika? Pardon me for saying so, but you don't look like the kind of person Marika socializes with in the States."

"She was a student in my political science class at the university. She was a very good student I might add. Why do you ask?"

"My question was a conversation opener when I started, but your answer prompts an additional thought now. If you taught political science when Marika was a student, you must have indoctrinated her into the Communist system, true?"

"That is true, but what is so remarkable about that?" Josip rebutted. "Everyone was a Communist in those days. Although Marshal Tito was not strongly aligned with the Kremlin, he ensured that Yugoslavia remained committed to the Communist philosophy until his death. Consequently, students received indoctrination into Communist political philosophy at all academic levels."

"I realize that, but what happened to Marika later is the most amusing aspect to me."

"What is that?" both Marika and Josip asked in unison and with rising irritation.

"Marika," I addressed her as I composed my answer, "Josip taught you Communist philosophy from his exalted European position as a university professor. Shortly thereafter, you departed Serbia and came to the United States, where you learned about democracy. Now you have returned to your native country as an American citizen, and Josip works for you. I find that a highly amusing advertisement for democracy, don't you?"

"I don't know how you can be amused when you see our former Yugoslavia torn apart by conflict between Serbians, Croatians, Slovenians, Bosnians, Albanians, Orthodox Christians, and Muslims with a United Nations peacekeeping force to keep the various nationalities and faiths from committing more atrocities against each other," Marika decreed harshly.

"You forgot one group—the highly organized and efficient international crime networks which, supposedly, is why we're here now. Speaking of that, when do I tour Milovan's house or any Sandzak facility in the neighborhood?"

HOUSE HUNTING

"Milovan has a city house and a villa in the country. Which one do you want to see?" Josip asked.

"I would like to see both of them, but if I can see only one today, I would like to see the one that is currently vacant. Is that possible?"

"If you and Josip are going Sandzak house hunting, drop me off at my brother's house first," Marika ordered.

"That suits me fine because I need to pick up my backpack before we go sightseeing," I stated agreeably, somewhat startling both of them with my 180-degree mood swing.

"You realize that Milovan's house guards will not let you tour the grounds of his country estate just because you want to—even in this weather," Marika admonished. "Besides, the river may be over its banks now, and you need to cross a bridge before you come anywhere near his property."

"I understand. Is his estate with other houses on the far side of the river, or does he crave complete privacy?" I asked more enthused with each passing second.

"His property backs up to a recreational area and forest," Marika advised passively. "I believe his house is the only one on the opposite side of the river in that area. Am I correct, Josip?"

"I have not been near there in several years," Josip answered. "Unless some new houses were built during that time, I agree that his house is the only one in the immediate area on that side of the river."

"So, his estate is isolated, right?" I almost betrayed my pleasure at hearing that as we turned into the driveway of Marika's family house. "How far from the river is Milovan's house?" I continued as we drove to the covered back entrance.

"Yes, definitely his is the only house in that area," Marika asserted. "If I recall correctly, the house is a kilometer or two east of the river. What is significant about that?"

"Nothing until I see the area for myself," I responded as I jumped out of the car before it came to a complete stop.

I was up to my room for my backpack and down again before Marika and Josip came inside.

"Can I change out of my wet clothes before we leave?" Josip asked.

"We don't have time to waste now, Professor. Besides, you will only get wet again when we reach Milovan's house. Ask the driver to turn the car heater on full blast. You can dry out on the way."

"What do you have in the bag?" Josip inquired attempting to delay me long enough to change my mind about giving him time to warm himself and get into dry clothes.

"Early Christmas presents whether or not Milovan believes in Father Christmas. I hope they are wrapped appropriately," I continued fabricating my Christmas theme.

"Yes, but, perhaps, you would make more of an impression on him if they were delivered personally to him at his city home," Josip declared leaving me unsure about Marika and her allegiance to the cause that had brought me to Belgrade. *Whose war was I fighting?*

"Dear Professor Josip, I generally appreciate counselors and friends like you who inform me about local customs and polite ways of conducting business, but I'll take my chances and deliver this present via my own code of conduct first. If that doesn't work, I'll use your approach if the opportunity arises later. Is that satisfactory to you?"

I grabbed Josip's arm, spun him around, hauled him outside, deposited him into the front seat of the car, and instructed him to tell the driver where we wanted to go as I jumped into the back seat to have room to organize my package for Milovan. As I looked back at the house from the rear window of the limousine, I saw Marika watching us from an upstairs window. That didn't bother me as much as seeing her with a phone in her hand. Despite being old school chums, I hoped that she wasn't warning Milovan or his henchmen about my interest in his country estate. But, I didn't have time to worry about that immediately. I was committed. Or as Caesar put it more profoundly, "*Alia jacta est.*" Indeed, the die was cast on my first move against the Sandzak network after being in town only a few hours.

We drove several miles or kilometers outside the city. The road was dark, deserted, and treacherous. The headlights barely penetrated the gloom, and the wind-driven ice pellets and rain beat on the car incessantly. Josip and I peered ahead as if we were lookouts on the next ship out of the harbor after learning that the Titanic went down while the driver skillfully kept the car on the road and seemed to have better vision and instincts than either Josip or I did. Eventually, we arrived at the bridge that I surmised led to Milovan's mansion on the other side of the river. For my limited demolition skills, it was the wrong bridge. I had seen stone and concrete bridges all day long. This one was constructed of steel girders. I had rigged my "*plastique*s" as Advari called them for the wrong type of charge. But, if I wanted to make a holiday impression on Milovan that night, I had no choice but to use what presents I had brought. We certainly didn't need to worry about traffic or dog walkers observing us with the storm swirling in all directions.

"Professor, tell the driver to stop here," I instructed.

"Tell him yourself; he's a university graduate and not deaf," Josip responded sharply, still angry with me for my shameful conduct in requiring him to sit in the car in his wet clothes.

"Badgering a guest in your country twice in one night is highly irregular, Josip," I muttered as the driver stopped the car in the middle of the road. "But, we'll discuss that later when it's your turn to sit in the chair at the mausoleum and I get to pound on your face."

NATURAL FORCES AT THE BRIDGE

The driver wisely had stopped based on his own survival skills as a huge chunk of ice pounded against the midstream support of the bridge causing a frightening metallic groan to emanate from the entire structure. I got out of the car and walked as quickly as I could on the slippery downward slope of the road to the bridge. Peering into the darkness, I witnessed the most powerful display of natural forces against a man-made structure I had seen in decades.

Apparently, the river had frozen sometime earlier. Now, the mixture of ice and heavy rain from this storm was flowing on top of the old river ice. Occasionally, the force of the new runoff caused chunks of old ice to dislodge and accelerate downstream moving everything out of their way while the flow of the rising water around the ice chunks gouged out the river banks on both sides. I watched the drama for a while, stupidly wondering how I should rig my C-4 explosives to take maximum advantage of the current and ice. A blast of wind served notice of the breakup of additional ice chunks. Within seconds, the jagged chunks slammed into the full length of the bridge. With a loud groan, the bridge surrendered to the superior forces of nature, crumpled on both ends, moved downstream a short distance, and then plunged to the bottom of the river. The soaked ground under the road gave way almost to where I stood, and I instinctively jumped back.

I hadn't allowed myself to react fearfully to any danger for many years, but I let fear take its course that night as I turned and unceremoniously ran back to the car. Heart pounding, I dove head first into the back seat scattering the web of C-4 explosives I had knitted. I wouldn't need to use them tonight on Milovan's bridge. My Guiding Hand had done the work for me.

"Are you finished?" Josip inquired. "Or, do you want to blow up the orchard over there while we are in the vicinity? It's the only thing of Milovan's still intact here."

"I had a long day," I answered, hoping to salvage some pride and camaraderie. "But, if you two are tired, we can go back to town now."

The drive back to town was a subdued event filled with many thankful prayers coming from the back seat. As we approached a warehouse district, I was attracted to a monolithic concrete building with a dragon logo in the shape of an "S" painted on it and several container cars with similar dragon logos on them parked on a rail siding nearby.

"What's that building, Josip?" I asked.

"That is a Sandzak warehouse," Josip answered crisply, still bitter that I hadn't allowed him to change into dry clothes earlier.

Interesting, I thought. My Chinese astrological Angry Dragon had presented another opportunity to challenge the Serbian Sandzak Dragon again that night.

Flaming the Dragon

"The rail cars too, Josip?" I asked for clarification.

"Yes, those are Sandzak container cars, but they are empty," Josip assured me.

"How do you distinguish the empties from the full ones, Josip? Do the empties always have their doors closed, or are they always parked on that particular track?"

"I have some knowledge of Sandzak operations. You know that. Otherwise, I would not be your guide. The full container cars are located at the loading platform around the rear of the building."

"Get me there," I instructed the driver with no variations included in the instruction manual.

Without additional prompting, the driver turned right to give me a view of the rear of the warehouse, aiming the front of the car directly into the teeth of the raging ice storm. The front and rear of the building looked the same except for an elevated wooden deck on the rear with windows jutting out from the main building to give anyone standing inside a clear view of loading or unloading operations.

"What do you plan to do?" Josip inquired, searching my face for signs of a concise answer.

"You're sitting on part of it," I pointed, causing Josip to bounce in several directions at once while he tried to untangle himself from my wiring.

"Where are the warehouse security guards at this time of night?" I asked Josip, not waiting for him to finish his gymnastics before testing the breadth of his knowledge of Sandzak operations.

"The same place as always. They are inside somewhere drunk, especially in this kind of weather. If you intend to attack the building, you have selected a good time. But one never knows. A stray guard could look out a window and see you at any time."

"If you help me, I can finish the job quicker."

"I know nothing about explosives. You will have to show me if you want my help. That will give the security guards more opportunity to discover and interrupt your plans," Josip intoned negatively.

"My wiring between the charges is almost finished. All we need to do is adjust the charges to the length of the freight cars."

"But the wires are all knotted. It will take too much time to untangle them. Surely, a guard will see us before then," Josip continued his negative litany.

"Josip, do I look like a demented demolitions demon? Listen to me. The knots are slip knots that adjust easily like this," I said as I showed him how to slide the line of charges.

"All right, I will help you. But, you must promise to do something for me if I survive this."

"Josip, you'd better have only one wish because this genie will run out of darkness and storm if you keep delaying me in setting the charges."

Without instruction, the driver stopped the car in back of a nearby warehouse. Josip and I bailed out with my prefabricated C-4 charges and wiring. During our ride from the bridge, I had forgotten how the sting of the wind-driven ice had felt on my face. On this escapade, Josip and I would face directly into the biting wind to set the *plastique* charges under the wheel carriages of the rail cars. My intent was to create a crater and buckle the rail under the cars. If *Santa Fortunata* smiled favorably on us, one or more of the cars would tip toward the building, causing immediate angst among the security guards, plus intermediate distress among managerial ranks in setting those container cars upright again and repairing the track before subsequent deliveries could arrive or depart. I thought this was a modest goal for Josip and me to accomplish at that late hour. The storm and the direction of our approach would hide us from any less-than-fully alert guards.

Having handled explosives in my military life, I finished wiring my three cars long before Josip was finished with the two rail cars I had assigned to him. I made only three steps in running back to the limo before Josip saw me.

"Please do not leave me here alone," Josip wailed.

"I wouldn't dream of it, Josip," I shouted over my shoulder. "Keep setting your charges. I need more detonator wire from the car. I'll be right back."

I intended to return promptly, but a guard dog attached by a leash to an overgrown Goliath in a security guard uniform blocked my way. I didn't have time to spare before this interruption let alone deal with this inconveniently located brute and his long-fanged associate. I stopped where I was and raised my hands in the generally accepted protocol of surrendering. As designed, this movement activated the spring to pop the derringer from my sleeve into my hand. I didn't stop to celebrate the advantages of technology but put the first round into Goliath's forehead. As he was about to clamp a jaw full of teeth into my leg, my second shot ended the dog's guard duty days as well. I finished my run to the car to find the driver dead. Based on a quick glance, it looked like Goliath had snapped the driver's neck. I didn't have time to perform an autopsy, so that cursory medical evaluation would have to do. I reloaded and reset my derringer on my inner forearm, grabbed a roll of detonator wire, and sprinted back to Josip and the rail cars.

"Where have you been?" Josip pleaded. "I thought I heard gunshots."

"As long as the guards inside didn't hear anything in this gale, we'll be okay," I told him, purposely not informing him of the condition of our driver and Goliath. "Take this wire and attach it to the charge on your first rail car, and I'll do the same with mine. When you finish, run the wire back here, and we'll return to the car uncoiling the wire as we go. We'll use the car battery as the power source to detonate the charges. Are you okay with that?"

"If it means we can leave, I am okay with anything," Josip responded more courageously than in any previous statement he had uttered.

As planned, we separated, wired the charges to our respective container cars, rejoined each other, and then trotted back to the limo letting the wire unwind itself from the spool as we went. Intent on what I was doing, I went head over heels over Josip, who had stopped suddenly when he saw Goliath and the dog lying in frozen pools of blood. I didn't intend to do a pratfall at this point in our activities. I was back on my feet quickly and unreeled wire with one hand and pushed Josip ahead of me with the other. As we turned the corner of the neighboring warehouse to reach our parked car, Josip saw the driver's head protruding out of the open side window where it was rapidly becoming encrusted with ice.

"What's the matter with you, Josip?" I admonished him. "Haven't you seen a dead chauffeur before? Move him out of the way if you need to and pop the hood of the car so that I can get to the battery," I commanded Josip, not caring if I hurt his feelings with my insensitivity to him and the deceased driver.

Josip obeyed robot-like, and I attached one wire to the positive terminal of the battery. Then, I touched the other wire to the negative terminal and expected to hear a big bang from the container cars. Nothing happened to the charges Josip had set. Then, I saw a puff of smoke in the first of my charges, then the second, and the third. In the next nanosecond, the three container cars that I had wired rose off their wheels and teetered toward the building. I thought that I had set the charges to dig a crater about two feet deep under the rail cars. Because of the frozen ground or, perhaps, because of a concrete apron under the dock area, the intended cratering to tip the cars was only borderline effective. Fortunately, a powerful gust of wind blew decisively in my favor. The middle car teetered further toward the warehouse dragging the other two rail cars with it. The first car leaned past the point of no return and deposited its container against the wood and glass observation deck of the building.

The deck was not constructed to withstand that amount of force and allowed the first car to lean further against the concrete building. With a loud crack of tearing wood accompanied by the crunch of breaking glass, the middle car container slid from its mooring, pounded against and through a large steel dock door, and deposited itself inside the warehouse. The container skidded across the warehouse floor taking everything in its path with it. The container did not stop until it severed a gas line and simultaneously activated an ignition source in the sparks it made while sliding across the warehouse floor. The initial explosion raised the container off floor level for a moment, sending sparks and flames in all directions while igniting a chain reaction of other flammable material inside the warehouse.

Within seconds, super-searing flames generated a second eruption inside the loading dock area blowing out all four dock doors and lighting up the interior of the first floor of the warehouse. The explosion cast a kaleidoscope of flaming colors on neighboring warehouses and factories. The flames engulfed Josip's and my two other cars that were now leaning against the building. In using the car battery as the ignition source for the C-4 charges, my Guiding Hand had taken us out of the deadly range of the fireworks. Otherwise, Josip and I could have been very crisp coffin cargo. We didn't see any security guards. We wouldn't have had time to rescue them if we had. Ironically, the containers as tools of Sandzak's illegal trade were now the means I had used to destroy a network storage facility. I didn't blame Josip for not wiring his charges correctly. From the look of things, we didn't need additional firepower to cause extensive damage to the building and the container cars.

Timely departure was the next agenda item. I made a mental note to check the contents of a container car, if possible, before I wired a similar demolition job in the future. Boxcars or containers loaded with firearms, ammunition, or other ordnance wouldn't need heavy-duty C-4 charges to rattle windows in any neighborhood.

If Josip's charges had ignited, the entire building might have collapsed or exploded, trapping us with falling or propelled debris. It was well past time to leave, but I stood transfixed as I watched the flames lick at the feet of the painted dragon symbolizing the Sandzak network. A few moments later, the entire dragon blistered and burned off the side of the building. I hoped this was a good omen. Only time would tell how successful I would be against Sandzak's personnel. Torching a building was simple when compared to fighting against live and aggressive people with superior firepower and resources who wanted me dead. Before my thought trolley derailed my enthusiasm for this project, Josip brought me back to reality.

"What will we do with him?" Josip asked, pointing to the driver.

"Take him with us," I answered trying not to be callous in my response this time. "Why?"

"I think I am going to be sick. I can't do this. I can't move him by myself."

I helped Josip shift the driver's body to the passenger side of the front seat and covered it with the blanket that the driver had wrapped around himself as he waited for us to complete our demolition exercise.

"Can we go now?" Josip pleaded.

"I know you've had a difficult day, Josip, but I need to do one more thing," I answered. Wait here. I won't be long."

I trotted back to where Goliath and the dog lay. I took a sheet of Calderon letterhead paper I had ripped from one of Advari's shipping lists and put it in the dog's mouth. Some might believe that my planting bogus evidence of Calderon's complicity in the destruction of the warehouse was callous, but this was war against killers and their suppliers. My personal feelings shifted into neutral and stayed there, allowing me to continue the business of war against Calderon and Sandzak. If I could pit the Calderon and Sandzak networks against each other, the postman might not have to keep ringing my solitary message of vengeance against them.

As I trotted back to the car in the light provided by the warehouse blaze, I became aware that the fireworks we had generated brought no response from anyone in the neighborhood or from any emergency or firefighting crews. My second surprise when I returned to the car was to see Josip behind the wheel and ready to move. He drove into a different part of town more quickly than I expected, considering we were sliding sideways on the icy streets most of the way. The first five minutes of our drive passed without conversation. I was willing to let Josip concentrate on his driving.

"He was a hero tonight in his own way," Josip finally announced. "Like me, he was not accustomed to the high life and activities of the Sandzak network. We were happy to avoid them and their crowd whenever we could."

"The quiet heroes make the world a better place," I said, guessing correctly that Josip was eulogizing the driver.

"And who are you, then?" Josip answered, half turning to look at me in the back seat, which was dangerous considering the condition of the roads and Josip's non-professional driving skills.

"I might have an answer for you someday when I know myself. Meanwhile, tell me what favor I owe you," I responded quickly to evade any self-analysis about doing this kind of work for an unknown organization long after my colleagues had retired or handed in their résumés to St. Peter.

Party Time

"I need help to force my daughter away from the Sandzak people," Josip declared as if he was ordering a pizza delivery.

"That's fair enough after the help you gave me tonight. When would you like me to do that?" I asked instead of giving him my sarcastic *"here we go with kids in trouble again"* response I internally felt like giving him.

"I am driving to Milovan's city house now. My daughter is probably there at a holiday party. How difficult would it be for you to bring her out of the house so that my wife and I can take care of her until she is well again?"

"Assuming I listen intently when you describe her and provide other information about where she might be in the house and the type of people at the party, I can assure you I have no idea how long such an extraction will take or how successful I will be. If I listen haphazardly or you don't tell me all I should know, I expect that your daughter and I will be carried out of the house within a half hour. So, tell me all the relevant information you can."

"My daughter is slender, about my height, and with dark hair usually in a braid. Sometimes, she winds the braid around the top of her head. She has dark eyes, uhmm, I do not know what else to tell you."

"What is her name, what might she be wearing, and what she does for Milovan would be helpful additional information for me," I outlined some basic recognition data for Josip to consider.

"Oh yes, her name is Katerina, and she is a cook. Tonight, she will be wearing a green uniform."

"At first, your description sounded like she was a princess. How did she land a cook's job? Did she fall out of bed? Oops, that was an uncharitable and unprofessional remark. I apologize."

"I wanted her to go to the university," Josip continued without recognition of my remark or my apology. "She is intelligent enough, but young people have their own way. They know everything. She is headstrong like her mother. She would not listen to me. She was invited to a party at Milovan's house last summer, and she decided to stay."

That description didn't sound right to me, but something else distracted me as we approached the outskirts of town. I rolled down my window to have a better look. In the driving ice and rain, I saw an extended camp of what appeared to be homeless people.

"What's that all about, Josip?" I asked, completely bewildered.

"Roma," he said. "Maybe you know them as Gypsies."

"Yes, we have Gypsy groups in the States. Sometimes, they follow the small carnivals around the country. But, this is an entire community. I know the various people who made up the former Socialist Federal Republics of Yugoslavia (SFR) have been at war with each other, and Gypsies don't have the best reputation around the world, but is this the best Serbia can do for these people?"

"We tried, but this is the kind of life they choose to live," Josip answered reflexively.

"I don't think so," I said in rebuttal. "Nobody chooses this kind of life, not in this weather, not for their families. Some only have tents and a few boards to call home. Look at that place there with the lantern—small kids, dogs, cats, garbage—that's no place for humans."

By that time, we had driven past the place, and Josip did not answer any of my questions. I didn't press him further. Neither of us spoke for the next fifteen or twenty minutes. My thoughts focused on his daughter. If I thought about the plight of the Gypsies at the same time, my brain would have shorted out without doing anyone any good.

"We are approaching Milovan's house over there," Josip said finally breaking the silence as he pointed to a mansion three times the size I could have imagined to delight Cinderella and any prince she selected.

A number of luxury cars were parked in the driveway and along the curb outside the wrought-iron fence enclosing the property. Valets and security guards were running in all directions ensuring that late-arriving guests were protected from the elements, and from potential intruders like me who probably would be escorted off the property after receiving the appropriate number of bruises.

"Do you want to enter here or go around to the back? The security people there know me so I have a better chance to get you inside from there."

Josip completed his solo dialogue without any signal one way or another from me.

"You know what, Josip, if you want me to rescue your daughter in that crowd, I need a clean shirt and some other equipment to get her out of the kitchen, if that's where she is. Take me to Marika's place—sorry—her brother's place, and we'll come back in the proper attire as soon as we can. Do you have any objections?"

Without comment, Josip stepped on the accelerator—ice or no ice—and headed toward the Kalemegdan Citadel area and Marika's brother's house a short distance away. The sound of the car's acceleration caused several heads attached to security bodies to look up which I didn't consider helpful to Katerina's rescue or my longevity. We'd have enough trouble entering and exiting Milovan's house party without prematurely announcing our presence or intentions. But we didn't generate any serious problems that I could detect. Later, I'd discover that we had other significant problems and hostile people to occupy our time. For example, if I had asked Josip to show me the rear entrance of the house, I would have learned that this side was the rear. In this line of work, one needs to verify hearsay evidence from a parent as much as a lawyer confirms the statements of an unreliable witness. My miscalculation on that topic was lost in the surprise I received when we arrived at Marika's family house. Both Advari and Shortcake greeted me as I slid across the tiled floor of the rear entrance in my wet shoes to meet them.

Uninvited Guests

"Advari, I'm so glad you're here. I really need you tonight," I exclaimed as I messed up his hair.

"Shortcake, I'm glad to see you too, but what are you doing here?" I asked incredulously.

"Marika sent for us," Amy responded with excitement. "Marika had already instructed me to follow you to Lisbon, so I came with Advari when Marika called us to help you with this operation. Is that okay? Besides, I need to tell you something important," Amy continued without giving me a chance to vote on the importance of her presence one way or another.

"If you can hold your information until we resolve another pressing problem, you may be able to help Josip and me a great deal," I told her. "Do you have a party dress in your luggage?"

"Strange that you should ask. Marika told me to bring party clothes. I have a red dress with me that I wore as a bridesmaid. It may be wrinkled a little. Is that okay? Marika said she arranged party invitations for us. I'm really excited."

"I wouldn't have guessed your excitement. If we bring the U.S. Marine Band and a ten-foot-long American flag in with us, probably nobody at the party will notice you in a red dress. Okay, get into whatever party clothes you have while I change my wet rags as I talk to Advari. Josip, this may be a good time for you to find dry clothes for yourself too, and arrange with the butler to get his colleague out of the car. Thanks for your help today. I'm sorry I kept you out in the bad weather so long."

"You have casualties already?" Amy asked with concern behind her inquiry.

"MAGENTA would call it collateral damage. We might call it a tragic death of a noncombatant. Either way, he's dead. Don't dwell on it now, Shortcake, or you'll lose your focus and have us join him before the night is over."

As the three of us ran upstairs to change clothes, the large clock in the foyer chimed midnight. I glanced back at Josip to see him still standing in the kitchen entrance looking at me.

"Josip," I said, "I'm sorry that we need you to help us a little more tonight. We'll do our best to rescue your daughter so that both of you can enjoy Christmas together."

Josip continued to stand in the foyer looking wistfully at me as I climbed the remaining stairs leading to my bedroom. Advari tried to hide behind the door to surprise me, but I saw his shadow and grabbed him as soon as I got in the room. Throwing him onto the bed, I told him what I needed him to do as I got into dry clothes and adjusted the shoulder holster for my big pistol. Advari's eyes got wider as he saw me pack both the heavy artillery and my derringer along with an ankle sheath for my commando knife. "Peace on earth, goodwill to men" would be deferred this Christmas season in Belgrade.

Advari and I were the first ones back downstairs. The taxi I had instructed the butler to call was waiting for Advari. He didn't waste any time running out to it as the ice and snowstorm continued. Advari understood the importance of what I needed from him later that night. Josip appeared in a well-tailored business suit. Maybe it was too fine for a professor's pay, but I didn't comment. As Amy came down the stairs, I recognized her ponytail, but little else. The All-American girl from the Iowa cornfields had grown up. It would take a Marine combat brigade and the band to keep Milovan's guests from noticing her tonight. One other thing was new and noteworthy. I saw the glint of a diamond engagement ring and matching earrings. My Scout was working on different job dimensions whether I was ready for that change or not. With a full-length party dress and an engagement ring, I dismissed any hope I had of ever seeing her knees. But tonight, she was still my Scout, and we had hard work to do.

The butler came inside after having removed the driver's corpse from the front seat of the car. I didn't ask where he stored the body. It would take everything I had to ensure that we didn't add to the collection before the night was over. We enlisted the butler as our replacement driver because Josip needed to arrive as Amy's escort to the party. Marika "volunteered" to stay home in case we needed a spare seat for Katerina on our return trip if we successfully extracted her from Milovan's clutches. Otherwise, I could have used Marika to identify Milovan for me. But, I agreed that her presence might remind the locals of her prior relationship with Milovan and bring unwelcome attention to our band of party crashers. In addition, I thought she would be headed for Budapest by now despite the storm. But, that was just one more item I couldn't let derail my thoughts from the immediate task.

As we approached Milovan's house for the second time that night, Josip leaned forward and whispered something in Serbian to the butler that I didn't catch. The butler nodded, and I assumed that Josip was reminding him to go to the front entrance. To my dismay, we returned to the same entrance that Josip had shown me earlier.

Initially, the entrance we used didn't matter because the house was wall-to-wall party. When Amy took off her coat and entered the ballroom on Josip's arm, the party stopped in its tracks as if she was Louis XIV's guest princess at a grand ball at Versailles. That was the impact I hoped she would have as I moved slowly along the wall to find my way to the kitchen. But, my good *karma* and the distraction Amy caused among the party-goers did not play long enough. Josip had misled me. Intentionally or unintentionally, the problem was the same. The back of the house was really the front, and I was nowhere near the kitchen. Already, I had attracted the attention of the basal dinosauromorph-like security guards who were moving discreetly through or around the guests to intercept me. I knew now why I wasn't searched when I arrived. Initially, the security muscles assumed that I was unarmed, well-mannered, and with

Josip. Now, they had a different perspective. I was a security threat they were paid to eliminate.

As I approached a hallway leading away from the ballroom, a dark-haired young lady with shining dark eyes grabbed me, and we started dancing. My dancing biorhythms were too busy at first noticing that her green "cook's" uniform was a little short on the top and bottom, but my feet gradually found a dancing gear that semi-synchronized to the music and her movements.

Dance Partner

"My name is Katerina," my dancing partner said in academically trained English. I saw you come in with my father. You are American, yes? Who is the young lady in red?"

"Although you are asking me a lot of questions for a new dancing partner, I am glad that you found me. Pardon me if I am confused. Your father told me that you were a cook here. I would have missed you entirely even if I had found my way to the kitchen. I am not acquainted with the Serbian custom of cooks dressing in green for Christmas and being allowed to mingle with invited guests. To answer your questions, the young lady in red is another American who I met in Belgrade through a mutual friend. Your father and Marika invited us to the party. Have I answered all your questions?"

"I have one more. Why are you carrying a gun under your jacket?"

"That's for my protection in case an attractive cook dances too close. Now, I have questions for you. Let's start with your presence here and why your father wants me to bring you home. Are you in trouble with Milovan?"

"Ooh, you also have many difficult questions," Katerina cooed. "I am here because Belgrade has few good jobs for women. I like excitement. So, I became, how you Americans say, 'arm candy' for Milovan. He takes me to the Riviera, to Monte Carlo, Paris—all the places I want to go. He gives me new cars and all the money I want."

"In return, I suppose he gives you all the cocaine or heroin you want if you are a good girl. Is that why your father wants you away from Milovan?"

"I told you I like excitement. Besides, my father worked for Milovan for many years. He cannot judge me or the life I want to have now."

"What did your father do for Milovan?"

"Surely you know, or you will soon learn. He finds people like you who are Milovan's enemies, and informs Milovan before you become a problem. See? The guards are coming for you now. But, I like you although you are a terrible dancer. Come with me. I will give you a chance to escape."

"Why are you doing this, Katerina?"

"I told you. I like excitement. I want to see if you can find a way out of this house when so many others have failed."

"In that case, put both your arms around my neck and take a step backward as we dance so that I have space between us to take the safety strap off my holster. When you feel my arm move to pull out the gun, take two quick steps to your right and drop to the floor. Can you do that?"

"Why should I?" Katerina pouted.

"With that attitude, I don't care if you enjoy my dancing or not. But, I had hoped to save your father the agony of seeing you in this condition so close to Christmas—that is, if you still care about him."

"Oh, so now you are an American cowboy who will preach to me about the spirit of Christmas. Or, will you shoot up the place to rescue me from my friends? You Americans are so naïve."

"Girl, I don't have time to play with your freaked-out brain," I whispered to her as I roughly pushed her out of the way and drew the big pistol just in time. Katerina landed roughly, but safely on the floor.

Love's Ultimate Sacrifice

I wasn't in time to win the luck of the draw, but I was in time to create a temporary standoff. A man I presumed to be Milovan approached with his arm firmly around Amy's neck, pinning her right arm to her left shoulder while bending her backwards toward him to keep her off balance, and to let me know unequivocally that she was his hostage and shield. All the security goons around the room had their weapons drawn and pointed at me. My big pistol was pointed directly at Milovan's forehead. I was surprised at how steady I held the big gun given my active day. Milovan stopped about ten feet from me, and drew Amy's head closer to his for additional cover. Had he realized how short she was, he might have selected another hostage whose vertical dimension provided better protection. I had seen many emotions in Amy's face since she became my Scout, but this was the first time she displayed deep fear. The sight wasn't pleasant watching her suffer that way, but I had to play out this hand even though I had drawn crummy cards.

"What will it be cowboy?" Milovan asked menacingly. "My men are excellent shots. They can kill you anytime I give the signal."

"I am pleased to meet you too, Milovan. If any of your men shoot me, you will not live to see me hit the floor. You will be in hell, or at least in line ahead of me. One of us needs to invent another plan. Do you have any suggestions?"

"You talk big, but you will not risk hitting your friend here, will you?" Milovan sneered as he pulled Amy's head back even closer to him forcing her to her tiptoes. "My grandfather was in World War II, and he told me that Americans talked big, but they would never risk shooting a woman hostage, even if it cost them their lives."

"I was too young to participate in that war, and etiquette lessons after it ended were never quite the same. So, at times like these, I've always taught Amy to use her head. Until now, that plan has succeeded."

"You are talking nonsense. Drop your gun, and I may let her live. You know you are a dead man, but you still have a chance to save her."

"You know that she's not your type, Milovan. She is attractive in her Midwest American way, but you know that she is not the flashy type who you want to show off at the casino or on your yacht. She will cause you trouble. Eventually, you will throw her away just like you did Katerina. So, we may as well finish our business here."

On cue, Amy went limp in Milovan's arms despite his stranglehold. She dug her heel into his shin, and then bolted back up to catch his chin with the top of her head. Simultaneously, she turned her head to scratch his eyes with her earrings. The latter was an innovative twist to the routine that all my Scouts had practiced a million times. Her moves were smooth. Normally, I would have had plenty of time and a big enough target to shoot. But this time, Milovan had partially turned his head to instruct his guards to close in on me. Amy's jawbreaker move only glanced off Milovan's cheek. She was still his prisoner. But, enough of his head was exposed, and, as I predicted, Milovan would precede me in line to hell.

In the same instant, all the windows in the grand ballroom shattered as the Gypsy army that I had instructed Advari to recruit broke through and flung themselves on the security guards with shovels, axes, knives, bricks, and whatever else they could find.

We could have used one more Gypsy, or a quicker stone from Advari's slingshot. One uncovered guard fired at Josip while he was bending over to help Katerina, who was still on the floor where I had pushed her. In her drugged state, Katerina saw the guard aim and flung herself in front of her father, taking the bullet intended for him in her back. The guard paid for that shot with his life as members of the Gypsy army flung him to the floor and exacted their brand of justice on the spot. Except for the continued screaming of the other lady guests, the battle was over in minutes. I stepped toward Amy to see if she needed attention but she was already moving toward Josip and Katerina.

"She was a good girl," Josip said as he looked into my eyes for approval as he held Katerina's body close.

"She had to be. She was your daughter, Josip," I tried to comfort him. "I'm sorry that we could not save her so that she could prove her love for you in other ways," I said quietly as I grabbed a server's towel to wipe Milovan's blood off Amy's neck and back with my left hand. That was a careless move. I still had the index finger of my right hand in the trigger guard of my pistol. Before I could react, Josip grabbed the gun barrel and pulled the gun toward him, jerking my finger against the trigger. The curse of modern technology worked against me in the double-action mechanism of my pistol. The revolver moved to the next chamber, the hammer cocked, and the gun fired, sending a bullet into Josip's chest.

"See, you were wrong," Josip muttered as he slid to the floor from his kneeling position despite holding onto my jacket and pant leg. "You helped me very much. Now, Katerina and I will be together for Christmas after all," he said as he slid the remaining way to the floor beside his daughter into a widening pool of blood.

I hoped that whatever father and daughter did voluntarily or involuntarily for Milovan was forgiven now in their last act of mutual love and anguish for each other.

"I hate this job! I hate you! I don't know why I ever let you talk me into doing this work!" Amy stormed at me after she saw Josip take his final breath.

"I'm almost glad that you do," I replied. "If more people understood and got angry about what some of us volunteer to do to shield society from the Milovans of the world, the Calderon and Sandzak networks would never exist. Fortunately for you," I said, taking her left hand and holding it up so that her engagement diamond caught the light, "you have a date with a better future than I can promise you as a Scout."

"We did well tonight, didn't we?" Advari exclaimed as he came over to our little group. "Oh, I am sorry. I did not see them—" his voice trailed off as he saw Josip cradling his daughter in death.

"It's almost Christmas—at least for some of us," I told him. "We did the best we could, little soldier. Tell your Roma army thank you, and tell them to take all the food and blankets that they need, but nothing else, okay? Tell them to leave something for the cooks and servants. They need to eat too," I called out after him.

Shortly after the Roma and guests left, the local police conveniently arrived. Amy, Advari, and I should have departed long ago, but I lingered to inspect Milovan's home office for anything that could help me identify the scope of the Sandzak network and people involved. I could have used Manco's cousin, Felipe, to crack the safe. As usual, I didn't take time to read the paperwork. I dumped the Christmas presents out of a shopping bag, and stuffed whatever documents that looked worthwhile for my review into the bag. The symbolism of that act wasn't lost on me either. We were leaving as the police arrived. Fortunately, I saw Interpol badges as well as the local police.

As the senior Interpol detective approached me, he asked, "What were you trying to do here tonight, start an ethnic war between your associates and Milovan's distinguished guests? Pitting Muslim Albanian Gypsies against Orthodox Serbian Christians in this country is an explosive combination that even the United Nations didn't handle correctly in the late 1990s. Do you realize that?"[2]

"Believe it or not, yes I do," I answered. "About a year ago, I did some insightful reading and training to prepare myself for any situation in the former Yugoslavia, particularly Kosovo, related to NATO's ineffectual peacekeeping forces, the Clinton administration's misconception of the genocidal nature of the war, and Russian intransigence concerning the entire Yugoslavian situation. Tonight, I needed an army that would not merely tap on the windows, but break through them when the situation demanded. Besides, this was a delayed present from my Guiding Hand in exchange for me not activating the 'avenger clause' of my employment agreement with him regarding some personal business I had a short time ago. My Guiding Hand was preparing me for this action, although I didn't know and appreciate it at the time. So, delivering this message to the Sandzak network tonight was a big deal for me. I leave to you and your courts to decide how distinguished Milovan's guests were. If nothing else, our barging in on his party tonight made Milovan remember something his grandfather told him a long time ago about Americans. I suppose Milovan thought that he was the only one here tonight who had a grandfather. My grandfather told me that Americans should always remember where they came from, and never forget whose sacrifice made it possible for them to be Americans. Apparently, that was the opposite of what Milovan's grandfather told him which might have been a major factor in his career choice and citizenship. But, I'm glad Marika informed you about our presence in Belgrade. In taking care of other business, I neglected to do that."

"On purpose?" the detective inquired.

"Maybe, but often I don't know how much help I need until the shooting starts. I'm certain you encounter similar situations in your work," I added in my defense.

"In that case, I recommend that you move your people out of here before the local police ask questions that both you and I might not want you to answer tonight, or at any other time. We have a private jet waiting at the airport to take you and your two assistants to Madrid. I suggest that you do not miss the flight. And thank you. We have tried to gain access to Milovan's house for years without success and you did it in one night."

"In the future, tell the locals and your people to give the Roma a chance to help gather information," I suggested. "The Roma see and understand everything that is wrong with the world. Quite possibly, the quality of your intelligence and your success rate against organized crime and traffickers may improve. But, for now, if one of your people can drive us to Marika's place to pick up my gear and then take us to the airport, we will be out of town within the hour."

ENOUGH FOR ONE NIGHT

Nobody spoke in the car on the way to Marika's family house or during the drive to the airport except Advari, who wanted to know if the plane would take him on to Lisbon. After the driver's short phone chat with Marika and her subsequent call to the airport, the pilot agreed to take Advari home and arrange safe transport for my gear that was not cleared to travel via commercial airlines. Otherwise, we were lost in our own thoughts.

> In my mind, I felt like a privateer in eighteenth century colonial days. At that time, the fledgling U.S. government did not have enough ships and men to protect American sailors from being impressed into the navies of larger countries such as England, France, and Spain. Under those conditions, U.S. privateers were given letters of marque and reprisal by the colonial government that commissioned them to attack any enemy vessel suspected of

having Americans aboard, and to do whatever damage they could for a share of any valuable booty that the enemy ship carried.[3]

The only difference in my operation was that I didn't receive a share of the booty. Then again, I recalled the biblical reading from Jeremiah the night I became Joe Legion. My life would be spared as part of my booty arrangement with my Guiding Hand. I was satisfied to continue that arrangement.

At the Madrid airport, I tried to contact Beth, who I thought was with Daniela in Slovakia, searching for Janosik's treasure and keeping an eye out for Hassan and Vasily. Daniela answered the phone.

"No, Yuri, Beth is not here. She left yesterday to go back home. Call her there. Do not delay. I think that something very important happened. We did not find any more clues concerning Janosik's treasure."

The short conversation was strange and disconcerting. Daniela had used the Russian version of my real name, which was our code that she had seen Vasily in the area. *So, why had Beth returned home when Vasily was in Slovakia?* Locating him was the entire purpose of her being with Daniela. As I listened to Daniela, I turned around in the phone cubicle and thought I saw Hassan standing in the far corner talking to a *Policia de Securitas* officer and two other men. I hoped whatever Beth thought important at home was equal to or greater than Vasily's presence in Slovakia and Hassan's presence in Madrid. At least, I knew Beth was away from immediate danger. I called her and found her at home.

"I'm glad you called," Beth answered almost before I finished dialing. "I've been waiting for your call for hours. Something terrible has happened to Aunt Agnes and Uncle Ted in California. You absolutely must come home now! Where are you?"

"I'm at the Madrid airport. I saw Hassan and some of his colleagues pass an envelope to the airport *vigilantes*. I'd like to find out what that's all about, and I'll see you in a few days. Okay? We had some success in Belgrade, and none of our people were hurt," I confirmed.

"I'm glad nobody was hurt. But I've heard your story of one more day or one more operation so many times that I'm not listening to it any more. This is really important! You're always chasing gangs, networks, or criminals around the world. Well, this time, the family needs you in California. They probably killed my Aunt Agnes and almost killed Uncle Ted before they were discovered. A lot of money is missing. You have to come home right now!" Beth added again with extreme emphasis.

"Who gave you the information? Are they reliable?" I quizzed her, hoping to determine the real level of urgency.

"I'll relate the details when you get home. I don't ask much from you on family matters when you're away, but you have to believe me and come home this time!"

"Okay, Beth, I'll come. Calm down. We'll catch the first plane out of here. Meanwhile, find out as much information as you can about what happened to your aunt and uncle," I said, trying to soothe her by giving her something to do.

"Who is the 'we' you keep referring to?" Beth asked, nowhere near being soothed.

"This time, the 'we' is my Scout Amy and I. Fortunately, Marika arranged for her and Advari to come to Belgrade without informing me. Advari is flying back to Lisbon on a private jet. I'll book a night flight and see you as soon as the plane arrives at O'Hare."

"Is Amy okay? Is Advari hurt?" Beth asked, forgetting that I told her earlier that everyone was okay. "I know you never get hurt, but everyone around you does eventually. Are they okay?" Beth repeated.

"Amy has an engagement ring, so something is wrong with her head. But, that happened before she arrived in Belgrade, and she used her head as a Sandzak jawbreaker tonight as she was trained to do. Otherwise, I'm not responsible for the condition of her head. She probably saved my life again, although she's ready to scratch my eyes out for ruining her party dress. If you don't have anything else, I'll hang up and run to the ticket counter. Hopefully, Hassan won't see me if I'm not ready to track him and his friends from here tonight."

"Good, because I don't know who or what Sandzak is. Just come home quickly, please!" Beth urged again.

HOME FOR THE HOLIDAYS

Catching a last minute holiday plane out of Madrid wasn't easy, but I was able to buy two remaining seats on the earliest flight. Both were middle seats, and, obviously, not together. However, the two gentlemen in Amy's row graciously moved over to give her an aisle seat. And they hadn't seen her knees or her party dress. I walked further back in the plane until I found my seat between two matronly ladies who obviously were twins and proud of it—both in dress and manners. I immediately lost all hope of negotiating a better seating arrangement. After a struggle to gain her feet, Ada stepped into the aisle to let me flop into the middle seat while her sister Abigail in the window seat coldly inspected me before introducing herself. After I learned that they were not from Iowa or the Chicago metropolitan area, I allowed my adrenalin level to lose interest in any enlightening conversation with them. However, they weren't ready to allow me to disengage myself from them without additional interaction.

I had really wanted to look at the documents I collected at Milovan's house, but the sisters maintained radar surveillance of my every move. I decided to amuse myself by closing my eyes to ponder where Janosik's treasure might be. One possibility was that it never existed other than in the folklore of the Slovak and Polish mountain people. Another possibility was that it existed, but hadn't been found. That meant it probably remained somewhere near the King's Plateau area of the Pieniny Mountains. Other possibilities might be that: one, it was found by Poles and taken north to Krakow; two, it was found by Czechs or Slovaks and never left the country; three, it was discovered by Hungarians and moved south to Budapest or Estergom; or four, whoever found it did not retain it through all the wars and movement of people across Europe for the last four centuries. The treasure may have been moved any number of times but never arrived at any of its intended destinations.

Thinking about the treasure was not the stress reducer I had intended it to be. I began thinking of all the invading armies that marched through that area of Europe since the early 1700s. I didn't arrive anywhere near World War I or II for the first hour of my cranial excursion. I had a major brain wreck when I pondered the 1805 Battle of Austerlitz in which Napoleon defeated the combined armies of Austria and Russia. Local Czechs and Moravians know Austerlitz by its non-Germanic name of Slavkov. Whichever name one selects, the fact remains that the town is about twenty kilometers east of the Moravian provincial capital of Brno with the actual battlefield another twenty kilometers further east. The French Army numbered 75,000 against the combined Austrian and Russian force of 73,000 men. That put a host of foragers in Janosik's yard as they hunted for food for themselves and their horses. If the French found the treasure, it could have traveled either to Moscow or Paris because Napoleon went to both cities as victor and vanquished. If the treasure remained hidden until World War I, it may have been found or destroyed then or in World War II, because Russian General Marikovsky used Napoleon's battle plan to defeat the Nazi Army in approximately the same location. Napoleon's plan was simple enough, I conceded as

I continued my mental warfare. He took the high ground on Stanton (Zuran) Hill to the north. Then, he suckered the Austrians and Russians to leave their position on the Pratzen Heights (Pracky Kopec) to the south and let them march toward him on the assumption that he had a weak right flank. When the Austro-Russian troops were in the valley and swamps between the two positions, Napoleon had the French Army circle around to the Pratzen Heights and attack the Austrians and Russians from the high ground in the rear and center.[4]

When their turn came against the Wehrmacht in World War II, the Russians resurrected Napoleon's battle plan while the Nazi general forgot his military history and paid the price for it. Well, nuts. Marikovsky's victory generated another possibility for the treasure to be located in the Kremlin's private collection, never to be seen in public again. The permutations and combinations of where the treasure could be were endless. I was really enjoying my mind game of treasure hunting when I received a poke in the arm from Ada.

In-Flight Inquisition

"I think this young lady wants to talk to you," Ada said, directing my gaze to Amy, who was standing in the aisle looking at me. Both of my traveling companions positioned themselves to obtain the best acoustical reception possible.

"I didn't mean what I said back there, you know," Amy confessed.

"What didn't you mean, dear?" the matronly pair asked in stereo while assuming they controlled both the seating arrangements and any conversations in their vicinity.

They also stamped me as the guilty party in whatever transpired before I had a chance to testify. In that environment, I made a few assumptions myself as I responded to Amy.

"Regardless of your intent, what did you say that requires your declaration of guilt and an apology in front of a planeload of people?" I asked, trying to ignore the stereophonic interruption from my traveling companions.

"Remember, I said I hated you?"

"Why does this young lady hate you?" the duo interrupted as if their entire existence was now directed to pronouncing their verdict against me, my heirs, and assigns forever.

"So do a lot of people," I replied to Amy. "Why do you consider yourself unique and in need of absolution?" I asked, attempting to overcome the preponderance of the evidence that the "inquisition sisters" attempted to heap upon me.

"Because you saved my life even though you scared me half to death by shooting so close to me. The bullet singed the top of my head."

"Remember our discussions about introducing you to firearms? I didn't say it would be pleasant or which end of the firearm I would introduce you to first. Congratulate yourself for having passed your introductory lesson in firearms."

"Well, it doesn't matter now. My fiancé wants me to quit as your Scout anyway."

Fiancé? Amy didn't make sudden moves without thinking. Perhaps, he is someone from Amy's past who she now recognizes as her Mr. Right. This development could also explain Amy's breaking up with Rick and hiding in Minneapolis with a "friend". I told Rick in our first meeting in the Quad Cities hospital that Amy is personable and has many friends. I'm sure I would learn more in time, but now wasn't the time with the sisters listening. So, I played it straight in our Scout-Operative conversation.

"That's perfectly understandable and reasonable. What can I do to make life easier for you and demonstrate that an apology is quite unnecessary given all the times you have helped me?"

"I only want to move on to my next phase in life. I don't think that includes remaining a Scout," Amy continued as if she still needed to justify her decision to me.

"This may surprise you, but I think you're right. Sooner or later, we all must decide who we are and who we want to be in life. Probably, it's time for both of us to take separate paths."

"Will you quit 'M'?" Amy asked in surprise. "That's unbelievable after all the years you worked with them. But, everything is unraveling in the world today! Are you sure? They probably need you more than ever!" Amy argued both sides of her internal debate.

Fortunately, Amy's conversation left Ada and Abigail totally confused and speechless.

"I may not stop doing what I'm doing given what's happening in the world now, as you say. But, maybe the big 'M' isn't the right format for me going forward. I believe my wife already found trouble for me to explore as a free agent. Otherwise, the only changes I see for myself are different faces and different places."

"You'll stay in touch, though, won't you?" Amy asked hopefully and confused at the same time.

"Sure, at least until your babies arrive. You'll be too busy for me then. By the time you start thinking about me again, I will have submitted my résumé and recommendation letter to St. Peter. Something less than full disclosure may be my best approach to salvation. But, if you put a good word in for me now and then and tell your grandchildren how you helped an old soldier, maybe I'll get time off for good behavior. Thanks for letting me know your plans. You'd better go back to your seat. You're holding up passengers and beverage carts. We'll talk again when we land at O'Hare."

At the time, I believed that conversation would be my last extended talk with Amy. When we landed, the most I expected was a "farewell and good luck" at the luggage carousel. But, by the time I unwound myself from Ada and Abigail, Amy was far ahead of me. I arrived at the baggage claim area in time to see Amy run into the arms of a fine-looking young man who gave her a big hug and kiss, took her luggage, and walked out the door with her to the parking lot without either of them looking back. That should have made our separation a lot simpler. Or, maybe, that was my way of dealing with losing another Scout and friend—first, Alice Bright Feather, then Jenny, and now Amy. Ron certainly was right. My Scouts were a part of my life, and they will remain in my thoughts for the remainder of my days. I might find time to analyze my feelings at greater length someday, but not that night. I needed to get home and find out what was causing Beth so much mental distress.

Chapter Notes

1. Sarah Johnston and others, *Europe on a Shoestring* (Melbourne: Lonely Planet Publications Pty. Ltd., 2005), p. 1008 *et. sec.* By permission of Lonely Planet Publications Pty. Ltd.

2. Wikipedia contributors, "Kosovo War," *Wikipedia, The Free Encyclopedia*, http://en.wikipedia.org/w/index.php?title=Kosovo_War&oldid=320084556 (accessed October 15, 2009). pp. 1–28.

3. Wikipedia contributors, "Letter of Marque," *Wikipedia, The Free Encyclopedia*, http://en.wikipedia.org/w/index.php?title=Letter_of_marque&oldid=315629748 (accessed September 28, 2009). pp. 1–3. Also, Max Boot, "Pirates, Then and Now How Piracy Was Defeated in the Past and Can Be Again," *Foreign Affairs,* Volume 88, Number 4 (July/August, 2009), p. 98.

4. Wikipedia contributors, "Battle of Austerlitz,"*Wikipedia,The Free Encyclopedia*, http://en.wikipedia.org/w/index.php?title=Battle_of_Austerlitz&oldid=315870369 (accessed September 9, 2009). pp. 1–13.

CHAPTER 22

TRANSITION TO NEW PROBLEMS

LATE ARRIVAL

As I picked up my luggage at the O'Hare carousel, I thought I heard several shots. In my line of work, the sound of gunfire resuscitates even my most comatose cranial cells. Nah, that couldn't be. O'Hare was too heavily guarded and patrolled for gunfire.

I was near the exit on the lower level of the terminal to catch a ride home when Amy came running back through the revolving door directly toward me. I couldn't help noticing her blood-spattered clothes.

"They killed him! They killed my Sean!" she screamed at me, turned, and ran back out the door.

By the time I dropped my luggage and followed her, all kinds of security and emergency people had converged on the scene. I had difficulty getting through the throng to be near Amy. I scanned the crowd but didn't observe anyone suspicious. The crowd murmured as Sean raised his head when the paramedics loaded his gurney into the ambulance. Whoever was assigned to erase Amy or Sean hadn't succeeded. Amy jumped aboard the ambulance, the doors shut, and the siren wailed to clear traffic for their drive to the nearest hospital. I wasn't helping anyone by merely standing there. I gathered Amy's luggage, went back into the terminal to retrieve mine, and walked outside to the limo line. As the next car in line pulled up, my cell phone rang. It was Ron.

"Get out of there, *muy pronto*," he instructed without giving any details.

"I'm about to get into a limo now. What's up?"

"Tell your driver to follow the dark blue car waiting at the front of the limo line."

"What kind of trouble am I facing? Do I need weapons?"

"You can get your cannon out if it makes you feel more secure on the way home. Another dark blue car will follow you out of the airport.

When you arrive home, stay there until we sort things out. I'll keep in touch. Your wife doesn't need to know about any of this."

"What's going on?" I asked again to a dead phone. Ron had hung up.

"Hey, buddy. Do you want a ride, or are you planning to hold up traffic all night?" the limo driver asked in a familiar voice.

I got in and looked more closely at the driver. It was Police Chief Dunbar from Aurora.

"What in blue blazes is happening, Chief?" I asked him.

"I was about to ask you the same thing. So far, you only have European *pistoleros* and the CIA on your heels. You must have really upset somebody in Europe. Don't worry; we'll keep your house under surveillance tonight. Don't say anything to your wife yet."

"That's the second time in two minutes I've heard that message. This may shock you, but first, I don't live in your jurisdiction, and second, my wife notices unusual events lately, especially when she knows that I'm involved somehow and I'm being less than candid with her. For example, she'll notice surveillance cars parked on the street with law enforcement people lounging in them. If it isn't premature to ask, what happens tomorrow after everyone leaves?"

"Your friend Ron will be able to answer those questions for you, and you should have your personal defenses in place by then. Meanwhile, relax and enjoy the ride. But, I need to turn the radio off."

I didn't respond to Chief Dunbar. If nobody would tell me what was happening, I didn't care if MAGENTA monitored my ride home or not. By that time, my brain was heavily engaged elsewhere.

During the trip home, four items replayed in my mind: *One, who was responsible for shooting Sean? Two, was the hit actually intended for Amy? Three, what should I do about it? Four, should I have followed the ambulance to the hospital to learn more about what had happened and to protect Amy?* Once again, my personal war against terrorists had erupted near home and generated collateral damage. If this kept up, I could learn to hate this work and myself as much as Amy said she did.

Not Quite an Auld Lang Syne Conversation

I arrived home long after Beth's normal bedtime, but she was waiting for me. Chief Dunbar didn't linger. His limo disappeared as fast as he could drive through the stop sign at the corner without stopping. Now that I was home, I knew I wouldn't get any sleep with my cranial software on overload, so I might as well chat with Beth if that fit her late night agenda.

"Merry Christmas," I greeted her without energy because I had none left.

"It doesn't feel like Christmas with our tree under the snow on the patio where the neighbors put it after we went to Europe."

"I feel bad about that. From here, the tree appears to be a good selection. Can I borrow your hair dryer to melt the snow before I bring it inside tomorrow? Or, will an angel lose his wings because I'm late putting it up?"

"It's already tomorrow, but you'll feel worse and drop your wings when I tell you about my aunt and uncle in California. For once, I'm glad you carry weapons. We may need guns to defend the elderly in our family from abuse and much worse," Beth spoke prophetically.

"If you make some hot tea while I start the fireplace, you can tell me what I should know," I responded with increasing interest although I was dead tired and worried about Amy and Sean and now the fate of Beth's Aunt Agnes and Uncle Ted.

"From what I've learned so far, you may want to take notes for your memoirs," Beth began. "You'll have unlimited material. Despite all your bizarre experiences over the years, you can't imagine what happened to my aunt and uncle simply because they're elderly and trying to live independently in their own home."

"Have they thrown in with a terrorist network from the comfort of their own living room?" I asked, testing again to determine how serious the situation really was.

"They didn't need to look for problems. The predators found them, their neighbors, and their assets."

"Terrorists attacking a retirement neighborhood in California are certainly newsworthy. But, for California, it's not good advertising in addition to increased wildfires, mudslides, and earthquakes. Why are you identifying whatever happened as terrorist activity rather than local crime?"

"I know you're tired, but bear with me. I checked things out, and my aunt and uncle are in deep trouble."

I sensed that whatever happened wasn't contrived by Beth to get me home for the holidays. "Have you called the police there? Is anyone helping them?" I asked.

"I haven't yet, and when you hear my story, I hope you'll agree that I was right not to involve the local police without more information."

"You know that every time you don't call the police at this time of year, Marley's ghost visits me for several nights thereafter."

"Never mind the attitude, Santa Hotshot," Beth replied a little vexed as she sat on the floor next to me. "This is serious."

"You're beginning to concern me that your story is truly more serious than me leaving Paolo, Chauncey, Hassan, Vasily, and the Calderon and Sandzak networks unattended and functioning on two or more continents. In addition, somebody tried to erase Amy and her fiancé at O'Hare tonight," I added, violating Ron's and everybody else's admonitions at the airport.

"I'm truly sorry about Amy. Is she all right?"

"For now, yes, but I don't know how soon before that may change."

"The way events are unfolding, your terrorists or related groups may be involved with the California bunch. Believe me, you won't be lonesome for playmates. Your regular adversaries and some new ones may be involved directly or indirectly. My experiences in North Africa certainly taught me to be more vigilant about the people around me. By the way, your stocking was too heavy to hang on the hearth because Mrs. Claus bought you two boxes of .44-caliber ammunition. That's how serious I think this situation is."

"After forty years, you finally went into a gun shop?" I exclaimed while choking on hot tea. "You are serious! Did anyone take photographs?"

"I used a proxy because I don't have a gun ID card, remember?"

"I hope you didn't ask the teenager down the street. He'll be a grand uncle by the time he's released from the federal hotel. Okay, I'm listening, I promise. No more angel wings, no more buffalo wings—maybe flamingo wings, but they aren't in season now. No more ghosts. Okay, I'm ready. Tell me the whole story, or the part that you know," I said as I straightened up long enough to throw another log on the fire because this conversation appeared to be an all-nighter.

"Before I start, how was Belgrade? If you tell me now, I'll have a better chance of retaining your interest when we get into the details of my story."

"After all these years, my habits don't surprise you anymore. On the plus side, we converted a Sandzak warehouse into a pile of rubble, and one of its proprietors named Milovan now is only a fading memory among his former business associates and party guests."

"Did you punch his ticket?"

"I was about to when someone co-opted me. When did you start using such language?"

"That's good isn't it? I mean Milovan's demise, not my language."

"I wish I could answer positively, but I believe Vasily beat me to the draw."

"Why would Vasily shoot Milovan when, according to what you told me earlier, you expected Vasily to approach the Calderon and Sandzak networks to sell weapons?"

"I thought about his motivation a while myself. It comes down to power and efficiency. If Vasily can control or rub out Ernesto Calderon, Vasily can eliminate a middleman, and take sole possession of that network. Similarly, if Vasily removes Kabrinovic and Zandar, the two remaining partners running the Sandzak network, he can set his own price and deal with whomever he wants in the South American, European, North African, and possibly Asian weapons markets. When I left Serbia, Marika was preparing to chase Kabrinovic and Zandar in Budapest. She unwittingly may help Vasily consolidate his empire if she eliminates those two targets. Now that I think about it, I may be helping Vasily gain control over both networks too."

"As an adjunct of my rehabilitation program for Chauncey, Paolo, and Advari, who were shaving profits off illegal Calderon cargo and selling some themselves, I have them busy diverting illegal shipments and fouling up the paperwork from both networks. I'll see if Ernesto is sharp enough to acquire the Sandzak empire, or whoever operates it after Marika or Vasily finish off Kabrinovic and Zandar. On the other hand, Vasily may dethrone Ernesto. Or, a third party may wipe out all of them. Save your bingo cards until all the numbers are verified on that game."

"You told me a long time ago that you consider Vasily your most dangerous opponent. Do you still feel that way?"

"Yeah, more than ever now."

"Can you use the police or military to capture him?"

"The local police and Interpol agents play a different game than I do when it comes to the intensity they have in pursuing criminals. Plus, network biggies invest heavily in their personal security. Nobody really knows what resources Vasily commands. No European police officer appears anxious to challenge Vasily and risk losing everything including life, limb, job, pension, home, and family."

"Are you sure that the shooter at the Belgrade party was Vasily?"

"Picture a smaller and wider Serbian version of the hall of mirrors at Versailles with four curtained hallways leading off it like spokes of a wheel. That was the size of the ballroom where the party was held. As I was about to nail Milovan, who was using Amy as a shield at the time, I thought I saw Vasily's reflection in one of the mirrored panels on the opposite wall an instant before he fired at Milovan and disappeared behind the curtain immediately thereafter. In the confusion and with me in everyone's view aiming my pistol at Milovan's head while waiting for Amy's jawbreaker move on him, I'm certain everyone, including Amy, believes I shot Milovan. She mentioned that the bullet parted her hair. Because Amy is short, I had enough of Milovan's head as a target to avoid spoiling her hairdo. If the police examine Milovan's entry wound closely, I'm sure they'll find that the bullet entered his skull from an angle rather than straight ahead if I had shot him. In addition, Vasily undoubtedly used a 9-mm pistol while I had my .44-caliber. If I had shot Milovan, his head would have exploded like a pumpkin all over Amy. More distressing than that, when I called Daniela, thinking that you were still with her, she gave me the code word to confirm that she had seen Vasily traveling west in Slovakia a few days earlier. Circumstantially, he certainly could have been in Belgrade visiting the Sandzak network czars when I was there."

"It sounds like you had a rough time again. I can understand why you're tired and frustrated."

"In addition to all that, Josip, Marika's old university professor, helped me torch the Sandzak warehouse. After we finished that project, he asked me to rescue his daughter, who was on Milovan's payroll as a cook, arm candy, and drug addict, among other jobs. That's how we wound up at Milovan's party. After Milovan was shot, one of his henchmen decided to end the professor's tenure on this planet, but his daughter jumped in front of him to take the bullet. We came so close to extracting her that the thought of her loss overwhelmed old Josip. I was careless with my weapon, even considering everything going on around me, and he pulled on the barrel of my pistol. I had my finger on the trigger at the time, the gun discharged, and we lost Josip too."

"Was Advari there? Is he okay?"

"Fortunately, yes. I had him requisition members of the local Roma encampment I had seen earlier in the day outside of town. Without his help, I wouldn't have been able to overcome Milovan's security force. As compensation, I allowed the Roma to raid Milovan's pantry and closets for food and blankets. Hopefully, we did some good for them. They live under very ugly conditions that you and I might not survive."

"Did Advari return to Lisbon safely?"

"Marika arranged a private flight for him, so be assured that he made the most of that trip. The sad part is that Chauncey and Paolo are involved in the Calderon network, and I'm not certain I can keep them out of jail, or if I really want to defend them against whatever legal penalties that may come their way."

"If Paolo is imprisoned, besides breaking his wife's heart, what happens to Advari?"

"Exactly, now you see my problem. If I turn him in, Paolo may be released from jail in time to see his baby graduate from the university, assuming he survives the prison environment. Then, what do I do with Chauncey? Will his mother suffer because he's not there to care for her? Do I find Chauncey an attorney, and who might that be? I don't have a clue. So far, the spirit of Christmas has eluded me this year. But, before I whine endlessly about my clients and their elves, give me more details about what's happening with your aunt and uncle."

"You said Vasily might become unstoppable if he gains control of the Calderon and Sandzak networks," Beth continued discussing my problem clients instead of taking the opening I gave her to move the conversation to her California relatives.

"Yes, that's why I have Chauncey and Paolo starting a war between the Calderon and Sandzak networks by diverting Calderon cargo shipments in the Cape Verde islands. If they're successful, maybe there won't be enough left of the networks to attract Vasily."

"Maybe you can devise a plan for Hassan to help you overcome Vasily while he waits for the internal fighting to stop among the various network candidates," Beth suggested.

"For Chauncey and Paolo, my approach is a modern version of a 'trial by ordeal' used by the gentry in the Dark Ages before lawyers invented trial by jury for their financial benefit. If the accused survived the ordeal, he or she was declared not guilty. Under my version, if Chauncey and Paolo don't get themselves killed by the Calderon or Sandzak networks, they might gain their freedom and redemption if they help me bring down Vasily. What are their chances for survival in that venture? I don't know. As for Advari, he knows that I want him involved in the diversion of shipments, not as punishment, but to keep an eye on Chauncey and Paolo. His survival skills are better than all of us combined, so I don't worry about him in that way."

"But, having Hassan help me against Vasily is a tougher question. Hassan is the wildcard in my deck. I don't know if he's playing both ends as a law enforcement agent, or if he's a rogue operator similar to Vasily. I need to gain more certainty about him. How's that for disrupting our Christmas spirit this year? But tell me about the trials and tribulations your aunt and uncle have encountered. I'm sorry I keep delaying or interrupting your story," I heaped blame on myself for re-routing the California discussion again.

The Alpha and the Omega

Beth hadn't exaggerated the seriousness of the trouble that had fallen upon her elderly relatives. In the first five minutes alone, she related events and acts, which, if true, included murder, attempted murder, conspiracy, bank and securities fraud, extortion, immigration violations, human trafficking, money laundering, elder abuse, and tax evasion. Of the pile of sins committed, I thought that tax evasion was the clear winner. One could cop a plea on the other charges, but tax evasion was a serious crime to the Internal Revenue Service. Beth was right on another item too. It will take another book for me to relate this new story. The more she told me, the more I began to perceive connections with the international networks I had already uncovered. Shakespeare didn't miss the mark when he wrote: "The web of our life is of a mingled yarn, good and ill together."[1]

"Daniela and Marek each sent us Christmas cards," Beth announced as she opened the stack of mail that had collected in our absence. "Marek asked if you want him to explore any other caves for Janosik's treasure during the slow tourist season. I thought he would see through your game of using the treasure hunt as an excuse for him to continue courting Daniela. No, that's not right. He will welcome any excuse to keep seeing Daniela, won't he—even soliciting your help to revive an old legend?"

"When you send our cards to them, ask Daniela to look for tire tracks in the mud or snow around the abandoned Tesla electrical factory south of Dolny Kubin. Depending on her answer, I'll know if Janosik's treasure is only a legend, or if I can re-market it to trap some adversaries," I answered with a second surge of adrenalin.

"What do you know about the treasure that you're not telling me?"

"Nothing that I can explain to you or anyone else without more information," I replied honestly.

Fully awake after that conversation, I left Beth to sort through the remainder of the mail while I gathered the Christmas decorations from the basement. Still fully charged, I put on my coat, retrieved the tree from the patio, shook as much snow off it as I could, and put the tree in the garage to thaw before I brought it inside to decorate later. Not satisfied with that exercise, I started cleaning my weapons and thinking about what I needed for a trip to California. In the course of my chores, I noticed three non-neighbor cars parked along the street. Chief Dunbar had been correct. Some law enforcement agency was providing a protective screen for my house through the night and early morning hours. *What was that all about, and why didn't someone tell me?*

Beth had gone to bed long ago, and only a few embers still glowed as I closed the fireplace doors and went upstairs. Falling asleep shouldn't have been a problem. *Why was my brain still trying to make connections between the terrorist networks, Hassan, Vasily, Calderon, Sandzak, Janosik's treasure, and Beth's relatives in California?* The connections between those organizations and people were tenuous at best, but the thoughts kept me awake. To induce sleep, I finally accepted the fact that this was not the end of my encounters with terrorist networks. It was the old alpha and omega trick. Thus far, I had only experienced the end of the beginning of a larger story that I would have to experience and record in my tardy MAGENTA performance reports and for my own enlightenment, if for no other reasons.

I had no sooner dispatched my demons and fallen asleep when the phone rang. It was Marika.

"You should be satisfied with yourself. You put Milovan in his family's cemetery plot earlier than I expected," she said. "I wasn't as fortunate. Both Kabrinovic and Zandar slipped through my fingers before I arrived in Budapest. Surprisingly, both were there at the same time. Probably, they're hiding now. But that's not why I called. Until those two surface again, I decided to pursue the possibility of networks in Southeast Asia. I told my supervisor about the information you had on Don Sak pier. If you're interested, he asked me to offer you a place on my team to find our agent's killers and eliminate illegal traffic in that area. Will you work with us—on either a contract or collaborative basis?"

"You're several hours too late or too early. Beth already instructed me to track down the people responsible for troubling her aunt and uncle in

California. From the few details she gave me, a South Pacific or Southeast Asian connection may be present in that activity. We may be collaborating no matter what. If I discover a connection, I definitely will call you for help, or pass on any information I have about those I believe are involved."

"Okay, but don't wait too long. Network gunners killed one of my agents already. You and a boy with a slingshot won't intimidate them, although they should be apprehensive after the results you produced. Somehow, you reduce the population wherever you go. Good luck."

I had no sooner hung up with Marika when the phone rang again. This time, it was Ron.

"I'm checking on how your night went after you left the airport," he opened.

"If you're asking if the police stakeout was successful, there were no incidents in my immediate neighborhood. If you're asking how I slept, I won't get a passing grade."

"Now you know how it feels when you wake me up early. Speaking of passing grades, I don't know what kind of performance evaluation MAGENTA will give you this year. I haven't forwarded much of anything we talked about during the past year to MAGENTA, and I don't intend to unless it's positive. You have wreckage all over the globe and a lot of unfinished business. On the positive side, you brought the missionaries and me home. You finished Barrantes but nailed only one of two Calderons. I know you have continuing troubles with your friends on both ends of the Southern Cross International Shipping Company and the flow of illegal goods continues. Certainly, Vasily is not contained in any way, and Hassan is a wildcard for everyone. Like you, I don't know if Hassan's son is a hostage, or if he voluntarily works for the Calderon network when he isn't doped out on drugs. Rescuing him isn't my top priority for the next year either. Do you need additional help in tying up your loose ends in the next few days?"

"Yesterday, I might have said yes, but Beth told me about troubles her aunt and uncle are having in California. We are flying there in the next day or so. From what she and Marika tell me, I might encounter additional network or gang-related activity, so right now, MAGENTA's performance ratings don't interest me. I can work with Marika or independently either MAGENTA-less and Scout-less, if necessary, although I won't turn away help from any source."

"You appear to be lining up an active new year. I'll do my best to support and inform you."

"If you tell me who or what MAGENTA is and the significance of what happened last night, I might spare you a lot of agony."

There was a long pause on Ron's end of the line. He cleared his throat, then spoke in a choked voice I had never heard from him.

"First, I can tell you that Amy is willing to continue as your Scout if you help her find her fiancé's shooter. By the way, the doctors plugged all the holes, and Sean will recover."

There was another long pause. I thought I'd intervene to move the conversation along.

"Usually, when there's a first, Ron, the next number is a second. Do you have a second item in mind?"

"I have a big second item. I don't know if you're ready for it, though."

"The only way to find out is to try me, I guess. What do you have?"

"All these years, I've never identified PURPLE or MAGENTA to you. Ready or not, I will tell you some of the story now. If you can absorb it, I'll tell you more."

"Fine, let's hear it."

"The leader of PURPLE and MAGENTA and the original Joe Legion are one and the same person. How does that strike you after all these years?"

"That would be credible if my brother hadn't died over forty years ago. Ron, are you saying Joe has been alive all these years? Where? What? Tell me the whole story! Is that why Colonel Andrews denied me permission to attend his funeral? But, our family buried somebody. Who was that? Ron, answer me! You can't start a story like that and not finish it!"

"It depends," Ron answered much too quickly to assure me that he actually would paint the entire picture.

"Depends on what?" I challenged him.

"It depends on if you want to take your brother's place again. Take some time, and let me know what you want to do."

I stood there in shock, holding the phone long after Ron ordinarily would have hung up. I finally got my mouth to work in conjunction with active brain waves.

"Ron, if Joe was alive all these years, where was he, and who killed him now?"

"Before you met her, Joe met and fell in love with Alice Bright Feather. She was his first Scout. I'll bet you never knew that. After she told him that she didn't love him in the same way, he was so heartbroken that he resigned his commission as an Army intelligence officer and went to Slovakia to become a priest. Later, when she wrote him that she loved you but you didn't return her love, he joined a cloistered monastery. But, talent like his didn't stay hidden for long, especially with a new Polish pope who wanted reliable intelligence from Eastern Europe. Joe was called to the Vatican, and, within a short time, he had full diplomatic status with Eastern European countries. Obviously, he couldn't participate in the fieldwork that still fills our lives, but he could pass on important information to the Pentagon and JASON under the aegis of PURPLE and MAGENTA in addition to the Vatican. He got the names from the color of his vestments. He suffered from the same red-green color deficiency you have. I'll bet you never would have made that connection either."

"I concede that point to you. How did he die?" I was about to say how would anyone dare kill a Vatican diplomat, but Pope John Paul II had been shot, so papal and priest-diplomat robes weren't bulletproof. Who got to Joe? Was Vasily responsible?"

"Everyone remembers when Pope John Paul II was shot by Mehmet Ali Agca in St. Peter's Square on May 13, 1981. But, few remember that a Spanish priest attempted to stab the pope with a bayonet at the Fatima Shrine on May 12, 1982. If you look closely at the security tape of that day, you'll see that Joe was one of the defenders who prevented the deranged priest from reaching Pope John Paul II."

"I assume you have the tape if I want to see it. Was Joe injured in defending the pope?"

"Yeah, I have a copy of the tape whenever you're ready to see it. No, Joe wasn't hurt that day. He kept himself in shape and could always defend himself physically. But remember when I told you that if anyone could die of a broken heart, Alice was a prime candidate? Well, that medical and emotional state isn't exclusive to women. When Joe learned of her death, it revived all the old memories and emotions he thought he had conquered years ago. A few days ago, his aides went into his room and found him in bed clutching his prayer book with a photo of Alice inside. Now that you know, how does it feel? Would you feel better if I had told you about your brother and Alice long ago?"

"I don't know. In one sense, I killed both of them without firing a shot, didn't I? The three sergeants taught me too well."

"I hope you're not going to drag that guilt boulder around for the remainder of your life because the top position of MAGENTA is available to you without requiring you to join the priesthood—assuming you want it. I'm sure your wife would enjoy having you sequestered in a monastery for the remainder of your days. I know we talked about you converting to freelance work, but think it over. I have a doctor's appointment. I'll contact you in a few days. By the way, Joe's casket will be transported back here now that you know. Old Jim can finish the inscription on Joe's tombstone for you and your sister now. She doesn't know any of this yet either, so you get to explain as much as you feel she can handle. Bye."

Ron hung up before I had a chance to ask who Joe's contact was in the Pentagon and within JASON. The nearest monastery and I were pleased that I didn't need to become a priest to continue intelligence work at MAGENTA, but knowing who the Pentagon contact was might be important to me in making a decision to take Joe's place again or to go it alone.

A REMINDER OF JEREMIAH'S PROMISE

Reminiscent of the night I sought silent counsel in the Post Chapel long ago after being told of Joe's alleged death, I again sought comfort and wisdom from the words of the prophets. I had no idea how to proceed on any front. Worse, I seemed no closer to understanding the promise of Jeremiah that I had read and remembered from so long ago.

In my aleatory shuffling through my Bible now, I came upon the words of Habacuc:

> "I will stand at my guard post, and station myself upon the rampart, and keep watch to see what he will say to me, and what answer he will give to my complaint. Then the Lord answered me and said: Write down the vision clearly upon the tablets so that one can read it readily. For the vision still has its time, presses on to fulfillment, and it will not disappoint; if it delays, wait for it, it will surely come, it will not be late." (Hab. 2:1-4)[2]

My future, my destiny, and Jeremiah's promise of my full understanding of my mission on earth were still ahead for me. I would not escape hardship and suffering, but my life would be spared to accomplish my mission and to tell its story, although the time had not yet arrived when I would fully understand it. On a more immediate basis, I would have to coordinate my activities with a federal administration that would not admit it had actionable intelligence on the 9/11 attackers until May 15, 2002, but it couldn't or wouldn't act on it prior to the attack. The same administration would initiate a war of choice on March 19, 2003, against a regime that we easily defeated in the desert a decade earlier, and that still did not have weapons of mass destruction to pose a threat to our country. With my brother no longer in his hidden role as the head of MAGENTA, with Marika off on separate operations with the CIA or FBI, and Ron unable to join me in field operations, I was on my own, and I knew it.

Chapter Notes

1. "All's Well That Ends Well Act IV Scene III," *William Shakespeare The Complete Works* (New York: Barnes & Noble Books,1994), p. 775.
2. The Holy Bible, *op. cit.*, p. 941.

APPENDIX

LIST OF CHARACTERS AND ORGANIZATIONS

Abigail—One of twin sisters with Joe Legion and Amy on the return flight from Belgrade.

Ada—Abigail's matronly twin sister.

Acrobats—Street performers in Marrakesh who help Joe Legion fight the Calderon network in Morocco.

Advari—Street urchin from Chennai, India who saves Joe Legion's life several times with his slingshot and street savvy.

Ahmed—Porter at the Marrakesh hotel who helps Joe Legion organize an attack on the Calderon villa in La Montagne, Morocco to rescue Ahmed's son, Ali.

Alexandra—Amy's younger sister who bargains with Joe Legion to protect Amy while she works as Joe's fourth Scout.

Ali—Ahmed's drug-addicted son who works for Calderon and is rescued by Joe Legion.

Alice Bright Feather—Colonel Redmond's secretary and Joe Legion's first Scout during his active military service.

Amy—Joe Legion's physical therapist and fourth Scout with the code name of Shortcake.

Andrews, Rick—Intern who helps Amy recover from her car accident injuries in the Quad cities hospital. He is also identified as Dr. Andrews, or Rick.

Anna—Marika's niece and receptionist.

Angry Dragon—Joe Legion's nom de guerre during Asian operations.

Aunt Maria—Beth's ninety-year-old aunt in Trstena, Slovakia who provides leads about the contents and location of Janosik's treasure.

Barrantes, Alfonso—Drug lord in Peru who operates a tea ranch in Quillabamba and a cocaine factory in Tingo Maria. He is also known as Señor Barrantes, or simply Barrantes.

Barrantes, Juanita—Alfonso's wife who helps Joe Legion oppose her husband's drug operations. She is also called Señora Barrantes, or Juanita.

Beth—Joe Legion's wife who helps him fight contraband networks in Europe, Morocco, and South America.

Bhabha Atomic Research Center—India's nuclear research center in Mumbai (Bombay).

Bill or "Pontius"—Private pilot for Barrantes who helps Joe Legion and Ron rescue three Mormon missionaries.

Cala—Ahmed's wife and mother of Ali who works as a maid at a hotel in Marrakesh.

Calderon, Ernesto—Gilberto's twin brother who directs the European and North African operations of their drug and smuggling network. He is also called the Red Hatband Man.

Calderon, Gilberto—Ernesto's twin brother who directs the South American operations of their drug and smuggling network.

Chauncey—Charge d'Affaires of the U.S. Embassy in Lima, Peru who vacillates between helping and interfering with Joe Legion's South American operations.

Chief Inspector Harley—Scotland Yard officer who interrogates Joe Legion about a lost camera bag and smuggled nuclear triggers at London's Heathrow Airport.

CIA Agent Turner—Injured agent in Guatemala who Joe Legion and Advari pick up on their return to the U.S. from Peru.

Colonel Andrews—Army Officer who recruits and trains Joe Legion to replace his brother, Joe following the latter's presumed death in Southeast Asia.

Colonel Redmond—Army Officer who initiates special operations assignments for Joe Legion following his training to replace his brother.

Colonel Sebastian—Commanding Officer of Spanish Military Operations in North Africa.

Colonel X—Army Officer and CIA Agent who both assists and frustrates Joe Legion in Joe's South American assignment to rescue three missionaries.

Conserje Alva—Foreman of the Quillabamba ranch.

Conserje Cerro—Foreman of the Tingo Maria ranch.

Customs Agent Tambos—Peruvian official who unwittingly aids Joe Legion in an operation against the Tingo Maria drug facilities.

Customs Director Pevas—Customs Agent Tambos's supervisor who also is duped into assisting Joe Legion in an operation against the Tingo Maria drug ranch.

Daniela—Joe Legion's unmarried cousin in Slovakia.

Dick—Joe Legion's Army partner from Iowa who helps Joe escape when their joint military assignment is unsuccessful.

Director Brujas–Director of the Costa Rican Immigration Office.

Director Rajiv—Director of the Bhabha Atomic Research Center in Mumbai, India.

Dottie—Joe Legion's neighbor who helps Joe rescue Amy from drug network enforcers.

Dr. Haynes—Military doctor who provides emergency care to help Joe Legion return to the U.S. from an overseas operation.

Dr. Murphy—Former MAGENTA physician who provides emergency care to Joe Legion following a neighborhood attack by network enforcers.

Dr. Scott—Civilian orthopedic surgeon who repairs major injuries to Joe Legion's shoulders.

Farid—Leader of a Berber horse troupe who helps Joe Legion avoid violence in an operation against the Calderons' villa in La Montagne, Morocco.

FBI Agent Sanders—Local FBI agent who tries to help Joe Legion against drug network enforcers, but whose actions are misinterpreted.

Felipe—Manco's cousin who cracks the Calderons' safe at the Tingo Maria ranch.

Hassan—Joe Legion's Kuwaiti friend who alternatively helps and interferes with Joe's assignments against drug and smuggling networks.

Heidi—Amy's roommate, who helps Joe Legion and Amy fight network enforcers.

Irina—Latvian interpreter during Joe Legion's consulting trip to Latvia and Russia.

Isadora   Youngest of the Barrantes' three daughters who playfully helps Joe Legion at the Quillabama ranch.

JASON—Group of elite U.S. scientists who provide classified information and advice to top government officials.

Jenny—Joe Legion's third Scout whose murder influences Joe's actions against network enforcers.

Joe Legion—Principal character who replaces his brother using the same nom de guerre.

Jorge—Peruvian law student who Joe Legion recruits to gain access to the Barrantes ranch.

Juraj—Joe Legion's real Slovak first name used by his cousin, Daniela.

Juraj Janosik—Early eighteenth century Slovak outlaw and national hero whose legendary treasure has never been found.
Josip—Marika's former university professor who helps Joe Legion fight the Sandzak network in Belgrade, Serbia.
Kabrinovic—One of the three chief operators of the Sandzak network in Serbia.
Katerina—Josip's daughter who Joe Legion attempts to rescue from the Sandzak network.
MAGENTA—Secret anti-terrorist organization that provides intelligence and logistic support to Joe Legion through its Operatives and Scouts; formerly named PURPLE.
Manco—Aymaran Indian guide who helps Joe Legion and Ron against Peruvian and Bolivian network enforcers and who assists Joe in his Quillabamba and Tingo Maria ranch operations.
Marek—Park Ranger in Slovakia who helps Daniela and Joe Legion explore caves and other possible hiding places for Janosik's treasure.
Marika—Joe Legion's second Scout, who becomes a MAGENTA Operative and CIA Agent. She later helps Joe fight the Sandzak network in Serbia.
Marshal Train—Air Marshal on Joe Legion's and Beth's flight to Madrid.
Maya—Manco's wife who helps Joe Legion against the Calderon network in Peru.
Metropolitan Cerveny—Archbishop of Slovakia in the early 1990s.
Miguel—One of three Portuguese brothers who operate the Southern Cross International Shipping Company.
Milovan—One of three chief operators of the Sandzak network in Serbia.
Mormon missionaries—Three young missionary students Jim, Scott, and Steve who become entangled in the Calderon drug network in Bolivia and Peru until extracted by Joe Legion and Ron.
Mr. Robbins—British MI-6 intelligence officer who with Chief Inspector Harley interrogates Joe Legion at London's Heathrow Airport about weapons trafficking.
Napokon—Joe Legion's code name during Russian and Eastern European operations.
Omar—Advari's Moroccan acrobat friend who helps Joe Legion rescue Beth from the Calderon network.

Paolo—Advari's guardian and one of the three Portuguese brothers who operate the SCI Shipping Company.

Philippine sergeants—Three former Philippine Scouts who survived the Bataan death march in World War II and trained Joe Legion to replace his brother in special operations.

Police Chief Dunbar—Chief of Aurora, Illinois police department.

Police Chief Franzen—Chief of the Lisle, Illinois police department who has divided loyalties in helping Joe Legion and Amy while the Calderon network holds his daughter hostage in South America.

Professor Palmer—Seismology professor from Iowa who aids Joe Legion in gaining access to the Calderon villa in Ceuta, Morocco.

PURPLE—Secret anti-terrorist organization that provides intelligence and logistic support to Joe Legion. PURPLE is the predecessor organization of MAGENTA.

Ravi—Police officer in Bhuj, India involved in the attempted kidnapping of Roberto.

Roberto—Sujaya's husband and nuclear scientist in India who Joe Legion rescues following an attempted kidnapping.

Ron—Former U.S. Army Ranger and friend who assists or advises Joe Legion in his special operations assignments.

Sam—Local cemetery custodian.

Sandzak—Smuggling network based in Serbia operated by three principal adversaries of Joe Legion.

Santiago—Manco's uncle who aids Joe Legion in his operations against the Quillabamba and Tingo Maria ranches in Peru.

Sean—Amy's fiancé who is shot at O'Hare International Airport.

Sergeant Biggens—Police officer who aids Joe Legion against drug network enforcers in Chicago's western suburbs.

Slick—Joe Legion's friend in the Personnel department of Joe Legion's U.S. Army unit.

Skaric—One of Marika's fellow CIA agents in Serbia.

Southern Cross International Shipping Company—Family shipping company owned by Paolo, Miguel, and Roberto who help or hinder Joe Legion's activities against drug lords in Europe, North Africa, and South America.

Sujaya—Indian gynecologist who provides emergency care to the earthquake victims in Bhuj, India who later helps Joe Legion rescue Roberto, her nuclear scientist husband.

Svetlana—Russian interpreter for the Human Resources consulting group in Moscow and St. Petersburg.

Tabriz—Amhed's cousin and bus driver carrying Joe Legion's acrobat army to raid Ernesto Calderon's La Montagne, Morocco villa.

"Transition"—A Russian organization intended to assist former Russian military officers to find civilian employment.

Vasily—Joe Legion's arch-enemy who attempts to sell stolen nuclear materials to terrorist networks.

Veronica—Beth's second cousin who lives in Trstena, Slovakia.

Water Man—Street performer in Marrakesh who helps Joe Legion and the acrobat army rescue Beth from the Calderon network in Morocco.

Yuri—Russian equivalent of Joe Legion's real first name used by Daniela to alert Joe Legion that Vasily is in the vicinity.

Zaki—Snake handler in Marrakesh marketplace who joins Joe Legion's acrobat army to rescue Beth.

Zandar—One of the three principals of the Sandzak network in Serbia.

BIBLIOGRAPHY

"Afghanistan, the Sequel," *Chicago Tribune* Editorial, July 30, 2009, p. 18.

Avial, Oscar. "A Cold Warrior's Revival," *Chicago Tribune*, November 3, 2006, pp. 1, 24.

Barnes, Julian E. "Resource Shift in Afghanistan," *Chicago Tribune*, July 30, 2009, p. 12.

Barnes, Julian E. and Greg Miller. "Obama Ditches Bush's Missile Shield," *Chicago Tribune*, September 18, 2009, p. 16.

Bartlett, John (compiler). *Familiar Quotations 13th Edition*. Boston: Little, Brown and Company, 1955.

"Biden to Reassure Poles During European Trip," *Associated Press*, October 20, 2009, p. 1.

Biello, David. "A Need for New Warheads," *Scientific American*, Volume 297 Number 5 (November, 2007), pp. 80-85.

Boot, Max. "Pirates, Then and Now How Piracy was Defeated in the Past and Can Be Again," *Foreign Affairs,* Volume 88, Number 4 (July/August, 2009), pp. 94–107.

Brummitt, Chris. "10,000 Marines Deploy in Start of Afghan Surge," *Chicago Tribune*, June 9, 2009, p. 12.

Burakovskaya, Alla and Grace Chung. "U.S. Russia Agree to Missile Cuts, But Tensions Remain," *The McClatchy Company*, July 6, 2009, pp. 1–4.

Butler, Desmond. "EU Report: Georgian Attack Started War with Russia," *Associated Press*, September 30, 2009, pp. 1–2.

Clancy, Tom. *Into the Storm*. New York: The Berkley Publishing Group, 1998.

Cleary, Thomas (translator). *Sun Tzu. The Art of War*. Boston: Shambhala Publications, Inc., 2003.

"Crazy Raspberry Ants Leave Sour Taste in Texas," *Chicago Tribune*, May 15, 2008, p. 3.

D 'Este, Carlo. *Patton A Genius for War*. New York. HarperCollins Publishers, Inc., 1995.

Dunlap, Fiona. *Fodor's Exploring India*. New York: Fodor's Travel Publications, 1998.

Dyomkin, Denis and Margarita Antizde. "Russia Says U.S. Mercenaries, Others Fought for Georgia," *Reuters*, November 24, 2008, pp. 1–3.

Emerick, Yahiya. *The Complete Idiot's Guide to Understanding Islam*. Indianapolis: Alpha Books, 2002.

"Europe: Proton Beams Circulate in Big Bang Machine," *Associated Press*, November 21, 2009, pp. 1–3.

Gach, Gary. *The Complete Idiot's Guide to Understanding Buddhism*. Indianapolis: Alpha Books, 2002.

Graham, Colonel J.J. (translator). Carl Von Clausewitz *On War*. New York: Barnes & Noble Publishing Co., 2004.

Hardy, Paula; Mara Vorhees; and others. *Morocco*, 7th Edition. Melbourne: Lonely Planet Publications Pty. Ltd., 2005.

Higgins, Alexander G. "Winter, Repairs Stall Atom Smasher Until Spring," *Associated Press*. September 23, 2008, pp. 1–3.

Johnsen, Linda. *The Complete Idiot's Guide to Hinduism*. Indianapolis: Alpha Books, 2002.

Johnson, Sarah and others. *Europe on a Shoestring*. Melbourne: Lonely Planet Publications Pty. Ltd., 2005.

Jordans, Frank. "Big Particle Collider Repairs to Cost $21 Million," *Associated Press*. November 17, 2008, pp. 1–3.

Kapstein, Ethan B. "The New Global Slave Trade," *Foreign Affairs*, Volume 85, Number 6 (November/December, 2006), pp. 103–115.

Karnow, Stanley. *Vietnam A History*. New York: Penguin Books, 1984.

Keller, Julia. "Fermilab's All-Night Pajama Party," *Chicago Tribune*, Metro Section, September 11, 2008, p. 1.

Kemp, Geoffrey and Robert Harkavy. *Strategic Geography and the Changing Middle East*. Washington, D.C.: Brookings Institution Press, 1997.

King, Laura. "General: We Must Protect Afghans," *Chicago Tribune*, June 16, 2009, p. 15.

King, Laura. "Afghan Race at the Wire," *Chicago Tribune*, August 18, 2009, p. 10.

King, Winston L. *Zen and the Way of the Sword*. New York: Oxford University Press, 1993.

Klapper, Bradley S., Frank Jordans, and Deborah Seward. "French Arrest Physicist Suspected of Al-Qaida Link," *Associated Press*, October 9, 2009, pp. 1–3.

"Kyrgyzstan: Deal Reached on U.S. Bases," *Chicago Tribune*, June 24, 2009, p. 17.

Paolo—Advari's guardian and one of the three Portuguese brothers who operate the SCI Shipping Company.

Philippine sergeants—Three former Philippine Scouts who survived the Bataan death march in World War II and trained Joe Legion to replace his brother in special operations.

Police Chief Dunbar—Chief of Aurora, Illinois police department.

Police Chief Franzen—Chief of the Lisle, Illinois police department who has divided loyalties in helping Joe Legion and Amy while the Calderon network holds his daughter hostage in South America.

Professor Palmer—Seismology professor from Iowa who aids Joe Legion in gaining access to the Calderon villa in Ceuta, Morocco.

PURPLE—Secret anti-terrorist organization that provides intelligence and logistic support to Joe Legion. PURPLE is the predecessor organization of MAGENTA.

Ravi—Police officer in Bhuj, India involved in the attempted kidnapping of Roberto.

Roberto—Sujaya's husband and nuclear scientist in India who Joe Legion rescues following an attempted kidnapping.

Ron—Former U.S. Army Ranger and friend who assists or advises Joe Legion in his special operations assignments.

Sam—Local cemetery custodian.

Sandzak—Smuggling network based in Serbia operated by three principal adversaries of Joe Legion.

Santiago—Manco's uncle who aids Joe Legion in his operations against the Quillabamba and Tingo Maria ranches in Peru.

Sean—Amy's fiancé who is shot at O'Hare International Airport.

Sergeant Biggens—Police officer who aids Joe Legion against drug network enforcers in Chicago's western suburbs.

Slick—Joe Legion's friend in the Personnel department of Joe Legion's U.S. Army unit.

Skaric—One of Marika's fellow CIA agents in Serbia.

Southern Cross International Shipping Company—Family shipping company owned by Paolo, Miguel, and Roberto who help or hinder Joe Legion's activities against drug lords in Europe, North Africa, and South America.

Sujaya—Indian gynecologist who provides emergency care to the earthquake victims in Bhuj, India who later helps Joe Legion rescue Roberto, her nuclear scientist husband.

Svetlana—Russian interpreter for the Human Resources consulting group in Moscow and St. Petersburg.
Tabriz—Amhed's cousin and bus driver carrying Joe Legion's acrobat army to raid Ernesto Calderon's La Montagne, Morocco villa.
"Transition"—A Russian organization intended to assist former Russian military officers to find civilian employment.
Vasily—Joe Legion's arch-enemy who attempts to sell stolen nuclear materials to terrorist networks.
Veronica—Beth's second cousin who lives in Trstena, Slovakia.
Water Man—Street performer in Marrakesh who helps Joe Legion and the acrobat army rescue Beth from the Calderon network in Morocco.
Yuri—Russian equivalent of Joe Legion's real first name used by Daniela to alert Joe Legion that Vasily is in the vicinity.
Zaki—Snake handler in Marrakesh marketplace who joins Joe Legion's acrobat army to rescue Beth.
Zandar—One of the three principals of the Sandzak network in Serbia.

MacDonald, Charles B. *A Time for Trumpets The Untold Story of the Battle of the Bulge.* New York: Bantam Books, 1985.

Malcolm, Noel. *Bosnia A Short History.* New York: New York University Press, 1994.

Manier, Jeremy and Jo Napolitano. "Fermilab Gears Up for New Project," *Chicago Tribune*, September 5, 2008, p. 2.

Martinez, Michael and Tom Hundley. "Moroccans Fear Spain's Crackdown," *Chicago Tribune*, March 17, 2004, p. 3.

Mason, Jeff, Guy Faulconbridge, and Michael Stott. "Russia Lets U.S. Fly Troops, Weapons to Afghanistan," *Reuters*, July 6, 2009, pp. 1–3.

Musser, George. *The Complete Idiot's Guide to String Theory.* Indianapolis: Alpha Books, 2008.

"Obama, Medvedev Agree to Pursue Nuclear Reduction," *Associated Press*, July 6, 2009, pp. 1–4.

"Obama: Missile Defense Decision Not About Russia," *Associated Press*, September 20, 2009, pp. 1–3.

"Obama's Iran Disclosure Likely Part of Clever Chess Game," *The McClatchy Company*, September 26, 2009, pp. 1–4.

Parsons, Christi and Megan Stack. "Summit Opens in Agreement," *Chicago Tribune*, July 7, 2009, p. 12.

Parsons, Christi. "Nations Set Goals to Cut Nuclear Arms," *Chicago Tribune*, September 25, 2009, p. 25.

Prange, Gordon G., Donald M. Goldstein, and Katherine V. Dillon. *Miracle at Midway.* New York: McGraw-Hill Book Company, 1982.

Rachowiecki, Rob and Charlotte Beech. *Peru.* Melbourne: Lonely Planet Publications Pty. Ltd., 1987.

Richardson, Bill. "A New Realism," *Foreign Affairs*, Volume 87 Number 1 (January/February, 2008), pp. 142–154.

Richissin, Todd. "Rush-Hour Blasts Kill 192 on Madrid Trains," *Chicago Tribune*, March 12, 2004, p. 1.

Richter, Paul and Christi Parsons. " U.S. , Russia Signs Arms Treaty," *Chicago Trubune*, April 9, 2010, p. 12.

Rodwell, John Medows (translator). *The Koran.* New York: Bantam Books, 2004.

"Russia: Putin Offers Ban on Nukes," *Chicago Tribune*, June 11, 2009, p. 18.

Salter, Mark and Gordon McLachlan. *Poland A Rough Guide.* London: Rough Guides Ltd., 1993.

Scislowska, Monika. "Putin Puts Blame on West for WWII," *Chicago Tribune*, September 1, 2009, p. 14.

Shanahan, John M. (editor). *The Most Brilliant Thoughts of All Time*. New York: HarperCollins Publishers, Inc., 1999.

Simons, Marlise. "Spain's New Premier Orders Pullout in Iraq," *Chicago Tribune*, April 19, 2004, p. 7.

Sly, Liz. "Milestone and Crucial Test," *Chicago Tribune*, June 30, 2009, p. 4.

Spolar, Christine. "Old Divides Plague Bosnia," *Chicago Tribune*, May 14, 2007, pp. 1, 16.

Stack, Megan K. "Report: Georgia, Russia Both at Fault," *Chicago Tribune*, October 1, 2009, p. 14.

Stannard, Dorothy. *Morocco Insight Pocket Guide*. New York: Langenscheidt Publishers, Inc., 2001.

Tellis, Ashley J. *India's Emerging Nuclear Posture*. Santa Monica: RAND, 2001.

The Holy Bible The New American Catholic Edition. New York: Benzinger Brothers, Inc., 1961.

The Commission on the Intelligence Capabilities of the United States Regarding Weapons of Mass Destruction. *Report to the President of the United States*. Washington, D.C.: U.S. Government Printing Office, 2005.

United States of America Department of State. *Treaty Between the Government of the United States of America and the Government of the Republic of Bolivia on Extradition Treaty*. Treaty Document 1104-22. Washington, D.C.: U.S. Government Printing Office, 1995.

Von Hippel, Frank N. "Rethinking Nuclear Fuel Recycling," *Scientific American*, Volume 298 Number 5, (May, 2008), pp. 88–93.

Whitehall, Harold (editor). *Webster's New Twentieth Century Dictionary of the English Language Unabridged*. New York: Standard Reference Works Publishing Company, Inc., 1956.

Williams, China and others. *Southeast Asia on a Shoestring* 13th Edition. Melbourne: Lonely Planet Publications Pty. Ltd., 2006.

William Shakespeare, The Complete Works. New York: Barnes and Noble Books, 1994.

"Work Begins on World's Deepest Underground Lab," *Associated Press*, June 22, 2009, pp. 1–3.

ABOUT THE AUTHOR

George Banas was born in Joliet, Illinois, and grew up in Michigan before returning to Illinois to attend high school. Following college, he enlisted in the Army, and is an early Vietnam-era veteran. He holds a Bachelor's degree in Marketing, a Master of Business Administration degree in Human Resources, and a Juris Doctor degree in Corporate Law. Following retirement after 28 years with a non-profit medical association, he served on the boards of his local wildlife foundation and library district. He lives with his wife in suburban Chicago.

Made in the USA
Charleston, SC
01 November 2014